THE
WINGS OF THE
DOVE

HENRY JAMES

THE
WINGS OF THE
DOVE

With a Preface by the Author

Introduction by Amy Bloom

Notes by Pierre A. Walker
SALEM STATE COLLEGE

THE MODERN LIBRARY

NEW YORK

2004 Modern Library Mass Market Edition

Biographical note © 1993 by Random House, Inc.
Introduction copyright © 2003 by Amy Bloom
Notes and reading group guide copyright © 2003 by Random House, Inc.

A trade paperback version of this work was originally published by
Modern Library, an imprint of The Random House Publishing Group, a
division of Random House, Inc., in 2003.

LIBRARY OF CONGRESS CATALOGING-IN-PUBLICATION DATA
James, Henry, 1843–1916.
The wings of the dove/Henry James.
p.   cm.
ISBN 0-8129-7211-2
I. Title.
PS2116.W5   1993
813'.4—dc20   93–15338

Modern Library website address: www.modernlibrary.com

Printed in the United States of America

2 4 6 8 9 7 5 3 1

HENRY JAMES

Henry James was born in New York City on April 15, 1843, of Scottish and Irish ancestry. His father, Henry James, Sr., was a whimsical, utterly charming, maddeningly open-minded parent—a Swedenborgian philosopher of considerable wealth who believed in a universal but wholly unformed society. He gave both Henry and his elder son, William, an infant baptism by taking them to Europe before they could even speak. In fact, Henry James later claimed that his first memory, dating from the age of two, was a glimpse of the column of the Place Vendôme framed by the window of the carriage in which he was riding. His peripatetic childhood took him to experimental schools in Geneva, Paris, and London. Even back in the United States he was shuffled from New York City to Albany to Newport to Boston and finally to Cambridge, where in 1862 he briefly attended Harvard Law School. "An obscure hurt," probably to his back, exempted him from service in the Civil War, and James felt he had failed as a man when it counted most to be one and vowed never to marry.

In search of a possible occupation, the young James turned to literature; within five years it had become his profession. His earliest story appeared in *The Atlantic Monthly* in 1865, when he was twenty-two. From the start of his career James supported himself as a writer, and over the next ten years he produced book reviews, drama and art criticism, newspaper columns, travel pieces and travel books, short stories, novelettes, a biography, and his first novel—*Roderick Hudson* (1876). Late in 1875, following two recent trips to Europe, James settled in Paris, where he met Turgenev, Flaubert, and Zola, and wrote *The American* (1877). In December 1876 he moved to London, where he produced *The Europeans* (1878). Soon afterward he achieved fame on both sides of the Atlantic with the publication of *Daisy Miller* (1879), the book that forever identified him with the "international theme" of the effect of Americans and Europeans on each other.

Yet Henry James aspired to more than the success of *Daisy Miller*. Determined to scale new literary heights, James abandoned the intense social life of his earlier years and, with Balzac as his role model, devoted himself all out to the craft of fiction. Although *The Portrait of a Lady* (1881) was critically acclaimed and sold well, the other novels of James's "Balzac" period—*Washington Square* (1881), *The Bostonians* (1886), *The Princess Casamassima* (1886), and *The Tragic Muse* (1890)—were not popular with the public. As a result, he decided to redirect his efforts and began writing for the stage. In 1895, the disastrous opening night of his play *Guy Domville*— when James came onstage only to be hissed and booed by the London audience—forever ended his career as a playwright.

Rededicating himself to fiction, he wrote *The Spoils of Poynton* (1897), *What Maisie Knew* (1897), *The Turn of the Screw* (1898), and *The Awkward Age* (1899). Then, as he approached and passed the age of sixty James's three greatest novels appeared in rapid succession: *The Wings of the Dove* (1902), *The Ambassadors* (1903), and *The Golden Bowl* (1904). He spent most of his remaining years at Lamb House, his ivy-covered home in Rye, writing his memoirs and revising his novels for the twenty-four-volume New York Edition of his lifework. When World War I broke out, he was eager to serve his adopted country and threw himself into the civilian war effort. In 1915, after four decades of living in England, James became a British subject, and King George V conferred the Order of Merit on him in January 1916. Henry James died in London on February 28, 1916, and his ashes were buried in the James family plot in Cambridge, Massachusetts.

Commenting on the enormous contemporary interest in James, novelist Louis Auchincloss said: "How he would have loved his posthumous fame! One can imagine Emily Brontë and Herman Melville shrugging shoulders, faintly scornful, but James would have bristled with pride at every mention of his name. . . . It is pleasant to think that in the end he had at least a whiff of it and

that the silent, grave, bearded young man should have
evolved into the portly figure of the rolling, resolute gait,
simple in emotion but quick and spontaneous in affection, leaving among his recording disciples a deep impression of majesty, beauty, and greatness."

CONTENTS

INTRODUCTION

LONELY DOVE

Amy Bloom

One is never set at rest by Mr. Henry James' novels. His books end as an episode in life ends. You remain with the sense of the life still going on; and even the subtle presence of the dead is felt in that silence that comes upon the artist-creation when the last word has been read. It is eminently satisfying, but it is not final. Mr. Henry James, great artist and faithful historian, never attempts the impossible.

That a sacrifice must be made, that something has to be given up, is the truth engraved in the innermost recesses of the fair temple built for our edification by the masters of fiction. There is no other secret behind the curtain. All adventure, all love, every success is resumed in the supreme energy of an act of renunciation.
—*FROM JOSEPH CONRAD'S NOTES ON LIFE AND LETTERS (J. M. DENT EDITION, 1921)*

Henry James understood want, and need, and he understood how terribly easy it is for wants to become needs and needs to become as compelling and necessary as air.

No one has ever written with more tenderness, more sympathy, or more steely understanding about liars, gamblers, cheaters, thieves, and everyone else who fights off shame, or succumbs to it. In his last great trio of novels (*The Ambassadors, The Golden Bowl* and *The Wings of the Dove*), James's rolling language, his passionate fussiness, and his brilliant evocations of Italy (and, above all, of non-Italians in Italy) all serve as intriguing backdrop to the relentless, clear-eyed, and compassionate portraits of people who abandon goodness, embrace their ambition, and survey wreckage when they do, finally, see. He sings, for this is prose that sings, in a self-consciously rich and operatic tone and, at other times, in a straightforward and unflinching voice, as frank and cool as any contemporary writer, but without the modern gloss of irony that hopes to disguise its sentimental heart. James waxes sentimental about all sorts of things, especially things and manners gone by, not the least of which was his own unlived life, but there is no plucking on heartstrings or hustling goodwill in his portraits of outsiders, of the hopelessly, awkwardly yearning, the self-deceiving, the desperate, the self-aware, and the weak-willed. And, as much as James paints aristocratic rogues and sterling gentlemen, genteel lady writers and watchful wives, his greatest portraits are of passive men and troubled women—upper-class women, in particular. James fills his novels with the women who matter to him: angels (who are, perhaps, just a bit tiresome in their celestial sweetness) and humans (who break our hearts with their bad choices and faulty vision). James's luminously innocent heroines are charming and often frail, all versions of his beloved cousin Minny Temple, "a young and shining apparition," with a "wonderful, ethereal brightness of presence," who walked with distinctively "long, light and yet almost sliding steps," which James will give directly to Milly Theale in these next pages. His troubled, complex women (like Kate Croy) are not even heroines, they are just women, women on the verge of consciousness, women on the verge of self-knowledge and painfully past it, women who know more than society wishes them to and try not to show it.

As Millicent Bell wrote of Henry James: "Physical action, public life—the modes of male heroism—were less interesting to him than the drama of feeling and intelligence in such unspectacular experience as a chaperoned American girl's journey to Europe. . . . James, however, felt he had no choice but to recognize the coincidence of his experience and outlook with a woman's. Temper and upbringing excluded him from masculine preoccupation. As a marginal man, excluded from domestic as well as public power, he could identify with the marginal role of women . . . he enunciated a feminism of his own."

It may be this—his own strong sense, from childhood, that he would always be a lesser being in thrall to greater ones (*Notes of a Son and Brother* captures it, I think): a stammering little brother with a forceful older one (so in awe of William James that at fifty he could still write a shrill letter defending his right to buy Lamb House and disregard his older brother's advice: "I do, strange as it may appear to you, in this matter know more or less what I'm about"—a note familiar to any younger sibling), twice uprooted from America to attend European schools in which he floundered, badly; the bookish observer, standing by softly as two younger, bolder brothers joined the Northern army; the tongue-tied suitor who could not compete with more dashing, masculine boys (whom he admired as much as the girl he courted); the bumbling, ill-suited law student—it may be that all this paved the way for the Master, who even more than he felt his genius, even as he bowed his head complacently to accept his place as *"cher Maître,"* always felt what it was *not* to be master.

The Wings of the Dove is a small, deeply felt tragedy, with big themes and grand sets. Kate Croy, ambitious and needy, has not that far to fall, but her steady, morally bankrupt collapse and the slide, rather than fall, of her complicit lover, Merton Densher, combine to make a greater tragedy of love undeserved and unrequited, of desire's miscalculation and of money's merciless, irresistible pull; for James, until *The Golden Bowl*, money stood in sex's usual place—glorious passion and blinding, even catastrophic, need.

The Wings of the Dove is also a novel of intimacy. James wrote to friends that in this book he had successfully married novelistic and theatrical techniques, creating a "key that . . . fits the complicated chambers of both the narrative and the dramatic lock." Intimacy is that key—unlocking the door between the author and his characters, between the characters, and between reader and story. Even the voice of the narrative itself—hesitant, dubious, roundabout, questioning, sarcastic—is the intimate voice of conversation, of people living and sorting out their lives. Scenes are alluded to but not always witnessed—because in life, one sometimes arrives late, or not at all, to the big scene, even though one feels its aftershocks for years. Conversations are overheard, but not always completely understood, and sometimes, even the eavesdropping must be abruptly curtailed—as in life. James creates something like, and totally different from, the traditional omniscient narrator. The narrator of *The Wings of the Dove* goes everywhere, from "the tall rich heavy house of Lancaster Gatton the other side of the Park" to the deceivingly "great gilded historic chamber" for which Lord Mark requires Milly Theale's fortune (as does almost everyone herein), to Milly's borrowed Palazzo Leporelli, in Venice, which "held history still in its great lap, even like a painted idol, a solemn puppet hung about with decorations." And, even in the course of traveling everywhere on the slightly bumpy, occasionally bumptious Jamesian prose, the narrator knows where he cannot, will not, go. He knows that one cannot know everything; that some motives remain obscure, although the narrator, like us, will take an educated guess; that some outcomes are unforeseen, although the narrator, like us, has suspected something, but not *this;* that life is lived, is not merely described, not even just understood, but is the thing that happens to us even as we are attempting to understand it. This great flow of event and understanding, of life yielding to analysis and defying it, of people reaching for what they think they want even as their fingers itch to take the prize and to drop it at once, is the intimate, intensely felt life of *The Wings of the Dove*.

The many ironies of the novel are the ironies we know from our own lives—ironies of loves unexpected and undeserved, ironies of devotion that turn into a trap and traps that become salvation; the ironies seem to spring from the complicated hearts of Merton, Kate, and even Milly the Dove, whose wings are powerful, beneath the soft and pretty feathers. We meet Kate, the least sympathetic protagonist ("the least little bit brutal . . . with a wild beauty in that") in circumstances that inspire not only sympathy, but admiration: she is trying to do right by her cruel, sponging, and profoundly disinterested father. She offers to turn down her aunt's proposal (that Kate live luxuriously with Aunt Maud, enjoy her patronage and support and never see her father again) and live modestly—more than modestly, meanly—with her father and look after him. His indifference is monumental and his grasp on opportunity unshakeable. If Kate has any true feeling for him—and he does not care if she does not—she will go along with Aunt Maud, marry a man of whom Aunt Maud approves, and when Kate is well settled, she will provide handsomely for her father. Kate makes it clear that she had hoped her father valued her more than money and that if he had set an example of love above money, she would be encouraged, emboldened, to follow suit. There is no redemption, no shining moment, and no forgiveness: "Do you know, dear," her father says, adamant in his refusal to have a poor daughter, furious that she shares her small inheritance with her widowed sister, rather than with him, "you make me sick? I've tried to be clear and it isn't fair."

Over and over, with greater theatrical skill than he ever showed as a playwright, James brings us to one painful, private moment after another, one true, revealing, ironic scene leading to another. Everyone's faults, lies, self-deceptions and missteps—Kate's wish that she can deceive Milly, swindle her out of a fortune, and be her best friend; Milly's firm, gentle insistence that no harm is being done, even as it kills her; Merton's hope and pretense that he has done nothing wrong, until it is too late, and he can only live with himself by doing more harm—come forward and we cannot escape them, any more than James's characters could.

The Wings of the Dove was written, as James wrote of Jeffrey Aspern, "free and general and not all afraid; to feel, understand and express everything." Henry James came rather lonely and rather late in life, I think, to passionate love, but he breathes passionate life into his mismatched, doomed lovers; he gives us passion, he gives us love in its terrible and enchanting forms, he gives everything he knew; and he knew "the only way to know is to have lived and loved and cursed and floundered and enjoyed and suffered." We cannot read this book without experiencing all of that, in Milly and Merton and Kate, and, because it is art, within ourselves.

———

AMY BLOOM is the author of *Normal, A Blind Man Can See How Much I Love You, Come to Me,* and a novel,

Love Invents Us. Her work has appeared in *The New Yorker, The Atlantic Monthly,* and *Harper's Bazaar,* among other publications, and in many anthologies, including *The Best American Short Stories; Prize Stories: The O. Henry Awards;* and *The Scribner Anthology of Contemporary Short Fiction.* She lives in Connecticut and teaches at Yale University.

A Note on the Text

The Wings of the Dove was first published in August 1902 in two volumes by Scribner's in New York and one volume by Constable in London. The differences between the two texts suggest that James was able to give more attention to correcting the final proof for Scribner's than for Constable, and this Modern Library edition of the novel follows the text of the 1902 Scribner's edition (with the addition of the Preface, which James wrote for the 1909 edition). In 1907, James undertook the preparation for Scribner's of a revised, definitive edition of twenty-four volumes (called the New York Edition) containing many of his short stories and novels; the revised version of *The Wings of the Dove* appeared in 1909 as volumes nineteen and twenty of the New York Edition. In preparing the New York Edition text of the novel, James made about 1,500 alterations, mostly of a stylistic nature (for instance, he inserted more Italian phrases in the novel's Venice chapters).

Since the New York Edition revisions do not drastically alter the novel, and because there are so many of them, the notes of this Modern Library edition only indicate those revisions which, in the editor's opinion, most warrant readers' attention, for example, corrections of probable errors in the 1902 text, significant clarifications or changes of meaning, or interesting alternative readings. Obvious typographical errors in the 1902 text have been replaced by the 1909 reading and are only annotated when the 1902 reading might be of special interest.

For all of the volumes of the New York Edition, James commissioned frontispieces from the photographer Alvin Langdon Coburn. For the first volume of *The Wings of the Dove* (volume nineteen of the New York Edition), James had Coburn photograph the front door of 143 Harley Street, London, and entitled the frontispiece: "The Doctor's Door." For the second volume (volume twenty of the New York Edition), Coburn photographed the Grand Canal facade of Palazzo Barbaro (see 450. 15–16), and James entitled this frontispiece: "The Venetian Palace." Volume nineteen contains James's 1909 preface to *The Wings of the Dove* and Books First through Fifth; volume twenty contains Books Sixth through Tenth.

THE
WINGS OF THE
DOVE

Preface

....

TO THE NEW YORK EDITION

"THE WINGS OF THE DOVE," published in 1902, represents to my memory a very old—if I should n't perhaps rather say a very young—motive; I can scarce remember the time when the situation on which this long-drawn fiction mainly rests was not vividly present to me. The idea, reduced to its essence, is that of a young person conscious of a great capacity for life, but early stricken and doomed, condemned to die under short respite, while also enamoured of the world; aware moreover of the condemnation and passionately desiring to "put in" before extinction as many of the finer vibrations as possible, and so achieve, however briefly and brokenly, the sense of having lived. Long had I turned it over, standing off from it, yet coming back to it; convinced of what might be done with it, yet seeing the theme as formidable. The image so figured would be, at best, but half the matter; the rest would be all the picture of the struggle involved, the adventure brought about, the gain recorded or the loss incurred, the precious experience somehow compassed. These things, I had from the first felt, would require much working-out;

that indeed was the case with most things worth working at all; yet there are subjects and subjects, and this one seemed particularly to bristle. It was formed, I judged, to make the wary adventurer walk round and round it—it had in fact a charm that invited and mystified alike that attention; not being somehow what one thought of as a "frank" subject, after the fashion of some, with its elements well in view and its whole character in its face. It stood there with secrets and compartments, with possible treacheries and traps; it might have a great deal to give, but would probably ask for equal services in return, and would collect this debt to the last shilling. It involved, to begin with, the placing in the strongest light a person infirm and ill—a case sure to prove difficult and to require much handling; though giving perhaps, with other matters, one of those chances for good taste, possibly even for the play of the very best in the world, that are not only always to be invoked and cultivated, but that are absolutely to be jumped at from the moment they make a sign.

Yes then, the case prescribed for its central figure a sick young woman, at the whole course of whose disintegration and the whole ordeal of whose consciousness one would have quite honestly to assist. The expression of her state and that of one's intimate relation to it might therefore well need to be discreet and ingenious; a reflection that fortunately grew and grew, however, in proportion as I focussed my image—roundabout which, as it persisted, I repeat, the interesting possibilities and the attaching wonderments, not to say the insoluble mysteries, thickened apace. Why had one to look so straight in the face and so closely to cross-question that idea of making one's protagonist "sick"?—as if to be menaced with death or danger had n't been from time immemorial, for heroine or hero, the very shortest of all cuts to the interesting state. Why should a figure be disqualified for a central position by the particular circumstance that might most quicken, that might crown with a fine intensity, its liability to many accidents, its consciousness of all relations? This circumstance, true enough, might disqualify it for many activities—even though we should have imputed to it the unsurpassable activity of passionate, of inspired resistance. This last fact was the real issue, for the way grew straight from the moment one recognised that the poet essentially *can't* be concerned with the act of dying. Let him deal with the sickest of the sick, it is still by the act of living that they appeal to him, and appeal the more as the conditions plot against them and prescribe the battle. The process of life gives way fighting, and often may so shine out on the lost ground as in no other connexion. One had had moreover, as a various chronicler, one's secondary physical weaklings and failures, one's accessory invalids—introduced with a complacency that made light of criticism. To Ralph Touchett in "The Portrait of a Lady," for instance, his deplorable state of health was not only no drawback; I had clearly been right in counting it, for any happy effect he should produce, a positive good mark, a direct aid to pleasantness and vividness. The reason of this

moreover could never in the world have been his fact of
sex; since men, among the mortally afflicted, suffer on
the whole more overtly and more grossly than women,
and resist with a ruder, an inferior strategy. I had thus
to take *that* anomaly for what it was worth, and I give
it here but as one of the ambiguities amid which my
subject ended by making itself at home and seating
itself quite in confidence.

With the clearness I have just noted, accordingly, the
last thing in the world it proposed to itself was to be
the record predominantly of a collapse. I don't mean to
say that my offered victim was not present to my imagination, constantly, as dragged by a greater force than
any she herself could exert; she had been given me from
far back as contesting every inch of the road, as catching
at every object the grasp of which might make for delay,
as clutching these things to the last moment of her
strength. Such an attitude and such movements, the
passion they expressed and the success they in fact represented, what were they in truth but the soul of
drama?—which is the portrayal, as we know, of a catastrophe determined in spite of oppositions. My young
woman would *herself* be the opposition—to the catastrophe announced by the associated Fates, powers conspiring to a sinister end and, with their command of
means, finally achieving it, yet in such straits really to
stifle the sacred spark that, obviously, a creature so animated, an adversary so subtle, could n't but be felt worthy, under whatever weaknesses, of the foreground and
the limelight. She would meanwhile wish, moreover, all

along, to live for particular things, she would found her
struggle on particular human interests, which would
inevitably determine, in respect to her, the attitude of
other persons, persons affected in such a manner as to
make them part of the action. If her impulse to wrest
from her shrinking hour still as much of the fruit of life
as possible, if this longing can take effect only by the aid
of others, their participation (appealed to, entangled and
coerced as they find themselves) becomes their drama
too—that of their promoting her illusion, under her
importunity, for reasons, for interests and advantages,
from motives and points of view, of their own. Some of
these promptings, evidently, would be of the highest
order—others doubtless might n't; but they would make
up together, for her, contributively, her sum of experience, represent to her somehow, in good faith or in bad,
what she should have *known*. Somehow, too, at such a
rate, one would see the persons subject to them drawn
in as by some pool of a Lorelei—see them terrified and
tempted and charmed; bribed away, it may even be,
from more prescribed and natural orbits, inheriting from
their connexion with her strange difficulties and still
stranger opportunities, confronted with rare questions
and called upon for new discriminations. Thus the
scheme of her situation would, in a comprehensive way,
see itself constituted; the rest of the interest would be
in the number and nature of the particulars. Strong
among these, naturally, the need that life should, apart
from her infirmity, present itself to our young woman as
quite dazzlingly liveable, and that if the great pang for

her is in what she must give up we shall appreciate it the more from the sight of all she has.

One would see her then as possessed of all things, all but the single most precious assurance; freedom and money and a mobile mind and personal charm, the power to interest and attach; attributes, each one, enhancing the value of a future. From the moment his imagination began to deal with her at close quarters, in fact, nothing could more engage her designer than to work out the detail of her perfect rightness for her part; nothing above all more solicit him than to recognise fifty reasons for her national and social status. She should be the last fine flower—blooming alone, for the fullest attestation of her freedom—of an "old" New York stem; the happy congruities thus preserved for her being matters, however, that I may not now go into, and this even though the fine association that shall yet elsewhere await me is of a sort, at the best, rather to defy than to encourage exact expression. There goes with it, for the heroine of "The Wings of the Dove," a strong and special implication of liberty, liberty of action, of choice, of appreciation, of contact—proceeding from sources that provide better for large independence, I think, than any other conditions in the world—and this would be in particular what we should feel ourselves deeply concerned with. I had from far back mentally projected a certain sort of young American as more the "heir of all the ages" than any other young person whatever (and precisely on those grounds I have just glanced at but to pass them by for the moment); so that here was a chance to confer on some such figure a supremely touching value. To be the heir of all the ages only to know yourself, as that consciousness should deepen, balked of your inheritance, would be to play the part, it struck me, or at least to arrive at the type, in the light on the whole the most becoming. Otherwise, truly, what a perilous part to play *out*—what a suspicion of "swagger" in positively attempting it! So at least I could reason—so I even think I *had* to—to keep my subject to a decent compactness. For already, from an early stage, it had begun richly to people itself: the difficulty was to see whom the situation I had primarily projected might, by this, that or the other turn, *not* draw in. My business was to watch its turns as the fond parent watches a child perched, for its first riding-lesson, in the saddle; yet its interest, I had all the while to recall, was just in its making, on such a scale, for developments.

What one had discerned, at all events, from an early stage, was that a young person so devoted and exposed, a creature with her security hanging so by a hair, could n't but fall somehow into some abysmal trap—this being, dramatically speaking, what such a situation most naturally implied and imposed. Did n't the truth and a great part of the interest also reside in the appearance that she would constitute for others (given her passionate yearning to live while she might) a complication as great as any they might constitute for herself?—which is what I mean when I speak of such matters as "natural." They would be as natural, these tragic, pathetic, ironic, these indeed for the most part sinister, liabilities, to her living associates, as they could be to herself as prime subject. If her story was to consist, as it could so little help doing, of her being let in, as we say, for this, that and the other irreducible anxiety, how could she not have put a premium on the acquisition, by any close sharer of her life, of a consciousness similarly embarrassed? I have named the Rhine-maiden, but our young friend's existence would create rather, all round her, very much that whirlpool movement of the waters produced by the sinking of a big vessel or the failure of a great business; when we figure to ourselves the strong narrowing eddies, the immense force of suction, the general engulfment that, for any neighbouring object, makes immersion inevitable. I need scarce say, however, that in spite of these communities of doom I saw the main dramatic complication much more prepared *for* my vessel of sensibility than by her—the work of other hands (though with her own imbrued too, after all, in the measure of their never not being, in some direction, generous and extravagant, and thereby provoking).

The great point was, at all events, that if in a predicament she was to be, accordingly, it would be of the essence to create the predicament promptly and build it up solidly, so that it should have for us as much as possible its ominous air of awaiting her. That reflexion I found, betimes, not less inspiring than urgent; one begins so, in such a business, by looking about for one's compositional key, unable as one can only be to move till one has found it. To start without it is to pretend to enter the train and, still more, to remain in one's seat, without a ticket. Well—in the steady light and for the continued charm of these verifications—I had secured my ticket over the tolerably long line laid down for "The Wings of the Dove" from the moment I had noted that there could be no full presentation of Milly Theale as *engaged* with elements amid which she was to draw her breath in such pain, should not the elements have been, with all solicitude, duly prefigured. If one had seen that her stricken state was but half her case, the correlative half being the state of others as affected by her (they too should have a "case," bless them, quite as much as she!) then I was free to choose, as it were, the half with which I should begin. If, as I had fondly noted, the little world determined for her was to "bristle"—I delighted in the term!—with meanings, so, by the same token, could I but make my medal hang free, its obverse and its reverse, its face and its back, would beautifully become optional for the spectator. I somehow wanted them correspondingly embossed, wanted them inscribed and figured with an equal salience; yet it was none the less visibly my "key," as I have said, that though my regenerate young New Yorker, and what might depend on her, should form my centre, my circumference was every whit as treatable. Therefore I must trust myself to know when to proceed from the one and when from the other. Preparatively and, as it were, yearningly—given the whole ground—one began, in the event, with the outer ring, approaching the centre thus by narrowing circumvallations. There, full-blown, accordingly, from one hour to the other, rose one's process—for which there remained all the while so many amusing formulae.

The medal *did* hang free—I felt this perfectly, I remember, from the moment I had comfortably laid the ground provided in my first Book, ground from which Milly is superficially so absent. I scarce remember perhaps a case—I like even with this public grossness to insist on it—in which the curiosity of "beginning far back," as far back as possible, and even of going, to the same tune, far "behind," that is behind the face of the subject, was to assert itself with less scruple. The free hand, in this connexion, was above all agreeable—the hand the freedom of which I owed to the fact that the work had ignominiously failed, in advance, of all power to see itself "serialised." This failure had repeatedly waited, for me, upon shorter fictions; but the considerable production we here discuss was (as "The Golden Bowl" was to be, two or three years later) born, not otherwise than a little bewilderedly, into a world of periodicals and editors, of roaring "successes" in fine, amid which it was well-nigh unnotedly to lose itself. There is fortunately something bracing, ever, in the alpine chill, that of some high icy *arête*, shed by the cold editorial shoulder; sour grapes may at moments fairly intoxicate and the story-teller worth his salt rejoice to feel again how many accommodations he can practise. Those addressed to "conditions of publication" have in a degree their interesting, or at least their provoking, side; but their charm is qualified by the fact that the prescriptions here spring from a soil often wholly alien to the ground of the work itself. They are almost always the fruit of another air altogether and conceived in a light liable to represent *within* the circle of the work itself little else than darkness. Still, when not too blighting, they often operate as a tax on ingenuity—that ingenuity of the expert craftsman which likes to be taxed very much to the same tune to which a well-bred horse likes to be saddled. The best and finest ingenuities, nevertheless, with all respect to that truth, are apt to be, not one's compromises, but one's fullest conformities, and I well remember, in the case before us, the pleasure of feeling my divisions, my proportions and general rhythm, rest all on permanent rather than in any degree on momentary proprieties. It was enough for my alternations, thus, that they were good in themselves; it was in fact so much for them that I really think any further account of the constitution of the book reduces itself to a just notation of the law they followed.

There was the "fun," to begin with, of establishing one's successive centres—of fixing them so exactly that the portions of the subject commanded by them as by happy points of view, and accordingly treated from them, would constitute, so to speak, sufficiently solid *blocks* of wrought material, squared to the sharp edge, as to have weight and mass and carrying power; to make for construction, that is, to conduce to effect and to provide for beauty. Such a block, obviously, is the whole preliminary presentation of Kate Croy, which, from the first, I recall, absolutely declined to enact itself save in terms of amplitude. Terms of amplitude, terms of atmosphere, those terms, and those terms only, in which images assert their fulness and roundness, their power to revolve, so that they have sides and backs, parts in the shade as true as parts in the sun—these were plainly to be my conditions, right and left, and I was so far from overrating the amount of expression the whole thing, as I saw and felt it, would require, that to retrace the way at present is, alas, more than anything else, but to mark the gaps and the lapses, to miss, one by one, the intentions that, with the best will in the world, were not to fructify. I have just said that the process of the general attempt is described from the moment the "blocks" are numbered, and that would be a true enough picture of my plan. Yet one's plan, alas, is one thing and one's result another; so I am perhaps nearer the point in saying that this last strikes me at present as most characterised by the happy features that *were*, under my first and most blest illusion, to have contributed to it. I meet them all, as I renew acquaintance, I mourn for them all as I remount the stream, the absent values, the palpable voids, the missing links, the mocking shadows, that reflect, taken together, the early bloom of one's good faith. Such cases are of course far from abnormal—so far from it that some acute mind ought surely to have worked out by this time the "law" of the degree in which the artist's energy fairly depends on his fallibility. How much and how often, and in what connexions and with what almost infinite variety, must he be a dupe, that of his prime object, to be at all measurably a master, that of his actual substitute for it—or in other words at all appreciably to exist? He places, after an earnest survey, the piers of his bridge—he has at least sounded deep enough, heaven knows, for their brave position; yet the bridge spans the stream, after the fact, in apparently complete independence of these properties, the principal grace of the original design. *They* were an illusion, for their necessary hour; but the span itself, whether of a single arch or of many, seems by the oddest chance in the world to be a reality; since, actually, the rueful builder, passing under it, sees figures and hears sounds above: he makes out, with his heart in his throat, that it bears and is positively being "used."

The building-up of Kate Croy's consciousness to the capacity for the load little by little to be laid on it was, by way of example, to have been a matter of as many hundred close-packed bricks as there are actually poor dozens. The image of her so compromised and compromising father was all effectively to have pervaded her life, was in a certain particular way to have tampered with her spring; by which I mean that the shame and the irritation and the depression, the general poisonous influence of him, were to have been *shown*, with a truth beyond the compass even of one's most emphasised "word of honour" for it, to do these things. But where do we find him, at this time of day, save in a beggarly scene or two which scarce arrives at the dignity of functional reference? He but "looks in," poor beautiful dazzling, damning apparition that he was to have been; he sees his place so taken, his company so little missed, that, cocking again that fine form of hat which has yielded him for so long his one effective cover, he turns away with a whistle of indifference that nobly misrepresents the deepest disappointment of his life. One's poor word of honour has *had* to pass muster for the show. Every one, in short, was to have enjoyed so much better a chance that, like stars of the theatre condescending to oblige, they have had to take small parts, to content themselves with minor identities, in order to come on at all. I have n't the heart now, I confess, to adduce the detail of so many lapsed importances; the explanation of most of which, after all, I take to have been in the crudity of a truth beating full upon me through these reconsiderations, the odd inveteracy with which picture, at almost any turn, is jealous of drama, and drama (though on the whole with a greater patience, I think) suspicious of picture. Between them, no doubt, they do much for the theme; yet each baffles insidiously the other's ideal and eats round the edges of its position; each is too ready to say "I can take the thing for 'done' only when done in *my* way." The residuum of comfort for the witness of these broils is of course meanwhile in the convenient reflexion, invented for him in the twilight of time and the infancy of art by the Angel, not to say by the Demon, of Compromise, that nothing is so easy to "do" as not to be thankful for almost any stray help in its getting done. It was n't, after this fashion, by making good one's dream of Lionel Croy that my structure was to stand on its feet—any more than it was by letting him go that I was to be left irretrievably lamenting. The who and the what, the how and the why, the whence and the whither of Merton Densher, these, no less, were quantities and attributes that should have danced about him with the antique grace of nymphs and fauns circling round a bland Hermes and crowning him with flowers. One's main anxiety, for each one's agents, is that the air of each shall be *given;* but what does the whole thing become, after all, as one goes, but a series of sad places at which the hand of generosity has been cautioned and stayed? The young man's situation, personal, professional, social, was to have been so decanted for us that we should get all the taste; we were to have been penetrated with Mrs. Lowder, by the same token, saturated with her presence, her "personality," and felt all her weight in the scale. We were to have revelled in Mrs. Stringham, my heroine's attendant friend, her fairly choral Bostonian, a subject for innumerable touches, and in an extended and above all an *animated* reflexion of Milly Theale's experience of English society; just as the strength and sense of the situation in Venice, for our gathered friends, was to have come to us in a deeper draught out of a larger cup, and just as the pattern of Densher's final position and fullest consciousness there was to have been marked in fine stitches, all silk and gold, all pink and silver, that have had to remain, alas, but entwined upon the reel.

It is n't, no doubt, however—to recover, after all, our critical balance—that the pattern didn't, for each compartment, get itself somehow wrought, and that we might n't thus, piece by piece, opportunity offering, trace it over and study it. The thing has doubtless, as a whole, the advantage that each piece is true to its pattern, and that while it pretends to make no simple statement it yet never lets go its scheme of clearness. Applications of this scheme are continuous and exemplary enough, though I scarce leave myself room to glance at them. The clearness is obtained in Book First—or otherwise, as I have said, in the first "piece," each Book having its subordinate and contributive pattern—through the associated consciousness of my two prime young persons, for whom I early recognised that I should have to consent, under stress, to a practical *fusion* of consciousness. It is into the young woman's "ken" that Merton Densher is represented as swimming; but her mind is not here, rigorously, the one reflector. There are occasions when it plays this part, just as there are others when his plays it, and an intelligible plan consists naturally not a little in fixing such occasions and making them, on one side and the other, sufficient to themselves. Do I sometimes in fact forfeit the advantage of that distinctness? Do I ever abandon one centre for another after the former has been postulated? From the moment we proceed by "centres"—and I have never, I confess, embraced the logic of any superior process— they must *be*, each, as a basis, selected and fixed; after which it is that, in the high interest of economy of treatment, they determine and rule. There is no economy of treatment without an adopted, a related point of view, and though I understand, under certain degrees of pressure, a represented community of vision between several parties to the action when it makes for concentration, I

understand no breaking-up of the register, no sacrifice
of the recording consistency, that does n't rather scatter
and weaken. In this truth resides the secret of the dis-
criminated occasion—that aspect of the subject which
we have our noted choice of treating either as picture or
scenically, but which is apt, I think, to show its fullest
worth in the Scene. Beautiful exceedingly, for that matter, those occasions or parts of an occasion when the
boundary line between picture and scene bears a little
the weight of the double pressure.

Such would be the case, I can't but surmise, for the
long passage that forms here before us the opening of
Book Fourth, where all the offered life centres, to intensity, in the disclosure of Milly's single throbbing consciousness, but where, for a due rendering, everything
has to be brought to a head. This passage, the view of
her introduction to Mrs. Lowder's circle, has its mate,
for illustration, later on in the book and at a crisis for
which the occasion submits to another rule. My registers
or "reflectors," as I so conveniently name them (bur-
nished indeed as they generally are by the intelligence,
the curiosity, the passion, the force of the moment,
whatever it be, directing them), work, as we have seen,
in arranged alternation; so that in the second connexion
I here glance at it is Kate Croy who is, "for all she is
worth," turned on. She is turned on largely at Venice,
where the appearances, rich and obscure and portentous
(another word I rejoice in) as they have by that time
become and altogether exquisite as they remain, are
treated almost wholly through her vision of them and

Densher's (as to the lucid interplay of which conspiring and conflicting agents there would be a great deal to say). It is in Kate's consciousness that at the stage in question the drama is brought to a head, and the occasion on which, in the splendid saloon of poor Milly's hired palace, she takes the measure of her friend's festal evening, squares itself to the same synthetic firmness as the compact constructional block inserted by the scene at Lancaster Gate. Milly's situation ceases at a given moment to be "renderable" in terms closer than those supplied by Kate's intelligence, or, in a richer degree, by Densher's, or, for one fond hour, by poor Mrs. Stringham's (since to that sole brief futility is this last participant, crowned by my original plan with the quaintest functions, in fact reduced); just as Kate's relation with Densher and Densher's with Kate have ceased previously, and are then to cease again, to be projected for us, so far as Milly is concerned with them, on any more responsible plate than that of the latter's admirable anxiety. It is as if, for these aspects, the impersonal plate—in other words the poor author's comparatively cold affirmation or thin guarantee—had felt itself a figure of attestation at once too gross and too bloodless, likely to affect us as an abuse of privilege when not as an abuse of knowledge.

Heaven forbid, we say to ourselves during almost the whole Venetian climax, heaven forbid we should "know" anything more of our ravaged sister than what Densher darkly pieces together, or than what Kate Croy pays, heroically, it must be owned, at the hour of her

visit alone to Densher's lodging, for her superior handling and her dire profanation of. For we have time,
while this passage lasts, to turn round critically; we have
time to recognise intentions and proprieties; we have
time to catch glimpses of an economy of composition, as
I put it, interesting in itself: all in spite of the author's
scarce more than half-dissimulated despair at the inveterate displacement of his general centre. "The Wings
of the Dove" happens to offer perhaps the most striking example I may cite (though with public penance for
it already performed) of my regular failure to keep the
appointed halves of my whole equal. Here the makeshift
middle—for which the best I can say is that it 's always
rueful and never impudent—reigns with even more than
its customary contrition, though passing itself off perhaps too with more than its usual craft. Nowhere, I
seem to recall, had the need of dissimulation been felt so
as anguish; nowhere had I condemned a luckless theme
to complete its revolution, burdened with the accumulation of its difficulties, the difficulties that grow with a
theme's development, in quarters so cramped. Of
course, as every novelist knows, it is difficulty that
inspires; only, for that perfection of charm, it must have
been difficulty inherent and congenital, and not difficulty
"caught" by the wrong frequentations. The latter half,
that is the false and deformed half, of "The Wings"
would verily, I think, form a signal object-lesson for a
literary critic bent on improving his occasion to the
profit of the budding artist. This whole corner of the
picture bristles with "dodges"—such as he should feel

himself all committed to recognise and denounce—for
disguising the reduced scale of the exhibition, for foreshortening at any cost, for imparting to patches the
value of presences, for dressing objects in an *air* as of
the dimensions they can't possibly have. Thus he would
have his free hand for pointing out what a tangled web
we weave when—well, when, through our mislaying or
otherwise trifling with our blest pair of compasses, we
have to produce the illusion of mass without the illusion of extent. *There* is a job quite to the measure of
most of our monitors—and with the interest for them
well enhanced by the preliminary cunning quest for the
spot where deformity has begun.

I recognise meanwhile, throughout the long earlier
reach of the book, not only no deformities but, I think,
a positively close and felicitous application of method,
the preserved consistencies of which, often illusive, but
never really lapsing, it would be of a certain diversion,
and might be of some profit, to follow. The author's
accepted task at the outset has been to suggest with
force the nature of the tie formed between the two
young persons first introduced—to give the full impression of its peculiar worried and baffled, yet clinging and
confident, ardour. The picture constituted, so far as may
be, is that of a pair of natures well-nigh consumed by a
sense of their intimate affinity and congruity, the reciprocity of their desire, and thus passionately impatient
of barriers and delays, yet with qualities of intelligence
and character that they are meanwhile extraordinarily
able to draw upon for the enrichment of their relation,

the extension of their prospect and the support of their "game." They are far from a common couple, Merton Densher and Kate Croy, as befits the remarkable fashion in which fortune was to waylay and opportunity was to distinguish them—the whole strange truth of their response to which opening involves also, in its order, no vulgar art of exhibition; but what they have most to tell us is that, all unconsciously and with the best faith in the world, all by mere force of the terms of their superior passion combined with their superior diplomacy, they are laying a trap for the great innocence to come. If I like, as I have confessed, the "portentous" look, I was perhaps never to set so high a value on it as for all this prompt provision of forces unwittingly waiting to close round my eager heroine (to the eventual deep chill of her eagerness) as the result of her mere lifting of a latch. Infinitely interesting to have built up the relation of the others to the point at which its aching restlessness, its need to affirm itself otherwise than by an exasperated patience, meets as with instinctive relief and recognition the possibilities shining out of Milly Theale. Infinitely interesting to have prepared and organised, correspondingly, that young woman's precipitations and liabilities, to have constructed, for Drama essentially to take possession, the whole bright house of her exposure.

These references, however, reflect too little of the detail of the treatment imposed; such a detail as I for instance get hold of in the fact of Densher's interview with Mrs. Lowder before he goes to America. It forms, in this preliminary picture, the one patch not strictly

seen over Kate Croy's shoulder; though it 's notable that
immediately after, at the first possible moment, we surrender again to our major convenience, as it happens to
be at the time, that of our drawing breath through the
young woman's lungs. Once more, in other words,
before we know it, Densher's direct vision of the scene
at Lancaster Gate is replaced by her apprehension, her
contributive assimilation, of his experience: it melts back
into that accumulation, which we have been, as it were,
saving up. Does my apparent deviation here count
accordingly as a muddle?—one of the muddles ever
blooming so thick in any soil that fails to grow reasons
and determinants. No, distinctly not; for I had definitely
opened the door, as attention of perusal of the first two
Books will show, to the subjective community of my
young pair. (Attention of perusal, I thus confess by the
way, is what I at every point, as well as here, absolutely
invoke and take for granted; a truth I avail myself of this
occasion to note once for all—in the interest of that variety of ideal reigning, I gather, in the connexion. The
enjoyment of a work of art, the acceptance of an irresistible illusion, constituting, to my sense, our highest
experience of "luxury," the luxury is not greatest, by my
consequent measure, when the work asks for as little
attention as possible. It is greatest, it is delightfully,
divinely great, when we feel the surface, like the thick
ice of the skater's pond, bear without cracking the
strongest pressure we throw on it. The sound of the
crack one may recognise, but never surely to call it a
luxury.) That I had scarce availed myself of the privilege

of seeing with Densher's eyes is another matter; the point is that I had intelligently marked my possible, my occasional need of it. So, at all events, the constructional "block" of the first two Books compactly forms itself. A new block, all of the squarest and not a little of the smoothest, begins with the Third—by which I mean of course a new mass of interest governed from a new centre. Here again I make prudent *provision*—to be sure to keep my centre strong. It dwells mainly, we at once see, in the depths of Milly Theale's "case," where, close beside it, however, we meet a supplementary reflector, that of the lucid even though so quivering spirit of her dedicated friend.

The more or less associated consciousness of the two women deals thus, unequally, with the next presented face of the subject—deals with it to the exclusion of the dealing of others; and if, for a highly particular moment, I allot to Mrs. Stringham the responsibility of the direct appeal to us, it is again, charming to relate, on behalf of that play of the portentous which I cherish so as a "value" and am accordingly for ever setting in motion. There is an hour of evening, on the alpine height, at which it becomes of the last importance that our young woman should testify eminently in this direction. But as I was to find it long since of a blest wisdom that no expense should be incurred or met, in any corner of picture of mine, without some concrete image of the account kept of it, that is of its being organically re-economised, so under that dispensation Mrs. Stringham has to register the transaction. Book Fifth is a new block mainly in its provision of a new set of occasions, which readopt, for their order, the previous centre, Milly's now almost full-blown consciousness. At my game, with renewed zest, of driving portents home, I have by this time all the choice of those that are to brush that surface with a dark wing. They are used, to our profit, on an elastic but a definite system; by which I mean that having to sound here and there a little deep, as a test, for my basis of method, I find it everywhere obstinately present. It draws the "occasion" into tune and keeps it so, to repeat my tiresome term; my nearest approach to muddlement is to have sometimes—but not too often—to break my occasions small. Some of them succeed in remaining ample and in really aspiring then to the higher, the sustained lucidity. The whole actual centre of the work, resting on a misplaced pivot and lodged in Book Fifth, pretends to a long reach, or at any rate to the larger foreshortening—though bringing home to me, on reperusal, what I find striking, charming and curious, the author's instinct everywhere for the *indirect* presentation of his main image. I note how, again and again, I go but a little way with the direct—that is with the straight exhibition of Milly; it resorts for relief, this process, whenever it can, to some kinder, some merciful indirection: all as if to approach her circuitously, deal with her at second hand, as an unspotted princess is ever dealt with; the pressure all round her kept easy for her, the sounds, the movements regulated, the forms and ambiguities made charming. All of which proceeds, obviously, from her painter's tenderness of imagination about her, which reduces him to watching her, as it were, through the successive windows of other people's interest in her. So, if we talk of princesses, do the balconies opposite the palace gates, do the coigns of vantage and respect enjoyed for a fee, rake from afar the mystic figure in the gilded coach as it comes forth into the great *place*. But my use of windows and balconies is doubtless at best an extravagance by itself, and as to what there may be to note, of this and other supersubtleties, other arch-refinements, of tact and taste, of design and instinct, in "The Wings of the Dove," I become conscious of overstepping my space without having brought the full quantity to light. The failure leaves me with a burden of residuary comment of which I yet boldly hope elsewhere to discharge myself.

Volume One

Book First

....

I

SHE WAITED, Kate Croy, for her father to come in, but he kept her unconscionably, and there were moments at which she showed herself, in the glass over the mantel, a face positively pale with the irritation that had brought her to the point of going away without sight of him. It was at this point, however, that she remained; changing her place, moving from the shabby sofa to the armchair upholstered in a glazed cloth that gave at once—she had tried it—the sense of the slippery and of the sticky. She had looked at the sallow prints on the walls and at the lonely magazine, a year old, that combined, with a small lamp in coloured glass and a knitted white centre-piece wanting in freshness, to enhance the effect of the purplish cloth on the principal table; she had above all, from time to time, taken a brief stand on the small balcony to which the pair of long windows gave access. The vulgar little street, in this view, offered scant relief from the vulgar little room; its main office was to suggest to her that the narrow black house-fronts, adjusted to a standard that would have been low even for backs, constituted quite the publicity implied by such privacies. One felt them in the room exactly as one felt the room—the hundred like it, or worse—in the street. Each time she turned in again, each time, in her impatience, she gave him up, it was to sound to a deeper depth, while she tasted the faint, flat emanation of things, the failure of fortune and of honour. If she continued to wait it was really, in a manner, that she might not add the shame of fear, of individual, personal collapse, to all the other shames. To feel the street, to feel the room, to feel the table-cloth and the centre-piece and the lamp, gave her a small, salutary sense, at least, of neither shirking nor lying. This whole vision was the worst thing yet—as including, in particular, the interview for which she had prepared herself; and for what had she come but for the worst? She tried to be sad, so as not to be angry; but it made her angry that she couldn't be sad. And yet where was misery, misery too beaten for blame and chalk-marked by fate like a "lot" at a common auction, if not in these merciless signs of mere mean, stale feelings?

Her father's life, her sister's, her own, that of her two lost brothers—the whole history of their house had the effect of some fine florid, voluminous phrase, say even a musical, that dropped first into words, into notes, without sense, and then, hanging unfinished, into no words, no notes at all. Why should a set of people have been put in motion, on such a scale and with such an air of being equipped for a profitable journey, only to break down without an accident, to stretch themselves in the wayside dust without a reason? The answer to these

questions was not in Chirk Street, but the questions
themselves bristled there, and the girl's repeated pause
before the mirror and the chimney-place might have
represented her nearest approach to an escape from
them. Was it not in fact the partial escape from this
"worst" in which she was steeped to be able to make
herself out again as agreeable to see? She stared into the
tarnished glass too hard indeed to be staring at her
beauty alone. She readjusted the poise of her black,
closely-feathered hat; retouched, beneath it, the thick
fall of her dusky hair; kept her eyes, aslant, no less on
her beautiful averted than on her beautiful presented
oval. She was dressed altogether in black, which gave
an even tone, by contrast, to her clear face and made her
hair more harmoniously dark. Outside, on the balcony,
her eyes showed as blue; within, at the mirror, they
showed almost as black. She was handsome, but the
degree of it was not sustained by items and aids; a circumstance moreover playing its part at almost any time
in the impression she produced. The impression was
one that remained, but as regards the sources of it no
sum in addition would have made up the total. She had
stature without height, grace without motion, presence
without mass. Slender and simple, frequently soundless,
she was somehow always in the line of the eye—she
counted singularly for its pleasure. More "dressed,"
often, with fewer accessories, than other women, or less
dressed, should occasion require, with more, she probably could not have given the key to these felicities.
They were mysteries of which her friends were con-

scious—those friends whose general explanation was to
say that she was clever, whether or no it were taken by
the world as the cause or as the effect of her charm. If
she saw more things than her fine face in the dull glass
of her father's lodgings, she might have seen that, after
all, she was not herself a fact in the collapse. She didn't
judge herself cheap, she didn't make for misery. Personally, at least, she was not chalk-marked for the auction. She hadn't given up yet, and the broken sentence,
if she was the last word, *would* end with a sort of meaning. There was a minute during which, though her eyes
were fixed, she quite visibly lost herself in the thought
of the way she might still pull things round had she only
been a man. It was the name, above all, she would take
in hand—the precious name she so liked and that, in
spite of the harm her wretched father had done it, was
not yet past praying for. She loved it in fact the more
tenderly for that bleeding wound. But what could a penniless girl do with it but let it go?

When her father at last appeared she became, as
usual, instantly aware of the futility of any effort to hold
him to anything. He had written her that he was ill, too
ill to leave his room, and that he must see her without
delay; and if this had been, as was probable, the sketch
of a design, he was indifferent even to the moderate finish required for deception. He had clearly wanted, for
perversities that he called reasons, to see her, just as she
herself had sharpened for a talk; but she now again felt,
in the inevitability of the freedom he used with her, all
the old ache, her poor mother's very own, that he

couldn't touch you ever so lightly without setting up.
No relation with him could be so short or so superficial
as not to be somehow to your hurt; and this, in the
strangest way in the world, not because he desired it to
be—feeling often, as he surely must, the profit for him
of its not being—but because there was never a mistake
for you that he could leave unmade or a conviction of
his impossibility in you that he could approach you
without strengthening. He might have awaited her on
the sofa in his sitting-room, or might have stayed in bed
and received her in that situation. She was glad to be
spared the sight of such *penetralia*, but it would have
reminded her a little less that there was no truth in him.
This was the weariness of every fresh meeting; he dealt
out lies as he might the cards from the greasy old pack
for the game of diplomacy to which you were to sit
down with him. The inconvenience—as always happens
in such cases—was not that you minded what was false,
but that you missed what was true. He might be ill, and
it might suit you to know it, but no contact with him,
for this, could ever be straight enough. Just so he even
might die, but Kate fairly wondered on what evidence of
his own she would some day have to believe it.

He had not at present come down from his room,
which she knew to be above the one they were in: he
had already been out of the house, though he would
either, should she challenge him, deny it or present it
as a proof of his extremity. She had, however, by this
time, quite ceased to challenge him; not only, face to
face with him, vain irritation dropped, but he breathed

upon the tragic consciousness in such a way that after a
moment nothing of it was left. The difficulty was not
less that he breathed in the same way upon the comic:
she almost believed that with this latter she might still
have found a foothold for clinging to him. He had
ceased to be amusing—he was really too inhuman. His
perfect look, which had floated him so long, was practically perfect still; but one had long since for every
occasion taken it for granted. Nothing could have better shown than the actual how right one had been. He
looked exactly as much as usual—all pink and silver as
to skin and hair, all straitness and starch as to figure and
dress—the man in the world least connected with anything unpleasant. He was so particularly the English
gentleman and the fortunate, settled, normal person.
Seen at a foreign *table d'hôte*, he suggested but one
thing: "In what perfection England produces them!" He
had kind, safe eyes, and a voice which, for all its clean
fulness, told, in a manner, the happy history of its having never had once to raise itself. Life had met him so,
half-way, and had turned round so to walk with him,
placing a hand in his arm and fondly leaving him to
choose the pace. Those who knew him a little said,
"How he does dress!"—those who knew him better said,
"How *does* he?" The one stray gleam of comedy just
now in his daughter's eyes was the funny feeling he
momentarily made her have of being herself "looked
up" by him in sordid lodgings. For a minute after he
came in it was as if the place were her own and he the
visitor with susceptibilities. He gave you funny feelings,

he had indescribable arts, that quite turned the tables: that had been always how he came to see her mother so long as her mother would see him. He came from places they had often not known about, but he patronised Lexham Gardens. Kate's only actual expression of impatience, however, was "I'm glad you're so much better!"

"I'm not so much better, my dear—I'm exceedingly unwell; the proof of which is, precisely, that I've been out to the chemist's—that beastly fellow at the corner." So Mr. Croy showed he could qualify the humble hand that assuaged him. "I'm taking something he has made up for me. It's just why I've sent for you—that you may see me as I really am."

"Oh papa, it's long since I've ceased to see you otherwise than as you really are! I think we've all arrived by this time at the right word for that: 'You're beautiful—*n'en parlons plus.*' You're as beautiful as ever—you look lovely." He judged meanwhile her own appearance, as she knew she could always trust him to do; recognising, estimating, sometimes disapproving, what she wore, showing her the interest he continued to take in her. He might really take none at all, yet she virtually knew herself the creature in the world to whom he was least indifferent. She had often enough wondered what on earth, at the pass he had reached, could give him pleasure, and she had come back, on these occasions, to that. It gave him pleasure that she was handsome, that she was, in her way, a sensible value. It was at least as marked, nevertheless, that he derived none from similar conditions, so far as they *were* similar, in his other child. Poor Marian might be handsome, but he certainly didn't care. The hitch here, of course, was that, with whatever beauty, her sister, widowed and almost in want, with four bouncing children, was not a sensible value. She asked him, the next thing, how long he had been in his actual quarters, though aware of how little it mattered, how little any answer he might make would probably have in common with the truth. She failed in fact to notice his answer, truthful or not, already occupied as she was with what she had on her own side to say to him. This was really what had made her wait— what superseded the small remainder of her resentment at his constant practical impertinence; the result of all of which was that, within a minute, she had brought it out. "Yes—even now I'm willing to go with you. I don't know what you may have wished to say to me, and even if you hadn't written you would within a day or two have heard from me. Things have happened, and I've only waited, for seeing you, till I should be quite sure. I *am* quite sure. I'll go with you."

It produced an effect. "Go with me where?"

"Anywhere. I'll stay with you. Even here." She had taken off her gloves and, as if she had arrived with her plan, she sat down.

Lionel Croy hung about in his disengaged way— hovered there as if, in consequence of her words, look-ing for a pretext to back out easily: on which she immediately saw she had discounted, as it might be called, what he had himself been preparing. He wished her not to come to him, still less to settle with him, and

had sent for her to give her up with some style and
state; a part of the beauty of which, however, was to
have been his sacrifice to her own detachment. There
was no style, no state, unless she wished to forsake him.
His idea had accordingly been to surrender her to her
wish with all nobleness; it had by no means been to
have positively to keep her off. She cared, however, not
a straw for his embarrassment—feeling how little, on
her own part, she was moved by charity. She had seen
him, first and last, in so many attitudes that she could
now deprive him quite without compunction of the luxury of a new one. Yet she felt the disconcerted gasp in
his tone as he said: "Oh my child, I can never consent
to that!"

"What then are you going to do?"

"I'm turning it over," said Lionel Croy. "You may
imagine if I'm not thinking."

"Haven't you thought then," his daughter asked, "of
what I speak of? I mean of my being ready."

Standing before her with his hands behind him and
his legs a little apart, he swayed slightly to and fro,
inclined toward her as if rising on his toes. It had an
effect of conscientious deliberation. "No. I haven't. I
couldn't. I wouldn't." It was so respectable a show that
she felt afresh, and with the memory of their old
despair, the despair at home, how little his appearance
ever by any chance told about him. His plausibility had
been the heaviest of her mother's crosses; inevitably so
much more present to the world than whatever it was
that was horrid—thank God they didn't really know!—

that he had done. He had positively been, in his way, by
the force of his particular type, a terrible husband not to
live with; his type reflecting so invidiously on the
woman who had found him distasteful. Had this thereby
not kept directly present to Kate herself that it might, on
some sides, prove no light thing for her to leave uncom-
panied a parent with·such a face and such a manner?
Yet if there was much she neither knew nor dreamed
of, it passed between them at this very moment that he
was quite familiar with himself as the subject of such
quandaries. If he recognised his younger daughter's
happy aspect as a sensible value, he had from the first
still more exactly appraised his own. The great wonder
was not that in spite of everything his own had helped
him; the great wonder was that it hadn't helped him
more. However, it was, to its old, eternal, recurrent
tune, helping him all the while; her drop into patience
with him showed how it was helping him at this
moment. She saw the next instant precisely the line he
would take. "Do you really ask me to believe you've
been making up your mind to that?"

She had to consider her own line. "I don't think I
care, papa, what you believe. I never, for that matter,
think of you as believing anything; hardly more," she
permitted herself to add, "than I ever think of you as
yourself believed. I don't know you, father, you see."

"And it's your idea that you may make that up?"

"Oh dear, no; not at all. That's no part of the question. If I haven't understood you by this time, I never
shall, and it doesn't matter. It has seemed to me that

you may be lived with, but not that you may be understood. Of course I've not the least idea how you get on."

"I don't get on," Mr. Croy almost gaily replied.

His daughter took in the place again, and it might well have seemed odd that in so little to meet the eye there should be so much to show. What showed was the ugliness—so positive and palpable that it was somehow sustaining. It was a medium, a setting, and to that extent, after all, a dreadful sign of life; so that it fairly put a point into her answer. "Oh, I beg your pardon. You flourish."

"Do you throw it up at me again," he pleasantly inquired, "that I've not made away with myself?"

She treated the question as needing no reply; she sat there for real things. "You know how all our anxieties, under mamma's will, have come out. She had still less to leave than she feared. We don't know how we lived. It all makes up about two hundred a year for Marian, and two for me, but I give up a hundred to Marian."

"Oh, you weak thing!" her father kindly sighed.

"For you and me together," she went on, "the other hundred would do something."

"And what would do the rest?"

"Can you yourself do nothing?"

He gave her a look; then, slipping his hands into his pockets and turning away, stood for a little at the window she had left open. She said nothing more—she had placed him there with that question, and the silence lasted a minute, broken by the call of an appealing costermonger, which came in with the mild March air, with the shabby sunshine, fearfully unbecoming to the room, and with the small homely hum of Chirk Street. Presently he moved nearer, but as if her question had quite dropped. "I don't see what has so suddenly wound you up."

"I should have thought you might perhaps guess. Let me at any rate tell you. Aunt Maud has made me a proposal. But she has also made me a condition. She wants to keep me."

"And what in the world else *could* she possibly want?"

"Oh, I don't know—many things. I'm not so precious a capture," the girl a little dryly explained. "No one has ever wanted to keep me before."

Looking always what was proper, her father looked now still more surprised than interested. "You've not had proposals?" He spoke as if that were incredible of Lionel Croy's daughter; as if indeed such an admission scarce consorted, even in filial intimacy, with her high spirit and general form.

"Not from rich relations. She's extremely kind to me, but it's time, she says, that we should understand each other."

Mr. Croy fully assented. "Of course it is—high time; and I can quite imagine what she means by it."

"Are you very sure?"

"Oh, perfectly. She means that she'll 'do' for you handsomely if you'll break off all relations with me. You speak of her condition. Her condition's of course that."

"Well then," said Kate, "it's what has wound me up. Here I am."

He showed with a gesture how thoroughly he had taken it in; after which, within a few seconds, he had, quite congruously, turned the situation about. "Do you really suppose me in a position to justify your throwing yourself upon me?"

She waited a little, but when she spoke it was clear. "Yes."

"Well then, you're a bigger fool than I should have ventured to suppose you."

"Why so? You live. You flourish. You bloom."

"Ah, how you've all always hated me!" he murmured with a pensive gaze again at the window.

"No one could be less of a mere cherished memory," she declared as if she had not heard him. "You're an actual person, if there ever was one. We agreed just now that you're beautiful. You strike me, you know, as—in your own way—much more firm on your feet than I am. Don't put it to me therefore as monstrous that the fact that we are, after all, parent and child should at present in some manner count for us. My idea has been that it should have some effect for each of us. I don't at all, as I told you just now," she pursued, "make out your life; but whatever it is I hereby offer you to accept it. And, on my side, I'll do everything I can for you."

"I see," said Lionel Croy. Then, with the sound of extreme relevance, "And what *can* you?" She only, at this, hesitated, and he took up her silence. "You can describe yourself—*to* yourself—as, in a fine flight, giving up your aunt for me; but what good, I should like to know, would your fine flight do me?" As she still said

nothing he developed a little. "We're not possessed of
so much, at this charming pass, please to remember, as
that we can afford not to take hold of any perch held out
to us. I like the way you talk, my dear, about 'giving up'!
One doesn't give up the use of a spoon because one's
reduced to living on broth. And your spoon, that is your
aunt, please consider, is partly mine as well." She rose
now, as if in sight of the term of her effort, in sight of the
futility and the weariness of many things, and moved
back to the poor little glass with which she had com-
muned before. She retouched here again the poise of her
hat, and this brought to her father's lips another
remark—in which impatience, however, had already
been replaced by a funny flare of appreciation. "Oh,
you're all right! Don't muddle yourself up with *me!*"

His daughter turned round to him. "The condition
Aunt Maud makes is that I shall have absolutely nothing to do with you; never see you, nor speak, nor write
to you, never go near you nor make you a sign, nor hold
any sort of communication with you. What she requires
is that you shall simply cease to exist for me."

He had always seemed—it was one of the marks of
what they called the "unspeakable" in him—to walk a
little more on his toes, as if for jauntiness, in the presence of offence. Nothing, however, was more wonderful than what he sometimes would take for offence,
unless it might be what he sometimes wouldn't. He
walked at any rate on his toes now. "A very proper
requirement of your Aunt Maud, my dear—I don't hesitate to say it!" Yet as this, much as she had seen, left

her silent at first from what might have been a sense of sickness, he had time to go on: "That's her condition then. But what are her promises? Just what does she engage to do? You must work it, you know."

"You mean make her feel," Kate asked after a moment, "how much I'm attached to you?"

"Well, what a cruel, invidious treaty it is for you to sign. I'm a poor old dad to make a stand about giving up—I quite agree. But I'm not, after all, quite the old dad not to get something *for* giving up."

"Oh, I think her idea," said Kate almost gaily now, "is that I shall get a great deal."

He met her with his inimitable amenity. "But does she give you the items?"

The girl went through the show. "More or less, I think. But many of them are things I dare say I may take for granted—things women can do for each other and that you wouldn't understand."

"There's nothing I understand so well, always, as the things I needn't! But what I want to do, you see," he went on, "is to put it to your conscience that you've an admirable opportunity; and that it's moreover one for which, after all, damn you, you've really to thank *me*."

"I confess I don't see," Kate observed, "what my 'conscience' has to do with it."

"Then, my dear girl, you ought simply to be ashamed of yourself. Do you know what you're a proof of, all you hard, hollow people together?" He put the question with a charming air of sudden spiritual heat. "Of the deplorably superficial morality of the age. The family

sentiment, in our vulgarised, brutalised life, has gone
utterly to pot. There was a day when a man like me—by
which I mean a parent like me—would have been for a
daughter like you a quite distinct value; what's called
in the business world, I believe, an 'asset.' " He continued sociably to make it out. "I'm not talking only of
what you might, with the right feeling do *for* me, but
of what you might—it's, what I call your opportunity—
do *with* me. Unless indeed," he the next moment imperturbably threw off, "they come a good deal to the same
thing. Your duty as well as your chance, if you're capable of seeing it, is to use me. Show family feeling by seeing what I'm good for. If you had it as *I* have it you'd
see I'm still good—well, for a lot of things. There's in
fact, my dear," Mr. Croy wound up, "a coach-and-four
to be got out of me." His drop, or rather his climax,
failed a little of effect, indeed, through an undue pre-
cipitation of memory. Something his daughter had said
came back to him. "You've settled to give away half
your little inheritance?"

Her hesitation broke into laughter. "No—I haven't
'settled' anything."

"But you mean, practically, to let Marian collar it?"
They stood there face to face, but she so denied herself
to his challenge that he could only go on. "You've a view
of three hundred a year for her in addition to what her
husband left her with? Is *that*," the remote progenitor of
such wantonness audibly wondered, "your morality?"

Kate found her answer without trouble. "Is it your
idea that I should give you everything?"

The "everything" clearly struck him—to the point even of determining the tone of his reply. "Far from it. How can you ask that when I refuse what you tell me you came to offer? Make of my idea what you can; I think I've sufficiently expressed it, and it's at any rate to take or to leave. It's the only one, I may nevertheless add; it's the basket with all my eggs. It's my conception, in short, of your duty."

The girl's tired smile watched the word as if it had taken on a small grotesque visibility. "You're wonderful on such subjects! I think I should leave you in no doubt," she pursued, "that if I were to sign my aunt's agreement I should carry it out, in honour, to the letter."

"Rather, my own love! It's just your honour that I appeal to. The only way to play the game *is* to play it. There's no limit to what your aunt can do for you."

"Do you mean in the way of marrying me?"

"What else should I mean? Marry properly——"

"And then?" Kate asked as he hung fire.

"And then—well, I *will* talk with you. I'll resume relations."

She looked about her and picked up her parasol. "Because you're not so afraid of any one else in the world as you are of *her*? My husband, if I should marry, would be, at the worst, less of a terror? If that's what you mean, there may be something in it. But doesn't it depend a little also on what you mean by my getting a proper one? However," Kate added as she picked out the frill of her little umbrella, "I don't suppose your idea of him is *quite* that he should persuade you to live with us."

"Dear no—not a bit." He spoke as not resenting either the fear or the hope she imputed; met both imputations, in fact, with a sort of intellectual relief. "I place the case for you wholly in your aunt's hands. I take her view, with my eyes shut; I accept in all confidence any man she selects. If he's good enough for *her*—elephantine snob as she is—he's good enough for me; and quite in spite of the fact that she'll be sure to select one who can be trusted to be nasty to me. My only interest is in your doing what she wants. You shan't be so beastly poor, my darling," Mr. Croy declared, "if I can help it."

"Well then, good-bye, papa," the girl said after a reflection on this that had perceptibly ended for her in a renunciation of further debate. "Of course you understand that it may be for long."

Her companion, hereupon, had one of his finest inspirations. "Why not, frankly, for ever? You must do me the justice to see that I don't do things, that I've never done them, by halves—that if I offer you to efface myself, it's for the final, fatal sponge that I ask, well saturated and well applied."

She turned her handsome, quiet face upon him at such length that it might well have been for the last time. "I don't know what you're like."

"No more do I, my dear. I've spent my life in trying, in vain, to discover. Like nothing—more's the pity. If there had been many of us, and we could have found each other out, there's no knowing what we mightn't have done. But it doesn't matter now. Good-bye, love."

He looked even not sure of what she would wish him to suppose on the subject of a kiss, yet also not embarrassed by his uncertainty.

She forbore in fact for a moment longer to clear it up. "I wish there were some one here who might serve—for any contingency—as a witness that I *have* put it to you that I'm ready to come."

"Would you like me," her father asked, "to call the landlady?"

"You may not believe me," she pursued, "but I came really hoping you might have found some way. I'm very sorry, at all events, to leave you unwell." He turned away from her, on this, and, as he had done before, took refuge, by the window, in a stare at the street. "Let me put it—unfortunately without a witness," she added after a moment, "that there's only one word you really need speak."

When he took this up it was still with his back to her. "If I don't strike you as having already spoken it, our time has been singularly wasted."

"I'll engage with you in respect to my aunt exactly to what she wants of me in respect to you. She wants me to choose. Very well, I *will* choose. I'll wash my hands of her for you to just that tune."

He at last brought himself round. "Do you know, dear, you make me sick? I've tried to be clear, and it isn't fair."

But she passed this over; she was too visibly sincere. "Father!"

"I don't quite see what's the matter with you," he

said, "and if you can't pull yourself together I'll—upon my honour—take you in hand. Put you into a cab and deliver you again safe at Lancaster Gate."

She was really absent, distant. "Father."

It was too much, and he met it sharply. "Well?"

"Strange as it may be to you to hear me say it, there's a good you can do me and a help you can render."

"Isn't it then exactly what I've been trying to make you feel?"

"Yes," she answered patiently, "but so in the wrong way. I'm perfectly honest in what I say, and I know what I'm talking about. It isn't that I'll pretend I could have believed a month ago in anything to call aid or support from you. The case is changed—that's what has happened; my difficulty's a new one. But even now it's not a question of anything I should ask you in a way to 'do.' It's simply a question of your not turning me away—taking yourself out of my life. It's simply a question of your saying: 'Yes then, since you will, we'll stand together. We won't worry in advance about how or where; we'll have a faith and find a way.' That's all— *that* would be the good you'd do me. I should *have* you, and it would be for my benefit. Do you see?"

If he didn't it was not for want of looking at her hard. "The matter with you is that you're in love, and that your aunt knows and—for reasons, I'm sure, perfect— hates and opposes it. Well she may! It's a matter in which I trust her with my eyes shut. Go, please." Though he spoke not in anger—rather in infinite sadness—he fairly turned her out. Before she took it up he had, as the fullest expression of what he felt, opened the door of the room. He had fairly, in his deep disapproval, a generous compassion to spare. "I'm sorry for her, deluded woman, if she builds on you."

Kate stood a moment in the draught. "She's not the person *I* pity most, for, deluded in many ways though she may be, she's not the person who's most so. I mean," she explained, "if it's a question of what you call building on me."

He took it as if what she meant might be other than her description of it. "You're deceiving *two* persons then, Mrs. Lowder and somebody else?"

She shook her head with detachment. "I've no intention of that sort with respect to any one now—to Mrs. Lowder least of all. If you fail me"—she seemed to make it out for herself—"that has the merit at least that it simplifies. I shall go my way—as I see my way."

"Your way, you mean then, will be to marry some blackguard without a penny?"

"You ask a great deal of satisfaction," she observed, "for the little you give."

It brought him up again before her as with a sense that she was not to be hustled; and, though he glared at her a little, this had long been the practical limit to his general power of objection. "If you're base enough to incur your aunt's disgust, you're base enough for my argument. What, if you're not thinking of an utterly improper person, do your speeches to me signify? Who *is* the beggarly sneak?" he demanded as her response failed.

Her response, when it came, was cold but distinct. "He has every disposition to make the best of you. He only wants in fact to be kind to you."

"Then he *must* be an ass! And how in the world can you consider it to improve him for me," her father pursued, "that he's also destitute and impossible? There are asses and asses, even—the right and the wrong—and you appear to have carefully picked out one of the wrong. Your aunt knows *them*, by good fortune; I perfectly trust, as I tell you, her judgment for them; and you may take it from me once for all that I won't hear of any one of whom *she* won't." Which led up to his last word. "If you should really defy us both——!"

"Well, papa?"

"Well, my sweet child, I think that—reduced to insignificance as you may fondly believe me—I should still not be quite without some way of making you regret it."

She had a pause, a grave one, but not, as appeared, that she might measure this danger. "If I shouldn't do it, you know, it wouldn't be because I'm afraid of you."

"Oh, if you don't do it," he retorted, "you may be as bold as you like!"

"Then you can do nothing at all for me?"

He showed her, this time unmistakably—it was before her there on the landing, at the top of the tortuous stairs and in the midst of the strange smell that seemed to _cling to them—how vain her appeal remained. "I've never pretended to do more than my duty; I've given you the best and the clearest advice."

And then came up the spring that moved him. "If it only displeases you, you can go to Marian to be consoled." What he couldn't forgive was her dividing with Marian her scant share of the provision their mother had been able to leave them. She should have divided it with *him*.

II

SHE HAD GONE to Mrs. Lowder on her mother's death—gone with an effort the strain and pain of which made her at present, as she recalled them, reflect on the long way she had travelled since then. There had been nothing else to do—not a penny in the other house, nothing but unpaid bills that had gathered thick while its mistress lay mortally ill, and the admonition that there was nothing she must attempt to raise money on, since everything belonged to the "estate." How the estate would turn out at best presented itself as a mystery altogether gruesome; it had proved, in fact, since then a residuum a trifle less scant than, with Marian, she had for some weeks feared; but the girl had had at the beginning rather a wounded sense of its being watched on behalf of Marian and her children. What on earth was it supposed that *she* wanted to do to it? She wanted in truth only to give up—to abandon her own interest, which she, no doubt, would already have done had not the point been subject to Aunt Maud's sharp intervention. Aunt Maud's intervention was all sharp now, and the other point, the great one, was that it was

to be, in this light, either all put up with or all declined.
Yet at the winter's end, nevertheless, she could scarce
have said what stand she conceived she had taken. It
wouldn't be the first time she had seen herself obliged to
accept with smothered irony other people's interpreta-
tion of her conduct. She often ended by giving up to
them—it seemed really the way to live—the version that
met their convenience.

The tall, rich, heavy house at Lancaster Gate, on the
other side of the Park and the long South Kensington
stretches, had figured to her, through childhood,
through girlhood, as the remotest limit of her vague
young world. It was further off and more occasional
than anything else in the comparatively compact circle
in which she revolved, and seemed, by a rigour early
marked, to be reached through long, straight, discouraging vistas, which kept lengthening and straightening,
whereas almost everything else in life was either, at the
worst, round about Cromwell Road, or, at the furthest,
in the nearer parts of Kensington Gardens. Mrs. Lowder was her only "real" aunt, not the wife of an uncle,
and had been thereby, both in ancient days and when
the greater trouble came, the person, of all persons,
properly to make some sign; in accord with which our
young woman's feeling was founded on the impression,
quite cherished for years, that the signs made across the
interval just mentioned had never been really in the note
of the situation. The main office of this relative, for the
young Croys—apart from giving them their fixed measure of social greatness—had struck them as being to

form them to a conception of what they were not to expect. When Kate came to think matters over with the aid of knowledge, she failed quite to see how Aunt Maud could have been different—she had rather perceived by this time how many other things might have been; yet she also made out that if they had all consciously lived under a liability to the chill breath of *ultima Thule* they couldn't, either, on the facts, very well have done less. What in the event appeared established was that if Mrs. Lowder had disliked them she had yet not disliked them so much as they supposed. It had at any rate been for the purpose of showing how she struggled with her aversion that she sometimes came to see them, that she at regular periods invited them to her house, and in short, as it now looked, kept them along on the terms that would best give her sister the perennial luxury of a grievance. This sister, poor Mrs. Croy, the girl knew, had always judged her resentfully, and had brought them up, Marian, the boys and herself, to the idea of a particular attitude, for signs of the practice of which they watched each other with awe. The attitude was to make plain to Aunt Maud, with the same regularity as her invitations, that they sufficed—thanks awfully—to themselves. But the ground of it, Kate lived to discern, was that this was only because *she* didn't suffice to them. The little she offered was to be accepted under protest, yet not, really, because it was excessive. It wounded them—there was the rub!—because it fell short.

The number of new things our young lady looked out

on from the high south window that hung over the
Pàrk—this number was so great (though some of the
things were only old ones altered and, as the phrase was
of other matters, done up), that life at present turned to
her view from week to week more and more the face of
a striking and distinguished stranger. She had reached
a great age—for it quite seemed to her that at twenty-
five it was late to reconsider; and her most general sense
was a shade of regret that she had not known earlier.
The world was different—whether for worse or for better—from her rudimentary readings, and it gave her the
feeling of a wasted past. If she had only known sooner
she might have arranged herself more to meet it. She
made, at all events, discoveries every day, some of which
were about herself and others about other persons. Two
of these—one under each head—more particularly
engaged, in alternation, her anxiety. She saw as she had
never seen before how material things spoke to her. She
saw, and she blushed to see, that if, in contrast with
some of its old aspects, life now affected her as a dress
successfully "done up," this was exactly by reason of the
trimmings and lace, was a matter of ribbons and silk
and velvet. She had a dire accessibility to pleasure from
such sources. She liked the charming quarters her aunt
had assigned her—liked them literally more than she
had in all her other days liked anything; and nothing
could have been more uneasy than her suspicion of her
relative's view of this truth. Her relative was prodigious—she had never done her relative justice. These
larger conditions all tasted of her, from morning till

night; but she was a person in respect to whom the growth of acquaintance could only—strange as it might seem—keep your heart in your mouth.

The girl's second great discovery was that, so far from having been for Mrs. Lowder a subject of superficial consideration, the blighted home in Lexham Gardens had haunted her nights and her days. Kate had spent, all winter, hours of observation that were not less pointed for being spent alone; recent events, which her mourning explained, assured her a measure of isolation, and it was in the isolation above all that her neighbour's influence worked. Sitting far downstairs Aunt Maud was yet a presence from which a sensitive niece could feel herself extremely under pressure. She knew herself now, the sensitive niece, as having been marked from far back. She knew more than she could have told you, by the upstairs fire, in a whole dark December afternoon. She knew so much that her knowledge was what fairly kept her there, making her at times circulate more endlessly between the small silk-covered sofa that stood for her in the firelight and the great grey map of Middlesex spread beneath her lookout. To go down, to forsake her refuge, was to meet some of her discoveries half-way, to have to face them or fly before them; whereas they were at such a height only like the rumble of a far-off siege heard in the provisioned citadel. She had almost liked, in these weeks, what had created her suspense and her stress: the loss of her mother, the submersion of her father, the discomfort of her sister, the confirmation of their shrunken prospects, the certainty, in especial, of her having to recognise that, should she behave, as she called it, decently—that is still do something for others—she would be herself wholly without supplies. She held that she had a right to sadness and stillness; she nursed them for their postponing power. What they mainly postponed was the question of a surrender—though she could not yet have said exactly of what: a general surrender of everything—that was at moments the way it presented itself—to Aunt Maud's looming "personality." It was by her personality that Aunt Maud was prodigious, and the great mass of it loomed because, in the thick, the foglike air of her arranged existence, there were parts doubtless magnified and parts certainly vague. They represented at all events alike, the dim and the distinct, a strong will and a high hand. It was perfectly present to Kate that she might be devoured, and she likened herself to a trembling kid, kept apart a day or two till her turn should come, but sure sooner or later to be introduced into the cage of the lioness.

The cage was Aunt Maud's own room, her office, her counting-house, her battlefield, her especial scene, in fine, of action, situated on the ground-floor, opening from the main hall and figuring rather to our young woman on exit and entrance as a guardhouse or a toll-gate. The lioness waited—the kid had at least that consciousness; was aware of the neighbourhood of a morsel she had reason to suppose tender. She would have been meanwhile a wonderful lioness for a show, an extraordinary figure in a cage or anywhere; majestic, magnificent, high-coloured, all brilliant gloss, perpetual satin,

twinkling bugles and flashing gems, with a lustre of
agate eyes, a sheen of raven hair, a polish of complexion that was like that of well-kept china and that—as if
the skin were too tight—told especially at curves and
corners. Her niece had a quiet name for her—she kept it
quiet; thinking of her, with a free fancy, as somehow
typically insular, she talked to herself of Britannia of the
Market Place—Britannia unmistakable, but with a pen
in her ear, and felt she should not be happy till she
might on some occasion add to the rest of the panoply
a helmet, a shield, a trident and a ledger. It wasn't in
truth, however, that the forces with which, as Kate felt,
she would have to deal were those most suggested by
an image simple and broad; she was learning after all
each day to know her companion, and what she had
already most perceived was the mistake of trusting to
easy analogies. There was a whole side of Britannia, the
side of her florid philistinism, her plumes and her train,
her fantastic furniture and heaving bosom, the false gods
of her taste and false notes of her talk, the sole contemplation of which would be dangerously misleading. She
was a complex and subtle Britannia, as passionate as she
was practical, with a reticule for her prejudices as deep
as that other pocket, the pocket full of coins stamped in
her image, that the world best knew her by. She carried
on, in short, behind her aggressive and defensive front,
operations determined by her wisdom. It was in fact,
we have hinted, as a besieger that our young lady, in the
provisioned citadel, had for the present most to think
of her, and what made her formidable in this character

was that she was unscrupulous and immoral. So, at all
events, in silent sessions and a youthful off-hand way,
Kate conveniently pictured her: what this sufficiently
represented being that her weight was in the scale of
certain dangers—those dangers that, by our showing,
made the younger woman linger and lurk above, while
the elder, below, both militant and diplomatic, covered
as much of the ground as possible. Yet what were the
dangers, after all, but just the dangers of life and of
London? Mrs. Lowder *was* London, *was* life—the roar
of the siege and the thick of the fray. There were some
things, after all, of which Britannia was afraid; but Aunt
Maud was afraid of nothing—not even, it would appear,
of arduous thought.

These impressions, none the less, Kate kept so much
to herself that she scarce shared them with poor Marian,
the ostensible purpose of her frequent visits to whom
yet continued to be to talk over everything. One of her
reasons for holding off from the last concession to Aunt
Maud was that she might be the more free to commit
herself to this so much nearer and so much less fortunate relative, with whom Aunt Maud would have,
directly, almost nothing to do. The sharpest pinch of
her state, meanwhile, was exactly that all intercourse
with her sister had the effect of casting down her
courage and tying her hands, adding daily to her sense
of the part, not always either uplifting or sweetening,
that the bond of blood might play in one's life. She was
face to face with it now, with the bond of blood; the
consciousness of it was what she seemed most clearly to

have "come into" by the death of her mother, much of
that consciousness as her mother had absorbed and carried away. Her haunting, harrassing father, her menacing, uncompromising aunt, her portionless little
nephews and nieces, were figures that caused the chord
of natural piety superabundantly to vibrate. Her manner
of putting it to herself—but more especially in respect to
Marian—was that she saw what you might be brought
to by the cultivation of consanguinity. She had taken,
in the old days, as she supposed, the measure of this liability; those being the days when, as the second-born,
she had thought no one in the world so pretty as Marian, no one so charming, so clever, so assured, in
advance, of happiness and success. The view was different now, but her attitude had been obliged, for many
reasons, to show as the same. The subject of this estimate was no longer pretty, as the reason for thinking her
clever was no longer plain; yet, bereaved, disappointed,
demoralised, querulous, she was all the more sharply
and insistently Kate's elder and Kate's own. Kate's most
constant feeling about her was that she would make her,
Kate, do things; and always, in comfortless Chelsea, at
the door of the small house the small rent of which she
couldn't help having on her mind, she fatalistically
asked herself, before going in, which thing it would
probably be this time. She noticed with profundity that
disappointment made people selfish; she marvelled at
the serenity—it was the poor woman's only one—of
what Marian took for granted: her own state of abasement as the second-born, her life reduced to mere inex-

haustible sisterhood. She existed, in that view, wholly for the small house in Chelsea; the moral of which moreover, of course, was that the more one gave oneself the less of one was left. There were always people to snatch at one, and it would never occur to *them* that they were eating one up. They did that without tasting.

There was no such misfortune, or at any rate no such discomfort, she further reasoned, as to be formed at once for being and for seeing. You always saw, in this case, something else than what you were, and you got, in consequence, none of the peace of your condition. However, as she never really let Marian see what she was, Marian might well not have been aware that she herself saw. Kate was accordingly, to her own vision, not a hypocrite of virtue, for she gave herself up; but she was a hypocrite of stupidity, for she kept to herself everything that was not herself. What she most kept was the particular sentiment with which she watched her sister instinctively neglect nothing that would make for her submission to their aunt; a state of the spirit that perhaps marked most sharply how poor you might become when you minded so much the absence of wealth. It was through Kate that Aunt Maud should be worked, and nothing mattered less than what might become of Kate in the process. Kate was to burn her ships, in short, so that Marian should profit; and Marian's desire to profit was quite oblivious of a dignity that had, after all, its reasons—if it had only cared for them—for keeping itself a little stiff. Kate, to be properly stiff for both of them, would therefore have had to be selfish, have had to prefer an ideal of behaviour—than which nothing, ever, was more selfish—to the possibility of stray crumbs for the four small creatures. The tale of Mrs. Lowder's disgust at her elder niece's marriage to Mr. Condrip had lost little of its point; the incredibly fatuous behaviour of Mr. Condrip, the parson of a dull suburban parish, with a saintly profile which was always in evidence, being so distinctly on record to keep criticism consistent. He had presented his profile on system, having, goodness knew, nothing else to present—nothing at all to full-face the world with, no imagination of the propriety of living and minding his business. Criticism had remained on Aunt Maud's part consistent enough; she was not a person to regard such proceedings as less of a mistake for having acquired more of the privilege of pathos. She had not been forgiving, and the only approach she made to overlooking them was by overlooking—with the surviving delinquent—the solid little phalanx that now represented them. Of the two sinister ceremonies that she lumped together, the marriage and the interment, she had been present at the former, just as she had sent Marian, before it, a liberal cheque; but this had not been for her more than the shadow of an admitted link with Mrs. Condrip's course. She disapproved of clamorous children for whom there was no prospect; she disapproved of weeping widows who couldn't make their errors good; and she had thus put within Marian's reach one of the few luxuries left when so much else had gone, an easy pretext for a constant grievance. Kate Croy remembered well what their mother, in a different quarter, had made of it; and it was Marian's marked failure to pluck the fruit of resentment that committed them, as sisters, to an almost equal fellowship in abjection. If the theory was that, yes, alas, one of the pair had ceased to be noticed, but that the other was noticed enough to make up for it, who would fail to see that Kate couldn't separate herself without a cruel pride? That lesson became sharp for our young lady the day after her interview with her father.

"I can't imagine," Marian on this occasion said to her, "how you can think of anything else in the world but the horrid way we're situated."

"And, pray, how do you know," Kate inquired in reply, "anything about my thoughts? It seems to me I give you sufficient proof of how much I think of *you*. I don't, really, my dear, know what else you've to do with!"

Marian's retort, on this, was a stroke as to which she had supplied herself with several kinds of preparation, but there was, none the less, something of an unexpected note in its promptitude. She had foreseen her sister's general fear; but here, ominously, was the special one. "Well, your own business is of course your own business, and you may say there's no one less in a position than I to preach to you. But, all the same, if you wash your hands of me for ever for it, I won't, for this once, keep back that I don't consider you've a right, as we all stand, to throw yourself away."

It was after the children's dinner, which was also their

mother's, but which their aunt mostly contrived to keep
from ever becoming her own luncheon; and the two
young women were still in the presence of the crumpled
table-cloth, the dispersed pinafores, the scraped dishes,
the lingering odour of boiled food. Kate had asked, with
ceremony, if she might put up a window a little, and
Mrs. Condrip had replied without it that she might do
as she liked. She often received such inquiries as if they
reflected in a manner on the pure essence of her little
ones. The four had retired, with much movement and
noise, under imperfect control of the small Irish gov-
erness whom their aunt had hunted out for them and
whose brooding resolve not to prolong so uncrowned a
martyrdom she already more than suspected. Their
mother had become for Kate—who took it just for the
effect of being their mother—quite a different thing
from the mild Marian of the past: Mr. Condrip's widow
expansively obscured that image. She was little more
than a ragged relic, a plain, prosaic result of him, as if
she had somehow been pulled through him as through
an obstinate funnel, only to be left crumpled and useless
and with nothing in her but what he accounted for. She
had grown red and almost fat, which were not happy
signs of mourning; less and less like any Croy, particularly a Croy in trouble, and sensibly like her husband's
two unmarried sisters, who came to see her, in Kate's
view, much too often and stayed too long, with the consequence of inroads upon the tea and bread-and-butter
—matters as to which Kate, not unconcerned with the
tradesmen's books, had feelings. About them, moreover,

Marian *was* touchy, and her nearer relative, who observed and weighed things, noted as an oddity that she would have taken any reflection on them as a reflection on herself. If that was what marriage necessarily did to you, Kate Croy would have questioned marriage. It was a grave example, at any rate, of what a man—and such a man!—might make of a woman. She could see how the Condrip pair pressed their brother's widow on the subject of Aunt Maud—who wasn't, after all, *their* aunt; made her, over their interminable cups, chatter and even swagger about Lancaster Gate, made her more vulgar than it had seemed written that any Croy could possibly become on such a subject. They laid it down, they rubbed it in, that Lancaster Gate was to be kept in sight, and that she, Kate, was to keep it; so that, curiously, or at all events sadly, our young woman was sure of being, in her own person, more permitted to them as an object of comment than they would in turn ever be permitted to herself. The beauty of which, too, was that Marian didn't love them. But they were Condrips—they had grown near the rose; they were almost like Bertie and Maudie, like Kitty and Guy. They talked of the dead to her, which Kate never did; it being a relation in which Kate could but mutely listen. She couldn't indeed too often say to herself that if that was what marriage did to you——! It may easily be guessed, therefore, that the ironic light of such reserves fell straight across the field of Marian's warning. "I don't quite see," she answered, "where, in particular, it strikes you that my danger lies. I'm not conscious, I assure you, of the least disposition to 'throw' myself anywhere. I feel as if, for the present, I have been quite sufficiently thrown."

"You don't feel"—Marian brought it all out—"as if you would like to marry Merton Densher?"

Kate took a moment to meet this inquiry. "Is it your idea that if I should feel so I would be bound to give you notice, so that you might step in and head me off? Is that your idea?" the girl asked. Then, as her sister also had a pause, "I don't know what makes you talk of Mr. Densher," she observed.

"I talk of him just because you don't. That you never do, in spite of what I know—that's what makes me think of him. Or rather perhaps it's what makes me think of *you*. If you don't know by this time what I hope for you, what I dream of—my attachment being what it is—it's no use my attempting to tell you." But Marian had in fact warmed to her work, and Kate was sure she had discussed Mr. Densher with the Miss Condrips. "If I name that person I suppose it's because I'm so afraid of him. If you want really to know, he fills me with terror. If you want really to know, in fact, I dislike him as much as I dread him."

"And yet don't think it dangerous to abuse him to me?"

"Yes," Mrs. Condrip confessed, "I do think it dangerous; but how can I speak of him otherwise? I dare say, I admit, that I shouldn't speak of him at all. Only I do want you for once, as I said just now, to know."

"To know what, my dear?"

"That I should regard it," Marian promptly

returned, "as far and away the worst thing that has happened to us yet."

"Do you mean because he hasn't money?"

"Yes, for one thing. And because I don't believe in him."

Kate was civil, but perfunctory. "What do you mean by not believing in him?"

"Well, being sure he'll never get it. And you *must* have it. You *shall* have it."

"To give it to you?"

Marian met her with a readiness that was practically pert. "To *have* it, first. Not, at any rate, to go on not having it. Then we should see."

"We should indeed!" said Kate Croy. It was talk of a kind she loathed, but if Marian chose to be vulgar what was one to do? It made her think of the Miss Condrips with renewed aversion. "I like the way you arrange things—I like what you take for granted. If it's so easy for us to marry men who want us to scatter gold, I wonder we any of us do anything else. I don't see so many of them about, nor what interest I might ever have for them. You live, my dear," she presently added, "in a world of vain thoughts."

"Not so much as you, Kate; for I see what I see, and you can't turn it off that way." The elder sister paused long enough for the younger's face to show, in spite of superiority, an apprehension. "I'm not talking of any man but Aunt Maud's man, nor of any money, even, if you like, but Aunt Maud's money. I'm not talking of anything but your doing what *she* wants. You're wrong if you speak of anything that I want of you; I want nothing but what she does. That's good enough for me!"— and Marian's tone struck her companion as dreadful. "If I don't believe in Merton Densher, I do at least in Mrs. Lowder."

"Your ideas are the more striking," Kate returned, "that they're the same as papa's. I had them from him, you may be interested to know—and with all the brilliancy you may imagine—yesterday."

Marian clearly was interested to know. "He has been to see you?"

"No, I went to him."

"Really?" Marian wondered. "For what purpose?"

"To tell him I'm ready to go to him."

Marian stared. "To leave Aunt Maud——?"

"For my father, yes."

She had fairly flushed, poor Mrs. Condrip, with horror. "You're ready——?"

"So I told him. I couldn't tell him less."

"And pray, could you tell him more?" Marian gasped in her distress. "What in the world is he *to* us? You bring out such a thing as that this way?"

They faced each other—the tears were in Marian's eyes. Kate watched them there a moment and then said: "I had thought it well over—over and over. But you needn't feel injured. I'm not going. He won't have me."

Her companion still panted—it took time to subside. "Well, *I* wouldn't have you—wouldn't receive you at all, I can assure you—if he had made you any other answer. I do feel injured—at your having been willing.

If you were to go to papa, my dear, you would have to stop coming to me." Marian put it thus, indefinably, as a picture of privation from which her companion might shrink. Such were the threats she could complacently make, could think herself masterful for making. "But if he won't take you," she continued, "he shows at least his sharpness."

Marian had always her views of sharpness; she was, as her sister privately commented, great on it. But Kate had her refuge from irritation. "He won't take me," she simply repeated. "But he believes, like you, in Aunt Maud. He threatens me with his curse if I leave her."

"So you *won't?*" As the girl at first said nothing her companion caught at it. "You won't, of course? I see you won't. But I don't see why, nevertheless, I shouldn't insist to you once for all on the plain truth of the whole matter. The truth, my dear, of your duty. Do you ever think about *that?* It's the greatest duty of all."

"There you are again," Kate laughed. "Papa's also immense on my duty."

"Oh, I don't pretend to be immense, but I pretend to know more than you do of life; more even perhaps than papa." Marian seemed to see that personage at this moment, nevertheless, in the light of a kinder irony. "Poor old papa!"

She sighed it with as many condonations as her sister's ear had more than once caught in her "Dear old Aunt Maud!" These were things that made Kate, for the time, turn sharply away, and she gathered herself now to go. They were the note again of the abject; it was hard

to say which of the persons in question had most shown
how little they liked her. The younger woman proposed,
at any rate, to let discussion rest, and she believed that,
for herself, she had done so during the ten minutes that,
thanks to her wish not to break off short, elapsed before
she could gracefully withdraw. It then appeared, however, that Marian had been discussing still, and there
was something that, at the last, Kate had to take up.
"Whom do you mean by Aunt Maud's young man?"

"Whom should I mean but Lord Mark?"

"And where do you pick up such vulgar twaddle?"
Kate demanded with her clear face. "How does such
stuff, in this hole, get to you?"

She had no sooner spoken than she asked herself what
had become of the grace to which she had sacrificed.
Marian certainly did little to save it, and nothing indeed
was so inconsequent as her ground of complaint. She
desired her to "work" Lancaster Gate as she believed
that scene of abundance could be worked; but she now
didn't see why advantage should be taken of the bloated
connection to put an affront on her own poor home. She
appeared in fact for the moment to take the position that
Kate kept her in her "hole" and then heartlessly
reflected on her being in it. Yet she didn't explain how
she had picked up the report on which her sister had
challenged her—so that it was thus left to her sister to
see in it, once more, a sign of the creeping curiosity of
the Miss Condrips. They lived in a deeper hole than
Marian, but they kept their ear to the ground, they
spent their days in prowling, whereas Marian, in gar-

ments and shoes that seemed steadily to grow looser and
larger, never prowled. There were times when Kate
wondered if the Miss Condrips were offered her by fate
as a warning for her own future—to be taken as showing her what she herself might become at forty if she
let things too recklessly go. What was expected of her
by others—and by so many of them—could, all the
same, on occasion, present itself as beyond a joke; and
this was just now the aspect it particularly wore. She
was not only to quarrel with Merton Densher to oblige
her five spectators—with the Miss Condrips there were
five; she was to set forth in pursuit of Lord Mark on
some preposterous theory of the premium attached to
success. Mrs. Lowder's hand had attached it, and it figured at the end of the course as a bell that would ring,
break out into public clamour, as soon as touched. Kate
reflected sharply enough on the weak points of this fond
fiction, with the result at last of a certain chill for her
sister's confidence; though Mrs. Condrip still took
refuge in the plea—which was after all the great point—
that their aunt would be munificent when their aunt
should be pleased. The exact identity of her candidate
was a detail; what was of the essence was her conception
of the kind of match it was open to her niece to make
with her aid. Marian always spoke of marriages as
"matches," but that was again a detail. Mrs. Lowder's
"aid" meanwhile awaited them—if not to light the way
to Lord Mark, then to somebody better. Marian would
put up, in fine, with somebody better; she only wouldn't
put up with somebody so much worse. Kate had, once

more, to go through all this before a graceful issue was reached. It was reached by her paying with the sacrifice of Mr. Densher for her reduction of Lord Mark to the absurd. So they separated softly enough. She was to be let off hearing about Lord Mark so long as she made it good that she wasn't underhand about anybody else. She had denied everything and every one, she reflected as she went away—and that was a relief; but it also made rather a clean sweep of the future. The prospect put on a bareness that already gave her something in common with the Miss Condrips.

Book Second

....

I

MERTON DENSHER, who passed the best hours of each night at the office of his newspaper, had at times, during the day, to make up for it, a sense, or at least an appearance, of leisure, in accordance with which he was not infrequently to be met, in different parts of the town, at moments when men of business are hidden from the public eye. More than once, during the present winter's end, he had deviated, toward three o'clock, or toward four, into Kensington Gardens, where he might for a while, on each occasion, have been observed to demean himself as a person with nothing to do. He made his way indeed, for the most part, with a certain directness, over to the north side; but once that ground was reached his behaviour was noticeably wanting in point. He moved seemingly at random from alley to alley; he stopped for no reason and remained idly agaze; he sat down in a chair and then changed to a bench; after which he walked about again, only again to repeat both the vagueness and the vivacity. Distinctly, he was a man either with nothing at all to do or with ever so much to think about; and it was not to be denied that

the impression he might often thus easily make had the
effect of causing the burden of proof, in certain directions, to rest on him. It was a little the fault of his
aspect, his personal marks, which made it almost impossible to name his profession.

He was a longish, leanish, fairish young Englishman,
not unamenable, on certain sides, to classification—as
for instance by being a gentleman, by being rather
specifically one of the educated, one of the generally
sound and generally pleasant; yet, though to that degree
neither extraordinary nor abnormal, he would have
failed to play straight into an observer's hands. He was
young for the House of Commons, he was loose for the
army. He was refined, as might have been said, for the
city, and, quite apart from the cut of his cloth, he was
sceptical, it might have been felt, for the church. On the
other hand he was credulous for diplomacy, or perhaps
even for science, while he was perhaps at the same time
too much in his mere senses for poetry, and yet too little in them for art. You would have got fairly near him
by making out in his eyes the potential recognition of
ideas; but you would have quite fallen away again on the
question of the ideas themselves. The difficulty with
Densher was that he looked vague without looking
weak—idle without looking empty. It was the accident,
possibly, of his long legs, which were apt to stretch
themselves; of his straight hair and his well-shaped
head, never, the latter, neatly smooth, and apt, into the
bargain, at the time of quite other calls upon it, to throw
itself suddenly back and, supported behind by his

uplifted arms and interlocked hands, place him for
unconscionable periods in communion with the ceiling,
the tree-tops, the sky. He was in short visibly absent-
minded, irregularly clever, liable to drop what was near
and to take up what was far; he was more a respecter,
in general, than a follower of custom. He suggested
above all, however, that wondrous state of youth in
which the elements, the metals more or less precious, are
so in fusion and fermentation that the question of the
final stamp, the pressure that fixes the value, must wait
for comparative coolness. And it was a mark of his
interesting mixture that if he was irritable it was by a
law of considerable subtlety—a law that, in intercourse
with him, it might be of profit, though not easy, to master. One of the effects of it was that he had for you surprises of tolerance as well as of temper.

He loitered, on the best of the relenting days, the several occasions we speak of, along the part of the Gardens
nearest to Lancaster Gate, and when, always, in due
time, Kate Croy came out of her aunt's house, crossed
the road and arrived by the nearest entrance, there was
a general publicity in the proceeding which made it
slightly anomalous. If their meeting was to be bold and
free it might have taken place within doors; if it was to
be shy or secret it might have taken place almost anywhere better than under Mrs. Lowder's windows. They
failed indeed to remain attached to that spot; they wandered and strolled, taking in the course of more than one
of these interviews a considerable walk, or else picked
out a couple of chairs under one of the great trees and

sat as much apart—apart from every one else—as possible. But Kate had, each time, at first, the air of wishing to expose herself to pursuit and capture if those
things were in question. She made the point that she
was not underhand, any more than she was vulgar; that
the Gardens were charming in themselves and this use
of them a matter of taste; and that, if her aunt chose to
glare at her from the drawing-room or to cause her to be
tracked and overtaken, she could at least make it convenient that this should be easily done. The fact was
that the relation between these young persons abounded
in such oddities as were not inaptly symbolised by assig-
nations that had a good deal more appearance than
motive. Of the strength of the tie that held them we
shall sufficiently take the measure; but it was meanwhile
almost obvious that if the great possibility had come up
for them it had done so, to an exceptional degree, under
the protection of the famous law of contraries. Any deep
harmony that might eventually govern them would not
be the result of their having much in common—having
anything, in fact, but their affection; and would really
find its explanation in some sense, on the part of each, of
being poor where the other was rich. It is nothing new
indeed that generous young persons often admire most
what nature hasn't given them—from which it would
appear, after all, that our friends were both generous.

Merton Densher had repeatedly said to himself—and
from far back—that he should be a fool not to marry a
woman whose value would be in her differences; and
Kate Croy, though without having quite so philoso-

phised, had quickly recognised in the young man a precious unlikeness. He represented what her life had never given her and certainly, without some such aid as his, never would give her; all the high, dim things she lumped together as of the mind. It was on the side of the mind that Densher was rich for her, and mysterious and strong; and he had rendered her in especial the sovereign service of making that element real. She had had, all her days, to take it terribly on trust; no creature she had ever encountered having been able in any degree to testify for it directly. Vague rumours of its existence had made their precarious way to her; but nothing had, on the whole, struck her as more likely than that she should live and die without the chance to verify them. The chance had come—it was an extraordinary one—on the day she first met Densher; and it was to the girl's lasting honour that she knew on the spot what she was in the presence of. That occasion indeed, for everything that straightway flowered in it, would be worthy of high commemoration; Densher's perception went out to meet the young woman's and quite kept pace with her own recognition. Having so often concluded on the fact of his weakness, as he called it, for life—his strength merely for thought—life, he logically opined, was what he must somehow arrange to annex and possess. This was so much a necessity that thought by itself only went on in the void; it was from the immediate air of life that it must draw its breath. So the young man, ingenious but large, critical but ardent too, made out both his case and Kate Croy's. They had

originally met before her mother's death—an occasion
marked for her as the last pleasure permitted by the
approach of that event; after which the dark months had
interposed a screen and, for all Kate knew, made the end
one with the beginning.

The beginning—to which she often went back—had
been a scene, for our young woman, of supreme brilliancy; a party given at a "gallery" hired by a hostess
who fished with big nets. A Spanish dancer, understood
to be at that moment the delight of the town, an American reciter, the joy of a kindred people, an Hungarian
fiddler, the wonder of the world at large—in the name
of these and other attractions the company in which, by
a rare privilege, Kate found herself had been freely con-
voked. She lived under her mother's roof, as she considered, obscurely, and was acquainted with few persons
who entertained on that scale; but she had had dealings
with two or three connected, as appeared, with such—
two or three through whom the stream of hospitality,
filtered or diffused, could thus now and then spread to
outlying receptacles. A good-natured lady in fine, a
friend of her mother and a relative of the lady of the
gallery, had offered to take her to the party in question
and had there fortified her, further, with two or three
of those introductions that, at large parties, lead to other
things—that had at any rate, on this occasion, culmi-
nated for her in conversation with a tall, fair, slightly
unbrushed and rather awkward, but on the whole not
dreary, young man. The young man had affected her as
detached, as—it was indeed what he called himself—

awfully at sea, as much more distinct from what surrounded them than any one else appeared to be, and even as probably quite disposed to be making his escape when pulled up to be placed in relation with her. He gave her his word for it indeed, that same evening, that only their meeting had prevented his flight, but that now he saw how sorry he should have been to miss it. This point they had reached by midnight, and though in respect to such remarks everything was in the tone, the tone was by midnight there too. She had had originally her full apprehension of his coerced, certainly of his vague, condition—full apprehensions often being with her immediate; then she had had her equal consciousness that, within five minutes, something between them had—well, she couldn't call it anything but *come*. It was nothing, but it was somehow everything—it was that something for each of them had happened.

They had found themselves looking at each other straight, and for a longer time on end than was usual even at parties in galleries; but that, after all, would have been a small affair, if there hadn't been something else with it. It wasn't, in a word, simply that their eyes had met; other conscious organs, faculties, feelers had met as well, and when Kate afterwards imaged to herself the sharp, deep fact she saw it, in the oddest way, as a particular performance. She had observed a ladder against a garden wall, and had trusted herself so to climb it as to be able to see over into the probable garden on the other side. On reaching the top she had found herself face to face with a gentleman engaged in a like calculation at the same moment, and the two inquirers had remained confronted on their ladders. The great point was that for the rest of that evening they had been perched—they had not climbed down; and indeed, during the time that followed, Kate at least had had the perched feeling—it was as if she were there aloft without a retreat. A simpler expression of all this is doubtless but that they had taken each other in with interest; and without a happy hazard six months later the incident would have closed in that account of it. The accident, meanwhile, had been as natural as anything in London ever is: Kate had one afternoon found herself opposite Mr. Densher on the Underground Railway. She had entered the train at Sloane Square to go to Queen's Road, and the carriage in which she had found a place was all but full. Densher was already in it—on the other bench and at the furthest angle; she was sure of him before they had again started. The day and the hour were darkness, there were six other persons, and she had been busy placing herself; but her consciousness had gone to him as straight as if they had come together in some bright level of the desert. They had on neither part a second's hesitation; they looked across the choked compartment exactly as if she had known he would be there and he had expected her to come in; so that, though in the conditions they could only exchange the greeting of movements, smiles, silence, it would have been quite in the key of these passages that they should have alighted for ease at the very next station. Kate was in fact sure that the very next station was the young man's true goal—

which made it clear that he was going on only from the
wish to speak to her. He had to go on, for this purpose,
to High Street, Kensington, as it was not till then that
the exit of a passenger gave him his chance.

His chance put him, however, in quick possession of
the seat facing her, the alertness of his capture of which
seemed to show her his impatience. It helped them,
moreover, with strangers on either side, little to talk;
though this very restriction perhaps made such a mark
for them as nothing else could have done. If the fact that
their opportunity had again come round for them could
be so intensely expressed between them without a word,
they might very well feel on the spot that it had not
come round for nothing. The extraordinary part of the
matter was that they were not in the least meeting where
they had left off, but ever so much further on, and that
these added links added still another between High
Street and Notting Hill Gate, and then between the latter station and Queen's Road an extension really inordinate. At Notting Hill Gate, Kate's right-hand
neighbour descended, whereupon Densher popped
straight into that seat; only there was not much gained
when a lady, the next instant, popped into Densher's.
He could say almost nothing to her—she scarce knew, at
least, what he said; she was so occupied with a certainty
that one of the persons opposite, a youngish man with
a single eyeglass, which he kept constantly in position,
had made her out from the first as visibly, as strangely
affected. If such a person made her out, what then did
Densher do?—a question in truth sufficiently answered

when, on their reaching her station, he instantly followed her out of the train. That had been the real beginning—the beginning of everything else; the other time,
the time at the party, had been but the beginning of
that. Never in life before had she so let herself go; for
always before—so far as small adventures could have
been in question for her—there had been, by the vulgar measure, more to go upon. He had walked with her
to Lancaster Gate, and then she had walked with him
away from it—for all the world, she said to herself, like
the housemaid giggling to the baker.

This appearance, she was afterwards to feel, had been
all in order for a relation that might precisely best be
described in the terms of the baker and the housemaid.
She could say to herself that from that hour they had
kept company; that had come to represent, technically
speaking, alike the range and the limit of their tie. He
had on the spot, naturally, asked leave to call upon
her—which, as a young person who wasn't really young,
who didn't pretend to be a sheltered flower, she as rationally gave. That—she was promptly clear about it—was
now her only possible basis; she was just the contemporary London female, highly modern, inevitably battered, honourably free. She had of course taken her aunt
straight into her confidence—had gone through the form
of asking her leave; and she subsequently remembered
that though, on this occasion, she had left the history
of her new alliance as scant as the facts themselves, Mrs.
Lowder had struck her at the time surprisingly mild. It
had been, in every way, the occasion, full of the

reminder that her hostess was deep: it was definitely
then that she had begun to ask herself what Aunt Maud
was, in vulgar parlance, "up to." "You may receive, my
dear, whom you like"—that was what Aunt Maud, who
in general objected to people's doing as they liked, had
replied; and it bore, this unexpectedness, a good deal of
looking into. There were many explanations, and they
were all amusing—amusing, that is, in the line of the
sombre and brooding amusement, cultivated by Kate in
her actual high retreat. Merton Densher came the very
next Sunday; but Mrs. Lowder was so consistently mag-
nanimous as to make it possible to her niece to see him
alone. She saw him, however, on the Sunday following,
in order to invite him to dinner; and when, after dining, he came again—which he did three times, she
found means to treat his visit as preponderantly to herself. Kate's conviction that she didn't like him made that
remarkable; it added to the evidence, by this time voluminous, that she was remarkable all round. If she had
been, in the way of energy, merely usual, she would
have kept her dislike direct; whereas it was now as if she
were seeking to know him in order to see best where to
"have" him. That was one of the reflections made in our
young woman's high retreat; she smiled from her look-
out, in the silence that was only the fact of hearing irrelevant sounds, as she caught the truth that you could
easily accept people when you wanted them so to be
delivered to you. When Aunt Maud wished them
despatched, it was not to be done by deputy; it was
clearly always a matter reserved for her own hand.

But what made the girl wonder most was the implications of so much diplomacy in respect to her own
value. What view might she take of her position in the
light of this appearance that her companion feared so, as
yet, to upset her? It was as if Densher were accepted
partly under the dread that if he hadn't been she would
act in resentment. Hadn't her aunt considered the danger that she would in that case have broken off, have
seceded? The danger was exaggerated—she would have
done nothing so gross; but that, it seemed, was the way
Mrs. Lowder saw her and believed her to be reckoned
with. What importance therefore did she really attach to
her, what strange interest could she take on their keeping on terms? Her father and her sister had their answer
to this—even without knowing how the question struck
her; they saw the lady of Lancaster Gate as panting to
make her fortune, and the explanation of that appetite
was that, on the accident of a nearer view than she had
before enjoyed, she had been charmed, been dazzled.
They approved, they admired in her one of the belated
fancies of rich, capricious, violent old women—the more
marked, moreover, because the result of no plot; and
they piled up the possible results for the person concerned. Kate knew what to think of her own power thus
to carry by storm; she saw herself as handsome, no
doubt, but as hard, and felt herself as clever but as cold;
and as so much too imperfectly ambitious, furthermore,
that it was a pity, for a quiet life, she couldn't settle to
be either finely or stupidly indifferent. Her intelligence
sometimes kept her still—too still—but her want of it

was restless; so that she got the good, it seemed to her, of neither extreme. She saw herself at present, none the less, in a situation, and even her sad, disillusioned mother, dying, but with Aunt Maud interviewing the nurse on the stairs, had not failed to remind her that it was of the essence of situations to be, under Providence, worked. The dear woman had died in the belief that she was actually working the one then produced.

Kate took one of her walks with Densher just after her visit to Mr. Croy; but most of it went, as usual, to their sitting in talk. They had, under the trees, by the lake, the air of old friends—phases of apparent earnestness, in particular, in which they might have been settling every question in their vast young world; and periods of silence, side by side, perhaps even more, when "a long engagement!" would have been the final reading of the signs on the part of a passer struck with them, as it was so easy to be. They would have presented themselves thus as very old friends rather than as young persons who had met for the first time but a year before and had spent most of the interval without contact. It was indeed for each, already, as if they were older friends; and though the succession of their meetings might, between them, have been straightened out, they only had a confused sense of a good many, very much alike, and a confused intention of a good many more, as little different as possible. The desire to keep them just as they were had perhaps to do with the fact that in spite of the presumed diagnosis of the stranger there had been for them as yet no formal, no final understanding. Densher had at the

very first pressed the question, but that, it had been easy
to reply, was too soon; so that a singular thing had afterwards happened. They had accepted their acquaintance
as too short for an engagement, but they had treated it as
long enough for almost anything else, and marriage was
somehow before them like a temple without an avenue.
They belonged to the temple and they met in the
grounds; they were in the stage at which grounds in general offered much scattered refreshment. But Kate had
meanwhile had so few confidants that she wondered at
the source of her father's suspicions. The diffusion of
rumour was of course, in London, remarkable, and for
Marian not less—as Aunt Maud touched neither
directly—the mystery had worked. No doubt she had
been seen. Of course she had been seen. She had taken
no trouble not to be seen, and it was a thing, clearly, she
was incapable of taking. But she had been seen how?—
and what *was* there to see? She was in love—she knew
that: but it was wholly her own business, and she had the
sense of having conducted herself, of still so doing, with
almost violent conformity.

"I've an idea—in fact I feel sure—that Aunt Maud
means to write to you; and I think you had better know
it." So much as this she said to him as soon as they met,
but immediately adding to it: "So as to make up your
mind how to take her. I know pretty well what she'll say
to you."

"Then will you kindly tell me?"

She thought a little. "I can't do that. I should spoil
it. She'll do the best for her own idea."

"Her idea, you mean, that I'm a sort of a scoundrel; or, at the best, not good enough for you?"

They were side by side again in their penny chairs, and Kate had another pause. "Not good enough for *her*."

"Oh, I see. And that's necessary."

He put it as a truth rather more than as a question; but there had been plenty of truths between them that each had contradicted. Kate, however, let this one sufficiently pass, only saying the next moment: "She has behaved extraordinarily."

"And so have we," Densher declared. "I think, you know, we've been awfully decent."

"For ourselves, for each other, for people in general, yes. But not for *her*. For her," said Kate, "we've been monstrous. She has been giving us rope. So if she does send for you," the girl repeated, "you must know where you are."

"That I always know. It's where *you* are that concerns me."

"Well," said Kate after an instant, "her idea of that is what you'll have from her." He gave her a long look, and whatever else people who wouldn't let her alone might have wished, for her advancement, his long looks were the thing in the world she could never have enough of. What she felt was that, whatever might happen, she must keep them, must make them most completely her possession; and it was already strange enough that she reasoned, or at all events began to act, as if she might work them in with other and alien things, privately cherish them, and yet, as regards the

rigour of it, pay no price. She looked it well in the face,
she took it intensely home, that they were lovers; she
rejoiced to herself and, frankly, to him, in their wearing of the name; but, distinguished creature that, in her
way, she was, she took a view of this character that
scarce squared with the conventional. The character
itself she insisted on as their right, taking that so for
granted that it didn't seem even bold; but Densher,
though he agreed with her, found himself moved to
wonder at her simplifications, her values. Life might
prove difficult—was evidently going to; but meanwhile
they had each other, and that was everything. This was
her reasoning, but meanwhile, for *him*, each other was
what they didn't have, and it was just the point.
Repeatedly, however, it was a point that, in the face of
strange and special things, he judged it rather awkwardly gross to urge. It was impossible to keep Mrs.
Lowder out of their scheme. She stood there too close
to it and too solidly; it had to open a gate, at a given
point, do what they would to take her in. And she came
in, always, while they sat together rather helplessly
watching her, as in a coach-in-four; she drove round
their prospect as the principal lady at the circus drives
round the ring, and she stopped the coach in the middle to alight with majesty. It was our young man's
sense that she was magnificently vulgar, but yet, quite,
that this wasn't all. It wasn't with her vulgarity that she
felt his want of means, though that might have helped
her richly to embroider it; nor was it with the same
infirmity that she was strong, original, dangerous.

His want of means—of means sufficient for any one but himself—was really the great ugliness, and was, moreover, at no time more ugly for him than when it rose there, as it did seem to rise, shameless, face to face with the elements in Kate's life colloquially and conveniently classed by both of them as funny. He sometimes indeed, for that matter, asked himself if these elements were as funny as the innermost fact, so often vivid to him, of his own consciousness—his private inability to believe he should ever be rich. His conviction on this head was in truth quite positive and a thing by itself; he failed, after analysis, to understand it, though he had naturally more lights on it than any one else. He knew how it subsisted in spite of an equal consciousness of his being neither mentally nor physically quite helpless, neither a dunce nor a cripple; he knew it to be absolute, though secret, and also, strange to say, about common undertakings, not discouraging, not prohibitive. Only now was he having to think if it were prohibitive in respect to marriage; only now, for the first time, had he to weigh his case in scales. The scales, as he sat with Kate, often dangled in the line of his vision; he saw them, large and black, while he talked or listened, take, in the bright air, singular positions. Sometimes the right was down and sometimes the left; never a happy equipoise—one or the other always kicking the beam. Thus was kept before him the question of whether it were more ignoble to ask a woman to take her chance with you, or to accept it from one's conscience that her chance could be at the best but one of the degrees of privation; whether, too, otherwise, marrying for money mightn't after all be a smaller cause of shame than the mere dread of marrying without. Through these variations of mood and view, all the same, the mark on his forehead stood clear; he saw himself remain without whether he married or not. It was a line on which his fancy could be admirably active; the innumerable ways of making money were beautifully present to him; he could have handled them, for his newspaper, as easily as he handled everything. He was quite aware how he handled everything; it was another mark on his forehead; the pair of smudges from the thumb of fortune, the brand on the passive fleece, dated from the primal hour and kept each other company. He wrote, as for print, with deplorable ease; since there had been nothing to stop him even at the age of ten, so there was as little at twenty; it was part of his fate in the first place and part of the wretched public's in the second. The innumerable ways of making money were, no doubt, at all events, what his imagination often was busy with after he had tilted his chair and thrown back his head with his hands clasped behind it. What would most have prolonged that attitude, moreover, was the reflection that the ways were ways only for others. Within the minute, now— however this might be—he was aware of a nearer view than he had yet quite had of those circumstances on his companion's part that made least for simplicity of relation. He saw above all how she saw them herself, for she spoke of them at present with the last frankness, telling him of her visit to her father and giving him, in an account of her subsequent scene with her sister, an instance of how she was perpetually reduced to patching up, in one way or another, that unfortunate woman's hopes.

"The tune," she exclaimed, "to which we're a failure as a family!" With which he had it again all from her—and this time, as it seemed to him, more than all: the dishonour her father had brought them, his folly and cruelty and wickedness; the wounded state of her mother, abandoned, despoiled and helpless, yet, for the management of such a home as remained to them, dreadfully unreasonable too; the extinction of her two young brothers—one, at nineteen, the eldest of the house, by typhoid fever, contracted at a poisonous little place, as they had afterwards found out, that they had taken for a summer; the other, the flower of the flock, a middy on the *Britannia*, dreadfully drowned, and not even by an accident at sea, but by cramp, unrescued, while bathing, too late in the autumn, in a wretched little river during a holiday visit to the home of a shipmate. Then Marian's unnatural marriage, in itself a kind of spiritless turning of the other cheek to fortune: her actual wretchedness and plaintiveness, her greasy children, her impossible claims, her odious visitors—these things completed the proof of the heaviness, for them all, of the hand of fate. Kate confessedly described them with an excess of impatience; it was much of her charm for Densher that she gave in general that turn to her descriptions, partly as if to amuse him by free and humorous colour, partly—and that charm was the greatest—as if to work off, for her own relief, her constant perception of the incongruity of things. She had seen the general show too early and too sharply, and she was so intelligent that she knew it and allowed for that misfortune; therefore when, in talk with him, she was violent and almost unfeminine, it was almost as if they had settled, for intercourse, on the short cut of the fantastic and the happy language of exaggeration. It had come to be definite between them at a primary stage that, if they could have no other straight way, the realm of thought at least was open to them. They could think whatever they liked about whatever they would—or, in other words, they could say it. Saying it for each other, for each other alone, only of course added to the taste. The implication was thereby constant that what they said when not together had no taste for them at all, and nothing could have served more to launch them, at special hours, on their small floating island than such an assumption that they were only making believe everywhere else. Our young man, it must be added, was conscious enough that it was Kate who profited most by this particular play of the fact of intimacy. It always seemed to him that she had more life than he to react from, and when she recounted the dark disasters of her house and glanced at the hard, odd offset of her present exaltation—since as exaltation it was apparently to be considered—he felt his own grey domestic annals to make little show. It was naturally, in all such reference, the question of her father's character that engaged him most, but her pic-

ture of her adventure in Chirk Street gave him a sense
of how little as yet that character was clear to him.
What was it, to speak plainly, that Mr. Croy had originally done?

"I don't know—and I don't want to. I only know
that years and years ago—when I was about fifteen—
something or other happened that made him impossible. I mean impossible for the world at large first, and
then, little by little, for mother. We of course didn't
know it at the time," Kate explained, "but we knew it
later; and it was, oddly enough, my sister who first
made out that he had done something. I can hear her
now—the way, one cold, black Sunday morning when,
on account of an extraordinary fog, we had not gone to
church, she broke it to me by the school-room fire. I
was reading a history-book by the lamp—when we
didn't go to church we had to read history-books—and
I suddenly heard her say, out of the fog, which was in
the room, and *apropos* of nothing: 'Papa has done
something wicked.' And the curious thing was that I
believed it on the spot and have believed it ever since,
though she could tell me nothing more—neither what
was the wickedness, nor how she knew, nor what would
happen to him, nor anything else about it. We had our
sense, always, that all sorts of things *had* happened,
were all the while happening, to him; so that when
Marian only said she was sure, tremendously sure, that
she had made it out for herself, but that that was
enough, I took her word for it—it seemed somehow so
natural. We were not, however, to ask mother—which

made it more natural still, and I said never a word. But mother, strangely enough, spoke of it to me, in time, of her own accord very much later on. He hadn't been with us for ever so long, but we were used to that. She must have had some fear, some conviction that I had an idea, some idea of her own that it was the best thing to do. She came out as abruptly as Marian had done, 'If you hear anything against your father—anything I mean, except that he's odious and vile—remember it's perfectly false.' That was the way I knew—it was true, though I recall that I said to her then that I of course knew it wasn't. She might have told me it was true, and yet have trusted me to contradict fiercely enough any accusation of him that I should meet—to contradict it much more fiercely and effectively, I think, than she would have done herself. As it happens, however," the girl went on, "I've never had occasion, and I've been conscious of it with a sort of surprise. It has made the world, at times, seem more decent. No one has so much as breathed to me. That has been a part of the silence, the silence that surrounds him, the silence that, for the world, has washed him out. He doesn't exist for people. And yet I'm as sure as ever. In fact, though I know no more than I did then, I'm more sure. And that," she wound up, "is what I sit here and tell you about my own father. If you don't call it a proof of confidence I don't know what will satisfy you."

"It satisfies me beautifully," Densher declared, "but it doesn't, my dear child, very greatly enlighten me. You don't, you know, really tell me anything. It's so vague that what am I to think but that you may very well be mistaken? What has he done, if no one can name it?"

"He has done everything."

"Oh—everything! Everything's nothing."

"Well then," said Kate, "he has done some particular thing. It's known—only, thank God, not to us. But it has been the end of him. *You* could doubtless find out with a little trouble. You can ask about."

Densher for a moment said nothing; but the next moment he made it up. "I wouldn't find out for the world, and I'd rather lose my tongue than put a question."

"And yet it's a part of me," said Kate.

"A part of you?"

"My father's dishonour." Then she sounded for him, but more deeply than ever yet, her note of proud, still pessimism. "How can such a thing as that not be the great thing in one's life?"

She had to take from him again, on this, one of his long looks, and she took it to its deepest, its headiest dregs. "I shall ask you, for the great thing in your life," he said, "to depend on *me* a little more." After which, just hesitating, "Doesn't he belong to some club?" he inquired.

She had a grave headshake. "He used to—to many."

"But he has dropped them?"

"They've dropped *him*. Of that I'm sure. It ought to do for you. I offered him," the girl immediately contin-ued—"and it was for that I went to him—to come and be with him, make a home for him so far as is possible. But he won't hear of it."

Densher took this in with visible, but generous, wonder. "You offered him—'impossible' as you describe him to me—to live with him and share his disadvantages?" The young man saw for the moment but the high beauty of it. "You *are* gallant!"

"Because it strikes you as being brave for him?" She wouldn't in the least have this. "It wasn't courage—it was the opposite. I did it to save myself—to escape."

He had his air, so constant at this stage, as of her giving him finer things than any one to think about. "Escape from what?"

"From everything."

"Do you by any chance mean from me?"

"No; I spoke to him of you, told him—or what amounted to it—that I would bring you, if he would allow it, with me."

"But he won't allow it," said Densher.

"Won't hear of it on any terms. He won't help me, won't save me, won't hold out a finger to me," Kate went on; "he simply wriggles away, in his inimitable manner, and throws me back."

"Back then, after all, thank goodness," Densher concurred, "on me."

But she spoke again as with the sole vision of the whole scene she had evoked. "It's a pity, because you'd like him. He's wonderful—he's charming." Her companion gave one of the laughs that marked in him, again, his feeling in her tone, inveterately, something that banished the talk of other women, so far as he knew other women, to the dull desert of the conventional, and she had already continued. "He would make himself delightful to you."

"Even while objecting to me?"

"Well, he likes to please," the girl explained—"personally. He would appreciate you and be clever with you. It's to *me* he objects—that is as to my liking you."

"Heaven be praised then," Densher exclaimed, "that you like me enough for the objection!"

But she met it after an instant with some inconsequence. "I don't. I offered to give you up, if necessary, to go to him. But it made no difference, and that's what I mean," she pursued, "by his declining me on any terms. The point is, you see, that I don't escape."

Densher wondered. "But if you didn't wish to escape *me?*"

"I wished to escape Aunt Maud. But he insists that it's through her and through her only that I may help him; just as Marian insists that it's through her, and through her only, that I can help *her*. That's what I mean," she again explained, "by their turning me back."

The young man thought. "Your sister turns you back too?"

"Oh, with a push!"

"But have you offered to live with your sister?"

"I would in a moment if she'd have me. That's all my virtue—a narrow little family feeling. I've a small stupid piety—I don't know what to call it." Kate bravely sustained it; she made it out. "Sometimes, alone, I've to

smother my shrieks when I think of my poor mother.
She went through things—they pulled her down; I know
what they were now—I didn't then, for I was a pig; and
my position, compared with hers, is an insolence of success. That's what Marian keeps before me; that's what
papa himself, as I say, so inimitably does. My position's
a value, a great value, for them both"—she followed and
followed. Lucid and ironic, she knew no merciful muddle. "It's *the* value—the only one they have."

Everything between our young couple moved today,
in spite of their pauses, their margin, to a quicker measure—the quickness and anxiety playing lightning-like
in the sultriness. Densher watched, decidedly, as he had
never done before. "And the fact you speak of holds
you!"

"Of course, it holds me. It's a perpetual sound in my
ears. It makes me ask myself if I've any right to personal
happiness, any right to anything but to be as rich and
overflowing, as smart and shining, as I can be made."

Densher had a pause. "Oh, you might, with good
luck, have the personal happiness too."

Her immediate answer to this was a silence like his
own; after which she gave him straight in the face, but
quite simply and quietly: "Darling!"

It took him another moment; then he was also quiet
and simple. "Will you settle it by our being married to-
morrow—as we can, with perfect ease, civilly?"

"Let us wait to arrange it," Kate presently replied,
"till after you've seen her."

"Do you call that adoring me?" Densher demanded.

They were talking, for the time, with the strangest mixture of deliberation and directness, and nothing could have been more in the tone of it than the way she at last said: "You're afraid of her yourself."

He gave a smile a trifle glassy. "For young persons of a great distinction and a very high spirit, we're a caution!"

"Yes," she took it straight up; "we're hideously intelligent. But there's fun in it too. We must get our fun where we can. I think," she added, and for that matter, not without courage, "our relation's beautiful. It's not a bit vulgar. I cling to some saving romance in things."

It made him break into a laugh which had more freedom than his smile. "How you must be afraid you'll chuck me!"

"No, no, *that* would be vulgar. But, of course, I do see my danger," she admitted, "of doing something base."

"Then what can be so base as sacrificing me?"

"I *shan't* sacrifice you; don't cry out till you're hurt. I shall sacrifice nobody and nothing, and that's just my situation, that I want and that I shall try for everything. That," she wound up, "is how I see myself, and how I see you quite as much, acting for them."

"For 'them'?" and the young man strongly, extravagantly marked his coldness. "Thank you!"

"Don't you care for them?"

"Why should I? What are they to me but a serious nuisance?"

As soon as he had permitted himself this qualification of the unfortunate persons she so perversely cherished, he repented of his roughness—and partly because he expected a flash from her. But it was one of her finest sides that she sometimes flashed with a mere mild glow. "I don't see why you don't make out a little more that if we avoid stupidity we may do *all*. We may keep her."

He stared. "Make her pension us?"

"Well, wait at least till we have seen."

He thought. "Seen what can be got out of her?"

Kate for a moment said nothing. "After all I never asked her; never, when our troubles were at the worst, appealed to her nor went near her. She fixed upon me herself, settled on me with her wonderful gilded claws."

"You speak," Densher observed, "as if she were a vulture."

"Call it an eagle—with a gilded beak as well, and with wings for great flights. If she's a thing of the air, in short—say at once a balloon—I never myself got into her car. I was her choice."

It had really, her sketch of the affair, a high colour and a great style; at all of which he gazed a minute as at a picture by a master. "What she must see in you!"

"Wonders!" And, speaking it loud, she stood straight up. "Everything. There it is."

Yes, there it was, and as she remained before him he continued to face it. "So that what you mean is that I'm to do my part in somehow squaring her?"

"See her, see her," Kate said with impatience.

"And grovel to her?"

"Ah, do what you like!" And she walked in her impatience away.

II

HIS EYES HAD FOLLOWED her at this time quite long
enough, before he overtook her, to make out more than
ever, in the poise of her head, the pride of her step—he
didn't know what best to call it—a part, at least, of Mrs.
Lowder's reasons. He consciously winced while he figured his presenting himself as a reason opposed to these;
though, at the same moment, with the source of Aunt
Maud's inspiration thus before him, he was prepared to
conform, by almost any abject attitude or profitable
compromise, to his companion's easy injunction. He
would do as *she* liked—his own liking might come off
as it would. He would help her to the utmost of his
power; for, all the rest of that day and the next, her easy
injunction, tossed off that way as she turned her beautiful back, was like the crack of a great whip in the blue
air, the high element in which Mrs. Lowder hung. He
wouldn't grovel perhaps—he wasn't quite ready for that;
but he would be patient, ridiculous, reasonable, unreasonable, and above all deeply diplomatic. He would be
clever, with all his cleverness—which he now shook
hard, as he sometimes shook his poor, dear, shabby, old
watch, to start it up again. It wasn't, thank goodness,
as if there weren't plenty of that, and with what they
could muster between them it would be little to the
credit of their star, however pale, that defeat and surrender—surrender so early, so immediate—should have
to ensue. It was not indeed that he thought of that dis-
aster as, at the worst, a direct sacrifice of their possibil-

ities: he imaged it—which was enough as some proved vanity, some exposed fatuity, in the idea of bringing Mrs. Lowder round. When, shortly afterwards, in this lady's vast drawing-room—the apartments at Lancaster Gate had struck him from the first as of prodigious extent—he awaited her, at her request, conveyed in a "reply-paid" telegram, his theory was that of their still clinging to their idea, though with a sense of the difficulty of it really enlarged to the scale of the place.

He had the place for a long time—it seemed to him a quarter of an hour—to himself; and while Aunt Maud kept him and kept him, while observation and reflection crowded on him, he asked himself what was to be expected of a person who could treat one like that. The visit, the hour were of her own proposing, so that her delay, no doubt, was but part of a general plan of putting him to inconvenience. As he walked to and fro, however, taking in the message of her massive, florid furniture, the immense expression of her signs and symbols, he had as little doubt of the inconvenience he was prepared to suffer. He found himself even facing the thought that he had nothing to fall back on, and that that was as great an humiliation in a good cause as a proud man could desire. It had not yet been so distinct to him that he made no show—literally not the smallest; so complete a show seemed made there all about him; so almost abnormally affirmative, so aggressively erect, were the huge, heavy objects that syllabled his hostess' story. "When all's said and done, you know, she's colossally vulgar"—he had once all but said that of Mrs.

Lowder to her niece; only just keeping it back at the last, keeping it to himself with all its danger about it. It mattered because it bore so directly, and he at all events quite felt it a thing that Kate herself would some day bring out to him. It bore directly at present, and really all the more that somehow, strangely, it didn't in the least imply that Aunt Maud was dull or stale. She was vulgar with freshness, almost with beauty, since there was beauty, to a degree, in the play of so big and bold a temperament. She was in fine quite the largest possible quantity to deal with; and he was in the cage of the lioness without his whip—the whip, in a word, of a supply of proper retorts. He had no retort but that he loved the girl—which in such a house as that was painfully cheap. Kate had mentioned to him more than once that her aunt was Passionate, speaking of it as a kind of offset and uttering it as with a capital P, marking it as something that he might, that he in fact ought to, turn about in some way to their advantage. He wondered at this hour to what advantage he could turn it; but the case grew less simple the longer he waited. Decidedly there was something he hadn't enough of. He stood as one fast.

His slow march to and fro seemed to give him the very measure; as he paced and paced the distance it became the desert of his poverty; at the sight of which expanse moreover he could pretend to himself as little as before that the desert looked redeemable. Lancaster Gate looked rich—that was all the effect; which it was unthinkable that any state of his own should ever

remotely resemble. He read more vividly, more critically, as has been hinted, the appearances about him;
and they did nothing so much as make him wonder at
his æsthetic reaction. He hadn't known—and in spite of
Kate's repeated reference to her own rebellions of
taste—that he should "mind" so much how an independent lady might decorate her house. It was the language
of the house itself that spoke to him, writing out for
him, with surpassing breadth and freedom, the associations and conceptions, the ideals and possibilities of the
mistress. Never, he flattered himself, had he seen anything so gregariously ugly—operatively, ominously so
cruel. He was glad to have found this last name for the
whole character; "cruel" somehow played into the subject for an article—that his impression put straight into
his mind. He would write about the heavy horrors that
could still flourish, that lifted their undiminished heads,
in an age so proud of its short way with false gods; and
it would be funny if what he should have got from Mrs.
Lowder were to prove, after all, but a small amount of
copy. Yet the great thing, really the dark thing, was
that, even while he thought of the quick column he
might add up, he felt it less easy to laugh at the heavy
horrors than to quail before them. He couldn't describe
and dismiss them collectively, call them either Mid-
Victorian or Early; not being at all sure they were range-
able under one rubric. It was only manifest they were
splendid and were furthermore conclusively British.
They constituted an order and they abounded in rare
material—precious woods, metals, stuffs, stones. He had

never dreamed of anything so fringed and scalloped, so buttoned and corded, drawn everywhere so tight, and curled everywhere so thick. He had never dreamed of so much gilt and glass, so much satin and plush, so much rosewood and marble and malachite. But it was, above all, the solid forms, the wasted finish, the misguided cost, the general attestation of morality and money, a good conscience and a big balance. These things finally represented for him a portentous negation of his own world of thought—of which, for that matter, in the presence of them, he became as for the first time hopelessly aware. They revealed it to him by their merciless difference.

His interview with Aunt Maud, none the less, took by no means the turn he had expected. Passionate though her nature, no doubt Mrs. Lowder, on this occasion, neither threatened nor appealed. Her arms of aggression, her weapons of defence, were presumably close at hand, but she left them untouched and unmentioned, and was in fact so bland that he properly perceived only afterwards how adroit she had been. He properly perceived something else as well, which complicated his case; he shouldn't have known what to call it if he hadn't called it her really imprudent goodnature. Her blandness, in other words, was not mere policy—he wasn't dangerous enough for policy; it was the result, he could see, of her fairly liking him a little. From the moment she did that she herself became more interesting; and who knew what might happen should he take to liking *her*? Well, it was a risk he naturally must face. She fought him, at any rate, but with one hand, with a few loose grains of stray powder. He recognised at the end of ten minutes, and even without her explaining it, that if she had made him wait it had not been to wound him; they had by that time almost directly met on the fact of her intention. She had wanted him to think for himself of what she proposed to say to him—not having otherwise announced it; wanted to let it come home to him on the spot, as she had shrewdly believed it would. Her first question, on appearing, had practically been as to whether he hadn't taken her hint, and this inquiry assumed so many things that it made discussion, immediately, frank and large. He knew, with the question put, that the hint was just what he *had* taken; knew that she had made him quickly forgive her the display of her power; knew that if he didn't take care he should understand her, and the strength of her purpose, to say nothing of that of her imagination, nothing of the length of her purse, only too well. Yet he pulled himself up with the thought, too, that he was not going to be afraid of understanding her; he was just going to understand and understand without detriment to the feeblest, even, of his passions. The play of one's mind let one in, at the best, dreadfully, in action, in the need of action, where simplicity was all; but when one couldn't prevent it the thing was to make it complete. There would never be mistakes but for the original fun of mistakes. What he must *use* his fatal intelligence for was to resist. Mrs. Lowder, meanwhile, might use it for whatever she liked.

It was after she had begun her statement of her own idea about Kate that he began, on his side, to reflect that—with her manner of offering it as really sufficient if he would take the trouble to embrace it—she couldn't half hate him. That was all, positively, she seemed to show herself for the time as attempting; clearly, if she did her intention justice, she would have nothing more disagreeable to do. "If I hadn't been ready to go very much further, you understand, I wouldn't have gone so far. I don't care what you repeat to her—the more you repeat to her, perhaps the better; and, at any rate, there's nothing she doesn't already know. I don't say it for her; I say it for you—when I want to reach my niece I know how to do it straight." So Aunt Maud delivered herself—as with homely benevolence, in the simplest, but the clearest terms; virtually conveying that, though a word to the wise was, doubtless, in spite of the advantage, *not* always enough, a word to the good could never fail to be. The sense our young man read into her words was that she liked him because he was good—was really, by her measure, good enough: good enough, that is, to give up her niece for her and go his way in peace. But *was* he good enough—by his own measure? He fairly wondered, while she more fully expressed herself, if it might be his doom to prove so. "She's the finest possible creature—of course you flatter yourself that you know it. But I know it, quite as well as you possibly can—by which I mean a good deal better yet; and the tune to which I'm ready to prove my faith compares favourably enough, I think, with anything *you* can do.

I don't say it because she's my niece—that's nothing to me: I might have had fifty nieces, and I wouldn't have brought one of them to this place if I hadn't found her to my taste. I don't say I wouldn't have done something else, but I wouldn't have put up with her presence. Kate's presence, by good fortune, I marked early; Kate's presence—unluckily for *you*—is everything I could possibly wish; Kate's presence is, in short, as fine as you know, and I've been keeping it for the comfort of my declining years. I've watched it long; I've been saving it up and letting it, as you say of investments, appreciate, and you may judge whether, now it has begun to pay so, I'm likely to consent to treat for it with any but a high bidder. I can do the best with her, and I've my idea of the best."

"Oh, I quite conceive," said Densher, "that your idea of the best isn't me."

It was an oddity of Mrs. Lowder's that her face in speech was like a lighted window at night, but that silence immediately drew the curtain. The occasion for reply allowed by her silence was never easy to take; yet she was still less easy to interrupt. The great glaze of her surface, at all events, gave her visitor no present help. "I didn't ask you to come to hear what it isn't—I asked you to come to hear what it *is*."

"Of course," Densher laughed, "it's very great indeed."

His hostess went on as if his contribution to the subject were barely relevant. "I want to see her high, high up—high up and in the light."

"Ah, you naturally want to marry her to a duke, and are eager to smooth away any hitch."

She gave him so, on this, the mere effect of the drawn blind that it quite forced him, at first, into the sense, possibly just, of having affected her as flippant, perhaps even as low. He had been looked at so, in blighted moments of presumptuous youth, by big cold public men, but never, so far as he could recall, by any private lady. More than anything yet it gave him the measure of his companion's subtlety, and thereby of Kate's possible career. "Don't be *too* impossible!"—he feared from his friend, for a moment, some such answer as that; and then felt, as she spoke otherwise, as if she were letting him off easily. "I want her to marry a great man." That was all; but, more and more, it was enough; and if it hadn't been her next words would have made it so. "And I think of her what I think. There you are."

They sat for a little face to face upon it, and he was conscious of something deeper still, of something she wished him to understand if he only would. To that extent she did appeal—appealed to the intelligence she desired to show she believed him to possess. He was meanwhile, at all events, not the man wholly to fail of comprehension. "Of course I'm aware how little I can answer to any fond, proud dream. You've a view—a magnificent one; into which I perfectly enter. I thoroughly understand what I'm not, and I'm much obliged to you for not reminding me of it in any rougher way." She said nothing—she kept that up; it might even have been to let him go further, if he was capable of it, in the

way of poorness of spirit. It was one of those cases in
which a man couldn't show, if he showed at all, save for
poor; unless indeed he preferred to show for asinine. It
was the plain truth: he *was*—on Mrs. Lowder's basis,
the only one in question—a very small quantity, and he
did know, damnably, what made quantities large. He
desired to be perfectly simple; yet in the midst of that
effort a deeper apprehension throbbed. Aunt Maud
clearly conveyed it, though he couldn't later on have
said how. "You don't really matter, I believe, so much
as you think, and I'm not going to make you a martyr
by banishing you. Your performances with Kate in the
Park are ridiculous so far as they're meant as consideration for me; and I had much rather see you myself—
since you're, in your way, my dear young man,
delightful—and arrange with you, count with you, as I
easily, as I perfectly should. Do you suppose me so stupid as to quarrel with you if it's not really necessary? It
won't—it would be too absurd!—*be* necessary. I can bite
your head off any day, any day I really open my mouth;
and I'm dealing with you now, see—and successfully
judge—without opening it. I do things handsomely all
round—I place you in the presence of the plan with
which, from the moment it's a case of taking you seriously, you're incompatible. Come then as near it as you
like, walk all round it—don't be afraid you'll hurt it!—
and live on with it before you."

He afterwards felt that if she hadn't absolutely
phrased all this it was because she so soon made him out
as going with her far enough. He was so pleasantly

affected by her asking no promise of him, her not proposing he should pay for her indulgence by his word of honour not to interfere, that he gave her a kind of general assurance of esteem. Immediately afterwards, then, he spoke of these things to Kate, and what then came back to him first of all was the way he had said to her—he mentioned it to the girl—very much as one of a pair of lovers says in a rupture by mutual consent: "I hope immensely, of course, that you'll always regard me as a friend." This had perhaps been going far—he submitted it all to Kate; but really there had been so much in it that it was to be looked at, as they might say, wholly in its own light. Other things than those we have presented had come up before the close of his scene with Aunt Maud, but this matter of her not treating him as a peril of the first order easily predominated. There was moreover plenty to talk about on the occasion of his subsequent passage with our young woman, it having been put to him abruptly, the night before, that he might give himself a lift and do his newspaper a service—so flatteringly was the case expressed—by going, for fifteen or twenty weeks, to America. The idea of a series of letters from the United States from the strictly social point of view had for some time been nursed in the inner sanctuary at whose door he sat, and the moment was now deemed happy for letting it loose. The imprisoned thought had, in a word, on the opening of the door, flown straight out into Densher's face, or perched at least on his shoulder, making him look up in surprise from his mere inky office-table. His account of the matter to Kate was that he couldn't refuse—not being in a position, as yet, to refuse anything; but that his being chosen for such an errand confounded his sense of proportion. He was definite as to his scarce knowing how to measure the honour, which struck him as equivocal; he had not quite supposed himself the man for the class of job. This confused consciousness, he intimated, he had promptly enough betrayed to his manager; with the effect, however, of seeing the question surprisingly clear up. What it came to was that the sort of twaddle that was not in his chords was, unexpectedly, just what they happened this time not to want. They wanted his letters, for queer reasons, about as good as he could let them come; he was to play his own little tune and not be afraid; that was the whole point.

It would have been the whole, that is, had there not been a sharper one still in the circumstance that he was to start at once. His mission, as they called it at the office, would probably be over by the end of June, which was desirable; but to bring that about he must now not lose a week; his inquiries, he understood, were to cover the whole ground, and there were reasons of State—reasons operating at the seat of empire in Fleet Street—why the nail should be struck on the head. Densher made no secret to Kate of his having asked for a day to decide; and his account of that matter was that he felt he owed it to her to speak to her first. She assured him on this that nothing so much as that scruple had yet shown her how they were bound together; she was clearly proud of his letting a thing of such importance depend on her; but she was clearer still as to his instant duty. She rejoiced in his prospect and urged him to his task; she should miss him intensely— of course she should miss him; but she made so little of it that she spoke with jubilation of what he would see and would do. She made so much of this last quantity that he laughed at her innocence, though also with scarce the heart to give her the real size of his drop in the daily bucket. He was struck at the same time with her happy grasp of what had really occurred in Fleet Street—all the more that it was his own final reading. He was to pull the subject up—that was just what they wanted; and it would take more than all the United States together, visit them each as he might, to let *him* down. It was just because he didn't nose about and wasn't the usual gossipmonger that they had picked him out; it was a branch of their correspondence with which they evidently wished a new tone associated, such a tone as, from now on, it would have always to take from his example.

"How you ought indeed, when you understand so well, to be a journalist's wife!" Densher exclaimed in admiration, even while she struck him as fairly hurrying him off.

But she was almost impatient of the praise. "What do you expect one *not* to understand when one cares for you?"

"Ah then, I'll put it otherwise and say 'How much you care for me!' "

"Yes," she assented; "it fairly redeems my stupidity.

I *shall*, with a chance to show it," she added, "have some imagination for you."

She spoke of the future this time as so little contingent, that he felt a queerness of conscience in taking her the report that he presently arrived at on what had passed for him with the real arbiter of their destiny. The way for that had been blocked a little by his news from Fleet Street; but in the crucible of their happy discussion this element soon melted into the other, and in the mixture that ensued the parts were not to be distinguished. The young man moreover, before taking his leave, was to see why Kate had just spoken of the future as if they now really possessed it, and was to come to the vision by a devious way that deepened the final cheer. Their faces were turned to the illumined quarter as soon as he had answered her question in respect to the appearance of their being able to play a waiting game with success. It was for the possibility of that appearance that she had, a few days before, so earnestly pressed him to see her aunt; and if after his hour with that lady it had not struck Densher that he had seen her to the happiest purpose the poor facts flushed with a better meaning as Kate, one by one, took them up.

"If she consents to your coming, why isn't that everything?"

"It *is* everything; everything *she* thinks it. It's the probability—I mean as Mrs. Lowder measures probability—that I may be prevented from becoming a complication for her by some arrangement, *any* arrangement, through which you shall see me often and easily. She's sure of my want of money, and that gives her time. She believes in my having a certain amount of delicacy, in my wishing to better my state before I put the pistol to your head in respect to sharing it. The time that will take figures for her as the time that will help her if she doesn't spoil her chance by treating me badly. She doesn't at all wish moreover," Densher went on, "to treat me badly, for I believe, upon my honour, funny as it may sound to you, that she personally rather likes me, and that if you weren't in question I might almost become her pet young man. She doesn't disparage intellect and culture—quite the contrary; she wants them to adorn her board and be named in her programme; and I'm sure it has sometimes cost her a real pang that I should be so desirable, at once, and so impossible." He paused a moment, and his companion then saw that a strange smile was in his face—a smile as strange even as the adjunct, in her own, of this informing vision. "I quite suspect her of believing that, if the truth were known, she likes me literally better than—deep down—you yourself do: wherefore she does me the honour to think that I may be safely left to kill my own cause. There, as I say, comes in her margin. I'm not the sort of stuff of romance that wears, that washes, that survives use, that resists familiarity. Once in any degree admit that, and your pride and prejudice will take care of the rest! the pride fed full, meanwhile, by the system she means to practise with you, and the prejudice excited by the comparison she'll enable you to make, from which I shall come off badly. She likes me, but she'll never like

me so much as when she succeeded a little better in
making me look wretched. For then *you'll* like me less."

Kate showed for this evocation a due interest, but no
alarm; and it was a little as if to pay his tender cynicism
back in kind that she after an instant replied: "I see, I
see; what an immense affair she must think me! One
was aware, but you deepen the impression."

"I think you'll make no mistake," said Densher, "in
letting it go as deep as it will."

He had given her indeed, she made no scruple of
showing, plenty to consider. "Her facing the music, her
making you boldly as welcome as you say—that's an
awfully big theory, you know, and worthy of all the
other big things that, in one's acquaintance with people, give her a place so apart."

"Oh, she's grand," the young man conceded; "she's
on the scale, altogether, of the car of Juggernaut—which
was a kind of image that came to me yesterday while I
waited for her at Lancaster Gate. The things in your
drawing-room there were like the forms of the strange
idols, the mystic excrescences, with which one may suppose the front of the car to bristle."

"Yes, aren't they?" the girl returned; and they had,
over all that aspect of their wonderful lady, one of those
deep and free interchanges that made everything but
confidence a false note for them. There were complications, there were questions; but they were so much more
together than they were anything else. Kate uttered for a
while no word of refutation of Aunt Maud's "big"
diplomacy, and they left it there, as they would have left

any other fine product, for a monument to her powers. But, Densher related further, he had had in other respects too the car of Juggernaut to face; he omitted nothing from his account of his visit, least of all the way Aunt Maud had frankly at last—though indeed only under artful pressure—fallen foul of his very type, his want of the right marks, his foreign accidents, his queer antecedents. She had told him he was but half a Briton, which, he granted Kate, would have been dreadful if he hadn't so let himself in for it.

"I was really curious, you see," he explained, "to find out from her what sort of queer creature, what sort of social anomaly, in the light of such conventions as hers, such an education as mine makes one pass for."

Kate said nothing for a little; but then, "Why should you care?" she asked.

"Oh," he laughed, "I like her so much; and then, for a man of my trade, her views, her spirit, are essentially a thing to get hold of; they belong to the great public mind that we meet at every turn and that we must keep setting up 'codes' with. Besides," he added, "I want to please her personally."

"Ah, yes, we must please her personally!" his companion echoed; and the words may represent all their definite recognition, at the time, of Densher's politic gain. They had in fact between this and his start for New York many matters to handle, and the question he now touched upon came up for Kate above all. She looked at him as if he had really told her aunt more of his immediate personal story than he had ever told her-

self. That, if it were so, was an accident, and it put him,
for half an hour, on as much of the picture of his early
years abroad, his migratory parents, his Swiss schools,
his German university, as she had easy attention for. A
man, he intimated, a man of their world, would have
spotted him straight as to many of these points; a man
of their world, so far as they had a world, would have
been through the English mill. But it was none the less
charming to make his confession to a woman; women
had, in fact, for such differences, so much more imagination. Kate showed at present all his case could require;
when she had had it from beginning to end she declared
that she now made out more than ever yet of what she
loved him for. She had herself, as a child, lived with
some continuity in the world across the Channel, coming home again still a child; and had participated after
that, in her teens, in her mother's brief but repeated
retreats to Dresden, to Florence, to Biarritz, weak and
expensive attempts at economy from which there stuck
to her—though in general coldly expressed, through the
instinctive avoidance of cheap raptures—the religion of
foreign things. When it was revealed to her how many
more foreign things were in Merton Densher than he
had hitherto taken the trouble to catalogue, she almost
faced him as if he were a map of the continent or a
handsome present of a delightful new "Murray." He
hadn't meant to swagger, he had rather meant to plead,
though with Mrs. Lowder he had meant also a little to
explain. His father had been, in strange countries, in
twenty settlements of the English, British chaplain, res-

ident or occasional, and had had for years the unusual
luck of never wanting a billet. His career abroad had
therefore been unbroken, and, as his stipend had never
been great, he had educated his children at the smallest
cost, in the schools nearest; which was also a saving of
railway fares. Densher's mother, it further appeared, had
practised on her side a distinguished industry, to the
success of which—so far as success ever crowned it—
this period of exile had much contributed: she copied,
patient lady, famous pictures in great museums, having
begun with a happy natural gift and taking in betimes
the scale of her opportunity. Copyists abroad of course
swarmed, but Mrs. Densher had had a sense and a hand
of her own, had arrived at a perfection that persuaded,
that even deceived, and that made the disposal of her
work blissfully usual. Her son, who had lost her, held
her image sacred, and the effect of his telling Kate all
about her, as well as about other matters until then
mixed and dim, was to render his history rich, his
sources full, his outline anything but common. He had
come round, he had come back, he insisted abundantly,
to being a Briton: his Cambridge years, his happy connection, as it had proved, with his father's college,
amply certified to that, to say nothing of his subsequent
plunge into London, which filled up the measure. But
brave enough though his descent to English earth, he
had passed, by the way, through zones of air that had
left their ruffle on his wings, had been exposed to initi-
ations ineffaceable. Something had happened to him that
could never be undone.

When Kate Croy said to him as much he besought her not to insist, declaring that this indeed was what was too much the matter with him, that he had been but too probably spoiled for native, for insular use. On which, not unnaturally, she insisted the more, assuring him, without mitigation, that if he was complicated and brilliant she wouldn't for the world have had him any thing less; so that he was reduced in the end to accusing her of putting the dreadful truth to him in the hollow guise of flattery. She was making out how abnormal he was in order that she might eventually find him impossible; and, as she could fully make it out but with his aid, she had to bribe him by feigned delight to help her. If her last word for him, in the connection, was that the way he saw himself was just a precious proof the more of his having tasted of the tree and being thereby prepared to assist her to eat, this gives the happy tone of their whole talk, the measure of the flight of time in the near presence of his settled departure. Kate showed, however, that she was to be more literally taken when she spoke of the relief Aunt Maud would draw from the prospect of his absence.

"Yet one can scarcely see why," he replied, "when she fears me so little."

His friend weighed his objection. "Your idea is that she likes you so much that she'll even go so far as to regret losing you?"

Well, he saw it in their constant comprehensive way. "Since what she builds on is the gradual process of your alienation, she may take the view that the process con-

stantly requires me. Mustn't I be there to keep it going?
It's in my exile that it may languish."

He went on with that fantasy, but at this point Kate
ceased to attend. He saw after a little that she had been
following some thought of her own, and he had been
feeling the growth of something determinant even
through the extravagance of much of the pleasantry, the
warm, transparent irony, into which their livelier intimacy kept plunging like a confident swimmer. Suddenly
she said to him with extraordinary beauty: "I engage
myself to you for ever."

The beauty was in everything, and he could have separated nothing—couldn't have thought of her face as distinct from the whole joy. Yet her face had a new light.
"And I pledge you—I call God to witness!—every spark
of my faith; I give you every drop of my life." That was
all, for the moment, but it was enough, and it was almost
as quiet as if it were nothing. They were in the open air,
in an alley of the Gardens; the great space, which seemed
to arch just then higher and spread wider for them,
threw them back into deep concentration. They moved
by a common instinct to a spot, within sight, that struck
them as fairly sequestered, and there, before their time
together was spent, they had extorted from concentration
every advance it could make them. They had exchanged
vows and tokens, sealed their rich compact, solemnized,
so far as breathed words and murmured sounds and
lighted eyes and clasped hands could do it, their agreement to belong only, and to belong tremendously, to
each other. They were to leave the place accordingly an

affianced couple; but before they left it other things still
had passed. Densher had declared his horror of bringing to a premature end her happy relation with her aunt;
and they had worked round together to a high level of
wisdom and patience. Kate's free profession was that she
wished not to deprive *him* of Mrs. Lowder's countenance, which, in the long run, she was convinced he
would continue to enjoy; and as, by a blessed turn, Aunt
Maud had demanded of him no promise that would tie
his hands, they should be able to cultivate their destiny
in their own way and yet remain loyal. One difficulty
alone stood out, which Densher named.

"Of course it will never do—we must remember
that—from the moment you allow her to found hopes of
you for any one else in particular. So long as her view
is content to remain as general as at present appears, I
don't see that we deceive her. At a given moment, you
see, she must be undeceived: the only thing therefore is
to be ready for the moment and to face it. Only, after
all, in that case," the young man observed, "one doesn't
quite make out what we shall have got from her."

"What she'll have got from *us?*" Kate inquired with a
smile. "What she'll have got from us," the girl went on,
"is her own affair—it's for *her* to measure. I asked her
for nothing," she added; "I never put myself upon her.
She must take her risks, and she surely understands
them. What we shall have got from her is what we've
already spoken of," Kate further explained; "it's that we
shall have gained time. And so, for that matter, will
she."

Densher gazed a little at all this clearness; his gaze was not at the present hour into romantic obscurity. "Yes; no doubt, in our particular situation, time's everything. And then there's the joy of it."

She hesitated. "Of our secret?"

"Not so much perhaps of our secret in itself, but of what's represented and, as we must somehow feel, protected and made deeper and closer by it." And his fine face, relaxed into happiness, covered her with all his meaning. "Our being as we are."

It was as if for a moment she let the meaning sink into her. "So gone?"

"So gone. So extremely gone. However," he smiled, "we shall go a good deal further." Her answer to which was only the softness of her silence—a silence that looked out for them both at the far reach of their prospect. This was immense, and they thus took final possession of it. They were practically united and they were splendidly strong; but there were other things— things they were precisely strong enough to be able successfully to count with and safely to allow for; in consequence of which they would, for the present, subject to some better reason, keep their understanding to themselves. It was not indeed, however, till after one more observation of Densher's that they felt the question completely straightened out. "The only thing of course is that she may any day absolutely put it to you."

Kate considered. "Ask me where, on my honour, we are? She may, naturally; but I doubt if in fact she will.

While you're away she'll make the most of it. She'll leave me alone."

"But there'll be my letters."

The girl faced his letters. "Very, very many?"

"Very, very, very many—more than ever; and you know what that is! And then," Densher added, "there'll be yours."

"Oh, I shan't leave mine on the hall-table. I shall post them myself."

He looked at her a moment. "Do you think then I had best address you elsewhere?" After which, before she could quite answer, he added with some emphasis: "I'd rather not, you know: It's straighter."

She might again have just waited. "Of course it's straighter. Don't be afraid I shan't be straight. Address me," she continued, "where you like. I shall be proud enough of its being known you write to me."

He turned it over for the last clearness. "Even at the risk of its really bringing down the inquisition?"

Well, the last clearness now filled her. "I'm not afraid of the inquisition. If she asks if there's any thing definite between us, I know perfectly what I shall say."

"That I *am*, of course, 'gone' for you?"

"That I love you as I shall never in my life love any one else, and that she can make what she likes of that." She said it out so splendidly that it was like a new profession of faith, the fulness of a tide breaking through; and the effect of that, in turn, was to make her companion meet her with such eyes that she had time again before he could otherwise speak. "Besides, she's just as likely to ask *you*."

"Not while I'm away."

"Then when you come back."

"Well then," said Densher, "we shall have had our particular joy. But what I feel is," he candidly added, "that, by an idea of her own, her superior policy, she *won't* ask me. She'll let me off. I shan't have to lie to her."

"It will be left all to me?" asked Kate.

"All to you!" he tenderly laughed.

But it was, oddly, the very next moment as if he had perhaps been a shade too candid. His discrimination seemed to mark a possible, a natural reality, a reality not wholly disallowed by the account the girl had just given of her own intention. There *was* a difference in the air— even if none other than the supposedly usual difference in truth between man and woman; and it was almost as if the sense of this provoked her. She seemed to cast about an instant, and then she went back a little resentfully to something she had suffered to pass a minute before. She appeared to take up rather more seriously than she need the joke about her freedom to deceive. Yet she did this too in a beautiful way. "Men are too stupid—even you. You didn't understand just now why, if I post my letters myself, it won't be for any thing so vulgar as to hide them."

"Oh, you said—for the pleasure."

"Yes; but you didn't, you don't understand what the

pleasure may be. There are refinements——!" she more patiently dropped. "I mean of consciousness, of sensation, of appreciation," she went on. "No," she sadly insisted—"men *don't* know. They know, in such matters, almost nothing but what women show them."

This was one of the speeches, frequent in her, that, liberally, joyfully, intensely adopted and, in itself, as might be, embraced, drew him again as close to her, and held him as long, as their conditions permitted. "Then that's exactly why we've such an abysmal need of you!"

Book Third

....

I

THE TWO LADIES WHO, in advance of the Swiss season, had been warned that their design was unconsidered, that the passes would not be clear, nor the air mild, nor the inns open—the two ladies who, characteristically, had braved a good deal of possibly interested remonstrance were finding themselves, as their adventure turned out, wonderfully sustained. It was the judgment of the head-waiters and other functionaries on the Italian lakes that approved itself now as interested; they themselves had been conscious of impatiences, of bolder dreams—at least the younger had; so that one of the things they made out together—making out as they did an endless variety—was that in those operatic palaces of the Villa d'Este, of Cadenabbia, of Pallanza and Stresa, lone women, however reinforced by a travelling-library of instructive volumes, were apt to be beguiled and undone. Their flights of fancy moreover had been modest; they had for instance risked nothing vital in hoping to make their way by the Brünig. They were making it in fact happily enough as we meet them, and were only wishing that, for the wondrous beauty of the

early high-climbing spring, it might have been longer
and the places to pause and rest more numerous.

Such at least had been the intimated attitude of Mrs.
Stringham, the elder of the companions, who had her
own view of the impatiences of the younger, to which,
however, she offered an opposition but of the most cir-
cuitous. She moved, the admirable Mrs. Stringham, in a
fine cloud of observation and suspicion; she was in the
position, as she believed, of knowing much more about
Milly Theale than Milly herself knew, and yet of having to darken her knowledge as well as make it active.
The woman in the world least formed by nature, as she
was quite aware, for duplicities and labyrinths, she found
herself dedicated to personal subtlety by a new set of circumstances, above all by a new personal relation; had
now in fact to recognise that an education in the occult—
she could scarce say what to call it—had begun for her
the day she left New York with Mildred. She had come
on from Boston for that purpose; had seen little of the
girl—or rather had seen her but briefly, for Mrs. Stringham, when she saw anything at all, saw much, saw
everything—before accepting her proposal; and had
accordingly placed herself, by her act, in a boat that she
more and more estimated as, humanly speaking, of the
biggest, though likewise, no doubt, in many ways, by
reason of its size, of the safest. In Boston, the winter
before, the young lady in whom we are interested had,
on the spot, deeply, yet almost tacitly, appealed to her,
dropped into her mind the shy conceit of some assistance, some devotion to render. Mrs. Stringham's little

life had often been visited by shy conceits—secret dreams that had fluttered their hour between its narrow walls without, for any great part, so much as mustering courage to look out of its rather dim windows. But this imagination—the fancy of a possible link with the remarkable young thing from New York—*had* mustered courage: had perched, on the instant, at the clearest look-out it could find, and might be said to have remained there till, only a few months later, it had caught, in surprise and joy, the unmistakable flash of a signal.

Milly Theale had Boston friends, such as they were, and of recent making; and it was understood that her visit to them—a visit that was not to be meagre—had been undertaken, after a series of bereavements, in the interest of the particular peace that New York could not give. It was recognised, liberally enough, that there were many things—perhaps even too many—New York *could* give; but this was felt to make no difference in the constant fact that what you had most to do, under the discipline of life, or of death, was really to feel your situation as grave. Boston could help you to that as nothing else could, and it had extended to Milly, by every presumption, some such measure of assistance. Mrs. Stringham was never to forget—for the moment had not faded, nor the infinitely fine vibration it set up in any degree ceased—her own first sight of the striking apparition, then unheralded and unexplained: the slim, constantly pale, delicately haggard, anomalously, agreeably angular young person, of not more than two-and-twenty in spite of her marks, whose hair was some-

how exceptionally red even for the real thing, which it
innocently confessed to being, and whose clothes were
remarkably black even for robes of mourning, which
was the meaning they expressed. It was New York
mourning, it was New York hair, it was a New York
history, confused as yet, but multitudinous, of the loss
of parents, brothers, sisters, almost every human
appendage, all on a scale and with a sweep that had
required the greater stage; it was a New York legend of
affecting, of romantic isolation, and, beyond everything,
it was by most accounts, in respect to the mass of
money so piled on the girl's back, a set of New York
possibilities. She was alone, she was stricken, she was
rich, and, in particular, she was strange—a combination
in itself of a nature to engage Mrs. Stringham's attention. But it was the strangeness that most determined
our good lady's sympathy, convinced as she was that it
was much greater than any one else—any one but the
sole Susan Stringham—supposed. Susan privately settled
it that Boston was not in the least seeing her, was only
occupied with her seeing Boston, and that any assumed
affinity between the two characters was delusive and
vain. *She* was seeing her, and she had quite the deepest
moment of her life in now obeying the instinct to conceal the vision. She couldn't explain it—no one would
understand. They would say clever Boston things—Mrs.
Stringham was from Burlington, Vermont, which she
boldly upheld as the real heart of New England, Boston
being "too far south"—but they would only darken
counsel.

There could be no better proof, than this quick intellectual split, of the impression made on our friend, who
shone, herself, she was well aware, with but the reflected
light of the admirable city. She too had had her discipline, but it had not made her striking; it had been prosaically usual, though doubtless a decent dose; and had
only made her usual to match it—usual, that is, as
Boston went. She had lost first her husband, and then
her mother, with whom, on her husband's death, she
had lived again; so that now, childless, she was but more
sharply single than before. But she sat rather coldly
light, having, as she called it, enough to live on—so far,
that is, as she lived by bread alone: how little indeed she
was regularly content with that diet appeared from the
name she had made—Susan Shepherd Stringham—as a
contributor to the best magazines. She wrote short stories, and she fondly believed she had her "note," the art
of showing New England without showing it wholly in
the kitchen. She had not herself been brought up in the
kitchen; she knew others who had not; and to speak for
them had thus become with her a literary mission. To *be*
in truth literary had ever been her dearest thought, the
thought that kept her bright little nippers perpetually
in position. There were masters, models, celebrities,
mainly foreign, whom she finely accounted so and in
whose light she ingeniously laboured; there were others
whom, however chattered about, she ranked with the
inane, for she was full of discrimination; but all cate-
gories failed her—they ceased at least to signify—as
soon as she found herself in presence of the real thing,

the romantic life itself. That was what she saw in Mildred—what positively made her hand a while tremble too much for the pen. She had had, it seemed to her, a revelation—such as even New England refined and grammatical couldn't give; and, all made up as she was of small neat memories and ingenuities, little industries and ambitions, mixed with something moral, personal, that was still more intensely responsive, she felt her new friend would have done her an ill turn if their friendship shouldn't develop, and yet that nothing would be left of anything else if it should. It was for the surrender of everything else that she was, however, quite prepared, and while she went about her usual Boston business with her usual Boston probity she was really all the while holding herself. She wore her "handsome" felt hat, so Tyrolese, yet somehow, though feathered from the eagle's wing, so truly domestic, with the same straightness and security; she attached her fur boa with the same honest precautions; she preserved her balance on the ice-slopes with the same practised skill; she opened, each evening, her "Transcript" with the same interfusion of suspense and resignation; she attended her almost daily concert with the same expenditure of patience and the same economy of passion; she flitted in and out of the Public Library with the air of conscientiously returning or bravely carrying off in her pocket the key of knowledge itself; and finally—it was what she most did—she watched the thin trickle of a fictive "love-interest" through that somewhat serpentine channel, in the magazines, which she mainly managed to keep clear for it. But the real thing, all the while, was elsewhere; the real thing had gone back to New York, leaving behind it the two unsolved questions, quite distinct, of why it *was* real, and whether she should ever be so near it again.

For the figure to which these questions attached themselves she had found a convenient description—she thought of it for herself, always, as that of a girl with a background. The great reality was in the fact that, very soon, after but two or three meetings, the girl with the background, the girl with the crown of old gold and the mourning that was not as the mourning of Boston, but at once more rebellious in its gloom and more frivolous in its frills, had told her she had never seen any one like her. They had met thus as opposed curiosities, and that simple remark of Milly's—if simple it was—became the most important thing that had ever happened to her; it deprived the love-interest, for the time, of actuality and even of pertinence; it moved her first, in short, in a high degree, to gratitude, and then to no small compassion. Yet in respect to this relation at least it was what did prove the key of knowledge; it lighted up as nothing else could do the poor young woman's history. That the potential heiress of all the ages should never have seen any one like a mere typical subscriber, after all, to the "Transcript" was a truth that—in especial as announced with modesty, with humility, with regret—described a situation. It laid upon the elder woman, as to the void to be filled, a weight of responsibility; but in particular it led her to ask whom poor Mildred *had* then seen, and what range of contacts it had taken to produce such queer surprises. That was really the inquiry that had ended by clearing the air: the key of knowledge was felt to click in the lock from the moment it flashed upon Mrs. Stringham that her friend had been starved for culture. Culture was what she herself represented for her, and it was living up to that principle that would surely prove the great business. She knew, the clever lady, what the principle itself represented, and the limits of her own store; and a certain alarm would have grown upon her if something else hadn't grown faster. This was, fortunately for her—and we give it in her own words—the sense of a harrowing pathos. That, primarily, was what appealed to her, what seemed to open the door of romance for her still wider than any, than a still more reckless, connection with the "picture-papers." For such was essentially the point: it was rich, romantic, abysmal, to have, as was evident, thousands and thousands a year, to have youth and intelligence and if not beauty, at least, in equal measure, a high, dim, charming, ambiguous oddity, which was even better, and then on top of all to enjoy boundless freedom, the freedom of the wind in the desert—it was unspeakably touching to be so equipped and yet to have been reduced by fortune to little humble-minded mistakes.

It brought our friend's imagination back again to New York, where aberrations were so possible in the intellectual sphere, and it in fact caused a visit she presently paid there to overflow with interest. As Milly had beautifully invited her, so she would hold out if she

could against the strain of so much confidence in her
mind; and the remarkable thing was that even at the end
of three weeks she *had* held out. But by this time her
mind had grown comparatively bold and free; it was
dealing with new quantities, a different proportion altogether—and that had made for refreshment: she had
accordingly gone home in convenient possession of her
subject. New York was vast, New York was startling,
with strange histories, with wild cosmopolite backward
generations that accounted for anything; and to have got
nearer the luxuriant tribe of which the rare creature was
the final flower, the immense, extravagant, unregulated
cluster, with free-living ancestors, handsome dead
cousins, lurid uncles, beautiful vanished aunts, persons
all busts and curls, preserved, though so exposed, in the
marble of famous French chisels—all this, to say nothing of the effect of closer growths of the stem, was to
have had one's small world-space both crowded and
enlarged. Our couple had at all events effected an
exchange; the elder friend had been as consciously intellectual as possible, and the younger, abounding in personal revelation, had been as unconsciously
distinguished. This was poetry—it was also history—
Mrs. Stringham thought, to a finer tune even than
Maeterlinck and Pater, than Marbot and Gregorovius.
She appointed occasions for the reading of these authors
with her hostess, rather perhaps than actually achieved
great spans; but what they managed and what they
missed speedily sank for her into the dim depths of the
merely relative, so quickly, so strongly had she clutched

her central clue. All her scruples and hesitations, all her
anxious enthusiasms, had reduced themselves to a single
alarm—the fear that she really might act on her companion clumsily and coarsely. She was positively afraid
of what she might do to her, and to avoid that, to avoid
it with piety and passion, to do, rather, nothing at all,
to leave her untouched because no touch one could
apply, however light, however just, however earnest and
anxious, would be half good enough, would be anything
but an ugly smutch upon perfection—this now imposed
itself as a consistent, an inspiring thought.

Less than a month after the event that had so determined Mrs. Stringham's attitude—close upon the heels,
that is, of her return from New York—she was reached
by a proposal that brought up for her the kind of question her delicacy might have to contend with. Would
she start for Europe with her young friend at the earliest
possible date, and should she be willing to do so without making conditions? The inquiry was launched
by wire; explanations, in sufficiency, were promised;
extreme urgency was suggested, and a general surrender invited. It was to the honour of her sincerity that she
made the surrender on the spot, though it was not perhaps altogether to that of her logic. She had wanted,
very consciously, from the first, to give something up
for her new acquaintance, but she had now no doubt
that she was practically giving up all. What settled this
was the fulness of a particular impression, the impression that had throughout more and more supported her
and which she would have uttered so far as she might

by saying that the charm of the creature was positively in the creature's greatness. She would have been content so to leave it; unless indeed she had said, more familiarly, that Mildred was the biggest impression of her life. That was at all events the biggest account of her, and none but a big, clearly, would do. Her situation, as such things were called, was on the grand scale; but it still was not that. It was her nature, once for all—a nature that reminded Mrs. Stringham of the term always used in the newspapers about the great new steamers, the inordinate number of "feet of water" they drew; so that if, in your little boat, you had chosen to hover and approach, you had but yourself to thank, when once motion was started, for the way the draught pulled you. Milly drew the feet of water, and odd though it might seem that a lonely girl, who was not robust and who hated sound and show, should stir the stream like a leviathan, her companion floated off with the sense of rocking violently at her side. More than prepared, however, for that excitement, Mrs. Stringham mainly failed of ease in respect to her own consistency. To attach herself for an indefinite time seemed a roundabout way of holding her hands off. If she wished to be sure of neither touching nor smutching, the straighter plan would doubtless have been not to keep her friend within reach. This in fact she fully recognised, and with it the degree to which she desired that the girl should lead her life, a life certain to be so much finer than that of anybody else. The difficulty, however, by good fortune, cleared away as soon as she had further recognised, as she was speedily able to do, that she, Susan Shepherd—the name with which Milly for the most part amused herself—was *not* anybody else. She had renounced that character; she had now no life to lead; and she honestly believed that she was thus supremely equipped for leading Milly's own. No other person whatever, she was sure, had to an equal degree this qualification, and it was really to assert it that she fondly embarked.

Many things, though not in many weeks, had come and gone since then, and one of the best of them, doubtless, had been the voyage itself, by the happy southern course, to the succession of Mediterranean ports, with the dazzled wind-up at Naples. Two or three others had preceded this; incidents, indeed rather lively marks, of their last fortnight at home, and one of which had determined on Mrs. Stringham's part a rush to New York, forty-eight breathless hours there, previous to her final rally. But the great sustained sea-light had drunk up the rest of the picture, so that for many days other questions and other possibilities sounded with as little effect as a trio of penny whistles might sound in a Wagner overture. It was the Wagner overture that practically prevailed, up through Italy, where Milly had already been, still further up and across the Alps, which were also partly known to Mrs. Stringham; only perhaps "taken" to a time not wholly congruous, hurried in fact on account of the girl's high restlessness. She had been expected, she had frankly promised, to be restless—that was partly why she was "great"—or was a consequence, at any rate, if not a cause; yet she had not perhaps altogether announced herself as straining so hard at the cord. It was familiar, it was beautiful to Mrs. Stringham that she had arrears to make up, the chances that had lapsed for her through the wanton ways of forefathers fond of Paris, but not of its higher sides, and fond almost of nothing else; but the vagueness, the openness, the eagerness without point and the interest without pause—all a part of the charm of her oddity as at first presented—had become more striking in proportion as they triumphed over movement and change. She had arts and idiosyncrasies of which no great account could have been given, but which were a daily grace if you lived with them; such as the art of being almost tragically impatient and yet making it as light as air; of being inexplicably sad and yet making it as clear as noon; of being unmistakably gay, and yet making it as soft as dusk. Mrs. Stringham by this time understood everything, was more than ever confirmed in wonder and admiration, in her view that it was life enough simply to feel her companion's feelings; but there were special keys she had not yet added to her bunch, impressions that, of a sudden, were apt to affect her as new.

This particular day on the great Swiss road had been, for some reason, full of them, and they referred themselves, provisionally, to some deeper depth than she had touched—though into two or three such depths, it must be added, she had peeped long enough to find herself suddenly draw back. It was not Milly's unpacified state, in short, that now troubled her—though certainly, as

Europe was the great American sedative, the failure was
to some extent to be noted: it was the suspected presence of something behind it—which, however, could
scarcely have taken its place there since their departure.
What any fresh motive of unrest could suddenly have
sprung from was, in short, not to be divined. It was but
half an explanation to say that excitement, for each of
them, had naturally dropped, and that what they had
left behind, or tried to—the great serious facts of life,
as Mrs. Stringham liked to call them—was once more
coming into sight as objects loom through smoke when
smoke begins to clear; for these were general appearances from which the girl's own aspect, her really larger
vagueness, seemed rather to disconnect itself. The nearest approach to a personal anxiety indulged in as yet by
the elder lady was on her taking occasion to wonder if
what she had more than anything else got hold of
mightn't be one of the finer, one of the finest, one of the
rarest—as she called it so that she might call it nothing
worse—cases of American intensity. She had just had a
moment of alarm—asked herself if her young friend
were merely going to treat her to some complicated
drama of nerves. At the end of a week, however, with
their further progress, her young friend had effectively
answered the question and given her the impression,
indistinct indeed as yet, of something that had a reality
compared with which the nervous explanation would
have been coarse. Mrs. Stringham found herself from
that hour, in other words, in presence of an explanation
that remained a muffled and intangible form, but that,

assuredly, should it take on sharpness, would explain
everything and more than everything, would become
instantly the light in which Milly was to be read.

Such a matter as this may at all events speak of the
style in which our young woman could affect those who
were near her, may testify to the sort of interest she
could inspire. She worked—and seemingly quite without
design—upon the sympathy, the curiosity, the fancy of
her associates, and we shall really ourselves scarce otherwise come closer to her than by feeling their impression and sharing, if need be, their confusion. She
reduced them, Mrs. Stringham would have said, reduced
them to a consenting bewilderment; which was precisely, for that good lady, on a last analysis, what was
most in harmony with her greatness. She exceeded,
escaped measure, was surprising only because *they* were
so far from great. Thus it was that on this wondrous day
on the Brünig the spell of watching her had grown more
than ever irresistible; a proof of what—or of a part of
what—Mrs. Stringham had, with all the rest, been
reduced to. She had almost the sense of tracking her
young friend as if at a given moment to pounce. She
knew she shouldn't pounce, she hadn't come out to
pounce; yet she felt her attention secretive, all the same,
and her observation scientific. She struck herself as hovering like a spy, applying tests, laying traps, concealing
signs. This would last, however, only till she should
fairly know what was the matter; and to watch was, after
all, meanwhile, a way of clinging to the girl, not less
than an occupation, a satisfaction in itself. The pleasure

of watching, moreover, if a reason were needed, came from a sense of her beauty. Her beauty hadn't at all originally seemed a part of the situation, and Mrs. Stringham had, even in the first flush of friendship, not named it, grossly, to any one; having seen early that, for stupid people—and who, she sometimes secretly asked herself, wasn't stupid?—it would take a great deal of explaining. She had learned not to mention it till it was mentioned first—which occasionally happened, but not too often; and then she was there in force. Then she both warmed to the perception that met her own perception, and disputed it, suspiciously, as to special items; while, in general, she had learned to refine even to the point of herself employing the word that most people employed. She employed it to pretend that she was also stupid and so have done with the matter; spoke of her friend as plain, as ugly even, in a case of especially dense insistence; but as, in appearance, so "awfully full of things." This was her own way of describing a face that, thanks, doubtless, to rather too much forehead, too much nose and too much mouth, together with too little mere conventional colour and conventional line, was expressive, irregular, exquisite, both for speech and for silence. When Milly smiled it was a public event—when she didn't it was a chapter of history. They had stopped, on the Brünig, for luncheon, and there had come up for them under the charm of the place the question of a longer stay.

Mrs. Stringham was now on the ground of thrilled recognitions, small sharp echoes of a past which she kept in a well-thumbed case, but which, on pressure of a spring and exposure to the air, still showed itself ticking as hard as an honest old watch. The embalmed "Europe" of her younger time had partly stood for three years of Switzerland, a term of continuous school at Vevey, with rewards of merit in the form of silver medals tied by blue ribbons and mild mountain-passes attacked with alpenstocks. It was the good girls who, in the holidays, were taken highest, and our friend could now judge, from what she supposed her familiarity with the minor peaks, that she had been one of the best. These reminiscences, sacred to-day because prepared in the hushed chambers of the past, had been part of the general train laid for the pair of sisters, daughters early fatherless, by their brave Vermont mother, who struck her at present as having apparently, almost like Columbus, worked out, all unassisted, a conception of the other side of the globe. She had focussed Vevey, by the light of nature, and with extraordinary completeness, at Burlington; after which she had embarked, sailed, landed, explored and, above all, made good her presence. She had given her daughters the five years in Switzerland and Germany that were to leave them ever afterwards a standard of comparison for all cycles of Cathay, and to stamp the younger in especial—Susan was the younger—with a character that, as Mrs. Stringham had often had occasion, through life, to say to herself, made all the difference. It made all the difference for Mrs. Stringham, over and over again and in the most remote connections, that, thanks to her parent's lonely,

thrifty, hardy faith, she was a woman of the world.
There were plenty of women who were all sorts of
things that she wasn't, but who, on the other hand, were
not that, and who didn't know *she* was (which she
liked—it relegated them still further) and didn't know,
either, how it enabled her to judge them. She had never
seen herself so much in this light as during the actual
phase of her associated, if slightly undirected, pilgrimage; and the consciousness gave perhaps to her plea for
a pause more intensity than she knew. The irrecoverable
days had come back to her from far off; they were part
of the sense of the cool upper air and of everything else
that hung like an indestructible scent to the torn gar-
ment of youth—the taste of honey and the luxury of
milk, the sound of cattle-bells and the rush of streams,
the fragrance of trodden balms and the dizziness of deep
gorges.

Milly clearly felt these things too, but they affected
her companion at moments—that was quite the way
Mrs. Stringham would have expressed it—as the
princess in a conventional tragedy might have affected
the confidant if a personal emotion had ever been permitted to the latter. That a princess could only be a
princess was a truth with which, essentially, a confidant,
however responsive, had to live. Mrs. Stringham was a
woman of the world, but Milly Theale was a princess,
the only one she had yet had to deal with, and this in
its way, too, made all the difference. It was a perfectly
definite doom for the wearer—it was for every one else
a perfectly palpable quality. It might have been, possi-

bly, with its involved loneliness and other mysteries, the weight under which she fancied her companion's admirable head occasionally, and ever so submissively, bowed. Milly had quite assented at luncheon to their staying over, and had left her to look at rooms, settle questions, arrange about their keeping on their carriage and horses; cares that had now moreover fallen to Mrs. Stringham as a matter of course and that yet for some reason, on this occasion particularly, brought home to her—all agreeably, richly, almost grandly—what it was to live with the great. Her young friend had, in a sublime degree, a sense closed to the general question of difficulty, which she got rid of, furthermore, not in the least as one had seen many charming persons do, by merely passing it on to others. She kept it completely at a distance: it never entered the circle; the most plaintive confidant couldn't have dragged it in; and to tread the path of a confidant was accordingly to live exempt. Service was in other words so easy to render that the whole thing was like court life without the hardships. It came back of course to the question of money, and our observant lady had by this time repeatedly reflected that if one were talking of the "difference," it was just this, this incomparably and nothing else, that when all was said and done most made it. A less vulgarly, a less obviously purchasing or parading person she couldn't have imagined; but it was, all the same, the truth of truths that the girl couldn't get away from her wealth. She might leave her conscientious companion as freely alone with it as possible and never ask a question, scarce even tolerate a reference; but it was in the fine folds of the helplessly expensive little black frock that she drew over the grass as she now strolled vaguely off; it was in the curious and splendid coils of hair, "done" with no eye whatever to the *mode du jour*, that peeped from under the corresponding indifference of her hat, the merely personal tradition that suggested a sort of noble inelegance; it lurked between the leaves of the uncut but antiquated Tauchnitz volume of which, before going out, she had mechanically possessed herself. She couldn't dress it away, nor walk it away, nor read it away, nor think it away; she could neither smile it away in any dreamy absence nor blow it away in any softened sigh. She couldn't have lost it if she had tried—that was what it was to be really rich. It had to be *the* thing you were. When at the end of an hour she had not returned to the house Mrs. Stringham, though the bright afternoon was yet young, took, with precautions, the same direction, went to join her in case of her caring for a walk. But the purpose of joining her was in truth less distinct than that of a due regard for a possibly preferred detachment: so that, once more, the good lady proceeded with a quietness that made her slightly "underhand" even in her own eyes. She couldn't help that, however, and she didn't care, sure as she was that what she really wanted was not to overstep, but to stop in time. It was to be able to stop in time that she went softly, but she had on this occasion further to go than ever yet, for she followed in vain, and at last with some anxiety, the footpath she believed Milly to have taken. It

wound up a hillside and into the higher Alpine mead-
ows in which, all these last days, they had so often
wanted, as they passed above or below, to stray; and
then it obscured itself in a wood, but always going up,
up, and with a small cluster of brown old high-perched
châlets evidently for its goal. Mrs. Stringham reached
in due course the châlets, and there received from a
bewildered old woman, a very fearful person to behold,
an indication that sufficiently guided her. The young
lady had been seen not long before passing further on,
over a crest and to a place where the way would drop
again, as our unappeased inquirer found it, in fact, a
quarter of an hour later, markedly and almost alarm-
ingly to do. It led somewhere, yet apparently quite into
space, for the great side of the mountain appeared, from
where she pulled up, to fall away altogether, though
probably but to some issue below and out of sight. Her
uncertainty moreover was brief, for she next became
aware of the presence on a fragment of rock, twenty
yards off, of the Tauchnitz volume that the girl had
brought out, and that therefore pointed to her shortly
previous passage. She had rid herself of the book, which
was an encumbrance, and meant of course to pick it up
on her return; but as she hadn't yet picked it up what on
earth had become of her? Mrs. Stringham, I hasten to
add, was within a few moments to see; but it was quite
an accident that she had not, before they were over,
betrayed by her deeper agitation the fact of her own
nearness.

The whole place, with the descent of the path and as

a sequel to a sharp turn that was masked by rocks and
shrubs, appeared to fall precipitously and to become a
"view" pure and simple, a view of great extent and
beauty, but thrown forward and vertiginous. Milly, with
the promise of it from just above, had gone straight
down to it, not stopping till it was all before her; and
here, on what struck her friend as the dizzy edge of it,
she was seated at her ease. The path somehow took care
of itself and its final business, but the girl's seat was a
slab of rock at the end of a short promontory or excres-
cence that merely pointed off to the right into gulfs of
air and that was so placed by good fortune, if not by
the worst, as to be at last completely visible. For Mrs.
Stringham stifled a cry on taking in what she believed to
be the danger of such a perch for a mere maiden; her
liability to slip, to slide, to leap, to be precipitated by a
single false movement, by a turn of the head—how
could one tell? into whatever was beneath. A thousand
thoughts, for the minute, roared in the poor lady's ears,
but without reaching, as happened, Milly's. It was a
commotion that left our observer intensely still and
holding her breath. What had first been offered her was
the possibility of a latent intention—however wild the
idea—in such a posture; of some betrayed accordance
of Milly's caprice with a horrible hidden obsession. But
since Mrs. Stringham stood as motionless as if a sound,
a syllable, must have produced the start that would be
fatal, so even the lapse of a few seconds had a partly
reassuring effect. It gave her time to receive the impression which, when she some minutes later softly retraced

her steps, was to be the sharpest she carried away. This was the impression that if the girl was deeply and recklessly meditating there, she was not meditating a jump; she was on the contrary, as she sat, much more in a state of uplifted and unlimited possession that had nothing to gain from violence. She was looking down on the kingdoms of the earth, and though indeed that of itself might well go to the brain, it wouldn't be with a view of renouncing them. Was she choosing among them, or did she want them all? This question, before Mrs. Stringham had decided what to do, made others vain; in accordance with which she saw, or believed she did, that if it might be dangerous to call out, to sound in any way a surprise, it would probably be safe enough to withdraw as she had come. She watched a while longer, she held her breath, and she never knew afterwards what time had elapsed.

Not many minutes probably, yet they had not seemed few, and they had given her so much to think of, not only while creeping home, but while waiting afterwards at the inn, that she was still busy with them when, late in the afternoon, Milly reappeared. She had stopped at the point of the path where the Tauchnitz lay, had taken it up and, with the pencil attached to her watchguard, had scrawled a word—*à bientôt!*—across the cover; then, even under the girl's continued delay, had measured time without a return of alarm. For she now saw that the great thing she had brought away was precisely a conviction that the future was not to exist for her princess in the form of any sharp or simple release from the human predicament. It wouldn't be for her a question of a flying leap and thereby of a quick escape. It would be a question of taking full in the face the whole assault of life, to the general muster of which indeed her face might have been directly presented as she sat there on her rock. Mrs. Stringham was thus able to say to herself, even after another interval of some length, that if her young friend still continued absent it wouldn't be because—whatever the opportunity—she had cut short the thread. She wouldn't have committed suicide; she knew herself unmistakably reserved for some more complicated passage; this was the very vision in which she had, with no little awe, been discovered. The image that thus remained with the elder lady kept the character of revelation. During the breathless minutes of her watch she had seen her companion afresh; the latter's type, aspect, marks, her history, her state, her beauty, her mystery, all unconsciously betrayed themselves to the Alpine air, and all had been gathered in again to feed Mrs. Stringham's flame. They are things that will more distinctly appear for us, and they are meanwhile briefly represented by the enthusiasm that was stronger on our friend's part than any doubt. It was a consciousness she was scarce yet used to carrying, but she had as beneath her feet a mine of something precious. She seemed to herself to stand near the mouth, not yet quite cleared. The mine but needed working and would certainly yield a treasure. She was not thinking, either, of Milly's gold.

THE GIRL SAID NOTHING, when they met, about the words scrawled on the Tauchnitz, and Mrs. Stringham then noticed that she had not the book with her. She had left it lying and probably would never remember it at all. Her comrade's decision was therefore quickly made not to speak of having followed her; and within five minutes of her return, wonderfully enough, the pre-occupation denoted by her forgetfulness further declared itself. "Should you think me quite abominable if I were to say that after all——?"

Mrs. Stringham had already thought, with the first sound of the question, everything she was capable of thinking, and had immediately made such a sign that Milly's words gave place to visible relief at her assent. "You don't care for our stop here—you'd rather go straight on? We'll start then with the peep of to-morrow's dawn—or as early as you like; it's only rather late now to take the road again." And she smiled to show how she meant it for a joke that an instant onward rush was what the girl would have wished. "I bullied you into stopping," she added; "so it serves me right."

Milly made in general the most of her good friend's jokes; but she humoured this one a little absently. "Oh yes, you do bully me." And it was thus arranged between them, with no discussion at all, that they would resume their journey in the morning. The younger tourist's interest in the detail of the matter—in spite of a declaration from the elder that she would consent to

be dragged anywhere—appeared almost immediately
afterwards quite to lose itself; she promised, however, to
think till supper of where, with the world all before
them, they might go—supper having been ordered for
such time as permitted of lighted candles. It had been
agreed between them that lighted candles at wayside
inns, in strange countries, amid mountain scenery, gave
the evening meal a peculiar poetry—such being the mild
adventures, the refinements of impression, that they, as
they would have said, went in for. It was now as if,
before this repast, Milly had designed to "lie down"; but
at the end of three minutes more she was not lying
down, she was saying instead, abruptly, with a transition
that was like a jump of four thousand miles: "What was
it that, in New York, on the ninth, when you saw him
alone, Dr. Finch said to you?"

It was not till later that Mrs. Stringham fully knew
why the question had startled her still more than its
suddenness explained; though the effect of it even at the
moment was almost to frighten her into a false answer.
She had to think, to remember the occasion, the
"ninth," in New York, the time she had seen Dr. Finch
alone, and to recall what he had then said to her; and
when everything had come back it was quite, at first, for
a moment, as if he had said something that immensely
mattered. He hadn't, however, in fact; it was only as if
he might perhaps after all have been going to. It was on
the sixth—within ten days of their sailing—that she had
hurried from Boston under the alarm, a small but a sufficient shock, of hearing that Mildred had suddenly

been taken ill, had had, from some obscure cause, such
an upset as threatened to stay their journey. The bearing of the accident had happily soon announced itself
as slight, and there had been, in the event, but a few
hours of anxiety; the journey had been pronounced
again not only possible, but, as representing "change,"
highly advisable; and if the zealous guest had had five
minutes by herself with the doctor, that was, clearly, no
more at his instance than at her own. Almost nothing
had passed between them but an easy exchange of
enthusiasms in respect to the remedial properties of
"Europe"; and this assurance, as the facts came back to
her, she was now able to give. "Nothing whatever, on
my word of honour, that you mayn't know or mightn't
then have known. I've no secret with him about you.
What makes you suspect it? I don't quite make out how
you know I did see him alone."

"No—you never told me," said Milly. "And I don't
mean," she went on, "during the twenty-four hours
while I was bad, when your putting your heads together
was natural enough. I mean after I was better—the last
thing before you went home."

Mrs. Stringham continued to wonder. "Who told you
I saw him then?"

"*He* didn't himself—nor did you write me it afterwards. We speak of it now for the first time. That's
exactly why!" Milly declared—with something in her
face and voice that, the next moment, betrayed for her
companion that she had really known nothing, had only
conjectured and, chancing her charge, made a hit. Yet

why had her mind been busy with the question? "But if you're not, as you now assure me, in his confidence," she smiled, "it's no matter."

"I'm not in his confidence, and he had nothing to confide. But are you feeling unwell?"

The elder woman was earnest for the truth, though the possibility she named was not at all the one that seemed to fit—witness the long climb Milly had just indulged in. The girl showed her constant white face, but that her friends had all learned to discount, and it was often brightest when superficially not bravest. She continued for a little mysteriously to smile. "I don't know—haven't really the least idea. But it might be well to find out."

Mrs. Stringham, at this, flared into sympathy. "Are you in trouble—in pain?"

"Not the least little bit. But I sometimes won-der——!"

"Yes"—she pressed: "wonder what?"

"Well, if I shall have much of it."

Mrs. Stringham stared. "Much of what? Not of pain?"

"Of everything. Of everything I have."

Anxiously again, tenderly, our friend cast about. "You 'have' everything; so that when you say 'much' of it——"

"I only mean," the girl broke in, "shall I have it for long? That is if I *have* got it."

She had at present the effect, a little, of confounding, or at least of perplexing her comrade, who was touched, who was always touched, by something helpless in her

grace and abrupt in her turns, and yet actually half
made out in her a sort of mocking light. "If you've got
an ailment?"

"If I've got everything," Milly laughed.

"Ah, *that*—like almost nobody else."

"Then for how long?"

Mrs. Stringham's eyes entreated her; she had gone
close to her, half enclosed her with urgent arms. "Do
you want to see some one?" And then as the girl only
met it with a slow headshake, though looking perhaps a
shade more conscious: "We'll go straight to the best
near doctor." This too, however, produced but a gaze
of qualified assent and a silence, sweet and vague, that
left everything open. Our friend decidedly lost herself.
"Tell me, for God's sake, if you're in distress."

"I don't think I've really *everything*," Milly said as if
to explain—and as if also to put it pleasantly.

"But what on earth can I do for you?"

The girl hesitated, then seemed on the point of being
able to say; but suddenly changed and expressed herself otherwise. "Dear, dear thing—I'm only too happy!"

It brought them closer, but it rather confirmed Mrs.
Stringham's doubt. "Then what's the matter?"

"That's the matter—that I can scarcely bear it."

"But what is it you think you haven't got?"

Milly waited another moment; then she found it, and
found for it a dim show of joy. "The power to resist the
bliss of what I *have!*"

Mrs. Stringham took it in—her sense of being "put
off" with it, the possible, probable irony of it—and her

tenderness renewed itself in the positive grimness of a long murmur. "Whom will you see?"—for it was as if they looked down from their height at a continent of doctors. "Where will you first go?"

Milly had for the third time her air of consideration; but she came back with it to her plea of some minutes before. "I'll tell you at supper—good-bye till then." And she left the room with a lightness that testified for her companion to something that again particularly pleased her in the renewed promise of motion. The odd passage just concluded, Mrs. Stringham mused as she once more sat alone with a hooked needle and a ball of silk, the "fine" work with which she had always provided—this mystifying mood had simply been precipitated, no doubt, by their prolonged halt, with which the girl really hadn't been in sympathy. One had only to admit that her complaint was in fact but the excess of the joy of life, and everything *did* then fit. She couldn't stop for the joy, but she could go on for it, and with the sense of going on she floated again, was restored to her great spaces. There was no evasion of any truth—so at least Susan Shepherd hoped—in one's sitting there while the twilight deepened and feeling still more finely that the position of this young lady was magnificent. The evening at that height had naturally turned to cold, and the travelers had bespoken a fire with their meal; the great Alpine road asserted its brave presence through the small panes of the low, clean windows, with incidents at the inn-door, the yellow *diligence*, the great waggons, the hurrying, hooded, private conveyances, reminders, for our fanciful friend, of old stories, old pictures, historic flights, escapes, pursuits, things that had happened, things indeed that by a sort of strange congruity helped her to read the meanings of the greatest interest into the relation in which she was now so deeply involved. It was natural that this record of the magnificence of her companion's position should strike her as, after all, the best meaning she could extract; for she herself was seated in the magnificence as in a court-carriage—she came back to that, and such a method of progression, such a view from crimson cushions, would evidently have a great deal more to give. By the time the candles were lighted for supper and the short, white curtains were drawn, Milly had reappeared, and the little scenic room had then all its romance. That charm moreover was far from broken by the words in which she, without further loss of time, satisfied her patient mate. "I want to go straight to London."

It was unexpected, corresponding with no view positively taken at her departure; when England had appeared, on the contrary, rather relgated and postponed—seen for the moment, as who should say, at the end of an avenue of preparations and introductions. London, in short, might have been supposed to be the crown, and to be achieved like a siege by gradual approaches. Milly's actual fine stride was therefore the more exciting, as any simplification almost always was to Mrs. Strigham; who, besides, was afterwards to recall as the very beginning of a drama the terms in which, between their smoky candles, the girl had put her preference and in which still other things had come up,

come while the clank of waggon-chains in the sharp air
reached their ears, with the stamp of hoofs, the rattle
of buckets and the foreign questions, foreign answers,
that were all alike the part of the cheery converse of the
road. The girl brought out in truth as she might have
brought a huge confession, something she admitted
herself shy about and that would seem to show her as
frivolous; it had rolled over her that what she wanted of
Europe was "people," so far as they were to be had, and
that if her friend really wished to know, the vision of
this same equivocal quantity was what had haunted her
during their previous days, in museums and churches,
and what was again spoiling for her the pure taste of
scenery. She was all for scenery—yes; but she wanted
it human and personal, and all she could say was that
there would be in London—wouldn't there?—more of
that kind than anywhere else. She came back to her idea
that if it wasn't for long—if nothing should happen to
be so for *her*—why, the particular thing she spoke of
would probably have most to give her in the time,
would probably be less than anything else a waste of
her remainder. She produced this last consideration
indeed with such gaiety that Mrs. Stringham was not
again disconcerted by it, was in fact quite ready—if talk
of early dying was in order—to match it from her own
future. Good, then; they would eat and drink because
of what might happen to-morrow; and they would
direct their course from that moment with a view to
such eating and drinking. They ate and drank that
night, in truth, as if in the spirit of this decision;

whereby the air, before they separated, felt itself the clearer.

It had cleared perhaps to a view only too extensive—extensive, that is, in proportion to the signs of life presented. The idea of "people" was not so entertained on Milly's part as to connect itself with particular persons, and the fact remained for each of the ladies that they would, completely unknown, disembark at Dover amid the completely unknowing. They had no relation already formed; this plea Mrs. Stringham put forward to see what it would produce. It produced nothing at first but the observation on the girl's side that what she had in mind was no thought of society nor of scraping acquaintance; nothing was further from her than to desire the opportunities represented for the compatriot in general by a trunkful of "letters." It wasn't a question, in short, of the people the compatriot was after; it was the human, the English picture itself, as they might see it in their own way—the world imagined always in what one had read and dreamed. Mrs. Stringham did every justice to this world, but when later on an occasion chanced to present itself, she made a point of not omitting to remark that it might be a comfort to know in advance even an individual. This still, however, failed in vulgar parlance, to "fetch" Milly, so that she had presently to go all the way. "Haven't I understood from you, for that matter, that you gave Mr. Densher something of a promise?"

There was a moment, on this, when Milly's look had to be taken as representing one of two things—either

that she was completely vague about the promise or that
Mr. Densher's name itself started no train. But she
really couldn't be so vague about the promise, her interlocutress quickly saw, without attaching it to something;
it had to be a promise to somebody in particular to be so
repudiated. In the event, accordingly, she acknowledged
Mr. Merton Densher, the so unusually clever young
Englishman who had made his appearance in New York
on some special literary business—wasn't it?—shortly
before their departure, and who had been three or four
times in her house during the brief period between her
visit to Boston and her companion's subsequent stay
with her; but she required much reminding before it
came back to her that she had mentioned to this companion just afterwards the confidence expressed by the
personage in question in her never doing so dire a thing
as to come to London without, as the phrase was, looking a fellow up. She had left him the enjoyment of his
confidence, the form of which might have appeared a
trifle free—that she now reasserted; she had done nothing either to impair or to enhance it; but she had also
left Mrs. Stringham, in the connection and at the time,
rather sorry to have missed Mr. Densher. She had
thought of him again after that, the elder woman; she
had likewise gone so far as to notice that Milly appeared
not to have done so—which the girl might easily have
betrayed; and, interested as she was in everything that
concerned her, she had made out for herself, for herself
only and rather idly, that, but for interruptions, the
young Englishman might have become a better acquain-

tance. His being an acquaintance at all was one of the signs that in the first days had helped to place Milly, as a young person with the world before her, for sympathy and wonder. Isolated, unmothered, unguarded, but with her other strong marks, her big house, her big fortune, her big freedom, she had lately begun to "receive," for all her few years, as an older woman might have done—as was done, precisely, by princesses who had public considerations to observe and who came of age very early. If it was thus distinct to Mrs. Stringham then that Mr. Densher had gone off somewhere else in connection with his errand before her visit to New York, it had been also not undiscoverable that he had come back for a day or two later on, that is after her own second excursion—that he had in fine reappeared on a single occasion on his way to the West: his way from Washington as she believed, though he was out of sight at the time of her joining her friend for their departure. It had not occurred to her before to exaggerate—it had not occurred to her that she could; but she seemed to become aware to-night that there had been just enough in this relation to meet, to provoke, the free conception of a little more.

She presently put it that, at any rate, promise or no promise, Milly would, at a pinch, be able, in London, to act on his permission to make him a sign; to which Milly replied with readiness that her ability, though evident, would be none the less quite wasted, inasmuch as the gentleman would, to a certainty, be still in America. He had a great deal to do there—which he would scarce have begun; and in fact she might very well not have thought of London at all if she hadn't been sure he wasn't yet near coming back. It was perceptible to her companion that the moment our young woman had so far committed herself she had a sense of having over-stepped; which was not quite patched up by her saying the next minute, possibly with a certain failure of pres-ence of mind, that the last thing she desired was the air of running after him. Mrs. Stringham wondered pri-vately what question there could be of any such appear-ance—the danger of which thus suddenly came up; but she said, for the time, nothing of it—she only said other things: one of which was, for instance, that if Mr. Den-sher was away he was away, and that this was the end of it; also that of course they must be discreet at any price. But what was the measure of discretion, and how was one to be sure? So it was that, as they sat there, she pro-duced her own case: *she* had a possible tie with London, which she desired as little to disown as she might wish to risk presuming on it. She treated her companion, in short, for their evening's end, to the story of Maud Manningham, the odd but interesting English girl who had formed her special affinity in the old days at the Vevey school; whom she had written to, after their sep-aration, with a regularity that had at first faltered and then altogether failed, yet that had been for the time quite a fine case of crude constancy; so that it had in fact flickered up again of itself on the occasion of the marriage of each. They had then once more fondly, scrupulously written—Mrs. Lowder first; and even

another letter or two had afterwards passed. This, however, had been the end—though with no rupture, only
a gentle drop: Maud Manningham had made, she
believed, a great marriage, while she herself had made
a small; on top of which, moreover, distance, difference,
diminished community and impossible reunion had
done the rest of the work. It was but after all these years
that reunion had begun to show as possible—if the other
party to it, that is, should be still in existence. That was
exactly what it now struck our friend as interesting to
ascertain, as, with one aid and another, she believed she
might. It was an experiment she would at all events now
make if Milly didn't object.

Milly in general objected to nothing, and, though she
asked a question or two, she raised no present plea. Her
questions—or at least her own answers to them—kindled, on Mrs. Stringham's part, a backward train: she
hadn't known till tonight how much she remembered, or
how fine it might be to see what had become of large,
high-coloured Maud, florid, exotic and alien—which
had been just the spell—even to the perceptions of
youth. There was the danger—she frankly touched it—
that such a temperament mightn't have matured, with
the years, all in the sense of fineness; it was the sort of
danger that, in renewing relations after long breaks, one
had always to look in the face. To gather in strayed
threads was to take a risk—for which, however, she was
prepared if Milly was. The possible "fun," she confessed, was by itself rather tempting; and she fairly
sounded, with this—wound up a little as she was—the

note of fun as the harmless final right of fifty years of
mere New England virtue. Among the things she was
afterwards to recall was the indescribable look dropped
on her, at this, by her companion; she was still seated
there between the candles and before the finished supper, while Milly moved about, and the look was long to
figure for her as an inscrutable comment on *her* notion
of freedom. Challenged, at any rate, as for the last wise
word, Milly showed perhaps, musingly, charmingly,
that, though her attention had been mainly soundless,
her friend's story—produced as a resource unsuspected,
a card from up the sleeve—half surprised, half beguiled
her. Since the matter, such as it was, depended on that,
she brought out, before she went to bed, an easy, a light
"Risk everything!"

This quality in it seemed possibly a little to deny
weight to Maud Lowder's evoked presence—as Susan
Stringham, still sitting up, became, in excited reflection,
a trifle more conscious. Something determinant, when
the girl had left her, took place in her—nameless but,
as soon as she had given way, coercive. It was as if she
knew again, in this fulness of time, that she had been,
after Maud's marriage, just sensibly outlived or, as people nowadays said, shunted. Mrs. Lowder had left her
behind, and on the occasion, subsequently, of the corresponding date in her own life—not the second, the sad
one, with its dignity of sadness, but the first, with the
meagreness of its supposed felicity—she had been, in
the same spirit, almost patronisingly pitied. If that suspicion, even when it had ceased to matter, had never

quite died out for her, there was doubtless some oddity in its now offering itself as a link, rather than as another break, in the chain; and indeed there might well have been for her a mood in which the notion of the development of patronage in her quondam schoolmate would have settled her question in another sense. It was actually settled—if the case be worth our analysis—by the happy consummation, the poetic justice, the generous revenge, of her having at last something to show. Maud, on their parting company, had appeared to have so much, and would now—for wasn't it also, in general, quite the rich law of English life?—have, with accretions, promotions, expansions, ever so much more. Very good; such things might be; she rose to the sense of being ready for them. Whatever Mrs. Lowder might have to show—and one hoped one did the presumptions all justice—she would have nothing like Milly Theale, who constituted the trophy producible by poor Susan. Poor Susan lingered late—till the candles were low, and as soon as the table was cleared she opened her neat portfolio. She had not lost the old clue; there were connections she remembered, addresses she could try; so the thing was to begin. She wrote on the spot.

Book Fourth

....

I

It HAD ALL GONE so fast after this that Milly uttered but the truth nearest to hand in saying to the gentleman on her right—who was, by the same token, the gentleman on her hostess's left—that she scarce even then knew where she was: the words marking her first full sense of a situation really romantic. They were already dining, she and her friend, at Lancaster Gate, and surrounded, as it seemed to her, with every English accessory; though her consciousness of Mrs. Lowder's existence, and still more of her remarkable identity, had been of so recent and so sudden a birth. Susie, as she was apt to call her companion for a lighter change, had only had to wave a neat little wand for the fairy-tale to begin at once; in consequence of which Susie now glittered—for, with Mrs. Stringham's new sense of success, it came to that—in the character of a fairy godmother. Milly had almost insisted on dressing her, for the present occasion, as one; and it was no fault of the girl's if the good lady had not now appeared in a peaked hat, a short petticoat and diamond shoe-buckles, brandishing the magic crutch. The good lady,

in truth, bore herself not less contentedly than if these
insignia had marked her work; and Milly's observation
to Lord Mark had just been, doubtless, the result of
such a light exchange of looks with her as even the great
length of the table had not baffled. There were twenty
persons between them, but this sustained passage was
the sharpest sequel yet to that other comparison of views
during the pause on the Swiss pass. It almost appeared
to Milly that their fortune had been unduly precipitated—as if, properly, they were in the position of having ventured on a small joke and found the answer out
of proportion grave. She could not at this moment, for
instance, have said whether, with her quickened perceptions, she were more enlivened or oppressed; and the
case might in fact have been serious had she not, by
good fortune, from the moment the picture loomed,
quickly made up her mind that what finally most concerned her was neither to seek nor to shirk, was not even
to wonder too much, but was to let things come as they
would, since there was little enough doubt of how they
would go.

Lord Mark had been brought to her before dinner—
not by Mrs. Lowder, but by the handsome girl, that
lady's niece, who was now at the other end and on the
same side as Susie; he had taken her in, and she meant
presently to ask him about Miss Croy, the handsome
girl, actually offered to her sight—though now in a
splendid way—but for the second time. The first time
had been the occasion—only three days before—of her
calling at their hotel with her aunt and then making, for

our other two heroines, a great impression of beauty and
eminence. This impression had remained so with Milly
that, at present, and although her attention was aware
at the same time of everything else, her eyes were
mainly engaged with Kate Croy when not engaged with
Susie. That wonderful creature's eyes moreover readily
met them—she ranked now as a wonderful creature; and
it seemed a part of the swift prosperity of the American visitors that, so little in the original reckoning, she
should yet appear conscious, charmingly, frankly conscious, of possibilities of friendship for them. Milly had
easily and, as a guest, gracefully generalised: English
girls had a special, strong beauty, and it particularly
showed in evening dress—above all when, as was strikingly the case with this one, the dress itself was what it
should be. That observation she had all ready for Lord
Mark when they should, after a little, get round to it.
She seemed even now to see that there might be a good
deal they would get round to; the indication being that,
taken up once for all with her other neighbour, their
hostess would leave them much to themselves. Mrs.
Lowder's other neighbour was the Bishop of Murrum—
a real bishop, such as Milly had never seen, with a complicated costume, a voice like an old-fashioned wind
instrument, and a face all the portrait of a prelate; while
the gentleman on our young lady's left, a gentleman
thick-necked, large and literal, who looked straight
before him and as if he were not to be diverted by vain
words from that pursuit, clearly counted as an offset to
the possession of Lord Mark. As Milly made out these

things—with a shade of exhilaration at the way she already fell in—she saw how she was justified of her plea for people and her love of life. It wasn't then, as the prospect seemed to show, so difficult to get into the current, or to stand, at any rate, on the bank. It was easy to get near—if they *were* near; and yet the elements were different enough from any of her old elements, and positively rich and strange.

She asked herself if her right-hand neighbour would understand what she meant by such a description of them, should she throw it off; but another of the things to which, precisely, her sense was awakened was that no, decidedly, he wouldn't. It was nevertheless by this time open to her that his line would be to be clever; and indeed, evidently, no little of the interest was going to be in the fresh reference and fresh effect both of people's cleverness and of their simplicity. She thrilled, she consciously flushed, and turned pale with the certitude—it had never been so present—that she should find herself completely involved: the very air of the place, the pitch of the occasion, had for her so positive a taste and so deep an undertone. The smallest things, the faces, the hands, the jewels of the women, the sound of words, especially of names, across the table, the shape of the forks, the arrangement of the flowers, the attitude of the servants, the walls of the room, were all touches in a picture and denotements in a play; and they marked for her, moreover, her alertness of vision. She had never, she might well believe, been in such a state of vibration; her sensibility was almost too sharp for her comfort:

there were, for example, more indications than she could reduce to order in the manner of the friendly niece, who struck her as distinguished and interesting, as in fact surprisingly genial. This young woman's type had, visibly, other possibilities; yet here, of its own free movement, it had already sketched a relation. Were they, Miss Croy and she, to take up the tale where their two elders had left it off so many years before?——were they to find they liked each other and to try for themselves if a scheme of constancy on more modern lines could be worked? She had doubted, as they came to England, of Maud Manningham, had believed her a broken reed and a vague resource, had seen their dependence on her as a state of mind that would have been shamefully silly—so far as it *was* dependence—had they wished to do any thing so inane as "get into society." To have made their pilgrimage all for the sake of such society as Mrs. Lowder might have in reserve for them—that didn't bear thinking of at all, and she herself had quite chosen her course for curiosity about other matters. She would have described this curiosity as a desire to see the places she had read about, and *that* description of her motive she was prepared to give her neighbour—even though, as a consequence of it, he should find how little she had read. It was almost at present as if her poor prevision had been rebuked by the majesty—she could scarcely call it less—of the event, or at all events by the commanding character of the two figures—she could scarcely call *that* less either—mainly presented. Mrs. Lowder and her niece, however dissimilar, had at least

in common that each was a great reality. That was true,
primarily, of the aunt—so true that Milly wondered
how her own companion had arrived, in other days, at
so odd an alliance; yet she none the less felt Mrs. Lowder as a person of whom the mind might in two or three
days roughly make the circuit. She would sit there massive, at least, while one attempted it; whereas Miss
Croy, the handsome girl, would indulge in incalculable
movements that might interfere with one's tour. She was
real, none the less, and everything and everybody were
real; and it served them right, no doubt, the pair of
them, for having rushed into their adventure.

Lord Mark's intelligence meanwhile, however, had
met her own quite sufficiently to enable him to tell her
how little he could clear up her situation. He explained,
for that matter—or at least he hinted—that there was no
such thing, to-day in London, as saying where any one
was. Every one was everywhere—nobody was anywhere.
He should be put to it—yes, frankly—to give a name
of any sort or kind to their hostess's "set." *Was* it a set
at all, or wasn't it, and were there not really no such
things as sets, in the place, any more?—was there any
thing but the senseless shifting tumble, like that of some
great greasy sea in mid-Channel, of an overwhelming
melted mixture? He threw out the question, which
seemed large; Milly felt that at the end of five minutes
he had thrown out a great many, though he followed
none more than a step or two; perhaps he would prove
suggestive, but he helped her as yet to no discriminations: he spoke as if he had given them up from too

much knowledge. He was thus at the opposite extreme
from herself, but, as a consequence of it, also wandering and lost; and he was furthermore, for all his temporary incoherence, to which she guessed there would be
some key, as great a reality as either Mrs. Lowder or
Kate. The only light in which he placed the former of
these ladies was that of an extraordinary woman—a
most extraordinary woman, and "the more extraordinary
the more one knows her," while of the latter he said
nothing, for the moment, but that she was tremendously, yes, quite tremendously, good-looking. It was
some time, she thought, before his talk showed his cleverness, and yet each minute she believed in it more,
quite apart from what her hostess had told her on first
naming him. Perhaps he was one of the cases she had
heard of at home—those characteristic cases of people in
England who concealed their play of mind so much
more than they showed it. Even Mr. Densher a little did
that. And what made Lord Mark, at any rate, so real
either, when this was a thing he so definitely insisted
on? His type somehow, as by a life, a need, an intention of its own, insisted *for* him; but that was all. It was
difficult to guess his age—whether he were a young man
who looked old or an old man who looked young; it
seemed to prove nothing, as against other things, that he
was bald and, as might have been said, slightly stale,
or, more delicately perhaps, dry: there was such a fine
little fidget of preoccupied life in him, and his eyes, at
moments—though it was an appearance they could suddenly lose—were as candid and clear as those of a pleas-

ant boy. Very neat, very light, and so fair that there was little other indication of his moustache than his constantly feeling it—which was again boyish—he would have affected her as the most intellectual person present if he had not affected her as the most frivolous. The latter quality was rather in his look than in anything else, though he constantly wore his double eyeglass, which was, much more, Bostonian and thoughtful.

The idea of his frivolity had, no doubt, to do with his personal designation, which represented—as yet, for our young woman, a little confusedly—a connection with an historic patriciate, a class that, in turn, also confusedly, represented an affinity with a social element that she had never heard otherwise described than as "fashion." The supreme social element in New York had never known itself but as reduced to that category, and though Milly was aware that, as applied to a territorial and political aristocracy, the label was probably too simple, she had for the time none other at hand. She presently, it is true, enriched her idea with the perception that her interlocutor was indifferent; yet this, indifferent as aristocracies notoriously were, saw her but little further, inasmuch as she felt that, in the first place, he would much rather get on with her than not, and in the second was only thinking of too many matters of his own. If he kept her in view on the one hand and kept so much else on the other—the way he crumbed up his bread was a proof—why did he hover before her as a potentially insolent noble? She couldn't have answered the question, and it was precisely one of those that swarmed. They were complicated, she might fairly have said, by his visibly knowing, having known from afar off, that she was a stranger and an American, and by his none the less making no more of it than if she and her like were the chief of his diet. He took her, kindly enough, but imperturbably, irreclaimably, for granted, and it wouldn't in the least help that she herself knew him, as quickly, for having been in her country and threshed it out. There would be nothing for her to explain or attenuate or brag about; she could neither escape nor prevail by her strangeness; he would have, for that matter, on such a subject, more to tell her than to learn from her. She might learn from *him* why she was so different from the handsome girl—which she didn't know, being merely able to feel it; or at any rate might learn from him why the handsome girl was so different from her.

On these lines, however, they would move later; the lines immediately laid down were, in spite of his vagueness for his own convenience, definite enough. She was already, he observed to her, thinking what she should say on her other side—which was what Americans were always doing. She needn't in conscience say anything at all; but Americans never knew that, nor ever, poor creatures, yes (*she* had interposed the "poor creatures!") what not to do. The burdens they took on—the things, positively, they made an affair of! This easy and, after all, friendly jibe at her race was really for her, on her new friend's part, the note of personal recognition so far as she required it; and she gave him a prompt and con-

scious example of morbid anxiety by insisting that her
desire to be, herself, "lovely" all round was justly
founded on the lovely way Mrs. Lowder had met her.
He was directly interested in that, and it was not till
afterwards that she fully knew how much more information about their friend he had taken than given. Here
again, for instance, was a pertinent note for her: she had,
on the spot, with her first plunge into the obscure
depths of a society constituted from far back, encountered the interesting phenomenon of complicated, of
possibly sinister motive. However, Maud Manningham
(her name, even in her presence, somehow still fed the
fancy) *had*, all the same, been lovely, and one was going
to meet her now quite as far on as one had one's self
been met. She had been with them at their hotel—they
were a pair—before even they had supposed she could
have got their letter. Of course indeed they had written
in advance, but they had followed that up very fast. She
had thus engaged them to dine but two days later, and
on the morrow again, without waiting for a return visit,
waiting for anything, she had called with her niece. It
was as if she really cared for them, and it was magnificent fidelity—fidelity to Mrs. Stringham, her own companion and Mrs. Lowder's former schoolmate, the lady
with the charming face and the rather high dress down
there at the end.

Lord Mark took in through his nippers these balanced attributes of Susie. "But isn't Mrs. Stringham's
fidelity then equally magnificent?"

"Well, it's a beautiful sentiment; but it isn't as if she had anything to *give*."

"Hasn't she got you?" Lord Mark presently asked.

"Me—to give Mrs. Lowder?" Milly had clearly not yet seen herself in the light of such an offering. "Oh, I'm rather a poor present; and I don't feel as if, even at that, I've as yet quite been given."

"You've been shown, and if our friend has jumped at you it comes to the same thing." He made his jokes, Lord Mark, without amusement for himself; yet it wasn't that he was grim. "To be seen you must recognise, *is*, for you, to be jumped at; and, if it's a question of being shown, here you are again. Only it has now been taken out of your friend's hands; it's Mrs. Lowder, already, who's getting the benefit. Look round the table and you'll make out, I think, that you're being, from top to bottom, jumped at."

"Well, then," said Milly, "I seem also to feel that I like it better than being made fun of."

It was one of the things she afterwards saw—Milly was for ever seeing things afterwards—that her companion had here had some way of his own, quite unlike any one's else, of assuring her of his consideration. She wondered how he had done it, for he had neither apologised nor protested. She said to herself, at any rate, that he had led her on; and what was most odd was the question by which he had done so. "Does she know much about you?"

"No, she just likes us."

Even for this his travelled lordship, seasoned and saturated, had no laugh. "I mean you particularly. Has that lady with the charming face, which *is* charming, told her?"

Milly hesitated. "Told her what?"

"Everything."

· This, with the way he dropped it, again considerably moved her—made her feel for a moment that, as a matter of course, she was a subject for disclosures. But she quickly found her answer. "Oh, as for that, you must ask *her*."

"Your clever companion?"

"Mrs. Lowder."

He replied to this that their hostess was a person with whom there were certain liberties one never took, but that he was none the less fairly upheld, inasmuch as she was for the most part kind to him and as, should he be very good for a while, she would probably herself tell him. "And I shall have, at any rate, in the meantime, the interest of seeing what she does with you. That will teach me more or less, you see, how much she knows."

Milly followed this—it was lucid; but it suggested something apart. "How much does she know about *you?*"

"Nothing," said Lord Mark serenely. "But that doesn't matter—for what she does with me." And then, as to anticipate Milly's question about the nature of such doing: "This, for instance—turning me straight on for *you.*"

The girl thought. "And you mean she wouldn't if she did know——?"

He met it as if it were really a point. "No. I believe, to do her justice, she still would. So you can be easy."

Milly had the next instant, then, acted on the permission. "Because you're even at the worst the best thing she has?"

With this he was at last amused. "I was till you came. You're the best now."

It was strange his words should have given her the sense of his knowing, but it was positive that they did so, and to the extent of making her believe them, though still with wonder. That, really, from this first of their meetings, was what was most to abide with her: she accepted almost helplessly, she surrendered to the inevitability of being the sort of thing, as he might have said, that he at least thoroughly believed he had, in going about, seen here enough of for all practical purposes. Her submission was naturally, moreover, not to be impaired by her learning later on that he had paid at short intervals, though at a time apparently just previous to her own emergence from the obscurity of extreme youth, three separate visits to New York, where his nameable friends and his contrasted contacts had been numerous. His impression, his recollection of the whole mixed quantity, was still visibly rich. It had helped him to place her, and she was more and more sharply conscious of having—as with the door sharply slammed upon her and the guard's hand raised in signal to the train—been popped into the compartment in which she was to travel for him. It was a use of her that many a girl would have been doubtless quick to resent; and the kind of mind that thus, in our young lady, made all for mere seeing and taking is precisely one of the charms of our subject. Milly had practically just learned from him, had made out, as it were, from her rumbling compartment, that he gave her the highest place among their friend's actual properties. She was a success, that was what it came to, he presently assured her, and that was what it was to be a success: it always happened before one could know it. One's ignorance was in fact often the greatest part of it. "You haven't had time yet," he said; "this is nothing. But you'll see. You'll see everything. You can, you know—everything you dream of."

He made her more and more wonder; she almost felt as if he were showing her visions while he spoke; and strangely enough, though it was visions that had drawn her on, she hadn't seen them in connection—that is in such preliminary and necessary connection—with such a face as Lord Mark's, such eyes and such a voice, such a tone and such a manner. He had for an instant the effect of making her ask herself if she were after all going to be afraid; so distinct was it for fifty seconds that a fear passed over her. There they were again—yes, certainly: Susie's overture to Mrs. Lowder had been their joke, but they had pressed in that gaiety an electric bell that continued to sound. Positively, while she sat there, she had the loud rattle in her ears, and she wondered, during these moments, why the others didn't hear it. They didn't stare, they didn't smile, and the fear in her that I speak of was but her own desire to stop it. That dropped, however, as if the alarm itself had ceased; she seemed to have seen in a quick, though tempered glare that there were two courses for her, one to leave London again the first thing in the morning, the other to do nothing at all. Well, she would do nothing at all; she was already doing it; more than that, she had already done it, and her chance was gone. She gave herself up—she had the strangest sense, on the spot, of so deciding; for she had turned a corner before she went on again with Lord Mark. Inexpressive, but intensely signicant, he met as no one else could have done the very question she had suddenly put to Mrs. Stringham on the Brünig. Should she have it, whatever she did have, that question had been, for long? "Ah, so possibly not," her neighbour appeared to reply; "therefore, don't you see? *I'm* the way." It was vivid that he might be, in spite of his absence of flourish; the way being doubtless just *in* that absence. The handsome girl, whom she didn't lose sight of and who, she felt, kept her also in view—Mrs. Lowder's striking niece would, perhaps, be the way as well, for in her too was the absence of flourish, though she had little else, so far as one could tell, in common with Lord Mark. Yet how indeed *could* one tell, what did one understand, and of what was one, for that matter, provisionally conscious but of their being somehow together in what they represented? Kate Croy, fine but friendly, looked over at her as really with a guess at Lord Mark's effect on her. If she could guess this effect what then did she know about it and in what degree had she felt it herself? Did that represent, as between them, anything particular, and should she have to count with them as duplicating, as intensifying by a mutual intelligence, the relation into which she was sinking? Nothing was so odd as that she should have to recognise so quickly in each of these glimpses of an instant the various signs of a relation; and this anomaly itself, had she had more time to give to it, might well, might almost terribly have suggested to her that her doom was to live fast. It was queerly a question of the short run and the consciousness proportionately crowded.

These were immense excursions for the spirit of a young person at Mrs. Lowder's mere dinner-party; but what was so significant and so admonitory as the fact of their being possible? What could they have been but just a part, already, of the crowded consciousness? And it was just a part, likewise, that while plates were changed and dishes presented and periods in the banquet marked; while appearances insisted and phenomena multiplied and words reached her from here and there like plashes of a slow, thick tide; while Mrs. Lowder grew somehow more stout and more instituted and Susie, at her distance and in comparison, more thinly improvised and more different—different, that is, from every one and everything: it was just a part that while this process went forward our young lady alighted, came back, taking up her destiny again as if she had been able by a wave or two of her wings to place herself briefly in sight of an alternative to it. Whatever it was it had showed in this brief interval as better than the alternative; and it now presented itself altogether in the image and in the place in which she had left it. The image was that of her being, as Lord Mark had declared, a success. This depended more or less of course on his idea of the thing—into which at present, however, she wouldn't go. But, renewing soon, she had asked him what he meant then that Mrs. Lowder would do with her, and she had replied that this might safely be left. "She'll get back," he pleasantly said, "her money." He could say it too—which was singular—without affecting her either as vulgar or as "nasty"; and he had soon explained himself by adding: "Nobody here, you know, does anything for nothing."

"Ah, if you mean that we shall reward her as hard as ever we can, nothing is more certain. But she's an idealist," Milly continued, "and idealists, in the long run, I think, *don't* feel that they lose."

Lord Mark seemed, within the limits of his enthusiasm, to find this charming. "Ah, she strikes you as an idealist?"

"She idealises *us*, my friend and me, absolutely. She sees us in a light," said Milly. "That's all I've got to hold on by. So don't deprive me of it."

"I wouldn't for the world. But do you think," he continued as if it were suddenly important for him—"do you think she sees *me* in a light?"

She neglected his question for a little, partly because her attention attached itself more and more to the handsome girl, partly because, placed so near their hostess, she wished not to show as discussing her too freely.

Mrs. Lowder, it was true, steering in the other quarter a course in which she called at subjects as if they were islets in an archipelago, continued to allow them their ease, and Kate Croy, at the same time, steadily revealed herself as interesting. Milly in fact found, of a sudden, her ease—found it all—as she bethought herself that what Mrs. Lowder was really arranging for was a report on her quality and, as perhaps might be said, her value from Lord Mark. She wished him, the wonderful lady, to have no pretext for not knowing what he thought of Miss Theale. Why his judgment so mattered remained to be seen; but it was this divination, in any case, that now determined Milly's rejoinder. "No. She knows you. She has probably reason to. And you all, here, know each other—I see that—so far as you know anything. You know what you're used to, and it's your being used to it—that, and that only—that makes you. But there are things you don't know."

He took it in as if it might fairly, to do him justice, be a point. "Things that I don't—with all the pains I take and the way I've run about the world to leave nothing unlearned?"

Milly thought, and it was perhaps the very truth of his claim—its not being negligible—that sharpened her impatience and thereby her wit. "You're blasé, but you're not enlightened. You're familiar with everything, but conscious, really, of nothing. What I mean is that you've no imagination."

Lord Mark, at this, threw back his head, ranging with his eyes the opposite side of the room and showing himself at last so much more completely as diverted that it fairly attracted their hostess's notice. Mrs. Lowder, however, only smiled on Milly for a sign that something racy was what she had expected, and resumed, with a splash of her screw, her cruise among the islands. "Oh, I've heard that," the young man replied, "before!"

"There it is then. You've heard everything before. You've heard *me* of course before, in my country, often enough."

"Oh, never too often," he protested; "I'm sure I hope I shall still hear you again and again."

"But what good then has it done you?" the girl went on as if now frankly to amuse him.

"Oh, you'll see when you know me."

"But, most assuredly, I shall never know you."

"Then that will be exactly," he laughed, "the good!"

If it established thus that they couldn't, or wouldn't, mix, why, none the less, did Milly feel, through it, a perverse quickening of the relation to which she had been, in spite of herself, appointed? What queerer consequence of their not mixing than their talking—for it was what they had arrived at—almost intimately? She wished to get away from him, or indeed, much rather, away from herself so far as she was present to him. She saw already—wonderful creature, after all, herself too— that there would be a good deal more of him to come for her, and that the special sign of their intercourse would be to keep herself out of the question. Everything else might come in—only never that; and with such an arrangement they might even go far. This in fact might

quite have begun, on the spot, with her returning again
to the topic of the handsome girl. If she was to keep herself out she could naturally best do so by putting in
somebody else. She accordingly put in Kate Croy, being
ready to that extent—as she was not at all afraid for
her—to sacrifice her if necessary. Lord Mark himself,
for that matter, had made it easy by saying a little while
before that no one among them did anything for nothing. "What then"—she was aware of being abrupt—
"does Miss Croy, if she's so interested, do it for? What
has she to gain by *her* lovely welcome? Look at her
now!" Milly broke out with characteristic freedom of
praise, though pulling herself up also with a compunctious "Oh!" as the direction thus given to their eyes
happened to coincide with a turn of Kate's face to them.
All she had meant to do was to insist that this face was
fine; but what she had in fact done was to renew again
her effect of showing herself to its possessor as conjoined
with Lord Mark for some interested view of it. He had,
however, promptly met her question.

"To gain? Why, your acquaintance."

"Well, what's my acquaintance to her? She can care
for me—she must feel that—only by being sorry for me;
and that's why she's lovely: to be already willing to take
the trouble to be. It's the height of the disinterested."

There were more things in this than one that Lord
Mark might have taken up; but in a minute he had
made his choice. "Ah then, I'm nowhere, for I'm afraid
I'm not sorry for you in the least. What do you make
then," he asked, "of your success?"

"Why, just the great reason of all. It's just because our friend there sees it that she pities me. She understands," Milly said; "she's better than any of you. She's beautiful."

He appeared struck with this at last—with the point the girl made of it; to which she came back even after a diversion created by a dish presented between them. "Beautiful in character, I see. *Is* she so? You must tell me about her."

Milly wondered. "But haven't you known her longer than I? Haven't you seen her for yourself?"

"No—I've failed with her. It's no use. I don't make her out. And I assure you I really should like to." His assurance had in fact for his companion a positive suggestion of sincerity; he affected her as now saying something that he felt; and she was the more struck with it as she was still conscious of the failure even of curiosity he had just shown in respect to herself. She had meant something—though indeed for herself almost only—in speaking of their friend's natural pity; it had been a note, doubtless, of questionable taste, but it had quavered out in spite of her; and he had not so much as cared to inquire "Why 'natural'?" Not that it wasn't really much better for her that he shouldn't: explanations would in truth have taken her much too far. Only she now perceived that, in comparison, her word about this other person really "drew" him; and there were things in that, probably, many things, as to which she would learn more and which glimmered there already as part and parcel of that larger "real"

with which, in her new situation, she was to be
beguiled. It was in fact at the very moment, this element, not absent from what Lord Mark was further
saying. "So you're wrong, you see, as to our knowing all
about each other. There are cases where we break
down. I at any rate give *her* up—up, that is, to you.
You must do her for me—tell me, I mean, when you
know more. You'll notice," he pleasantly wound up,
"that I've confidence in you."

"Why shouldn't you have?" Milly asked, observing
in this, as she thought, a fine, though, for such a man,
a surprisingly artless, fatuity. It was as if there might
have been a question of her falsifying for the sake of her
own show—that is of her honesty not being proof
against her desire to keep well with him herself. She
didn't, none the less, otherwise protest against his
remark; there was something else she was occupied in
seeing. It was the handsome girl alone, one of his own
species and his own society, who had made him feel
uncertain; of his certainties about a mere little American, a cheap exotic, imported almost wholesale, and
whose habitat, with its conditions of climate, growth,
and cultivation, its immense profusion, but its few vari-
eties and thin development, he was perfectly satisfied.
The marvel was, too, that Milly understood his satisfaction—feeling that she expressed the truth in presently
saying: "Of course; I make out that she must be difficult; just as I see that I myself must be easy." And that
was what, for all the rest of this occasion, remained with
her—as the most interesting thing that could remain.

She was more and more content herself to be easy; she would have been resigned, even had it been brought straighter home to her, to passing for a cheap exotic. Provisionally, at any rate, that protected her wish to keep herself, with Lord Mark, in abeyance. They *had* all affected her as inevitably knowing each other, and if the handsome girl's place among them was something even their initiation couldn't deal with—why, then, she would indeed be a quantity.

II

THAT SENSE OF QUANTITIES, separate or mixed, was indeed doubtless what most prevailed at first for our slightly gasping American pair; it found utterance for them in their frequent remark to each other that they had no one but themselves to thank. It dropped from Milly more than once that if she had ever known it was so easy—! though her exclamation mostly ended without completing her idea. This, however, was a trifle to Mrs. Stringham, who cared little whether she meant that in this case she would have come sooner. She couldn't have come sooner, and she perhaps, on the contrary, meant— for it would have been like her—that she wouldn't have come at all; why it was so easy being at any rate a matter as to which her companion had begun quickly to pick up views. Susie kept some of these lights for the present to herself, since, freely communicated, they might have been a little disturbing; with which, more- over, the quantities that we speak of as surrounding the

two ladies were, in many cases, quantities of things—
and of other things—to talk about. Their immediate lesson, accordingly, was that they just had been caught up
by the incalculable strength of a wave that was actually
holding them aloft and that would naturally dash them
wherever it liked. They meanwhile, we hasten to add,
make the best of their precarious position, and if Milly
had had no other help for it she would have found not
a little in the sight of Susan Shepherd's state. The girl
had had nothing to say to her, for three days, about the
"success" announced by Lord Mark—which they saw,
besides, otherwise established; she was too taken up, too
touched, by Susie's own exaltation. Susie glowed in the
light of her justified faith; everything had happened that
she had been acute enough to think least probable; she
had appealed to a possible delicacy in Maud Manningham—a delicacy, mind you, but *barely* possible—and
her appeal had been met in a way that was an honour
to human nature. This proved sensibility of the lady of
Lancaster Gate performed verily, for both our friends,
during these first days, the office of a fine floating gold-
dust, something that threw over the prospect a harmon-
ising blur. The forms, the colours behind it were strong
and deep—we have seen how they already stood out for
Milly; but nothing, comparatively, had had so much of
the dignity of truth as the fact of Maud's fidelity to a
sentiment. That was what Susie was proud of, much
more than of her great place in the world, which she was
moreover conscious of not as yet wholly measuring.
That was what was more vivid even than her being—in

senses more worldly and in fact almost in the degree of
a revelation—English and distinct and positive, with
almost no inward, but with the finest outward resonance.

Susan Shepherd's word for her, again and again, was
that she was "large"; yet it was not exactly a case, as to
the soul, of echoing chambers: she might have been
likened rather to a capacious receptacle, originally perhaps loose, but now drawn as tightly as possible over
its accumulated contents—a packed mass, for her American admirer, of curious detail. When the latter good
lady, at home, had handsomely figured her friends as
not small—which was the way she mostly figured
them—there was a certain implication that they were
spacious because they were empty. Mrs. Lowder, by a
different law, was spacious because she was full, because
she had something in common, even in repose, with a
projectile, of great size, loaded and ready for use. That
indeed, to Susie's romantic mind, announced itself as
half the charm of their renewal—a charm as of sitting
in springtime, during a long peace, on the daisied,
grassy bank of some great slumbering fortress. True to
her psychological instincts, certainly, Mrs. Stringham
had noted that the "sentiment" she rejoiced in on her
old schoolmate's part was all a matter of action and
movement, was not, save for the interweaving of a more
frequent plump "dearest" than she would herself perhaps have used, a matter of much other embroidery. She
brooded, with interest, on this further remark of race,
feeling in her own spirit a different economy. The joy,
for her, was to know *why* she acted—the reason was half

the business; whereas with Mrs. Lowder there might have been no reason: "why" was the trivial seasoning-substance, the vanilla or the nutmeg, omittable from the nutritive pudding without spoiling it. Mrs. Lowder's desire was clearly sharp that their young companions should also prosper together; and Mrs. Stringham's account of it all to Milly, during the first days, was that when, at Lancaster Gate, she was not occupied in telling, as it were, about her, she was occupied in hearing much of the history of her hostess's brilliant niece.

They had plenty, on these lines, the two elder women, to give and to take, and it was even not quite clear to the pilgrim from Boston that what she should mainly have arranged for in London was not a series of thrills for herself. She had a bad conscience, indeed almost a sense of immorality, in having to recognise that she was, as she said, carried away. She laughed to Milly when she also said that she didn't know where it would end; and the principal of her uneasiness was that Mrs. Lowder's life bristled for her with elements that she was really having to look at for the first time. They represented, she believed, the world, the world that, as a consequence of the cold shoulder turned to it by the Pilgrim Fathers, had never yet boldly crossed to Boston—it would surely have sunk the stoutest Cunarder—and she couldn't pretend that she faced the prospect simply because Milly had had a caprice. She was in the act herself of having one, directed precisely to their present spectacle. She could but seek strength in the thought that she had never had one—or had never yielded to one, which came to the same thing—before. The sustaining sense of it all, moreover, as literary material—that quite dropped from her. She must wait, at any rate, she should see: it struck her, so far as she had got, as vast, obscure, lurid. She reflected in the watches of the night that she was probably just going to love it for itself—that is for itself and Milly. The odd thing was that she could think of Milly's loving it without dread—or with dread, at least not on the score of conscience, only on the score of peace. It was a mercy, at all events, for the hour, that their fancies jumped together.

While, for this first week that followed their dinner, she drank deep at Lancaster Gate, her companion was no less happily, appeared to be indeed on the whole quite as romantically, provided for. The handsome English girl from the heavy English house had been as a figure in a picture stepping by magic out of its frame: it was a case, in truth, for which Mrs. Stringham presently found the perfect image. She had lost none of her grasp, but quite the contrary, of that other conceit in virtue of which Milly was the wandering princess: so what could be more in harmony now than to see the princess waited upon at the city gate by the worthiest maiden, the chosen daughter of the burgesses? It was the real again, evidently, the amusement of the meeting for the princess too; princesses living for the most part, in such an appeased way, on the plane of mere elegant representation. That was why they pounced, at city gates, on deputed flower-strewing damsels; that was why, after effigies, processions, and other stately games, frank

human company was pleasant to them. Kate Croy really
presented herself to Milly—the latter abounded for Mrs.
Stringham in accounts of it—as the wondrous London
girl in person, by what she had conceived, from far back,
of the London girl; conceived from the tales of travellers
and the anecdotes of New York, from old porings over
Punch and a liberal acquaintance with the fiction of the
day. The only thing was that she was nicer, for the creature in question had rather been, to our young woman,
an image of dread. She had thought of her, at her best, as
handsome just as Kate was, with turns of head and tones
of voice, felicities of stature and attitude, things "put on"
and, for that matter, put off, all the marks of the product of a packed society who should be at the same time
the heroine of a strong story. She placed this striking
young person from the first in a story, saw her, by a
necessity of the imagination, for a heroine, felt it the only
character in which she wouldn't be wasted; and this in
spite of the heroine's pleasant abruptness, her forbearance from gush, her umbrellas and jackets and shoes—
as these things sketched themselves to Milly—and
something rather of a breezy boy in the carriage of her
arms and the occasional freedom of her slang.

When Milly had settled that the extent of her goodwill itself made her shy, she had found for the moment
quite a sufficient key, and they were by that time thoroughly afloat together. This might well have been the
happiest hour they were to know, attacking in friendly
independence their great London—the London of
shops and streets and suburbs oddly interesting to

Milly, as well as of museums, monuments, "sights" oddly unfamiliar to Kate, while their elders pursued a separate course, both rejoicing in their intimacy and each thinking the other's young woman a great acquisition for her own. Milly expressed to Susan Shepherd more than once that Kate had some secret, some smothered trouble, besides all the rest of her history; and that if she had so good-naturedly helped Mrs. Lowder to meet them this was exactly to create a diversion, to give herself something else to think about. But on the case thus postulated our young American had as yet had no light: she only felt that when the light should come it would greatly deepen the colour; and she liked to think she was prepared for anything. What she already knew, moreover, was full to her vision, of English, of eccentric, of Thackerayan character, Kate Croy having gradually become not a little explicit on the subject of her situation, her past, her present, her general predicament, her small success, up to the present hour, in contenting at the same time her father, her sister, her aunt and herself. It was Milly's subtle guess, imparted to her Susie, that the girl had somebody else as well, as yet unnamed, to content, it being manifest that such a creature couldn't help having; a creature not perhaps, if one would, exactly formed to inspire passions, since that always implied a certain silliness, but essentially seen, by the admiring eye of friendship, under the clear shadow of some probably eminent male interest. The clear shadow, from whatever source projected, hung, at any rate, over Milly's companion the whole week, and

Kate Croy's handsome face smiled out of it, under
bland skylights, in the presence alike of old masters
passive in their glory and of thoroughly new ones, the
newest, who bristled restlessly with pins and bran-
dished snipping shears.

It was meanwhile a pretty part of the intercourse of
these young ladies that each thought the other more
remarkable than herself—that each thought herself, or
assured the other she did, a comparatively dusty object
and the other a favourite of nature and of fortune. Kate
was amused, amazed at the way her friend insisted on
"taking" her, and Milly wondered if Kate were sincere
in finding her the most extraordinary—quite apart from
her being the most charming—person she had come
across. They had talked, in long drives, and quantities
of history had not been wanting—in the light of which
Mrs. Lowder's niece might superficially seem to have
had the best of the argument. Her visitor's American
references, with their bewildering immensities, their
confounding moneyed New York, their excitements of
high pressure, their opportunities of wild freedom, their
record of used-up relatives, parents, clever, eager, fair,
slim brothers—these the most loved—all engaged, as
well as successive superseded guardians, in a high
extravagance of speculation and dissipation that had left
this exquisite being her black dress, her white face and
her vivid hair as the mere last broken link: such a picture quite threw into the shade the brief biography,
however sketchily amplified, of a mere middle-class
nobody in Bayswater. And though that indeed might be

but a Bayswater way of putting it, in addition to which Milly was in the stage of interest in Bayswater ways, this critic so far prevailed that, like Mrs. Stringham herself, she fairly got her companion to accept from her that she was quite the nearest approach to a practical princess Bayswater could hope ever to know. It was a fact—it became one at the end of three days—that Milly actually began to borrow from the handsome girl a sort of view of her state; the handsome girl's impression of it was clearly so sincere. This impression was a tribute, a tribute positively to power, power the source of which was the last thing Kate treated as a mystery. There were passages, under all their skylights, the succession of their shops being large, in which the latter's easy, yet the least bit dry manner sufficiently gave out that if *she* had had so deep a pocket——!

It was not moreover by any means with not having the imagination of expenditure that she appeared to charge her friend, but with not having the imagination of terror, of thrift, the imagination or in any degree the habit of a conscious dependence on others. Such moments, when all Wigmore Street, for instance, seemed to rustle about and the pale girl herself to be facing the different rustlers, usually so undiscriminated, as individual Britons too, Britons personal, parties to a relation and perhaps even intrinsically remarkable—such moments in especial determined in Kate a perception of the high happiness of her companion's liberty. Milly's range was thus immense; she had to ask nobody for anything, to refer nothing to any one; her freedom, her for-

tune and her fancy were her law; an obsequious world
surrounded her, she could sniff up at every step its
fumes. And Kate, in these days, was altogether in the
phase of forgiving her so much bliss; in the phase moreover of believing that, should they continue to go on
together, she would abide in that generosity. She had,
at such a point as this, no suspicion of a rift within the
lute—by which we mean not only none of anything's
coming between them, but none of any definite flaw in
so much clearness of quality. Yet, all the same, if Milly,
at Mrs. Lowder's banquet, had described herself to
Lord Mark as kindly used by the young woman on the
other side because of some faintly-felt special propriety
in it, so there really did match with this, privately, on
the young woman's part, a feeling not analysed but
divided, a latent impression that Mildred Theale was
not, after all, a person to change places, to change even
chances with. Kate, verily, would perhaps not quite have
known what she meant by this reservation, and she
came near naming it only when she said to herself that,
rich as Milly was, one probably wouldn't—which was
singular—ever hate her for it. The handsome girl had,
with herself, these felicities and crudities: it wasn't
obscure to her that, without some very particular reason to help, it might have proved a test of one's philosophy not to be irritated by a mistress of millions, or
whatever they were, who, as a girl, so easily might have
been, like herself, only vague and fatally female. She was
by no means sure of liking Aunt Maud as much as *she*
deserved, and Aunt Maud's command of funds was

obviously inferior to Milly's. There was thus clearly, as
pleading for the latter, some influence that would later
on become distinct; and meanwhile, decidedly, it was
enough that she was as charming as she was queer and
as queer as she was charming—all of which was a rare
amusement; as well, for that matter, as further sufficient
that there were objects of value she had already pressed
on Kate's acceptance. A week of her society in these
conditions—conditions that Milly chose to sum up as
ministering immensely, for a blind, vague pilgrim, to aid
and comfort—announced itself from an early hour as
likely to become a week of presents, acknowledgments,
mementos, pledges of gratitude and admiration that
were all on one side. Kate as promptly embraced the
propriety of making it clear that she must forswear
shops till she should receive some guarantee that the
contents of each one she entered as a humble companion
should not be placed at her feet; yet that was in truth
not before she had found herself in possession, under
whatever protests, of several precious ornaments and
other minor conveniences.

Great was the absurdity, too, that there should have
come a day, by the end of the week, when it appeared
that all Milly would have asked in definite "return," as
might be said, was to be told a little about Lord Mark
and to be promised the privilege of a visit to Mrs. Condrip. Far other amusements had been offered her, but
her eagerness was shamelessly human, and she seemed
really to count more on the revelation of the anxious
lady of Chelsea than on the best nights of the opera.

Kate admired, and showed it, such an absence of fear: to
the fear of being bored, in such a connection, she would
have been so obviously entitled. Milly's answer to this
was the plea of her curiosities—which left her friend
wondering as to their odd direction. Some among them,
no doubt, were rather more intelligible, and Kate had
heard without wonder that she was blank about Lord
Mark. This young lady's account of him, at the same
time, professed itself as frankly imperfect; for what they
best knew him by at Lancaster Gate was a thing difficult to explain. One knew people in general by something they had to show, something that, either for them
or against, could be touched or named or proved; and
she could think of no other case of a value taken as so
great and yet flourishing untested. His value was his
future, which had somehow got itself as accepted by
Aunt Maud as if it had been his good cook or his steam-
launch. She, Kate, didn't mean she thought him a humbug; he might do great things—but they were all, as yet,
so to speak, he had done. On the other hand it was of
course something of an achievement, and not open to
every one, to have got one's self taken so seriously by
Aunt Maud. The best thing about him, doubtless, on
the whole, was that Aunt Maud believed in him. She
was often fantastic, but she knew a humbug, and—no,
Lord Mark wasn't that. He had been a short time in the
House, on the Tory side, but had lost his seat on the
first opportunity, and this was all he had to point to.
However, he pointed to nothing; which was very possibly just a sign of his real cleverness, one of those that

the really clever had in common with the really void. Even Aunt Maud frequently admitted that there was a good deal, for her view of him, to come up in the rear. And he wasn't meanwhile himself indifferent—indifferent to himself—for he was working Lancaster Gate for all it was worth: just as it was, no doubt, working *him*, and just as the working and the worked were in London, as one might explain, the parties to every relation.

Kate did explain, for her listening friend: every one who had anything to give—it was true they were the fewest—made the sharpest possible bargain for it, got at least its value in return. The strangest thing, furthermore, was that this might be, in cases, a happy understanding. The worker in one connection was the worked in another; it was as broad as it was long—with the wheels of the system, as might be seen, wonderfully oiled. People could quite like each other in the midst of it, as Aunt Maud, by every appearance, quite liked Lord Mark, and as Lord Mark, it was to be hoped, liked Mrs. Lowder, since if he didn't he was a greater brute than one could believe. She, Kate, had not yet, it was true, made out what he was doing for her—besides which the dear woman needed him, even at the most he could do, much less than she imagined; so far as all of which went, moreover, there were plenty of things on every side she had not yet made out. She believed, on the whole, in any one Aunt Maud took up; and she gave it to Milly as worth thinking of that, whatever wonderful people this young lady might meet in the land, she would meet no more extraordinary woman. There were greater celebrities by the million, and of course greater swells, but a bigger *person*, by Kate's view, and a larger natural handful every way, would really be far to seek. When Milly inquired with interest if Kate's belief in *her* was primarily on the lines of what Mrs. Lowder "took up," her interlocutress could handsomely say yes, since by the same principle she believed in herself. Whom but Aunt Maud's niece, pre-eminently, had Aunt Maud taken up, and who was thus more in the current, with her, of working and of being worked? "You may ask," Kate said, "what in the world I have to give; and that indeed is just what I'm trying to learn. There must be something, for her to think she can get it out of me. She *will* get it—trust her; and then I shall see what it is; which I beg you to believe I should never have found out for myself." She declined to treat any question of Milly's own "paying" power as discussable; that Milly would pay a hundred per cent.—and even to the end, doubtless, through the nose—was just the beautiful basis on which they found themselves.

These were fine facilities, pleasantries, ironies, all these luxuries of gossip and philosophies of London and of life, and they became quickly, between the pair, the common form of talk, Milly professing herself delighted to know that something was to be done with her. If the most remarkable woman in England was to do it, so much the better, and if the most remarkable woman in England had them both in hand together, why, what could be jollier for each? When she reflected indeed a little on the oddity of her wanting two at once, Kate had

the natural reply that it was exactly what showed her
sincerity. She invariably gave way to feeling, and feeling had distinctly popped up in her on the advent of her
girlhood's friend. The way the cat would jump was
always, in presence of anything that moved her, interesting to see; visibly enough, moreover, for a long time,
it hadn't jumped anything like so far. This, in fact, as
we already know, remained the marvel for Milly Theale,
who, on sight of Mrs. Lowder, found fifty links in
respect to Susie absent from the chain of association. She
knew so herself what she thought of Susie that she
would have expected the lady of Lancaster Gate to think
something quite different; the failure of which endlessly
mystified her. But her mystification was the cause for
her of another fine impression, inasmuch as when she
went so far as to observe to Kate that Susan Shepherd—
and especially Susan Shepherd emerging so uninvited
from an irrelevant past—ought, by all the proprieties,
simply to have bored Aunt Maud, her confidant agreed
with her without a protest and abounded in the sense
of her wonder. Susan Shepherd at least bored the
niece—that was plain; this young woman saw nothing in
her—nothing to account for anything, not even for
Milly's own indulgence: which little fact became in turn
to the latter's mind a fact of significance. It was a light
on the handsome girl—representing more than merely
showed—that poor Susie was simply as nought to her.
This was, in a manner too, a general admonition to poor
Susie's companion, who seemed to see marked by it the
direction in which she had best most look out. It just

faintly rankled in her that a person who was good
enough and to spare for Milly Theale shouldn't be good
enough for another girl; though, oddly enough, she
could easily have forgiven Mrs. Lowder herself the
impatience. Mrs. Lowder didn't feel it, and Kate Croy
felt it with ease; yet in the end, be it added, she grasped
the reason, and the reason enriched her mind. Wasn't
it sufficiently the reason that the handsome girl was,
with twenty other splendid qualities, the least bit brutal too, and didn't she suggest, as no one yet had ever
done for her new friend, that there might be a wild
beauty in that, and even a strange grace? Kate wasn't
brutally brutal—which Milly had hitherto benightedly
supposed the only way; she wasn't even aggressively so,
but rather indifferently, defensively and, as might be
said, by the habit of anticipation. She simplified in
advance, was beforehand with her doubts, and knew
with singular quickness what she wasn't, as they said in
New York, going to like. In that way at least people
were clearly quicker in England than at home; and Milly
could quite see, after a little, how such instincts might
become usual in a world in which dangers abounded.
There were more dangers, clearly, round about Lancaster Gate than one suspected in New York or could
dream of in Boston. At all events, with more sense of
them, there were more precautions, and it was a remarkable world altogether in which there could be precautions, on whatever ground, against Susie.

III

SHE CERTAINLY MADE up with Susie directly, however, for any allowance she might have had privately to extend to tepid appreciation; since the late and long talks of these two embraced not only everything offered and suggested by the hours they spent apart, but a good deal more besides. She might be as detached as the occasion required at four o'clock in the afternoon, but she used no such freedom to any one about anything as she habitually used about everything to Susan Shepherd at midnight. All the same, it should with much less delay than this have been mentioned, she had not yet—had not, that is, at the end of six days—produced any news for her comrade to compare with an announcement made her by the latter as a result of a drive with Mrs. Lowder, for a change, in the remarkable Battersea Park. The elder friends had sociably revolved there while the younger ones followed bolder fancies in the admirable equipage appointed to Milly at the hotel—a heavier, more emblazoned, more amusing chariot than she had ever, with "stables" notoriously mismanaged, known at home; whereby, in the course of the circuit, more than once repeated, it had "come out," as Mrs. Stringham said, that the couple at Lancaster Gate were, of all people, acquainted with Mildred's other English friend— the gentleman, the one connected with the English newspaper (Susie hung fire a little over his name) who had been with her in New York so shortly previous to present adventures. He had been named of course in

Battersea Park—else he couldn't have been identified;
and Susie had naturally, before she could produce her
own share in the matter as a kind of confession, to make
it plain that her allusion was to Mr. Merton Densher.
This was because Milly had at first a little air of not
knowing whom she meant; and the girl really kept, as
well, a certain control of herself while she remarked that
the case was surprising, the chance one in a thousand.
They knew him, both Maud and Miss Croy knew him,
she gathered too, rather well, though indeed it was not
on any show of intimacy that he had happened to be
mentioned. It had not been—Susie made the point—she
herself who brought him in: he had in fact not been
brought in at all, but only referred to as a young journalist known to Mrs. Lowder and who had lately gone
to their wonderful country—Mrs. Lowder always said
"your wonderful country"—on behalf of his journal. But
Mrs. Stringham had taken it up—with the tips of her
fingers indeed; and that was the confession: she had,
without meaning any harm, recognised Mr. Densher as
an acquaintance of Milly's, though she had also pulled
herself up before getting in too far. Mrs. Lowder had
been struck, clearly—it wasn't too much to say; then she
also, it had rather seemed, had pulled herself up; and
there had been a little moment during which each might
have been keeping something from the other. "Only,"
said Milly's mate, "I luckily remembered in time that I
had nothing whatever to keep—which was much simpler and nicer. I don't know what Maud has, but there
it is. She was interested, distinctly, in your knowing

him—in his having met you over there with so little loss of time. But I ventured to tell her it hadn't been so long as to make you as yet great friends. I don't know if I was right."

Whatever time this explanation might have taken, there had been moments enough in the matter now—before the elder woman's conscience had done itself justice—to enable Milly to reply that although the fact in question doubtless had its importance she imagined they wouldn't find the importance overwhelming. It *was* odd that their one Englishman should so instantly fit; it wasn't, however, miraculous—they surely all had often seen that, as every one said, the world was extraordinarily "small." Undoubtedly, too, Susie had done just the plain thing in not letting his name pass. Why in the world should there be a mystery?—and what an immense one they would appear to have made if he should come back and find they had concealed their knowledge of him! "I don't know, Susie dear," the girl observed, "what you think I have to conceal."

"It doesn't matter, at a given moment," Mrs. Stringham returned, "what you know or don't know as to what I think; for you always find out the very next moment, and when you do find out, dearest, you never *really* care. Only," she presently asked, "have you heard of him from Miss Croy?"

"Heard of Mr. Densher? Never a word. We haven't mentioned him. Why should we?"

"That *you* haven't, I understand; but that she hasn't," Susie opined, "may mean something."

"May mean what?"

"Well," Mrs. Stringham presently brought out, "I tell
you all when I tell you that Maud asks me to suggest
to you that it may perhaps be better for the present not
to speak of him: not to speak of him to her niece, that is,
unless she herself speaks to you first. But Maud thinks
she won't."

Milly was ready to engage for anything; but in
respect to the facts—as they so far possessed them—it
all sounded a little complicated. "Is it because there's
anything between them?"

"No—I gather not; but Maud's state of mind is pre-
cautionary. She's afraid of something. Or perhaps it
would be more correct to say she's afraid of everything."

"She's afraid, you mean," Milly asked, "of their—a—
liking each other?"

Susie had an intense thought and then an effusion.
"My dear child, we move in a labyrinth."

"Of course we do. That's just the fun of it!" said
Milly with a strange gaiety. Then she added: "Don't tell
me that—in this for instance—there are not abysses. I
want abysses."

Her friend looked at her—it was not unfrequently the
case—a little harder than the surface of the occasion
seemed to require; and another person present at such
times might have wondered to what inner thought of her
own the good lady was trying to fit the speech. It was
too much her disposition, no doubt, to treat her young
companion's words as symptoms of an imputed malady.
It was none the less, however, her highest law to be light

when the girl was light. She knew how to be quaint with the new quaintness—the great Boston gift; it had been, happily, her note in the magazines; and Maud Lowder, to whom it was new indeed and who had never heard anything remotely like it, quite cherished her, as a social resource, for it. It should not therefore fail her now; with it in fact one might face most things. "Ah, then let us hope we shall sound the depths—I'm prepared for the worst—of sorrow and sin! But she would like her niece—we're not ignorant of that, are we?—to marry Lord Mark. Hasn't she told you so?"

"Hasn't Mrs. Lowder told me?"

"No; hasn't Kate? It isn't, you know, that she doesn't know it."

Milly had, under her comrade's eyes, a minute of mute detachment. She had lived with Kate Croy for several days in a state of intimacy as deep as it had been sudden, and they had clearly, in talk, in many directions, proceeded to various extremities. Yet it now came over her as in a clear cold way that there was a possible account of their relations in which the quantity her new friend had told her might have figured as small, as smallest, beside the quantity she hadn't. She couldn't say, at any rate, whether or no she had made the point that her aunt designed her for Lord Mark: it had only sufficiently come out—which had been, moreover, eminently guessable—that she was involved in her aunt's designs. Somehow, for Milly, brush it over nervously as she might and with whatever simplifying hand, this abrupt extrusion of Mr. Densher altered all proportions, had an effect on all values. It was fantastic of her to let it make a difference that she couldn't in the least have defined—and she was at least, even during these instants, rather proud of being able to hide, on the spot, the difference it did make. Yet, all the same, the effect for her was, almost violently, of Mr. Densher's having been there—having been where she had stood till now in her simplicity—before her. It would have taken but another free moment to make her see abysses—since abysses were what she wanted—in the mere circumstance of his own silence, in New York, about his English friends. There had really been in New York little time for anything; but, had she liked, Milly could have made it out for herself that he had avoided the subject of Miss Croy, and that Miss Croy was yet a subject it could never be natural to avoid. It was to be added at the same time that even if his silence had been a labyrinth—which was absurd in view of all the other things too he couldn't possibly have spoken of—this was exactly what must suit her, since it fell under the head of the plea she had just uttered to Susie. These things, however, came and went, and it set itself up between the companions, for the occasion, in the oddest way, both that their happening all to know Mr. Densher—except indeed that Susie didn't, but probably would,—was a fact belonging, in a world of rushing about, to one of the common orders of chance; and yet further that it was amusing—oh, awfully amusing!—to be able fondly to hope that there was "something *in*" its having been left to crop up with such suddenness. There seemed somehow a possibility that the ground or, as it were, the air might, in a manner, have undergone some pleasing preparation; though the question of this possibility would probably, after all, have taken some threshing out. The truth, moreover—and there they were, already, our pair, talking about it, the "truth!"—had not in fact quite cropped out. This, obviously, in view of Mrs. Lowder's request to her old friend.

It was accordingly on Mrs. Lowder's recommendation that nothing should be said to Kate—it was on this rich attitude of Aunt Maud's that the idea of an interesting complication might best hope to perch; and when, in fact, after the colloquy we have reported Milly saw Kate again without mentioning any name, her silence succeeded in passing muster with her as the beginning of a new sort of fun. The sort was all the newer by reason of its containing a small element of anxiety: when she had gone in for fun before it had been with her hands a little more free. Yet it *was*, none the less, rather exciting to be conscious of a still sharper reason for interest in the handsome girl, as Kate continued, even now, pre-eminently to remain for her; and a reason—this was the great point—of which the young woman herself could have no suspicion. Twice over, thus, for two or three hours together, Milly found herself seeing Kate, quite fixing her in the light of the knowledge that it was a face on which Mr. Densher's eyes had more or less familiarly rested and which, by the same token, had looked, rather *more* beautifully than less, into his own. She pulled herself up indeed with the thought that it had inevitably looked, as beautifully as one would, into thousands of faces in which one might one's self never trace it; but just the odd result of the thought was to intensify for the girl that side of her friend which she had doubtless already been more prepared than she quite knew to think of as the "other," the not wholly calculable. It was fantastic, and Milly was aware of this; but the other side was what had, of a sudden, been turned straight towards her by the show of Mr. Densher's propinquity. She hadn't the excuse of knowing it for Kate's own, since nothing whatever as yet proved it particularly to be such. Never mind; it was with this other side now fully presented that Kate came and went, kissed her for greeting and for parting, talked, as usual, of everything but—as it had so abruptly become for Milly—*the* thing. Our young woman, it is true, would doubtless not have tasted so sharply a difference in this pair of occasions had she not been tasting so peculiarly her own possible betrayals. What happened was that afterwards, on separation, she wondered if the matter had not mainly been that she herself was so "other," so taken up with the unspoken; the strangest thing of all being, still subsequently, that when she asked herself how Kate could have failed to feel it she became conscious of being here on the edge of a great darkness. She should never know how Kate truly felt about anything such a one as Milly Theale should give her to feel. Kate would never—and not from ill-will, nor from duplicity, but from a sort of failure of common terms—reduce it to such a one's comprehension or put it within her convenience.

It was as such a one, therefore, that, for three or four days more, Milly watched Kate as just such another; and it was presently as such a one that she threw herself into their promised visit, at last achieved, to Chelsea, the quarter of the famous Carlyle, the field of exercise of his ghost, his votaries, and the residence of "poor Marian," so often referred to and actually a somewhat incongruous spirit there. With our young woman's first view of poor Marian everything gave way but the sense of how, in England, apparently, the social situation of sisters could be opposed, how common ground, for a place in the world, could quite fail them: a state of things sagely perceived to be involved in an hierarchical, an aristocratic order. Just whereabouts in the order Mrs. Lowder had established her niece was a question not wholly void, as yet, no doubt, of ambiguity—though Milly was withal sure Lord Mark could exactly have fixed the point if he would, fixing it at the same time for Aunt Maud herself; but it was clear that Mrs. Condrip was, as might have been said, in quite another geography. She would not, in short, have been to be found on the same social map, and it was as if her visitors had turned over page after page together before the final relief of their benevolent "Here!" The interval was bridged, of course, but the bridge, verily, was needed, and the impression left Milly to wonder whether, in the general connection, it were of bridges or of intervals that the spirit not locally disciplined would find itself most conscious. It was as if at home, by contrast, there were neither—neither the difference

itself, from position to position, nor, on either side, and
particularly on one, the awfully good manner, the conscious sinking of a consciousness, that made up for it.
The conscious sinking, at all events, and the awfully
good manner, the difference, the bridge, the interval, the
skipped leaves of the social atlas—these, it was to be
confessed, had a little, for our young lady, in default of
stouter stuff, to work themselves into the light literary
legend—a mixed, wandering echo of Trollope, of
Thackeray, perhaps mostly of Dickens—under favour of
which her pilgrimage had so much appealed. She could
relate to Susie later on, late the same evening, that the
legend, before she had done with it, had run clear, that
the adored author of *The Newcomes*, in fine, had been
on the whole the note: the picture lacking thus more
than she had hoped, or rather perhaps showing less than
she had feared, a certain possibility of Pickwickian outline. She explained how she meant by this that Mrs.
Condrip had not altogether proved another Mrs. Nickleby, nor even—for she might have proved almost anything, from the way poor worried Kate had spoken—a
widowed and aggravated Mrs. Micawber.

Mrs. Stringham, in the midnight conference, intimated rather yearningly that, however the event might
have turned, the side of English life such experiences
opened to Milly were just those she herself seemed
"booked"—as they were all, roundabout her now,
always saying—to miss: she had begun to have a little,
for her fellow-observer, these moments of fanciful reaction—reaction in which she was once more all Susan

Shepherd—against the high sphere of colder conventions into which her overwhelming connection with Maud Manningham had rapt her. Milly never lost sight, for long, of the Susan Shepherd side of her, and was always there to meet it when it came up and vaguely, tenderly, impatiently to pat it, abounding in the assurance that they would still provide for it. They had, however, to-night, another matter in hand; which proved to be presently, on the girl's part, in respect to her hour of Chelsea, the revelation that Mrs. Condrip, taking a few minutes when Kate was away with one of the children, in bed upstairs for some small complaint, had suddenly, without its being in the least "led up to," broken ground on the subject of Mr. Densher, mentioned him with impatience as a person in love with her sister. "She wished me, if I cared for Kate, to know," Milly said— "for it would be quite too dreadful, and one might do something."

Susie wondered. "Prevent anything coming of it? That's easily said. Do what?"

Milly had a dim smile. "I think that what she would like is that I should come a good deal to see *her* about it."

"And doesn't she suppose you've anything else to do?"

The girl had by this time clearly made it out. "Nothing but to admire and make much of her sister—whom she doesn't, however, herself in the least understand—and give up one's time, and everything else, to it." It struck the elder friend that she spoke with an almost unprecedented approach to sharpness; as if Mrs. Con-

drip had been rather specially disconcerting. Never yet
so much as just of late had Mrs. Stringham seen her
companion as exalted, and by the very play of something within, into a vague golden air that left irritation
below. That was the great thing with Milly—it was her
characteristic poetry; or at least it was Susan Shepherd's.
"But she made a point," the former continued, "of my
keeping what she says from Kate. I'm not to mention
that she has spoken."

"And why," Mrs. Stringham presently asked, "is Mr.
Densher so dreadful?"

Milly had, she thought, an hesitation—something
that suggested a fuller talk with Mrs. Condrip than she
inclined perhaps to report. "It isn't so much he himself." Then the girl spoke a little as for the romance of
it; one could never tell, with her, where romance would
come in. "It's the state of his fortunes."

"And is that very bad?"

"He has no 'private means,' and no prospect of any.
He has no income, and no ability, according to Mrs.
Condrip, to make one. He's as poor, she calls it, as
'poverty,' and she says she knows what that is."

Again Mrs. Stringham considered, and it presently
produced something. "But isn't he brilliantly clever?"

Milly had also then an instant that was not quite
fruitless. "I haven't the least idea."

To which, for the time, Susie only answered "Oh!"—
though by the end of a minute she had followed it with
a slightly musing "I see"; and that in turn with: "It's
quite what Maud Lowder thinks."

"That he'll never do anything?"

"No—quite the contrary: that he's exceptionally able."

"Oh yes; I know"—Milly had again, in reference to what her friend had already told her of this, her little tone of a moment before. "But Mrs. Condrip's own great point is that Aunt Maud herself won't hear of any such person. Mr. Densher, she holds—that's the way, at any rate, it was explained to me—won't ever be either a public man or a rich man. If he were public she'd be willing, as I understand, to help him; if he were rich—without being anything else—she'd do her best to swallow him. As it is, she taboos him."

"In short," said Mrs. Stringham as with a private purpose, "she told you, the sister, all about it. But Mrs. Lowder likes him," she added.

"Mrs. Condrip didn't tell me that."

"Well, she does, all the same, my dear, extremely."

"Then there it is!" On which, with a drop and one of those sudden, slightly sighing surrenders to a vague reflux and a general fatigue that had recently more than once marked themselves for her companion, Milly turned away. Yet the matter was not left so, that night, between them, albeit neither perhaps could afterwards have said which had first come back to it. Milly's own nearest approach, at least, for a little, to doing so, was to remark that they appeared all—every one they saw—to think tremendously of money. This prompted in Susie a laugh, not untender, the innocent meaning of which was that it came, as a subject for indifference, money

did, easier to some people than to others: she made the
point in fairness, however, that you couldn't have told,
by any too crude transparency of air, what place it held
for Maud Manningham. She did her worldliness with
grand proper silences—if it mightn't better be put perhaps that she did her detachment with grand occasional
pushes. However Susie put it, in truth, she was really, in
justice to herself, thinking of the difference, as favourites
of fortune, between her old friend and her new. Aunt
Maud sat somehow in the midst of her money, founded
on it and surrounded by it, even if with a clever high
manner about it, her manner of looking, hard and
bright, as if it weren't there. Milly, about hers, had no
manner at all—which was possibly, from a point of
view, a fault: she was at any rate far away on the edge of
it, and you hadn't, as might be said, in order to get at
her nature, to traverse, by whatever avenue, any piece of
her property. It was clear, on the other hand, that Mrs.
Lowder was keeping her wealth as for purposes, imagi-
nations, ambitions, that would figure as large, as honourably unselfish, on the day they should take effect.
She would impose her will, but her will would be only
that a person or two shouldn't lose a benefit by not submitting if they could be made to submit. To Milly, as so
much younger, such far views couldn't be imputed:
there was nobody she was supposable as interested for.
It was too soon, since she wasn't interested for herself.
Even the richest woman, at her age, lacked motive, and
Milly's motive doubtless had plenty of time to arrive.
She was meanwhile beautiful, simple, sublime without

it—whether missing it and vaguely reaching out for it or not; and with it, for that matter, in the event, would really be these things just as much. Only then she might very well have, like Aunt Maud, a manner. Such were the connections, at all events, in which the colloquy of our two ladies freshly flickered up—in which it came round that the elder asked the younger if she had herself, in the afternoon, named Mr. Densher as an acquaintance.

"Oh no—I said nothing of having seen him. I remembered," the girl explained, "Mrs. Lowder's wish."

"But that," her friend observed after a moment, "was for silence to Kate."

"Yes—but Mrs. Condrip would immediately have told Kate."

"Why so?—since she must dislike to talk about him."

"Mrs. Condrip must?" Milly thought. "What she would like most is that her sister should be brought to think ill of him; and if anything she can tell her will help that—" But Milly dropped suddenly here, as if her companion would see.

Her companion's interest, however, was all for what she herself saw. "You mean she'll immediately speak?" Mrs. Stringham gathered that this was what Milly meant, but it left still a question. "How will it be against him that you know him?"

"Oh, I don't know. It won't be so much one's knowing him as one's having kept it out of sight."

"Ah," said Mrs. Stringham, as if for comfort, "*you*

haven't kept it out of sight. Isn't it much rather Miss Croy herself who has?"

"It isn't my acquaintance with him," Milly smiled, "that she has dissimulated."

"She has dissimulated only her own? Well then, the responsibility's hers."

"Ah but," said the girl, not perhaps with marked consequence, "she has a right to do as she likes."

"Then so, my dear, have you!" smiled Susan Shepherd.

Milly looked at her as if she were almost venerably simple, but also as if this were what one loved her for. "We're not quarrelling about it, Kate and I, *yet*."

"I only meant," Mrs. Stringham explained, "that I don't see what Mrs. Condrip would gain."

"By her being able to tell Kate?" Milly thought. "I only meant that I don't see what I myself should gain."

"But it will have to come out—that he knows you both—some time."

Milly scarce assented. "Do you mean when he comes back?"

"He'll find you both here, and he can hardly be looked to, I take it, to 'cut' either of you for the sake of the other."

This placed the question at last on a basis more distinctly cheerful. "I might get at him somehow beforehand," the girl suggested; "I might give him what they call here the tip—that he's not to know me when we meet. Or, better still, I mightn't be here at all."

"Do you want to run away from him?"

It was, oddly enough, an idea Milly seemed half to accept. "I don't know *what* I want to run away from!"

It dispelled, on the spot—something, to the elder woman's ear, in the sad, sweet sound of it—any ghost of any need of explaining. The sense was constant for her that their relation was as if afloat, like some island of the south, in a great warm sea that made, for every conceivable chance, a margin, an outer sphere of general emotion; and the effect of the occurrence of anything in particular was to make the sea submerge the island, the margin flood the text. The great wave now for a moment swept over. "I'll go anywhere else in the world you like."

But Milly came up through it. "Dear old Susie—how I do work you!"

"Oh, this is nothing yet."

"No indeed—to what it will be."

"You're not—and it's vain to pretend," said dear old Susie, who had been taking her in, "as sound and strong as I insist on having you."

"Insist, insist—the more the better. But the day I *look* as sound and strong as that, you know," Milly went on—"on that day I shall be just sound and strong enough to take leave of you sweetly for ever. That's where one is," she continued thus agreeably to embroider, "when even one's *most* 'beaux moments' aren't such as to qualify, so far as appearance goes, for anything gayer than a handsome cemetery. Since I've lived all these years as if I were dead, I shall die, no doubt, as if I were alive—which will happen to be as you want me.

So, you see," she wound up, "you'll never really know where I am. Except indeed when I'm gone; and then you'll only know where I'm not."

"I'd die *for* you," said Susan Shepherd after a moment.

" 'Thanks awfully'! Then stay here for me."

"But we can't be in London for August, nor for many of all these next weeks."

"Then we'll go back."

Susie blenched. "Back to America?"

"No, abroad—to Switzerland, Italy, anywhere. I mean by your staying 'here' for me," Milly pursued, "your staying with me wherever I may be, even though we may neither of us know at the time where it is. No," she insisted, "I *don't* know where I am, and you never will, and it doesn't matter—and I dare say it's quite true," she broke off, "that everything will have to come out." Her friend would have felt of her that she joked about it now, had not her scale from grave to gay been a thing of such unnamable shades that her contrasts were never sharp. She made up for failures of gravity by failures of mirth; if she hadn't, that is, been at times as earnest as might have been liked, so she was certain not to be at other times as easy as she would like herself. "I must face the music. It isn't, at any rate, its 'coming out,' " she added; "it's that Mrs. Condrip would put the fact before her to his injury."

Her companion wondered. "But how to *his*?"

"Why, if he pretends to love her——!"

"And does he only 'pretend'?"

"I mean if, trusted by her in strange countries, he forgets her so far as to make up to other people."

The amendment, however, brought Susie in, as if with gaiety, for a comfortable end. "Did he make up, the false creature, to *you*?"

"No—but the question isn't of that. It's of what Kate might be made to believe."

"That, given the fact that he evidently more or less followed up his acquaintance with you, to say nothing of your obvious weird charm, he must have been all ready if you had at all led him on?"

Milly neither accepted nor qualified this; she only said, after a moment, as with a conscious excess of the pensive: "No, I don't think she'd quite wish to suggest that I made up to *him;* for that I should have had to do so would only bring out his constancy. All I mean is," she added—and now at last, as with a supreme impatience—"that her being able to make him out a little a person who could give cause for jealousy would evidently help her, since she's afraid of him, to do him in her sister's mind a useful ill turn."

Susan Shepherd perceived in this explanation such signs of an appetite for motive as would have sat gracefully even on one of her own New England heroines. It was seeing round several corners; but that was what New England heroines did, and it was moreover interesting for the moment to make out how many really her young friend had undertaken to see round. Finally, too, weren't they braving the deeps? They got their amusement where they could. "Isn't it only," she asked, "rather probable she'd see that Kate's knowing him as (what's the pretty old word?) *volage*—?"

"Well?" She hadn't filled out her idea, but neither, it seemed, could Milly.

"Well, might but do what that often does—by all *our* blessed little laws and arrangements at least; excite Kate's own sentiment instead of depressing it."

The idea was bright, yet the girl but beautifully stared. "Kate's own sentiment? Oh, she didn't speak of that. I don't think," she added as if she had been unconsciously giving a wrong impression, "I don't think Mrs. Condrip imagines *she's* in love."

It made Mrs. Stringham stare in turn. "Then what's her fear?"

"Well, only the fact of Mr. Densher's possibly himself keeping it up—the fear of some final result from *that*."

"Oh," said Susie, intellectually a little disconcerted—"she looks far ahead!"

At this, however, Milly threw off another of her sudden vague "sports." "No—it's only we who do."

"Well, don't let us be more interested for them than they are for themselves!"

"Certainly not"—the girl promptly assented. A certain interest nevertheless remained; she appeared to wish to be clear. "It wasn't of anything on Kate's own part she spoke."

"You mean she thinks her sister does *not* care for him?"

It was still as if, for an instant, Milly had to be sure

of what she meant; but there it presently was. "If she did care Mrs. Condrip would have told me."

What Susan Shepherd seemed hereupon for a little to wonder was why then they had been talking so. "But did you ask her?"

"Ah, no!"

"Oh!" said Susan Shepherd.

Milly, however, easily explained that she wouldn't have asked her for the world.

Book Fifth
....

I

LORD MARK LOOKED at her to-day in particular as if
to wring from her a confession that she had originally
done him injustice; and he was entitled to whatever
there might be in it of advantage or merit that his intention really in a manner took effect: he cared about something, that is, after all, sufficiently to make her feel
absurdly as if she *were* confessing—all the while it was
quite the case that neither justice nor injustice was what
had been in question between them. He had presented
himself at the hotel, had found her and had found Susan
Shepherd at home, had been "civil" to Susan—it was
just that shade, and Susan's fancy had fondly caught it;
and then had come again and missed them, and then
had come and found them once more: besides letting
them easily see that if it hadn't by this time been the
end of everything—which they could feel in the
exhausted air, that of the season at its last gasp—the
places they might have liked to go to were such as they
would have had only to mention. Their feeling was—or
at any rate their modest general plea—that there was no
place they would have liked to go to; there was only the

sense of finding they liked, wherever they were, the
place to which they had been brought. Such was highly
the case as to their current consciousness—which could
be indeed, in an equally eminent degree, but a matter
of course; impressions this afternoon having by a happy
turn of their wheel been gathered for them into a splendid cluster, an offering like an armful of the rarest flowers. They were in presence of the offering—they had
been led up to it; and if it had been still their habit to
look at each other across distances for increase of unanimity his hand would have been silently named
between them as the hand applied to the wheel. He had
administered the touch that, under light analysis, made
the difference—the difference of their not having lost, as
Susie on the spot and at the hour phrased it again and
again, both for herself and for such others as the question might concern, so beautiful and interesting an experience; the difference also, in fact, of Mrs. Lowder's not
having lost it either, though it was with Mrs. Lowder,
superficially, they had come, and though it was further
with that lady that our young woman was directly
engaged during the half-hour or so of her most agreeably inward response to the scene.

The great historic house had, for Milly, beyond ter-
race and garden, as the centre of an almost extravagantly
grand Watteau-composition, a tone as of old gold kept
"down" by the quality of the air, summer full-flushed,
but attuned to the general perfect taste. Much, by her
measure, for the previous hour, appeared, in connection
with this revelation of it, to have happened to her—a

quantity expressed in introductions of charming new
people, in walks through halls of armour, of pictures, of
cabinets, of tapestry, of tea-tables, in an assault of
reminders that this largeness of style was the sign of
appointed felicity. The largeness of style was the great
containing vessel, while everything else, the pleasant
personal affluence, the easy, murmurous welcome, the
honoured age of illustrious host and hostess, all at once
so distinguished and so plain, so public and so shy,
became but this or that element of the infusion. The
elements melted together and seasoned the draught, the
essence of which might have struck the girl as distilled
into the small cup of iced coffee she had vaguely
accepted from somebody, while a fuller flood, somehow,
kept bearing her up—all the freshness of response of her
young life the freshness of the first and only prime.
What had perhaps brought on just now a kind of climax
was the fact of her appearing to make out, through Aunt
Maud, what was really the matter. It couldn't be less
than a climax for a poor shaky maiden to find it put to
her of a sudden that she herself was the matter—for that
was positively what, on Mrs. Lowder's part, it came to.
Everything was great, of course, in great pictures, and
it was doubtless precisely a part of the brilliant life—
since the brilliant life, as one had faintly figured it,
clearly *was* humanly led—that all impressions within its
area partook of its brilliancy; still, letting that pass, it
fairly stamped an hour as with the official seal for one to
be able to take in so comfortably one's companion's
broad blandness. "You must stay among us—you must

stay; anything else is impossible and ridiculous; you don't know yet, no doubt—you can't; but you will soon enough: you can stay in *any* position." It had been as the murmurous consecration to follow the murmurous welcome; and even if it were but part of Aunt Maud's own spiritual ebriety—for the dear woman, one could see, was spiritually "keeping" the day—it served to Milly, then and afterwards, as a high-water mark of the imagination.

It was to be the end of the short parenthesis which had begun but the other day at Lancaster Gate with Lord Mark's informing her that she was a "success"—the key thus again struck; and though no distinct, no numbered revelations had crowded in, there had, as we have seen, been plenty of incident for the space and the time. There had been thrice as much, and all gratuitous and genial—if, in portions, not exactly hitherto *the* revelation—as three unprepared weeks could have been expected to produce. Mrs. Lowder had improvised a "rush" for them, but out of elements, as Milly was now a little more freely aware, somewhat roughly combined. Therefore if at this very instant she had her reasons for thinking of the parenthesis as about to close—reasons completely personal—she had on behalf of her companion a divination almost as deep. The parenthesis would close with this admirable picture, but the admirable picture still would show Aunt Maud as not absolutely sure either if she herself were destined to remain in it. What she was doing, Milly might even not have escaped seeming to see, was to talk herself into a sublimer seren-

ity while she ostensibly talked Milly. It was fine, the girl
fully felt, the way she did talk *her*, little as, at bottom,
our young woman needed it or found other persuasions
at fault. It was in particular during the minutes of her
grateful absorption of iced coffee—qualified by a sharp
doubt of her wisdom—that she most had in view Lord
Mark's relation to her being there, or at least to the
question of her being amused at it. It wouldn't have
taken much by the end of five minutes quite to make
her feel that this relation was charming. It might, once
more, simply have been that everything, anything, was
charming when one was so justly and completely
charmed; but, frankly, she had not supposed anything
so serenely sociable could define itself between them as
the friendly understanding that was at present somehow
in the air. They were, many of them together, near the
marquee that had been erected on a stretch of sward as
a temple of refreshment and that happened to have the
property—which was all to the good—of making Milly
think of a "durbar"; her iced coffee had been a consequence of this connection, in which, further, the bright
company scattered about fell thoroughly into place. Certain of its members might have represented the contingent of "native princes"—familiar, but scarce the less
grandly gregarious term!—and Lord Mark would have
done for one of these even though for choice he but presented himself as a supervisory friend of the family. The
Lancaster Gate family, he clearly intended, in which he
included its American recruits, and included above all
Kate Croy—a young person blessedly easy to take care

of. She knew people, and people knew her, and she was
the handsomest thing there—this last a declaration made
by Milly, in a sort of soft mid-summer madness, a
straight skylark-flight of charity, to Aunt Maud.

Kate had, for her new friend's eyes, the extraordinary
and attaching property of appearing at a given moment
to show as a beautiful stranger, to cut her connections
and lose her identity, letting the imagination for the
time make what it would of them—make her merely a
person striking from afar, more and more pleasing as
one watched, but who was above all a subject for curiosity. Nothing could have given her, as a party to a relation, a greater freshness than this sense—which sprang
up at its own hours—of being as curious about her as
if one hadn't known her. It had sprung up, we have
gathered, as soon as Milly had seen her after hearing
from Mrs. Stringham of her knowledge of Merton Densher; she had *looked* then other and, as Milly knew the
real critical mind would call it, more objective; and our
young woman had foreseen it of her, on the spot, that
she would often look so again. It was exactly what she
was doing this afternoon; and Milly, who had amusements of thought that were like the secrecies of a little
girl playing with dolls when conventionally "too big,"
could almost settle to the game of what one would suppose her, how one would place her, if one didn't know
her. She became thus, intermittently, a figure condi-
tioned only by the great facts of aspect, a figure to be
waited for, named and fitted. This was doubtless but a
way of feeling that it was of her essence to be peculiarly

what the occasion, whatever it might be, demanded
when its demand was highest. There were probably
ways enough, on these lines, for such a consciousness;
another of them would be, for instance, to say that she
was made for great social uses. Milly was not wholly
sure that she herself knew what great social uses might
be—unless, as a good example, exerting just that sort
of glamour in just that sort of frame were one of them:
she would have fallen back on knowing sufficiently that
they existed at all events for her friend. It imputed a
primness, all round, to be reduced but to saying, by way
of a translation of one's amusement, that she was always
so *right*—since that, too often, was what the *insupportables* themselves were; yet it was, in overflow to Aunt
Maud, what she had to content herself withal—save for
the lame enhancement of saying she was lovely. It
served, all the same, the purpose, strengthened the bond
that for the time held the two ladies together, distilled in
short its drop of rosecolour for Mrs. Lowder's own
view. That was really the view Milly had, for most of
the rest of the occasion, to give herself to immediately
taking in; but it didn't prevent the continued play of
those swift crosslights, odd beguilements of the mind, at
which we have already glanced.

Mrs. Lowder herself found it enough simply to reply,
in respect to Kate, that she was indeed a luxury to take
about the world: she expressed no more surprise than
that at her "rightness" to-day. Wasn't it by this time
sufficiently manifest that it was precisely *as* the very
luxury she was proving that she had, from far back,

been appraised and waited for? Crude elation, however,
might be kept at bay, and the circumstance none the less
demonstrated that they were all swimming together in
the blue. It came back to Lord Mark again, as he
seemed slowly to pass and repass and conveniently to
linger before them; he was personally the note of the
blue—like a suspended skein of silk within reach of the
broiderer's hand. Aunt Maud's free-moving shuttle took
a length of him at rhythmic intervals; and one of the
intermixed truths that flickered across to Milly was that
he ever so consentingly knew he was being worked in.
This was almost like an understanding with her at Mrs.
Lowder's expense, which she would have none of; she
wouldn't for the world have had him make any such
point as that he wouldn't have launched them at
Matcham—or whatever it was he *had* done—only for
Aunt Maud's *beaux yeux*. What he had done, it would
have been guessable, was something he had for some
time been desired in vain to do; and what they were all
now profiting by was a change comparatively sudden,
the cessation of hope delayed. What had caused the cessation easily showed itself as none of Milly's business;
and she was luckily, for that matter, in no real danger
of hearing from him directly that her individual weight
had been felt in the scale. Why then indeed was it an
effect of his diffused but subdued participation that he
might absolutely have been saying to her "Yes, let the
dear woman take her own tone? Since she's here she
may stay," he might have been adding—"for whatever
she can make of it. But you and I are different." Milly

knew *she* was different in truth—his own difference was his own affair; but also she knew that, after all, even at their distinctest, Lord Mark's "tips" in this line would be tacit. He practically placed her—it came round again to that—under no obligation whatever. It was a matter of equal ease, moreover, her letting Mrs. Lowder take a tone. She might have taken twenty—they would have spoiled nothing.

"You must stay on with us; you *can*, you know, in any position you like; any, any, *any*, my dear child"— and her emphasis went deep. "You must make your home with us; and it's really open to you to make the most beautiful one in the world. You mustn't be under a mistake—under any of any sort; and you must let us all think for you a little, take care of you and watch over you. Above all you must help me with Kate, and you must stay a little *for* her; nothing for a long time has happened to me so good as that you and she should have become friends. It's beautiful; it's great; it's every- thing. What makes it perfect is that it should have come about through our dear delightful Susie, restored to me, after so many years, by such a miracle. No—that's more charming to me than even your hitting it off with Kate. God has been good to one—positively; for I couldn't, at my age, have made a new friend—undertaken, I mean, out of whole cloth, the real thing. It's like chang- ing one's bankers—after fifty: one doesn't do that. That's why Susie has been kept for me, as you seem to keep people in your wonderful country, in lavender and pink paper—coming back at last as straight as out of a

fairy-tale and with you as an attendant fairy." Milly
hereupon replied appreciatively that such a description
of herself made her feel as if pink paper were her dress
and lavender its trimming; but Aunt Maud was not to
be deterred by a weak joke from keeping it up. Her
interlocutress could feel besides that she kept it up in
perfect sincerity. She was somehow at this hour a very
happy woman, and a part of her happiness might precisely have been that her affections and her views were
moving as never before in concert. Unquestionably she
loved Susie; but she also loved Kate and loved Lord
Mark, loved their funny old host and hostess, loved
every one within range, down to the very servant who
came to receive Milly's empty ice-plate—down, for that
matter, to Milly herself, who was, while she talked,
really conscious of the enveloping flap of a protective
mantle, a shelter with the weight of an eastern carpet.
An eastern carpet, for wishing-purposes of one's own,
was a thing to be on rather than under; still, however,
if the girl should fail of breath it wouldn't be, she could
feel, by Mrs. Lowder's fault. One of the last things she
was afterwards to recall of this was Aunt Maud's going
on to say that she and Kate must stand together because
together they could do anything. It was for Kate of
course she was essentially planning; but the plan,
enlarged and uplifted now, somehow required Milly's
prosperity too for its full operation, just as Milly's prosperity at the same time involved Kate's. It was nebu-
lous yet, it was slightly confused, but it was
unmistakably free and genial, and it made our young

woman understand things Kate had said of her aunt's possibilities as well as characterisations that had fallen from Susan Shepherd. One of the most frequent on the lips of the latter had been that dear Maud was a natural force.

II

A PRIME REASON, we must add, why sundry impressions were not to be fully present to the girl till later on was that they yielded at this stage, with an effect of sharp supersession, to a detached quarter of an hour—her only one—with Lord Mark. "Have you seen the picture in the house, the beautiful one that's so like you?"—he was asking that as he stood before her; having come up at last with his smooth intimation that any wire he had pulled and yet wanted not to remind her of wasn't quite a reason for his having no joy at all.

"I've been through rooms and I've seen pictures. But if I'm 'like' anything so beautiful as most of them seemed to me—!" It needed in short for Milly some evidence, which he only wanted to supply. She was the image of the wonderful Bronzino, which she must have a look at on every ground. He had thus called her off and led her away; the more easily that the house within was above all what had already drawn round her its mystic circle. Their progress, meanwhile, was not of the straightest; it was an advance, without haste, through innumerable natural pauses and soft concussions, determined for the most part by the appearance before them of ladies and gentlemen, singly, in couples, in groups, who brought them to a stand with an inveterate "I say, Mark." What they said she never quite made out; it was their all so domestically knowing him, and his knowing them, that mainly struck her, while her impression, for the rest, was but of fellow-strollers more vaguely afloat than themselves, supernumeraries mostly a little battered, whether as jaunty males or as ostensibly elegant women. They might have been moving a good deal by a momentum that had begun far back, but they were still brave and personable, still warranted for continuance as long again, and they gave her, in especial collectively, a sense of pleasant voices, pleasanter than those of actors, of friendly, empty words and kind, lingering eyes. The lingering eyes looked her over, the lingering eyes were what went, in almost confessed simplicity, with the pointless "I say, Mark"; and what was really most sensible of all was that, as a pleasant matter of course, if she didn't mind, he seemed to suggest their letting people, poor dear things, have the benefit of her.

The odd part was that he made her herself believe, for amusement, in the benefit, measured by him in mere manner—for wonderful, of a truth, was, as a means of expression, his slightness of emphasis—that her present good-nature conferred. It was, as she could easily see, a mild common carnival of good-nature—a mass of London people together, of sorts and sorts, but who mainly knew each other and who, in their way, did, no doubt, confess to curiosity. It had gone round that she was there; questions about her would be passing; the easiest

thing was to run the gauntlet with *him*—just as the easiest thing was in fact to trust him generally. Couldn't
she know for herself, passively, how little harm they
meant her?—to that extent that it made no difference
whether or not he introduced them. The strangest thing
of all for Milly was perhaps the uplifted assurance and
indifference with which she could simply give back the
particular bland stare that appeared in such cases to
mark civilisation at its highest. It was so little her fault,
this oddity of what had "gone round" about her, that
to accept it without question might be as good a way as
another of feeling life. It was inevitable to supply the
probable description—that of the awfully rich young
American who was so queer to behold, but nice, by all
accounts, to know; and she had really but one instant
of speculation as to fables or fantasies perchance originally launched. She asked herself once only if Susie
could, inconceivably, have been blatant about her; for
the question, on the spot, was really blown away for
ever. She knew in fact on the spot and with sharpness
just why she had "elected" Susan Shepherd: she had had
from the first hour the conviction of her being precisely
the person in the world least possibly a trumpeter. So it
wasn't their fault, it wasn't their fault, and anything
might happen that would, and everything now again
melted together, and kind eyes were always kind eyes—
if it were never to be worse than that! She got with her
companion into the house; they brushed, beneficently,
past all their accidents. The Bronzino was, it appeared,
deep within, and the long afternoon light lingered for

them on patches of old colour and waylaid them, as they
went, in nooks and opening vistas.

It was all the while for Milly as if Lord Mark had
really had something other than this spoken pretext in
view; as if there were something he wanted to say to her
and were only—consciously yet not awkwardly, just delicately—hanging fire. At the same time it was as if the
thing had practically been said by the moment they
came in sight of the picture; since what it appeared to
amount to was "Do let a fellow who isn't a fool take care
of you a little." The thing somehow, with the aid of the
Bronzino, was done; it hadn't seemed to matter to her
before if he were a fool or no; but now, just where they
were, she liked his not being; and it was all moreover
none the worse for coming back to something of the
same sound as Mrs. Lowder's so recent reminder. She
too wished to take care of her—and wasn't it, à peu près,
what all the people with the kind eyes were wishing?
Once more things melted together—the beauty and the
history and the facility and the splendid midsummer
glow: it was a sort of magnificent maximum, the pink
dawn of an apotheosis, coming so curiously soon. What
in fact befell was that, as she afterwards made out, it
was Lord Mark who said nothing in particular—it was
she herself who said all. She couldn't help that—it came;
and the reason it came was that she found herself, for
the first moment, looking at the mysterious portrait
through tears. Perhaps it was her tears that made it just
then so strange and fair—as wonderful as he had said:
the face of a young woman, all magnificently drawn,

down to the hands, and magnificently dressed; a face almost livid in hue, yet handsome in sadness and crowned with a mass of hair rolled back and high, that must, before fading with time, have had a family resemblance to her own. The lady in question, at all events, with her slightly Michaelangelesque squareness, her eyes of other days, her full lips, her long neck, her recorded jewels, her brocaded and wasted reds, was a very great personage—only unaccompanied by a joy. And she was dead, dead, dead. Milly recognised her exactly in words that had nothing to do with her. "I shall never be better than this."

He smiled for her at the portrait. "Than she? You'd scarce need to be better, for surely that's well enough. But you *are*, one feels, as it happens, better; because, splendid as she is, one doubts if she was good."

He hadn't understood. She was before the picture, but she had turned to him, and she didn't care if, for the minute, he noticed her tears. It was probably as good a moment as she should ever have with him. It was perhaps as good a moment as she should have with any one, or have in any connection whatever. "I mean that everything this afternoon has been too beautiful, and that perhaps everything together will never be so right again. I'm very glad therefore you've been a part of it."

Though he still didn't understand her he was as nice as if he had; he didn't ask for insistence, and that was just a part of his looking after her. He simply protected her now from herself, and there was a world of practice in it. "Oh, we must talk about these things!"

Ah, they had already done that, she knew, as much as she ever would; and she was shaking her head at her pale sister the next moment with a world, on her side, of slowness. "I wish I could see the resemblance. Of course her complexion's green," she laughed; "but mine's several shades greener."

"It's down to the very hands," said Lord Mark.

"Her hands are large," Milly went on, "but mine are larger. Mine are huge."

"Oh, you go her, all round, 'one better'—which is just what I said. But you're a pair. You must surely catch it," he added as if it were important to his character as a serious man not to appear to have invented his plea.

"I don't know—one never knows one's self. It's a funny fancy, and I don't imagine it would have occurred——"

"I see it *has* occurred"—he has already taken her up. She had her back, as she faced the picture, to one of the doors of the room, which was open, and on her turning, as he spoke, she saw that they were in the presence of three other persons, also, as appeared, interested inquirers. Kate Croy was one of these; Lord Mark had just become aware of her, and she, all arrested, had immediately seen, and made the best of it, that she was far from being first in the field. She had brought a lady and a gentleman to whom she wished to show what Lord Mark was showing Milly, and he took her straightway as a reinforcement. Kate herself had spoken, however, before he had had time to tell her so.

"*You* had noticed too?"—she smiled at him without looking at Milly. "Then I'm not original—which one always hopes one has been. But the likeness is so great." And now she looked at Milly—for whom again it was, all round indeed, kind, kind eyes. "Yes, there you are, my dear, if you want to know. And you're superb." She took now but a glance at the picture, though it was enough to make her question to her friends not too straight. "Isn't she superb?"

"I brought Miss Theale," Lord Mark explained to the latter, "quite off my own bat."

"I wanted Lady Aldershaw," Kate continued to Milly, "to see for herself."

"*Les grands esprits se rencontrent!*" laughed her attendant gentleman, a high, but slightly stooping, shambling and wavering person, who represented urbanity by the liberal aid of certain prominent front teeth and whom Milly vaguely took for some sort of great man.

Lady Aldershaw meanwhile looked at Milly quite as if Milly had been the Bronzino and the Bronzino only Milly. "Superb, superb. Of course I had noticed you. It *is* wonderful," she went on with her back to the picture, but with some other eagerness which Milly felt gathering, directing her motions now. It was enough—they were introduced, and she was saying "I wonder if you could give us the pleasure of coming——" She was not fresh, for she was not young, even though she denied at every pore that she was old; but she was vivid and much bejewelled for the midsummer daylight; and she was all in the palest pinks and blues. She didn't think, at

this pass, that she could "come" anywhere—Milly
didn't; and she already knew that somehow Lord Mark
was saving her from the question. He had interposed,
taking the words out of the lady's mouth and not caring at all if the lady minded. That was clearly the right
way to treat her—at least for him; as she had only
dropped, smiling, and then turned away with him. She
had been dealt with—it would have done an enemy
good. The gentleman still stood, a little helpless,
addressing himself to the intention of urbanity as if it
were a large loud whistle; he had been signing sympathy, in his way, while the lady made her overture; and
Milly had, in this light, soon arrived at their identity.
They were Lord and Lady Aldershaw, and the wife was
the clever one. A minute or two later the situation had
changed, and she knew it afterwards to have been by the
subtle operation of Kate. She was herself saying that she
was afraid she must go now if Susie could be found; but
she was sitting down on the nearest seat to say it. The
prospect, through opened doors, stretched before her
into other rooms, down the vista of which Lord Mark
was strolling with Lady Aldershaw, who, close to him
and much intent, seemed to show from behind as peculiarly expert. Lord Aldershaw, for his part, had been left
in the middle of the room, while Kate, with her back to
him, was standing before her with much sweetness of
manner. The sweetness was all for *her*; she had the sense
of the poor gentleman's having somehow been handled
as Lord Mark had handled his wife. He dangled there,
he shambled a little; then he bethought himself of the

Bronzino, before which, with his eyeglass, he hovered. It drew from him an odd, vague sound, not wholly distinct from a grunt, and a "Humph—most remarkable!" which lighted Kate's face with amusement. The next moment he had creaked away, over polished floors, after the others, and Milly was feeling as if *she* had been rude. But Lord Aldershaw was in every way a detail, and Kate was saying to her that she hoped she wasn't ill.

Thus it was that, aloft there in the great gilded historic chamber and the presence of the pale personage on the wall, whose eyes all the while seemed engaged with her own, she found herself suddenly sunk in something quite intimate and humble and to which these grandeurs were strange enough witnesses. It had come up, in the form in which she had had to accept it, all suddenly, and nothing about it, at the same time, was more marked than that she had in a manner plunged into it to escape from something else. Something else, from her first vision of her friend's appearance three minutes before, had been present to her even through the call made by the others on her attention; something that was perversely *there*, she was more and more uncomfortably finding, at least for the first moments and by some spring of its own, with every renewal of their meeting. "Is it the way she looks to *him*?" she asked herself—the perversity being that she kept in remembrance that Kate was known to him. It wasn't a fault in Kate—nor in him assuredly; and she had a horror, being generous and tender, of treating either of them as if it had been. To Densher himself she couldn't make it up—he was too

far away; but her secondary impulse was to make it up
to Kate. She did so now with a strange soft energy—the
impulse immediately acting. "Will you render me to-
morrow a great service?"

"Any service, dear child, in the world."

"But it's a secret one—nobody must know. I must be
wicked and false about it."

"Then I'm your woman," Kate smiled, "for that's the
kind of thing I love. *Do* let us do something bad. You're
impossibly without sin, you know."

Milly's eyes, on this, remained a little with their companion's. "Ah, I shan't perhaps come up to your idea.
It's only to deceive Susan Shepherd."

"Oh!" said Kate as if this were indeed mild.

"But thoroughly—as thoroughly as I can."

"And for cheating," Kate asked, "my powers will
contribute? Well, I'll do my best for you." In accordance with which it was presently settled between them
that Milly should have the aid and comfort of her presence for a visit to Sir Luke Strett. Kate had needed a
minute for enlightenment, and it was quite grand for her
comrade that this name should have said nothing to her.
To Milly herself it had for some days been secretly saying much. The personage in question was, as she
explained, the greatest of medical lights—if she had got
hold, as she believed (and she had used to this end the
wisdom of the serpent) of the right, the special man. She
had written to him three days before, and he had named
her an hour, eleven-twenty; only it had come to her, on
the eve, that she couldn't go alone. Her maid, on the

other hand, wasn't good enough, and Susie was too good. Kate had listened, above all, with high indulgence. "And I'm betwixt and between, happy thought! Too good for what?"

Milly thought. "Why, to be worried if it's nothing. And to be still more worried—I mean before she need be—if it isn't."

Kate fixed her with deep eyes. "What in the world is the matter with you?" It had inevitably a sound of impatience, as if it had been a challenge really to produce something; so that Milly felt her for the moment only as a much older person, standing above her a little, doubting the imagined ailments, suspecting the easy complaints, of ignorant youth. It somewhat checked her, further, that the matter with her was what exactly as yet she wanted knowledge about; and she immediately declared, for conciliation, that if she were merely fanciful Kate would see her put to shame. Kate vividly uttered, in return, the hope that, since she could come out and be so charming, could so universally dazzle and interest, she wasn't all the while in distress or in anxiety—didn't believe herself, in short, to be in any degree seriously menaced. "Well, I want to make out—to make out!" was all that this consistently produced. To which Kate made clear answer: "Ah then, let us by all means!"

" I thought," Milly said, "you would like to help me. But I must ask you, please, for the promise of absolute silence."

"And how, if you *are* ill, can your friends remain in ignorance?"

"Well, if I am, it must of course finally come out. But I can go for a long time." Milly spoke with her eyes again on her painted sister's—almost as if under their suggestion. She still sat there before Kate, yet not without a light in her face. "That will be one of my advantages. I think I could die without its being noticed."

"You're an extraordinary young woman," her friend, visibly held by her, declared at last. "What a remarkable time to talk of such things!"

"Well, we won't talk, precisely"—Milly got herself together again. "I only wanted to make sure of you."

"Here in the midst of——!" But Kate could only sigh for wonder—almost visibly too for pity.

It made a moment during which her companion waited on her word; partly as if from a yearning, shy but deep, to have her case put to her just as Kate was struck by it; partly as if the hint of pity were already giving a sense to her whimsical "shot," with Lord Mark, at Mrs. Lowder's first dinner. Exactly this—the handsome girl's compassionate manner, her friendly descent from her own strength—was what she had then foretold. She took Kate up as if positively for the deeper taste of it. "Here in the midst of what?"

"Of everything. There's nothing you can't have. There's nothing you can't do."

"So Mrs. Lowder tells me."

It just kept Kate's eyes fixed as possibly for more of that; then, however, without waiting, she went on. "We all adore you."

"You're wonderful—you dear things!" Milly laughed.

"No, it's *you*." And Kate seemed struck with the real interest of it. "In three weeks!"

Milly kept it up. "Never were people on such terms! All the more reason," she added, "that I shouldn't needlessly torment you."

"But me? what becomes of *me*?" said Kate.

"Well, you—" Milly thought—"if there's anything to bear, you'll bear it."

"But I won't bear it!" said Kate Croy.

"Oh yes, you will: all the same! You'll pity me awfully, but you'll help me very much. And I absolutely trust you. So there we are." There they were, then, since Kate had so to take it; but there, Milly felt, she herself in particular was; for it was just the point at which she had wished to arrive. She had wanted to prove to herself that she didn't horribly blame her friend for any reserve; and what better proof could there be than this quite special confidence? If she desired to show Kate that she really believed the latter liked her, how could she show it more than by asking her for help?

III

WHAT IT REALLY CAME TO, on the morrow, this first time—the time Kate went with her—was that the great man had, a little, to excuse himself; had, by a rare accident—for he kept his consulting-hours in general rigorously free—but ten minutes to give her; ten mere minutes which he yet placed at her service in a manner that she admired even more than she could meet it:

so crystal-clean the great empty cup of attention that he
set between them on the table. He was presently to
jump into his carriage, but he promptly made the point
that he must see her again, see her within a day or two;
and he named for her at once another hour—easing her
off beautifully too even then in respect to her possibly
failing of justice to her errand. The minutes affected
her in fact as ebbing more swiftly than her little army
of items could muster, and they would probably have
gone without her doing much more than secure another
hearing, had it not been for her sense, at the last, that
she had gained above all an impression. The impression—all the sharp growth of the final few moments—
was neither more nor less than that she might make, of
a sudden, in quite another world, another straight
friend, and a friend who would moreover be, wonderfully, the most appointed, the most thoroughly adjusted
of the whole collection, inasmuch as he would somehow
wear the character scientifically, ponderably, prove-
ably—not just loosely and sociably. Literally, furthermore, it wouldn't really depend on herself, Sir Luke
Strett's friendship, in the least; perhaps what made her
most stammer and pant was its thus queerly coming
over her that she might find she had interested him
even beyond her intention, find she was in fact
launched in some current that would lose itself in the
sea of science. At the same time that she struggled,
however, she also surrendered; there was a moment at
which she almost dropped the form of stating, of
explaining, and threw herself, without violence, only

with a supreme pointless quaver that had turned, the next instant, to an intensity of interrogative stillness, upon his general goodwill. His large, settled face, though firm, was not, as she had thought at first, hard; he looked, in the oddest manner, to her fancy, half like a general and half like a bishop, and she was soon sure that, within some such handsome range, what it would show her would be what was good, what was best for her. She had established, in other words, in this time-saving way, a relation with it; and the relation was the special trophy that, for the hour, she bore off. It was like an absolute possession, a new resource altogether, something done up in the softest silk and tucked away under the arm of memory. She hadn't had it when she went in, and she had it when she came out; she had it there under her cloak, but dissimulated, invisibly carried, when smiling, smiling, she again faced Kate Croy. That young lady had of course awaited her in another room, where, as the great man was to absent himself, no one else was in attendance; and she rose for her with such a face of sympathy as might have graced the vestibule of a dentist. "Is it out?" she seemed to ask as if it had been a question of a tooth; and Milly indeed kept her in no suspense at all.

"He's a dear. I'm to come again."

"But what does he say?"

Milly was almost gay. "That I'm not to worry about anything in the world, and that if I'll be a good girl and do exactly what he tells me, he'll take care of me for ever and ever."

·　Kate wondered as if things scarce fitted. "But does he allow then that you're ill?"

"I don't know what he allows, and I don't care. I *shall* know, and whatever it is it will be enough. He knows all about me, and I like it. I don't hate it a bit."

Still, however, Kate stared. "But could he, in so few minutes, ask you enough——?"

"He asked me scarcely anything—he doesn't need to do anything so stupid," Milly said. "He can tell. He knows," she repeated; "and when I go back—for he'll have thought me over a little—it will be all right."

Kate, after a moment, made the best of this. "Then when are we to come?"

It just pulled her friend up, for even while they talked—at least it was one of the reasons—she stood there suddenly, irrelevantly, in the light of her *other* identity, the identity she would have for Mr. Densher. This was always, from one instant to another, an incalculable light, which, though it might go off faster than it came on, necessarily disturbed. It sprang, with a perversity all its own, from the fact that, with the lapse of hours and days, the chances themselves that made for his being named continued so oddly to fail. There were twenty, there were fifty, but none of them turned up. This, in particular, was of course not a juncture at which the least of them would naturally be present; but it would make, none the less, Milly saw, another day practically all stamped with avoidance. She saw in a quick glimmer, and with it all Kate's unconsciousness; and then she shook off the obsession. But it had lasted long enough to qualify her response. No, she had shown Kate how she trusted her; and that, for loyalty, would somehow do. "Oh, dear thing, now that the ice is broken I shan't trouble *you* again."

"You'll come alone?"

"Without a scruple. Only I shall ask you, please, for your absolute discretion still."

Outside, before the door, on the wide pavement of the great square, they had to wait again while their carriage, which Milly had kept, completed a further turn of exercise, engaged in by the coachman for reasons of his own. The footman was there, and had indicated that he was making the circuit; so Kate went on while they stood. "But don't you ask a good deal, darling, in proportion to what you give?"

This pulled Milly up still shorter—so short in fact that she yielded as soon as she had taken it in. But she continued to smile. "I see. Then you *can* tell."

"I don't want to 'tell,' " said Kate. "I'll be as silent as the tomb if I can only have the truth from you. All I want is that you shouldn't keep from me how you find out that you really are."

"Well then, I won't, ever. But you see for yourself," Milly went on, "how I really am. I'm satisfied. I'm happy."

Kate looked at her long. "I believe you like it. The way things turn out for you——!"

Milly met her look now without a thought of anything but the spoken. She had ceased to be Mr. Densher's image; she was all her own memento and she was none the less fine. Still, still, what had passed was a fair bargain, and it would do. "Of course I like it. I feel—I can't otherwise describe it—as if I had been, on my knees, to the priest. I've confessed and I've been absolved. It has been lifted off."

Kate's eyes never quitted her. "He must have liked *you.*"

"Oh—doctors!" Milly said. "But I hope," she added, "he didn't like me too much." Then as if to escape a little from her friend's deeper sounding, or as impatient for the carriage, not yet in sight, her eyes, turning away, took in the great stale square. As its staleness, however, was but that of London fairly fatigued, the late hot London with its dance all danced and its story all told, the air seemed a thing of blurred pictures and mixed echoes, and an impression met the sense—an impression that broke, the next moment, through the girl's tightened lips. "Oh, it's a beautiful big world, and everyone, yes, everyone——!" It presently brought her back to Kate, and, she hoped she didn't actually look as much as if she were crying as she must have looked to Lord Mark among the portraits at Matcham.

Kate at all events understood. "Everyone wants to be so nice?"

"So nice," said the grateful Milly.

"Oh," Kate laughed, "we'll pull you through! And won't you now bring Mrs. Stringham?"

But Milly after an instant was again clear about that. "Not till I've seen him once more."

She was to have found this preference, two days later,

abundantly justified; and yet when, in prompt accordance with what had passed between them, she reappeared before her distinguished friend—that character having, for him, in the interval, built itself up still higher—the first thing he asked her was whether she had been accompanied. She told him, on this, straightway, everything; completely free at present from her first embarrassment, disposed even—as she felt she might become—to undue volubility, and conscious moreover of no alarm from his thus perhaps wishing that she had not come alone. It was exactly as if, in the forty-eight hours that had passed, her acquaintance with him had somehow increased, and his own knowledge in particular received mysterious additions. They had been together, before, scarce ten minutes; but the relation, the one the ten minutes had so beautifully created, was there to take straight up: and this not, on his own part, from mere professional heartiness, mere bedside manner, which she would have disliked—much rather from a quiet, pleasant air in him of having positively asked about her, asked here and there and found out. Of course he couldn't in the least have asked, or have wanted to; there was no source of information to his hand, and he had really needed none: he had found out simply by his genius—and found out, she meant, literally everything. Now she knew not only that she didn't dislike this—the state of being found out about; but that, on the contrary, it was truly what she had come for, and that, for the time at least, it would give her something firm to stand on. She struck herself as aware,

aware as she had never been, of really not having had from the beginning anything firm. It would be strange for the firmness to come, after all, from her learning in these agreeable conditions that she was in some way doomed; but above all it would prove how little she had hitherto had to hold her up. If she was now to be held up by the mere process—since that was perhaps on the cards—of being let down, this would only testify in turn to her queer little history. *That* sense of loosely rattling had been no process at all; and it was ridiculously true that her thus sitting there to see her life put into the scales represented her first approach to the taste of orderly living. Such was Milly's romantic version—that her life, especially by the fact of this second interview, *was* put into the scales; and just the best part of the relation established might have been, for that matter, that the great grave charming man knew, had known at once, that it was romantic, and in that measure allowed for it. Her only doubt, her only fear, was whether he perhaps wouldn't even take advantage of her being a little romantic to treat her as romantic altogether. This doubtless was her danger with him; but she should see, and dangers in general meanwhile dropped and dropped.

The very place, at the end of a few minutes, the commodious, "handsome" room, far back in the fine old house, soundless from position, somewhat sallow with years of celebrity, somewhat sombre even at midsummer—the very place put on for her a look of custom and use, squared itself solidly round her as with promises

and certainties. She had come forth to see the world, and
this then was to be the world's light, the rich dusk of a
London "back," these the world's walls, those the
world's curtains and carpet. She should be intimate with
the great bronze clock and mantel-ornaments, conspicuously presented in gratitude and long ago; she should
be as one of the circle of eminent contemporaries, photographed, engraved, signatured, and in particular
framed and glazed, who made up the rest of the deco-
ration, and made up as well so much of the human comfort; and while she thought of all the clean truths,
unfringed, unfingered, that the listening stillness,
strained into pauses and waits, would again and again,
for years, have kept distinct, she also wondered what *she*
would eventually decide upon to present in gratitude.
She would give something better at least than the
brawny Victorian bronzes. This was precisely an
instance of what she felt he knew of her before he had
done with her: that she was secretly romancing at that
rate, in the midst of so much else that was more urgent,
all over the place. So much for her secrets with him,
none of which really required to be phrased. It would
have been, for example, a secret for her from any one
else that without a dear lady she had picked up just
before coming over she wouldn't have a decently near
connection, of any sort, for such an appeal as she was
making, to put forward: no one in the least, as it were,
to produce for respectability. But *his* seeing it she didn't
mind a scrap, and not a scrap either his knowing how
she had left the dear lady in the dark. She had come

alone, putting her friend off with a fraud: giving a pretext of shops, of a whim, of she didn't know what—the
amusement of being for once in the streets by herself.
The streets by herself were new to her—she had always
had in them a companion, or a maid; and he was never
to believe, moreover, that she couldn't take full in the
face anything he might have to say. He was softly
amused at her account of her courage; though he yet
showed it somehow without soothing her too grossly.
Still, he did want to know whom she had. Hadn't there
been a lady with her on Wednesday?

"Yes—a different one. Not the one who's travelling
with me. I've told *her*."

Distinctly he was amused, and it added to his air—
the greatest charm of all—of giving her lots of time.
"You've told her what?"

"Well," said Milly, "that I visit you in secret."

"And how many persons will she tell?"

"Oh, she's devoted. Not one."

"Well, if she's devoted doesn't that make another
friend for you?"

It didn't take much computation, but she nevertheless had to think a moment, conscious as she was that he
distinctly *would* want to fill out his notion of her—even
a little, as it were, to warm the air for her. That, however—and better early than late—he must accept as of
no use; and she herself felt for an instant quite a competent certainty on the subject of any such warming.
The air, for Milly Theale, was, from the very nature of
the case, destined never to rid itself of a considerable

chill. This she could tell him with authority, if she could tell him nothing else; and she seemed to see now, in short, that it would importantly simplify. "Yes, it makes another; but they all together wouldn't make—well, I don't know what to call it but the difference. I mean when one *is*—really alone. I've never seen anything like the kindness." She pulled up a minute while he waited—waited again as if with his reasons for letting her, for almost making her, talk. What she herself wanted was not, for the third time, to cry, as it were, in public. She *had* never seen anything like the kindness, and she wished to do it justice; but she knew what she was about, and justice was not wronged by her being able presently to stick to her point. "Only one's situation is what it is. It's *me* it concerns. The rest is delightful and useless. Nobody can really help. That's why I'm by myself to-day. I *want* to be—in spite of Miss Croy, who came with me last. If you can help, so much the better—and also of course if one can, a little, one's self. Except for that—you and me doing our best—I like you to see me just as I am. Yes, I like it—and I don't exaggerate. Shouldn't one, at the start, show the worst—so that anything after that may be better? It wouldn't make any real difference—it *won't* make any, anything that may happen won't—to any one. Therefore I feel myself, this way, with you, just as I am; and—if you do in the least care to know—it quite positively bears me up."

She put it as to his caring to know, because his manner seemed to give her all her chance, and the impression was there for her to take. It was strange and deep for her,

this impression, and she did, accordingly, take it straight
home. It showed him—showed him in spite of himself—
as allowing, somewhere far within, things comparatively
remote, things in fact quite, as she would have said, outside, delicately to weigh with him; showed him as interested, on her behalf, in other questions beside the
question of what was the matter with her. She accepted
such an interest as regular in the highest type of scientific
mind—his *being* the even highest, magnificently—
because otherwise, obviously, it wouldn't be there; but
she could at the same time take it as a direct source of
light upon herself, even though that might present her a
little as pretending to equal him. Wanting to know more
about a patient than how a patient was constructed or
deranged couldn't be, even on the part of the greatest of
doctors, anything but some form or other of the desire to
let the patient down easily. When that was the case the
reason, in turn, could only be, too manifestly, pity; and
when pity held up its tell-tale face like a head on a pike,
in a French revolution, bobbing before a window, what
was the inference but that the patient was bad? He might
say what he would now—she would always have seen the
head at the window; and in fact from this moment she
only wanted him to say what he would. He might say it
too with the greater ease to himself as there wasn't one of
her divinations that—*as* her own—he would in any way
put himself out for. Finally, if he was making her talk
she *was* talking; and what it could, at any rate, come to
for him was that she wasn't afraid. If he wanted to do the
dearest thing in the world for her he would show her he

believed she wasn't; which undertaking of hers—not to
have misled him—was what she counted at the moment
as her presumptuous little hint to him that she was as
good as himself. It put forward the bold idea that he
could really *be* misled; and there actually passed between
them for some seconds a sign, a sign of the eyes only,
that they knew together where they were. This made, in
their brown old temple of truth, its momentary flicker;
then what followed it was that he had her, all the same,
in his pocket; and the whole thing wound up, for that
consummation, with its kind dim smile. Such kindness
was wonderful with such dimness; but brightness—that
even of sharp steel—was of course for the other side of
the business, and it would all come in for her in one way
or another. "Do you mean," he asked, "that you've no
relations at all?—not a parent, not a sister, not even a
cousin nor an aunt?"

She shook her head as with the easy habit of an inter-
viewed heroine or a freak of nature at a show. "Nobody
whatever." But the last thing she had come for was to be
dreary about it. "I'm a survivor—a survivor of a general wreck. You see," she added, "how that's to be taken
into account—that everyone else *has* gone. When I was
ten years old there were, with my father and my mother,
six of us. I'm all that's left. But they died," she went on,
to be fair all round, "of different things. Still, there it
is. And, as I told you before, I'm American. Not that I
mean that makes me worse. However, you'll probably
know what it makes me."

"Yes," he discreetly indulged her; "I know perfectly

what it makes you. It makes you, to begin with, a capital case."

She sighed, though gratefully, as if again before the social scene. "Ah, there you are!"

"Oh, no; there 'we' aren't at all. There I am only— but as much as you like. I've no end of American friends: there *they* are, if you please, and it's a fact that you couldn't very well be in a better place than in their company. It puts you with plenty of others—and that isn't pure solitude." Then he pursued: "I'm sure you've an excellent spirit; but don't try to bear more things than you need." Which after an instant he further explained. "Hard things have come to you in youth, but you mustn't think life will be for you all hard things. You've the right to be happy. You must make up your mind to it. You must accept any form in which happiness may come."

"Oh, I'll accept any whatever!" she almost gaily returned. "And it seems to me, for that matter, that I'm accepting a new one every day. Now *this!*" she smiled.

"This is very well so far as it goes. You can depend on me," the great man said, "for unlimited interest. But I m only, after all, one element in fifty. We must gather in plenty of others. Don't mind who knows. Knows, I mean, that you and I are friends."

"Ah, you do want to see some one!" she broke out. "You want to get at some one who cares for me." With which, however, as he simply met this spontaneity in a manner to show that he had often had it from young persons of her race, and that he was familiar even with the possibilities of *their* familiarity, she felt her freedom rendered vain by his silence, and she immediately tried to think of the most reasonable thing she could say. This would be, precisely, on the subject of that freedom, which she now quickly spoke of as complete. "That's of course by itself a great boon; so please don't think I don't know it. I can do exactly what I like—anything in all the wide world. I haven't a creature to ask—there's not a finger to stop me. I can shake about till I'm black and blue. That perhaps isn't *all* joy; but lots of people, I know, would like to try it." He had appeared about to put a question, but then had let her go on, which she promptly did, for she understood him the next moment as having thus taken it from her that her means were as great as might be. She had simply given it to him so, and this was all that would ever pass between them on the odious head. Yet she couldn't help also knowing that an important effect, for his judgment, or at least for his amusement—which was his feeling, since, marvellously, he did have feeling—was produced by it. All her little pieces had now then fallen together for him like the morsels of coloured glass that used to make combinations, under the hand, in the depths of one of the polygonal peepshows of childhood. "So that if it's a question of my doing anything under the sun that will help——!"

"You'll *do* anything under the sun? Good." He took that beautifully, ever so pleasantly, for what it was worth; but time was needed—ten minutes or so were needed on the spot—to deal even provisionally with the substantive question. It was convenient, in its degree,

that there was nothing she wouldn't do; but it seemed
also highly and agreeably vague that she should have to
do anything. They thus appeared to be taking her,
together, for the moment, and almost for sociability, as
prepared to proceed to gratuitous extremities; the upshot
of which was in turn, that after much interrogation, aus-
cultation, exploration, much noting of his own
sequences and neglecting of hers, had duly kept up the
vagueness, they might have struck themselves, or may at
least strike us, as coming back from an undeterred but
useless voyage to the north pole. Milly was ready, under
orders, for the north pole; which fact was doubtless
what made a blinding anticlimax of her friend's actual
abstention from orders. "No," she heard him again distinctly repeat it, "I don't want you for the present to do
anything at all; anything, that is, but obey a small pre-
scription or two that will be made clear to you, and let
me within a few days come to see you at home."

It was at first heavenly. "Then you'll see Mrs. Stringham." But she didn't mind a bit now.

"Well, I shan't be afraid of Mrs. Stringham." And he
said it once more as she asked once more: "Absolutely
not; I 'send' you nowhere. England's all right—anywhere that's pleasant, convenient, decent, will be all
right. You say you can do exactly as you like. Oblige me
therefore by being so good as to do it. There's only one
thing: you ought of course, now, as soon as I've seen
you again, to get out of London."

Milly thought. "May I then go back to the continent?"

"By all means back to the continent. Do go back to the continent."

"Then how will you keep seeing me? But perhaps," she quickly added, "you won't want to keep seeing me."

He had it all ready; he had really everything all ready. "I shall follow you up; though if you mean that I don't want you to keep seeing *me*——"

"Well?" she asked.

It was only just here that he struck her the least bit as stumbling. "Well, see all you can. That's what it comes to. Worry about nothing. You *have* at least no worries. It's a great, rare chance."

She had got up, for she had had from him both that he would send her something and would advise her promptly of the date of his coming to her, by which she was virtually dismissed. Yet, for herself, one or two things kept her. "May I come back to England too?"

"Rather! Whenever you like. But always, when you do come, immediately let me know."

"Ah," said Milly, "it won't be a great going to and fro."

"Then if you'll stay with us, so much the better."

It touched her, the way he controlled his impatience of her; and the fact itself affected her as so precious that she yielded to the wish to get more from it. "So you don't think I'm out of my mind?"

"Perhaps that *is*," he smiled, "all that's the matter."

She looked at him longer. "No, that's too good. Shall I, at any rate, suffer?"

"Not a bit."

"And yet then live?"

"My dear young lady," said her distinguished friend, "isn't to 'live' exactly what I'm trying to persuade you to take the trouble to do?"

IV

SHE HAD GONE OUT with these last words so in her ears that when once she was well away—back this time in the great square alone—it was as if some instant application of them had opened out there before her. It was positively, this effect, an excitement that carried her on; she went forward into space under the sense of an impulse received—an impulse simple and direct, easy above all to act upon. She was borne up for the hour, and now she knew why she had wanted to come by herself. No one in the world could have sufficiently entered into her state; no tie would have been close enough to enable a companion to walk beside her without some disparity. She literally felt, in this first flush, that her only company must be the human race at large, present all round her, but inspiringly impersonal, and that her only field must be, then and there, the grey immensity of London. Grey immensity had somehow of a sudden become her element; grey immensity was what her distinguished friend had, for the moment, furnished her world with and what the question of "living," as he put it to her, living by option, by volition, inevitably took on for its immediate face. She went

straight before her, without weakness, altogether with
strength; and still as she went she was more glad to be
alone, for nobody—not Kate Croy, not Susan Shepherd
either—would have wished to rush with her as she
rushed. She had asked him at the last whether, being on
foot, she might go home so, or elsewhere, and he had
replied as if almost amused again at her extravagance:
"You're active, luckily, by nature—it's beautiful: therefore rejoice in it. *Be* active, without folly—for you're
not foolish: be as active as you can and as you like."
That had been in fact the final push, as well as the
touch that most made a mixture of her consciousness—
a strange mixture that tasted at one and the same time
of what she had lost and what had been given her. It
was wonderful to her, while she took her random
course, that these quantities felt so equal: she had been
treated—hadn't she?—as if it were in her power to live;
and yet one wasn't treated so—was one?—unless it
came up, quite as much, that one might die. The
beauty of the bloom had gone from the small old sense
of safety—that was distinct: she had left it behind her
there forever. But the beauty of the idea of a great
adventure, a big dim experiment or struggle in which
she might, more responsibly than ever before, take a
hand, had been offered her instead. It was as if she had
had to pluck off her breast, to throw away, some
friendly ornament, a familiar flower, a little old jewel,
that was part of her daily dress; and to take up and
shoulder as a substitute some queer defensive weapon,
a musket, a spear, a battle-axe—conducive possibly in a

higher degree to a striking appearance, but demanding all the effort of the military posture.

She felt this instrument, for that matter, already on her back, so that she proceeded now in very truth as a soldier on a march—proceeded as if, for her initiation, the first charge had been sounded. She passed along unknown streets, over dusty littery ways, between long rows of fronts not enhanced by the August light; she felt good for miles and only wanted to get lost; there were moments at corners, where she stopped and chose her direction, in which she quite lived up to his injunction to rejoice that she was active. It was like a new pleasure to have so new a reason; she would affirm, without delay, her option, her volition; taking this personal possession of what surrounded her was a fair affirmation to start with; and she really didn't care if she made it at the cost of alarms for Susie. Susie would wonder in due course "whatever," as they said at the hotel, had become of her; yet this would be nothing either, probably, to wonderments still in store. Wonderments in truth, Milly felt, even now attended her steps: it was quite as if she saw in people's eyes the reflection of her appearance and pace. She found herself moving at times in regions visibly not haunted by odd-looking girls from New York, duskily draped, sable-plumed, all but incongruously shod and gazing about them with extravagance; she might, from the curiosity she clearly excited in byways, in side-streets peopled with grimy children and costermongers' carts, which she hoped were slums, literally have had her musket on her shoulder, have announced herself as freshly on the warpath. But for the fear of overdoing this character she would here and there have begun conversation, have asked her way; in spite of the fact that, as that would help the requirements of adventure, her way was exactly what she wanted not to know. The difficulty was that she at last accidentally found it; she had come out, she presently saw, at the Regent's Park, round which, on two or three occasions with Kate Croy, her public chariot had solemnly rolled. But she went into it further now; this was the real thing; the real thing was to be quite away from the pompous roads, well within the centre and on the stretches of shabby grass. Here were benches and smutty sheep; here were idle lads at games of ball, with their cries mild in the thick air; here were wanderers, anxious and tired like herself; here doubtless were hundreds of others just in the same box. Their box, their great common anxiety, what was it, in this grim breathing-space, but the practical question of life? They could live if they would; that is, like herself, they had been told so; she saw them all about her, on seats, digesting the information, feeling it altered, assimilated, recognising it again as something, in a slightly different shape, familiar enough, the blessed old truth that they would live if they could. All she thus shared with them made her wish to sit in their company; which she so far did that she looked for a bench that was empty, eschewing a still emptier chair that she saw hard by and for which she would have paid, with superiority, a fee.

The last scrap of superiority had soon enough left

her, if only because she before long knew herself for
more tired than she had proposed. This and the charm,
after a fashion, of the situation in itself made her linger
and rest; there was a sort of spell in the sense that
nobody in the world knew where she was. It was the
first time in her life that this had happened; somebody,
everybody appeared to have known before, at every
instant of it, where she was; so that she was now suddenly able to put it to herself that that hadn't been a life.
This present kind of thing therefore might be—which
was where precisely her distinguished friend seemed to
be wishing her to come out. He wished her also, it was
true, not to make, as she was perhaps doing now, too
much of her isolation; at the same time however as he
clearly desired to deny her no decent source of interest.
He was interested—she arrived at that—in her appealing
to as many sources as possible; and it fairly filtered into
her, as she sat and sat, that he was essentially propping
her up. Had she been doing it herself she would have
called it bolstering—the bolstering that was simply for
the weak; and she thought and thought as she put
together the proofs that it was as one of the weak he was
treating her. It was of course as one of the weak that
she had gone to him—but, oh, with how sneaking a
hope that he might pronounce her, as to all indispens-
ables, a veritable young lioness! What indeed she was
really confronted with was the consciousness that he had
not, after all, pronounced her anything: she nursed herself into the sense that he had beautifully got out of it.
Did he think, however, she wondered, that he could

keep out of it to the end?—though, as she weighed the
question, she yet felt it a little unjust. Milly weighed,
in this extraordinary hour, questions numerous and
strange; but she had, happily, before she moved, worked
round to a simplification. Stranger than anything, for
instance, was the effect of its rolling over her that, when
one considered it, he might perhaps have "got out" by
one door but to come in with a beautiful, beneficent dis-
honesty by another. It kept her more intensely motionless there that what he might fundamentally be "up to"
was some disguised intention of standing by her as a
friend. Wasn't that what women always said they
wanted to do when they deprecated the addresses of
gentlemen they couldn't more intimately go on with? It
was what they, no doubt, sincerely fancied they could
make of men of whom they couldn't make husbands.
And she didn't even reason that it was, by a similar law,
the expedient of doctors in general for the invalids of
whom they couldn't make patients: she was somehow so
sufficiently aware that *her* doctor was—however fatuous
it might sound—exceptionally moved. This was the
damning little fact—if she could talk of damnation: that
she could believe herself to have caught him in the act
of irrelevantly liking her. She hadn't gone to him to be
liked, she had gone to him to be judged; and he was
quite a great enough man to be in the habit, as a rule,
of observing the difference. She could like *him*, as she
distinctly did—that was another matter; all the more
that her doing so was now, so obviously for herself,
compatible with judgment. Yet it would have been all

portentously mixed had not, as we say, a final, merciful
wave, chilling rather, but washing clear, come to her
assistance.

It came, of a sudden, when all other thought was
spent. She had been asking herself why, if her case was
grave—and she knew what she meant by that—he
should have talked to her at all about what she might
with futility "do"; or why on the other hand, if it were
light, he should attach an importance to the office of
friendship. She had him, with her little lonely acuteness—as acuteness went during the dog-days in the
Regent's Park—in a cleft stick: she either mattered, and
then she was ill; or she didn't matter, and then she was
well enough. Now he was "acting," as they said at
home, as if she did matter—until he should prove the
contrary. It was too evident that a person at his high
pressure must keep his inconsistencies, which were
probably his highest amusements, only for the very
greatest occasions. Her prevision, in fine, of just where
she should catch him furnished the light of that judgment in which we describe her as daring to indulge.
And the judgment it was that made her sensation simple. He *had* distinguished her—that was the chill. He
hadn't known—how could he?—that she was devilishly
subtle, subtle exactly in the manner of the suspected,
the suspicious, the condemned. He in fact confessed to
it, in his way, as to an interest in her combinations, her
funny race, her funny losses, her funny gains, her funny
freedom, and, no doubt, above all, her funny manners—
funny, like those of Americans at their best, without

being vulgar, legitimating amiability and helping to pass it off. In his appreciation of these redundancies he dressed out for her the compassion he so signally permitted himself to waste; but its operation for herself was as directly divesting, denuding, exposing. It reduced her to her ultimate state, which was that of a poor girl— with her rent to pay for example—staring before her in a great city. Milly had her rent to pay, her rent for her future; everything else but how to meet it fell away from her in pieces, in tatters. This was the sensation the great man had doubtless not purposed. Well, she must go home, like the poor girl, and see. There might after all be ways; the poor girl too would be thinking. It came back for that matter perhaps to views already presented. She looked about her again, on her feet, at her scattered, melancholy comrades—some of them so melancholy as to be down on their stomachs in the grass, turned away, ignoring, burrowing; she saw once more, with them, those two faces of the question between which there was so little to choose for inspiration. It was perhaps superficially more striking that one could live if one would; but it was more appealing, insinuating, irresistible, in short, that one would live if one could.

She found after this, for the day or two, more amusement than she had ventured to count on in the fact, if it were not a mere fancy, of deceiving Susie; and she presently felt that what made the difference was the mere fancy—as this *was* one—of a countermove to her great man. His taking on himself—should he do so—to get at her companion made her suddenly, she held, irre-

sponsible, made any notion of her own all right for her;
though indeed at the very moment she invited herself
to enjoy this impunity she became aware of new matter
for surprise, or at least for speculation. Her idea would
rather have been that Mrs. Stringham would have
looked at her hard—her sketch of the grounds of her
long, independent excursion showing, she could feel, as
almost cynically superficial. Yet the dear woman so
failed, in the event, to avail herself of any right of criticism that it was sensibly tempting, for an hour, to wonder if Kate Croy had been playing perfectly fair. Hadn't
she possibly, from motives of the highest benevolence,
promptings of the finest anxiety, just given poor Susie
what she would have called the straight tip? It must
immediately be mentioned, however, that, quite apart
from a remembrance of the distinctness of Kate's
promise, Milly, the next thing, found her explanation
in a truth that had the merit of being general. If Susie,
at this crisis, suspiciously spared her, it was really that
Susie was always suspiciously sparing her—yet occasionally, too, with portentous and exceptional mercies.
The girl was conscious of how she dropped at times into
inscrutable, impenetrable deferences—attitudes that,
though without at all intending it, made a difference for
familiarity, for the ease of intimacy. It was as if she
recalled herself to manners, to the law of court-
etiquette—which last note above all helped our young
woman to a just appreciation. It was definite for her,
even if not quite solid, that to treat her as a princess was
a positive need of her companion's mind; wherefore she

couldn't help it if this lady had her transcendent view of
the way the class in question were treated. Susan had
read history, had read Gibbon and Froude and Saint-
Simon; she had high-lights as to the special allowances
made for the class, and, since she saw them, when
young, as effete and overtutored, inevitably ironic and
infinitely refined, one must take it for amusing if she
inclined to an indulgence verily Byzantine. If one *could*
only be Byzantine!—wasn't *that* what she insidiously led
one on to sigh? Milly tried to oblige her—for it really
placed Susan herself so handsomely to be Byzantine
now. The great ladies of that race—it would be somewhere in Gibbon—weren't, apparently, questioned
about their mysteries. But oh, poor Milly and hers!
Susan at all events proved scarce more inquisitive than if
she had been a mosaic at Ravenna. Susan was a porcelain monument to the odd moral that consideration
might, like cynicism, have abysses. Besides, the Puritan
finally disencumbered——! What starved generations
wasn't Mrs. Stringham, ill fancy, going to make up for?

Kate Croy came straight to the hotel—came that
evening shortly before dinner; specifically and publicly
moreover, in a hansom that, driven apparently very
fast, pulled up beneath their windows almost with the
clatter of an accident, a "smash." Milly, alone, as happened, in the great garnished void of their sitting-room,
where, a little, really, like a caged Byzantine, she had
been pacing through the queer, long-drawn, almost sinister delay of night, an effect she yet liked—Milly, at
the sound, one of the French windows standing open,

passed out to the balcony that overhung, with preten-
sions, the general entrance, and so was in time for the
look that Kate, alighting, paying her cabman, happened
to send up to the front. The visitor moreover had a
shilling back to wait for, during which Milly, from the
balcony, looked down at her, and a mute exchange, but
with smiles and nods, took place between them on what
had occurred in the morning. It was what Kate had
called for, and the tone was thus, almost by accident,
determined for Milly before her friend came up. What
was also, however, determined for her was, again, yet
irrepressibly again, that the image presented to her, the
splendid young woman who looked so particularly
handsome in impatience, with the fine freedom of her
signal, was the peculiar property of somebody else's
vision, that this fine freedom in short was the fine freedom she showed Mr. Densher. Just so was how she
looked to him, and just so was how Milly was held by
her—held as by the strange sense of seeing through that
distant person's eyes. It lasted, as usual, the strange
sense, but fifty seconds; yet in so lasting it produced
an effect. It produced in fact more than one, and we
take them in their order. The first was that it struck our
young woman as absurd to say that a girl's looking so
to a man could possibly be without connections; and
the second was that by the time Kate had got into the
room Milly was in mental possession of the main connection it must have for herself.

She produced this commodity on the spot—produced
it, that is, in straight response to Kate's frank "Well,

what?" The inquiry bore of course, with Kate's eagerness, on the issue of the morning's scene, the great man's latest wisdom, and it doubtless affected Milly a little as the cheerful demand for news is apt to affect troubled spirits when news is not, in one of the neater forms, prepared for delivery. She couldn't have said what it was exactly that, on the instant, determined her; the nearest description of it would perhaps have been as the more vivid impression of all her friend took for granted. The contrast between this free quantity and the maze of possibilities through which, for hours, she had herself been picking her way, put on, in short, for the moment, a grossness that even friendly forms scarce lightened: it helped forward in fact the revelation to herself that she absolutely had nothing to tell. Besides which, certainly, there was something else—an influence, at the particular juncture, still more obscure. Kate had lost, on the way upstairs, the look—*the* look—that made her young hostess so subtly think and one of the signs of which was that she never kept it for many moments at once; yet she stood there, none the less, so in her bloom and in her strength, so completely again the "handsome girl" beyond all others, the "handsome girl" for whom Milly had at first gratefully taken her, that to meet her now with the note of the plaintive would amount somehow to a surrender, to a confession. *She* would never in her life be ill; the greatest doctor would keep her, at the worst, the fewest minutes; and it was as if she had asked just *with* all this practical impeccability for all that was most mortal in her friend. These things, for Milly,

inwardly danced their dance; but the vibration produced
and the dust kicked up had lasted less than our account
of them. Almost before she knew it she was answering,
and answering, beautifully, with no consciousness of
fraud, only as with a sudden flare of the famous "will-
power" she had heard about, read about, and which was
what her medical adviser had mainly thrown her back
on. "Oh, it's all right. He's lovely."

Kate was splendid, and it would have been clear for
Milly now, had the further presumption been needed,
that she had said no word to Mrs. Stringham. "You
mean you've been absurd?"

"Absurd." It was a simple word to say, but the consequence of it, for our young woman, was that she felt
it, as soon as spoken, to have done something for her
safety.

And Kate really hung on her lips. "There's nothing
at all the matter?"

"Nothing to worry about. I shall take a little watching, but I shan't have to do anything dreadful, or even,
in the least, inconvenient. I can do in fact as I like." It
was wonderful for Milly how just to put it so made all
its pieces fall at present quite properly into places.

Yet even before the full effect came Kate had seized,
kissed, blessed her. "My love, you're too sweet! It's too
dear! But it's as I was sure." Then she grasped the full
beauty. "You can do as you like?"

"Quite. Isn't it charming?"

"Ah, but catch you," Kate triumphed with gaiety,
"*not* doing——! And what *shall* you do?"

"For the moment simply enjoy it. Enjoy"—Milly was completely luminous—"having got out of my scrape."

"Learning, you mean, so easily, that you *are* well."

It was as if Kate had but too conveniently put the words into her mouth. "Learning, I mean, so easily, that I *am* well."

"Only, no one's of course well enough to stay in London now. He can't," Kate went on, "want this of you."

"Mercy, no—I'm to knock about. I'm to go to places."

"But not beastly 'climates'—Engadines, Rivieras, boredoms?"

"No; just, as I say, where I prefer. I'm to go in for pleasure."

"Oh, the duck!"—Kate, with her own shades of familiarity, abounded. "But what kind of pleasure?"

"The highest," Milly smiled.

Her friend met it as nobly. "Which *is* the highest?"

"Well, it's just our chance to find out. You must help me."

"What have I wanted to do but help you," Kate asked, "from the moment I first laid eyes on you?" Yet with this too Kate had her wonder. "I like your talking, though, about that. What help, with your luck all round, do you want?"

V

MILLY INDEED AT LAST couldn't say; so that she had really for the time brought it along to the point so oddly

marked for her by her visitor's arrival, the truth that she
was enviably strong. She carried this out, from that
evening, for each hour still left her, and the more easily
perhaps that the hours were now narrowly numbered.
All she actually waited for was Sir Luke Strett's
promised visit; as to her proceeding on which, however,
her mind was quite made up. Since he wanted to get at
Susie he should have the freest access, and then perhaps
he would see how he liked it. What was between *them*
they might settle as between them, and any pressure it
should lift from her own spirit they were at liberty to
convert to their use. If the dear man wished to fire
Susan Shepherd with a still higher ideal, he would only
after all, at the worst, have Susan on his hands. If devotion, in a word, was what it would come up for the
interested pair to organise, she was herself ready to consume it as the dressed and served dish. He had talked
to her of her "appetite," her account of which, she felt,
must have been vague. But for devotion, she could now
see, this appetite would be of the best. Gross, greedy,
ravenous—these were doubtless the proper names for
her: she was at all events resigned in advance to the
machinations of sympathy. The day that followed her
lonely excursion was to be the last but two or three of
their stay in London; and the evening of that day practically ranked for them as, in the matter of outside relations, the last of all. People were by this time quite
scattered, and many of those who had so liberally man-
ifested in calls, in cards, in evident sincerity about visits,
later on, over the land, had positively passed in music

out of sight; whether as members, these latter, more especially, of Mrs. Lowder's immediate circle or as members of Lord Mark's—our friends being by this time able to make the distinction. The general pitch had thus, decidedly, dropped, and the occasions still to be dealt with were special and few. One of these, for Milly, announced itself as the doctor's call already mentioned, as to which she had now had a note from him: the single other, of importance, was their appointed leave-taking—for the shortest separation—in respect to Mrs. Lowder and Kate. The aunt and the niece were to dine with them alone, intimately and easily—as easily as should be consistent with the question of their afterwards going on together to some absurdly belated party, at which they had had it from Aunt Maud that they would do well to show. Sir Luke was to make his appearance on the morrow of this, and in respect to that complication Milly had already her plan.

The night was, at all events, hot and stale, and it was late enough by the time the four ladies had been gathered in, for their small session, at the hotel, where the windows were still open to the high balconies and the flames of the candles, behind the pink shades—disposed as for the vigil of watchers—were motionless in the air in which the season lay dead. What was presently settled among them was that Milly, who betrayed on this occasion a preference more marked than usual, should not hold herself obliged to climb that evening the social stair, however it might stretch to meet her, and that, Mrs. Lowder and Mrs. Stringham facing the ordeal

together, Kate Croy should remain with her and await
their return. It was a pleasure to Milly, ever, to send
Susan Shepherd forth; she saw her go with complacency,
liked, as it were, to put people off with her, and noted
with satisfaction, when she so moved to the carriage, the
further denudation—a markedly ebbing tide—of her little benevolent back. If it wasn't quite Aunt Maud's
ideal, moreover, to take out the new American girl's
funny friend instead of the new American girl herself,
nothing could better indicate the range of that lady's
merit than the spirit in which—as at the present hour
for instance—she made the best of the minor advantage.
And she did this with a broad, cheerful absence of illusion; she did it—confessing even as much to poor
Susie—because, frankly, she *was* good-natured. When
Mrs. Stringham observed that her own light was too
abjectly borrowed and that it was as a link alone, fortunately not missing, that she was valued, Aunt Maud
concurred to the extent of the remark: "Well, my dear,
you're better than nothing." To-night, furthermore, it
came up for Milly that Aunt Maud had something particular in mind. Mrs. Stringham, before adjourning with
her, had gone off for some shawl or other accessory, and
Kate, as if a little impatient for their withdrawal, had
wandered out to the balcony, where she hovered, for the
time, unseen, though with scarce more to look at than
the dim London stars and the cruder glow, up the street,
on a corner, of a small public-house, in front of which
a fagged cab-horse was thrown into relief. Mrs. Lowder made use of the moment: Milly felt as soon as she

had spoken that what she was doing was somehow for use.

"Dear Susan tells me that you saw, in America, Mr. Densher—whom I've never till now, as you may have noticed, asked you about. But do you mind at last, in connection with him, doing something for me?" She had lowered her fine voice to a depth, though speaking with all her rich glibness; and Milly, after a small sharpness of surprise, was already guessing the sense of her appeal. "Will you name him, in any way you like, to *her*"—and Aunt Maud gave a nod at the window; "so that you may perhaps find out whether he's back?"

Ever so many things, for Milly, fell into line at this; it was a wonder, she afterwards thought, that she could be conscious of so many at once. She smiled hard, however, for them all. "But I don't know that it's important to me to 'find out.' " The array of things was further swollen, however, even as she said this, by its striking her as too much to say. She therefore tried as quickly to say less. "Except you mean, of course, that it's important to *you*." She fancied Aunt Maud was looking at her almost as hard as she was herself smiling, and that gave her another impulse. "You know I never *have* yet named him to her; so that if I should break out now——"

"Well?"—Mrs. Lowder waited.

"Why, she may wonder what I've been making a mystery of. She hasn't mentioned him, you know," Milly went on, "herself."

"No"—her friend a little heavily weighed it—"she

wouldn't. So it's she, you see then, who has made the mystery."

Yes, Milly but wanted to see; only there was so much. "There has been of course no particular reason." Yet that indeed was neither here nor there. "Do you think," she asked, "he *is* back?"

"It will be about his time, I gather, and rather a comfort to me definitely to know."

"Then can't you ask her yourself?"

"Ah, we never speak of him!"

It helped Milly for the moment to the convenience of a puzzled pause. "Do you mean he's an acquaintance of whom you disapprove for her?"

Aunt Maud, as well, just hung fire. "I disapprove of *her* for the poor young man. She doesn't care for him."

"And *he* cares so much——?"

"Too much, too much. And my fear is," said Mrs. Lowder, "that he privately besets her. She keeps it to herself, but I don't want her worried. Neither, in truth," she both generously and confidentially concluded, "do I want *him*."

Milly showed all her own effort to meet the case. "But what can *I* do?"

"You can find out where they are. If I myself try," Mrs. Lowder explained, "I shall appear to treat them as if I supposed them deceiving me."

"And you don't. You don't," Milly mused for her, "suppose them deceiving you."

"Well," said Aunt Maud, whose fine onyx eyes failed to blink, even though Milly's questions might have been

taken as drawing her rather further than she had originally meant to go—"well, Kate is thoroughly aware of
my views for her, and that I take her being with me, at
present, in the way she *is* with me, if you know what I
mean, as a loyal assent to them. Therefore as my views
don't happen to provide a place, at all, for Mr. Densher,
much, in a manner, as I like him"—therefore, therefore
in short she had been prompted to this step, though she
completed her sense, but sketchily, with the rattle of her
large fan.

It assisted them perhaps, however, for the moment,
that Milly was able to pick out of her sense what might
serve as the clearest part of it. "You do like him then?"

"Oh dear, yes. Don't you?"

Milly hesitated, for the question was somehow as the
sudden point of something sharp on a nerve that
winced. She just caught her breath, but she had ground
for joy afterwards, she felt, in not really having failed
to choose with quickness sufficient, out of fifteen possible answers, the one that would best serve her. She was
then almost proud, as well, that she had cheerfully
smiled. "I did—three times—in New York." So came
and went for her, in these simple words, the speech that
was to figure for her, later on, that night, as the one she
had ever uttered that cost her most. She was to lie
awake, at all events, half the night, for the gladness of
not having taken any line so really inferior as the denial
of a happy impression.

For Mrs. Lowder also, moreover, her simple words
were the right ones; they were at any rate, that lady's

laugh showed, in the natural note of the racy. "You dear American thing! But people may be very good, and yet not good for what one wants."

"Yes," the girl assented, "even I suppose when what one wants is something very good."

"Oh, my child, it would take too long just now to tell you all *I* want! I want everything at once and together—and ever so much for you too, you know. But you've seen us," Aunt Maud continued; "you'll have made out."

"Ah," said Milly, "I *don't* make out"; for again—it came that way in rushes—she felt an obscurity in things. "Why, if our friend here doesn't like him——"

"Should I conceive her interested in keeping things from me?" Mrs. Lowder did justice to the question. "My dear, how can you ask? Put yourself in her place. She meets me, but on *her* terms. Proud young women are proud young women. And proud old ones are—well, what *I* am. Fond of you as we both are, you can help us."

Milly tried to be inspired. "Does it come back then to my asking her straight?"

At this, however, finally, Aunt Maud threw her up. "Oh, if you've so many reasons not——!"

"I've not so many," Milly smiled—"but I've one. If I break out so suddenly as knowing him, what will she make of my not having spoken before?"

Mrs. Lowder looked blank at it. "Why should you care what she makes? You may have only been decently discreet."

"Ah, I *have* been," the girl made haste to say.

"Besides," her friend went on, "I suggested to you, through Susan, your line."

"Yes, that reason's a reason for *me*."

"And for *me*," Mrs. Lowder insisted. "She's not therefore so stupid as not to do justice to grounds so marked. You can tell her perfectly that I had asked you to say nothing."

"And may I tell her that you've asked me now to speak?"

Mrs. Lowder might well have thought, yet, oddly, this pulled her up. "You can't do it without——?"

Milly was almost ashamed to be raising so many difficulties. "I'll do what I can if you'll kindly tell me one thing more." She faltered a little—it was so prying; but she brought it out. "Will he have been writing to her?"

"It's exactly, my dear, what I should like to know." Mrs. Lowder was at last impatient. "Push in for yourself, and I dare say she'll tell you."

Even now, all the same, Milly had not quite fallen back. "It will be pushing in," she continued to smile, "for *you*." She allowed her companion, however, no time to take this up. "The point will be that if he *has* been writing she may have answered."

"But what point, you subtle thing, is that?"

"It isn't subtle, it seems to me, but quite simple," Milly said, "that if she has answered she has very possibly spoken of me."

"Very certainly indeed. But what difference will it make?"

The girl had a moment, at this, of thinking it natural
that her interlocutress herself should so fail of subtlety.
"It will make the difference that he will have written to
her in answer that he knows me. And that, in turn," our
young woman explained, "will give an oddity to my
own silence."

"How so, if she's perfectly aware of having given you
no opening? The only oddity," Aunt Maud lucidly professed, "is for yourself. It's in *her* not having spoken."

"Ah, there we are!" said Milly.

And she had uttered it, evidently, in a tone that
struck her friend. "Then it *has* troubled you?"

But ah, the inquiry had only to be made to bring the
rare colour with fine inconsequence, to her face. "Not,
really, the least little bit!" And, quickly feeling the need
to abound in this sense, she was on the point, to cut
short, of declaring that she cared, after all, no scrap how
much she obliged. Only she felt at this instant too the
intervention of still other things. Mrs. Lowder was, in
the first place, already beforehand, already affected as by
the sudden vision of her having herself pushed too far.
Milly could never judge from her face of her uppermost
motive—it was so little, in its hard, smooth sheen, that
kind of human countenance. She looked hard when she
spoke fair; the only thing was that when she spoke hard
she likewise didn't look soft. Something, none the less,
had arisen in her now—a full appreciable tide, entering
by the rupture of some bar. She announced that if what
she had asked was to prove in the least a bore her young
friend was not to dream of it; making her young friend at

the same time, by the change in her tone, dream on the
spot more profusely. She spoke with a belated light,
Milly could apprehend—she could always apprehend—
from pity; and the result of that perception, for the girl,
was singular: it proved to her as quickly that Kate, keeping her secret, had been straight with her. From Kate
distinctly then, as to why she was to be pitied, Aunt
Maud knew nothing, and was thereby simply putting in
evidence the fine side of her own character. This fine
side was that she could almost at any hour, by a kindled
preference or a diverted energy, glow for another interest than her own. She exclaimed as well, at this moment,
that Milly must have been thinking, round the case,
much more than she had supposed; and this remark
could, at once, affect the girl as sharply as any other form
of the charge of weakness. It was what everyone, if she
didn't look out, would soon be saying—"There's something the matter with you!" What one was therefore
one's self concerned immediately to establish was that
there was nothing at all. "I shall like to help you; I shall
like, so far as that goes, to help Kate herself," she made
such haste as she could to declare; her eyes wandering
meanwhile across the width of the room to that dusk of
the balcony in which their companion perhaps a little
unaccountably lingered. She suggested hereby her impatience to begin; she almost overtly wondered at the
length of the opportunity this friend was giving them—
referring it, however, so far as words went, to the other
friend, breaking off with an amused: "How tremendously Susie must be beautifying!"

It only marked Aunt Maud, none the less, as too pre-occupied for her allusion. The onyx eyes were fixed upon her with a polished pressure that must signify some enriched benevolence. "Let it go, my dear. We shall, after all, soon enough see."

"If he *has* come back we shall certainly see," Milly after a moment replied; "for he'll probably feel that he can't quite civilly not come to see me. Then *there*," she remarked, "we shall be. It wouldn't then, you see, come through Kate at all—it would come through him. Except," she wound up with a smile, "that he won't find me."

She had the most extraordinary sense of interesting her interlocutress, in spite of herself, more than she wanted; it was as if her doom so floated her on that she couldn't stop—by very much the same trick it had played her with her doctor. "Shall you run away from him?"

She neglected the question, wanting only now to get off. "Then," she went on, "you'll deal with Kate directly."

"Shall you run away from *her*?" Mrs. Lowder profoundly inquired, while they became aware of Susie's return through the room, opening out behind them, in which they had dined.

This affected Milly as giving her but an instant; and suddenly, with it, everything she felt in the connection rose to her lips in a question that, even as she put it, she knew she was failing to keep colourless. "Is it your own belief that he *is* with her?"

Aunt Maud took it in—took in, that is, everything of
the tone that she just wanted her not to; and the result
for some seconds, was but to make their eyes meet in
silence. Mrs. Stringham had rejoined them and was asking if Kate had gone—an inquiry at once answered by
this young lady's reappearance. They saw her again in
the open window, where, looking at them, she had
paused—producing thus, on Aunt Maud's part, almost
too impressive a "Hush!" Mrs. Lowder indeed, without
loss of time, smothered any danger in a sweeping retreat
with Susie; but Milly's words to her, just uttered, about
dealing with her niece directly, struck our young woman
as already recoiling on herself. Directness, however
evaded, would be, fully, for *her*; nothing in fact would
ever have been for her so direct as the evasion. Kate had
remained in the window, very handsome and upright,
the outer dark framing in a highly favourable way her
summery simplicities and lightnesses of dress. Milly had,
given the relation of space, no real fear she had heard
their talk; only she hovered there as with conscious eyes
and some added advantage. Then indeed, with small
delay, her friend sufficiently saw. The conscious eyes,
the added advantage were but those she had now always
at command—those proper to the person Milly knew as
known to Merton Densher. It was for several seconds
again as if the *total* of her identity had been that of the
person known to him—a determination having for result
another sharpness of its own. Kate had positively but to
be there just as she was to tell her he had come back. It
seemed to pass between them, in fine, without a word,

that he was in London, that he was perhaps only round the corner; and surely therefore no dealing of Milly's with her would yet have been so direct.

VI

IT WAS DOUBTLESS because this queer form of directness had in itself, for the hour, seemed so sufficient that Milly was afterwards aware of having really, all the while—during the strange, indescribable session before the return of their companions—done nothing to intensify it. If she was most aware only afterwards, under the long, discurtained ordeal of the morrow's dawn, that was because she had really, till their evening's end came, ceased, after a little, to miss anything from their ostensible comfort. What was behind showed but in gleams and glimpses; what was in front never at all confessed to not holding the stage. Three minutes had not passed before Milly quite knew she should have done nothing Aunt Maud had just asked her. She knew it moreover by much the same light that had acted for her with that lady and with Sir Luke Strett. It pressed upon her then and there that she was still in a current determined, through her indifference, timidity, bravery, generosity— she scarce could say which—by others; that not she but the current acted, and that somebody else, always, was the keeper of the lock or the dam. Kate for example had but to open the flood-gate: the current moved in its mass—the current, as it had been, of her doing as Kate wanted. What, somehow, in the most extraordinary way in the world, *had* Kate wanted but to be, of a sudden, more interesting than she had ever been? Milly, for their evening then, quite held her breath with the appreciation of it. If she hadn't been sure her companion would have had nothing, from her moments with Mrs. Lowder, to go by, she would almost have seen the admirable creature "cutting in" to anticipate a danger. This fantasy indeed, while they sat together, dropped after a little; even if only because other fantasies multiplied and clustered, making fairly, for our young woman, the buoyant medium in which her friend talked and moved. They sat together, I say, but Kate moved as much as she talked; she figured there, restless and charming, just perhaps a shade perfunctory, repeatedly quitting her place, taking slowly, to and fro, in the trailing folds of her light dress, the length of the room, and almost avowedly performing for the pleasure of her hostess.

Mrs. Lowder had said to Milly at Matcham that she and her niece, as allies, could practically conquer the world; but though it was a speech about which there had even then been a vague, grand glamour, the girl read into it at present more of an approach to a meaning. Kate, for that matter, by herself, could conquer anything, and *she*, Milly Theale, was probably concerned with the "world" only as the small scrap of it that most impinged on her and that was therefore first to be dealt with. On this basis of being dealt with she would doubtless herself do her share of the conquering: she would have something to supply, Kate something to take— each of them thus, to that tune, something for squaring

with Aunt Maud's ideal. This in short was what it came
to now—that the occasion, in the quiet late lamplight,
had the quality of a rough rehearsal of the possible big
drama. Milly knew herself dealt with—handsomely,
completely: she surrendered to the knowledge, for so it
was, she felt, that she supplied her helpful force. And
what Kate had to take Kate took as freely and, to all
appearance, as gratefully; accepting afresh, with each of
her long, slow walks, the relation between them so
established and consecrating her companion's surrender
simply by the interest she gave it. The interest to Milly
herself we naturally mean; the interest to Kate Milly felt
as probably inferior. It easily and largely came for their
present talk, for the quick flight of the hour before the
breach of the spell—it all came, when considered, from
the circumstance, not in the least abnormal, that the
handsome girl was in extraordinary "form." Milly
remembered her having said that she was at her best late
at night; remembered it by its having, with its fine
assurance, made her wonder when *she* was at her best
and how happy people must be who had such a fixed
time. She had no time at all; she was never at her best—
unless indeed it were exactly, as now, in listening,
watching, admiring, collapsing. If Kate moreover, quite
mercilessly, had never been so good, the beauty and the
marvel of it was that she had never really been so frank:
being a person of such a calibre, as Milly would have
said, that, even while "dealing" with you and thereby, as
it were, picking her steps, she could let herself go, could,

in irony, in confidence, in extravagance, tell you things she had never told before. That was the impression—that she was telling things, and quite conceivably for her own relief as well; almost as if the errors of vision, the mistakes of proportion, the residuary innocence of spirit still to be remedied on the part of her auditor had their moments of proving too much for her nerves. She went at them just now, these sources of irritation, with an amused energy that it would have been open to Milly to regard as cynical and that was nevertheless called for—as to this the other was distinct—by the way that in certain connections the American mind broke down. It seemed at least—the American mind as sitting there thrilled and dazzled in Milly—not to understand English society without a separate confrontation with *all* the cases. It couldn't proceed by—there was some technical term she lacked until Milly suggested both analogy and induction, and then, differently, instinct, none of which were right: it had to be led up and introduced to each aspect of the monster, enabled to walk all round it, whether for the consequent exaggerated ecstasy or for the still more—as appeared to this critic—disproportionate shock. It might, the monster, Kate conceded, loom large for those born amid forms less developed and therefore no doubt less amusing; it might on some sides be a strange and dreadful monster, calculated to devour the unwary, to abase the proud, to scandalise the good; but if one had to live with it one must, not to be for ever sitting up, learn how: which was virtually in short

to-night what the handsome girl showed herself as
teaching.

She gave away publicly, in this process, Lancaster
Gate and everything it contained; she gave away, hand
over hand, Milly's thrill continued to note, Aunt Maud
and Aunt Maud's glories and Aunt Maud's complacen-
cies; she gave herself away most of all, and it was naturally what most contributed to her candour. She didn't
speak to her friend once more, in Aunt Maud's strain, of
how they could scale the skies; she spoke, by her bright,
perverse preference on this occasion, of the need, in the
first place, of being neither stupid nor vulgar. It might
have been a lesson, for our young American, in the art
of seeing things as they were—a lesson so various and so
sustained that the pupil had, as we have shown, but
receptively to gape. The odd thing furthermore was that
it could serve its purpose while explicitly disavowing
every personal bias. It wasn't that she disliked Aunt
Maud, who was everything she had on other occasions
declared; but the dear woman, ineffaceably stamped by
inscrutable nature and a dreadful art, wasn't—how *could*
she be?—what she wasn't. She wasn't any one. She
wasn't anything. She wasn't anywhere. Milly mustn't
think it—one couldn't, as a good friend, let her. Those
hours at Matcham were *inespérées*, were pure manna
from heaven; or if not wholly that perhaps, with hum-
bugging old Lord Mark as a backer, were vain as a
ground for hopes and calculations. Lord Mark was very
well, but he wasn't *the* cleverest creature in England,

and even if he had been he still wouldn't have been the most obliging. He weighed it out in ounces, and indeed each of the pair was really waiting for what the other would put down.

"She has put down *you*," said Milly, attached to the subject still; "and I think what you mean is that, on the counter, she still keeps hold of you."

"Lest"—Kate took it up—"he should suddenly grab me and run? Oh, as he isn't ready to run, he's much less ready, naturally, to grab. I *am*—you're so far right as that—on the counter, when I'm not in the shop-window; in and out of which I'm thus conveniently, commercially whisked: the essence, all of it, of my position, and the price, as properly, of my aunt's protection." Lord Mark was substantially what she had begun with as soon as they were alone; the impression was even yet with Milly of her having sounded his name, having imposed it, as a topic, in direct opposition to the other name that Mrs. Lowder had left in the air and that all her own look, as we have seen, kept there at first for her companion. The immediate strange effect had been that of her consciously needing, as it were, an alibi—which, successfully, she so found. She had worked it to the end, ridden it to and fro across the course marked for Milly by Aunt Maud, and now she had quite, so to speak, broken it in. "The bore is that if she wants him so much—wants him, heaven forgive her! for *me*—he has put us all out, since your arrival, by wanting somebody else. I don't mean somebody else than you."

Milly threw off the charm sufficiently to shake her head. "Then I haven't made out who it is. If I'm any part of his alternative he had better stop where he is."

"Truly, truly?—always, always?"

Milly tried to insist with an equal gaiety. "Would you like me to swear?"

Kate appeared for a moment—though that was doubtless but gaiety too—to think. "Haven't we been swearing enough?"

"You have perhaps, but I haven't, and I ought to give you the equivalent. At any rate there it is. 'Truly, truly' as you say—'always, always.' So I'm not in the way."

"Thanks," said Kate—"but that doesn't help me."

"Oh, it's as simplifying for *him* that I speak of it."

"The difficulty really is that he's a person with so many ideas that it's particularly hard to simplify for him. That's exactly of course what Aunt Maud has been trying. He won't," Kate firmly continued, "make up his mind about me."

"Well," Milly smiled, "give him time."

Her friend met it in perfection. "One is *doing* that—one *is*. But one remains, all the same, but one of his ideas."

"There's no harm in that," Milly returned, "if you come out in the end as the best of them. What's a man," she pursued, "especially an ambitious one, without a variety of ideas?"

"No doubt. The more the merrier." And Kate looked at her grandly. "One can but hope to come out, and do nothing to prevent it."

All of which made for the impression, fantastic or not, of the *alibi*. The splendour, the grandeur were, for Milly, the bold ironic spirit behind it, so interesting too in itself. What, moreover, was not less interesting was the fact, as our young woman noted it, that Kate confined her point to the difficulties, so far as *she* was concerned, raised only by Lord Mark. She referred now to none that her own taste might present; which circumstance again played its little part. She was doing what she liked in respect to another person, but she was in no way committed to the other person, and her furthermore talking of Lord Mark as not young and not true were only the signs of her clear self-consciousness, were all in the line of her slightly hard, but scarce the less graceful extravagance. She didn't wish to show too much her consent to be arranged for, but that was a different thing from not wishing sufficiently to give it. There was something moreover, on it all, that Milly still found occasion to say, "If your aunt has been, as you tell me, put out by me, I feel that she has remained remarkably kind."

"Oh, but she has—whatever might have happened in that respect—plenty of use for you! You put her in, my dear, more than you put her out. You don't half see it, but she has clutched your petticoat. You can do anything—you can do, I mean, lots that *we* can't. You're an outsider, independent and standing by yourself; you're not hideously relative to tiers and tiers of others." And Kate, facing in that direction, went further and further; wound up, while Milly gaped, with extraordinary

words. "We're of no use to you—it's decent to tell you.
You'd be of use to us, but that's a different matter. My
honest advice to you would be—" she went indeed all
lengths—"to drop us while you can. It would be funny
if you didn't soon see how awfully better you can do.
We've not really done for you the least thing worth
speaking of—nothing you mightn't easily have had in
some other way. Therefore you're under no obligation.
You won't want us next year; we shall only continue to
want you. But that's no reason for you, and you mustn't
pay too dreadfully for poor Mrs. Stringham's having let
you in. She has the best conscience in the world; she's
enchanted with what she has done; but you shouldn't
take your people from *her*. It has been quite awful to see
you do it."

Milly tried to be amused, so as not—it was too
absurd—to be fairly frightened. Strange enough
indeed—if not natural enough—that, late at night thus,
in a mere mercenary house, with Susie away, a want of
confidence should possess her. She recalled, with all the
rest of it, the next day, piecing things together in the
dawn, that she had felt herself alone with a creature who
paced like a panther. That was a violent image, but it
made her a little less ashamed of having been scared.
For all her scare, none the less, she had now the sense to
find words. "And yet without Susie I shouldn't have
had *you*."

It had been at this point, however, that Kate flickered
highest. "Oh, you may very well loathe me yet!"

Really at last, thus, it had been too much; as, with

her own least feeble flare, after a wondering watch,
Milly had shown. She hadn't cared; she had too much
wanted to know; and, though a small solemnity of
reproach, a sombre strain, had broken into her tone, it
was to figure as her nearest approach to serving Mrs.
Lowder. "Why do you say such things to me?"

This unexpectedly had acted, by a sudden turn of
Kate's attitude, as a happy speech. She had risen as she
spoke, and Kate had stopped before her, shining at her
instantly with a softer brightness. Poor Milly hereby
enjoyed one of her views of how people, wincing oddly,
were often touched by her. "Because you're a dove."
With which she felt herself ever so delicately, so considerately, embraced; not with familiarity or as a liberty
taken, but almost ceremonially and in the manner of an
accolade; partly as if, though a dove who could perch
on a finger, one were also a princess with whom forms
were to be observed. It even came to her, through the
touch of her companion's lips, that this form, this cool
pressure, fairly sealed the sense of what Kate had just
said. It was moreover, for the girl, like an inspiration:
she found herself accepting as the right one, while she
caught her breath with relief, the name so given her. She
met it on the instant as she would have met the revealed
truth; it lighted up the strange dusk in which she lately
had walked. *That* was what was the matter with her. She
was a dove. Oh, *wasn't* she?—it echoed within her as
she became aware of the sound, outside, of the return
of their friends. There was, the next thing, little enough
doubt about it after Aunt Maud had been two minutes

in the room. She had come up, Mrs. Lowder, with
Susan—which she needn't have done, at that hour,
instead of letting Kate come down to her; so that Milly
could be quite sure it was to catch hold, in some way, of
the loose end they had left. Well, the way she did catch
was simply to make the point that it didn't now in the
least matter. She had mounted the stairs for this, and
she had her moment again with her younger hostess
while Kate, on the spot, as the latter at the time noted,
gave Susan Shepherd unwonted opportunities. Kate was
in other words, as Aunt Maud engaged her friend, listening with the handsomest response to Mrs. Stringham's impression of the scene they had just quitted. It
was in the tone of the fondest indulgence—almost,
really, that of dove cooing to dove—that Mrs. Lowder
expressed to Milly the hope that it had all gone beautifully. Her "all" had an ample benevolence; it soothed
and simplified; she spoke as if it were the two young
women, not she and her comrade, who had been facing
the town together. But Milly's answer had prepared
itself while Aunt Maud was on the stair; she had felt in
a rush all the reasons that would make it the most dove-
like; and she gave it, while she was about it, as earnest,
as candid. "I don't *think*, dear lady, he's here."

It gave her straightway the measure of the success she
could have as a dove: that was recorded in the long look
of deep criticism, a look without a word, that Mrs. Lowder poured forth. And the word, presently, bettered it
still. "Oh, you exquisite thing!" The luscious innuendo
of it, almost startling, lingered in the room, after the vis-

itors had gone, like an oversweet fragrance. But left alone with Mrs. Stringham Milly continued to breathe it: she studied again the dovelike and so set her companion to mere rich reporting that she averted all inquiry into her own case.

That, with the new day, was once more her law— though she saw before her, of course, as something of a complication, her need, each time, to decide. She should have to be clear as to how a dove *would* act. She settled it, she thought, well enough this morning by quite re- adopting her plan in respect to Sir Luke Strett. That, she was pleased to reflect, had originally been pitched in the key of a merely iridescent drab; and although Mrs. Stringham, after breakfast, began by staring at it as if it had been a priceless Persian carpet suddenly unrolled at her feet, she had no scruple, at the end of five min- utes, in leaving her to make the best of it. "Sir Luke Strett comes, by appointment, to see me at eleven, but I'm going out on purpose. He's to be told, please, deceptively, that I'm at home, and, you, as my repre- sentative, when he comes up, are to see him instead. He will like that, this time, better. So do be nice to him." It had taken, naturally, more explanation, and the men- tion, above all, of the fact that the visitor was the great- est of doctors; yet when once the key had been offered Susie slipped it on her bunch, and her young friend could again feel her lovely imagination operate. It oper- ated in truth very much as Mrs. Lowder's, at the last, had done the night before: it made the air heavy once more with the extravagance of assent. It might, afresh,

almost have frightened our young woman to see how
people rushed to meet her: *had* she then so little time
to live that the road must always be spared her? It was
as if they were helping her to take it out on the spot.
Susie—she couldn't deny, and didn't pretend to—
might, of a truth, on *her* side, have treated such news
as a flash merely lurid; as to which, to do Susie justice,
the pain of it was all there. But, none the less, the margin always allowed her young friend was all there as
well; and the proposal now made her—what was it in
short but Byzantine? The vision of Milly's perception of
the propriety of the matter had, at any rate, quickly
engulfed, so far as her attitude was concerned, any surprise and any shock; so that she only desired, the next
thing, perfectly to possess the facts. Milly could easily
speak, on this, as if there were only one: she made nothing of such another as that she had felt herself menaced.
The great fact, in fine, was that she *knew* him to desire
just now, more than anything else, to meet, quite apart,
some one interested in her. Who therefore so interested
as her faithful Susan? The only other circumstance that,
by the time she had quitted her friend, she had treated
as worth mentioning was the circumstance of her having
at first intended to keep quiet. She had originally best
seen herself as sweetly secretive. As to that she had
changed, and her present request was the result. She
didn't say why she had changed, but she trusted her
faithful Susan. Their visitor would trust her not less,
and she herself would adore their visitor. Moreover he
wouldn't—the girl felt sure—tell her anything dreadful.

The worst would be that he was in love and that he needed a confidant to work it. And now she was going to the National Gallery.

VII

THE IDEA of the National Gallery had been with her from the moment of her hearing from Sir Luke Strett about his hour of coming. It had been in her mind as a place so meagrely visited, as one of the places that had seemed at home one of the attractions of Europe and one of its highest aids to culture, but that—the old story—the typical frivolous always ended by sacrificing to vulgar pleasures. She had had perfectly, at those whimsical moments on the Brünig, the half-shamed sense of turning her back on such opportunities for real improvement as had figured to her, from of old, in connection with the continental tour, under the general head of "pictures and things"; and now she knew for what she had done so. The plea had been explicit—she had done so for life, as opposed to learning; the upshot of which had been that life was now beautifully provided for. In spite of those few dips and dashes into the many-coloured stream of history for which of late Kate Croy had helped her to find time, there were possible great chances she had neglected, possible great moments she should, save for to-day, have all but missed. She might still, she had felt, overtake one or two of them among the Titians and the Turners; she had been honestly nursing the hour, and, once she was in the benignant halls, her faith knew itself justified. It was the air she wanted and the world she would now exclusively choose; the quiet chambers, nobly overwhelming, rich but slightly veiled, opened out round her and made her presently say "If I could lose myself *here!*" There were people, people in plenty, but, admirably, no personal question. It was immense, outside, the personal question; but she had blissfully left it outside, and the nearest it came, for a quarter of an hour, to glimmering again into sight was when she watched for a little one of the more earnest of the lady-copyists. Two or three in particular, spectacled, aproned, absorbed, engaged her sympathy to an absurd extent, seemed to show her for the time the right way to live. She should have been a lady-copyist—it met so the case. The case was the case of escape, of living under water, of being at once impersonal and firm. There it was before one—one had only to stick and stick.

Milly yielded to this charm till she was almost ashamed; she watched the lady-copyists till she found herself wondering what would be thought by others of a young woman, of adequate aspect, who should appear to regard them as the pride of the place. She would have liked to talk to them, to get, as it figured to her, into their lives, and was deterred but by the fact that she didn't quite see herself as purchasing imitations and yet feared she might excite the expectation of purchase. She really knew before long that what held her was the mere refuge, that something within her was after all too weak for the Turners and Titians. They joined hands about her in a circle too vast, though a circle that a year before she would only have desired to trace. They were truly for the larger, not for the smaller life, the life of which the actual pitch, for example, was an interest, the interest of compassion, in misguided efforts. She marked absurdly her little stations, blinking, in her shrinkage of curiosity, at the glorious walls, yet keeping an eye on vistas and approaches, so that she shouldn't be flagrantly caught. The vistas and approaches drew her in this way from room to room, and she had been through many parts of the show, as she supposed, when she sat down to rest. There were chairs in scant clusters, places from which one could gaze. Milly indeed at present fixed her eyes more than elsewhere on the appearance, first, that she couldn't quite, after all, have accounted to an examiner for the order of her "schools," and then on that of her being more tired than she had meant, in spite of her having been so much less intelligent. They found, her eyes, it should be added, other occupation as well, which she let them freely follow: they rested largely, in her vagueness, on the vagueness of other visitors; they attached themselves in especial, with mixed results, to the surprising stream of her compatriots. She was struck with the circumstance that the great museum, early in August, was haunted with these pilgrims, as also with that of her knowing them from afar, marking them easily, each and all, and recognising not less promptly that they had ever new lights for her— new lights on their own darkness. She gave herself up at last, and it was a consummation like another: what

she should have come to the National Gallery for to-day
would be to watch the copyists and reckon the Baedekers. That perhaps was the moral of a menaced state of
health—that one would sit in public places and count
the Americans. It passed the time in a manner; but it
seemed already the second line of defence, and this
notwithstanding the pattern, so unmistakable, of her
country-folk. They were cut out as by scissors, coloured,
labelled, mounted; but their relation to her failed to
act—they somehow did nothing for her. Partly, no
doubt, they didn't so much as notice or know her, didn't
even recognise their community of collapse with her, the
sign on her, as she sat there, that for her too Europe was
"tough." It came to her idly thus—for her humour
could still play—that she didn't seem then the same success with them as with the inhabitants of London, who
had taken her up on scarce more of an acquaintance. She
could wonder if they would be different should she go
back with that glamour attached; and she could also
wonder, if it came to that, whether she should ever go
back. Her friends straggled past, at any rate, in all the
vividness of their absent criticism, and she had even at
last the sense of taking a mean advantage.

There was a finer instant, however, at which three
ladies, clearly a mother and daughters, had paused
before her under compulsion of a comment apparently
just uttered by one of them and referring to some object
on the other side of the room. Milly had her back to the
object, but her face very much to her young compatriot,
the one who had spoken and in whose look she per-

ceived a certain gloom of recognition. Recognition, for
that matter, sat confessedly in her own eyes: she *knew*
the three, generically, as easily as a schoolboy with a crib
in his lap would know the answer in class; she felt, like
the schoolboy, guilty enough—questioned, as honour
went, as to her right so to possess, to dispossess, people
who hadn't consciously provoked her. She would have
been able to say where they lived, and how, had the
place and the way been but amenable to the positive;
she bent tenderly, in imagination, over marital, paternal Mr. Whatever-he-was, at home, eternally named,
with all the honours and placidities, but eternally unseen
and existing only as some one who could be financially
heard from. The mother, the puffed and composed
whiteness of whose hair had no relation to her apparent
age, showed a countenance almost chemically clean and
dry; her companions wore an air of vague resentment
humanised by fatigue; and the three were equally
adorned with short cloaks of coloured cloth surmounted
by little tartan hoods. The tartans were doubtless conceivable as different, but the cloaks, curiously, only
thinkable as one. "Handsome? Well, if you choose to
say so." It was the mother who had spoken, who herself added, after a pause during which Milly took the
reference as to a picture: "In the English style." The
three pair of eyes had converged, and their possessors
had for an instant rested, with the effect of a drop of
the subject, on this last characterisation—with that, too,
of a gloom not less mute in one of the daughters than
murmured in the other. Milly's heart went out to them

while they turned their backs; she said to herself that they ought to have known her, that there was something between them they might have beautifully put together. But she had lost *them* also—they were cold; they left her in her weak wonder as to what they had been looking at. The "handsome" disposed her to turn—all the more that the "English style" would be the English school, which she liked; only she saw, before moving, by the array on the side facing her, that she was in fact among small Dutch pictures. The action of this was again appreciable—the dim surmise that it wouldn't then be by a picture that the spring in the three ladies had been pressed. It was at all events time she should go, and she turned as she got on her feet. She had had behind her one of the entrances and various visitors who had come in while she sat, visitors single and in pairs—by one of the former of whom she felt her eyes suddenly held.

This was a gentleman in the middle of the place, a gentleman who had removed his hat and was for a moment, while he glanced, absently, as she could see, at the top tier of the collection, tapping his forehead with his pocket-handkerchief. The occupation held him long enough to give Milly time to take for granted—and a few seconds sufficed—that his face was the object just observed by her friends. This could only have been because she concurred in their tribute, even qualified, and indeed "the English style" of the gentleman—perhaps by instant contrast to the American—was what had had the arresting power. This arresting power, at the same time—and that was the marvel—had already

sharpened almost to pain, for in the very act of judging
the bared head with detachment she felt herself shaken
by a knowledge of it. It was Merton Densher's own, and
he was standing there, standing long enough unconscious for her to fix him and then hesitate. These suc-
cessions were swift, so that she could still ask herself in
freedom if she had best let him see her. She could still
reply to that that she shouldn't like him to catch her in
the effort to prevent this; and she might further have
decided that he was too preoccupied to see anything had
not a perception intervened that surpassed the first in
violence. She was unable to think afterwards how long
she had looked at him before knowing herself as otherwise looked at; all she was coherently to put together
was that she had had a second recognition without his
having noticed her. The source of this latter shock was
nobody less than Kate Croy—Kate Croy who was suddenly also in the line of vision and whose eyes met her
eyes at their next movement. Kate was but two yards
off—Mr. Densher wasn't alone. Kate's face specifically
said so, for after a stare as blank at first as Milly's it
broke into a far smile. That was what, wonderfully—in
addition to the marvel of their meeting—passed from
her for Milly; the instant reduction to easy terms of the
fact of their being there, the two young women,
together. It was perhaps only afterwards that the girl
fully felt the connection between this touch and her
already established conviction that Kate was a prodigious person; yet on the spot she none the less, in a
degree, knew herself handled and again, as she had been

the night before, dealt with—absolutely even dealt with
for her greater pleasure. A minute in fine hadn't elapsed
before Kate had somehow made her provisionally take
everything as natural. The provisional was just the
charm—acquiring that character from one moment to
the other; it represented happily so much that Kate
would explain on the very first chance. This left moreover—and that was the greatest wonder—all due margin
for amusement at the way things happened, the monstrous oddity of their turning up in such a place on the
very heels of their having separated without allusion to
it. The handsome girl was thus literally in control of the
scene by the time Merton Densher was ready to exclaim
with a high flush, or a vivid blush—one didn't distinguish the embarrassment from the joy—"Why, Miss
Theale: fancy!" and "Why, Miss Theale: what luck!"

Miss Theale had meanwhile the sense that for him
too, on Kate's part, something wonderful and unspoken
was determinant; and this although, distinctly, his companion had no more looked at him with a hint than he
had looked at her with a question. He had looked and he
was looking only at Milly herself, ever so pleasantly and
considerately—she scarce knew what to call it; but without prejudice to her consciousness, all the same, that
women got out of predicaments better than men. The
predicament of course wasn't definite or phraseable—
and the way they let all phrasing pass was presently to
recur to our young woman as a characteristic triumph of
the civilised state; but she took it for granted, insistently, with a small private flare of passion, because the

one thing she could think of to do for him was to show him how she eased him off. She would really, tired and nervous, have been much disconcerted, were it not that the opportunity in question had saved her. It was what had saved her most, what had made her, after the first few seconds, almost as brave for Kate as Kate was for her, had made her only ask herself what their friend would like of her. That he was at the end of three minutes, without the least complicated reference, so smoothly "their" friend was just the effect of their all being sublimely civilised. The flash in which he saw this was, for Milly, fairly inspiring—to that degree in fact that she was even now, on such a plane, yearning to be supreme. It took, no doubt, a big dose of inspiration to treat as not funny—or at least as not unpleasant—the anomaly, for Kate, that *she* knew their gentleman, and for herself, that Kate was spending the morning with him; but everything continued to make for this after Milly had tasted of her draught. She was to wonder in subsequent reflection what in the world they had actually said, since they had made such a success of what they didn't say; the sweetness of the draught for the time, at any rate, was to feel success assured. What depended on this for Mr. Densher was all obscurity to her, and she perhaps but invented the image of his need as a short cut to service. Whatever were the facts, their perfect manners, all round, saw them through. The finest part of Milly's own inspiration, it may further be mentioned, was the quick perception that what would be of most service was, so to speak, her own native wood-note. She had long been conscious with shame for her thin blood, or at least for her poor economy, of her unused margin as an American girl—closely indeed as, in English air, the text might appear to cover the page. She still had reserves of spontaneity, if not of comicality; so that all this cash in hand could now find employment. She became as spontaneous as possible and as American as it might conveniently appeal to Mr. Densher, after his travels, to find her. She said things in the air, and yet flattered herself that she struck him as saying them not in the tone of agitation but in the tone of New York. In the tone of New York agitation was beautifully discounted, and she had now a sufficient view of how much it might accordingly help her.

The help was fairly rendered before they left the place; when her friends presently accepted her invitation to adjourn with her to luncheon at her hotel, it was in the Fifth Avenue that the meal might have waited. Kate had never been there so straight, but Milly was at present taking her; and if Mr. Densher had been he had at least never had to come so fast. She proposed it as the natural thing—proposed it as the American girl; and she saw herself quickly justified by the pace at which she was followed. The beauty of the case was that to do it all she had only to appear to take Kate's hint. This had said, in its fine first smile, "Oh yes, our look is queer— but give me time;" and the American girl could give time as nobody else could. What Milly thus gave she therefore made them take—even if, as they might surmise, it was rather more than they wanted. In the porch of the museum she expressed her preference for a four-wheeler; they would take their course in that guise precisely to multiply the minutes. She was more than ever justified by the positive charm that her spirit imparted even to their use of this conveyance; and she touched her highest point—that is, certainly, for herself—as she ushered her companions into the presence of Susie. Susie was there with luncheon, with her return, in prospect; and nothing could now have filled her own consciousness more to the brim than to see this good friend take in how little she was abjectly anxious. The cup itself actually offered to this good friend might in truth well be startling, for it was composed beyond question of ingredients oddly mixed. She caught Susie fairly looking at her as if to know whether she had brought in guests to hear Sir Luke Strett's report. Well, it was better her companion should have too much than too little to wonder about; she had come out "anyway," as they said at home, for the interest of the thing; and interest truly sat in her eyes. Milly was none the less, at the sharpest crisis, a little sorry for her; she could of necessity extract from the odd scene so comparatively little of a soothing secret. She saw Mr. Densher suddenly popping up, but she saw nothing else that had happened. She saw in the same way her young friend indifferent to her young friend's doom, and she lacked what would explain it. The only thing to keep her in patience was the way, after luncheon, Kate almost, as might be said, made up to her. This was actually perhaps as well what most kept Milly herself in patience.

It had in fact for our young woman a positive beauty—was so marked as a deviation from the handsome girl's previous courses. Susie had been a bore to the handsome girl, and the change was now suggestive. The two sat together, after they had risen from table, in the apartment in which they had lunched, making it thus easy for the other guest and his entertainer to sit in the room adjacent. This, for the latter personage, was the beauty; it was almost, on Kate's part, like a prayer to be relieved. If she honestly liked better to be "thrown with" Susan Shepherd than with their other friend, why that said practically everything. It didn't perhaps altogether say why she had gone out with him for the morning, but it said, as one thought, about as much as she could say to his face.

Little by little indeed, under the vividness of Kate's behaviour, the probabilities fell back into their order. Merton Densher was in love, and Kate couldn't help it—could only be sorry and kind: wouldn't that, without wild flurries, cover everything? Milly at all events tried it as a cover, tried it hard, for the time; pulled it over her, in the front, the larger room, drew it up to her chin with energy. If it didn't, so treated, do everything for her, it did so much that she could herself supply the rest. She made that up by the interest of her great question, the question of whether, seeing him once more, with all that, as she called it to herself, had come and gone, her impression of him would be different from the impression received in New York. That had held her from the moment of their leaving the museum; it kept her company through their drive and during luncheon; and now that she was a quarter of an hour alone with him it became acute. She was to feel at this crisis that no clear, no common answer, no direct satisfaction on this point, was to reach her; she was to see her question itself simply go to pieces. She couldn't tell if he were different or not, and she didn't know nor care if *she* were: these things had ceased to matter in the light of the only thing she did know. This was that she liked him, as she put it to herself, as much as ever; and if that were to amount to liking a new person the amusement would be but the greater. She had thought him at first very quiet, in spite of recovery from his original confusion; though even the shade of bewilderment, she yet perceived, had not been due to such vagueness on the subject of her reintensified identity as the probable sight, over there, of many thousands of her kind would sufficiently have justified. No, he was quiet, inevitably, for the first half of the time, because Milly's own lively line—the line of spontaneity—made everything else relative; and because too, so far as Kate was spontaneous, it was ever so finely in the air among them that the normal pitch must be kept. Afterwards, when they had got a little more used, as it were, to each other's separate felicity, he had begun to talk more, clearly bethought himself, at a given moment, of what *his* natural lively line would be. It would be to take for granted she must wish to hear of the States, and to give her, in its order, everything he had seen and done there. He abounded, of a sudden—he almost insisted; he returned, after breaks, to the charge; and the

effect was perhaps the more odd as he gave no clue
whatever to what he had admired, as he went, or to
what he hadn't. He simply drenched her with his sociable story—especially during the time they were away
from the others. She had stopped then being American—all to let him be English; a permission of which
he took, she could feel, both immense and unconscious
advantage. She had really never cared less for the
"States" than at this moment; but that had nothing to
do with the matter. It would have been the occasion of
her life to learn about them, for nothing could put him
off, and he ventured on no reference to what had happened for herself. It might have been almost as if he had
known that the greatest of all these adventures was her
doing just what she did then.

It was at this point that she saw the smash of her
great question as complete, saw that all she had to do
with was the sense of being there with him. And there
was no chill for this in what she also presently saw—
that, however he had begun, he was now acting from a
particular desire, determined either by new facts or new
fancies, to be like everyone else, simplifyingly "kind" to
her. He had caught on already as to manner—fallen into
line with everyone else; and if his spirits verily *had* gone
up it might well be that he had thus felt himself lighting
on the remedy for all awkwardness. Whatever he did or
he didn't, Milly knew she should still like him—there
was no alternative to that; but her heart could none the
less sink a little on feeling how much his view of her was
destined to have in common with—as she now sighed

over it—*the* view. She could have dreamed of his not
having *the* view, of his having something or other, if
need be quite viewless, of his own; but he might have
what he could with least trouble, and *the* view wouldn't
be, after all, a positive bar to her seeing him. The defect
of it in general—if she might so ungraciously criticise—
was that, by its sweet universality, it made relations
rather prosaically a matter of course. It anticipated and
superseded the—likewise sweet—operation of real affini-
ties. It was this that was doubtless marked in her power
to keep him now—this and her glassy lustre of attention to his pleasantness about the scenery in the Rockies. She was in truth a little measuring her success in
detaining him by Kate's success in "standing" Susan. It
would not be, if she could help it, Mr. Densher who
should first break down. Such at least was one of the
forms of the girl's inward tension; but beneath even this
deep reason was a motive still finer. What she had left
at home on going out to give it a chance was meanwhile
still, was more sharply and actively, there. What had
been at the top of her mind about it and then been violently pushed down—this quantity was again working
up. As soon as their friends should go Susie would break
out, and what she would break out upon wouldn't be—
interested in that gentleman as she had more than once
shown herself—the personal fact of Mr. Densher. Milly
had found in her face at luncheon a feverish glitter, and
it told what she was full of. She didn't care now for Mr.
Densher's personal fact. Mr. Densher had risen before
her only to find his proper place in her imagination

already, of a sudden, occupied. His personal fact failed,
so far as she was concerned, to *be* personal, and her
companion noted the failure. This could only mean that
she was full to the brim, of Sir Luke Strett, and of what
she had had from him. What *had* she had from him? It
was indeed now working upward again that Milly would
do well to know, though knowledge looked stiff in the
light of Susie's glitter. It was therefore, on the whole,
because Densher's young hostess was divided from it by
so thin a partition that she continued to cling to the
Rockies.

Volume Two

Book Sixth

....

I

"I SAY, you know, Kate—you *did* stay!" had been Merton Densher's punctual remark on their adventure after they had, as it were, got out of it; an observation which she not less promptly, on her side, let him see that she forgave in him only because he was a man. She had to recognise, with whatever disappointment, that it was doubtless the most helpful he could make in this character. The fact of the adventure was flagrant between them; they had looked at each other, on gaining the street, as people look who have just rounded together a dangerous corner, and there was therefore already enough unanimity sketched out to have lighted, for her companion, anything equivocal in her action. But the amount of light men *did* need!—Kate could have been eloquent at this moment about that. What, however, on his seeing more, struck him as most distinct in her was her sense that, reunited after his absence and having been now half the morning together, it behooved them to face without delay the question of handling their immediate future. That it would require some handling, that they should still have to deal, deal in a subtle spirit, with

difficulties and delays, was the great matter he had come
back to, greater than any but the refreshed consciousness of their personal need of each other. This need had
had twenty minutes, the afternoon before, to find out
where it stood, and the time was fully accounted for by
the charm of the demonstration. He had arrived at
Euston at five, having wired her from Liverpool the
moment he landed, and she had quickly decided to meet
him at the station, whatever publicity might attend such
an act. When he had praised her for it on alighting from
his train she had answered frankly enough that such
things should be taken at a jump. She didn't care to-day
who saw her, and she profited by it for her joy. To-
morrow, inevitably, she should have time to think and
then, as inevitably, would become a creature of precautions. It was none the less for to-morrow at an early hour
that she had appointed their next meeting, keeping in
mind for the present a particular obligation to show at
Lancaster Gate by six o'clock. She had given, with
imprecations, her reason—people to tea, eternally, and a
promise to Aunt Maud; but she had been liberal enough
on the spot and had suggested the National Gallery for
the morning quite as with an idea that had ripened in
expectancy. They might be seen there too, but nobody
would know them; just as, for that matter, now, in the
refreshment-room to which they had adjourned, they
would incur the notice but, at the worst, of the unac-
quainted. They would "have something" there for the
facility it would give. Thus had it already come up for
them again that they had no place of convenience.

He found himself on English soil with all sorts of feelings, but he had not quite faced having to reckon with a certain ruefulness on that subject as one of the strongest. He was aware later on that there were questions his impatience had shirked; whereby it actually rather smote him, for want of preparation and assurance, that he had nowhere to "take" his love. He had taken it thus, at Euston—and on Kate's own suggestion—into the place where people had beer and buns, and had ordered tea at a small table in the corner; which, no doubt, as they were lost in the crowd, did well enough for a stopgap. It perhaps did as well as her simply driving with him to the door of his lodging, which had had to figure as the sole device of his own wit. That wit, the truth was, had broken down a little at the sharp prevision that once at his door they would have to hang back. She would have to stop there, wouldn't come in with him, couldn't possibly; and he shouldn't be able to ask her, would feel he couldn't without betraying a deficiency of what would be called, even at their advanced stage, respect for her: that again was all that was clear except the further fact that it was maddening. Compressed and concentrated, confined to a single sharp pang or two, but none the less in wait for him there on the Euston platform and lifting its head as that of a snake in the garden, was the disconcerting sense that "respect," in their game, seemed somehow—he scarce knew what to call it—a fifth wheel to the coach. It was properly an inside thing, not an outside, a thing to make love greater, not to make happiness less. They had met again for happiness, and he distinctly felt, during his most lucid moment or two, how he must keep watch on anything that really menaced that boon. If Kate had consented to drive away with him and alight at his house, there would probably enough have occurred for them, at the foot of his steps, one of those strange instants between man and woman that blow upon the red spark, the spark of conflict, ever latent in the depths of passion. She would have shaken her head—oh sadly, divinely—on the question of coming in; and he, though doing all justice to her refusal, would have yet felt his eyes reach further into her own than a possible word, at such a time, could reach. This would have meant the suspicion, the dread of the shadow, of an adverse will. Lucky therefore, in the actual case, that the scant minutes took another turn and that by the half-hour she did in spite of everything contrive to spend with him Kate showed so well how she could deal with the maddening. She seemed to ask him, to beseech him, and all for his better comfort, to leave her, now and henceforth, to meet it in her own way.

She had still met it in naming so promptly, for their early convenience one of the great museums; and indeed with such happy art that his fully seeing where she had placed him had not been till after he left her. His absence from her for so many weeks had had such an effect upon him that his demands, his desires had grown; and only the night before, as his ship steamed, beneath summer stars, in sight of the Irish coast, he had felt all the force of his particular necessity. He had not in other words at any point, doubted he was on his way to say to her that really their mistake must end. Their mistake was to have believed that they *could* hold out—hold out, that is, not against Aunt Maud, but against an impatience that, prolonged, made a man ill. He had known more than ever, on their separating in the court of the station, how ill a man, and even a woman, could be with it; but he struck himself as also knowing that he had already suffered Kate to begin finely to manipulate it. It had a vulgar sound—as throughout, in love, the names of things, the verbal terms of intercourse, were, compared with love itself, vulgar; but it was as if, after all, he might have come back to find himself "put off," though it would take him of course a day or two to see. His letters from the States had pleased whom it concerned, though not so much as he had meant they should; and he should be paid according to agreement and would now take up his money. It was not in truth very much to take up, so that he hadn't in the least come back flourishing a cheque-book; that new motive for bringing his mistress to terms he couldn't therefore pretend to show. The ideal certainty would have been to be able to present a change of prospect as a warrant for the change of philosophy, and without it he should have to make shift but with the pretext of the lapse of time. The lapse of time—not so many weeks, after all, she might always of course say—couldn't at any rate have failed to do something for him; and that consideration it was that had just now tided him over, all the more that he had his vision of what it had done personally for

Kate. This had come out for him with a splendour that almost scared him even in their small corner of the room at Euston—almost scared him because it just seemed to blaze at him that waiting was the game of dupes. Not yet had she been so the creature he had originally seen; not yet had he felt so soundly, safely sure. It was all there for him, playing on his pride of possession as a hidden master, in a great dim church, might play on the grandest organ. His final sense was that a woman couldn't be like that and then ask of one the impossible.

She had been like that afresh on the morrow; and so for the hour they had been able to float in the mere joy of contact—such contact as their situation, in pictured public halls, permitted. This poor makeshift for closeness confessed itself in truth, by twenty small signs of unrest even on Kate's part inadequate; so little could a decent interest in the interesting place presume to remind them of its claims. They had met there in order not to meet in the streets and not again, with a want of fancy, at a railway-station; not again, either, in Kensington Gardens, which, they could easily and tacitly agree, would have had too much of the taste of their old frustrations. The present taste, the taste that morning in the pictured halls, had been a variation; yet Densher had at the end of a quarter of an hour fully known what to conclude from it. This fairly consoled him for their awkwardness, as if he had been watching it affect her. She might be as nobly charming as she liked, and he had seen nothing to touch her in the States; she couldn't pretend that in such conditions as those she herself *believed*

it enough for him. She couldn't pretend she believed he
would believe it enough for herself. It was not enough
for herself—she showed him it was not. That was what
he could be glad, by demonstration, to have brought her
to. He would have said to her had he put it crudely and
on the spot: "*Now* am I to understand you that you consider this-sort of thing can go on?" It would have been
open to her, no doubt, to reply that to have him with
her again, to have him all so dear and so perfectly
proved and attested as she had held him in their yearning interval, was a sort of thing that he must allow her
to have no quarrel about; but that would be a mere gesture of her grace, a mere sport of her subtlety. She knew
as well as he what they wanted; in spite of which indeed
he scarce could have said how beautifully he mightn't
once more have named it and urged it if she hadn't, at
a given moment, blurred, as it were, the accord. They
had soon seated themselves for better talk, and so they
had remained awhile, intimate and superficial. The
immediate things to say had been many, for they had
not exhausted them at Euston. They drew upon them
freely now, and Kate appeared quite to forget—which
was amazingly becoming to her—to look about for surprises. He was to try afterwards, and try in vain, to
remember what speech or what silence of his own, what
natural sign of the eyes or accidental touch of the hand,
had precipitated for her, in the midst of this, a sudden
different impulse. She had got up, with inconsequence,
as if to break the charm, though he was not aware of
what he had done at the moment to make the charm a

danger. She had patched it up agreeably enough the next minute by some odd remark about some picture, to which he had not so much as replied; it being quite independently of this that he had himself exclaimed on the dreadful closeness of the rooms. He had observed that they must go out again to breathe; and it was as if their common consciousness, while they passed into another part, was that of persons who, infinitely engaged together, had been startled and were trying to look natural. It was probably while they were so occupied—as the young man subsequently reconceived—that they had stumbled upon his little New York friend. He thought of her for some reason as little, though she was of about Kate's height, to which, any more than to any other felicity in his mistress, he had never applied the diminutive.

What was to be in the retrospect more distinct to him was the process by which he had become aware that Kate's acquaintance with her was greater than he had gathered. She had written of it in due course as a new and amusing one, and he had written back that he had met over there, and that he much liked, the young person, whereupon she had rejoined that he must find out about her at home. Kate, in the event, however, had not returned to that, and he had of course, with so many things to find out about, been otherwise taken up. Little Miss Theale's history was not stuff for his paper; besides which, moreover, he was seeing but too many little Miss Theales. They even went so far as to impose themselves as one of the groups of social phenomena that fell into the scheme of his public letters. For this group in especial perhaps—the irrepressible, the supereminent young persons—his best pen was ready. Thus it was that there could come back to him in London, an hour or two after their luncheon with the American pair, the sense of a situation for which Kate had not wholly prepared him. Possibly indeed as marked as this was his recovered perception that preparations, of more than one kind, had been exactly what, both yesterday and to-day, he felt her as having in hand. This in fact now became for him so sharp an apprehension as to require some brushing away. He to some extent shook it off, on their separating first from their hostesses and then from each other, by a long and rather aimless walk. He was to go to the office later, but he had the next two or three hours, and he gave himself as a pretext that he had eaten much too much. After Kate had asked him to put her into a cab—which, as an announced, a resumed policy on her part, he found himself deprecating—he stood awhile by a corner and looked vaguely forth at his London. There was always doubtless a moment for the absentee recaptured—*the* moment, that of the reflux of the first emotion—at which it was beyond disproof that one was back. His full parenthesis was closed, and he was once more but a sentence, of a sort, in the general text, the text that, from his momentary street-corner, showed as a great grey page of print that somehow managed to be crowded without being "fine." The grey, however, was more or less the blur of a point of view not yet quite seized again; and there would be colour

enough to come out. He was back, flatly enough, but
back to possibilities and prospects, and the ground he
now somewhat sightlessly covered was the act of
renewed possession.

He walked northward without a plan, without suspicion, quite in the direction his little New York friend, in
her restless ramble, had taken a day or two before. He
reached, like Milly, the Regent's Park; and though he
moved further and faster he finally sat down, like Milly,
from the force of thought. For him too in this position,
be it added—and he might positively have occupied the
same bench—various troubled fancies folded their
wings. He had no more yet said what he really wanted
than Kate herself had found time. She should hear
enough of that in a couple of days. He had practically
not pressed her as to what most concerned them; it had
seemed so to concern them during these first hours but
to hold each other, spiritually speaking, close. This at
any rate was palpable, that there were at present more
things rather than fewer between them. The explanations about the two ladies would be part of the lot; these
could wait with all the rest. They were not meanwhile,
certainly, what most made him roam—the missing
explanations were not. That was what she had so often
said before, and always with the effect of suddenly
breaking off: "Now, please, call me a good cab." Their
previous encounters, the times when they had reached in
their stroll the south side of the park, had had a way of
winding up with his special irrelevance. It was, effectively, what most divided them, for he would generally,

but for her reasons, have been able to jump in with her. What did she think he wished to do to her?—it was a question he had had occasion to put. A small matter, however, doubtless—since when it came to that they didn't depend on cabs, good or bad, for the sense of union: its importance was less from the particular loss than as a kind of irritating mark of her expertness. This expertness, under providence, had been great from the first, so far as joining him was concerned; and he was critical only because it had been still greater, even from the first too, in respect to leaving him. He had reminded her of this, that afternoon, on the repetition of her appeal—had asked her once more what she supposed he wished to do. He recalled, on his bench in the Regent's Park, the freedom of fancy, funny and pretty, with which she had answered; the moment itself, while the usual hansom charged them, during which he felt himself, disappointed as he was, grimacing back at the superiority of her very "humour," in its added grace of gaiety, to the celebrated solemn American. Their fresh appointment had been at all events by that time made, and he should see what her choice in respect to it—a surprise as well as a relief—would do toward really simplifying. It meant either new help or new hindrance, though it took them at least out of the streets. And her naming this privilege had naturally made him ask if Mrs. Lowder knew of his return.

"Not from me," Kate had replied. "But I shall speak to her now." And she had argued, as with rather a quick, fresh view, that it would now be quite easy.

"We've behaved for months so properly that I've margin surely for my mention of you. You'll come to see *her*, and she'll leave you with me; she'll show her goodnature, and her want of betrayed fear, in that. With her, you know, you've never broken, quite the contrary, and she likes you as much as ever. We're leaving town; it will be the end, just now; therefore it's nothing to ask. I'll ask tonight," Kate had wound up, "and if you'll leave it to me—my cleverness, I assure you, has grown infernal—I'll make it all right."

He had of course thus left it to her and he was wondering more about it now than he had wondered there in Brook Street. He repeated to himself that if it wasn't in the line of triumph it was in the line of muddle. This indeed, no doubt, was as a part of his wonder for still other questions. Kate had really got off without meeting his little challenge about the terms of their intercourse with her dear Milly. Her dear Milly, it was sensible, *was* somehow in the picture. Her dear Milly, popping up in his absence, occupied—he couldn't have said quite why he felt it—more of the foreground than one would have expected her in advance to find clear. She took up room, and it was almost as if room had been made for her. Kate had appeared to take for granted he would know why it had been made; but that was just the point. It was a foreground in which he himself, in which his connection with Kate, scarce enjoyed a space to turn round. But Miss Theale was perhaps at the present juncture a possibility of the same sort as the softened, if not the squared, Aunt Maud. It might be true of her also that if she weren't a bore she'd be a convenience. It rolled over him of a sudden, after he had resumed his walk, that this might easily be what Kate had meant. The charming girl adored her—Densher had for himself made out that—and would protect, would lend a hand, to their interviews. These might take place in other words, on her premises, which would remove them still better from the streets. *That* was an explanation which did hang together. It was impaired a little, of a truth, by this fact that their next encounter was rather markedly not to depend upon her. Yet this fact in turn would be accounted for by the need of more preliminaries. One of the things he conceivably should gain on Thursday at Lancaster Gate would be a further view of that propriety.

II

IT WAS EXTRAORDINARY enough that he should actually be finding himself, when Thursday arrived, none so wide of the mark. Kate had not come all the way to this for him, but she had come to a good deal by the end of a quarter of an hour. What she had begun with was her surprise at her appearing to have left him on Tuesday anything more to understand. The parts, as he now saw, under her hand, did fall more or less together, and it was not even as if she had spent the interval in twisting and fitting them. She was bright and handsome, not fagged and worn, with the general clearness; for it certainly stuck out enough that if the American ladies

themselves were not to be squared, which was absurd,
they fairly imposed the necessity of trying Aunt Maud
again. One couldn't say to them, kind as she had been
to them: "We'll meet, please, whenever you'll let us, at
your house; but we count on you to help us to keep it
secret." They must in other terms inevitably speak to
Aunt Maud—it would be of the last awkwardness to ask
them not to: Kate had embraced all this in her choice
of speaking first. What Kate embraced altogether was
indeed wonderful to-day to Densher, though he perhaps
struck himself rather as getting it out of her piece by
piece than as receiving it in a steady light. He had
always felt, however, that the more he asked of her the
more he found her prepared, as he imaged it, to hand
out. He had said to her more than once even before his
absence: "You keep the key of the cupboard, and I fore-
see that when we're married you'll dole me out my
sugar by lumps." She had replied that she rejoiced in his
assumption that sugar would be his diet, and the domestic arrangement so prefigured might have seemed
already to prevail. The supply from the cupboard at this
hour was doubtless, of a truth, not altogether cloyingly
sweet; but it met, in a manner, his immediate requirements. If her explanations, at any rate, prompted questions, the questions no more exhausted them than they
exhausted her patience. And they were naturally, of the
series, the simpler; as for instance in his taking it from
her that Miss Theale then could do nothing for them.
He frankly brought out what he had ventured to fancy.
"If we can't meet here and we've really exhausted the

charms of the open air and the crowd, some such little raft in the wreck, some occasional opportunity like that of Tuesday, has been present to me these two days as better than nothing. But if our friends are so accountable to this house of course there's no more to be said. And it's one more nail, thank God, in the coffin of our odious delay." He was but too glad without more ado to point the moral. "Now I hope you see we can't work it anyhow."

If she laughed for this—and her spirits seemed really high—it was because of the opportunity that, at the hotel, he had most shown himself as enjoying. "Your idea's beautiful when one remembers that you hadn't a word except for Milly." But she was as beautifully good-humoured. "You might of course get used to her—you *will*. You're quite right—so long as they're with us or near us." And she put it, lucidly, that the dear things couldn't *help*, simply as charming friends, giving them a lift. "They'll speak to Aunt Maud, but they won't shut their doors to us: that would be another matter. A friend always helps—and she's a friend." She had left Mrs. Stringham by this time out of the question; she had reduced it to Milly. "Besides, she particularly likes us. She particularly likes *you*. I say, old boy, make something of that." He felt her dodging the ultimatum he had just made sharp, his definite reminder of how little, at the best, they could work it; but there were certain of his remarks—those mostly of the sharper penetration—that it had been quite her practice from the first not formally, not reverently to notice. She

showed the effect of them in ways less trite. This was
what happened now: he didn't think in truth that she
wasn't really minding. She took him up, none the less,
on a minor question. "You say we can't meet here, but
you see it's just what we do. What could be more lovely
than this?"

It wasn't to torment him—that again he didn't
believe; but he had to come to the house in some discomfort, so that he frowned a little at her calling it thus
a luxury. Wasn't there an element in it of coming back
into bondage? The bondage might be veiled and var-
nished, but he knew in his bones how little the very
highest privileges of Lancaster Gate could ever be a sign
of their freedom. They were upstairs, in one of the
smaller apartments of state, a room arranged as a
boudoir, but visibly unused—it defied familiarity—and
furnished in the ugliest of blues. He had immediately
looked with interest at the closed doors, and Kate had
met his interest with the assurance that it was all right,
that Aunt Maud did them justice—so far, that was, as
this particular time was concerned; that they should be
alone and have nothing to fear. But the fresh allusion
to this that he had drawn from her acted on him now
more directly, brought him closer still to the question.
They *were* alone—it *was* all right: he took in anew the
shut doors and the permitted privacy, the solid stillness
of the great house. They connected themselves on the
spot with something made doubly vivid in him by the
whole present play of her charming strong will. What
it amounted to was that he couldn't have her—hanged if

he could!—evasive. He couldn't and he wouldn't—
wouldn't have her elusive. He didn't want her deeper
than himself, fine as it might be as wit or as character;
he wanted to keep her where their communications
would be straight and easy and their intercourse independent. The effect of this was to make him say in a
moment: "Will you take me just as I am?"

She turned a little pale for the tone of truth in it—
which qualified to his sense delightfully the strength of
her will; and the pleasure he found in this was not the
less for her breaking out after an instant into a strain
that stirred him more than any she had ever used with
him. "Ah, do let me try myself! I assure you I see my
way—so don't spoil it: wait for me and give me time.
Dear man," Kate said, "only believe in me, and it will
be beautiful."

He hadn't come back to hear her talk of his believing in her as if he didn't; but he had come back—and
it all was upon him now—to seize her with a sudden
intensity that her manner of pleading with him had
made, as happily appeared, irresistible. He laid strong
hands upon her to say, almost in anger, "Do you love
me, love me, love me?" and she closed her eyes as with
the sense that he might strike her but that she could
gratefully take it. Her surrender was her response, her
response her surrender; and, though scarce hearing what
she said, he so profited by these things that it could for
the time be solid to him that he was keeping her. The
long embrace in which they held each other was the rout
of evasion, and he took from it the certitude that what

she had from him was real. It was stronger than an
uttered vow, and the name he was to give it in after-
thought was that she had been sublimely sincere. *That*
was all he asked—sincerity making a basis that would
bear almost anything. This settled so much, and settled
it so thoroughly, that there was nothing left to ask her to
swear to. Oaths and vows apart, now they could talk. It
seemed in fact only now that their questions were put on
the table. He had taken up more expressly at the end of
five minutes her plea for her own plan, and it was
marked that the difference made by the passage just
enacted was a difference in favour of her choice of
means. They had somehow suddenly become a detail—
her province and her care; it had grown more consistently vivid that her intelligence was one with her
passion. "I certainly don't want," he said—and he could
say it with a smile of indulgence—"to be all the while
bringing it up that I don't trust you."

"I should hope not! What do you think I want to do?"

He had really at this to make out a little what he
thought, and the first thing that put itself in evidence
was of course the oddity, after all, of their game, to
which he could but frankly allude. "We're doing, at the
best, in trying to temporise in so special a way, a thing
most people would call us fools for." But his visit
passed, all the same, without his again attempting to
make "just as he was" serve. He had no more money
just as he was than he had had just as he had been, or
than he would have, probably, when it came to that, just
as he always would be; whereas she, on her side, in com-

parison with her state of some months before, had measurably more to relinquish. He easily saw how their
meeting at Lancaster Gate gave more of an accent to
that quantity than their meeting at stations or in parks;
and yet, on the other hand, he couldn't urge this against
it. If Mrs. Lowder was indifferent her indifference
added in a manner to what Kate's taking him as he was
would call on her to sacrifice. Such, in fine, was her art
with him that she seemed to put the question of their
still waiting into quite other terms than the terms of
ugly blue, of florid Sèvres, of complicated brass, in
which their boudoir expressed it. She said almost all in
fact in saying, in respect to Aunt Maud, as to whom he
had once more pressed her, that when he should see her,
as must inevitably soon happen, he would understand.
"Do you mean," he asked on this, "that there's any *definite* sign of her coming round? I'm not talking," he
explained, "of mere hypocrisies in her, or mere brave
duplicities. Remember, after all, that supremely clever
as we are, and as strong a team, I admit, as there is
going—remember that she can play with us quite as
much as we play with her."

"She doesn't want to play with *me*, my dear," Kate
lucidly replied; "she doesn't want to make me suffer a
bit more than she need. She cares for me too much, and
everything she does, or doesn't do, has a value. *This* has
a value—her being as she has been about to-day. I
believe she's in her own room, where she's keeping
strictly to herself while you're here with me. But that
isn't 'playing'—not a bit."

"What is it then," the young man inquired—"from the moment it isn't her blessing and a cheque?"

Kate was complete. "It's simply her absence of smallness. There *is* something in her above trifles. She *generally* trusts us; she doesn't propose to hunt us into corners; and if we frankly ask a thing—why," said Kate, "she shrugs, but she lets it go. She has really but one fault—she's indifferent, on such ground as she has taken about us, to details. However," the girl cheerfully went on, "it isn't in detail we fight her."

"It seems to me," Densher said after a moment's thought of this, "that it's in detail we deceive her"—a speech that, as soon as he had uttered it, applied itself for him, as also visibly for his companion, to the circumstances of their recent embrace.

Any confusion attaching to it, however, dropped from Kate, whom, as he could see with sacred joy, it must take more than that to make compunctious. "I don't say we can do it again. I mean," she explained, "meet here."

Densher indeed had been wondering where they could do it again. If Lancaster Gate was so limited that issue reappeared. "I mayn't come back at all?"

"Certainly—to see her. It's she, really," his companion smiled, "who's in love with you."

But it made him—a trifle more grave—look at her a moment. "Don't make out, you know, that everyone's in love with me."

She hesitated. "I don't say everyone."

"You said just now Miss Theale."

"I said she liked you—yes."

"Well, it comes to the same thing." With which, however, he pursued. "Of course, I ought to thank Mrs. Lowder in person. I mean for this—as from myself."

"Ah but, you know, not too much!" She had an ironic gaiety for the implications of his "this," besides wishing to insist on a general prudence. "She'll wonder what you're thanking her for!"

Densher did justice to both considerations. "Yes, I can't very well tell her all."

It was perhaps because he said it so gravely that Kate was again in a manner amused. Yet she gave out light. "You can't very well 'tell' her anything, and that doesn't matter. Only be nice to her. Please her; make her see how clever you are—only without letting her see that you're trying. If you're charming to her you've nothing else to do."

But she oversimplified too. "I can be 'charming' to her, so far as I see, only by letting her suppose I give you up—which I'll be hanged if I do! It is," he said with feeling, "a game."

"Of course it's a game. But she'll never suppose you give me up—or I give *you*—if you keep reminding her how you enjoy our interviews."

"Then if she has to see us as obstinate and constant," Densher asked, "what good does it do?"

Kate was for a moment checked. "What good does what——?"

"Does my pleasing her—does anything. I *can't*," he impatiently declared, "please her."

Kate looked at him hard again, disappointed at his want of consistency; but it appeared to determine in her something better than a mere complaint. "Then *I* can! Leave it to me." With which she came to him under the compulsion, again, that had united them shortly before, and took hold of him in her urgency to the same tender purpose. It was her form of entreaty renewed and repeated, which made after all, as he met it, their great fact clear. And it somehow clarified *all* things so to possess each other. The effect of it was that, once more, on these terms, he could only be generous. He had so on the spot then left everything to her that she came back in the course of a few moments to one of her previous— and as positively seemed—her most precious ideas. "You accused me just now of saying that Milly's in love with you. Well, if you come to that, I do say it. So there you are. That's the good she'll do us. It makes a basis for her seeing you—so that she'll help us to go on."

Densher stared—she was wondrous all round. "And what sort of a basis does it make for my seeing *her?*"

"Oh, I don't mind!" Kate smiled.

"Don't mind my leading her on?"

She put it differently. "Don't mind her leading *you.*"

"Well, she won't—so it's nothing not to mind. But how can that 'help,' " he pursued, "with what she knows?"

"What she knows? That needn't prevent."

He wondered. "Prevent her loving us?"

"Prevent her helping you. She's *like* that," Kate Croy explained.

It took indeed some understanding. "Making nothing of the fact that I love another?"

"Making everything," said Kate. "To console you."

"But for what?"

"For not getting your other."

He continued to stare. "But how does she know——?"

"That you *won't* get her? She doesn't; but on the other hand she doesn't know you will. Meanwhile she sees you baffled, for she knows of Aunt Maud's stand. *That*"—Kate was lucid—"gives her the chance to be nice to you."

"And what does it give *me*," the young man none the less rationally asked, "the chance to be? A brute of a humbug to her?"

Kate so possessed her facts, as it were, that she smiled at his violence. "You'll extraordinarily like her. She's exquisite. And there are reasons. I mean others."

"What others?"

"Well, I'll tell you another time. Those I give you," the girl added, "are enough to go on with."

"To go on to what?"

"Why, to seeing her again—say as soon as you can: which, moreover, on all grounds, is no more than decent of you."

He of course took in her reference, and he had fully in mind what had passed between them in New York. It had been no great quantity, but it had made distinctly at the time for his pleasure; so that anything in the nature of an appeal in the name of it could have a slight kindling consequence. "Oh, I shall naturally call again without delay. Yes," said Densher, "her being in love with me is nonsense; but I must, quite independently of that, make every acknowledgment of favours received."

It appeared practically all Kate asked. "Then you see. I shall meet you there."

"I don't quite see," he presently returned, "why she should wish to receive *you* for it."

"She receives me for myself—that is for *her* self. She thinks no end of me. That I should have to drum it into you!"

Yet still he didn't take it. "Then I confess she's beyond me."

Well, Kate could but leave it as she saw it. "She regards me as already—in these few weeks—her dearest friend. It's quite separate. We're in, she and I, ever so deep." And it was to confirm this that, as if it had flashed upon her that he was somewhere at sea, she threw out at last her own real light. "She doesn't, of course, know I care for *you*. She thinks I care so little that it's not worth speaking of." That he *had* been somewhere at sea these remarks made quickly clear, and Kate hailed the effect with surprise. "Have you been supposing that she does know——?"

"About our situation? Certainly, if you're such friends as you show me—and if you haven't otherwise represented it to her." She uttered at this such a sound of impatience that he stood artlessly vague. "You *have* denied it to her?"

She threw up her arms at his being so backward.

" 'Denied it?' My dear man, we've never spoken of you."

"Never, never?"

"Strange as it may appear to your glory—never."

He couldn't piece it together. "But won't Mrs. Lowder have spoken?"

"Very probably. But of *you*. Not of me."

This struck him as obscure. "How does she know me but as part and parcel of you?"

"How?" Kate triumphantly asked. "Why, exactly to make nothing of it, to have nothing to do with it, to stick consistently to her line about it. Aunt Maud's line is to keep all reality out of our relation—that is out of my being in danger from you—by not having so much as suspected or heard of it. She'll get rid of it, as she believes, by ignoring it and sinking it—if she only does so hard enough. Therefore *she* in her manner 'denies' it, if you will. That's how she knows you otherwise than as part and parcel of me. She won't for a moment have allowed either to Mrs. Stringham or to Milly that I've in any way, as they say, distinguished you."

"And you don't suppose," said Densher, "that they must have made it out for themselves?"

"No, my dear, I don't; not even," Kate declared, "after Milly's so funnily bumping against us on Tuesday."

"She doesn't see from *that*——?"

"That you're, so to speak, mad about me. Yes, she sees, no doubt, that you regard me with a complacent eye—for you show it, I think, always too much. But nothing beyond that. I don't show it too much; I don't perhaps—to please you completely where others are concerned—show it enough."

"Can you show it or not as you like?" Densher demanded.

It pulled her up a little, but she came out resplendent. "Not where *you* are concerned. Beyond seeing that you're rather gone," she went on, "Milly only sees that I'm decently good to you."

"Very good indeed she must think it!"

"Very good indeed then. She easily sees me," Kate smiled, "as very good indeed."

The young man brooded. "But in a sense to take some explaining."

"Then I explain." She was really fine; it came back to her essential plea for her freedom of action and his beauty of trust. "I mean," she added, "I *will* explain."

"And what will *I* do?"

"Recognise the difference it will make if she thinks." But here in truth Kate faltered. It was his silence alone that, for the moment, took up her apparent meaning; and before he again spoke she had returned to remembrance and prudence. They were now not to forget that, Aunt Maud's liberality having put them on their honour, they mustn't spoil their case by abusing it. He must leave her in time; they should probably find it would help them. But she came back to Milly too. "Mind you go to see her."

Densher still, however, took up nothing of this. "Then I may come again?"

"For Aunt Maud—as much as you like. But we can't again," said Kate, "play her *this* trick. I can't see you here alone."

"Then where?"

"Go to see Milly," she, for all satisfaction, repeated.

"And what good will that do me?"

"Try it, and you'll see."

"You mean you'll manage to be there?" Densher asked. "Say you are, how will that give us privacy?"

"Try it—you'll see," the girl once more returned. "We must manage as we can."

"That's precisely what *I* feel. It strikes me we might manage better." His idea of this was a thing that made him for an instant hesitate; yet he brought it out with conviction. "Why won't you come to *me?*"

It was a question her troubled eyes seemed to tell him that he was scarce generous in expecting her definitely to answer, and in looking to him to wait at least she appealed to something that she presently made him feel as his pity. It was on that special shade of tenderness that he thus found himself thrown back; and while he asked of his spirit and of his flesh just what concession they could arrange she pressed him yet again on the subject of her singular remedy for their embarrassment. It might have been irritating had she ever struck him as having in her mind a stupid corner. "You'll see," she said, "the difference it will make."

Well, since she was not stupid she was intelligent; it was he that was stupid—the proof of which was that he would do what she liked. But he made a last effort to

understand, her allusion to the "difference" bringing
him round to it. He indeed caught at something subtle
but strong even as he spoke. "Is what you meant a
moment ago that the difference will be in her being
made to believe you hate me?"

Kate, however, had simply, for this gross way of
putting it, one of her more marked shows of impatience;
with which in fact she sharply closed their discussion.
He opened the door on a sign from her, and she accompanied him to the top of the stairs with an air of having so put their possibilities before him that questions
were idle and doubts perverse. "I verily believe I *shall*
hate you if you spoil for me the beauty of what I see!"

III

HE WAS REALLY, notwithstanding, to hear more from
her of what she saw; and the very next occasion had for
him still other surprises than that. He received from
Mrs. Lowder on the morning after his visit to Kate the
telegraphic expression of a hope that he might be free
to dine with them that evening; and his freedom affected
him as fortunate even though in some degree qualified
by her missive. "Expecting American friends, whom I'm
so glad to find you know!" His knowledge of American
friends was clearly an accident of which he was to taste
the fruit to the last bitterness. This apprehension, however, we hasten to add, enjoyed for him, in the immediate event, a certain merciful shrinkage; the immediate
event being that, at Lancaster Gate, five minutes after

his due arrival, prescribed him for eight-thirty, Mrs.
Stringham came in alone. The long daylight, the postponed lamps, the habit of the hour, made dinners late
and guests still later; so that, punctual as he was, he had
found Mrs. Lowder alone, with Kate herself not yet in
the field. He had thus had with her several bewildering
moments—bewildering by reason, fairly, of their tacit
invitation to him to be supernaturally simple. This was
exactly, goodness knew, what he wanted to be; but he
had never had it so largely and freely—*so* supernaturally
simply, for that matter—imputed to him as of easy
achievement. It was a particular in which Aunt Maud
appeared to offer herself as an example, appeared to say
quite agreeably: "What I want of you, don't you see? is
to be just exactly as *I* am." The quantity of the article
required was what might especially have caused him to
stagger—he liked so, in general, the quantities in which
Mrs. Lowder dealt. He would have liked as well to ask
her how feasible she supposed it for a poor young man
to resemble her at any point; but he had after all soon
enough perceived that he was doing as she wished by
letting his wonder show just a little as silly. He was conscious moreover of a small strange dread of the results of
discussion with her—strange, truly, because it was her
good-nature, not her asperity, that he feared. Asperity
might have made him angry—in which there was always
a comfort; good-nature, in his conditions, had a ten-
dency to make him ashamed—which Aunt Maud
indeed, wonderfully, liking him for himself, quite struck
him as having guessed. To spare him therefore she also

avoided discussion; she kept him down by refusing to quarrel with him. This was what she now proposed to him to enjoy, and his secret discomfort was his sense that on the whole it was what would best suit him. Being kept down was a bore, but his great dread, verily, was of being ashamed, which was a thing distinct; and it mattered but little that he was ashamed of that too.

It was of the essence of his position that in such a house as this the tables could always be turned on him. "What do you offer, what do you offer?"—the place, however muffled in convenience and decorum, constantly hummed for him with that thick irony. The irony was a renewed reference to obvious bribes, and he had already seen how little aid came to him from denouncing the bribes as ugly in form. That was what the precious metals—they alone—could afford to be; it was vain enough for him accordingly to try to impart a gloss to his own comparative brummagem. The humiliation of this impotence was precisely what Aunt Maud sought to mitigate for him by keeping him down; and as her effort to that end had doubtless never yet been so visible he had probably never felt so definitely placed in the world as while he waited with her for her half-dozen other guests. She welcomed him genially back from the States, as to his view of which her few questions, though not coherent, were comprehensive, and he had the amusement of seeing in her, as through a clear glass, the outbreak of a plan and the sudden consciousness of a curiosity. She became aware of America, under his eyes, as a possible scene for social operations; the idea of a visit to the wonderful country had clearly but just occurred to her, yet she was talking of it, at the end of a minute, as her favourite dream. He didn't believe in it, but he pretended to; this helped her as well as anything else to treat him as a harmless young man. She was so engaged, with the further aid of a complete absence of allusions, when the highest effect was given her method by the beautiful entrance of Kate. The method therefore received support all round, for no young man could have been more harmless than the person to the relief of whose shyness her niece ostensibly came. The ostensible, in Kate, struck him altogether, on this occasion, as prodigious; while scarcely less prodigious, for that matter, was his own reading, on the spot, of the relation between his companions—a relation lighted for him by the straight look, not exactly loving nor lingering, yet searching and soft, that, on the part of her aunt, the girl had to reckon with as she advanced. It took her in from head to foot, and in doing so it told a story that made poor Densher again the least bit sick: it marked so something with which Kate habitually and consummately reckoned.

That was the story—that she was always, for her beneficent dragon, under arms; living up, every hour, but especially at festal hours, to the "value" Mrs. Lowder had attached to her. High and fixed, this estimate ruled, on each occasion, at Lancaster Gate, the social scene; so that our young man now recognised in it something like the artistic idea, the plastic substance, imposed by tradition, by genius, by criticism, in respect to a given character, on a distinguished actress. As such a person was to dress the part, to walk, to look, to speak, in every way to express, the part, so all this was what Kate was to do for the character she had undertaken, under her aunt's roof, to represent. It was made up, the character, of definite elements and touches—things all perfectly ponderable to criticism; and the way for her to meet criticism was evidently at the start to be sure her make-up was exact and that she looked at least no worse than usual. Aunt Maud's appreciation of that to-night was indeed managerial, and Kate's own contribution fairly that of the faultless soldier on parade. Densher saw himself for the moment as in his purchased stall at the play; the watchful manager was in the depths of a box and the poor actress in the glare of the footlights. But she *passed*, the poor actress—he could see how she always passed; her wig, her paint, her jewels, every mark of her expression impeccable, and her entrance accordingly greeted with the proper round of applause. Such impressions as we thus note for Densher come and go, it must be granted, in very much less time than notation demands; but we may none the less make the point that there was, still further, time among them for him to feel almost too scared to take part in the ovation. He struck himself as having lost, for the minute, his presence of mind—so that, at any rate, he only stared in silence at the older woman's technical challenge and at the younger one's disciplined face. It was as if the drama—it thus came to him, for the fact of a drama there was no blinking—was between *them*, them quite preponderantly; with Merton

Densher relegated to mere spectatorship, a paying place in front, and one of the most expensive. This was why his appreciation had turned for the instant to fear—had just turned, as we have said, to sickness; and in spite of the fact that the disciplined face did offer him over the footlights, as he believed, the small gleam, fine, faint, but exquisite, of a special intelligence. So might a practised performer, even when raked by double-barrelled glasses, seem to be all in her part and yet convey a sign to the person in the house she loved best.

The drama, at all events, as Densher saw it, meanwhile went on—amplified soon enough by the advent of two other guests, stray gentlemen both, stragglers in the rout of the season, who visibly presented themselves to Kate, during the next moments, as subjects for a like impersonal treatment and sharers in a like usual mercy. At opposite ends of the social course, they displayed, in respect to the "figure" that each, in his way, made, one the expansive, the other the contractile effect of the perfect white waistcoat. A scratch company of two innocuous youths and a pacified veteran was therefore what now offered itself to Mrs. Stringham, who rustled in a little breathless and full of the compunction of having had to come alone. Her companion, at the last moment, had been indisposed—positively not well enough, and so had packed her off, insistently, with excuses, with wild regrets. This circumstance of their charming friend's illness was the first thing Kate took up with Densher on their being able after dinner, without bravado, to have ten minutes "naturally," as she called it—which wasn't what *he* did—together; but it was already as if the young man had, by an odd impression, throughout the meal, not been wholly deprived of Miss Theale's participation. Mrs. Lowder had made dear Milly the topic, and it proved, on the spot, a topic as familiar to the enthusiastic younger as to the sagacious older man. Any knowledge they might lack Mrs. Lowder's niece was moreover alert to supply, while Densher himself was freely appealed to as the most privileged, after all, of the group. Wasn't it he who had in a manner invented the wonderful creature—through having seen her first, caught her in her native jungle? Hadn't he more or less paved the way for her by his prompt recognition of her rarity, by preceding her, in a friendly spirit—as he had the "ear" of society—with a sharp flashlight or two?

He met, poor Densher, these inquiries as he could, listening with interest, yet with discomfort; wincing in particular, dry journalist as he was, to find it seemingly supposed of him that he had put his pen—oh, his "pen!"—at the service of private distinction. The ear of society?—they were talking, or almost, as if he had publicly paragraphed a modest young lady. They dreamt dreams, in truth, he appeared to perceive, that fairly waked *him* up, and he settled himself in his place both to resist his embarrassment and to catch the full revelation. His embarrassment came, naturally, from the fact that if he could claim no credit for Miss Theale's success, so neither could he gracefully insist on his not having been concerned with her. What touched him most nearly was that the occasion took on somehow the air of a commemorative banquet, a feast to celebrate a brilliant if brief career. There was of course more said about the heroine than if she had not been absent, and he found himself rather stupefied at the range of Milly's triumph. Mrs. Lowder had wonders to tell of it; the two wearers of the waistcoat, either with sincerity or with hypocrisy, professed in the matter an equal expertness; and Densher at last seemed to know himself in presence of a social "case." It was Mrs. Stringham, obviously, whose testimony would have been most invoked had she not been, as her friend's representative, rather confined to the function of inhaling the incense; so that Kate, who treated her beautifully, smiling at her, cheering and consoling her across the table, appeared benevolently both to speak and to interpret for her. Kate spoke as if she wouldn't perhaps understand *their* way of appreciating Milly, but would let them none the less, in justice to their goodwill, express it in their coarser fashion. Densher himself was not unconscious in respect to this of a certain broad brotherhood with Mrs. Stringham; wondering indeed, while he followed the talk, how it might move American nerves. He had only heard of them before, but in his recent tour he had caught them in the fact, and there was now a moment or two when it came to him that he had perhaps—and not in the way of an escape—taken a lesson from them.

They quivered, clearly, they hummed and drummed, they leaped and bounded in Mrs. Stringham's typical organism—this lady striking him as before all things

excited, as, in the native phrase, keyed-up, to a perception of more elements in the occasion than he was himself able to count. She was accessible to sides of it, he
imagined, that were as yet obscure to him; for, though
she unmistakably rejoiced and soared, he none the less
saw her at moments as even more agitated than pleasure required. It was a state of emotion in her that could
scarce represent simply an impatience to report at home.
Her little dry New England brightness—he had "sam-
pled" all the shades of the American complexity, if complexity it were—had its actual reasons for finding relief
most in silence; so that before the subject was changed
he perceived—with surprise at the others—that they had
given her enough of it. He had quite had enough of it
himself by the time he was asked if it were true that
their friend had really not made in her own country the
mark she had chalked so large in London. It was Mrs.
Lowder herself who addressed him that inquiry; while
he scarce knew if he were the more impressed with her
launching it under Mrs. Stringham's nose or with her
hope that he would allow to London the honour of discovery. The innocuous young man propounded the theory that they saw in London—for all that was
said—much further than in the States: it wouldn't be the
first time, he urged, that they had taught the Americans
to appreciate—especially when it was funny—some
native product. He didn't mean that Miss Theale was
funny—though she was weird, and this was precisely
her magic; but it might very well be that New York, in
having her to show, hadn't been aware of its luck. There

were plenty of people who were nothing over there and yet were awfully taken up in England; just as—to make the balance right, thank goodness—they sometimes sent out beauties and celebrities who left the Briton cold. The Briton's temperature in truth was not to be calculated—a formulation of the matter that was not reached, however, without producing in Mrs. Stringham a final feverish sally. She announced that if the point of view for a proper admiration of her young friend *had* seemed to fail a little in New York, there was no manner of doubt of her having carried Boston by storm. It pointed the moral that Boston, for the finer taste, left New York nowhere; and the good lady, as the exponent of this doctrine—which she set forth at a certain length—made, obviously, to Densher's mind, her nearest approach to supplying the weirdness in which Milly's absence had left them deficient. She made it indeed effective for him by suddenly addressing him.

"You know nothing, sir—but not the least little bit—about my friend."

He hadn't pretended he did, but there was a purity of reproach in Mrs. Stringham's face and tone, a purity charged apparently with solemn meanings; so that for a little, small as had been his claim, he couldn't but feel that she exaggerated. He wondered what she did mean, but while doing so he defended himself. "I certainly don't know enormously much—beyond her having been most kind to me, in New York, as a poor bewildered and newly landed alien, and my having tremendously appreciated it." To which he added, he scarce knew why, what had an immediate success. "Remember, Mrs. Stringham, that you weren't then present."

"Ah, there you are!" said Kate with a pleasant spirit, though whether for his own or for Mrs. Stringham's benefit he failed at the time to make out.

"You weren't present *then*, dearest," Mrs. Lowder richly concurred. "You don't know," she continued with mellow gaiety, "how far things may have gone."

It made the little woman, he could see, really lose her head. She had more things in mind than any of them, unless perhaps it were Kate, whom he felt as indirectly watching him during this foolish passage, though it pleased him—and because of the foolishness—not to meet her eyes. He met Mrs. Stringham's, which affected him: with her he could on occasion clear it up—a sense produced by the mute communion between them and really the beginning, as the event was to show, of something extraordinary. It was even already a little the effect of this communion that Mrs. Stringham perceptibly faltered in her retort to Mrs. Lowder's joke. "Oh, it's precisely my point that Mr. Densher *can't* have had vast opportunities." And then she smiled at him. "I wasn't away, you know, long."

It made everything, in the oddest way in the world, immediately right for him. "And I wasn't *there* long, either." He positively saw, with it, that nothing, for him, so far as she was concerned, would again be wrong. "She's beautiful, but I don't say she's easy to know."

"Ah, she's a thousand and one things!" replied the good lady, as if now to keep well with him.

He asked nothing better. "She was off with you, to these parts, before I knew it. I myself was off too— away off to wonderful parts, where I had endlessly more to see."

"But you didn't forget her!" Aunt Maud interposed, with almost menacing archness.

"No, of course I didn't forget her. One doesn't forget such charming impressions. But I never," he lucidly maintained, "chattered to others about her."

"She'll thank you for that, sir," said Mrs. Stringham with a flushed firmness.

"Yet doesn't silence in such a case," Aunt Maud blandly inquired, "very often quite prove the depth of the impression?"

He would have been amused, had he not been slightly displeased, at all they seemed to want to fasten on him. "Well, the impression was as deep as you like. But I really want Miss Theale to know," he pursued for Mrs. Stringham, "that I don't figure by any consent of my own as an authority about her."

Kate came to his assistance—if assistance it was— before their friend had had time to meet this charge. "You're right about her not being easy to know. One *sees* her, with intensity—sees her more than one sees almost any one; but then one discovers that that isn't knowing her and that one may know better a person whom one doesn't 'see,' as I say, half so well."

The discrimination was interesting, but it brought them back to the fact of her success; and it was at that comparatively gross circumstance, now so fully placed

before them, that Milly's anxious companion sat and
looked—looked very much as some spectator in an old-
time circus might have watched the oddity of a Chris-
tian maiden, in the arena, mildly, caressingly, martyred.
It was the nosing and fumbling not of lions and tigers
but of domestic animals let loose as for the joke. Even
the joke made Mrs. Stringham uneasy, and her mute
communion with Densher, to which we have alluded,
was more and more determined by it. He wondered
afterwards if Kate had made this out; though it was not
indeed till much later on that he found himself, in
thought, dividing the things she might have been conscious of from the things she must have missed. If she
actually missed, at any rate, Mrs. Stringham's discomfort, that but showed how her own idea held her. Her
own idea was, by insisting on the fact of the girl's
prominence as a feature of the season's end, to keep
Densher in relation, for the rest of them, both to present
and to past. "It's everything that has happened since
that makes you naturally a little shy about her. You
don't know what has happened since, but we do; we've
seen it and followed it; we've a little been *of* it." The
great thing for him, at this, as Kate gave it, *was* in fact
quite irresistibly that the case was a real one—the kind
of thing that, when one's patience was shorter than one's
curiosity, one had vaguely taken for possible in London,
but in which one had never been, even to this small
extent, concerned. The little American's sudden social
adventure, her happy and, no doubt, harmless flourish,
had probably been favoured by several accidents, but it

had been favoured above all by the simple spring-board
of the scene, by one of those common caprices of the
numberless foolish flock, gregarious movements as
inscrutable as ocean-currents. The huddled herd had
drifted to her blindly—it might as blindly have drifted
away. There had been of course a signal, but the great
reason was probably the absence at the moment of a
larger lion. The bigger beast would come and the
smaller would then vanish. It was at all events characteristic, and what was of the essence of it was grist to his
scribbling mill, matter for his journalising hand. That
hand already, in intention, played over it—the
"motive," as a sign of the season, a feature of the time,
of the purely expeditious and rough-and-tumble nature
of the social boom. The boom as in *itself* required—that
would be the note; the subject of the process a comparatively minor question. Anything was boomable enough
when nothing else was more so: the author of the "rot-
ten" book, the beauty who was no beauty, the heiress
who was only that, the stranger who was for the most
part saved from being inconveniently strange but by
being inconveniently familiar, the American whose
Americanism had been long desperately discounted, the
creature in fine as to whom spangles or spots of any sufficiently marked and applied sort could be loudly
enough predictated.

So he judged, at least, within his limits, and the idea
that what he had thus caught in the fact was the trick of
fashion and the tone of society went so far as to make
him take up again his sense of independence. He

had supposed himself civilised; but if this was civilisation——! One could smoke one's pipe outside when
twaddle was within. He had rather avoided, as we have
remarked, Kate's eyes, but there came a moment when
he would fairly have liked to put it, across the table, to
her: "I say, light of my life, is *this* the great world?"
There came another, it must be added—and doubtless
as a result of something that, over the cloth, did hang
between them—when she struck him as having quite
answered: "Dear no—for what do you take me? Not the
least little bit: only a poor silly, though quite harmless,
imitation." What she might have passed for saying,
however, was practically merged in what she did say,
for she came overtly to his aid, very much as if guessing some of his thoughts. She enunciated, to relieve his
bewilderment, the obvious truth that you couldn't leave
London for three months at that time of the year and
come back to find your friends just where they were. As
they had *of course* been jigging away they might well
be so red in the face that you wouldn't know them. She
reconciled in fine his disclaimer about Milly with that
honour of having discovered her which it was vain for
him modestly to shirk. He *had* unearthed her, but it
was they, all of them together, who had developed her.
She was always a charmer, one of the greatest ever seen,
but she wasn't the person he had "backed."

Densher was to feel sure afterwards that Kate had
had in these pleasantries no conscious, above all no
insolent purpose of making light of poor Susan Shepherd's property in their young friend—which property,

by such remarks, was very much pushed to the wall;
but he was also to know that Mrs. Stringham had
secretly resented them, Mrs. Stringham holding the
opinion, of which he was ultimately to have a glimpse,
that all the Kate Croys in Christendom were but dust
for the feet of her Milly. That, it was true, would be
what she must reveal only when driven to her last
entrenchments and well cornered in her passion—the
rare passion of friendship, the sole passion of her little
life save the one other, more imperturbably cerebral,
that she entertained for the art of Guy de Maupassant.
She slipped in the observation that her Milly was incapable of change, was just exactly, on the contrary, the
same Milly; but this made little difference in the drift
of Kate's contention. She was perfectly kind to Susie:
it was as if she positively knew her as handicapped for
any disagreement by feeling that she, Kate, had "type,"
and by being committed to admiration of type. Kate
had occasion subsequently—she found it somehow—to
mention to our young man Milly's having spoken to
her of this view on the good lady's part. She would
like—Milly had had it from her—to put Kate Croy in
a book and see what she could so do with her. "Chop
me up fine or serve me whole"—it was a way of being
got at that Kate professed she dreaded. It would be
Mrs. Stringham's, however, she understood, because
Mrs. Stringham, oddly, felt that with such stuff as the
strange English girl was made of, stuff that (in spite of
Maud Manningham, who was full of sentiment) she
had never known, there was none other to be employed.

These things were of later evidence, yet Densher might even then have felt them in the air. They were practically in it already when Kate, waiving the question of her friend's chemical change, wound up with the comparatively unobjectionable proposition that he must now, having missed so much, take them all up, on trust, further on. He met it peacefully, a little perhaps as an example to Mrs. Stringham—"Oh, as far on as you like!" This even had its effect: Mrs. Stringham appropriated as much of it as might be meant for herself. The nice thing about her was that she could measure how much; so that by the time dinner was over they had really covered ground.

IV

THE YOUNGER of the other men, it afterwards appeared, was most in his element at the piano; so that they had coffee and comic songs upstairs—the gentlemen, temporarily relinquished, submitting easily in this interest to Mrs. Lowder's parting injunction not to sit too tight. Our especial young man sat tighter when restored to the drawing-room; he made it out perfectly with Kate that they might, off and on, foregather without offence. He had perhaps stronger needs in this general respect than she; but she had better names for the scant risks to which she consented. It was the blessing of a big house that intervals were large and, of an August night, that windows were open; whereby, at a given moment, on the wide balcony, with the songs sufficiently sung, Aunt

Maud could hold her little court more freshly. Densher and Kate, during these moments, occupied, side by side, a small sofa—a luxury formulated by the latter as the proof, under criticism, of their remarkably good conscience. "To seem not to know each other—once you're here—would be," the girl said, "to overdo it"; and she arranged it charmingly that they *must* have some passage to put Aunt Maud off the scent. She would be wondering otherwise what in the world they found their account in. For Densher, none the less, the profit of snatched moments, snatched contacts, was partial and poor; there were in particular at present more things in his mind than he could bring out while watching the windows. It was true, on the other hand, that she suddenly met most of them—and more than he could see on the spot—by coming out for him with a reference to Milly that was not in the key of those made at dinner. "She's not a bit right, you know. I mean in health. Just see her to-night. I mean it looks grave. For you she would have come, you know, if it had been at all possible."

He took this in such patience as he could muster. "What's the matter with her?"

But Kate continued without saying. "Unless indeed your being here has been just a reason for her funking it."

"What's the matter with her?" Densher asked again.

"Why, just what I've told you—that she likes you so much."

"Then why should she deny herself the joy of meeting me?"

Kate had an hesitation—it would take so long to explain. "And perhaps it's true that she *is* bad. She easily may be."

"Quite easily, I should say, judging by Mrs. Stringham, who's visibly preoccupied and worried."

"Visibly enough. Yet it mayn't," said Kate, "be only for that."

"For what then?"

But this question too, on thinking, she neglected. "Why, if it's anything real, doesn't she go home? She would be anxious, and she has done all she need to be civil."

"I think," Densher remarked, "she has been quite beautifully civil."

It made Kate, he fancied, look at him the least bit harder; but she was already, in a manner, explaining "Her preoccupation is probably on two different heads. One of them would make her hurry back, but the other makes her stay. She's commissioned to tell Milly all about you."

"Well, then," said the young man between a laugh and a sigh, "I'm glad I felt, downstairs, a kind of 'drawing' to her. Wasn't I rather decent to her?"

"Awfully nice. You've instincts, you fiend. It's all," Kate declared, "as it should be."

"Except perhaps," he after a moment cynically suggested, "that she isn't getting much good of me now. Will she report to Milly on *this*?" And then as Kate seemed to wonder what "this" might be, "On our present disregard for appearances."

"Ah, leave appearances to me!" She spoke in her high way. "I'll make them all right. Aunt Maud, moreover," she added, "has her so engaged that she won't notice." Densher felt, with this, that his companion had indeed perceptive flights that he couldn't hope to match—had for instance another when she still subjoined: "And Mrs. Stringham's appearing to respond just in order to make that impression."

"Well," Densher dropped with some humour, "life's very interesting! I hope it's really as much so for you as you make it for others; I mean judging by what you make it for me. You seem to me to represent it as thrilling for *ces dames,* and in a different way for each: Aunt Maud, Susan Shepherd, Milly. But what *is,*" he wound up, "the matter? Do you mean she's as ill as she looks?"

Kate's face struck him as replying at first that his derisive speech deserved no satisfaction; then she appeared to yield to a need of her own—the need to make the point that "as ill as she looked" was what Milly scarce could be. If she were as ill as she looked she could scarce be a question with them, for her end would in that case be near. She believed herself nevertheless—and Kate couldn't help believing her too—seriously menaced. There was always the fact that they had been on the point of leaving town, the two ladies, and had suddenly been pulled up. "We bade them good-bye—or all but—Aunt Maud and I, the night before Milly, popping so very oddly into the National Gallery for a farewell look, found you and me together. They were then to get off a day or two later. But they've not got off—they're not getting off. When I see them—and I saw them this morning—they have showy reasons. They do mean to go, but they've postponed it." With which the girl brought out: "They've postponed it for *you*." He protested so far as a man might without fatuity, since a protest was itself credulous; but Kate, as ever, understood herself. "You've made Milly change her mind. She wants not to miss you—though she wants also not to show she wants you; which is why, as I hinted a moment ago, she may consciously have hung back to-night. She doesn't know when she may see you again—she doesn't know she ever may. She doesn't see the future. It has opened out before her in these last weeks as a dark, confused thing."

Densher wondered. "After the tremendous time you've all been telling me she has had?"

"That's it. There's a shadow across it."

"That of what you allude to as some physical break-up?"

"Some physical break-down. Nothing less. She's scared. She has so much to lose. And she wants more."

"Ah, well," said Densher, with a sudden strange sense of discomfort, "couldn't one say to her that she can't have everything?"

"No—for one wouldn't want to. She really," Kate went on, "has been somebody here. Ask Aunt Maud—you may think me prejudiced," the girl oddly smiled. "Aunt Maud will tell you—the world's before her. It has all come since you saw her, and it's a pity you've

missed it, for it certainly would have amused you. She
has really been a perfect success—I mean of course so
far as possible in the scrap of time—and she has taken it
like a perfect angel. If you can imagine an angel with a
thumping bank-account you'll have the simplest expression of the kind of thing. Her fortune's absolutely huge;
Aunt Maud has had all the facts, or enough of them, in
the last confidence, from 'Susie,' and Susie speaks by
book. Take them then, in the last confidence, from *me*.
There she is." Kate expressed above all what it most
came to. "It's open to her to make, you see, the very
greatest marriage. I assure you we're not vulgar about
her. Her possibilities are quite plain."

Densher showed he neither disbelieved nor grudged
them. "But what good then, on earth, can I do her?"

Well, she had it ready. "You can console her."

"And for what?"

"For all that, if she's stricken, she must see swept
away. I shouldn't care for her if she hadn't so much,"
Kate very simply said. And then as it made him laugh
not quite happily: "I shouldn't trouble about her if there
were one thing she did have." The girl spoke indeed
with a noble compassion. "She has nothing."

"Not all the young dukes?"

"Well we must see—see if anything can come of
them. She at any rate does love life. To have met a person like you," Kate further explained, "is to have felt
you become, with all the other fine things, a part of life.
Oh, she has you arranged!"

"You have, it strikes me, my dear"—and he looked

both detached and rueful. "Pray, what am I to do with
the dukes?"

"Oh, the dukes will be disappointed!"

"Then why shan't I be?"

"You'll have expected less," Kate wonderfully smiled.
"Besides, you will be. You'll have expected enough for
that."

"Yet it's what you want to let me in for?"

"I want," said the girl, "to make things pleasant for
her. I use, for the purpose, what I have. You're what I
have of most precious, and you're therefore what I use
most."

He looked at her long. "I wish I could use *you* a little more." After which, as she continued to smile at
him, "Is it a bad case of lungs?" he asked.

Kate showed for a little as if she wished it might be.
"Not lungs, I think. Isn't consumption, taken in time,
now curable?"

"People are, no doubt, patched up." But he wondered. "Do you mean she has something that's past
patching?" And before she could answer, "It's really as
if her appearance put her outside of such things—being,
in spite of her youth, that of a person who has been
through all it's conceivable she should be exposed to.
She affects one, I should say, as a creature saved from
a shipwreck. Such a creature may surely, in these days,
on the doctrine of chances, go to sea again with confidence. She has *had* her wreck—she has met her adventure."

"Oh, I grant you her wreck!"—Kate was all response

so far. "But do let her have still her adventure. There are wrecks that are not adventures."

"Well—if there be also adventures that are not wrecks!" Densher in short was willing, but he came back to his point. "What I mean is that she has none of the effect—on one's nerves or whatever—of an invalid."

Kate on her side did this justice. "No—that's the beauty of her."

"The beauty——?"

"Yes, she's so wonderful. She won't show for that, any more than your watch, when it's about to stop for want of being wound up, gives you convenient notice or shows as different from usual. She won't die, she won't live, by inches. She won't smell, as it were, of drugs. She won't taste, as it were, of medicine. No one will know."

"Then what," he demanded, frankly mystified now, "are we talking about? In what extraordinary state is she?"

Kate went on as if, at this, making it out, in a fashion, for herself. "I believe that if she's ill at all she's very ill. I believe that if she's bad she's not a *little* bad. I can't tell you why, but that's how I see her. She'll really live or she'll really not. She'll have it all or she'll miss it all. Now I don't think she'll have it all."

Densher had followed this, with his eye upon her—her own having thoughtfully wandered—as if it were more impressive than lucid. "You 'think,' and you 'don't think,' and yet you remain all the while without an inkling of her complaint?"

"No, not without an inkling; but it's a matter in which I don't want knowledge. She moreover herself doesn't want one to want it: she has, as to what may be preying upon her, a kind of ferocity of modesty, a kind of—I don't know what to call it—intensity of pride. And then, and then——" But with this she faltered.

"And then what?"

"I'm a brute about illness. I hate it. It's well for you, my dear," Kate continued, "that you're as sound as a bell."

"Thank you!" Densher laughed. "It's rather good then for yourself too that you're as strong as the sea."

She looked at him now a moment as for the selfish gladness of their young immunities. It was all they had together, but they had it at least without a flaw—each had the beauty, the physical felicity, the personal virtue, love and desire of the other. Yet it was as if this very consciousness threw them back the next moment into pity for the poor girl who had everything else in the world, the great genial good they, alas, didn't have, but failed, on the other hand, of this. "How we're talking about her!" Kate compunctiously sighed. But there were the facts. "From illness I keep away."

"But you don't—since here you are, in spite of all you say, in the midst of it."

"Ah, I'm only watching——!"

"And putting me forward in your place? Thank you!"

"Oh," said Kate, "I'm breaking you in. Let it give you the measure of what I shall expect of you. One can't begin too soon."

She drew away, as if under the impression of a stir on the balcony, the hand of which he had a minute before possessed himself; and the warning brought him back to attention. "You haven't even an idea if it's a case for surgery?"

"I dare say it may be; that is that if it comes to anything it may come to that. Of course she's in the highest hands."

"The doctors are after her then?"

"She's after *them*—it's the same thing. I think I'm free to say it now—she sees Sir Luke Strett."

It made him quickly wince. "Ah, fifty thousand knives!" Then after an instant: "One seems to guess." Yes, but she waved it away. "Don't guess. Only do as I tell you."

For a moment now, in silence, he took it all in, might have had it before him. "What you want of me then is to make up to a sick girl."

"Ah, but you admit yourself that she doesn't affect you as sick. You understand moreover just how much—and just how little."

"It's amazing," he presently answered, "what you think I understand."

"Well, if you've brought me to it, my dear," she returned, "that has been your way of breaking *me* in. Besides which, so far as making up to her goes, plenty of others will."

Densher for a little, under this suggestion, might have been seeing their young friend, on a pile of cushions and in a perpetual teagown, amid flowers and with drawn blinds, surrounded by the higher nobility. "Others can follow their tastes. Besides, others are free."

"But so are you, my dear!"

She had spoken with impatience, and her suddenly quitting him had sharpened it; in spite of which he kept his place, only looking up at her. "You're prodigious!"

"Of course I'm prodigious!"—and, as immediately happened, she gave a further sign of it that he fairly sat watching. The door from the lobby had, as she spoke, been thrown open for a gentleman who, immediately finding her within his view, advanced to greet her before the announcement of his name could reach her companion. Densher none the less felt himself brought quickly into relation; Kate's welcome to the visitor became almost precipitately an appeal to her friend, who slowly rose to meet it. "I don't know whether you know Lord Mark." And then for the other party: "Mr. Merton Densher—who has just come back from America."

"Oh!" said the other party, while Densher said nothing—occupied as he mainly was on the spot with weighing the sound in question. He recognised it in a moment as less imponderable than it might have appeared, as having indeed positive claims. It wasn't, that is, he knew the "Oh!" of the idiot, however great the superficial resemblance: it was that of the clever, the accomplished man; it was the very specialty of the speaker, and a deal of expensive training and experience had gone to producing it. Densher felt somehow that, as a thing of value accidentally picked up, it would retain an interest of curiosity. The three stood for a little together in an awkwardness to which he was conscious of contributing his share; Kate failing to ask Lord Mark to be seated, but letting him know that he would find Mrs. Lowder, with some others, on the balcony.

"Oh, and Miss Theale I suppose?—as I seemed to hear outside, from below, Mrs. Stringham's unmistakable voice."

"Yes, but Mrs. Stringham's alone. Milly's unwell," the girl explained, "and was compelled to disappoint us."

"Ah, 'disappoint'—rather!" And, lingering a little, he had his eyes on Densher while he inquired further. "She isn't really bad, I trust?"

Densher, after all he had heard, easily supposed him interested in Milly; but he could imagine him also interested in the young man with whom he had found Kate engaged and whom he yet considered without visible intelligence. Densher was sure, however, in a moment, that he was doing what he wanted, satisfying himself as to each. To this he was aided by Kate, who produced a prompt: "Oh dear no; I think not. I've just been reassuring Mr. Densher," she added—"who's as concerned as the rest of us. I've been calming his fears."

"Oh!" said Lord Mark again—and again it was just as good. That was for Densher, the latter could see, or think he saw. And then for the others: "*My* fears would want calming. We must take great care of her. This way?"

She went with him a few steps, and while Densher, hanging about, gave them frank attention, presently paused again for some further colloquy. What passed

between them our young man lost, but she was
presently with him again, Lord Mark joining the rest.
Densher was by this time quite ready for her. "It's *he*
who's your aunt's man?"

"Oh, immensely."

"I mean for *you*."

"That's what I mean too," Kate smiled. "There he is.
Now you can judge."

"Judge of what?"

"Judge of him."

"Why should I judge of him?" Densher asked. "I've
nothing to do with him."

"Then why do you ask about him?"

"To judge of you—which is different."

Kate, for a little, seemed to look at the difference.
"To take the measure, do you mean, of my danger?"

He hesitated; then he said: "I'm thinking, I dare say,
of Miss Theale's. How does your aunt reconcile his
interest in her——?"

"With his interest in me?"

"With her own interest in you," Densher said while
she reflected. "If that interest—Mrs. Lowder's—takes
the form of Lord Mark, hasn't he rather to look out for
the forms *he* takes?"

Kate seemed interested in the question, but "Oh, he
takes them easily," she answered. "The beauty is that
she doesn't trust him."

"That Milly doesn't?"

"Yes—Milly either. But I mean Aunt Maud. Not
really."

Densher gave it his wonder. "Takes him to her heart and yet thinks he cheats?"

"Yes," said Kate—"that's the way people are. What they think of their enemies, goodness knows, is bad enough; but I'm still more struck with what they think of their friends. Milly's own state of mind, however," she went on, "is lucky. That's Aunt Maud's security, though she doesn't yet fully recognise it—besides being Milly's own."

"You conceive it a real escape then not to care for him?"

She shook her head in beautiful grave deprecation. "You oughtn't to make me say too much. But I'm glad I don't."

"Don't say too much?"

"Don't care for Lord Mark."

"Oh!" Densher answered with a sound like his lordship's own. To which he added: "You absolutely hold that that poor girl doesn't?"

"Ah, you know what I hold about that poor girl!" It had made her again impatient.

Yet he stuck a minute to the subject. "You scarcely call him, I suppose, one of the dukes."

"Mercy, no—far from it. He's not, compared with other possibilities, 'in' it. Milly, it's true," she said, to be exact, "has no natural sense of social values, doesn't in the least understand our differences or know who's who or what's what."

"I see. That," Densher laughed, "is her reason for liking *me*."

"Precisely. She doesn't resemble me," said Kate, "who at least know what I lose."

Well, it had all risen for Densher to a considerable interest. "And Aunt Maud—why shouldn't *she* know? I mean that your friend there isn't really anything. Does she suppose him of ducal value?"

"Scarcely; save in the sense of being uncle to a duke. That's undeniably something. He's the best moreover we can get."

"Oh, oh!" said Densher; and his doubt was not all derisive.

"It isn't Lord Mark's grandeur," she went on without heeding this; "because perhaps in the line of that alone—as he has no money—more could be done. But she's not a bit sordid; she only counts with the sordidness of others. Besides, he's grand enough, with a duke in his family and at the other end of the string. *The* thing's his genius."

"And do you believe in that?"

"In Lord Mark's genius?" Kate, as if for a more final opinion than had yet been asked of her, took a moment to think. She looked indeed so that one would scarce have known what to expect; but she came out in time with a very sufficient "Yes!"

"Political?"

"Universal. I don't know at least," she said, "what else to call it when a man is able to make himself without effort, without violence, without machinery of any sort, so intensely felt. He has somehow an effect without his being in any traceable way a cause."

"Ah, but if the effect," said Densher with conscious superficiality, "isn't agreeable——?"

"Oh, but it is!"

"Not, surely, for everyone."

"If you mean not for you," Kate returned, "you may have reasons—and men don't count. Women don't know if it's agreeable or not."

"Then there you are!"

"Yes, precisely—that takes, on his part, genius."

Densher stood before her as if he wondered what everything she thus promptly, easily and, above all, amusingly met him with, would have been found, should it have come to an analysis, to "take." Something suddenly, as if under a last determinant touch, welled up in him and overflowed—the sense of his good fortune and her variety, of the future she promised, the interest she supplied. "All women but you are stupid. How can I look at another? You're different and different—and then you're different again. No marvel Aunt Maud builds on you—except that you're so much too good for what she builds *for*. Even 'society' won't know how good for it you are; it's too stupid, and you're beyond it. You'd have to pull it uphill—it's you yourself who are at the top. The women one meets—what are they but books one has already read? You're a whole library of the unknown, the uncut." He almost moaned, he ached, from the depth of his content. "Upon my word, I've a subscription!"

She took it from him with her face again, in answer, giving out all it had, and they remained once more confronted and united in their essential wealth of life. "It's you who draw me out. I exist in you. Not in others."

It had been, however, as if the thrill of their association itself pressed in him, as great felicities do, the sharp spring of fear. "See here, you know: don't, *don't*——!"

"Don't what?"

"Don't fail me. It would kill me."

She looked at him a minute with no response but her eyes. "So you think you'll kill me, in time, to prevent it?" She smiled, but he saw her the next instant as smiling through tears; and the instant after this she had got, in respect to the particular point, quite off. She had come back to another, which was one of her own; her own were so closely connected that Densher's were at best but parenthetic. Still, she had a distance to go. "You do then see your way?" She put it to him before they joined—as was high time—the others. And she made him understand that she meant his way with Milly.

He had dropped a little in presence of the explanation; then she had brought him up to a sort of recognition. He could make out by this light something of what he saw, but a dimness also there was, undispelled since his return. "There's something you must definitely tell me. If our friend knows that, all the while——?"

She came straight to his aid, formulating for him his anxiety, though quite to smooth it down. "All the while she and I, here, were growing intimate, you and I were in unmentioned relation? If she knows that, yes, she knows our relation consisted in your writing to me."

"Then how could she suppose you weren't answering?"

"She doesn't suppose it."

"How then can she imagine you never named her?"

"She doesn't. She knows now I did name her. I've told her everything. She's in possession of reasons which will perfectly do."

Still he just brooded. "She takes things from you exactly as I do?"

"Exactly as you do."

"She's just such another victim?"

"Just such another. You're a pair."

"Then if anything happens," said Densher, "we can console each other?"

"Ah, something *may* indeed happen," she exclaimed, "if you'll only go straight!"

He watched the others an instant through the window. "What do you mean by going straight?"

"Not worrying. Doing as you like. Try, as I've told you before, and you'll see. You'll have me perfectly, always, to refer to."

"Oh, rather, I hope! But if she's going away?"

It pulled Kate up but a moment. "I'll bring her back. There you are. You won't be able to say that I've not made it smooth for you."

He faced it all, and certainly it was queer. But it was not the queerness that, after another minute, was uppermost. He was in a wondrous silken web, and it *was* amusing. "You spoil me!"

He was not sure if Mrs. Lowder, who at this juncture

reappeared, had caught his word as it dropped from him; probably not, he thought, her attention being given to Mrs. Stringham, with whom she came through and who was now, none too soon, taking leave of her. They were followed by Lord Mark and by the other men, but two or three things happened before any dispersal of the company began. One of these was that Kate found time to say to him with furtive emphasis: "You must go now!" Another was that she next addressed herself in all frankness to Lord Mark, drew near to him with an almost reproachful "Come and talk to *me!*"—a challenge resulting after a minute for Densher in a consciousness of their installation together in an out-of-the-way corner, though not the same he himself had just occupied with her. Still another was that Mrs. Stringham, in the random intensity of her farewells, affected him as looking at him with a small grave intimation, something into which he afterwards read the meaning that if he had happened to desire a few words with her after dinner he would have found her ready. This impression was naturally light, but it just left him with the sense of something by his own act overlooked, unappreciated. It gathered perhaps a slightly sharper shade from the mild formality of her "Good-night, sir!" as she passed him; a matter as to which there was now nothing more to be done, thanks to the alertness of the young man whom he by this time had made out as even more harmless than himself. This personage had forestalled him in opening the door for her and was evidently—with a

view, Densher might have judged, to ulterior designs on
Milly—proposing to attend her to her carriage. What
further occurred was that Aunt Maud, having released
her, immediately had a word for himself. It was an
imperative "Wait a minute," by which she both detained
and dismissed him; she was particular about her minute,
but he had not yet given her, as happened, a sign of
withdrawal.

"Return to our little friend. You'll find her really
interesting."

"If you mean Miss Theale," he said, "I shall certainly
not forget her. But you must remember that, so far as
her 'interest' is concerned, I myself discovered, I—as
was said at dinner—invented her."

"Well, one seemed rather to see that you hadn't taken
out the patent. Don't, I only mean, in the press of other
things, too much neglect her."

Affected, surprised, by the coincidence of her appeal
with Kate's, he asked himself quickly if it mightn't help
him with her. He at any rate could but try. "You're all
looking after my manners. That's exactly, you know,
what Miss Croy has been saying to me. *She* keeps me
up—she has had so much to say about it."

He found pleasure in being able to give his hostess an
account of his passage with Kate that, while quite veracious, might be reassuring to herself. But Aunt Maud,
wonderfully and facing him straight, took it as if her
confidence were supplied with other props. If she saw
his intention in it she yet blinked neither with doubt nor

with acceptance; she only said imperturbably: "Yes, she'll herself do anything for her friend; so that she but preaches what she practises."

Densher really quite wondered if Aunt Maud knew how far Kate's devotion went. He was moreover a little puzzled by this special harmony; in face of which he quickly asked himself if Mrs. Lowder had bethought herself of the American girl as a distraction for him, and if Kate's intensity were therefore but an appearance addressed to her aunt. What might really become, in all this, of the American girl was therefore a question that, on the latter contingency, would lose none of its sharpness. However, questions could wait, and it was easy, so far as he understood, to meet Mrs. Lowder. "It isn't a bit, all the same, you know, that I resist. I find Miss Theale charming."

Well, it was all she wanted. "Then don't miss a chance."

"The only thing is," he went on, " that she's—naturally now—leaving town and, as I take it, going abroad."

Aunt Maud looked indeed an instant as if she herself had been dealing with this difficulty. "She won't go," she smiled in spite of it, "till she has seen you. Moreover, when she does go——" She paused, leaving him uncertain. But the next minute he was still more at sea. "We shall go too."

He gave a smile that he himself felt as slightly strange. "And what good will that do *me*?"

"We shall be near them somewhere, and you'll come out to us."

"Oh!" he said a little awkwardly.

"I'll see that you do. I mean I'll write to you."

"Ah, thank you, thank you!" Merton Densher laughed. She was indeed putting him on his honour, and his honour winced a little at the use he rather helplessly saw himself suffering her to believe she could make of it. "There are all sorts of things," he vaguely remarked, "to consider."

"No doubt. But there's above all the great thing."

"And, pray, what's that?"

"Why, the importance of your not losing the occasion of your life. I'm treating you handsomely, I'm looking after it for you. I *can*—I can smooth your path. She's charming, she's clever and she's good. And her fortune's a real fortune."

Ah, there she was, Aunt Maud! The pieces fell together for him as he felt her thus buying him off, and buying him—it would have been funny if it hadn't been so grave—with Miss Theale's money. He ventured, derisive, fairly to treat it as extravagant. "I'm much obliged to you for the handsome offer——"

"Of what doesn't belong to me?" She wasn't abashed. "I don't say it does—but there's no reason it shouldn't to *you*. Mind you, moreover"—she kept it up—"I'm not one who talks in the air. And you owe me something— if you want to know why."

Distinctly, he felt her pressure; he felt, given her basis, her consistency; he even felt, to a degree that was immediately to receive an odd confirmation, her truth. Her truth, for that matter, was that she believed him bribeable: a belief that for his own mind as well as they stood there, lighted up the impossible. What then in this light did Kate believe him? But that was not what he asked aloud. "Of course I know I owe you thanks for a deal of kind treatment. Your inviting me, for instance, tonight——!"

"Yes, my inviting you to-night is a part of it. But you don't know," she added, "how far I've gone for you."

He felt himself red, and as if his honour were colouring up; but he laughed again as he could. "I see how far you're going."

"I'm the most honest woman in the world; but I've nevertheless done for you what was necessary." And then, as her now quite sombre gravity only made him stare: "To start you, it *was* necessary. From *me* it has the weight." He but continued to stare, and she met his blankness with surprise. "Don't you understand me? I've told the proper lie for you." Still he only showed her his flushed, strained smile; in spite of which, speaking with force and as if he must with a minute's reflection see what she meant, she turned away from him. "I depend upon you now to make me right!"

The minute's reflection he was of course more free to take after he had left the house. He walked up the Bayswater Road, but he stopped short, under the murky stars, before the modern church, in the middle of the square that, going eastward, opened out on his left. He had had his brief stupidity, but now he understood. She had guaranteed to Milly Theale through Mrs. Stringham that Kate didn't care for him. She had affirmed through the same source that the attachment was only his. He made it out, he made it out, and he could see what she meant by its starting him. She had described Kate as merely compassionate, so that Milly might be compassionate too. "Proper" indeed it was, her lie—the very properest possible and the most deeply, richly diplomatic. So Milly was successfully deceived.

V

TO SEE HER ALONE, the poor girl, he none the less promptly felt, was to see her after all very much on the old basis, the basis of his three visits in New York; the new element, when once he was again face to face with her, not really amounting to much more than a recognition, with a little surprise, of the positive extent of the old basis. Everything but that, everything embarrassing fell away after he had been present five minutes: it was in fact wonderful that their excellent, their pleasant, their permitted and proper and harmless American relation— the legitimacy of which he could thus scarce express in names enough—should seem so unperturbed by other matters. They had both since then had great adventures—such an adventure for him was his mental annexation of her country; and it was now, for the moment, as if the greatest of them all were this acquired consciousness of reasons other than those that had already served. Densher had asked for her, at her hotel, the day after Aunt Maud's dinner, with a rich, that is with a

highly troubled, preconception of the part likely to be
played for him at present, in any contact with her, by
Kate's and Mrs. Lowder's so oddly conjoined and so
really superfluous attempts to make her interesting. She
had been interesting enough without them—that
appeared today to come back to him; and, admirable and
beautiful as was the charitable zeal of the two ladies, it
might easily have nipped in the bud the germs of a
friendship inevitably limited but still perfectly workable.
What had happily averted the need of his breaking off,
what would as happily continue to avert it, was his own
good sense and good humour, a certain spring of mind in
him which ministered, imagination aiding, to under-
standings and allowances and which he had positively
never felt such an occasion as just now to rejoice in the
possession of. Many men—he practically made the
reflection—wouldn't have taken the matter that way,
would have lost patience, finding the appeal in question
irrational, exorbitant; and, thereby making short work
with it, would have let it render any further acquaintance
with Miss Theale impossible. He had talked with Kate of
this young woman's being "sacrificed," and that would
have been one way, so far as he was concerned, to sacrifice her. Such, however, had not been the tune to which
his at first bewildered view had, since the night before,
cleared itself up. It wasn't so much that he failed of
being the kind of man who "chucked," for he knew himself as the kind of man intelligent enough to recognise
the cases in which chucking might be the minor evil and
the least cruelty. It was that he liked too much everyone

concerned willingly to show himself merely impractica-
ble. He liked Kate, goodness knew, and he also, clearly
enough, liked Mrs. Lowder. He liked in particular Milly
herself; and hadn't it come up for him the evening before
that he quite liked even Susan Shepherd? He had never
known himself so generally merciful. It was a footing, at
all events, whatever accounted for it, on which he would
surely be rather a muff not to manage on one line or
another to escape disobliging. Should he find he couldn't
work it there would still be time enough. The idea of
working it crystallised before him in such guise as not
only to promise much interest—fairly, in case of success,
much excitement; but positively to impart to failure an
appearance of barbarity.

Arriving thus in Brook Street both with the best
intentions and with a margin consciously left for some
primary awkwardness, he found his burden, to his great
relief, unexpectedly light. The awkwardness involved in
the responsibility so newly and so ingeniously traced for
him turned round on the spot to present him another
face. This was simply the face of his old impression,
which he now fully recovered—the impression that
American girls, when, rare case, they were as charming
as Milly, were clearly the easiest people in the world.
Had what had happened been that this specimen of the
class was from the first so committed to ease that nothing subsequent *could* ever make her difficult? This
affected him now as still more probable than on the occasion of the hour or two lately passed with her in Kate's
society. Milly Theale had recognised no complication,

to Densher's view, while bringing him, with his companion, from the National Gallery and entertaining them at luncheon; it need therefore scarce be supposed that complications had become so soon too much for her. His pretext for presenting himself was fortunately of the best and simplest; the least he could decently do, given their happy acquaintance, was to call with an inquiry after learning that she had been prevented by illness from meeting him at dinner. And then there was the beautiful accident of her other demonstration; he must at any rate have given a sign as a sequel to the hospitality he had shared with Kate. Well, he was giving one now— such as it was; he was finding her, to begin with, accessible, and very naturally and prettily glad to see him. He had come, after luncheon, early, though not so early but that she might already be out if she were well enough; and she was well enough and yet was still at home. He had an inner glimpse, with this, of the comment Kate would have made on it: it was not absent from his thought that Milly would have been at home by *her* account because expecting, after a talk with Mrs. Stringham, that a certain person might turn up. He even—so pleasantly did things go—enjoyed freedom of mind to welcome, on that supposition, a fresh sign of the beautiful hypocrisy of women. He went so far as to enjoy believing the girl *might* have stayed in for him; it helped him to enjoy her behaving as if she hadn't. She expressed, that is, exactly the right degree of surprise; she didn't a bit overdo it: the lesson of which was, perceptibly, that, so far as his late lights had opened the

door to any want of the natural in their meetings, he
might trust her to take care of it for him as well as for
herself.

She had begun this, admirably, on his entrance, with
her turning away from the table at which she had apparently been engaged in letter-writing; it was the very possibility of his betraying a concern for her as one of the
afflicted that she had within the first minute conjured
away. She was never, never—did he understand?—to be
one of the afflicted for him; and the manner in which he
understood it, something of the answering pleasure that
he couldn't help knowing he showed, constituted, he was
very soon after to acknowledge, something like a start for
intimacy. When things like that could pass, people had
in truth to be equally conscious of a relation. It soon
made one, at all events, when it didn't find one made.
She had let him ask—there had been time for that, his
allusion to her friend's explanatory arrival at Lancaster
Gate without her being inevitable; but she had blown
away, and quite as much with the look in her eyes as
with the smile on her lips, every ground for anxiety and
every chance for insistence. How was she?—why, she
was as he thus saw her and as she had reasons of her
own, the business of nobody else, for desiring to appear.
Kate's account of her as too proud for pity, as fiercely
shy about so personal a secret, came back to him; so that
he rejoiced he could take a hint, especially when he
wanted to. The question the girl had quickly disposed
of—"Oh, it was nothing: I'm all right, thank you!"—was
one he was glad enough to be able to banish. It was not

at all, in spite of the appeal Kate had made to him on it,
his affair; for his interest had been invoked in the name
of compassion, and the name of compassion was exactly
what he felt himself at the end of two minutes forbidden so much as to whisper. He had been sent to see her
in order to be sorry for her, and how sorry he might be,
quite privately, he was yet to make out. Didn't that signify, however, almost not at all?—inasmuch as, whatever
his upshot, he was never to let her know it. Thus the
ground was unexpectedly cleared; though it was not till a
slightly longer time had passed that he made sure, at first
with amusement and then with a sort of respect, of what
had most operated. Extraordinarily, quite amazingly, he
began to see that if his pity hadn't had to yield to still
other things it would have had to yield quite definitely to
her own. That was the way the case had turned round:
he had made his visit to be sorry for her, but he would
repeat it—if he did repeat it—in order that she might be
sorry for *him*. His situation made him, she judged—
when once one liked him—a subject for that tenderness:
he felt this judgment in her, and felt it as something he
should really, in decency, in dignity, in common honesty, have very soon to reckon with.

Odd enough was it certainly that the question originally before him, the question placed there by Kate,
should so of a sudden find itself quite dislodged by
another. This other, it was easy to see, came straight up
with the fact of her beautiful delusion and her wasted
charity; the whole thing preparing for him as pretty a
case of conscience as he could have desired, and one at

the prospect of which he was already wincing. If he was interesting it was because he was unhappy; and if he was unhappy, it was because his passion for Kate had spent itself in vain; and if Kate was indifferent, inexorable, it was because she had left Milly in no doubt of it. That, above all, was what came up for him—how clear an impression of this attitude, how definite an account of his own failure, Kate must have given her friend. His immediate quarter of an hour there with the girl lighted up for him almost luridly such an inference; it was almost as if the other party to their remarkable understanding had been with them as they talked, had been hovering about, had dropped in, to look after her work. The value of the work affected him as different from the moment he saw it so expressed in poor Milly. Since it was false that he wasn't loved, so his right was quite quenched to figure on that ground as important; and if he didn't look out he would find himself liking in a way quite at odds with straightness the good faith of Milly's benevolence. *There* was the place for scruples; there the need, absolutely, to mind what he was about. If it wasn't proper for him to enjoy consideration on a perfectly false footing, where was the guarantee that, if he kept on, he wouldn't himself pretend to the grievance in order not to miss the sweet? Consideration—from a charming girl—was soothing on whatever theory; and it didn't take him far to remember that he had himself as yet done nothing deceptive. It was Kate's description of him, his defeated state, it was none of his own; his responsibility would begin, as he might say, only with acting it out.

The sharp point was, however, in the difference between acting and not acting; this difference in fact it was that made the case of conscience. He saw it with a certain alarm rise before him that everything was acting that was not speaking the particular word. "If you like me because you think *she* doesn't, it isn't a bit true: she *does* like me, awfully!"—that would have been the particular word; which, at the same time, but too palpably, there were difficulties about one's uttering. Wouldn't it be as indelicate, in a way, to challenge her as to leave her deluded?—and this quite apart from the exposure, so to speak, of Kate, as to whom it would constitute a kind of betrayal. Kate's design was something so extraordinarily special to Kate that he felt himself shrink from the complications involved in judging it. Not to give away the woman one loved, but to back her up in her mistakes— once they had gone a certain length—that was perhaps chief among the inevitabilities of the abjection of love. Loyalty was, of course, sovereignty prescribed in presence of any design on her part, however roundabout, to do one nothing but good.

Densher had quite to steady himself not to be awestruck at the immensity of the good his own friend must on all this evidence have wanted to do him. Of one thing indeed meanwhile he was sure: Milly Theale wouldn't herself precipitate his necessity of intervention. She would absolutely never say to him: "*Is* it so impossible she shall ever care for you seriously?"—without which nothing could well be less delicate than for him aggressively to set her right. Kate would be free to do

that if Kate, in some prudence, some contrition, for some
better reason in fine, should revise her plan; but he asked
himself what, failing this, *he* could do that wouldn't be,
after all, more gross than doing nothing. This brought
him round again to the acceptance of the fact that the
poor girl liked him. She put it, for reasons of her own, on
a simple, a beautiful ground, a ground that already supplied her with the pretext she required. The ground was
there, that is, in the impression she had received,
retained, cherished; the pretext, over and above it, was
the pretext for acting on it. That she now believed as she
did made her sure at last that she might act; so that what
Densher therefore would have struck at would be the
root, in her soul, of a pure pleasure. It positively lifted its
head and flowered, this pure pleasure, while the young
man now sat with her, and there were things she seemed
to say that took the words out of his mouth. These were
not all the things she did say; they were rather what such
things meant in the light of what he knew. Her warning
him for instance of the question of how she was, the
quick, brave little art with which she did that, represented to his fancy a truth she didn't utter. "I'm well for
you—that's all you have to do with or need trouble
about: I shall never be anything so horrid as ill for you.
So there you are; worry about me, spare me, please, as
little as you can. Don't be afraid, in short, to ignore my
'interesting' side. It isn't, you see, even now while you sit
here, that there are not lots of others. Only do *them* justice and we shall get on beautifully." This was what was
folded finely up in her talk—all quite ostensibly about

her impressions and her intentions. She tried to put Densher again on his American doings, but he wouldn't have
that to-day. As he thought of the way in which, the other
afternoon, before Kate, he had sat complacently "jaw-
ing," he accused himself of excess, of having overdone it,
made—at least apparently—more of a "set" at his interlocutress than he was at all events then intending. He
turned the tables, drawing her out about London, about
her vision of life there, and only too glad to treat her as
a person with whom he could easily have other topics
than her aches and pains. He spoke to her, above all, of
the evidence offered him at Lancaster Gate that she had
come but to conquer; and when she had met this with
full and gay assent—"How could I help being the feature
of the season, the what-do-you-call-it, the theme of every
tongue?"—they fraternised freely over all that had come
and gone for each since their interrupted encounter in
New York.

At the same time, while many things, in quick succession, came up for them, came up in particular for
Densher, nothing perhaps was just so sharp as the odd
influence of their present conditions on their view of
their past ones. It was as if they hadn't known how
"thick" they had originally become, as if, in a manner,
they had really fallen to remembering more passages of
intimacy than there had in fact at the time quite been
room for. They were in a relation now, whether from
what they said or from what they didn't say, so complicated that it might have been seeking to justify its speedy
growth by reaching back to one of those fabulous periods

in which prosperous states place their beginnings. He
recalled what had been said at Mrs. Lowder's about the
steps and stages, in people's careers, that absence caused
one to miss, and about the resulting frequent sense of
meeting them further on; which, with some other matters
also recalled, he took occasion to communicate to Milly.
The matters he couldn't mention mingled themselves
with those he did; so that it would doubtless have been
hard to say which of the two groups now played most
of a part. He was kept face to face with this young lady
by a force absolutely resident in their situation and operating, for his nerves, with the swiftness of the forces
commonly regarded by sensitive persons as beyond their
control. The current thus determined had positively
become for him, by the time he had been ten minutes
in the room, something that, but for the absurdity of
comparing the very small with the very great, he would
freely have likened to the rapids of Niagara. An uncriti-
cised acquaintance between a clever young man and a
responsive young woman could do nothing more, at the
most, than go, and his actual experiment went and went
and went. Nothing probably so conduced to make it go
as the marked circumstance that they had spoken all the
while not a word about Kate; and this in spite of the fact
that, if it were a question for them of what had occurred
in the past weeks, nothing had occurred comparable to
Kate's predominance. Densher had but the night before
appealed to her for instruction as to what he must do
about her; but he fairly winced to find how little this
came to. She had told him of course how little; but it was

a truth that looked different when shown him by Milly. It proved to him that the latter had in fact been dealt with, but it produced in him the thought that Kate might perhaps again conveniently be questioned. He would have liked to speak to her before going further—to make sure she really meant him to succeed quite so much. With all the difference that, as we say, came up for him, it came up afresh, naturally, that he might make his visit brief and never renew it; yet the strangest thing of all was that the argument against that issue would have sprung precisely from the beautiful little eloquence involved in Milly's avoidances.

Precipitate these well might be, since they emphasised the fact that she was proceeding in the sense of the assurances she had taken. Over the latter she had visibly not hesitated, for hadn't they had the merit of giving her a chance? Densher quite saw her, felt her take it; the chance, neither more nor less, of helping him according to her freedom. It was what Kate had left her with: "Listen to him, *I*? Never! So do as you like." What Milly "liked" was to do, it thus appeared, as she was doing: our young man's glimpse of which was just what would have been for him not less a glimpse of the peculiar brutality of shaking her off. The choice exhaled its shy fragrance of heroism, for it was not aided by any question of parting with Kate. She would be charming to Kate as well as to Kate's adorer; she would incur whatever pain could dwell for her in the sight—should she continue to be exposed to the sight—of the adorer thrown with the adored. It

wouldn't really have taken much more to make him
wonder if he hadn't before him one of those rare cases
of exaltation—food for fiction, food for poetry—in
which a man's fortune with the woman who doesn't
care for him is positively promoted by the woman who
does. It was as if Milly had said to herself: "Well, he
can at least meet her in my society, if that's anything
to him; so that my line can only be to make my society attractive." She certainly couldn't have made a different impression if she *had* so reasoned. All of which,
none the less, didn't prevent his soon enough saying to
her, quite as if she were to be whirled into space: "And
now, then, what becomes of you? Do you begin to rush
about on visits to country-houses?"

She disowned the idea with a headshake that, put on
what face she would, couldn't help betraying to him
something of her suppressed view of the possibility—
ever, ever perhaps—of any such proceedings. They
weren't, at any rate, for her now. "Dear no—we go
abroad—for a few weeks, somewhere, of high air. That
has been before us for many days; we've only been kept
on by last necessities here. However, everything's done,
and the wind's in our sails."

"May you scud then happily before it! But when,"
he asked, "do you come back?"

She looked ever so vague; then as if to correct it: "Oh,
when the wind turns. And what do you do with your
summer

"Ah, I spend it in sordid toil. I drench it with mercenary ink. My work in your country counts for play as

well. You see what's thought of the pleasure your country can give. My holiday's over."

"I'm sorry you had to take it," said Milly, "at such
a different time from ours. If you could but have worked
while we've been working——"

"I might be playing while you play? Oh, the distinction isn't so great with me. There's a little of each for
me, of work and of play, in either. But you and Mrs.
Stringham, with Miss Croy and Mrs. Lowder—you
all," he went on, "have been given up, like navvies or
niggers, to real physical toil. Your rest is something
you've earned and you need. My labour's comparatively light."

"Very true," she smiled; "but, all the same, I like
mine."

"It doesn't leave you spent? "

"Not a bit. I don't get tired when I'm interested. Oh,
I could go far."

He bethought himself. "Then why don't you?—since
you've got here, as I learn, the whole place in your
pocket."

"Well, it's a kind of economy—I'm saving things up.
I've enjoyed so what you speak of—though your
account of it's fantastic—that I'm watching over its
future, that I can't help being anxious and careful. I
want—in the interest itself of what I've had, and may
still have—not to make any mistakes. The way not to
make them is to get off again to a distance and see the
situation from there. I shall keep it fresh," she wound
up as if herself rather pleased with the ingenuity of her

statement—"I shall keep it fresh, by that prudence, for my return."

"Ah, then, you *will* return? Can you promise one that?"

Her face fairly lighted at his asking for a promise; but she made as if bargaining a little. "Isn't London rather awful in winter?"

He had been going to ask her if she meant for the invalid; but he checked the infelicity of this and took the inquiry as referring to social life. "No—I like it, with one thing and another; it's less of a mob than later on; and it would have for *us* the merit—should you come here then—that we should probably see more of you. So do reappear for us—if it isn't a question of climate."

She looked at that a little graver. "If what isn't a question——?"

"Why, the determination of your movements. You spoke just now of going somewhere for that."

"For better air?"—she remembered. "Oh yes, one certainly wants to get out of London in August."

"Rather, of course!"—he fully understood. "Though I'm glad you've hung on long enough for me to catch you. Try us, at any rate," he continued, "once more."

"Whom do you mean by 'us'?" she presently asked.

It pulled him up an instant—representing, as he saw it might have seemed, an allusion to himself as conjoined with Kate, whom he was proposing not to mention any more than his hostess did. But the issue was easy. "I mean all of us together, everyone you'll find ready to surround you with sympathy."

It made her, none the less, in her odd, charming way, challenge him afresh. "Why do you say sympathy?"

"Well, it is doubtless, a pale word. What we *shall* feel for you will be much nearer worship."

"As near then as you like!" With which at last Kate's name was sounded. "The people I'd most come back for are the people you know. I'd do it for Mrs. Lowder, who has been beautifully kind to me."

"So she has to *me*," said Densher. "I feel," he added as she at first answered nothing, "that, quite contrary to anything I originally expected, I've made a good friend of her."

"*I* didn't expect it either—its turning out as it has. But I did," said Milly, "with Kate. I shall come back for her too. I'd do anything"—she kept it up—"for Kate."

Looking at him as with conscious clearness while she spoke, she might for the moment have effectively laid a trap for whatever remains of the ideal straightness in him were still able to pull themselves together and operate. He was afterwards to say to himself that something had at that moment hung for him by a hair. "Oh, I know what one would do for Kate!"—it had hung for him by a hair to break out with that, which he felt he had really been kept from by an element in his consciousness stronger still. The proof of the truth in question was precisely in his silence; resisting the impulse to break out was what he *was* doing for Kate. This at the time moreover came and went quickly enough; he was trying the next minute but to make Milly's allusion easy for herself. "Of course I know what friends you are—and of course I understand," he permitted himself to add, "any amount of devotion to a person so charming. That's the good turn then she'll do us all—I mean her working for your return."

"Oh, you don't know," said Milly, "how much I'm really on her hands."

He could but accept the appearance of wondering how much he might show he knew. "Ah, she's very masterful."

"She's great. Yet I don't say she bullies me."

"No—that's not the way. At any rate it isn't hers," he smiled. He remembered, however, then that an undue acquaintance with Kate's ways was just what he mustn't show; and he pursued the subject no further than to remark with a good intention that had the further merit of representing a truth: "I don't feel as if I knew her—really to call know."

"Well, if you come to that, I don't either!" she laughed. The words gave him, as soon as they were uttered, a sense of responsibility for his own; though during a silence that ensued for a minute he had time to recognise that his own contained, after all, no element of falsity. Strange enough therefore was it that he could go too far—if it *was* too far—without being false. His observation was one he would perfectly have made to Kate herself. And before he again spoke, and before Milly did, he took time for more still—for feeling that just here it was that he must break short off if his mind was really made up not to go further. It was as if he had been at a corner—and fairly put there by his last speech; so that it depended on him whether or no to turn it. The silence if prolonged but an instant might even have given him a sense of her waiting to see what he would do. It was filled for them, the next thing, by the sound, rather voluminous for the August afternoon, of the approach, in the street below them, of heavy carriage-wheels and of horses trained to "step." A rumble, a great shake, a considerable effective clatter, had been apparently succeeded by a pause at the door of the hotel, which was in turn accompanied by a due proportion of diminished prancing and stamping. "You've a visitor," Densher laughed, "and it must be at least an ambassador."

"It's only my own carriage; it does that—isn't it wonderful?—every day. But we find it, Mrs. Stringham and I, in the innocence of our hearts, very amusing." She had got up, as she spoke, to assure herself of what she said; and at the end of a few steps they were together on the balcony and looking down at her waiting chariot, which made indeed a brave show. "Is it very awful?"

It was to Densher's eyes—save for its absurd heaviness—only pleasantly pompous. "It seems to me delightfully rococo. But how do I know? You're mistress of these things, in contact with the highest wisdom. You occupy a position, moreover, thanks to which your carriage—well, by this time, in the eye of London, also occupies one." But she was going out, and he mustn't stand in her way. What had happened the next minute was, first, that she had denied she was going out, so that he might prolong his stay; and second, that she had said she would go out with pleasure if he would like to drive—that in fact there were always things to do, that there had been a question for her to-day of several in particular, and that this, in short, was why the carriage had been ordered so early. They perceived, as she said these things, that an inquirer had presented himself, and, coming back, they found Milly's servant announcing the carriage and prepared to accompany her. This appeared to have for her the effect of settling the matter—on the basis, that is, of Densher's happy response. Densher's happy response, however, had as yet hung fire, the process we have described in him operating by this time with extreme intensity. The system of not pulling up, not breaking off, had already brought him headlong, he seemed to feel, to where they actually stood; and just now it was, with a vengeance, that he must do either one thing or the other. He had been waiting for some moments, which probably seemed to him longer than they were; this was because he was anxiously watching himself wait. He couldn't keep that up for ever; and since one thing or the other was what he must do, it was for the other that he presently became conscious of having decided. If he had been drifting it settled itself in the manner of a bump, of considerable violence, against a firm object in the stream. "Oh yes; I'll go with you with pleasure. It's a charming idea."

She gave no look to thank him—she rather looked away; she only said at once to her servant, "In ten minutes"; and then to her visitor, as the man went out, "We'll go somewhere—I shall like that. But I must ask of you time—as little as possible—to get ready." She looked over the room to provide for him, keep him there. "There are books and things—plenty; and I dress very quickly." He caught her eyes only as she went, on which he thought them pretty and touching.

Why especially touching at that instant he could certainly scarce have said; it was involved, it was lost in the sense of her wishing to oblige him. Clearly what had occurred was her having wished it so that she had made him simply wish, in civil acknowledgment, to oblige *her;* which he had now fully done, by turning his corner. He was quite round it, his corner, by the time the door had closed upon her and he stood there alone. Alone he remained for three minutes more—remained with several very living little matters to think about. One of these was the phenomenon—typical, highly American, he would have said—of Milly's extreme spontaneity. It was perhaps rather as if he had sought refuge—refuge from another question—in the almost exclusive contemplation of this. Yet this, in its way, led him nowhere; not even to a sound generalisation about American girls. It was spontaneous for his young friend to have asked him to drive with her alone—since she hadn't mentioned her companion; but she struck him, after all, as no more advanced in doing it than Kate, for instance, who was not an American girl, might have struck him in not doing it. Besides, Kate *would* have done it, though Kate wasn't at all, in the same sense as Milly, spontaneous. And then, in addition, Kate *had* done it—or things very much like it. Furthermore, he was engaged to Kate—

even if his ostensibly not being put her public freedom on other grounds. On all grounds, at any rate, the relation between Kate and freedom, between freedom and Kate, was a different one from any he could associate, as to anything, with the girl who had just left him to prepare to give herself up to him. It had never struck him before, and he moved about the room while he thought of it, touching none of the books placed at his disposal. Milly was forward, as might be said, but not advanced; whereas Kate was backward—backward still, comparatively, as an English girl—and yet advanced in a high degree. However—though this didn't straighten it out— Kate was, of course, two or three years older; which at their time of life considerably counted.

Thus ingeniously discriminating, Densher continued slowly to wander; yet without keeping at bay for long the sense again that his corner was turned. It was so turned that he felt himself to have lost even the option of taking advantage of Milly's absence to retrace his steps. If he might have turned tail, vulgarly speaking, five minutes before, he couldn't turn tail now; he must simply wait there with his consciousness charged to the brim. Quickly enough, moreover, that issue was closed from without; in the course of three minutes more Miss Theale's servant had returned. He preceded a visitor, whom he had met, obviously, at the foot of the stairs, and whom, throwing open the door, he loudly announced as Miss Croy. Kate, on following him in, stopped short at sight of Densher—only after an instant, as the young man saw, with free amusement, not from

surprise, and still less from discomfiture. Densher
immediately gave his explanation—Miss Theale had
gone to prepare to drive—on receipt of which the servant effaced himself.

"And you're going with her?" Kate asked.

"Yes—with your approval; which I've taken, as you
see, for granted."

"Oh," she laughed, "my approval is complete!" She
was thoroughly consistent and handsome about it.

"What I mean is of course," he went on—for he was
sensibly affected by her gaiety—"at your so lively instigation."

She had looked about the room—she might have been
vaguely looking for signs of the duration, of the character, of his visit, a momentary aid in taking a decision.
"Well, instigation then, as much as you like." She
treated it as pleasant, the success of her plea with him;
she made a fresh joke of this direct impression of it. "So
much so as that? Do you know I think I won't wait?"

"Not to see her—after coming?"

"Well, with you in the field—! I came for news of
her, but she must be all right. If she is——"

But he took her straight up. "Ah, how do I know?"
He was moved to say more. "It's not I who am responsible for her, my dear. It seems to me it's you." She
struck him as making light of a matter that had been
costing him sundry qualms; so that they couldn't both
be quite just. Either she was too easy or he had been too
anxious. He didn't want, at all events, to feel a fool for

that. "I'm doing nothing—and shall not, I assure you, do anything but what I'm told."

Their eyes met, with some intensity, over the emphasis he had given his words; and he had taken it from her the next moment that he really needn't get into a state. What in the world was the matter? She asked it, with interest, for all answer. "Isn't she better—if she's able to see you?"

"She assures me she's in perfect health."

Kate's interest grew. "I knew she would." On which she added: "It won't have been really for illness that she stayed away last night."

"For what then?"

"Well—for nervousness."

"Nervousness about what?"

"Oh, you know!" She spoke with a hint of impatience, smiling, however, the next moment. "I've told you that."

He looked at her to recover in her face what she had told him; then it was as if what he saw there prompted him to say: "What have you told *her*?"

She gave him her controlled smile, and it was all as if they remembered where they were, liable to surprise, talking with softened voices, even stretching their opportunity, by such talk, beyond a quite right feeling. Milly's room would be close at hand, and yet they were saying things——! For a moment, none the less, they kept it up. "Ask *her*, if you like; you're free—she'll tell you. Act as you think best; don't trouble about what you think I may, or mayn't, have told. I'm all right with her," said Kate. "So there you are."

"If you mean *here I* am," he answered, "it's unmistakable. If you also mean that her believing in you is all I have to do with, you're so far right as that she certainly does believe in you."

"Well, then, take example by her."

"She's really doing it for you," Densher continued. "She's driving me out for you."

"Well, then," said Kate, with her soft tranquillity, "you can do it a little for *her*. I'm not afraid," she smiled.

He stood before her a moment, taking in again the face she put on it and affected again, as he had already so often been, by more things in this face, and in her whole person and presence, than he was, to his relief, obliged to find words for. It wasn't, under such impressions, a question of words. "I do nothing for any one in the world but you. But for you I'll do anything."

"Good, good," said Kate. "That's how I like you."

He waited again an instant. "Then you swear to it?"

"To 'it'? To what?"

"Why, that you do 'like' me. For it's only for that, you know, that I'm letting you do—well, God knows what with me."

She gave at this, with a stare, a disheartened gesture—the sense of which she immediately further expressed. "If you don't believe in me then, after .all, hadn't you better break off, before you've gone further?"

"Break off with you?"

"Break off with Milly. You might go now," she said, "and I'll stay and explain to her why it is."

He wondered—as if it struck him. "What would you say?"

"Why, that you find you can't stand her, and that there's nothing for me but to bear with you as I best may."

He considered of this. "How much do you abuse me to her? "

"Exactly enough. As much as you see by her attitude."

Again he thought. "It doesn't seem to me I ought to mind her attitude."

"Well, then, just as you like. I'll stay and do my best for you."

He saw she was sincere, was really giving him a chance; and that of itself made things clearer. The feeling of how far he had gone came back to him not in repentance, but in this very vision of an escape; and it was not of what he had done, but of what Kate offered, that he now weighed the consequence. "Won't it make her—her not finding me here—be rather more sure there's something between us?"

Kate thought. "Oh, I don't know. It will of course greatly upset her. But you needn't trouble about that. She won't die of it."

"Do you mean she *will?*" Densher presently asked.

"Don't put me questions when you don't believe what I say. You make too many conditions."

She spoke now with a sort of rational weariness that

made the want of pliancy, the failure to oblige her, look poor and ugly; so that what it suddenly came back to for him was his deficiency in the things a man of any taste, so engaged, so enlisted, would have liked to make sure of being able to show—imagination, tact, positively even humour. The circumstance is doubtless odd, but the truth is none the less that the speculation uppermost with him at this juncture was: "What if I should begin to bore this creature?" And that, within a few seconds, had translated itself. "If you'll swear again you love me——!"

She looked about, at door and window, as if he were asking for more than he said. "Here? There's nothing between us here," Kate smiled.

"Oh, *isn't* there?" Her smile itself, with this, had so settled something for him that he had come to her pleadingly and holding out his hands, which she immediately seized with her own, as if both to check him and to keep him. It was by keeping him thus for a minute that she did check him; she held him long enough; while, with their eyes deeply meeting, they waited in silence for him to recover himself and renew his discretion. He coloured, as with a return of the sense of where they were, and that gave her precisely one of her usual victories, which immediately took further form. By the time he had dropped her hands he had again taken hold, as it were, of Milly's. It was not, at any rate, with Milly he had broken. "I'll do all you wish," he declared as if to acknowledge the acceptance of his condition that he

had, practically, after all, drawn from her—a declaration
on which she then, recurring to her first idea, promptly
acted.

"If you *are* as good as that, I go. You'll tell her that,
finding you with her, I wouldn't wait. Say that, you
know, from yourself. She'll understand."

She had reached the door with it—she was full of
decision; but he had, before she left him, one more
doubt. "I don't see how she can understand enough, you
know, without understanding too much."

"You don't need to see."

He required then a last injunction. "I must simply
go it blind? "

"You must simply be kind to her."

"And leave the rest to you? "

"Leave the rest to *her*, " said Kate disappearing.

It came back then afresh to that, as it had come
before. Milly, three minutes after Kate had gone,
returned in her array—her big black hat, so little super-
stitiously in the fashion, her fine black garments
throughout, the swathing of her throat, which Densher
vaguely took for an infinite number of yards of priceless lace, and which, its folded fabric kept in place by
heavy rows of pearls, hung down to her feet like the
stole of a priestess. He spoke to her at once of their
friend's visit and flight. "She hadn't known she would
find me," he said—and said at present without difficulty. His corner was so turned that it wasn't a question of a word more or less.

She took this account of the matter as quite sufficient; she glossed over whatever might be awkward. "I'm sorry—but I, of course, often see *her*." He felt the discrimination in his favour, and how it justified Kate. This was Milly's tone when the matter was left to her. Well, it should now be wholly left.

Book Seventh
....

I

WHEN KATE AND DENSHER abandoned her to Mrs. Stringham on the day of her meeting them together and bringing them into luncheon, Milly, face to face with that companion, had had one of those moments in which the warned, the anxious fighter of the battle of life, as if once again feeling for the sword at his side, carries his hand straight to the quarter of his courage. She laid hers firmly on her heart, and the two women stood there showing each other a strange face. Susan Shepherd had received their great doctor's visit, which had been clearly no small affair for her; but Milly had since then, with insistence, kept standing, as against communication and betrayal, as she now practically confessed, the barrier of their invited guests. "You've been too dear. With what I see you're full of, you treated them beautifully. *Isn't* Kate charming when she wants to be?"

Poor Susie's expression, contending at first, as in a high, fine spasm, with different dangers, had now quite let itself go. She had to make an effort to reach a point in space already so remote. "Miss Croy? Oh, she was

pleasant and clever. She knew," Mrs. Stringham added.
"She knew."

Milly braced herself—but conscious, above all, for
the moment, of a high compassion for her mate. She
made her out as struggling—struggling in all her nature
against the betrayal of pity, which in itself, given her
nature, could only be a torment. Milly gathered from
the struggle how much there was of the pity, and how
therefore it was both in her tenderness and in her conscience that Mrs. Stringham suffered. Wonderful and
beautiful it was that this impression instantly steadied
the girl. Ruefully asking herself on what basis of ease,
with the drop of their barrier, they were to find themselves together, she felt the question met with a relief
that was almost joy. The basis, the inevitable basis, was
that she was going to be sorry for Susie, who, to all
appearance, had been condemned, in so much more
uncomfortable a manner, to be sorry for _her_. Mrs.
Stringham's sorrow would hurt Mrs. Stringham; but
how could her own ever hurt? She had, the poor girl, at
all events, on the spot, five minutes of exaltation in
which she turned the tables on her friend with a pass of
the hand, a gesture of an energy that made a wind in the
air. "Kate knew" she asked, "that you were full of Sir
Luke Strett?"

"She spoke of nothing, but she was gentle and nice;
she seemed to want to help me through." Which the
good lady had no sooner said, however, than she almost
tragically gasped at herself. She glared at Milly with a
pretended pluck. "'What I mean is that she saw one had

been taken up with something. When I say she knows I should say she's a person who guesses." And her grimace was also, on its side, heroic. "But *she* doesn't matter, Milly."

The girl felt she by this time could face anything. "Nobody matters, Susie—nobody." Which her next words, however, rather contradicted. "Did he take it ill that I wasn't here to see him? Wasn't it really just what he wanted—to have it out, so much more simply, with *you?*"

"We didn't have anything 'out,' Milly," Mrs. Stringham delicately quavered.

"Didn't he awfully like you," Milly went on, "and didn't he think you the most charming person I could possibly have referred him to for an account of me? Didn't you hit it off tremendously together and in fact fall quite in love, so that it will really be a great advantage for you to have me as a common ground? You're going to make, I can see, no end of a good thing of me."

"My own child, my own child!" Mrs. Stringham pleadingly murmured; yet showing as she did so that she feared the effect even of deprecation.

"Isn't he beautiful and good too himself?—altogether, whatever he may say, a lovely acquaintance to have made? You're just the right people for me—I see it now; and do you know what, between you, you must do?" Then as Susie still but stared, wonderstruck and holding herself: "You must simply see me through. Any way you choose. Make it out together. I, on my side, will be

beautiful too, and we'll be—the three of us, with whatever others, oh, as many as the case requires, any one
you like!—a sight for the gods. I'll be as easy for you
as carrying a feather." Susie took it for a moment in
such silence that her young friend almost saw her—and
scarcely withheld the observation—as taking it for "a
part of the disease." This accordingly helped Milly to
be, as she judged, definite and wise. "He is, at any rate,
awfully interesting, isn't he?—which is so much to the
good. We haven't at least—as we might have, with the
way we tumbled into it—got hold of one of the dreary."

"Interesting, dearest?"—Mrs. Stringham felt her feet
firmer. "I don't know if he's interesting or not; but I do
know, my own," she continued to quaver, "that he's just
as much interested as you could possibly desire."

"Certainly—that's it. Like all the world."

"No, my precious, not like all the world. Very much
more deeply and intelligently."

"Ah, there you are!" Milly laughed. "That's the way,
Susie, I want you. So 'buck' up, my dear. We'll have
beautiful times with him. Don't worry."

"I'm not worrying, Milly." And poor Susie's face reg-
istered the sublimity of her lie.

It was at this that, too sharply penetrated, her companion went to her, met by her with an embrace in
which things were said that exceeded speech. Each held
and clasped the other as if to console her for this
unnamed woe, the woe for Mrs. Stringham of learning
the torment of helplessness, the woe for Milly of having *her*, at such a time, to think of. Milly's assumption

was immense, and the difficulty for her friend was that of not being able to gainsay it without bringing it more to the proof than tenderness and vagueness could permit. Nothing in fact came to the proof between them but that they could thus cling together—except indeed that, as we have indicated, the pledge of protection and support was all the younger woman's own. "I don't ask you," she presently said, "what he told you for yourself, nor what he told you to tell me, nor how he took it, really, that I had left him to you, nor what passed between you about me in any way. It wasn't to get that out of you that I took my means to make sure of your meeting freely—for there are things I don't want to know. I shall see him again and again, and I shall know more than enough. All I do want is that you shall see me through on *his* basis, whatever it is; which it's enough—for the purpose—that you yourself should know: that is with him to show you how. I'll make it charming for you—that's what I mean; I'll keep you up to it in such a way that half the time you won't know you're doing it. And for that you're to rest upon me. There. It's understood. We keep each other going, and you may absolutely feel of me that I shan't break down. So, with the way you haven't so much as a dig of the elbow to fear, how could you be safer?"

"He told me I *can* help you—of course, he told me that," Susie, on her side, eagerly contended. "Why shouldn't he, and for what else have I come out with you? But he told me nothing dreadful—nothing, nothing, nothing," the poor lady passionately protested.

"Only that you must do as you like and as he tells you—which *is* just simply to do as you like."

"I must keep in sight of him. I must from time to time go to him. But that's of course doing as I like. It's lucky," Milly smiled, "that I like going to him."

Mrs. Stringham was here in agreement; she gave a clutch at the account of their situation that most showed it as workable. "That's what *will* be charming for me, and what I'm sure he really wants of me—to help you to do as you like."

"And also a little, won't it be," Milly laughed, "to save me from the consequences? Of course," she added, "there must first *be* things I like."

"Oh, I think you'll find some," Mrs. Stringham more bravely said. "I think there *are* some—as for instance just this one. I mean," she explained, "really having us so."

Milly thought. "Just as I wanted you comfortable about *him*, and him the same about you? Yes—I shall get the good of it."

Susan Shepherd appeared to wander from this into a slight confusion. "Which of them are you talking of?"

Milly wondered an instant—then had a light. "I'm not talking of Mr. Densher." With which moreover she showed amusement. "Though if you can be comfortable about Mr. Densher too, so much the better."

"Oh, you meant Sir Luke Strett? Certainly, he's a fine type. Do you know," Susie continued, "whom he reminds me of? Of *our* great man—Dr. Buttrick of Boston."

Milly recognised Dr. Buttrick of Boston, but she dropped him after a tributary pause. "What do you think, now that you've seen him, of Mr. Densher?"

It was not till after consideration, with her eyes fixed on her friend's, that Susie produced her answer. "I think he's very handsome."

Milly remained smiling at her, though putting on a little the manner of a teacher with a pupil. "Well, that will do for the first time. I *have* done," she went on, "what I wanted."

"Then that's all *we* want. You see there are plenty of things."

Milly shook her head for the "plenty." "The best is not to know—that includes them all. I don't—I don't know. Nothing about anything—except that you're *with* me. Remember that, please. There won't be anything that, on my side, for you, I shall forget. So it's all right."

The effect of it by this time was fairly, as intended, to sustain Susie who dropped in spite of herself into the reassuring. "Most certainly it's all right. I think you ought to understand that he sees no reason——"

"Why I shouldn't have a grand long life?" Milly had taken it straight up as if to understand it and for a moment consider it. But she disposed of it otherwise. "Oh, of course, I know *that*." She spoke as if her friend's point were small.

Mrs. Stringham tried to enlarge it. "Well, what I mean is that he didn't say to me anything that he hasn't said to yourself."

"Really?—I would in his place." She might have been

disappointed, but she had her good humour. "He tells
me to *live*"—and she oddly limited the word.

It left Susie a little at sea. "Then what do you want
more?"

"My dear," the girl presently said, "I don't 'want,'
as I assure you, anything. Still," she added, "I *am* living.
Oh yes, I'm living."

It put them again face to face, but it had wound Mrs.
Stringham up. "So am I then, you'll see!"—she spoke
with the note of her recovery. Yet it was her wisdom
now—meaning by it as much as she did—not to say
more than that. She had risen by Milly's aid to a certain command of what was before them; the ten minutes
of their talk had, in fact, made her more distinctly aware
of the presence in her mind of a new idea. It was really
perhaps an old idea with a new value; it had at all events
begun during the last hour, though at first but feebly, to
shine with a special light. That was because, in the
morning, darkness had so suddenly descended—a sufficient shade of night to bring out the power of a star.
The dusk might be thick yet, but the sky had comparatively cleared; and Susan Shepherd's star, from this
time on, continued to twinkle for her. It was for the
moment, after her passage with Milly, the one spark left
in the heavens. She recognised, as she continued to
watch it, that it had really been set there by Sir Luke
Strett's visit and that the impressions immediately following had done no more than fix it. Milly's reappearance with Mr. Densher at her heels—or, so oddly
perhaps, at Miss Croy's heels, Miss Croy being at

Milly's—had contributed to this effect, though it was
ónly with the lapse of the greater obscurity that Susie
made that out. The obscurity had reigned during the
hour of their friends' visit, faintly clearing indeed while,
in one of the rooms, Kate Croy's remarkable advance to
her intensified the fact that Milly and the young man
were conjoined in the other. If it hadn't acquired on the
spot all the intensity of which it was capable, this was
because the poor lady still sat in her primary gloom, the
gloom the great benignant doctor had practically left
behind him.

The intensity the circumstance in question *might*
wear to the informed imagination would have been sufficiently revealed for us, no doubt—and with other
things to our purpose—in two or three of those confi-
dential passages with Mrs. Lowder that she now permitted herself. She had not yet been so glad that she
believed in her old friend; for if she had not had, at such
a pass, somebody or other to believe in she would certainly have stumbled by the way. Discretion had ceased
to consist of silence; silence was gross and thick; whereas
wisdom should taper, however tremulously, to a point.
She betook herself to Lancaster Gate the morning after
the colloquy just noted; and there, in Maud Manningham's own sanctum, she gradually found relief in giving
an account of herself. An account of herself was one of
the things that she had long been in the habit of expecting herself regularly to give—the regularity depending
of course much on such tests of merit as might, by laws
beyond her control, rise in her path. She never

spared herself in short a proper sharpness of conception
of how she had behaved, and it was a statement that she
for the most part found herself able to make. What had
happened at present was that nothing, as she felt, was
left of her to report to; she was all too sunk in the
inevitable, and the abysmal. To give an account of herself she must give it to somebody else, and her first
instalment of it to her hostess was that she must please
let her cry. She couldn't cry, with Milly in observation,
at the hotel, which she had accordingly left for that purpose; and the power happily came to her with the good
opportunity. She cried and cried at first—she confined
herself to that; it was for the time the best statement of
her business. Mrs. Lowder moreover intelligently took it
as such, though knocking off a note or two more, as she
said, while Susie sat near her table. She could resist the
contagion of tears, but her patience did justice to her
visitor's most vivid plea for it. "I shall never be able,
you know, to cry again—at least not ever with *her;* so I
must take it out when I can. Even if she does herself, it
won't be for me to give away; for what would that be
but a confession of despair? I'm not with her for that—
I'm with her to be regularly sublime. Besides, Milly
won't cry herself."

"I'm sure I hope," said Mrs. Lowder, "that she won't
have occasion to."

"She won't even if she does have occasion. She won't
shed a tear. There's something that will prevent her.".

"Oh!" said Mrs. Lowder.

"Yes, her pride," Mrs. Stringham explained in spite

of her friend's doubt, and it was with this that her communication took consistent form. It had never been
pride, Maud Manningham had hinted, that kept *her*
from crying when other things made for it; it had only
been that these same things, at such times, made still
more for business, arrangements, correspondence, the
ringing of bells, the marshalling of servants, the taking
of decisions. "I might be crying now," she said, "if I
weren't writing letters"—and this quite without harsh-
ness for her anxious companion, to whom she allowed
just the administrative margin for difference. She had
interrupted her no more than she would have interrupted the piano-tuner. It gave poor Susie time; and
when Mrs. Lowder, to save appearances and catch the
post, had, with her addressed and stamped notes, met at
the door of the room the footman summoned by the
pressure of a knob, the facts of the case were sufficiently
ready for her. It took but two or three, however, given
their importance, to lay the ground for the great one—
Mrs. Stringham's interview of the day before with Sir
Luke, who had wished to see her about Milly.

"He had wished it himself?"

"I think he was glad of it. Clearly indeed he was. He
stayed a quarter of an hour. I could see that for *him* it
was long. He's interested," said Mrs. Stringham.

"Do you mean in her case?"

"He says it *isn't* a case."

"What then is it?"

"It isn't, at least," Mrs. Stringham explained, "the
case she believed it to be—thought it at any rate *might*

be—when, without my knowledge, she went to see him.
She went because there was something she was afraid of,
and he examined her thoroughly—he has made sure.
She's wrong—she hasn't what she thought."

"And what did she think?" Mrs. Lowder demanded.

"He didn't tell me."

"And you didn't ask?"

"I asked nothing," said poor Susie—"I only took
what he gave me. He gave me no more than he had to—
he was beautiful," she went on. "He *is,* thank God,
interested."

"He must have been interested in *you,* dear," Maud
Manningham observed with kindness.

Her visitor met it with candour. "Yes, love, I think
he *is.* I mean that he sees what he can do with me."

Mrs. Lowder took it rightly. "For *her.*"

"For her. Anything in the world he will or he must.
He can use me to the last bone, and he likes at least
that. He says the great thing for her is to be happy."

"It's surely the great thing for everyone. Why, therefore," Mrs. Lowder handsomely asked, "should we cry
so hard about it?"

"Only," poor Susie wailed, "that it's so strange, so
beyond us. I mean if she can't be."

"She must be." Mrs. Lowder knew no impossibles.
"She *shall* be."

"Well—if you'll help. He thinks, you know, we *can*
help."

Mrs. Lowder faced a moment, in her massive way,
what Sir Luke Strett thought. She sat back there, her

knees apart, not unlike a picturesque ear-ringed matron at a market-stall; while her friend, before her, dropped their items, tossed the separate truths of the matter one by one, into her capacious lap. "But is that all he came to you for—to tell you she must be happy?"

"That she must be *made* so—that's the point. It seemed enough, as he told me," Mrs. Stringham went on; "he makes it, somehow, such a grand, possible affair."

" Ah, well, if he makes it possible!"

"I mean especially he makes it grand. He gave it to me, that is, as my part. The rest's his own."

"And what is the rest?" Mrs. Lowder asked.

"I don't know. *His* business. He means to keep hold of her."

"Then why do you say it isn't a 'case'? It must be very much of one."

Everything in Mrs. Stringham confessed to the extent of it. "It's only that it isn't *the* case she herself supposed."

"It's another?"

"It's another."

"Examining her for what she supposed, he finds something else?"

"Something else."

"And what does he find?"

"Ah," Mrs. Stringham cried, "God keep me from knowing!"

"He didn't tell you that?"

But poor Susie had recovered herself. "What I mean

is that if it's there I shall know in time. He's considering, but I can trust him for it—because he does, I feel, trust me. He's considering," she repeated.

"He's, in other words, not sure?"

"Well, he's watching. I think that's what he means. She's to get away now, but to come back to him in three months."

"Then I think," said Maud Lowder, "that he oughtn't meanwhile to scare us."

It roused Susie a little, Susie being already enrolled in the great doctor's cause. This came out at least in her glimmer of reproach. "Does it scare us to enlist us for her happiness?"

Mrs. Lowder was rather stiff for it. "Yes; it scares *me*. I'm always scared—I may call it so—till I understand. What happiness is he talking about?"

Mrs. Stringham at this came straight. "Oh, you know!"

She had really said it so that her friend had to take it; which the latter in fact after a moment, showed herself as having done. A strange light humour in the matter even perhaps suddenly aiding, she met it with a certain accommodation. "Well, say one seems to see. The point is——" But, fairly too full now of her question, she dropped.

"The point is will it *cure?*"

"Precisely. Is it absolutely a remedy—*the* specific?"

"Well, I should think we might know!" Mrs. Stringham delicately declared.

"Ah, but we haven't the complaint."

"Have you never, dearest, been in love?" Susan Shepherd inquired.

"Yes, my child; but not by the doctor's direction."

Maud Manningham had spoken perforce with a break into momentary mirth, which operated—and happily too—as a challenge to her visitor's spirit. "Oh, of course we don't ask his leave to fall. But it's something to know he thinks it good for us."

"My dear woman," Mrs. Lowder cried, "it strikes me we know it without him. So that when *that's* all he has to tell us——!"

"Ah," Mrs. Stringham interposed, "it isn't all. I feel Sir Luke will have more; he won't have put me off with anything inadequate. I'm to see him again; he as good as told me that he'll wish it. So it won't be for nothing."

"Then what will it be for? Do you mean he has somebody of his own to propose? Do you mean you told him nothing?"

Mrs. Stringham dealt with these questions. "I showed him I understood him. That was all I could do. I didn't feel at liberty to be explicit; but I felt, even though his visit so upset me, the comfort of what I had from you night before last."

"What I spoke to you of in the carriage when we had left her with Kate?"

"You had *seen*, apparently, in three minutes. And now that he's here, now that I've met him and had my impression of him, I feel," said Mrs. Stringham, "that you've been magnificent."

"Of course I've been magnificent. When," asked

Maud Manningham, "was I anything else? But Milly won't be, you know, if she marries Merton Densher."

"Oh, it's always magnificent to marry the man one loves. But we're going fast!" Mrs. Stringham woefully smiled.

"The thing *is* to go fast if I see the case right. What had I, after all, but my instinct of that on coming back with you, night before last, to pick up Kate? I felt what I felt—I knew in my bones the man had returned."

"That's just where, as I say, you're magnificent. But wait," said Mrs. Stringham, "till you've seen him."

"I shall see him immediately"—Mrs. Lowder took it up with decision. "What *is* then," she asked, "your impression?"

Mrs. Stringham's impression seemed lost in her doubts. "How can he ever care for her?"

Her companion, in her companion's heavy manner, sat on it. "By being put in the way of it."

"For God's sake then," Mrs. Stringham wailed, "*put* him in the way. You have him, one feels, in your hand."

Maud Lowder's eyes at this rested on her friend's. "Is that your impression of him?"

"It's my impression, dearest, of you. You handle everyone."

Mrs. Lowder's eyes still rested, and Susan Shepherd now felt, for a wonder, not less sincere by seeing that she pleased her. But there was a great limitation. "I don't handle Kate."

It suggested something that her visitor had not yet

had from her—something the sense of which made Mrs. Stringham gasp. "Do you mean Kate cares for *him*?"

That fact the lady of Lancaster Gate had up to this moment, as we know, enshrouded, and her friend's quick question had produced a change in her face. She blinked—then looked at the question hard; after which, whether she had inadvertently betrayed herself or had only taken a decision and then been affected by the quality of Mrs. Stringham's surprise, she accepted all results. What took place in her for Susan Shepherd was not simply that she made the best of them, but that she suddenly saw more in them to her purpose than she could have imagined. A certain impatience in fact marked in her this transition: she had been keeping back, very hard, an important truth, and wouldn't have liked to hear that she had not concealed it cleverly. Susie nevertheless felt herself passing as something of a fool with her for not having thought of it. What Susie indeed, however, most thought of at present, in the quick, new light of it, was the wonder of Kate's dissimulation. She had time for that view while she waited for an answer to her cry. "Kate thinks she cares. But she's mistaken. And no one knows it." These things, distinct and responsible, were Mrs. Lowder's retort. Yet they were not all of it. "*You* don't know it—that must be your line. Or rather your line must be that you deny it utterly."

"Deny that she cares for him?"

"Deny that she so much as thinks that she does. Positively and absolutely. Deny that you've so much as heard of it."

Susie faced this new duty. "To Milly, you mean—if she asks?"

"To Milly, naturally. No one else *will* ask."

"Well," said Mrs. Stringham after a moment, "Milly won't."

Mrs. Lowder wondered. "Are you sure?"

"Yes, the more I think of it. And luckily for *me*. I lie badly."

"*I* lie well, thank God," Mrs. Lowder almost snorted, "when, as sometimes will happen, there's nothing else so good. One must always do the best. But without lies then," she went on, "perhaps we can work it out." Her interest had risen; her friend saw her as, within some minutes, more enrolled and inflamed—presently felt in her what had made the difference. Mrs. Stringham, it was true, descried this at the time but dimly; she only made out at first that Maud had found a reason for helping her. The reason was that, strangely, she might help Maud too, for which she now desired to profess herself ready even to lying. What really perhaps most came out for her was that her hostess was a little disappointed at her doubt of the social solidity of this appliance; and that in turn was to become a steadier light. The truth about Kate's delusion, as her aunt presented it, the delusion about the state of her affections, which might be removed—this was apparently the ground on which they now might more intimately meet. Mrs. Stringham saw herself recruited for the removal of Kate's delusion—by arts, however, in truth, that she as yet quite failed to compass. Or was it perhaps to be only

for the removal of Mr. Densher's?—success in which
indeed might entail other successes. Before that job,
unfortunately, her heart had already failed. She felt that
she believed in her bones what Milly believed, and what
would now make working for Milly such a dreadful
upward tug. All this, within her, was confusedly present—a cloud of questions out of which Maud Manningham's large seated self loomed, however, as a mass
more and more definite, taking in fact for the consulta-
tive relation something of the form of an oracle. From
the oracle the sound did come—or at any rate the sense
did, a sense all accordant with the insufflation she had
just seen working. "Yes," the sense was, "I'll help you
for Milly because if that comes off I shall be helped, by
its doing so, for Kate"—a view into which Mrs. Stringham could now sufficiently enter. She found herself of
a sudden, strange to say, quite willing to operate to
Kate's harm, or at least to Kate's good as Mrs. Lowder
with a noble anxiety measured it. She found herself in
short not caring what became of Kate—only convinced
at bottom of the predominance of Kate's star. Kate
wasn't in danger, Kate wasn't pathetic; Kate Croy,
whatever happened, would take care of Kate Croy. She
saw moreover by this time that her friend was travelling even beyond her own speed. Mrs. Lowder had
already, in mind, drafted a rough plan of action, a plan
vividly enough thrown off, as she said: "You must stay
on a few days, and you must immediately, both of you,
meet him at dinner." In addition to which Maud
claimed the merit of having by an instinct of pity, of

prescient wisdom, done much, two nights before, to prepare that ground. "The poor child, when I was with her there while you were getting your shawl, quite gave herself away to me."

"Oh, I remember how you afterwards put it to me. Though it was nothing more," Susie did herself the justice to observe, "than what I too had quite felt."

But Mrs. Lowder fronted her so on this that she wondered what she had said. "I suppose I ought to be edified at what you can so beautifully give up."

"Give up?" Mrs. Stringham echoed. "Why, I give up nothing—I cling."

Her hostess showed impatience, turning again with some stiffness to her great brass-bound cylinder-desk and giving a push to an object or two disposed there. "*I* give up then. You know how little such a person as Mr. Densher was to be my idea for her. You know what I've been thinking perfectly possible."

"Oh, you've been great"—Susie was perfectly fair. "A duke, a duchess, a princess, a palace: you've made me believe in them too. But where we break down is that *she* doesn't believe in them. Luckily for her—as it seems to be turning out—she doesn't want them. So what's one to do? I assure you I've had many dreams. But I've only one dream now."

Mrs. Stringham's tone in these last words gave so fully her meaning that Mrs. Lowder could but show herself as taking it in. They sat a moment longer confronted on it. "Her having what she does want?"

"If it *will* do anything for her."

Mrs. Lowder seemed to think what it might do; but she spoke for the instant of something else. "It does provoke me a bit, you know—for of course I'm a brute. And I had thought of all sorts of things. Yet it doesn't prevent the fact that we must be decent."

"We must take her"—Mrs. Stringham carried that out—"as she is."

"And we must take Mr. Densher as *he* is." With which Mrs. Lowder gave a sombre laugh. "It's a pity he isn't better!"

"Well, if he were better," her friend rejoined, "you would have liked him for your niece; and in that case Milly would interfere. I mean," Susie added, "interfere with *you*."

"She interferes with me as it is—not that it matters now. But I saw Kate and her—really as soon as you came to me—set up side by side. I saw your girl—I don't mind telling you—helping my girl; and when I say that," Mrs. Lowder continued, "you'll probably put in for yourself that it was part of the reason of my welcome to you. So you see what I give up. I do give it up. But when I take that line," she further set forth, "I take it handsomely. So good-bye to it all. Good-day to Mrs. Densher! Heavens!" she growled.

Susie held herself a minute. "Even as Mrs. Densher my girl will be somebody."

"Yes, she won't be nobody. Besides," said Mrs. Lowder, "we're talking in the air."

Her companion sadly assented. "We're leaving everything out."

"It's nevertheless interesting." And Mrs. Lowder had another thought. "*He's* not quite nobody either." It brought her back to the question she had already put and which her friend had not at the time met. "What, in fact, do you make of him?"

Susan Shepherd, at this, for reasons not clear even to herself was moved a little to caution. So she remained general. "He's charming."

She had met Mrs. Lowder's eyes with that extreme pointedness in her own to which people resort when they are not quite candid—a circumstance that had its effect. "Yes; he's charming."

The effect of the words, however, was equally marked; they almost determined in Mrs. Stringham a return of amusement. "I thought you didn't like him!"

"I don't like him for Kate."

"But you don't like him for Milly either."

Mrs. Stringham rose as she spoke, and her friend also got up. "I like him, my dear, for myself."

"Then that's the best way of all."

"Well, it's one way. He's not good enough for my niece, and he's not good enough for you. One's an aunt, one's a wretch and one's a fool."

"Oh, *I'm* not—not either," Susie declared.

But her companion kept on. "One lives for others. *You* do that. If I were living for myself I shouldn't at all mind him."

But Mrs. Stringham was sturdier. "Ah, if I find him charming it's however I'm living."

Well, it broke Mrs. Lowder down. She hung fire but

an instant, giving herself away with a laugh. "Of course he's all right in himself."

"That's all I contend," Susie said with more reserve; and the note in question—what Merton Densher was "in himself"—closed practically, with some inconsequence, this first of their councils.

II

IT HAD AT LEAST made the difference for them, they could feel, of an informed state in respect to the great doctor, whom they were now to take as watching, waiting, studying, or at any rate as proposing to himself some such process before he should make up his mind. Mrs. Stringham understood him as considering the matter meanwhile in a spirit that, on this same occasion, at Lancaster Gate, she had come back to a rough notation of before retiring. She followed the course of his reckoning. If what they had talked of *could* happen—if Milly, that is, could have her thoughts taken off herself—it wouldn't do any harm and might conceivably do much good. If it couldn't happen—if, anxiously, though tactfully working, they themselves, conjoined, could do nothing to contribute to it—they would be in no worse a box than before. Only in this latter case the girl would have had her free range for the summer, for the autumn; she would have done her best in the sense enjoined on her, and, coming back at the end to her eminent man, would—besides having more to show him—find him more ready to go on with her. It was visible further to

Susan Shepherd—as well as being ground for a second report to her old friend—that Milly did her part for a working view of the general case, inasmuch as she mentioned frankly and promptly that she meant to go and say good-bye to Sir Luke Strett and thank him. She even specified what she was to thank him for, his having been so easy about her behaviour.

"You see I didn't know that—for the liberty I took— I shouldn't afterwards get a stiff note from him."

So much Milly had said to her, and it had made her a trifle rash. "Oh, you'll never get a stiff note from him in your life."

She felt her rashness, the next moment, at her young friend's question. "Why not, as well as any one else who has played him a trick?"

"Well, because he doesn't regard it as a trick. He could understand your action. It's all right, you see."

"Yes—I do see. It *is* all right. He's easier with me than with any one else, because that's the way to let me down. He's only making believe, and I'm not worth hauling up."

Rueful at having provoked again this ominous flare, poor Susie grasped at her only advantage. "Do you really accuse a man like Sir Luke Strett of trifling with you?"

She couldn't blind herself to the look her companion gave her—a strange, half-amused perception of what she made of it. "Well, so far as it's trifling with me to pity me so much."

"He doesn't pity you," Susie earnestly reasoned. "He just—the same as any one else—likes you."

"He has no business then to like me. He's not the same as any one else."

"Why not, if he wants to work for you?"

Milly gave her another look, but this time a wonderful smile. "Ah, there you are!" Mrs. Stringham coloured, for there indeed she was again. But Milly let her off. "Work for me, all the same—work for me! It is of course what I want." Then, as usual, she embraced her friend. "I'm not going to be as nasty as this to *him*."

"I'm sure I hope not!"—and Mrs. Stringham laughed for the kiss. "I've no doubt, however, he'd take it from you! It's you, my dear, who are not the same as any one else."

Milly's assent to which, after an instant, gave her the last word. "No, so that people can take anything from me." And what Mrs. Stringham did indeed resignedly take after this was the absence, on her part, of any account of the visit then paid. It was the beginning in fact, between them, of an odd independence—an independence positively of action and custom—on the subject of Milly's future. They went their separate ways, with the girl's intense assent; this being really nothing but what she had so wonderfully put in her plea for after Mrs. Stringham's first encounter with Sir Luke. She fairly favoured the idea that Susie had or was to have other encounters—private, pointed, personal; she favoured every idea, but most of all the idea that she herself was to go on as if nothing were the matter. Since she was to be worked for, that would be her way; and though her companion learned from herself nothing of it, that was in the event her way with her medical adviser. She put her visit to him on the simplest ground; she had just come to tell him how touched she had been by his good nature. This required little explaining, for, as Mrs. Stringham had said, he quite understood, he could but reply that it was all right.

"I had a charming quarter of an hour with that clever lady. You've got good friends."

"So each one of them thinks—of all the others. But so I also think," Milly went on, "of all of them together. You're excellent for each other. And it's in that way, I dare say, that you're best for me."

There came to her on this occasion one of the strangest of her impressions, which was at the same time one of the finest of her alarms—the glimmer of a vision that if she should go, as it were, too far, she might perhaps deprive their relation of facility if not of value. Going too far was failing to try at least to remain simple. He would be quite ready to hate her if she did, by heading him off at every point, embarrass his exercise of a kindness that, no doubt, in a way, constituted for him a high method. Susie wouldn't hate her because Susie positively wanted to suffer for her; Susie had a noble idea that she might somehow so do her good. Such, however, was not the way in which the greatest of London doctors was to be expected to wish to do it. He wouldn't have time even if he should wish; whereby, in a word, Milly felt herself intimately warned. Face to face there with her smooth, strong director, she enjoyed at a given moment quite such another lift of feeling as she

had known in her crucial talk with Susie. It came round
to the same thing; him too she would help to help her
if that could possibly be; but if it couldn't possibly be
she would assist also to make this right. It wouldn't
have taken many minutes more, on the basis in question, almost to reverse for her their characters of patient
and physician. What *was* he, in fact, but patient, what
was she but physician, from the moment she embraced
once for all the necessity, adopted once for all the policy,
of saving him alarms about her subtlety? She would
leave the subtlety to him; he would enjoy his use of it;
and she herself, no doubt, would in time enjoy his
enjoyment. She went so far as to imagine that the
inward success of these reflections flushed her for the
minute, to his eyes, with a certain bloom, a comparative appearance of health; and what verily next occurred
was that he gave colour to the presumption. "Every little helps, no doubt!"—he noticed good-humouredly her
harmless sally. "But, help or no help, you're looking,
you know, remarkably well."

"Oh, I thought I was," she answered; and it was as if
already she saw his line. Only she wondered what he
would have guessed. If he had guessed anything at all it
would be rather remarkable of him. As for what there
was to guess, he couldn't—if this was present to him—
have arrived at it save by his own acuteness. This acuteness was therefore immense; and if it supplied the
subtlety she thought of leaving him to, his portion would
be none so bad. Neither, for that matter, would hers
be—which she was even actually enjoying. She wondered

if really then there mightn't be something for her. She
hadn't been sure in coming to him that she was "better,"
and he hadn't used, he would be awfully careful not to
use, that compromising term about her; in spite of all of
which she would have been ready to say, for the amiable
sympathy of it, "Yes, I *must* be," for he had this unaided
sense of something that had happened to her. It was a
sense unaided, because who could have told him of anything? Susie, she was certain, had not yet seen him again,
and there were things it was impossible she could have
told him the first time. Since such was his penetration,
therefore, why shouldn't she gracefully, in recognition
of it, accept the new circumstance, the one he was clearly
wanting to congratulate her on, as a sufficient cause? If
one nursed a cause tenderly enough it might produce an
effect; and this, to begin with, would be a way of nursing. "You gave me the other day," she went on, "plenty
to think over, and I've been doing that—thinking it
over—quite as you'll have probably wished me. I think
I must be pretty easy to treat," she smiled, "since you've
already done me so much good."

The only obstacle to reciprocity with him was that
he looked in advance so closely related to all one's possibilities that one missed the pleasure of really improving it. "Oh no, you're extremely difficult to treat. I've
need with you, I assure you, of all my wit."

"Well, I mean, I do come up." She hadn't meanwhile
a bit believed in his answer, convinced as she was that
if she *had* been difficult it would be the last thing he
would have told her. "I'm doing," she said, "as I like."

"Then it's as *I* like. But you must really, though we're having such a decent month, get straight away." In pursuance of which, when she had replied with promptitude that her departure—for the Tyrol and then for Venice—was quite fixed for the fourteenth, he took her up with alacrity. "For Venice? That's perfect, for we shall meet there. I've a dream of it for October, when I'm hoping for three weeks off; three weeks during which, if I can get them clear, my niece, a young person who has quite the whip hand of me, is to take me where she prefers. I heard from her only yesterday that she expects to prefer Venice."

"That's lovely then. I shall expect you there. And anything that, in advance or in any way, I can do for you——!"

"Oh, thank you. My niece, I seem to feel, does for me. But it will be capital to find you there."

"I think it ought to make you feel," she said after a moment, "that I *am* easy to treat."

But he shook his head again; he wouldn't have it. "You've not come to that *yet*."

"One has to be so bad for it?"

"Well, I don't think I've ever come to it—to 'ease' of treatment. I doubt if it's possible. I've not, if it is, found any one bad enough. The ease, you see, is for *you*."

"I see—I see."

They had an odd, friendly but perhaps the least bit awkward pause on it; after which Sir Luke asked: "And that clever lady—*she* goes with you?"

"Mrs. Stringham? Oh dear, yes. She'll stay with me, I hope, to the end."

He had a cheerful blankness. "To the end of what?"

"Well—of everything."

"Ah then," he laughed, "you're in luck. The end of everything is far off. This, you know, I'm hoping," said Sir Luke, "is only the beginning." And the next question he risked might have been a part of his hope. "Just you and she together?"

"No, two other friends; two ladies of whom we've seen more here than of any one and who are just the right people for us."

He thought a moment. "You'll be four women together then?"

"Ah," said Milly, "we're widows and orphans. But I think," she added as if to say what she saw would reassure him, "that we shall not be unattractive, as we move, to gentlemen. When you talk of 'life' I suppose you mean, mainly, gentlemen."

"When I talk of 'life,' " he made answer after a moment during which he might have been appreciating her raciness—"when I talk of life I think I mean more than anything else the beautiful show of it, in its freshness, made by young persons of your age. So go on as you are. I see more and more *how* you are. You can't," he went so far as to say for pleasantness, "better it."

She took it from him with a great show of peace. "One of our companions will be Miss Croy, who came with me here first. It's in *her* that life is splendid; and a part of that is even that she's devoted to me. But she's, above all, magnificent in herself. So that if you'd like," she freely threw out, "to see *her*——"

"Oh, I shall like to see any one who's devoted to you, for, clearly, it will be jolly to be 'in' it. So that if she's to be at Venice I *shall* see her?"

"We must arrange it—I shan't fail. She moreover has a friend who may also be there"—Milly found herself going on to this. "He's likely to come, I believe, for he always follows her."

Sir Luke wondered. "You mean they're lovers?"

"*He* is," Milly smiled; "but not she. She doesn't care for him."

Sir Luke took an interest. "What's the matter with him?"

"Nothing but that she doesn't like him."

Sir Luke kept it up. "Is he all right?"

"Oh, he's very nice. Indeed he's remarkably so."

"And he's to be in Venice?"

"So she tells me she fears. For if he is there he'll be constantly about with her."

"And she'll be constantly about with you?"

"As we're great friends—yes."

"Well, then," said Sir Luke, "you won't be four women alone."

"Oh, no; I recognise the chance of gentlemen. But he won't," Milly pursued in the same wondrous way, "have come, you see, for *me*."

"No—I see. But can't you help him?"

"Can't *you*?" Milly after a moment quaintly asked.

Then for the joke of it she explained. "I'm putting you, you see, in relation with my *entourage.*"

It might have been for the joke of it too, by this time, that her eminent friend fell in. "But if this gentleman *isn't* of your *entourage?* I mean if he's of—what do you call her?—Miss Croy's. Unless indeed you also take an interest in him."

"Oh, certainly I take an interest in him!"

"You think there may be then some chance for him?"

"I like him," said Milly, "enough to hope so."

"Then that's all right. But what, pray," Sir Luke next asked, "have I to do with him?"

"Nothing," said Milly, "except that if you're to be there, so may he be. And also that we shan't in that case be simply four dreary women."

He considered her as if at this point she a little tried his patience. "*You're* the least 'dreary' woman I've ever, ever seen. Ever, do you know? There's no reason why you shouldn't have a really splendid life."

"So everyone tells me," she promptly returned.

"The conviction—strong already when I had seen you once—is strengthened in me by having seen your friend. There's no doubt about it. The world's before you."

"What did my friend tell you?" Milly asked.

"Nothing that wouldn't have given you pleasure. We talked about you—and freely. I don't deny that. But it shows me I don't require of you the impossible."

She was now on her feet. "I think I know what you require of me."

"Nothing, for you," he went on, "*is* impossible. So go on." He repeated it again—wanting her so to feel that to-day he saw it. "You're all right."

"Well," she smiled—"keep me so."

"Oh, you'll get away from me."

"Keep me, keep me," she simply continued with her gentle eyes on him.

She had given him her hand for good-bye, and he thus for a moment did keep her. Something then, while he seemed to think if there were anything more, came back to him; though something of which there was not too much to be made. "Of course if there's anything I *can* do for your friend: I mean the gentleman you speak of——" He gave out in short that he was ready.

"Oh, Mr. Densher?" It was as if she had forgotten.

"Mr. Densher—is that his name?"

"Yes—but his case isn't so dreadful." She had within a minute got away from that.

"No doubt—if *you* take an interest." She had got away, but it was as if he made out in her eyes—though they also had rather got away—a reason for calling her back. "Still, if there's anything one can do——?"

She looked at him while she thought, while she smiled. "I'm afraid there's really nothing one can do."

III

NOT YET SO MUCH as this morning had she felt herself sink into possession; gratefully glad that the warmth of the southern summer was still in the high, florid rooms, palatial chambers where hard, cool pavements took reflections in their lifelong polish, and where the sun on the stirred sea-water, flickering up through open windows, played over the painted "subjects" in the splendid ceilings—medallions of purple and brown, of brave old melancholy colour, medals as of old reddened gold, embossed and beribboned, all toned with time and all flourished and scolloped and gilded about, set in their great moulded and figured concavity (a nest of white cherubs, friendly creatures of the air), and appreciated by the aid of that second tier of smaller lights, straight openings to the front, which did everything, even with the Baedekers and photographs of Milly's party dreadfully meeting the eye, to make of the place an apartment of state. This at last only, though she had enjoyed the palace for three weeks, seemed to count as effective occupation; perhaps because it was the first time she had been alone—really to call alone—since she had left London, her first full and unembarrassed sense of what the great Eugenio had done for her. The great Eugenio, recommended by grand-dukes and Americans, had entered her service during the last hours of all—had crossed from Paris, after multiplied *pourparlers* with Mrs. Stringham, to whom she had allowed more than ever a free hand, on purpose to escort her to the continent and encompass her there, and had dedicated to her, from the moment of their meeting, all the treasures of his experience. She had judged him in advance, polyglot and universal, very dear and very deep, as probably but a swindler finished to the finger-tips; for he was forever

carrying one well-kept Italian hand to his heart and
plunging the other straight into her pocket, which, as
she had instantly observed him to recognise, fitted it like
a glove. The remarkable thing was that these elements
of their common consciousness had rapidly gathered
into an indestructible link, formed the ground of a
happy relation; being by this time, strangely,
grotesquely, delightfully, what most kept up confidence
between them and what most expressed it.

She had seen quickly enough what was happening—
the usual thing again, yet once again. Eugenio had, in an
interview of five minutes, understood her, had got hold,
like all the world, of the idea not so much of the care
with which she must be taken up as of the ease with
which she must be let down. All the world understood
her, all the world had got hold; but for nobody yet, she
felt, would the idea have been so close a tie or won from
herself so patient a surrender. Gracefully, respectfully,
consummately enough—always with hands in position
and the look, in his thick, neat, white hair, smooth, fat
face and black, professional, almost theatrical eyes, as
of some famous tenor grown too old to make love, but
with an art still to make money—did he, on occasion,
convey to her that she was, of all the clients of his glorious career, the one in whom his interest was most personal and paternal. The others had come in the way of
business, but for her his sentiment was special. Confidence rested thus on her completely believing that: there
was nothing of which she felt more sure. It passed
between them every time they conversed; he was

abysmal, but this intimacy lived on the surface. He had taken his place already for her among those who were to see her through, and meditation ranked him, in the constant perspective, for the final function, side by side with poor Susie—whom she was now pitying more than ever for having to be herself so sorry and to say so little about it. Eugenio had the general tact of a residuary legatee—which was a character that could be definitely worn; whereas she could see Susie, in the event of her death, in no character at all, Susie being insistently, exclusively concerned in her mere make-shift duration. This principle, for that matter, Milly at present, with a renewed flare of fancy, felt that she should herself have liked to believe in. Eugenio had really done for her more than he probably knew—he didn't after all know everything—in having, for the wind-up of the autumn, on a weak word from her, so admirably, so perfectly established her. Her weak word, as a general hint, had been: "At Venice, please, if possible, no dreadful, no vulgar hotel; but, if it can be at all managed—you know what I mean—some fine old rooms, wholly independent, for a series of months. Plenty of them, too, and the more interesting the better: part of a palace, historic and picturesque, but strictly inodorous, where we shall be to ourselves, with a cook, don't you know?—with servants, frescoes, tapestries, antiquities, the thorough make-believe of a settlement."

The proof of how he better and better understood her was in all the place; as to his masterly acquisition of which she had from the first asked no questions. She

had shown him enough what she thought of it, and her
forbearance pleased him; with the part of the transaction
that mainly concerned her she would soon enough
become acquainted, and his connection with such values
as she would then find noted could scarce help growing, as it were, still more residuary. Charming people,
conscious Venice-lovers, evidently, had given up their
house to her, and had fled to a distance, to other countries, to hide their blushes alike over what they had,
however briefly, alienated, and over what they had,
however durably, gained. They had preserved and consecrated, and she now—her part of it was shameless—
appropriated and enjoyed. Palazzo Leporelli held its
history still in its great lap, even like a painted idol, a
solemn puppet hung about with decorations. Hung
about with pictures and relics, the rich Venetian past,
the ineffaceable character, was here the presence revered
and served: which brings us back to our truth of a
moment ago—the fact that, more than ever, this October morning, awkward novice though she might be,
Milly moved slowly to and fro as the priestess of the
worship. Certainly it came from the sweet taste of solitude, caught again and cherished for the hour; always a
need of her nature, moreover, when things spoke to her
with penetration. It was mostly in stillness that they
spoke to her best; amid voices she lost the sense. Voices
had surrounded her for weeks, and she had tried to listen, had cultivated them and had answered back; these
had been weeks in which there were other things they
might well prevent her from hearing. More than the

prospect had at first promised or threatened, she had felt
herself going on in a crowd and with a multiplied escort;
the four ladies pictured by her to Sir Luke Strett as a
phalanx comparatively closed and detached had in fact
proved a rolling snowball, condemned from day to day
to cover more ground. Susan Shepherd had compared
this portion of the girl's excursion to the Empress
Catherine's famous progress across the steppes of Russia; improvised settlements appeared at each turn of the
road, villagers waiting with addresses drawn up in the
language of London. Old friends, in fine, were in
ambush, Mrs. Lowder's, Kate Croy's, her own; when
the addresses were not in the language of London they
were in the more insistent idioms of the American centres. The current was swollen even by Susie's social connections; so that there were days, at hotels, at Dolomite
picnics, on lake steamers, when she could almost repay
to Aunt Maud and Kate, with interest, the debt contracted by the London "success" to which they had
opened the door.

Mrs. Lowder's success and Kate's, amid the shock of
Milly's and Mrs. Stringham's compatriots, failed but little, really, of the concert-pitch; it had gone almost as
fast as the boom, over the sea, of the last great native
novel. Those ladies were "so different"—different,
observably enough, from the ladies so appraising them;
it being, throughout, a case mainly of ladies, of a dozen
at once, sometimes, in Milly's apartment, pointing, also
at once, that moral and many others. Milly's companions were acclaimed not only as perfectly fascinating in

themselves, the nicest people yet known to the
acclaimers, but as obvious helping hands, socially speaking, for the eccentric young woman, evident initiators
and smoothers of her path, possible subduers of her
eccentricity. Short intervals, to her own sense, stood now
for great differences, and this renewed inhalation of her
native air had somehow left her to feel that she already,
that she mainly, struck the compatriot as queer and dis-
sociated. She moved such a critic, it would appear, as
to rather an odd suspicion, a benevolence induced by a
want of complete trust: all of which showed her in the
light of a person too plain and too ill-clothed for a thorough good time, and yet too rich and too befriended—
an intuitive cunning within her managing this last—for
a thorough bad one. The compatriots, in short, by what
she made out, approved her friends for their expert wisdom with her; in spite of which judicial sagacity it was
the compatriots who recorded themselves as the innocent parties. She saw things in these days that she had
never seen before, and she couldn't have said why save
on a principle too terrible to name; whereby she saw
that neither Lancaster Gate was what New York took
it for, nor New York what Lancaster Gate fondly fancied it in coquetting with the plan of a series of American visits. The plan might have been, humorously, on
Mrs. Lowder's part, for the improvement of her social
position—and it had verily, in that direction, lights that
were perhaps but half-a-century too prompt; at all of
which Kate Croy assisted with the cool, controlled facility that went so well, as the others said, with her par-

ticular kind of good looks, the kind that led you to expect the person enjoying them *would* dispose of disputations, speculations, aspirations, in a few very neatly and brightly uttered words, so simplified in sense, however, that they sounded, even when guiltless, like rather aggravated slang. It wasn't that Kate hadn't pretended too that *she* would like to go to America; it was only that with this young woman Milly had constantly proceeded, and more than ever of late, on the theory of intimate confessions, private, frank ironies that made up for their public grimaces and amid which, face to face, they wearily put off the mask.

These puttings-off of the mask had finally quite become the form taken by their moments together, moments indeed not increasingly frequent and not prolonged, thanks to the consciousness of fatigue on Milly's side whenever, as she herself expressed it, she got out of harness. They flourished their masks, the independent pair, as they might have flourished Spanish fans; they smiled and sighed on removing them; but the gesture, the smiles, the sighs, strangely enough, might have been suspected the greatest reality in the business. Strangely enough, we say, for the volume of effusion in general would have been found by either on measurement to be scarce proportional to the paraphernalia of relief. It was when they called each other's attention to their ceasing to pretend, it was then that what they were keeping back was most in the air. There was a difference, no doubt, and mainly to Kate's advantage: Milly didn't quite see what her friend could keep back, was

possessed of, in fine, that would be so subject to reten-
tion; whereas it was comparatively plain sailing for Kate
that poor Milly had a treasure to hide. This was not the
treasure of a shy, abject affection—concealment, on that
head, belonging to quite another phase of such states;
it was much rather a principle of pride relatively bold
and hard, a principle that played up like a fine steel
spring at the lightest pressure of too near a footfall.
Thus insuperably guarded was the truth about the girl's
own conception of her validity; thus was a wondering,
pitying sister condemned wistfully to look at her from
the far side of the moat she had dug round her tower.
Certain aspects of the connection of these young women
show for us, such is the twilight that gathers about
them, in the likeness of some dim scene in a Maeterlinck
play; we have positively the image, in the delicate dusk,
of the figures so associated and yet so opposed, so mutu-
ally watchful: that of the angular, pale princess, ostrich-
plumed, black robed, hung about with amulets,
reminders, relics, mainly seated, mainly still, and that of
the upright, restless, slow-circling lady of her court, who
exchanges with her, across the black water streaked with
evening gleams, fitful questions and answers. The
upright lady, with thick, dark braids down her back,
drawing over the grass a more embroidered train, makes
the whole circuit, and makes it again, and the broken
talk, brief and sparingly allusive, seems more to cover
than to free their sense. This is because, when it fairly
comes to not having others to consider, they meet in an
air that appears rather anxiously to wait for their words.

Such an impression as that was in fact grave, and might be tragic; so that, plainly enough, systematically at last, they settled to a care of what they said.

There could be no gross phrasing to Milly, in particular, of the probability that if she wasn't so proud she might be pitied with more comfort—more to the person pitying; there could be no spoken proof, no sharper demonstration than the consistently considerate attitude, that this marvellous mixture of her weakness and of her strength, her peril, if such it were, and her option, made her, kept her, irresistibly interesting. Kate's predicament in the matter was, after all, very much Mrs. Stringham's own, and Susan Shepherd herself indeed, in our Maeterlinck picture, might well have hovered in the gloaming by the moat. It may be declared for Kate, at all events, that her sincerity about her friend, through this time, was deep, her compassionate imagination strong; and that these things gave her a virtue, a good conscience, a credibility for herself, so to speak, that were later to be precious to her. She grasped with her keen intelligence the logic of their common duplicity, went unassisted through the same ordeal as Milly's other hushed follower, easily saw that for the girl to be explicit was to betray divinations, gratitudes, glimpses of the felt contrast between her fortune and her fear—all of which would have contradicted her systematic bravado. That was it, Kate wonderingly saw: to recognise was to bring down the avalanche—the avalanche Milly lived so in watch for and that might be started by the lightest of breaths; though less possibly the breath of her own stifled plaint than that of the vain sympathy, the mere helpless, gaping inference of others. With so many suppressions as these, therefore, between them, their withdrawal together to unmask had to fall back, as we have hinted, on a nominal motive—which was decently represented by a joy at the drop of chatter. Chatter had in truth all along attended their steps, but they took the despairing view of it on purpose to have ready, when face to face, some view or other of something. The relief of getting out of harness—that was the moral of their meetings; but the moral of this, in turn, was that they couldn't so much as ask each other why harness need be worn. Milly wore it as a general armour.

She was out of it at present, for some reason, as she had not been for weeks; she was always out of it, that is, when alone, and her companions had never yet so much as just now affected her as dispersed and suppressed. It was as if still again, still more tacitly and wonderfully, Eugenio had understood her, taking it from her without a word, and just bravely and brilliantly in the name, for instance, of the beautiful day: "Yes, get me an hour alone; take them off—I don't care where; absorb, amuse, detain them; drown them, kill them if you will: so that I may just a little, all by myself, see where I am." She was conscious of the dire impatience of it, for she gave up Susie as well as the others to him—Susie who would have drowned her very self for her; gave her up to a mercenary monster through whom she thus purchased respites. Strange were the turns of life and the moods of weakness; strange the flickers of fancy and the cheats

of hope; yet lawful, all the same—weren't they?—those
experiments tried with the truth that consisted, at the
worst, but in practising on one's self. She was now playing with the thought that Eugenio might *inclusively*
assist her: he had brought home to her, and always by
remarks that were really quite soundless, the conception,
hitherto ungrasped, of some complete use of her wealth
itself, some use of it as a counter-move to fate. It had
passed between them as preposterous that with so much
money she should just stupidly and awkwardly *want*—
any more want a life, a career, a consciousness, than
want a house, a carriage, or a cook. It was as if she had
had from him a kind of expert professional measure of
what he was in a position, at a stretch, to undertake for
her; the thoroughness of which, for that matter, she
could closely compare with a looseness on Sir Luke
Strett's part that—at least in Palazzo Leporelli, when
mornings were fine—showed as almost amateurish. Sir
Luke hadn't said to her "Pay enough money and leave
the rest to *me*"—which was distinctly what Eugenio did
say. Sir Luke had appeared indeed to speak of purchase
and payment, but in reference to a different sort of cash.
Those were amounts not to be named nor reckoned, and
such moreover as she wasn't sure of having at her command. Eugenio—this was the difference—could name,
could reckon, and prices of *his* kind were things she had
never suffered to scare her. She had been willing, goodness knew, to pay enough for anything, for everything,
and here was simply a new view of the sufficient quantity. She amused herself—for it came to that, since

Eugenio was there to sign the receipt—with possibilities of meeting the bill. She was more prepared than ever to pay enough, and quite as much as ever to pay too much. What else—if such were points at which your most trusted servant failed—was the use of being, as the dear Susies of earth called you, a princess in a palace?

She made now, alone, the full circuit of the place, noble and peaceful while the summer sea, stirring here and there a curtain or an outer blind, breathed into its veiled spaces. She had a vision of clinging to it; that perhaps Eugenio could manage. She was *in* it, as in the ark of her deluge, and filled with such a tenderness for it that why shouldn't this, in common mercy, be warrant enough? She would never, never leave it—she would engage to that; would ask nothing more than to sit tight in it and float on and on. The beauty and intensity, the real momentary relief of this conceit, reached their climax in the positive purpose to put the question to Eugenio on his return as she had not yet put it; though the design, it must be added, dropped a little when, coming back to the great saloon from which she had started on her pensive progress, she found Lord Mark, of whose arrival in Venice she had been unaware, and who had now—while a servant was following her through empty rooms—been asked, in her absence, to wait. He had waited then, Lord Mark, he was waiting—oh, unmistakably; never before had he so much struck her as the man to do that on occasion with patience, to do it indeed almost as with gratitude for the chance, though at the same time with a sort of notifying firmness. The

odd thing, as she was afterwards to recall, was that her
wonder for what had brought him was not immediate,
but had come at the end of five minutes; and also, quite
incoherently, that she felt almost as glad to see him, and
almost as forgiving of his interruption of her solitude, as
if he had already been in her thought or acting at her
suggestion. He was somehow, at the best, the end of a
respite; one might like him very much, and yet feel that
his presence tempered precious solitude more than any
other known to one: in spite of all of which, as he had
neither dear Susie, nor dear Kate, nor dear Aunt Maud,
nor even, for the least, dear Eugenio in person, the sight
of him did no damage to her sense of the dispersal of
her friends. She had not been so thoroughly alone with
him since those moments of his showing her the great
portrait at Matcham, the moments that had exactly
made the high-water-mark of her security, the moments
during which her tears themselves, those she had been
ashamed of, were the sign of her consciously rounding
her protective promontory, quitting the blue gulf of
comparative ignorance and reaching her view of the
troubled sea. His presence now referred itself to his
presence then, reminding her how kind he had been,
altogether, at Matcham, and telling her, unexpectedly, at
a time when she could particularly feel it, that, for such
kindness, and for the beauty of what they remembered
together, she hadn't lost him—quite the contrary. To
receive him handsomely, to receive him there, to see
him interested and charmed, as well, clearly, as
delighted to have found her without some other person

to spoil it—these things were so pleasant, for the first minutes, that they might have represented on her part some happy foreknowledge.

She gave an account of her companions, while he, on his side, failed to press her about them, even though describing his appearance, so unheralded, as the result of an impulse obeyed on the spot. He had been shivering at Carlsbad, belated there and blue, when taken by it; so that, knowing where they all were, he had simply caught the first train. He explained how he had known where they were; he had heard—what more natural?—from their friends, Milly's and his. He mentioned this betimes, but it was with his mention, singularly, that the girl became conscious of her inner question about his reason. She noticed his plural, which added to Mrs. Lowder, or added to Kate; but she presently noticed also that it didn't affect her as explaining. Aunt Maud had written to him; Kate apparently—and this was interesting—had written to him; but their design presumably hadn't been that he should come and sit there as if rather relieved, so far as *they* were concerned, at postponements. He only said "Oh!" and again "Oh!" when she sketched their probable morning for him, under Eugenio's care and Mrs. Stringham's—sounding it quite as if any suggestion that he should overtake them at the Rialto or the Bridge of Sighs would leave him temporarily cold. This precisely it was that, after a little, operated for Milly as an obscure but still fairly direct check to confidence. He had known where they all were from the others, but it was not for the others that, in

his actual dispositions, he had come. That, strange to
say, was a pity; for, stranger still to say, she could have
shown him more confidence if he himself had had less
intention. His intention so chilled her, from the moment
she found herself divining it, that, just for the pleasure
of going on with him fairly, just for the pleasure of their
remembrance together of Matcham and the Bronzino,
the climax of her fortune, she could have fallen to pleading with him and to reasoning, to undeceiving him in
time. There had been, for ten minutes, with the directness of her welcome to him and the way this clearly
pleased him, something of the grace of amends made,
even though he couldn't know it—amends for her not
having been originally sure, for instance at that first dinner of Aunt Maud's, that he was adequately human.
That first dinner of Aunt Maud's added itself to the
hour at Matcham, added itself to other things, to con-
solidate, for her present benevolence, the ease of their
relation, making it suddenly delightful that he had thus
turned up. He exclaimed, as he looked about, on the
charm of the place: "What a temple to taste and an
expression of the pride of life, yet, with all that, what a
jolly *home!*"—so that, for his entertainment, she could
offer to walk him about, though she mentioned that she
had just been, for her own purposes, in a general prowl,
taking everything in more susceptibly than before. He
embraced her offer without a scruple and seemed to
rejoice that he was to find her susceptible.

SHE COULDN'T HAVE said what it was, in the conditions, that renewed the whole solemnity, but by the end of twenty minutes a kind of wistful hush had fallen upon them, as if before something poignant in which her visitor also participated. That was nothing, verily, but the perfection of the charm—or nothing, rather, but their excluded, disinherited state in the presence of it. The charm turned on them a face that was cold in its beauty, that was full of a poetry never to be theirs, that spoke, with an ironic smile, of a possible but forbidden life. It all rolled afresh over Milly: "Oh, the impossible romance——!" The romance for her, yet once more, would be to sit there for ever, through all her time, as in a fortress; and the idea became an image of never going down, of remaining aloft in the divine, dustless air, where she would hear but the plash of the water against stone. The great floor on which they moved was at an altitude, and this prompted the rueful fancy. "Ah, not to go down—never, never to go down!" she strangely sighed to her friend.

"But why shouldn't you," he asked, "with that tremendous old staircase in your court? There ought of course always to be people at top and bottom, in Veronese costumes, to watch you do it."

She shook her head both lightly and mournfully enough at his not understanding. "Not even for people in Veronese costumes. I mean that the positive beauty is that one needn't go down. I don't move in fact," she added—"now. I've not been out, you know. I stay up. That's how you happily found me."

Lord Mark wondered—he was, oh yes, adequately human. "You don't go about?"

She looked over the place, the storey above the apartments in which she had received him, the *sala* corresponding to the *sala* below and fronting the great canal with its gothic arches. The casements between the arches were open, the ledge of the balcony broad, the sweep of the canal, so overhung, admirable, and the flutter toward them of the loose white curtain an invitation to she scarce could have said what. But there was no mystery, after a moment; she had never felt so invited to anything as to make that, and that only, just where she was, her adventure. It would be—to this it kept coming back—the adventure of not stirring. "I go about just here."

"Do you mean," Lord Mark presently asked, "that you're really not well?"

They were at the window, pausing, lingering, with the fine old faded palaces opposite and the slow Adriatic tide beneath; but after a minute, and before she answered, she had closed her eyes to what she saw and, unresistingly, dropped her face into her arms, which rested on the coping. She had fallen to her knees on the cushion of the window-place, and she leaned there, in a long silence, with her forehead down. She knew that her silence was itself too straight an answer, but it was beyond her now to say that she saw her way. She would have made the question itself impossible to others—

impossible, for example, to such a man as Merton Densher; and she could wonder even on the spot what it was a sign of in her feeling for Lord Mark that, from his lips, it almost tempted her to break down. This was doubtless really because she cared for him so little; to let herself go with him thus, suffer his touch to make her cup overflow, would be the relief—since it was actually, for her nerves, a question of relief—that would cost her least. If he had come to her moreover with the intention she believed, or even if this intention had but been determined in him by the spell of their situation, he mustn't be mistaken about her value—for what value did she now have? It throbbed within her as she knelt there that she had none at all; though, holding herself, not yet speaking, she tried, even in the act, to recover what might be possible of it. With that there came to her a light: wouldn't her value, for the man who should marry her, be precisely in the ravage of her disease? *She* mightn't last, but her money would. For a man in whom the vision of her money should be intense, in whom it should be most of the ground for "making up" to her, any prospective failure on her part to be long for this world might easily count as a positive attraction. Such a man, proposing to please, persuade, secure her, appropriate her for such a time, shorter or longer, as nature and the doctors should allow, would make the best of her, ill, damaged, disagreeable though she might be, for the sake of eventual benefits: she being clearly a person of the sort esteemed likely to do the handsome thing by a stricken and sorrowing husband.

She had said to herself betimes, in a general way, that
whatever habits her youth might form, that of seeing an
interested suitor in every bush should certainly never
grow to be one of them—an attitude she had early
judged as ignoble, as poisonous. She had had accordingly, in fact, as little to do with it as possible, and she
scarce knew why, at the present moment, she should
have had to catch herself in the act of imputing an ugly
motive. It didn't sit, the ugly motive, in Lord Mark's
cool English eyes; the darker side of it, at any rate,
showed, to her imagination, but briefly. Suspicion moreover, with this, simplified itself: there was a beautiful
reason—indeed there were two—why her companion's
motive shouldn't matter. One was that even should he
desire her without a penny she wouldn't marry him for
the world; the other was that she felt him, after all, per-
ceptively, kindly, very pleasantly and humanly, concerned for her. They were also two things, his wishing
to be well, to be very well, with her, and his beginning
to feel her as threatened, haunted, blighted; but they
were melting together for him, making him, by their
combination, only the more sure that, as he probably
called it to himself, he liked her. That was presently
what remained with her—his really doing it; and with
the natural and proper incident of being conciliated by
her weakness. Would she really have had him—she
could ask herself that—disconcerted or disgusted by it?
If he could only be touched enough to do what she preferred, not to raise, not to press any question, he might
render her a much better service than by merely

enabling her to refuse him. Again, again it was strange, but he figured to her for the moment as the one safe sympathiser. It would have made her worse to talk to others, but she wasn't afraid with him of how he might wince and look pale. She would keep him, that is, her one easy relation—in the sense of easy for himself. Their actual outlook had meanwhile such charm, what surrounded them within and without did so much toward making appreciative stillness as natural as at the opera, that she could consider she had not made him hang on her lips when at last, instead of saying if she were well or ill, she repeated: "I go about here. I don't get tired of it. I never should—it suits me so. I adore the place," she went on, "and I don't want in the least to give it up."

"Neither should I, if I had your luck. Still, with that luck, for one's *all*—! Should you positively like to live here?"

"I think I should like," said poor Milly after an instant, "to die here."

Which made him, precisely, laugh. That was what she wanted—when a person did care: it was the pleasant human way, without depths of darkness. "Oh, it's not good enough for *that*! That requires picking. But can't you keep it? It is, you know, the sort of place to see you in; you carry out the note, fill it, people it, quite by yourself, and you might do much worse—I mean for your friends—than show yourself here a while, three or four months, every year. But it's not my notion for the rest of the time. One has quite other uses for you."

"What sort of a use for me is it," she smilingly inquired, "to kill me?"

"Do you mean we should kill you in England?"

"Well, I've seen you, and I'm afraid. You're too much for me—too many. England bristles with questions. This is more, as you say there, my form."

"Oho, oho!"—he laughed again as if to humour her. "Can't you then buy it—for a price? Depend upon it that they'll treat, for money. That is, for money enough."

"I've exactly," she said, "been wondering if they won't. I think I shall try. But if I get it I shall cling to it." They were talking sincerely. "It will be my life—paid for as that. It will become my great gilded shell; so that those who wish to find me must come and hunt me up."

"Ah then, you *will* be alive," said Lord Mark.

"Well, not quite extinct perhaps, but shrunken, wasted, wizened; rattling about here like the dried kernel of a nut."

"Oh," Lord Mark returned, "we, much as you mistrust us, can do better for you than that."

"In the sense that you'll feel it better for me really to have it over?"

He let her see now that she worried him, and after a look at her, of some duration, without his glasses—which always altered the expression of his eyes—he resettled the nippers on his nose and went back to the view. But the view, in turn, soon enough released him. "Do you remember something I said to you that day at Matcham—or at least fully meant to?"

"Oh yes, I remember everything at Matcham. It's another life."

"Certainly it will be—I mean the kind of thing: what I then wanted it to represent for you. Matcham, you know," he continued, "is symbolic. I think I tried to rub that into you a little."

She met him with the full memory of what he had tried—not an inch, not an ounce of which was lost to her. "What I meant is that it seems a hundred years ago."

"Oh, for me it comes in better. Perhaps a part of what makes me remember it," he pursued, "is that I was quite aware of what might have been said about what I was doing. I wanted you to take it from me that I should perhaps be able to look after you—well, rather better. Rather better, of course, than certain other persons in particular."

"Precisely—than Mrs. Lowder, than Miss Croy, even than Mrs. Stringham."

"Oh, Mrs. Stringham's all right!" Lord Mark promptly amended.

It amused her, even with what she had else to think of; and she could show him, at all events, how little, in spite of the hundred years, she had lost what he alluded to. The way he was with her at this moment made in fact the other moment so vivid as almost to start again the tears it had started at the time. "You could do so much for me, yes. I perfectly understood you."

"I wanted, you see," he all the same explained, "to *fix* your confidence; I mean, you know, in the right place."

"Well, Lord Mark, you did—it's just exactly now, my confidence, where you put it then. The only difference," said Milly, "is that I seem now to have no use for it. Besides," she then went on, "I do seem to feel you disposed to act in a way that would undermine it a little."

He took no more notice of these last words than if she had not said them, only watching her at present as with a gradual new light. "Are you *really* in any trouble?"

To this, on her side, she gave no heed. Making out his light was a little a light for herself. "Don't say don't try to say, anything that's impossible. There are much better things you can do."

He looked straight at it and then straight over it. "It's too monstrous that one can't ask you as a friend what one wants so to know."

"What is it you want to know?" She spoke, as by a sudden turn, with a slight hardness. "Do you want to know if I'm badly ill?"

The sound of it in truth, though from no raising of her voice, invested the idea with a kind of terror, but a terror all for others. Lord Mark winced and flushed—clearly couldn't help it; but he kept his attitude together and spoke with even unwonted vivacity. "Do you imagine I can see you suffer and not say a word?"

"You won't see me suffer—don't be afraid. I shan't be a public nuisance. That's why I should have liked *this:* it's so beautiful in itself, and yet it's out of the gangway. You won't know anything about anything," she added; and then, as if to make with decision an end,

"And you *don't!* No, not even you." He faced her through it with the remains of his expression, and she saw him as clearly—for *him*—bewildered; which made her wish to be sure not to have been unkind. She would be kind once for all; that would be the end. "I'm very badly ill."

"And you don't do anything?"

"I do everything. Everything's *this*," she smiled; "I'm doing it now. One can't do more than live."

"Ah, than live in the right way, no. But is *that* what you do? Why haven't you advice?"

He had looked about at the rococo elegance as if there were fifty things it didn't give her, so that he suggested with urgency the most absent. But she met his remedy with a smile. "I've the best advice in the world. I'm acting under it now. I act upon it in receiving you, in talking with you thus. One can't, as I tell you, do more than live."

"Oh, live!" Lord Mark ejaculated.

"Well, it's immense for *me*." She finally spoke as if for amusement; now that she had uttered her truth, that he had learnt it from herself as no one had yet done, her emotion had, by the fact, dried up. There she was; but it was as if she would never speak again. "I shan't," she added, "have missed everything."

"Why should you have missed *anything*?" She felt, as he sounded this, to what, within the minute, he had made up his mind. "You're the person in the world for whom that's least necessary; for whom one would call it in fact most impossible; for whom 'missing' at all will surely require an extraordinary amount of misplaced goodwill. Since you believe in advice, for God's sake take *mine*. I know what you want."

Oh, she knew he would know it. But she had brought it on herself—or almost. Yet she spoke with kindness. "I think I want not to be too much worried."

"You want to be adored." It came at last straight. "Nothing would worry you less. I mean as I shall do it. It *is* so"—he firmly kept it up. "You're not loved enough."

"Enough for what, Lord Mark?"

"Why, to get the full good of it."

Well, she didn't after all mock at him. "I see what you mean. That full good of it which consists in finding one's self forced to love in return." She had grasped it, but she hesitated. "Your idea is that I might find myself forced to love *you*?"

"Oh, 'forced'——!" He was so fine and so expert, so awake to anything the least ridiculous, and of a type with which the preaching of passion somehow so ill consorted—he was so much all these things that he had absolutely to take account of them himself. And he did so, in a single intonation, beautifully. Milly liked him again, liked him for such shades as that, liked him so that it was woeful to see him spoiling it, and still more woeful to have to rank him among those minor charms of existence that she gasped, at moments, to remember she must give up. "Is it inconceivable to you that you might try?"

"To be so favourably affected by you——?"

"To believe in me. To believe in me," Lord Mark repeated.

Again she hesitated. "To 'try' in return for your trying?"

"Oh, I shouldn't have to!" he quickly declared. The prompt, neat accent, however, his manner of disposing of her question, failed of real expression, as he himself, the next moment, intelligently, helplessly, almost comically saw—a failure pointed moreover by the laugh into which Milly was immediately startled. As a suggestion to her of a healing and uplifting passion it *was* in truth deficient; it wouldn't do as the communication of a force that should sweep them both away. And the beauty of him was that he too, even in the act of persuasion, of self-persuasion, could understand that, and could thereby show but the better as fitting into the pleasant commerce of prosperity. The way she let him see that she looked at him was a thing to shut him out, of itself, from services of danger, a thing that made a discrimination against him never yet made—made at least to any consciousness of his own. Born to float in a sustaining air, this would be his first encounter with a judgment formed in the sinister light of tragedy. The gathering dusk of *her* personal world presented itself to him, in her eyes, as an element in which it was vain for him to pretend he could find himself at home, since it was charged with depressions and with dooms, with the chill of the losing game. Almost without her needing to speak, and simply by the fact that there could be, in such a case, no decent substitute for a felt intensity, he had to take it from her that

practically he was afraid—whether afraid to protest
falsely enough, or only afraid of what might be eventually disagreeable in a compromised alliance, being a
minor question. She believed she made out besides, wonderful girl, that he had never quite expected to have to
protest, about anything, beyond his natural convenience—more, in fine, than his disposition and habits,
his education as well, his personal *moyens* in short, permitted. His predicament was therefore one he couldn't
like, and also one she willingly would have spared him
had he not brought it on himself. No man, she was quite
aware, could enjoy thus having it from her that he was
not good for what she would have called her reality. It
wouldn't have taken much more to enable her positively
to make out in him that he was virtually capable of hint-
ing—had his innermost feeling spoken—at the propriety
rather, in his interest, of some cutting down, some dressing up, of the offensive real. He would meet that half-
way, but the real must also meet *him*. Milly's sense of it
for herself, which was so conspicuously, so financially
supported, couldn't, or wouldn't, so accommodate him,
and the perception of that fairly showed in his face, after
a moment, like the smart of a blow. It had marked the
one minute during which he could again be touching to
her. By the time he had tried once more, after all, to
insist, he had quite ceased to be so.

By this time she had turned from their window to
make a diversion, had walked him through other rooms,
appealing again to the inner charm of the place, going
even so far for that purpose as to point afresh her inde-

pendent moral, to repeat that if one only had such a house for one's own and loved it and cherished it enough, it would pay one back in kind, would close one in from harm. He quite grasped for the quarter of an hour the perch she held out to him—grasped it with one hand, that is, while she felt him attached to his own clue with the other; he was by no means either so sore or so stupid, to do him all justice, as not to be able to behave more or less as if nothing had happened. It was one of his merits, to which she did justice too, that both his native and his acquired notion of behaviour rested on the general assumption that nothing—nothing to make a deadly difference for him—ever *could* happen. It was, socially, a working view like another, and it saw them easily enough through the greater part of the rest of their adventure. Downstairs, again, however, with the limit of his stay in sight, the sign of his smarting, when all was said, reappeared for her, breaking out moreover, with an effect of strangeness, in another quite possibly sincere allusion to her state of health. He might, for that matter, have been seeing what he could do in the way of making it a grievance that she should snub him for a charity, on his own part, exquisitely roused. "It's true, you know, all the same, and I don't care a straw for your trying to freeze one up." He seemed to show her, poor man, bravely, how little he cared. "Everybody knows affection often makes things out when indifference doesn't notice. And that's why I know that *I* notice."

"Are you sure you've got it right?" the girl smiled.

"I thought rather that affection was supposed to be blind."

"Blind to faults, not to beauties," Lord Mark promptly rejoined.

"And are my extremely private worries, my entirely domestic complications, which I'm ashamed to have given you a glimpse of—are they beauties?"

"Yes, for those who care for you—as everyone does. Everything about you is a beauty. Besides which I don't believe," he declared, "in the seriousness of what you tell me. It's too absurd you should have *any* trouble about which something can't be done. If you can't get the right thing, who *can*, in all the world, I should like to know? You're the first young woman of your time. I mean what I say." He looked, to do him justice, quite as if he did; not ardent, but clear—simply so competent, in such a position, to compare, that his quiet assertion had the force not so much perhaps of a tribute as of a warrant. "We're all in love with you. I'll put it that way, dropping any claim of my own, if you can bear it better. I speak as one of the lot. You weren't born simply to torment us—you were born to make us happy. Therefore you must listen to us."

She shook her head with her slowness, but this time with all her mildness. "No, I mustn't listen to you—that's just what I mustn't do. The reason is, please, that it simply kills me. I must be as attached to you as you will, since you give that lovely account of yourselves. I give you in return the fullest possible belief of what it would be——" And she pulled up a little. "I give and

give and give—there you are; stick to me as close as you
like, and see if I don't. Only I can't listen or receive or
accept—I can't *agree*. I can't make a bargain. I can't
really. You must believe that from me. It's all I've
wanted to say to you, and why should it spoil anything?"

He let her question fall—though clearly, it might
have seemed, because, for reasons or for none, there was
so much that *was* spoiled. "You want somebody of your
own." He came back, whether in good faith or in bad, to
that; and it made her repeat her headshake. He kept it
up as if his faith were of the best. "You want somebody,
you want somebody."

She was to wonder afterwards if she had not been, at
this juncture, on the point of saying something emphatic
and vulgar—"Well, I don't at all events want *you!*"
What somehow happened, however, the pity of it being
greater than the irritation—the sadness, to her vivid
sense, of his being so painfully astray, wandering in a
desert in which there was nothing to nourish him—was
that his error amounted to positive wrongdoing. She was
moreover so acquainted with quite another sphere of
usefulness for him that her having suffered him to insist
almost convicted her of indelicacy. Why hadn't she
stopped him off with her first impression of his purpose? She could do so now only by the allusion she had
been wishing not to make. "Do you know I don't think
that you're doing very right?—and as a thing quite
apart, I mean, from my listening to you. That's not
right either—except that I'm *not* listening. You oughtn't

to have come to Venice to see *me*—and in fact you've
not come, and you mustn't behave as if you had. You've
much older friends than I, and ever so much better.
Really, if you've come at all, you can only have come—
properly, and if I may say so honourably—for the best
one, as I believe her to be, that you have in the world."

When once she had said it he took it, oddly enough,
as if he had been more or less expecting it. Still, he
looked at her very hard, and they had a moment of this
during which neither pronounced a name, each apparently determined that the other should. It was Milly's
fine coercion, in the event, that was the stronger. "Miss
Croy?" Lord Mark asked.

It might have been difficult to make out that she
smiled. "Mrs. Lowder." He did make out something,
and then fairly coloured for its attestation of his comparative simplicity. "I call *her* on the whole the best. I
can't imagine a man's having a better."

Still with his eyes on her he turned it over. "Do you
want me to marry Mrs. Lowder?"

At which it seemed to her that it was he who was
almost vulgar! But she wouldn't in any way have that.
"You know, Lord Mark, what I mean. One isn't in the
least turning you out into the cold world. There's no
cold world for you at all, I think," she went on; "nothing but a very warm and watchful and expectant world
that's waiting for you at any moment you choose to take
it up."

He never budged, but they were standing on the polished concrete and he had within a few minutes pos-

sessed himself again of his hat. "Do you want me to marry Kate Croy?"

"Mrs. Lowder wants it—I do no wrong, I think, in saying that; and she understands moreover that you know she does."

Well, he showed how beautifully he could take it; and it was not obscure to her, on her side, that it was a comfort to deal with a gentleman. "It's ever so kind of you to see such opportunities for me. But what's the use of my tackling Miss Croy?"

Milly rejoiced on the spot to be so able to demonstrate. "Because she's the handsomest and cleverest and most charming creature I ever saw, and because if I were a man I should simply adore her. In fact I do as it is." It was a luxury of response.

"Oh, my dear lady, plenty of people adore her. But that can't further the case of *all*."

"Ah," she went on, "I know about 'people.' If the case of one's bad, the case of another's good. I don't see what you have to fear from any one else," she said, "save through your being foolish, this way, about *me*."

So she said, but she was aware the next moment of what he was making of what she didn't see. "Is it your idea—since we're talking of these things in these ways— that the young lady you describe in such superlative terms is to be had for the asking?"

"Well, Lord Mark, try. She *is* a great person. But don't be humble." She was almost gay.

It was this apparently, at last, that was too much for him. "But don't you really *know*?"

As a challenge, practically, to the commonest intelligence she could pretend to, it made her of course wish to be fair. "I 'know,' yes, that a particular person is very much in love with her."

"Then you must know, by the same token, that she's very much in love with a particular person."

"Ah, I beg your pardon!"—and Milly quite flushed at having so crude a blunder imputed to her. "You're wholly mistaken."

"It's not true?"

"It's not true."

His stare became a smile. "Are you very, very sure?"

"As sure as one can be"—and Milly's manner could match it—"when one has every assurance. I speak on the best authority."

He hesitated. "Mrs. Lowder's?"

"No. I don't call Mrs. Lowder's the best."

"Oh, I thought you were just now saying," he laughed, "that everything about her is so good."

"Good for you"—she was perfectly clear. "For you," she went on, "let her authority be the best. She doesn't believe what you mention, and you must know yourself how little she makes of it. So you can take it from her. *I* take it——" But Milly, with the positive tremor of her emphasis, pulled up.

"You take it from Kate?"

"From Kate herself."

"That she's thinking of no one at all?"

"Of no one at all." Then, with her intensity, she went on. "She has given me her word for it."

"Oh!" said Lord Mark. To which he next added: "And what do you call her word?"

It made Milly, on her side, stare—though perhaps partly but with the instinct of gaining time for the consciousness that she was already a little further "in" than she had designed. "Why, Lord Mark, what should *you* call her word?"

"Ah, I'm not obliged to say. I've not asked her. You apparently have."

Well, it threw her on her defence—a defence that she felt, however, as especially of Kate. "We're very intimate," she said in a moment; "so that, without prying into each other's affairs, she naturally tells me things."

Lord Mark smiled as at a lame conclusion. "You mean then she made you of her own movement the declaration you quote?"

Milly thought again, though with hindrance rather than help in her sense of the way their eyes now met—met as for their each seeing in the other more than either said. What she most felt that she herself saw was the strange disposition on her companion's part to disparage Kate's veracity. She could be only concerned to "stand up" for that.

"I mean what I say: that when she spoke of her having no private interest——"

"She took her oath to you?" Lord Mark interrupted.

Milly didn't quite see why he should so catechise her; but she met it again for Kate. "She left me in no doubt whatever of her being free."

At this Lord Mark did look at her, though he continued to smile. "And thereby in no doubt of *your* being too?" It was as if as soon as he had said it, however, he felt it as something of a mistake, and she couldn't herself have told by what queer glare at him she had instantly signified that. He at any rate gave her glare no time to act further; he fell back on the spot and with a light enough movement, within his rights. "That's all very well, but why in the world, dear lady, should she be swearing to you?"

She had to take this "dear lady" as applying to herself; which disconcerted her when he might now, so gracefully, have used it for the aspersed Kate. Once more it came to her that she must claim her own part of the aspersion. "Because, as I've told you, we're such tremendous friends."

"Oh," said Lord Mark, who for the moment looked as if that might have stood rather for an absence of such rigours. He was going, however, as if he had, in a manner, at the last, got more or less what he wanted. Milly felt, while he addressed his next few words to leavetaking, that she had given rather more than she intended or than she should be able, when once more getting herself into hand, theoretically to defend. Strange enough in fact that he had had from her, about herself—and, under the searching spell of the place, infinitely straight—what no one else had had: neither Kate, nor Aunt Maud, nor Merton Densher, nor Susan Shepherd. He had made her within a minute, in particular, she was

aware, lose her presence of mind, and she now wished
that he would get off quickly, so that she might either
recover it or bear the loss better in solitude. If he
paused, however, she almost at the same time saw, it
was because of his watching the approach, from the end
of the *sala*, of one of the gondoliers, who, whatever
excursions were appointed for the party with the attendance of the others, always, as the most decorative, most
besashed and bestarched, remained at the palace on the
theory that she might whimsically want him—which she
never, in her caged freedom, had yet done. Brown
Pasquale, slipping in white shoes over the marble and
suggesting to her perpetually charmed vision she could
scarce say what, either a mild Hindoo, too noiseless
almost for her nerves, or simply a barefooted seaman on
the deck of a ship—Pasquale offered to sight a small
salver, which he obsequiously held out to her with its
burden of a visiting-card. Lord Mark—and as if also for
admiration of him—delayed his departure to let her
receive it; on which she read it with the instant effect
of another blow to her presence of mind. This precarious quantity was indeed now so gone that even for dealing with Pasquale she had to do her best to conceal its
disappearance. The effort was made, none the less, by
the time she had asked if the gentleman were below and
had taken in the fact that he had come up. He had followed the gondolier and was waiting at the top of the
staircase.

"I'll see him with pleasure." To which she added for

her companion, while Pasquale went off: "Mr. Merton Densher."

"Oh!" said Lord Mark—in a manner that, making it resound through the great, cool hall, might have carried it even to Densher's ear as a judgment of his identity heard and noted once before.

Book Eighth
....

I

DENSHER BECAME AWARE, afresh, that he disliked his hotel—and all the more promptly that he had had occasion of old to make the same discrimination. The establishment, choked at that season with the polyglot herd, cockneys of all climes, mainly German, mainly American, mainly English, it appeared as the corresponding sensitive nerve was touched, sounded loud and not sweet, sounded anything and everything but Italian, but Venetian. The Venetian was all a dialect, he knew; yet it was pure Attic beside some of the dialects at the bustling inn. It made, "abroad," both for his pleasure and his pain that he had to feel at almost any point how he had been through everything before. He had been three or four times, in Venice, in the other years, through this pleasant irritation of paddling away—away from the concert of false notes in the vulgarised hall, away from the amiable American families and overfed German porters. He had in each case made terms for a lodging more private and not more costly, and he recalled with tenderness these shabby but friendly asylums, the windows of which he should easily know again in passing on canal or through campo. The shabbiest now failed of an appeal to him, but he found himself at the end of forty-eight hours forming views in respect to a small independent *quartiere*, far down the Grand Canal, which he had once occupied for a month with a sense of pomp and circumstance, and yet also with a sense of initiation into the homelier Venetian mysteries. The humour of those days came back to him for an hour, and what further befell in this interval, to be brief, was that, emerging on a traghetto in sight of the house in question, he recognised on the green shutters of his old, of his young windows the strips of white pasted paper that figure in Venice as an invitation to tenants. This was in the course of his very first walk apart, a walk replete with impressions to which he responded with force. He had been almost without cessation, since his arrival, at Palazzo Leporelli, where, as happened, a turn of bad weather, on the second day, had kept the whole party continuously at home. The episode had passed for him like a series of hours in a museum, though without the fatigue of that; and it had also resembled something that he was still, with a stirred imagination, to find a name for. He might have been looking for the name while he gave himself up, subsequently, to the ramble—he saw that even after years he couldn't lose his way—crowned with his stare across the water at the little white papers.

He was to dine at the palace in an hour or two, and he had lunched there, at an early luncheon, that morning. He had then been out with the three ladies, the three being Mrs. Lowder, Mrs. Stringham and Kate, and had kept afloat with them, under a sufficient Venetian spell, until Aunt Maud had directed him to leave them and return to Miss Theale. Of two circumstances connected with this disposition of his person he was even now not unmindful; the first being that the lady of Lancaster Gate had addressed him with high publicity and as if expressing equally the sense of her companions, who had not spoken, but who might have been taken—yes, Susan Shepherd quite equally with Kate—for inscrutable parties to her plan. What he could as little contrive to forget was that he had, before the two others, as it struck him—that was to say especially before Kate—done exactly as he was bidden; gathered himself up without a protest and retraced his way to the palace. Present with him still was the question of whether he looked like a fool for it, of whether the awkwardness he felt as the gondola rocked with the business of his leaving it—they could but make, in submission, for a landing-place that was none of the best—had furnished his friends with such entertainment as was to cause them, behind his back, to exchange intelligent smiles. He had found Milly Theale twenty minutes later alone, and he had sat with her till the others returned to tea. The strange part of this was that it had been very easy, extraordinarily easy. He knew it for strange only when he was away from her, because when he was away from her he was in contact with particular things that made it so. At the time, in her presence, it was as simple as sitting with his sister might have been, and not, if the point were urged, very much more thrilling. He continued to see her as he had first seen her—that remained ineffaceably behind. Mrs. Lowder, Susan Shepherd, his own Kate, might, each in proportion, see her as a princess, as an angel, as a star, but for himself, luckily, she hadn't as yet complications to any point of discomfort: the princess, the angel, the star were muffled over, ever so lightly and brightly, with the little American girl who had been kind to him in New York and to whom, certainly—though without making too much of it for either of them—he was perfectly willing to be kind in return. She appreciated his coming in on purpose, but there was nothing in that—from the moment she was always at home—that they couldn't easily keep up. The only note the least bit high that had even yet sounded between them was this admission on her part that she found it best to remain within. She wouldn't let him call it keeping quiet, for she insisted that her palace—with all its romance and art and history—had set up round her a whirlwind of suggestion that never dropped for an hour. It wasn't, therefore, within such walls, confinement, it was the freedom of all the centuries: in respect to which Densher granted good-humouredly that they were then blown together, she and he, as much as she liked, through space.

Kate had found on the present occasion a moment to say to him that he suggested a clever cousin calling on a cousin afflicted, and bored for his pains; and though he denied on the spot the "bored," he could so far see it as an impression he might make that he wondered if

the same image wouldn't have occurred to Milly. As
soon as Kate appeared again the difference came up—
the oddity, as he then instantly felt it, of his having sunk
so deep. It was sinking because it was all doing what
Kate had conceived for him; it was not in the least
doing—and that had been his notion of his life—anything he himself had conceived. The difference, accordingly, renewed, sharp, sore, was the irritant under which
he had quitted the palace and under which he was to
make the best of the business of again dining there. He
said to himself that he must make the best of everything; that was in his mind, at the traghetto, even while,
with his preoccupation about changing quarters, he
studied, across the canal, the look of his former abode.
It had done for the past, would it do for the present?
would it play in any manner into the general necessity of
which he was conscious? That necessity of making the
best was the instinct—as he indeed himself knew—of a
man somehow aware that if he let go at one place he
should let go everywhere. If he took off his hand, the
hand that at least helped to hold it together, the whole
queer fabric that built him in would fall away in a
minute and admit the light. It was really a matter of
nerves; it was exactly because he was nervous that he
could go straight; yet if that condition should increase he
must surely go wild. He was walking, in short, on a high
ridge, steep down on either side, where the proprieties—
once he could face at all remaining there—reduced
themselves to his keeping his head. It was Kate who had
so perched him, and there came up for him at moments,

as he found himself planting one foot exactly before another, a sensible sharpness of irony as to her management of him. It wasn't that she had put him in danger— to be in real danger with her would have had another quality. There glowed for him in fact a kind of rage for what he was not having; an exasperation, a resentment, begotten truly by the very impatience of desire, in respect to his postponed and relegated, his so extremely manipulated state. It was beautifully done of her, but what was the real meaning of it unless that he was perpetually bent to her will? His idea from the first, from the very first of his knowing her, had been to be, as the French called it, *bon prince* with her, mindful of the good humour and generosity, the contempt, in the matter of confidence, for small outlays and small savings, that belonged to the man who wasn't generally afraid. There were things enough, goodness knew—for it was the moral of his plight—that he couldn't afford; but what had had a charm for him if not the notion of living handsomely, to make up for it, in another way? of not at all events reading the romance of his existence in a cheap edition. All he had originally felt in her came back to him, was indeed actually as present as ever—how he had admired and envied what he called to himself her direct talent for life, as distinguished from his own, a poor weak thing of the occasion, amateurishly patched up; only it irritated him the more that this was exactly what was now, ever so characteristically, standing out in her.

It was thanks to her direct talent for life, verily, that

he was just where he was, and that he was above all just
how he was. The proof of a decent reaction in him
against so much passivity was, with no great richness,
that he at least knew—knew, that is, how he was, and
how little he liked it as a thing accepted in mere helplessness. He was, for the moment, wistful—that above
all described it; that was so large a part of the force that,
as the autumn afternoon closed in, kept him, on his
traghetto, positively throbbing with his question. His
question connected itself, even while he stood, with his
special smothered soreness, his sense almost of shame;
and the soreness and the shame were less as he let himself, with the help of the conditions about him, regard
it as serious. It was born, for that matter, partly of the
conditions, those conditions that Kate had so almost
insolently braved, had been willing, without a pang, to
see him ridiculously—ridiculously so far as just complacently—exposed to. How little it *could* be complacently he was to feel with the last thoroughness before
he had moved from his point of vantage. His question,
as we have called it, was the interesting question of
whether he had really no will left. How could he
know—that was the point—without putting the matter
to the test? It had been right to be *bon prince*, and the
joy, something of the pride, of having lived, in spirit,
handsomely was even now compatible with the impulse
to look into their account; but he held his breath a little as it came home to him with supreme sharpness that,
whereas he had done absolutely everything that Kate
had wanted, she had done nothing whatever that he had.

So it was, in fine, that his idea of the test by which he must try that possibility kept referring itself, in the warm, early dusk, the approach of the southern night—"conditions" these, such as we just spoke of—to the glimmer, more and more ghostly as the light failed, of the little white papers on his old green shutters. By the time he looked at his watch he had been for a quarter-of-an-hour at this post of observation and reflection; but by the time he walked away again he had found his answer to the idea that had grown so importunate. Since a proof of his will was wanted it was indeed very exactly in wait for him, lurking there on the other side of the Canal. A ferryman at the little pier had from time to time accosted him; but it was a part of the play of his nervousness to turn his back on that facility. He would go over, but he walked, very quickly, round and round, crossing finally by the Rialto. The rooms, in the event, were unoccupied; the ancient *padrona* was there, with her smile all a light, but her recognition all a fable; the ancient rickety objects too, refined in their shabbiness, amiable in their decay, as to which, on his side, demonstrations were tenderly veracious; so that, before he took his way again, he had arranged to come in on the morrow.

He was amusing about it that evening at dinner—in spite of an odd first impulse, which at the palace quite melted away, to treat it merely as matter for his own satisfaction. This need, this propriety, he had taken for granted even up to the moment of suddenly perceiving, in the course of talk, that the incident would minister

to innocent gaiety. Such was quite its effect, with the aid
of his picture—an evocation of the quaint, of the hum-
blest rococo, of a Venetian interior in the true old note.
He made the point for his hostess that her own high
chambers, though they were a thousand grand things,
weren't really this; made it in fact with such success that
she presently declared it his plain duty to invite her, on
some near day, to tea. She had expressed as yet—he
could feel it as felt among them all—no such clear wish
to go anywhere, not even to make an effort for a parish
feast, or an autumn sunset, nor to descend her staircase
for Titian or Gianbellini. It was constantly Densher's
view that, as between himself and Kate, things were
understood without saying, so that he could catch in
her, as she but too freely could in him, innumerable
signs of it, the whole soft breath of consciousness meeting and promoting consciousness. This view was so far
justified to-night as that Milly's offer to him of her
company was, to his sense, taken up by Kate in spite of
her doing nothing to show it. It fell in so perfectly with
what she had desired and foretold that she was—and
this was what most struck him—sufficiently gratified
and blinded by it not to know, from the false quality of
his response, from his tone and his very look, which for
an instant instinctively sought her own, that he had
answered, inevitably, almost shamelessly, in a mere
time-gaining sense. It gave him on the spot, her failure
of perception, almost a beginning of the advantage he
had been planning for—that is, at least, if she too were
not darkly dishonest. She might, he was not unaware,

have made out, from some deep part of her, the bearing, in respect to herself, of the little fact he had announced; for she was after all capable of that, capable of guessing and yet of simultaneously hiding her guess. It wound him up a turn or two further, none the less, to impute to her now a weakness of vision by which he could himself feel the stronger. Whatever apprehension of his motive in shifting his abode might have brushed her with its wings, she at all events certainly didn't guess that he was giving their friend a hollow promise. That was what she had herself imposed on him; there had been from the first, in the prospect, a definite particular point at which hollowness, to call it by its least compromising name, would have to begin. Therefore its hour had now charmingly sounded.

Whatever in life he had recovered his old rooms for, he had not recovered them to receive Milly Theale: which made no more difference in his expression of happy readiness than if he had been—just what he was trying not to be—fully hardened and fully base. So rapid in fact was the rhythm of his inward drama that the quick vision of impossibility produced in him by his hostess' direct and unexpected appeal had the effect, slightly sinister, of positively scaring him. It gave him a measure of the intensity, the reality of his now mature motive. It prompted in him certainly no quarrel with these things, but it made them as vivid as if they already flushed with success. It was before the flush of success that his heart beat almost to dread. The dread was but the dread of the happiness to be compassed; only that was in itself a symptom. That a visit from Milly should, in this projection of necessities, strike him as of the last incongruity, quite as a hateful idea, and above all as spoiling, should one put it grossly, his game—the adoption of such a view might of course have an identity with one of those numerous ways of being a fool that seemed so to abound for him. It would remain, none the less, the way to which he should be in advance most reconciled. His mature motive, as to which he allowed himself no grain of illusion, had thus in an hour taken imaginative possession of the place: that precisely was how he saw it seated there, already unpacked and settled, for Milly's innocence, for Milly's beauty, no matter how short a time, to be housed with. There were things she would never recognise, never feel, never catch in the air, but this made no difference in the fact that her brushing against them would do nobody any good. The discrimination and the scruple were for *him*. So he felt all the parts of the case together, while Kate showed, admirably, as feeling none of them. Of course, however—when hadn't it to be his last word?—Kate was always sublime.

That came up in all connections during the rest of these first days; came up in especial under pressure of the fact that each time our plighted pair snatched, in its passage, at the good fortune of half-an-hour together, they were doomed—though Densher felt it as all by *his* act—to spend a part of the rare occasion in wonder at their luck and in study of its queer character. This was the case after he might be supposed to have got, in a

manner, used to it; it was the case even after the girl—
ready always, as we say, with the last word—had given
him the benefit of her righting of every wrong appearance, a support familiar to him now in reference to other
phases. It was still the case after he possibly might, with
a little imagination, as she freely insisted, have made
out, by the visible working of the crisis, what idea, on
Mrs. Lowder's part, had determined it. Such as the idea
was—and that it suited Kate's own book she openly
professed—he had only to see how things were turning
out to feel it strikingly justified. Densher's reply to all
this vividness was that of course Aunt Maud's intervention had not been occult, even for *his* vividness, from
the moment she had written him, with characteristic
concentration, that if he should see his way to come to
Venice for a fortnight she should engage he would find
it no blunder. It took Aunt Maud, really, to do such
things in such ways; just as it took him, he was ready
to confess, to do such others as he must now strike them
all—didn't he?—as committed to. Mrs. Lowder's admonition had been of course a direct reference to what she
had said to him at Lancaster Gate, on his withdrawing,
the night Milly had failed them through illness; only it
had at least matched that remarkable outbreak in respect
to the quantity of good nature it attributed to him. The
young man's discussions of his situation—which were
confined to Kate; he had none with Aunt Maud herself—suffered a little, it may be divined, by the sense
that he couldn't put everything off, as he privately
expressed it, on other people. His ears, in solitude, were

apt to burn with the reflection that Mrs. Lowder had simply sounded him, seen him as he was and made out what could be done with him. She had had but to whistle for him and he had come. If she had taken for granted his good nature she was as justified as Kate declared. This awkwardness of his conscience, both in respect to his general plasticity, the fruit of his feeling plasticity, within limits, to be a mode of life like another—certainly better than some, and particularly in respect to such confusion as might reign about what he had really come for—this inward ache was not wholly dispelled by the style, charming as that was, of Kate's poetic versions. Even the high wonder and delight of Kate couldn't set him right with himself when there was something quite distinct from these things that kept him wrong.

In default of being right with himself he had meanwhile, for one thing, the interest of seeing—and quite for the first time in his life—whether, on a given occasion, that might be quite so necessary to happiness as was commonly assumed and as he had up to this moment never doubted. He was engaged distinctly in an adventure—he who had never thought himself cut out for them, and it fairly helped him that he was able at moments to say to himself that he mustn't fall below it. At his hotel, alone, at night, or in the course of the few late strolls he was finding time to take through dusky labyrinthine alleys and empty *campi*, overhung with mouldering palaces, where he paused in disgust at his want of ease and where the sound of a rare footstep on

the enclosed pavement was like that of a retarded dancer
in a banquet-hall deserted—during these interludes he
entertained cold views, even to the point, at moments,
on the principle that the shortest follies are the best, of
thinking of immediate departure as not only possible
but as indicated. He had, however, only to cross again
the threshold of Palazzo Leporelli to see all the elements
of the business compose, as painters called it, differently. It began to strike him then that departure
wouldn't curtail, but would signally coarsen his folly,
and that, above all, as he hadn't really "begun" anything, had only submitted, consented, but too generously indulged and condoned the beginnings of others,
he had no call to treat himself with superstitious rigour.
The single thing that was clear, in complications, was
that, whatever happened, one was to behave as a gentleman—to which was added indeed the perhaps slightly
less shining truth that complications might sometimes
have their tedium beguiled by a study of the question
how a gentleman would behave. This question, I hasten to add, was not in the last resort Densher's greatest
worry. Three women were looking to him at once, and,
though such a predicament could never be, from the
point of view of facility, quite the ideal, it yet had, thank
goodness, its immediate workable law. The law was not
to be a brute—in return for amiabilities. He hadn't
come all the way out from England to be a brute. He
hadn't thought of what it might give him to have a fortnight, however handicapped, with Kate in Venice, to be
a brute. He hadn't treated Mrs. Lowder as if in

responding to her suggestion he had understood her—he hadn't done that either to be a brute. And what he had prepared least of all for such an anti-climax was the prompt and inevitable, the achieved surrender—*as* a gentleman, oh that indubitably!—to the unexpected impression made by poor pale exquisite Milly as the mistress of a grand old palace and the dispenser of an hospitality more irresistible, thanks to all the conditions, than any ever known to him.

This spectacle had for him an eloquence, an authority, a felicity—he scarce knew by what strange name to call it—for which he said to himself that he had not consciously bargained. Her welcome, her frankness, sweetness, sadness, brightness, her disconcerting poetry, as he made shift at moments to call it, helped as it was by the beauty of her whole setting and by the perception, at the same time, on the observer's part, that this element gained from her, in a manner, for effect and harmony, as much as it gave—her whole attitude had, to his imagination, meanings that hung about it, waiting upon her, hovering, dropping and quavering forth again, like vague, faint snatches, mere ghosts of sound, of old-fashioned melancholy music. It was positively well for him, he had his times of reflecting, that he couldn't put it off on Kate and Mrs. Lowder, as a gentleman so conspicuously wouldn't, that—well, that he had been rather taken in by not having known in advance! There had been now five days of it all without his risking even to Kate alone any hint of what he ought to have known and of what in particular therefore had taken him in.

The truth was doubtless that really, when it came to any free handling and naming of things, they were living together the five of them, in an air in which an ugly effect of "blurting out" might easily be produced. He came back with his friend on each occasion to the blessed miracle of renewed propinquity, which had a double virtue in that favouring air. He breathed on it as if he could scarcely believe it, yet the time had passed, in spite of this privilege, without his quite committing himself, for her ear, to any such comment on Milly's high style and state as would have corresponded with the amount of recognition it had produced in him. Behind everything, for him, was his renewed remembrance, which had fairly become a habit, that he had been the first to know her. This was what they had all insisted on, in her absence, that day at Mrs. Lowder's; and this was in especial what had made him feel its influence on his immediately paying her a second visit. Its influence was all there, was in the high-hung, rumbling carriage with them, from the moment she took him to drive, covering them in together as if it had been a rug of softest silk. It had worked as a clear connection with something lodged in the past, something already their own. He had more than once recalled how he had said to himself even at that moment, at some point in the drive, that he was not *there*, not just as he was in so doing it, through Kate and Kate's idea, but through Milly and Milly's own, and through himself and *his* own, unmistakably, as well as through the little facts, whatever they had amounted to, of his time in New York.

THERE WAS AT LAST, with everything that made for it, an occasion when he got from Kate, on what she now spoke of as his eternal refrain, an answer of which he was to measure afterwards the precipitating effect. His eternal refrain was the way he came back to the riddle of Mrs. Lowder's view of her profit—a view so hard to reconcile with the chances she gave them to meet. Impatiently, at this, the girl denied the chances, wanting to know from him, with a fine irony that smote him rather straight, whether he felt their opportunities as anything so grand. He looked at her deep in the eyes when she had sounded this note; it was the least he could let her off with for having made him visibly flush. For some reason then, with it, the sharpness dropped out of her tone, which became sweet and sincere. " 'Meet,' my dear man," she expressively echoed; "does it strike you that we get, after all, so very much out of our meetings?"

"On the contrary—they're starvation diet. All I mean is—and all I have meant from the day I came—that we at least get more than Aunt Maud."

"Ah, but you see," Kate replied, "you don't understand what Aunt Maud gets."

"Exactly so—and it's what I don't understand that keeps me so fascinated with the question. _She_ gives me no light; she's prodigious. She takes everything as of a natural——!"

"She takes it as 'of a natural' that, at this rate, I shall be making my reflections about you. There's every appearance for her," Kate went on, "that what she had made up her mind to as possible *is* possible; that what she had thought more likely than not to happen *is* happening. The very essence of her, as you surely by this time have made out for yourself, is that, when she adopts a view, she—well, to her own sense, really brings the thing about, fairly terrorises, with her view, any other, any opposite view, and those with it who represent it. I've often thought success comes to her"—Kate continued to study the phenomenon—"by the spirit in her that dares and defies her idea not to prove the right one. One has seen it so again and again, in the face of everything, *become* the right one."

Densher had for this, as he listened, a smile of the largest response. "Ah, my dear child, if you can *explain*, I of course needn't not 'understand.' I'm condemned to that," he on his side presently explained, "only when understanding fails." He took a moment; then he pursued: "Does she think she terrorises *us?*" To which he added while, without immediate speech, Kate but looked over the place: "Does she believe anything so stiff as that you've really changed about me?" He knew now that he was probing the girl deep—something told him so; but that was a reason the more. "Has she got it into her head that you dislike me?"

To this, of a sudden, Kate's answer was strong. "You could yourself easily put it there!"

He wondered. "By telling her so?"

"No," said Kate as with amusement at his simplicity; "I don't ask that of you."

"Oh, my dear," Densher laughed, "when you ask, you know, so little——!"

There was a full irony in this, on his own part, that he saw her resist the impulse to take up. "I'm perfectly justified in what I've asked," she quietly returned. "It's doing beautifully for you." Their eyes again intimately met, and the effect was to make her proceed. "You're not a bit unhappy."

"Oh, ain't I?" he brought out very roundly.

"It doesn't practically show—which is enough for Aunt Maud. You're wonderful, you're beautiful," Kate said; "and if you really want to know whether I believe you're doing it, you may take from me, perfectly, that I see it coming." With which, by a quick transition, as if she had settled the case, she asked him the hour.

"Oh, only twelve-ten"—he had looked at his watch. "We've taken but thirteen minutes; we've time yet."

"Then we must walk. We must go toward them."

Densher, from where they had been standing, measured the long reach of the Square. "They're still in their shop. They're safe for half-an-hour."

"That shows then, that shows!" said Kate.

This colloquy had taken place in the middle of Piazza San Marco, always, as a great social saloon, a smooth-floored, blue-roofed chamber of amenity, favourable to talk; or rather, to be exact, not in the middle, but at the point where our pair had paused by a common impulse after leaving the great mosque-like church. It rose now, domed and pinnacled, but a little way behind them, and they had in front the vast empty space, enclosed by its arcades, to which at that hour movement and traffic were mostly confined. Venice was at breakfast, the Venice of the visitor and the possible acquaintance, and, except for the parties of importunate pigeons picking up the crumbs of perpetual feasts, their prospect was clear and they could see their companions had not yet been, and were not for a while longer likely to be, disgorged by the laceshop, in one of the *loggie*, where, shortly before, they had left them for a look-in—the expression was artfully Densher's—at St. Mark. Their morning had happened to take such a turn as brought this chance to the surface; yet his allusion, just made to Kate, had not been an overstatement of their general opportunity. The worst that could be said of their general opportunity was that it was essentially in presence—in presence of everyone; everyone consisting at this juncture, in a peopled world, of Susan Shepherd, Aunt Maud and Milly. But the proof how, even in presence, the opportunity could become special was furnished precisely by this view of the compatibility of their comfort with a certain amount of lingering. The others had assented to their not waiting in the shop; it was the least, of course, the others could do. What had really helped them this morning was the fact that, on his turning up, as he always called it, at the palace, Milly had not, as before, been able to present herself. Custom and use had hitherto seemed fairly established; on his coming round, day after day— eight days had been now so conveniently marked—their friends, Milly's and his, conveniently dispersed and left him to sit with her till luncheon. Such was the perfect

operation of the scheme on which he had been, as he
phrased it to himself, had out; so that certainly there
was that amount of justification for Kate's vision of success. He *had*, for Mrs. Lowder—he couldn't help having, while sitting there—the air, which was the thing to
be desired, of no absorption in Kate sufficiently deep to
be alarming. He had failed their young hostess, each
morning, as little as she had failed him; it was only to-
day that she hadn't been well enough to see him.

That had made a mark, all round; the mark was in
the way in which, gathered in the room of state, with
the place, from the right time, all bright and cool and
beflowered, as always, to receive her descent, they—the
rest of them—simply looked at each other. It was
lurid—lurid, in all probability, for each of them privately—that they had uttered no common regrets. It was
strange for our young man above all that, if the poor girl
was indisposed to *that* degree, the hush of gravity, of
apprehension, of significance of some sort, should be the
most the case—that of the guests—could permit itself.
The hush, for that matter, continued after the party of
four had gone down to the gondola and taken their
places in it. Milly had sent them word that she hoped
they would go out and enjoy themselves, and this indeed
had produced a second remarkable look, a look as of
their knowing, one quite as well as the other, what such
a message meant as provision for the alternative beguile-
ment of Densher. She wished not to have spoiled his
morning, and he had therefore, in civility, to take it as
pleasantly patched up. Mrs. Stringham had helped the

affair out, Mrs. Stringham who, when it came to that, knew their friend better than any of them. She knew her so well that she knew herself as acting in exquisite compliance with conditions comparatively obscure, approximately awful to them, by not thinking it necessary to stay at home. She had corrected that element of the perfunctory which was the slight fault, for all of them, of the occasion; she had invented a preference for Mrs. Lowder and herself; she had remembered the fond dreams of the visitation of lace that had hitherto always been brushed away by accidents, and it had come up as well for her that Kate had, the day before, spoken of the part played by fatality in her own failure of real acquaintance with the inside of St. Mark's. Densher's sense of Susan Shepherd's conscious intervention had by this time a corner of his mind all to itself; something that had begun for them at Lancaster Gate was now a sentiment clothed in a shape; her action, ineffably discreet, had at all events a way of affecting him as for the most part subtly, even when not superficially, in his own interest. They were not, as a pair, as a "team," really united; there were too many persons, at least three, and too many things, between them; but meanwhile something was preparing that would draw the closer. He scarce knew what: probably nothing but his finding, at some hour when it would be a service to do so, that she had all the while understood him. He even had a presentiment of a juncture at which the understanding of everyone else would fail and this deep little person's alone survive.

Such was to-day, in its freshness, the moral air, as we
may say, that hung about our young friends; these had
been the small accidents and quiet forces to which they
owed the advantage we have seen them in some sort
enjoying. It seemed in fact fairly to deepen for them as
they stayed their course again; the splendid Square,
which had so notoriously, in all the years, witnessed
more of the joy of life than any equal area in Europe,
furnished them, in their remoteness from earshot, with
solitude and security. It was as if, being in possession,
they could say what they liked; and it was also as if, in
consequence of that, each had an apprehension of what
the other wanted to say. It was most of all, for them,
moreover, as if this very quantity, seated on their lips
in the bright, historic air, where the only sign for their
ears was the flutter of the doves, begot in the heart of
each a fear. There might have been a betrayal of that in
the way Densher broke the silence that had followed her
last words. "What did you mean just now that I can do
to make Mrs. Lowder believe? For myself, stupidly, if
you will, I don't see, from the moment I can't lie to her,
what else there *is* but lying."

Well, she could tell him. "You can say something
both handsome and sincere to her about Milly—whom
you honestly like so much. That wouldn't be lying; and,
coming from you, it would have an effect. You don't,
you know, say much about her." And Kate put before
him the fruit of observation. "You don't, you know,
speak of her at all."

"And has Aunt Maud," Densher asked, "told you

so?" Then as the girl, for answer, only hesitated, "You must have extraordinary conversations!" he exclaimed.

Yes, she had hesitated. But she decided. "We have extraordinary conversations."

His look, while their eyes met, marked him as disposed to hear more about them; but there was something in her own, apparently, that defeated the opportunity. He asked in a moment for something else instead, something that had been in his mind for a week, yet in respect to which he had had no chance so good as this. "Do you happen to know then, as such wonderful things pass between you, what she makes of the incident, the other day, of Lord Mark's so very superficial visit?—his having spent here, as I gather, but the two or three hours necessary for seeing our friend and yet taken no time at all, since he went off by the same night's train, for seeing any one else? What can she make of his not having waited to see *you*, or to see herself—with all he owes her?"

"Oh, of course," said Kate, "she understands. He came to make Milly his offer of marriage—he came for nothing but that. As Milly wholly declined it his business was for the time at an end. He couldn't quite on the spot turn round to make up to *us*."

Kate had looked surprised that, as a matter of taste on such an adventurer's part, Densher shouldn't see it. But Densher was lost in another thought. "Do you mean that when, turning up myself, I found him leaving her, that was what had been taking place between them?"

"Didn't you make it out, my dear?" Kate inquired.

"What sort of a blundering weathercock then *is* he?" the young man went on in his wonder.

"Oh, don't make too little of him!" Kate smiled. "Do you pretend that Milly didn't tell you?"

"How great an ass he had made of himself?"

Kate continued to smile. "You *are* in love with her, you know."

He gave her another long look. "Why, since she has refused him, should my opinion of Lord Mark show it? I'm not obliged, however, to think well of him for such treatment of the other persons I've mentioned, and I feel I don't understand from you why Mrs. Lowder should."

"She doesn't—but she doesn't care," Kate explained. "You know perfectly the terms on which lots of London people live together even when they are supposed to live very well. He's not committed to us—he was having his try. Mayn't an unsatisfied man," she asked, "always have his try?"

"And come back afterwards, with confidence in a welcome, to the victim of his inconstancy?"

Kate consented, as for argument, to be thought of as a victim. "Oh, but he has *had* his try at *me*. So it's all right."

"Through your also having, you mean, refused him?"

She balanced an instant during which Densher might have just wondered if pure historic truth were to suffer a slight strain. But she dropped on the right side. "I haven't let it come to that. I've been too discouraging. Aunt Maud," she went on—now as lucid as ever—"considers, no doubt, that she has a pledge from him in

respect to me; a pledge that would have been broken if
Milly had accepted him. As the case stands, that makes
no difference."

Densher laughed out. "It isn't *his* merit that he has
failed."

"It's still his merit, my dear, that he's Lord Mark.
He's just what he was, and what he knew he was. It's not
for me either to reflect on him after I've so treated him."

"Oh," said Densher impatiently, "you've treated him
beautifully."

"I'm glad," she smiled, "that you can still be jealous." But before he could take it up she had more to
say. "I don't see why it need puzzle you that Milly's so
marked line gratifies Aunt Maud more than anything
else can displease her. What does she see but that Milly
herself recognises her situation with you as too precious
to be spoiled? Such a recognition as that can't but seem
to her to involve in some degree your own recognition.
Out of which she therefore gets it that the more you
have for Milly the less you have for me."

There were moments again—we know that from the
first they had been numerous—when he felt with a
strange mixed passion the mastery of her mere way of
putting things. There was something in it that bent him
at once to conviction and to reaction. And this effect,
however it be named, now broke into his tone. "Oh, if
she began to know what I have for you——!"

It was not ambiguous, but Kate stood up to it.
"Luckily for us we may really consider that she doesn't.
So successful have we been."

"Well," he presently said, "I take from you what you give me, and I suppose that, to be consistent—to stand on my feet where I do stand at all—I ought to thank you. Only, you know, what you give me seems to me, more than anything else, the larger and larger size of my job. It seems to me more than anything else what you expect of me. It never seems to me, somehow, what I may expect of *you*. There's so much you *don't* give me."

"And pray what is it?"

"I give you proof," said Densher. "You give me none."

"What then do you call proof?" she after a moment ventured to ask.

"Your doing something for me."

She considered with surprise. "Am I not doing *this* for you? Do you call this nothing?"

"Nothing at all."

"Ah, I risk, my dear, everything for it."

They had strolled slowly further, but he was brought up short. "I thought you exactly contend that, with your aunt so beguiled, you risk nothing!"

It was the first time since the launching of her wonderful idea that he had seen her at a loss. He judged the next instant moreover that she didn't like it—either the being so or the being seen, for she soon spoke with an impatience that showed her as wounded; an appearance that produced in himself, he no less quickly felt, a sharp pang of indulgence. "What then do you wish me to risk?"

The appeal from danger touched him, but all to make

him, as he would have said, worse. "What I wish is to be loved. How can I feel at this rate that I *am*?" Oh, she understood him, for all she might so bravely disguise it, and that made him feel straighter than if she hadn't. Deep, always, was his sense of life with her—deep as it had been from the moment of those signs of life that in the dusky London of two winters ago they had originally exchanged. He had never taken her for unguarded, ignorant, weak; and if he put to her a claim for some intenser faith between them it was because he believed it could reach her and she could meet it. "I can go on perhaps," he said, "with help. But I can't go on without."

She looked away from him now, and it showed him how she understood. "We ought to be there—I mean when they come out."

"They *won't* come out—not yet. And I don't care if they do." To which he straightway added, as if to deal with the charge of selfishness that his words, sounding for himself, struck him as enabling her to make: "Why not have done with all and face the music as we are?" It broke from him in perfect sincerity. "Good God, if you'd only *take* me!"

It brought her eyes round to him again, and he could see how, after all, somewhere deep within, she tasted his rebellion as more sweet than bitter. Its effect on her spirit and her sense was visibly to hold her for an instant. "We've gone too far," she none the less pulled herself together to reply. "Do you want to kill her?"

He had an hesitation that was not all candid. "Kill, you mean, Aunt Maud?"

"You know whom I mean. We've told too many lies."

Oh, at this his head went up. "I, my dear, have told none!"

He had brought it out with a sharpness that did him good, but he had naturally, none the less, to take the look it made her give him. "Thank you very much."

Her expression, however, failed to check the words that had already risen to his lips. "Rather than lay myself open to the least appearance of it I'll go this very night."

"Then go," said Kate Croy.

He knew after a little, while they walked on again together, that what was in the air for him, and disconcertingly, was not the violence, but much rather the cold quietness, of the way this had come from her. They walked on together, and it was quite, for a minute, as if their difference had become, of a sudden, in all truth, a split—as if the basis of his departure had been settled. Then, incoherently and still more suddenly, recklessly moreover, since they now might easily, from under the arcades, be observed, he passed his hand into her arm with a force that produced for them another pause. "I'll tell any lie you want, any your idea requires, if you'll only come to me."

"Come to you?" She spoke low.

"Come to me."

"How? Where?"

She spoke low, but there was somehow, for his uncertainty, a wonder in her being so equal to him. "To my rooms, which are perfectly possible, and in taking which, the other day, I had you, as you must have felt, in view. We can arrange it—with two grains of courage. People in our case always arrange it." She listened as for the good information, and there was support for him— since it was a question of his going step by step—in the way she took no refuge in showing herself shocked. He had in truth not expected of her that particular vulgarity but the absence of it only added the thrill of a deeper reason to his sense of possibilities. For the knowledge of what she was he had absolutely to *see* her now, incapable of refuge, stand there for him in all the light of the day and of his admirable, merciless meaning. Her mere listening in fact made him even understand himself as he had not yet done. Idea for idea, his own was thus already, and in the germ, beautiful. "There's nothing for me possible but to feel that I'm not a fool. It's all I have to say, but you must know what it means. *With* you I can do it—I'll go as far as you demand, or as you will yourself. Without you—I'll be hanged! And I must be sure."

She listened so well that she was really listening after he had ceased to speak. He had kept his grasp of her, drawing her close, and though they had again, for the time, stopped walking, his talk—for others at a distance—might have been, in the matchless place, that of any impressed tourist to any slightly more detached companion. On possessing himself of her arm he had made her turn, so that they faced afresh to St. Mark's, over the great presence of which his eyes moved while she twiddled her parasol. She now, however, made a

motion that confronted them finally with the opposite
end. Then only she spoke—"Please take your hand out
of my arm." He understood at once: she had made out in
the shade of the gallery the issue of the others from their
place of purchase. So they went to them side by side, and
it was all right. The others had seen them as well and
waited for them, complacent enough, under one of the
arches. They themselves too—he argued that Kate would
argue—looked perfectly ready, decently patient, properly
accommodating. They suggested nothing worse—always
by Kate's system—than a pair of the children of a super-
civilised age making the best of an awkwardness. They
didn't nevertheless hurry—that would overdo it; so he
had time to feel, as it were what he felt. He felt, ever so
distinctly—it was with this he faced Mrs. Lowder—that
he was already, in a sense, possessed of what he wanted.
There was more to come—everything; he had by no
means, with his companion, had it all out. Yet what he
was possessed of was real—the fact that she hadn't
thrown over his lucidity the horrid shadow of cheap
reprobation. Of this he had had so sore a fear that its
being dispelled was in itself of the nature of bliss. The
danger had dropped—it was behind him there in the
great sunny space. So far she was good.

III

SHE WAS GOOD ENOUGH, as it proved, for him to put
to her that evening, and with further ground for it, the
next sharpest question that had been on his lips in the

morning—which his other preoccupation had then, to
his consciousness, crowded out. His opportunity was
again made, as befell, by his learning from Mrs. Stringham, on arriving, as usual, with the close of day, at the
palace, that Milly must fail them again at dinner, but
would to all appearance be able to come down later. He
had found Susan Shepherd alone in the great saloon,
where even more candles than their friend's large common allowance—she grew daily more splendid; they
were all struck with it and chaffed her about it—lighted
up the pervasive mystery of Style. He had thus five
minutes with the good lady before Mrs. Lowder and
Kate appeared—minutes illumined indeed to a longer
reach than by the number of Milly's candles.

"*May* she come down—ought she if she isn't really
up to it?"

He had asked that in the wonderment that was always
with him before glimpses—rare as were these—of the
inner truth about the girl. There was of course a question of health—it was in the air, it was in the ground
he trod, in the food he tasted, in the sounds he heard,
it was everywhere. But it was everywhere with the effect
of a request to him—to his very delicacy, to the common discretion of others as well as himself—that no
allusion to it should be made. There had practically
been none, that morning, on her explained non-
appearance—the absence of it, as we know, quite unnatural; and this passage with Mrs. Stringham offered him
his first licence to open his eyes. He had gladly enough
held them closed; all the more that his doing so per-

formed for his own spirit a useful function. If he positively wanted not to be brought up with his nose against
Milly's facts, what better proof could he have that his
conduct was marked by straightness? It was perhaps
pathetic for her, and for himself it was perhaps even
ridiculous; but he hadn't even the amount of curiosity
that he would have had about an ordinary friend. He
might have shaken himself at moments to try, for a sort
of dry decency, to have it; but that too, it appeared,
wouldn't come. Where, therefore, was the duplicity? He
was at least sure about his feelings—it being so established that he had none at all. They were all for Kate,
without a feather's weight to spare. He was acting for
Kate, and not, by the deviation of an inch, for her
friend. He was accordingly not interested, for had he
been interested he would have cared, and had he cared
he would have wanted to know. Had he wanted to know
he wouldn't have been purely passive, and it was his
pure passivity that had to represent his honour. His
honour, at the same time, let us add, fortunately fell
short, to-night, of spoiling his little talk with Susan
Shepherd. One glimpse—it was as if she had wished to
give him that; and it was as if, for himself, on current
terms, he could oblige. She not only permitted, she
fairly invited him to open his eyes. "I'm so glad you're
here." It was no answer to his question, but it had, for
the moment, to do. And the rest was fully to come.

He smiled at her, and he presently found himself, as
a kind of consequence of communion with her, talking
her own language. "It's a very wonderful experience."

"Well"—and her raised face shone up at him—
"that's all I want you to feel about it. If I weren't
afraid," she added, "there are things I should like to say
to you."

"And what are you afraid of, please?" he encourag-
ingly asked.

"Of other things that I may possibly spoil. Besides,
I don't, you know, seem to have the chance. You're
always, you know, *with* her."

He was strangely supported, it struck him, in his
fixed smile; which was the more fixed as he felt in these
last words an exact description of his course. It was an
odd thing to have come to, but he *was* always with her.
"Ah," he none the less smiled, "I'm not with her now."

"No—and I'm so glad, since I get this from it. She's
ever so much better."

"Better? Then she *has* been worse?"

Mrs. Stringham waited. "She has been marvellous—
that's what she has been. She *is* marvellous. But she's
really better."

"Oh then, if she's really better——!" But he checked
himself, wanting only to be easy about it and above all
not to show as engaged to the point of mystification.
"We shall miss her the more at dinner."

Susan Shepherd, however, was all there for him.
"She's keeping herself. You'll see. You'll not really need
to miss anything. There's to be a little party."

"Ah, I do see—by this aggravated grandeur."

"Well, it *is* lovely, isn't it? I want the whole thing.
She's lodged for the first time as she ought, from her

type, to be; and doing it—I mean bringing out all the
glory of the place—makes her really happy. It's a
Veronese picture, as near as can be—with me as the
inevitable dwarf, the small blackamoor, put into a corner
of the foreground for effect. If I only had a hawk or a
hound or something of that sort I should do the scene
more honour. The old housekeeper, the woman in
charge here, has a big red cockatoo that I might borrow
and perch on my thumb for the evening." These explanations and sundry others Mrs. Stringham gave, though
not all with the result of making him feel that the picture closed him in. What part was there for *him*, with
his attitude that lacked the highest style, in a composition in which everything else would have it? "They
won't, however, be at dinner, the few people she
expects; they come round afterwards, from their respec-
tive hotels; and Sir Luke Strett and his niece, the principal ones, will have arrived from London but an hour
or two ago. It's for *him* she has wanted to do something—just, this evening, to begin. We shall see more of
him, because she likes him; and I'm so glad—she'll be
glad too—that *you're* to see him." The good lady, in
connection with it, was urgent, was almost unnaturally
bright. "So I greatly hope——!" But her hope fairly lost
itself in the wide light of her cheer.

He considered a little this appearance, while she let
him, he thought, into still more knowledge than she
uttered. "What is it you hope?"

"Well, that you'll stay on."

"Do you mean after dinner?" She meant, he seemed

to feel, so much that he could scarce tell where it ended or began.

"Oh that, of course. Why, we're to have music—beautiful instruments and songs; and not Tasso declaimed as in the guide-books either. She has arranged it—or at least I have. That is Eugenio has. Besides, you're in the picture."

"Oh—I!" said Densher almost with the gravity of a real protest.

"You'll be the grand young man who surpasses the others and holds up his head and the wine-cup. What we hope," Mrs. Stringham pursued, "is that you'll be faithful to us—that you've not come for a mere foolish few days."

Densher's more private and particular shabby realities turned, without comfort, he was conscious, at this touch, in the artificial repose he had but half managed to induce. The way smooth ladies, travelling for their pleasure and housed in Veronese pictures, talked to plain, embarrassed working-men, engaged in an unprecedented sacrifice of time and of the opportunity of modest acquisition! The things they took for granted and the general misery of explaining! He couldn't tell them how he had tried to work, how it was partly what he had moved into rooms for, only to find himself, almost for the first time in his life, stricken and sterile; because that would give them a false view of the source of his restlessness, if not of the degree of it. It would operate indirectly perhaps, but infallibly, to add to that weight, on his heart, of conscious responsibility which these very

moments with Mrs. Stringham caused more and more to
settle. He had incurred it, conscious responsibility; the
thing was done, and there was no use talking; again,
again the cold breath of it was in the air. So there he
was. And at best he floundered. "I'm afraid you won't
understand when I say I've very tiresome things to consider. Botherations, necessities at home. The pinch, the
pressure in London."

But she understood in perfection; she rose to the
pinch and the pressure and showed how they had been
her own very element. "Oh, the daily task and the daily
wage, the golden guerdon or reward? No one knows better than I how they haunt one in the flight of the precious, deceiving days. Aren't they just what I myself
have given up? I've given up all to follow *her.* I wish you
could feel as I do. And can't you," she inquired, "write
about Venice?"

He very nearly wished, for the minute, that he could
feel as she did; and he smiled for her kindly. "Do *you*
write about Venice?"

"No; but I would—oh, wouldn't I?—if I hadn't so
completely given up. She's, you know, my princess, and
to one's princess——"

"One makes the whole sacrifice?"

"Precisely. There you are!"

It pressed on him with this that never had a man
been in so many places at once. "I quite understand that
she's yours. Only, you see, she's not mine." He felt he
could somehow, for honesty, risk that, as he had the
moral certainty that she wouldn't repeat it, least of all to

Mrs. Lowder, who would find in it a disturbing implication. This was part of what he liked in the good lady,
that she didn't repeat, and that she gave him moreover
a delicate sense of her shyly wishing him to know it.
That was in itself a hint of possibilities between them,
of a relation, beneficent and elastic for him, which
wouldn't engage him further than he could see. Yet even
as he afresh made this out he felt how strange it all was.
She wanted, Susan Shepherd then, as appeared, the same
thing that Kate wanted, only she wanted it, as still further appeared, in so different a way and from a motive
so different, even though scarce less deep. Then Mrs.
Lowder wanted, by so odd an evolution of her exuber-
ance, exactly what each of the others did; and he was
between them all, he was in the midst. Such perceptions
made occasions—well, occasions for fairly wondering if
it mightn't be best just to consent, luxuriously, to *be* the
ass the whole thing involved. Trying not to be and yet
keeping in it was of the two things the more asinine. He
was glad there was no male witness; it was a circle of
petticoats; he shouldn't have liked a man to see him. He
only had for a moment a sharp thought of Sir Luke
Strett, the great master of the knife whom Kate in London had spoken of Milly as in commerce with, and
whose renewed intervention, at such a distance, just
announced to him, required some accounting for. He
had a vision of great London surgeons—if this one was
a surgeon—as incisive all round; so that he should perhaps after all not wholly escape the ironic attention of
his own sex. The most he might be able to do was not

to care; while he was trying not to he could take that in. It was a train, however, that brought up the vision of Lord Mark as well. Lord Mark had caught him twice in the fact—the fact of his absurd posture; and that made a second male. But it was comparatively easy not to mind Lord Mark.

His companion had before this taken him up, and in a tone to confirm her discretion, on the matter of Milly's not being his princess. "Of course she's not. You must do something first."

Densher gave it his thought. "Wouldn't it be rather *she* who must?"

It had more than he intended the effect of bringing her to a stand. " I see. No doubt, if one takes it so." Her cheer was for the time in eclipse, and she looked over the place, avoiding his eyes, as if in the wonder of what Milly could do. "And yet she has wanted to be kind."

It made him feel on the spot like a brute. "Of course she has. No one could be more charming. She has treated me as if *I* were somebody. Call her my hostess as I've never had nor imagined a hostess, and I'm with you altogether. Of course," he added in the right spirit for her, "I do see that it's quite court life."

She promptly showed that this was almost all she wanted of him. "That's all I mean, if you understand it of such a court as never was: one of the courts of heaven, the court of an angel. That will do perfectly."

"Oh well then, I grant it. Only court life as a general thing, you know," he observed, "isn't supposed to pay."

"Yes, one has read; but this is beyond any book. That's just the beauty here; it's why she's the great and only princess. With her, at her court," said Mrs. Stringham, "it does pay." Then as if she had quite settled it for him: "You'll see for yourself."

He waited a moment, but said nothing to discourage her. "I think you were right just now. One must do something first."

"Well, you've done something."

"No—I don't see that. I can do more."

Oh, well, she seemed to say, if he would have it so! "You can do everything, you know."

"Everything" was rather too much for him to take up gravely, and he modestly let it alone, speaking the next moment, to avert fatuity, of a different but a related matter. "Why has she sent for Sir Luke Strett if, as you tell me, she's so much better?"

"She hasn't sent. He has come of himself," Mrs. Stringham explained. "He has wanted to come."

"Isn't that rather worse then—if it shows him as not easy?"

"He was coming, from the first, for his holiday. She has known that these several weeks." After which Mrs. Stringham added: "You can *make* him easy."

"*I* can?" he candidly wondered. It was truly the circle of petticoats. "What have I to do with it for a man like that?"

"How do you know," said his friend, "what he's like? He's not like any one you've ever seen. He's a great beneficent being."

"Ah, then he can do without me. I've no call, as an outsider, to meddle."

"Tell him, all the same," Mrs. Stringham urged, "what you think."

"What I think of Miss Theale?" Densher stared. It was, as they said, a large order. But he found the right note. "It's none of his business."

It did seem a moment, for Mrs. Stringham too, the right note. She fixed him at least with an expression still bright, but searching, that showed almost to excess what she saw in it; though what this might be he was not to make out till afterwards. "Say *that* to him then. Anything will do for him as a means of getting at you."

"And why should he get at me?"

"Give him a chance to. Let him talk to you. Then you'll see."

All of which, on Mrs. Stringham's part, sharpened his sense of immersion in an element rather more strangely than agreeably warm—a sense that was moreover, during the next two or three hours, to be fed to satiety by several other impressions. Milly came down after dinner, half-a-dozen friends—objects of interest mainly, it appeared, to the ladies of Lancaster Gate—having by that time arrived; and with this call on her attention, the further call of her musicians ushered by Eugenio, but personally and separately welcomed, and the supreme opportunity offered in the arrival of the great doctor, who came last of all, he felt her as diffusing, in wide warm waves, the spell of a general, a kind of beatific mildness. There was a deeper depth of it, doubtless, for some than for others; what he, at any rate, in particular knew of it was that he seemed to stand in it up to his neck. He moved about in it, and it made no plash; he floated, he noiselessly swam in it; and they were all together, for that matter, like fishes in a crystal pool. The effect of the place, the beauty of the scene, had probably much to do with it; the golden grace of the high rooms, chambers of art in themselves, took care, as an influence, of the general manner, and made people bland without making them solemn. They were only people, as Mrs. Stringham had said, staying for the week or two at the inns, people who during the day had fingered their Baedekers, gaped at their frescoes and differed, over fractions of francs, with their gondoliers. But Milly, let loose among them in a wonderful white dress, brought them somehow into relation with something that made them more finely genial; so that if the Veronese picture of which he had talked with Mrs. Stringham was not quite constituted, the comparative prose of the previous hours, the traces of insensibility qualified by "beating down," were at last almost nobly disowned. There was perhaps something for him in the accident of his seeing her for the first time in white, but she had not yet had occasion—circulating with a clearness intensified—to strike him as so happily pervasive. She was different, younger, fairer, with the colour of her braided hair more than ever a not altogether lucky challenge to attention; yet he was loath wholly to explain it by her having quitted this once, for some obscure, yet doubtless charming reason, her almost monastic, her

hitherto inveterate black. Much as the change did for
the value of her presence, she had never yet, when all
was said, made it for *him*; and he was not to fail of the
further amusement of seeing her as determined in the
matter by Sir Luke Strett's visit. If he could in this connection have felt jealous of Sir Luke Strett, whose strong
face and type, less assimilated by the scene perhaps than
any others, he was anon to study from the other side of
the saloon, that would doubtless have been most amusing of all. But he couldn't be invidious, even to profit by
so high a tide; he felt himself too much "in" it, as he
might have said: a moment's reflection put him more in
than any one. The way Milly neglected him for other
cares while Kate and Mrs. Lowder, without so much as
the attenuation of a joke, introduced him to English
ladies—that was itself a proof; for nothing really of so
close a communion had up to this time passed between
them as the single bright look and the three gay words—
all ostensibly of the last lightness—with which her confessed consciousness brushed by him.

She was acquitting herself to-night as hostess, he
could see, under some supreme idea, an inspiration
which was half her nerves and half an inevitable harmony; but what he especially recognised was the character that had already several times broken out in her
and that she so oddly appeared able by choice or by
instinctive affinity, to keep down or to display. She was
the American girl as he had originally found her—found
her at certain moments, it was true, in New York, more
than at certain others; she was the American girl as, still

more than then, he had seen her on the day of her meeting him, in London, in Kate's company. It affected him as a large though queer social resource in her—such as a man, for instance, to his diminution, would never in the world be able to command; and he wouldn't have known whether to see it in an extension or a contraction of "personality," taking it as he did most directly for a confounding extension of surface. Clearly too it was the right thing, this evening, all round: that came out for him in a word from Kate as she approached him to wreak on him a second introduction. He had, under cover of the music, melted away from the lady toward whom she had first pushed him; and there was something in her that he made out as telling, evasively, a tale of their talk in the Piazza. To what did she want to coerce him as a form of payment for what he had done to her there? It was thus, in contact, uppermost for him that he had done something; not only caused her perfect intelligence to act in his interest, but left her unable to get away, by any mere private effort, from his inattackable logic. With him thus in presence, and near him—and it had been so unmistakably through dinner—there was no getting away for her at all, there was less of it than ever: so that she could only either deal with the question straight, either frankly yield or ineffectually struggle or insincerely argue, or else merely express herself by following up the advantage she did possess. It was part of that advantage, for the hour—a brief, fallacious makeweight to his pressure—that there were plenty of things left in which he must feel her will.

They only told him, these indications, how much she was, in such close quarters, feeling his; and it was enough for him again that her very aspect, as great a variation, in its way, as Milly's own, gave him back the sense of his action. It had never yet in life been granted him to know, almost materially to taste, as he could do in these minutes, the state of what was vulgarly called victory. He had lived long enough to have been on occasion "liked," but it had never begun to be allowed him to be liked to any such tune in any such quarter. It was a liking greater than Milly's—or it would be: he felt it in him to answer for that. So at all events he read the case while he noted that Kate was somehow—for Kate—wanting in lustre. As a striking young presence she was practically superseded; of the mildness that Milly diffused she had assimilated all her share; she might fairly have been dressed tonight in the little black frock, superficially indistinguishable, that Milly had laid aside. This represented, he perceived, the opposite pole from such an effect as that of her wonderful entrance, under her aunt's eyes—he had never forgotten it—the day of their younger friend's failure at Lancaster Gate. She was, in her accepted effacement—it was actually her acceptance that made the beauty and repaired the damage—under her aunt's eyes now; but whose eyes were not effectually preoccupied? It struck him, none the less, certainly, that almost the first thing she said to him showed an exquisite attempt to appear if not unconvinced, at least self-possessed.

"Don't you think her good enough *now?*"

She looked at Milly from where they stood, noted her
in renewed talk, over her further wishes, with her little
orchestra, who had approached her with demonstrations
of deference enlivened by native freedoms that were
quite in the note of old Venetian comedy. The girl's idea
of music had been happy—a real solvent of shyness, yet
not drastic; thanks to the intermissions, discretions, a
general habit of mercy to gathered barbarians, that
reflected the good manners of its interpreters, represen-
tatives though these might be but of the order in which
taste was natural and melody rank. It was easy, at all
events, to answer Kate. "Ah, my dear, you know how
good I think her!"

"But she's *too* nice," Kate returned with appreciation.
"Everything suits her so—especially her pearls. They go
so with her old lace. I'll trouble you really to look at
them." Densher, though aware he had seen them before,
had perhaps not "really" looked at them, and had thus
not done justice to the embodied poetry—his mind, for
Milly's aspects, kept coming back to that—which owed
them part of its style. Kate's face, as she considered
them, struck him; the long, priceless chain, wound twice
round the neck, hung, heavy and pure, down the front
of the wearer's breast—so far down that Milly's trick,
evidently unconscious, of holding and vaguely finger-
ing and entwining a part of it, conduced presumably to
convenience. "She's a dove," Kate went on, "and one
somehow doesn't think of doves as bejewelled. Yet they
suit her down to the ground."

"Yes—down to the ground is the word." Densher

saw now how they suited her, but was perhaps still more aware of something intense in his companion's feeling about them. Milly was indeed a dove; this was the figure, though it most applied to her spirit. But he knew in a moment that Kate was just now, for reasons hidden from him, exceptionally under the impression of that element of wealth in her which was a power, which was a great power, and which was dove-like only so far as one remembered that doves have wings and wondrous flights, have them as well as tender tints and soft sounds. It even came to Densher dimly that such wings could in a given case—*had*, in fact, in the case in which he was concerned—spread themselves for protection. Hadn't they, for that matter, lately taken an inordinate reach, and weren't Kate and Mrs. Lowder, weren't Susan Shepherd and he, wasn't *he* in particular, nestling under them to a great increase of immediate ease? All this was a brighter blur in the general light, out of which he heard Kate presently going on.

"Pearls have such a magic that they suit everyone."

"They would uncommonly suit you," he frankly returned.

"Oh yes, I see myself!"

As she saw herself, suddenly, he saw her—she would have been splendid; and with it he felt more what she was thinking of. Milly's royal ornament had—under pressure now not wholly occult—taken on the character of a symbol of differences, differences of which the vision was actually in Kate's face. It might have been in her face too that, well as she certainly would look in pearls, pearls were exactly what Merton Densher would never be able to give her. Wasn't *that* the great difference that Milly to-night symbolised? She unconsciously represented to Kate, and Kate took it in at every pore, that there was nobody with whom she had less in common than a remarkably handsome girl married to a man unable to make her on any such lines as that the least little present. Of these absurdities, however, it was not till afterwards that Densher thought. He could think now, to any purpose, only of what Mrs. Stringham had said to him before dinner. He could but come back to his friend's question of a minute ago. "She's certainly good enough, as you call it, in the sense that I'm assured she's better. Mrs. Stringham, an hour or two since, was gay to me about it. She evidently believes her better."

"Well, if they choose to call it so——!"

"And what do *you* call it—as against them?"

"I don't call it anything to any one but you. I'm not 'against' them!" Kate added as with just a fresh breath of impatience for all he had to be taught.

"That's what I'm talking about," he said. "What do you call it to me?"

It made her wait a little. "She isn't better. She's worse. But that has nothing to do with it."

"Nothing to do?" He wondered.

But she was clear. "Nothing to do with *us*. Except of course that we're doing our best for her. We're making her want to live." And Kate again watched her. "To-night she does want to live." She spoke with a kindness that had the strange property of striking him as inconsequent—so much, and doubtless so unjustly, had all her clearness been an implication of the hard. "It's wonderful. It's beautiful."

"It's beautiful indeed."

He hated somehow the helplessness of his own note; but she had given it no heed. "She's doing it for *him*"— and she nodded in the direction of Milly's medical visitor. "She wants to be for him at her best. But she can't deceive him."

Densher had been looking too; which made him say in a moment: "And do you think *you* can? I mean, if he's to be with us here, about your sentiments. If Aunt Maud's so thick with him——!"

Aunt Maud now occupied in fact a place at his side, and was visibly doing her best to entertain him, though this failed to prevent such a direction of his own eyes— determined, in the way such things happen, precisely by the attention of the others—as Densher became aware of and as Kate promptly noted. "He's looking at *you*. He wants to speak to you."

"So Mrs. Stringham," the young man laughed, "advised me he would."

"Then let him. Be right with him. I don't need," Kate went on in answer to the previous question, "to deceive him. Aunt Maud, if it's necessary, will do that. I mean that, knowing nothing about me, he can see me only as she sees me. She sees me now so well. He has nothing to do with me."

"Except to reprobate you," Densher suggested.

"For not caring for *you*? Perfectly. As a brilliant

young man driven by it into your relation with Milly—
as all *that* I leave you to him."

"Well," said Densher sincerely enough, "I think I
can thank you for leaving me to some one easier perhaps
with me than yourself."

She had been looking about again meanwhile, the
lady having changed her place, for the friend of Mrs.
Lowder's to whom she had spoken of introducing him.
"All the more reason why I should commit you then to
Lady Mills."

"Oh, but wait." It was not only that he distinguished
Lady Mills from afar, that she inspired him with no
eagerness, and that, somewhere at the back of his head,
he was fairly aware of the question, in germ, of whether
this was the kind of person he should be involved with
when they were married. It was furthermore that the
consciousness of something he had not got from Kate in
the morning, and that logically much concerned him,
had been made more keen by these very moments—to
say nothing of the consciousness that, with their general
smallness of opportunity, he must squeeze each stray
instant hard. If Aunt Maud, over there with Sir Luke,
noted him as a little "attentive," that might pass for a
futile demonstration on the part of a gentleman who had
to confess to having, not very gracefully, changed his
mind. Besides, just now, he didn't care for Aunt Maud
except in so far as he was immediately to show. "How
can Mrs. Lowder think me disposed of, with any final-
ity, if I'm disposed of only to a girl who's dying? If
you're right about that—about the true state of the case,

you're wrong about Mrs. Lowder's being squared. If Milly, as you say," he lucidly pursued, "can't deceive a great surgeon, or whatever, the great surgeon won't deceive other people—not those, that is, who are closely concerned. He won't at any rate deceive Mrs. Stringham, who's Milly's greatest friend; and it will be very odd if Mrs. Stringham deceives Aunt Maud, who's her own."

Kate showed him at this the cold glow of an idea that really was worth his having kept her for. "Why will it be odd? I marvel at how little you see your way."

Mere curiosity, even, about his companion had now for him its quick, its slightly quaking intensities. He had compared her once, we know, to a "new book," an uncut volume of the highest, the rarest quality; and his emotion, to justify that, was again and again like the thrill of turning the page. "Well, you know how deeply I marvel at the way *you* see it!"

"It doesn't in the least follow," Kate went on, "that anything in the nature of what you call deception on Mrs. Stringham's part will be what you call odd. Why shouldn't she hide the truth?"

"From Mrs. Lowder?" Densher stared. "Why should she?"

"To please you."

"And how in the world can it please me?"

Kate turned her head away as if really at last almost tired of his density. But she looked at him again as she spoke. "Well then, to please Milly." And before he could question: "Don't you feel by this time that there's nothing Susan Shepherd won't do for you?"

He had in truth, after an instant, to take it in, so sharply it corresponded with the good lady's recent reception of him. It was queerer than anything again, the way they all came together round him. But that was an old story, and Kate's multiplied lights led him on and on. It was with a reserve, however, that he confessed this. "She's ever so kind. Only her view of the right thing may not be the same as yours."

"How can it be anything different if it's the view of serving you?"

Densher for an instant, but only for an instant, hung fire. "Oh, the difficulty is that I don't, upon my honour, even yet, quite make out how yours does serve me."

"It helps you—put it then," said Kate very simply—"to serve *me*. It gains you time."

"Time for what?"

"For everything!" She spoke at first, once more, with impatience; then, as usual, she qualified. "For anything that may happen."

Densher had a smile, but he felt it himself as strained. "You're cryptic, my love!"

It made her keep her eyes on him, and he could thus see that, by one of those incalculable motions in her without which she wouldn't have been a quarter so interesting, they half filled with tears from some source he had too roughly touched. "I'm taking a trouble for you I never dreamed I should take for any human creature."

Oh, it went home, making him flush for it; yet he soon enough felt his reply on his lips. "Well, isn't my whole insistence to you now that I can conjure trouble away?" And he let it, his insistence, come out again; it had so constantly had, all the week, but its step or two to make. "There *need* be none whatever between us. There need be nothing but our sense of each other."

It had only the effect, at first, that her eyes grew dry while she took up again one of the so numerous links in her close chain. "You can tell her anything you like, anything whatever."

"Mrs. Stringham? I *have* nothing to tell her."

"You can tell her about *us*. I mean," she wonderfully pursued, "that you do still like me."

It was indeed so wonderful that it amused him. "Only not that you still like me."

She let his amusement pass. "I'm absolutely certain she wouldn't repeat it."

"I see. To Aunt Maud."

"You don't quite see. Neither to Aunt Maud nor to any one else." Kate then, he saw, was always seeing Milly much more, after all, than he was; and she showed it again as she went on. "*There*, accordingly, is your time."

She did at last make him think, and it was fairly as if light broke, though not quite all at once. "You must let me say I *do* see. Time for something in particular that, I understand, you regard as possible. Time too that, I further understand, is time for you as well."

"Time indeed for me as well." And, encouraged, visibly, by his glow of concentration, she looked at him as through the air she had painfully made clear. Yet she was still on her guard. "Don't think, however, I'll do *all* the work for you. If you want things named you must name them."

He had quite, within the minute, been turning names over; and there was only one, which at last stared at him there dreadful, that properly fitted. "Since she's to die I'm to marry her?"

It struck him even at the moment as fine in her that she met it with no wincing nor mincing. She might, for the grace of silence, for favour to their conditions, have only answered him with her eyes. But her lips bravely moved. "To marry her."

"So that when her death has taken place I shall in the natural course have money?"

It was before him enough now, and he had nothing more to ask; he had only to turn, on the spot, considerably cold with the thought that all along—to his stupidity, his timidity—it had been, it had been only what she meant. Now that he was in possession, moreover, she couldn't forbear, strangely enough, to pronounce the words she had not pronounced: they broke through her controlled and colourless voice as if she should be ashamed, to the very end, to have flinched. "You'll in the natural course have money. We shall in the natural course be free."

"Oh, oh, oh!" Densher softly murmured.

"Yes, yes, yes." But she broke off. "Come to Lady Mills."

He never budged—there was too much else. "I'm to propose it then, marriage, on the spot?"

There was no ironic sound he needed to give it; the more simply he spoke the more he seemed ironic. But she remained consummately proof. "Oh, I can't go into that with you, and from the moment you don't wash your hands of me I don't think you ought to ask me. You must act as you like and as you can."

He thought again. "I'm far—as I sufficiently showed you this morning—from washing my hands of you."

"Then," said Kate, "it's all right."

"All right?" His eagerness flamed. "You'll come?"

But he had had to see in a moment that it wasn't what she meant. "You'll have a free hand, a clear field, a chance—well, quite ideal."

"Your descriptions"—her "ideal" was such a touch!—"are prodigious. And what I don't make out is how, caring for me, you can like it."

"I don't like it, but I'm a person, thank goodness, who can do what I don't like."

It was not till afterwards that, going back to it, I was to read into this speech a kind of heroic ring, a note of character that belittled his own incapacity for action. Yet he saw indeed even at the time the greatness of knowing so well what one wanted. At the time, too, moreover, he next reflected that he after all knew what *he* did. But something else, on his lips, was uppermost. "What I don't make out then is how you can even bear it."

"Well, when you know me better you'll find out how much I can bear." And she went on before he could take up, as it were, her too many implications. That it was left to him to know her, spiritually, "better" after his

long sacrifice to knowledge—this, for instance, was a
truth he hadn't been ready to receive so full in the face.
She had mystified him enough, heaven knew, but that
was rather by his own generosity than by hers. And
what, with it, did she seem to suggest she might incur at
his hands? In spite of these questions she was carrying
him on. "All you'll have to do will be to stay."

"And proceed to my business under your eyes?"

"Oh dear, no—we shall go."

" 'Go?' " he wondered. "Go when, go where?"

"In a day or two—straight home. Aunt Maud wishes
it now."

It gave him all he could take in to think of. "Then
what becomes of Miss Theale?"

"What I tell you. She stays on, and you stay with
her."

He stared. "All alone?"

She had a smile that was apparently for his tone.
"You're old enough—with plenty of Mrs. Stringham."

Nothing might have been so odd for him now, could
he have measured it, as his being able to feel, quite
while he drew from her these successive cues, that he
was essentially "seeing what she would say"—an
instinct compatible for him therefore with that absence
of a need to know her better to which she had a moment
before done injustice. If it hadn't been appearing to him
in gleams that she would somewhere break down, he
probably couldn't have gone on. Still, as she wasn't
breaking down there was nothing for him but to continue. "Is your going Mrs. Lowder's idea?"

"Very much indeed. Of course again you see what it does for us. And I don't," she added, "refer only to our going, but to Aunt Maud's view of the general propriety of it."

"I see again, as you say," Densher said after a moment. "It makes everything fit."

"Everything."

The word, for a little, held the air, and he might have seemed the while to be looking, by no means dimly now, at all it stood for. But he had in fact been looking at something else. "You leave her here then to die?"

"Ah, she believes she won't die. Not if you stay. I mean," Kate explained, "Aunt Maud believes."

"And that's all that's necessary?"

Still, indeed, she didn't break down. "Didn't we long ago agree that what she believes is the principal thing for us?"

He recalled it, under her eyes, but it came as from long ago. "Oh yes. I can't deny it." Then he added: "So that if I stay——"

"It won't"—she was prompt—"be our fault."

"If Mrs. Lowder still, you mean, suspects us?"

"If she still suspects us. But she won't."

Kate gave it an emphasis that might have appeared to leave him nothing more; and he might in fact well have found nothing if he had not presently found: "But what if she doesn't accept me?"

It produced in her a look of weariness that made the patience of her tone the next moment touch him. "You can but try."

"Naturally, I can but try. Only, you see, one has to try a little hard to propose to a dying girl."

"She isn't for you as if she's dying." It had determined in Kate the flash of *justesse* that he could perhaps most, on consideration, have admired, for her retort touched the truth. There before him was the fact of how Milly to-night impressed him, and his companion, with her eyes in his own and pursuing his impression to the depths of them, literally now perched on the fact in triumph. She turned her head to where their friend was again in range, and it made him turn his, so that they watched a minute in concert. Milly, from the other side, happened at the moment to notice them, and she sent across toward them in response all the candour of her smile, the lustre of her pearls, the value of her life, the essence of her wealth. It brought them, with faces made fairly grave by the reality she put into their plan, together again; Kate herself grew a little pale for it, and they had for a time only a silence. The music, however, gay and vociferous, had broken out afresh and protected more than interrupted them. When Densher at last spoke it was under cover.

"I might stay, you know, without trying."

"Oh, to stay *is* to try."

"To have for herself, you mean, the appearance of it?"

"I don't see how you can have the appearance more."

Densher waited. "You think it then possible she may *offer* marriage?"

"I can't think—if you really want to know—what she may *not* offer!"

"In the manner of princesses, who do such things?"

"In any manner you like. So be prepared."

Well, he looked as if he almost were. "It will be for me then to accept. But that's the way it must come."

Kate's silence, so far, let it pass; but she presently said: "You'll, on your honour, stay then?"

His answer made her wait, but when it came it was distinct. "Without you, you mean?"

"Without us."

"And you go yourselves, at latest——?"

"Not later than Thursday."

It made three days. "Well," he said, "I'll stay, on my honour, if you'll come to me. On *your* honour."

Again, as before, this made her momentarily rigid, with a rigour out of which, at a loss, she vaguely cast about her. Her rigour was more to him, nevertheless, than all her readiness; for her readiness was the woman herself, and this other thing was a mask, a "dodge." She cast about, however, as happened, not, for the instant, in vain. Her eyes, turned over the room, caught at a pretext. "Lady Mills is tired of waiting: she's coming—see—to *us*."

Densher saw in fact, but there was a distance for their visitor to cross, and he still had time. "If you decline to understand me I wholly decline to understand you. I'll do nothing."

"Nothing?" It was as if she tried for the minute to plead.

"I'll do nothing. I'll leave before you. I'll leave to-morrow."

He was to have afterwards the sense of her having then, as the phrase was—and for vulgar triumphs too—seen he meant it. She looked again at Lady Mills, who was nearer, but she quickly came back. "And if I do understand?"

"I'll do everything."

She found anew a pretext in her approaching friend: he was fairly playing with her pride. He had never, he then knew, tasted, in all his relation with her, of anything so sharp—too sharp for mere sweetness—as the vividness with which he saw himself master in the conflict. "Well, I understand."

"On your honour?"

"On my honour."

"You'll come?"

"I'll come."

Book Ninth

I

IT WAS AFTER they had gone that he truly felt the difference, which was most to be felt moreover in his faded old rooms. He had recovered from the first a part of his attachment to this scene of contemplation, within sight, as it was, of the Rialto bridge, on the hither side of that arch of associations and the left going up the Canal; he had seen it in a particular light, to which, more and more, his mind and his hands adjusted it; but the interest the place now wore for him had risen at a bound, becoming a force that, on the spot, completely engaged and absorbed him, and relief from which—if relief was the name—he could find only by getting away and out of reach. What had come to pass within his walls lingered there as an obsession importunate to all his senses; it lived again, as a cluster of pleasant memories, at every hour and in every object; it made everything but itself irrelevant and tasteless. It remained, in a word, a conscious, watchful presence, active on its own side, forever to be reckoned with, in face of which the effort at detachment was scarcely less futile than frivolous. Kate had come to him; it was only once—and this not from any failure of their need, but from such impossibilities, for bravery alike and for subtlety, as there was at the last no blinking; yet she had come, that once, to stay, as people called it; and what survived of her, what reminded and insisted, was something he couldn't have banished if he had wished. Luckily he didn't wish, even though there might be for a man almost a shade of the awful in so unqualified a consequence of his act. It had simply *worked*, his idea, the idea he had made her accept; and all erect before him, really covering the ground as far as he could see, was the fact of the gained success that this represented. It was, otherwise, but the fact of the idea as directly applied, as converted from a luminous conception into an historic truth. He had known it before but as desired and urged, as convincingly insisted on for the help it would render; so that at present, *with* the help rendered, it seemed to acknowledge its office and to set up, for memory and faith, an insistence of its own. He had, in fine, judged his friend's pledge in advance as an inestimable value, and what he must not know his case for was that of a possession of the value to the full. Wasn't it perhaps even rather the value that possessed *him*, kept him thinking of it and waiting on it, turning round and round it and making sure of it again from this side and that.

It played for him—certainly in this prime afterglow— the part of a treasure kept, at home, in safety and sanctity, something he was sure of finding in its place when, with each return, he worked his heavy old key in the lock. The door had but to open for him to be with it

again and for it to be all there; so intensely there that, as
we say, no other act was possible to him than the
renewed act, almost the hallucination, of intimacy.
Wherever he looked or sat or stood, to whatever aspect
he gave for the instant the advantage, it was in view as
nothing of the moment, nothing begotten of time or of
chance could be, or ever would; it was in view as, when
the curtain has risen, the play on the stage is in view,
night after night, for the fiddlers. He remained thus, in
his own theatre, in his single person, perpetual orchestra
to the ordered drama, the confirmed "run"; playing low
and slow, moreover, in the regular way, for the situations of most importance. No other visitor was to come
to him; he met, he bumped occasionally, in the Piazza or
in his walks, against claimants to acquaintance, remembered or forgotten, at present mostly effusive, sometimes
even inquisitive; but he gave no address and encouraged
no approach; he couldn't, for his life, he felt, have
opened his door to a third person. Such a person would
have interrupted him, would have profaned his secret
or perhaps have guessed it; would at any rate have broken the spell of what he conceived himself—in the
absence of anything "to show"—to be inwardly doing.
He was giving himself up—that was quite enough—to
the general feeling of his renewed engagement to
fidelity. The force of the engagement, the quantity of
the article to be supplied, the special solidity of the con-
tract, the way, above all, as a service for which the price
named by him had been magnificently paid, his equivalent office was to take effect—such items might well fill

his consciousness when there was nothing from outside
to interfere. Never was a consciousness more rounded
and fastened down over what filled it; which is precisely
what we have spoken of as, in its degree, the oppression
of success, the somewhat chilled state—tending to the
solitary—of supreme recognition. If it was lightly awful
to feel so justified, this was by the loss of the warmth
of the element of mystery. The lucid reigned instead of
it, and it was into the lucid that he sat and stared. He
shook himself out of it a dozen times a day, tried to
break by his own act his constant still communion. It
wasn't still communion she had meant to bequeath him;
it was the very different business of that kind of fidelity
of which the other name was careful action.

Nothing, he perfectly knew, was less like careful
action than the immersion he enjoyed at home. The
actual grand queerness was that to be faithful to Kate he
had positively to take his eyes, his arms, his lips straight
off her—he had to let her alone. He had to remember
it was time to go to the palace—which, in truth, was a
mercy, since the check was imperative. What it came to,
fortunately, as yet, was that when he closed the door
behind him for an absence he always shut her in. Shut
her out—it came to that rather, when once he had got
a little away; and before he reached the palace, much
more after hearing at his heels the bang of the greater
portone, he felt free enough not to know his position as
oppressively false. As Kate was *all* in his poor rooms,
and not a ghost of her left for the grander, it was only
on reflection that the falseness came out; so long as he

left it to the mercy of beneficent chance it offered him
no face and made of him no claim that he couldn't meet
without aggravation of his inward sense. This aggravation had been his original horror; yet what—in Milly's
presence, each day—was horror doing with him but virtually letting him off? He shouldn't perhaps get off to
the end; there was time enough still for the possibility of
shame to pounce. Still, however, he did constantly a little more what he liked best, and that kept him, for the
time, more safe. What he liked best was, in any case,
to know *why* things were as he felt them; and he knew
it pretty well, in this case, ten days after the retreat of
his other friends. He then fairly perceived that—even
putting their purity of motive at its highest—it was neither Kate nor he who made his strange relation to Milly,
who made her own, so far as it might be, innocent; it
was neither of them who practically purged it—if practically purged it was. Milly herself did everything—so
far at least as he was concerned—Milly herself, and
Milly's house, and Milly's hospitality, and Milly's manner, and Milly's character, and, perhaps still more than
anything else, Milly's imagination, Mrs. Stringham and
Sir Luke indeed a little aiding: whereby he knew the
blessing of a fair pretext to ask himself what more he
had to do. Something incalculable wrought for them—
for him and Kate; something outside, beyond, above
themselves, and doubtless ever so much better, than
they: which wasn't a reason, however—its being so
much better—for them not to profit by it. Not to profit
by it, so far as profit could be reckoned, would have

been to go directly against it; and the spirit of generosity at present engendered in Densher could have felt no greater pang than by his having to go directly against Milly.

To go *with* her was the thing, so far as she could herself go; which, from the moment her tenure of her loved palace was prolonged, was only possible by his remaining near her. This remaining was of course, on the face of it, the most "marked" of demonstrations—which was exactly why Kate had required it; it was so marked that on the very evening of the day it had taken effect Milly herself had not been able not to reach out to him, with an exquisite awkwardness, for some account of it. It was as if she had wanted from him some name that, now they were to be almost alone together, they could, for their further ease, know it and call it by—it being, after all, almost rudimentary that his presence, of which the absence of the others made quite a different thing, couldn't but have for himself some definite basis. She only wondered about the basis it would have for himself, and how he would describe it; that would quite do for her—it even would have done for her, he could see, had he produced some reason merely common, had he said he was waiting for money, or for clothes, or for letters, or for orders from Fleet Street, without which, as she might have heard, newspaper men never took a step. He hadn't, in the event, quite sunk to that; but he had none the less had there with her, that night, on Mrs. Stringham's leaving them alone—Mrs. Stringham proved really prodigious—his acquaintance with a shade of awkwardness darker than any Milly could know. He had supposed himself, beforehand, on the question of what he was doing or pretending, in possession of some tone that would serve; but there were three minutes in which he found himself incapable of promptness quite as a gentleman whose pocket has been picked finds himself incapable of purchase. It even didn't help him, oddly, that he was sure Kate would in some way have spoken for him—or, rather, not so much in some way as in one very particular way. He hadn't asked her, at the last, what she might, in the connection, have said; nothing would have induced him to ask, after she had been to see him: his lips were so sealed by that passage, his spirit in fact so hushed, in respect to any charge upon her freedom. There was something he could only therefore read back into the probabilities, and when he left the palace, an hour afterwards, it was with a sense of having breathed there, in the very air, the truth he imagined.

Just this perception it was, however, that had made him, for the time, ugly to himself in his awkwardness. It was horrible, with this creature, to *be* awkward; it was odious to be seeking excuses for the relation that involved it. Any relation that involved it was by the very fact as much discredited as a dish would be at dinner if one had to take medicine as a sauce. What Kate would have said in one of the young women's last talks was that—if Milly absolutely must have the truth about it—Mr. Densher was staying because she had really seen no way but to require it of him. If he stayed he

didn't follow her—or didn't appear to her aunt to be
doing so; and when she kept him from following her
Mrs. Lowder couldn't pretend, in scenes, the renewal
of which at this time of day was painful, that she after
all didn't snub him as she might. She did nothing in fact
but snub him—wouldn't that have been part of the
story?—only Aunt Maud's suspicions were of the sort
that had repeatedly to be dealt with. He had been, by
the same token, reasonable enough—as he now, for that
matter, well might; he had consented to oblige them,
aunt and niece, by giving the plainest sign possible that
he could exist away from London. To exist away from
London was to exist away from Kate Croy—which was
a gain, much appreciated, to the latter's comfort. There
was a minute, at this hour, out of Densher's three, during which he knew the terror of Milly's bringing out
some such allusion to their friend's explanation as he
must meet with words that wouldn't destroy it. To
destroy it was to destroy everything, to destroy probably
Kate herself, to destroy in particular by a breach of faith
still uglier than anything else, the beauty of their own
last passage. He had given her his word of honour that
if she would come to him he would act absolutely in her
sense, and he had done so with a full enough vision of
what her sense implied. What it implied, for one thing,
was that, tonight, in the great saloon, noble in its half-
lighted beauty, and straight in the white face of his
young hostess, divine in her trust, or at any rate
inscrutable in her mercy—what it implied was that he
should lie with his lips. The single thing, of all things,

that could save him from it would be Milly's letting him off after having thus scared him. What made her mercy inscrutable was that if she had already more than once saved him it was yet apparently without knowing how nearly he was lost.

These were transcendent motions, not the less blessed for being obscure; whereby, yet once more, he was to feel the pressure lighten. He was kept on his feet, in short, by the felicity of her not presenting him with Kate's version as a version to adopt. He couldn't stand up to lie—he felt as if he would have to go down on his knees. As it was he just sat there shaking a little for nervousness the leg he had crossed over the other. She was sorry for his snub, but he had nothing more to subscribe to, to perjure himself about, than the three or four inanities he had, on his own side, feebly prepared for the crisis. He scrambled a little higher than the reference to money and clothes, letters and directions from his manager; but he brought out the beauty of the chance for him—there before him like a temptress painted by Titian—to do a little quiet writing. He was vivid, for a moment, on the difficulty of writing quietly in London; and he was precipitate, almost explosive, on his idea, long cherished, of a book.

The explosion lighted her face. "You'll do your book here?"

"I hope to begin it."

"It's something you haven't begun?"

"Well, only just."

"And since you came?"

She was so full of interest that he shouldn't perhaps after all be too easily let off. "I tried to think a few days ago that I had broken ground."

Scarcely anything, it was indeed clear, could have let him in deeper. "I'm afraid we've made an awful mess of your time."

"Of course you have. But what I'm hanging on for now is precisely to repair that ravage."

"Then you mustn't mind me, you know."

"You'll see," he tried to say with ease, "how little I shall mind anything."

"You'll want"—Milly had thrown herself into it—"the best part of your days."

He thought a moment; he did what he could to wreathe it in smiles. "Oh, I shall make shift with the worst part. The best will be for *you*." And he wished Kate could hear him. It didn't help him moreover that he visibly, even pathetically, imaged to her by such touches his quest for comfort against discipline. He was to sink Kate's snub, and also the hard law she had now laid on him, in a high intellectual effort. This at least was his crucifixion—that Milly was so interested. She was so interested that she presently asked him if he found his rooms propitious, while he felt that in just decently answering her he put on a brazen mask. He should need it quite particularly were she to express again her imagination of coming to tea with him—an extremity that he saw he was not to be spared. "We depend on you, Susie and I, you know, not to forget we're coming"—the extremity was but to face that

remainder, yet it demanded all his tact. Facing their
visit itself—to this, no matter what he might have to do,
he would never consent, as we know, to be pushed; and
that even though it might be exactly such a demonstration as would figure for him at the top of Kate's list of
his proprieties. He could wonder freely enough, deep
within, if Kate's view of that especial propriety had not
been modified by a subsequent occurrence; but his
deciding that it was quite likely not to have been had
no effect on his own preference for tact. It pleased him
to think of "tact" as his present prop in doubt; that
glossed his predicament over, for it was of application
among the sensitive and the kind. He wasn't inhuman,
in fine, so long as it would serve. It had to serve now,
accordingly, to help him not to sweeten Milly's hopes.
He didn't want to be rude to them, but he still less
wanted them to flower again in the particular connection; so that, casting about him, in his anxiety, for a
middle way to meet her, he put his foot, with unhappy
effect, just in the wrong place. "Will it be safe for you
to break into your custom of not leaving the house?"

"'Safe'——?" She had for twenty seconds an exquisite pale glare. Oh, but he didn't need it, by that time,
to wince; he had winced, for himself, as soon as he had
made his mistake. He had done what, so unforgettably,
she had asked him in London not to do; he had
touched, all alone with her here, the supersensitive nerve
of which she had warned him. He had not, since the
occasion in London, touched it again till now; but he
saw himself freshly warned that it was able to bear still

less. So for the moment he knew as little what to do as he had ever known it in his life. He couldn't emphasise that he thought of her as dying, yet he couldn't pretend he thought of her as indifferent to precautions. Meanwhile too she had narrowed his choice. "You suppose me so awfully bad?"

He turned, in his pain, within himself; but by the time the colour had mounted to the roots of his hair he had found what he wanted. "I'll believe whatever you tell me."

"Well then, I'm splendid."

"Oh, I don't need you to tell me that."

"I mean I'm capable of life."

"I've never doubted it."

"I mean," she went on, "that I want so to live——!"

"Well?" he asked while she paused with the intensity of it.

"Well, that I know I *can*."

"Whatever you do?" He shrank from solemnity about it.

"Whatever I do. If I want to."

"If you want to do it?"

"If I want to live. I *can*," Milly repeated.

He had clumsily brought it on himself, but he hesitated with all the pity of it. "Ah then, *that* I believe."

"I will, I will," she declared; yet with the weight of it somehow turned for him to mere light and sound.

He felt himself smiling through a mist. "You simply must!"

It brought her straight again to the fact. "Well then, if you say it, why mayn't we pay you our visit?"

"Will it help you to live?"

"Every little helps," she laughed; "and it's very little for me, in general, to stay at home. Only I shan't want to miss it——!"

"Yes?"—she had dropped again.

"Well, on the day you give us a chance."

It was amazing what this brief exchange had at this point done with him. His great scruple suddenly broke, giving way to something inordinately strange, something of a nature clear to him only when he had left her. "You can come," he said, "when you like."

What had taken place for him, however—the drop, almost with violence, of everything but a sense of her own reality—apparently showed in his face or his manner, and even so vividly that she could take it for something else. "I see how you feel—that I'm an awful bore about it and that, sooner than have any such upset, you'll go. So it's no matter."

"No matter? Oh!"—he quite protested now.

"If it drives you away to escape us. We want you not to go."

It was beautiful how she spoke for Mrs. Stringham. Whatever it was, at any rate, he shook his head. "I won't go."

"Then I won't go!" she brightly declared.

"You mean you won't come to me?"

"No—never now. It's over. But it's all right. I mean,

....

apart from that," she went on, "that I won't do anything that I oughtn't, or that I'm not forced to."

"Oh, who can ever force you?" he asked with his hand-to-mouth way, at all times, of speaking for her encouragement. "You're the least coercible of creatures."

"Because, you think, I'm so free?"

"The freest person probably now in the world. You've got everything."

"Well," she smiled, "call it so. I don't complain."

On which again, in spite of himself, it let him in. "No, I know you don't complain."

As soon as he had said it he had himself heard the pity in it. His telling her she had "everything" was extravagant kind humour, whereas his knowing so tenderly that she didn't complain was terrible kind gravity. Milly felt, he could see, the difference; he might as well have praised her outright for looking death in the face. She looked *him* again, for the moment, and it made nothing better for him that she took him up more gently than ever. "It isn't a merit—when one sees one's way."

"To peace and plenty? Well, I dare say not."

"I mean to keeping what one has."

"Oh, that's success. If what one has is good," Densher said at random, "it's enough to try for."

"Well, it's my limit. I'm not trying for more." To which then she added with a change: "And now about your book."

"My book——?" He had got, in a moment, far from it.

"The one you're now to understand that nothing will induce either Susie or me to run the risk of spoiling."

He hesitated, but he made up his mind. "I'm not doing a book."

"Not what you said?" she asked in a wonder. "You're not writing?"

He already felt relieved. "I don't know, upon my honour, what I'm doing."

It made her visibly grave; so that, disconcerted in another way, he was afraid of what she would see in it. She saw in fact exactly what he feared, but again his honour, as he called it, was saved even while she didn't know she had threatened it. Taking his words for a betrayal of the sense that he, on his side, *might* complain, what she clearly wanted was to urge on him some such patience as he should be perhaps able to arrive at with her indirect help. Still more clearly, however, she wanted to be sure of how far she might venture; and he could see her make out in a moment that she had a sort of test. "Then if it's not for your book——?"

"What *am* I staying for?"

"I mean with your London work—with all you have to do. Isn't it rather empty for you?"

"Empty for me?" He remembered how Kate had said that she might propose marriage, and he wondered if this were the way she would naturally begin it. It would leave him, such an incident, he already felt, at a loss, and the note of his finest anxiety might have been in the vagueness of his reply. "Oh, well——!"

"I ask too many questions?" She settled it for herself before he could protest. "You stay because you've got to."

He grasped at it. "I stay because I've got to." And he couldn't have said when he had uttered it if it were loyal to Kate or disloyal. It gave her, in a manner, away; it showed the tip of the ear of her plan. Yet Milly took it, he perceived, but as a plain statement of his truth. He was waiting for what Kate would have told her of—the permission, from Lancaster Gate, to come any nearer. To remain friends with either niece or aunt he mustn't stir without it. All this Densher read in the girl's sense of the spirit of his reply; so that it made him feel he was lying, and he had to think of something to correct it. What he thought of was, in an instant, "Isn't it enough, whatever may be one's other complications, to stay, after all, for *you?*"

"Oh, you must judge."

He was on his feet, by this time, to take leave, and also because he was at last too restless. The speech in question, at least, wasn't disloyal to Kate; that was the very tone of their bargain. So was it, by being loyal, another kind of lie, the lie of the uncandid profession of a motive. He was staying so little "for" Milly that he was staying positively against her. He didn't, none the less, know, and at last, thank goodness, he didn't care. The only thing he could say might make it either better or worse. "Well then, so long as I don't go, you must think of me all *as* judging!"

HE DIDN'T GO HOME, on leaving her—he didn't want to; he walked, instead, through his narrow ways and his *campi* with gothic arches, to a small and comparatively sequestered café where he had already more than once found refreshment and comparative repose, together with solutions that consisted, mainly and pleasantly, of further indecisions. It was a literal fact that those awaiting him there to-night, while he leaned back on his velvet bench with his head against a florid mirror and his eyes not looking further than the fumes of his tobacco, might have been regarded by him as a little less limp than usual. This was not because, before he had got to his feet again, there was a step he had seen his way to; it was simply because the acceptance of his position took sharper effect from his sense of what he had just had to deal with. When he had turned about, to Milly, at the palace, half-an-hour before, on the question of the impossibility he had so strongly felt, turned about on the spot and under her eyes, he had acted, of a sudden, as a consequence of seeing much further, seeing how little, how not at all, impossibilities mattered. It wasn't a case for pedantry; when people were at *her* pass everything was allowed. And her pass was now, as by the sharp click of a spring, just completely his own—to the extent, as he felt, of her deep dependence on him. Anything he should do, or he shouldn't, would have reference, directly, to her life, which was thus absolutely in his hands—and ought never to have reference to anything else. It was on the cards for him that he might kill her—that was the way he read the cards as he sat in his customary corner. The fear in this thought made him let everything go, kept him there, actually, motionless, for three hours on end. He renewed his consumption and smoked more cigarettes than he had ever done in the time. What had come out for him had come out, with this first intensity, as a terror; so that action itself, of any sort, the right as well as the wrong—if the difference even survived—had heard in it a vivid "Hush!" the injunction, from that moment, to keep intensely still. He thought, in fact, while his vigil lasted, of the different ways of doing so, and the hour might have served him as a lesson in going on tip-toe.

What he finally took home, when he ventured to leave the place, was the perceived truth that he might on any other system go straight to destruction. Destruction was represented for him by the idea of his really bringing to a point, on Milly's side, anything whatever. Nothing so "brought," he easily argued, but *must* be in one way or another a catastrophe. He was mixed up in her fate, or her fate, if that were better, was mixed up in *him*, so that a single false motion might, either way, snap the coil. They helped him, it was true, these considerations, to a degree of eventual peace, for what they luminously amounted to was that he was to do nothing, and that fell in, after all, with the burden laid on him by Kate. He was only not to budge without the girl's leave—not, oddly enough, at the last, to move without it, whether further or nearer, any more than without

Kate's. It was to this his wisdom reduced itself—to the need again simply to be kind. That was the same as being still—as creating, studiously, the minimum of vibration. He felt himself, as he smoked, shut up to a room, on the wall of which something precious was too precariously hung. A false step would bring it down, and it must hang as long as possible. He was aware when he walked away again that even Fleet Street, at this juncture, wouldn't successfully touch him. His manager might wire that he was wanted, but he could easily be deaf to his manager. His money, for the idle life, might be none to much; happily, however, Venice was cheap, and it was moreover the queer fact that Milly in a manner supported him. The greatest of his expenses really was to walk to the palace to dinner. He didn't want, in short, to give that up, and he could probably, he felt, be still enough.

He tried it then for three weeks, and with the sense, after a little, of not having failed. There had to be a delicate art in it, for he was not trying—quite the contrary—to be either distant or dull. That would not have been being "nice"; which, in its own form, was the real law. That too might just have produced the vibration he desired to avert; so that he best kept everything in place by not hesitating or fearing, as it were, to let himself go—go in the direction, that is to say, of staying. It depended on where he went; which was what he meant by taking care. When one went on tip-toe one could turn off for retreat without betraying the manœuvre. Perfect tact—the necessity for which he had from the first, as we know, happily recognised—was to keep all intercourse in the key of the absolutely settled. It was settled thus, for instance, that they were indissoluble good friends, and settled as well that her being the American girl was, just in time, and for the relation which they found themselves concerned in, a boon inappreciable. If, at least, as the days went on, she was to fall short of her prerogative of the great national feminine and juvenile ease, if she didn't, diviningly, responsively, desire and labour to record herself as possessed of it, this would not have been for want of Densher's keeping her, with his idea, well up to it, for want, in fine, of his encouragement and reminder. He didn't perhaps in so many words speak to her of the quantity itself as of the thing she was least to intermit; but he talked of it, freely, in what he flattered himself was an impersonal way, and this held it there before her—since he was careful also to talk pleasantly. It was at once their idea, when all was said, and the most marked of their conveniences. The type was so elastic that it could be stretched to almost anything; and yet, not stretched, it kept down, remained normal, remained properly within bounds. And he *had* meanwhile, thank goodness, without being too much disconcerted, the sense, for the girl's part of the business, of the queerest conscious compliance, of her doing very much what he wanted, even though without her quite seeing why. She fairly touched this once in saying: "Oh yes, you like us to be as we are because it's a kind of facility to you that we don't quite measure: I think one would have to be English to measure it!"—

and that too, strangely enough, without prejudice to her good nature. She might have been conceived as doing—that is of being—what he liked, if only to judge where it would take them. They really, as it went on, *saw* each other at the game; she knowing he tried to keep her in tune with his notion, and he knowing she thus knew it. Add that he, again, knew she knew, and yet that nothing was spoiled by it, and we get a fair impression of their most completely workable line. The strangest fact of all for us must be that the success he himself thus promoted was precisely what figured, to his gratitude, as the something above and beyond him, above and beyond Kate, that made for daily decency. There would scarce have been felicity—certainly too little of the right lubricant—had not the national character so invoked been, not less inscrutably than completely, in Milly's chords. It made her unity and was the one thing he could unlimitedly take for granted in her.

He did so then, daily, for twenty days, without deepened fear of the undue vibration that was keeping him watchful. He was living at best, he knew, in his nervousness, from day to day, and from hand to mouth; but he had succeeded, he believed, in avoiding a mistake. All women had alternatives, and Milly's would doubtless be shaky too; but the national character was firm in her, whether as all of her, practically, by this time, or as but a part; the national character that, in a woman who was young, made of the air breathed a virtual non-conductor. It was not till a certain occasion when the twenty days had passed that, going to the

palace at tea-time, he was met by the information that
the signorina padrona was not "receiving." The
announcement was made him, in the court, by one of
the gondoliers, and made, he thought, with such a conscious eye as the knowledge of his freedoms of access,
hitherto conspicuously shown, could scarce fail to beget.
Densher had not been, at Palazzo Leporelli, among the
receivable, but had taken his place once for all among
the involved and included, so that on being so flagrantly
braved he recognised after a moment the propriety of a
further appeal. Neither of the two ladies, it appeared,
received, and yet Pasquale was not prepared to say that
either was not well. He was yet not prepared to say that
either *was* well, and he would have been blank, Densher mentally observed, if the term could ever apply to
members of a race in whom vacancy was but a nest of
darknesses—not a vain surface, but a place of withdrawal in which something obscure, something always
ominous, indistinguishably lived. He felt afresh indeed,
at this hour, the force of the veto laid, in the house, on
any mention, any cognition, of the liabilities of its mistress. Her health, or her illness, was not confessed to
there as a reason. Whether it was inwardly known as
one was another matter; of which he grew fully aware on
carrying his inquiry further. His appeal was to his friend
Eugenio, whom he immediately sent for, with whom,
for three rich minutes, protected from the weather, he
was confronted in the gallery that led from the water-
steps to the court, and whom he always called, in meditation, his friend because it was unmistakable that he

would have put an end to him if he could. That produced a relation which required a name of its own, an
intimacy of consciousness, in truth, for each—an intimacy of eye, of ear, of general sensibility, of everything
but tongue. It had been, in other words, for the five
weeks, far from occult to our young man that Eugenio
took a vulgar view of him, which was at the same time
a view he was definitely hindered from preventing. It
was all in the air now again; it was as much between
them as ever while Eugenio waited on him in the court.

The weather, from early morning, had turned to
storm, the first sea-storm of the autumn, and Densher
had almost invidiously brought him down the outer
staircase—the massive ascent, the great feature of the
court, to Milly's *piano nobile*. This was to pay him—it
was the one chance—for the vulgar view; the view that,
clever and not rich, the young man from London was—
by the obvious way—after Miss Theale's fortune. It was
to pay him for the further implication that he must take
the young lady's most devoted servant (interested
scarcely less in the high attraction) for a strangely superficial person if he counted, in such a connection, on
impunity and prosperity. The view was a vulgar one for
Densher because it was but the view that might have
been taken of another man, and three things alone,
accordingly, had kept him from righting himself. One of
these was that his critic sought expression only in an
impersonality, a positive inhumanity, of politeness; the
second was that refinements of expression in a friend's
servant were not a thing a visitor could take action on;

and the third was the fact that the particular attribution
of motive did him, after all, no wrong. It was his own
fault if the vulgar view and the view that might have
been taken of another man happened so incorrigibly to
fit him. He apparently wasn't so different from another
man as that came to. If therefore, in fine, Eugenio figured to him as "my friend" because he was conscious
of his seeing so much in him, what he made him see,
on the same lines, in the course of their present interview was ever so much more. Densher felt that he
marked himself, no doubt, as insisting, by dissatisfaction
with the gondolier's answer, on the pursuit imputed to
him; and yet felt it only in the augmented, the exalted
distance that was by this time established between them.
Eugenio had of course reflected that a word to Miss
Theale, from such a pair of lips, would cost him his
place; but he could also bethink himself that, so long as
the word never came—and it was, on the basis he had
arranged, impossible—he enjoyed the imagination of
mounting guard. He had never so mounted guard, Densher could see, as during these minutes in the damp *loggia*, where the storm-gusts were strong; and there came
in fact for our young man, as a result of his presence, a
sudden sharp sense that everything had turned to the
dismal. Something had happened—he didn't know
what; and it wasn't Eugenio who would tell him. What
Eugenio told him was that he thought the ladies—as if
their liability had been equal—were a "leetle" fatigued,
just a "leetle leetle," and without any cause named for it.
It was one of the signs of what Densher felt in him that,

by a refinement of resource, he always met the latter's
Italian with English and his English with Italian. He
now, as usual, slightly smiled at him in the process—but
ever so slightly, this time, his manner also being
attuned, our young man made out, to the thing, whatever it was, that constituted the rupture of peace.

This manner, while they stood for a long minute facing each other over all they didn't say, played a part as
well in the sudden jar to Densher's protected state. It
was a Venice all of evil that had broken out for them
alike, so that they were together in their anxiety, if they
really could have met on it; a Venice of cold, lashing
rain from a low black sky, of wicked wind raging
through narrow passes, of general arrest and interruption, with the people engaged in all the water-life huddled, stranded and wageless, bored and cynical, under
archways and bridges. Our young man's mute exchange
with his friend contained meanwhile such a depth of reference that, had the pressure been but slightly prolonged, they might have reached a point at which they
were equally weak. Each had verily something in mind
that would have made a hash of mutual suspicion and in
the presence of which, as a possibility, they were more
united than disjoined. But it was to have been a
moment, for Densher, that nothing could ease off—not
even the formal propriety with which his interlocutor
finally attended him to the *portone* and bowed upon his
retreat. Nothing had passed about his coming back, and
the air had made itself felt as a non-conductor of mes-
sages. Densher knew of course, as he took his way again,

that Eugenio's invitation to return was not what he
missed; yet he knew at the same time that what had
happened to him was part of his punishment. Out in the
square beyond the *fondamenta* that gave access to the
land-gate of the palace, out where the wind was higher,
he fairly, with the thought of it, pulled his umbrella
closer down. It couldn't be, his consciousness, unseen
enough by others—the base predicament of having, by a
concatenation, just to *take* such things: such things as
the fact that one very acute person in the world, whom
he couldn't dispose of as an interested scoundrel,
enjoyed an opinion of him that there was no attacking,
no disproving, no—what was worst of all—even noticing. One had come to a queer pass when a servant's
opinion mattered. Eugenio's would have mattered even
if, as founded on a low vision of appearances, it had
been quite wrong. It was the more disagreeable, accordingly, that the vision of appearances was quite right, and
yet was scarcely less low.

Such as it was, at any rate, Densher shook it off with
the more impatience that he was independently restless.
He had to walk in spite of weather, and he took his
course, through crooked ways, to the Piazza, where he
should have the shelter of the galleries. Here, in the high
arcade, half Venice was crowded close, while, on the
Molo, at the limit of the expanse, the old columns of
St. Mark and of the Lion were like the lintels of a door
wide open to the storm. It was odd for him, as he
moved, that it should have made such a difference—if
the difference wasn't only that the palace had for the

first time failed of a welcome. There was more, but it came from that; that gave the harsh note and broke the spell. The wet and the cold were now to reckon with, and it was precisely, to Densher, as if he had seen the obliteration, at a stroke, of the margin on a faith in which they were all living. The margin had been his name for it—for the thing that, though it had held out, could bear no shock. The shock, in some form, had come, and he wondered about it while, threading his way among loungers as vague as himself, he dropped his eyes sightlessly on the rubbish in shops. There were stretches of the gallery paved with squares of red marble, greasy now with the salt spray; and the whole place, in its huge elegance, the grace of its conception and the beauty of its detail, was more than ever like a great drawing-room, the drawing-room of Europe, profaned and bewildered by some reverse of fortune. He brushed shoulders with brown men whose hats askew, and the loose sleeves of whose pendent jackets, made them resemble melancholy maskers. The tables and chairs that overflowed from the cafés were gathered, still with a pretence of service, into the arcade, and here and there a spectacled German, with his coat-collar up, partook publicly of food and philosophy. These were impressions for Densher too, but he had made the whole circuit thrice before he stopped short, in front of Florian's, with the force of his sharpest. His eye had caught a face within the café—he had spotted an acquaintance behind the glass. The person he had thus paused long enough to look at twice was seated, well within range, at a small

table on which a tumbler, half emptied and evidently
neglected, still remained; and though he had on his
knee, as he leaned back, a copy of a French newspaper—the heading of the *Figaro* was visible—he stared
straight before him at the little opposite rococo wall.
Densher had him for a minute in profile, had him for a
time during which his identity produced, however
quickly, all the effect of establishing connections—connections startling and direct; and then, as if it were the
one thing more needed, took in the look, determined by
a turn of the head, that might have been a prompt result
of the sense of being noticed. This wider view showed
him *all* Lord Mark—Lord Mark as encountered, several
weeks before, the day of the first visit of each to Palazzo
Leporelli. For it had been all Lord Mark that was going
out, on that occasion, as he came in—he had felt it, in
the hall, at the time; and he was accordingly the less at
a loss to recognise in a few seconds, as renewed meeting brought it to the surface, the same potential quantity.

It was a matter, the whole passage—it could only
be—but of a few seconds; for as he could neither stand
there to stare nor on the other hand make any advance
from it, he had presently resumed his walk—and this
time to another pace. It had been, for all the world, during his pause, as if he had caught his answer to the riddle of the day. Lord Mark had simply faced him—as he
had faced *him*, not placed by him, not at first—as one of
the damp, shuffling crowd. Recognition, though hanging fire, had then clearly come; yet no light of saluta-
tion had been struck from these certainties.

Acquaintance between them was scant enough for neither to take it up. That neither had done so was not, however, what now mattered, but that the gentleman at Florian's was in the place at all. He couldn't have been in it long; Densher, as inevitably a haunter of the great meeting-ground, would in that case have seen him before. He paid short visits; he was on the wing; the question for him even as he sat there was of his train or of his boat. He had come back for something—as a sequel to his earlier visit; and whatever he had come back for it had had time to be done. He might have arrived but last night or that morning; he had already made the difference. It was a great thing for Densher to get this answer. He held it close, he hugged it, quite leaned on it as he continued to circulate. It kept him going and going—it made him no less restless. But it explained—and that was much, for with explanations he might somehow deal. The vice in the air, otherwise, was too much like the breath of fate. The weather had changed, the rain was ugly, the wind wicked, the sea impossible, *because* of Lord Mark. It was because of him, *a fortiori*, that the palace was closed. Densher went round again twice, and found the visitor each time as he had found him first. Once, that is, he was staring before him; the next time he was looking over his *Figaro*, which he had opened out. Densher didn't again stop, but he left him apparently unconscious of his passage—on another repetition of which Lord Mark had disappeared. He had spent but the day; he would be off that night; he had now gone to his hotel for arrangements. These things were as plain to Densher as if he had had them in words. The obscure had cleared for him—if cleared it was; there was something he didn't see, the great thing; but he saw so round it and so close to it that this was almost as good. He had been looking at a man who had done what he had come for, and for whom, as done, it temporarily sufficed. The man had come again to see Milly, and Milly had received him. His visit would have taken place just before or just after luncheon, and it was the reason why he himself had found her door shut.

He said to himself that evening, he still said even on the morrow, that he only wanted a reason, and that with this perception of one he could now mind, as he called it, his business. His business, he had settled, as we know, was to keep thoroughly still; and he asked himself why it should prevent this that he could feel, in connection with the crisis, so remarkably blameless. He gave the appearances before him all the benefit of being critical, so that if blame were to accrue he shouldn't feel he had dodged it. But it wasn't a bit he who, that day, had touched her, and if she was upset it wasn't a bit his act. The ability so to think about it amounted for Densher, during several hours, to a kind of exhilaration. The exhilaration was heightened fairly, besides, by the visible conditions—sharp, striking, ugly to him—of Lord Mark's return. His constant view of it, for all the next hours, of which there were many, was as a demonstration on the face of it sinister even to his own actual ignorance. He didn't need, for seeing it as evil, seeing

it as, to a certainty, in a high degree "nasty," to know
more about it than he had so easily and so wonderfully
picked up. You couldn't drop on the poor girl that way
without, by the fact, being brutal. Such a visit was a
descent, an invasion, an aggression, constituting precisely one or other of the stupid shocks that he himself
had so decently sought to spare her. Densher had indeed
drifted, by the next morning, to the reflection—which,
positively, with the occasion, he might have brought
straight out—that the only delicate and honourable way
of treating a person in such a state was to treat her as he,
Merton Densher, did. With time, actually—for the
impression but deepened—this sense of the contrast, to
the advantage of Merton Densher, became a sense of
relief, and that, in turn, a sense of escape. It was for all
the world—and he drew a long breath on it—as if a special danger for him had passed. Lord Mark had, without
in the least intending such a service, got it straight out
of the way. It was *he*, the brute, who had stumbled into
just the wrong inspiration, and who had therefore produced, for the very person he had wished to hurt, an
impunity that was comparative innocence, that was
almost like purification. The person he had wished to
hurt could only be the person so unaccountably hanging
about. To keep still, meanwhile, was, for this person,
more comprehensively, to keep it all up; and to keep it
all up was, if that seemed on consideration best, not, for
the day or two, to go back to the palace.

The day or two passed—stretched to three days; and
with the effect extraordinarily, that Densher felt himself,

in the course of them, washed but the more clean. Some
sign would come if his presence there were better; and
he was at all events, in absence, without the particular
scruple. It wouldn't have been meant for him by either
of the women that he was to return but to face Eugenio. That was impossible—the being again denied; for it
made him, practically, answerable, and answerable was
what he was not. There was no neglect, either, in
absence, inasmuch as, from the moment he didn't get
in, the one message he could send up would be some
hope on the score of health. Since, accordingly, that sort
of expression was definitely forbidden him he had only
to wait—which he was actually helped to do by his feeling, with the lapse of each day, more and more wound
up to it. The days in themselves were anything but
sweet; the wind and the weather lasted, the fireless cold
hinted at worse; the broken charm of the world about
was broken into smaller pieces. He walked up and down
his rooms and listened to the wind—listened also to tin-
kles of bells and watched for some servant of the palace.
He might get a note, but the note never came; there
were hours when he stayed at home not to miss it.
When he was not at home he was in circulation again
as he had been at the hour of his seeing Lord Mark. He
strolled about the Square with the herd of refugees; he
raked the approaches and the cafés on the chance the
brute, as he now regularly imaged him, *might* be still
there. He could only be there, he knew, to be received
afresh; and that—one had but to think of it—would be
indeed stiff. He had gone, however—it was proved;

though Densher's care for the question, either way, only added to what was of least savour in the taste of his present ordeal. It all came round to what he was doing for Milly—spending days that neither relief nor escape could purge of a smack of the abject. What was it but abject for a man of his parts to be reduced to such pastimes? What was it but sordid for him, shuffling about in the rain, to have to peep into shops and to consider possible meetings? What was it but odious to find himself wondering what, as between him and another man, a possible meeting would produce? There recurred moments when, in spite of everything, he felt no straighter than another man. And yet even on the third day, when still nothing had come, he more than ever knew that he wouldn't have budged for the world.

He thought of the two women, in their silence, at last—he at all events thought of Milly—as probably, for her reasons, now intensely wishing him to go. The cold breath of her reasons was, with everything else, in the air; but he didn't care for them any more than for her wish itself, and he would stay in spite of her, stay in spite of odium, stay in spite perhaps of some final experience that would be, for the pain of it, all but unbearable. That would be his one way, purified though he was, to mark his virtue beyond any mistake. It would be accepting the disagreeable, and the disagreeable would be a proof; a proof of his not having stayed for the thing—the agreeable, as it were—that Kate had named. The thing Kate had named was not to have been the odium of staying in spite of hints. It was part

of the odium, as actual, too, that Kate was, for her comfort, just now well aloof. These were the first hours,
since her flight, in which his sense of what she had
done for him on the eve of that event was to incur a
qualification. It was strange, it was perhaps base, to be
thinking such things so soon; but one of the intimations
of his solitude was that she had provided for herself.
She was out of it all, by her act, as much as he was in
it; and this difference grew, positively, as his own intensity increased. She had said in their last sharp snatch
of talk—sharp though thickly muffled, and with every
word in it final and deep, unlike even the deepest words
they had ever yet spoken: "Letters? Never—*now*. Think
of it. Impossible." So that as he had sufficiently caught
her sense—into which he read, all the same, a strange
inconsequence—they had practically wrapped their
understanding in the breach of their correspondence.
He had moreover, on losing her, done justice to her law
of silence; for there was doubtless a finer delicacy in
his not writing to her than in his writing as he must
have written had he spoken of themselves. That would
have been a turbid strain, and her idea had been to be
noble; which, in a degree, was a manner. Only it left
her, for the pinch, comparatively at ease. And it left
him, in the conditions, peculiarly alone. He was alone,
that is, till, on the afternoon of his third day, in gathering dusk and renewed rain, with his shabby rooms
looking, doubtless, in their confirmed dreariness, for
the mere eyes of others, at their worst, the grinning
padrona threw open the door and introduced Mrs.

Stringham. That made, at a bound, a difference, especially when he saw that his visitor was weighted. It appeared a part of her weight that she was in a wet waterproof, that she allowed her umbrella to be taken from her by the good woman without consciousness or care, and that her face, under her veil, richly rosy with the driving wind, was—and the veil too—as splashed as if the rain were her tears.

III

THEY CAME TO IT almost immediately; he was to wonder afterwards at the fewness of their steps. "She has turned her face to the wall."

"You mean she's worse?"

The poor lady stood there as she had stopped; Densher had, in the instant flare of his eagerness, his curiosity, all responsive at sight of her, waved away, on the spot, the padrona, who had offered to relieve her of her mackintosh. She looked vaguely about through her wet veil, intensely conscious now of the step she had taken and wishing it not to have been in the dark, but clearly, as yet, seeing nothing. "I don't know *how* she is—and it's why I've come to you."

"I'm glad enough you've come," he said, "and it's quite—you make me feel—as if I had been wretchedly waiting for you."

She showed him again her blurred eyes—she had caught at his word. "Have you been wretched?"

Now, however, on his lips, the word expired. It

would have sounded for him like a complaint, and
before something he already made out in his visitor he
knew his own trouble as small. Hers, under her damp
draperies, which shamed his lack of a fire, was great,
and he felt she had brought it all with her. He answered
that he had been patient and above all that he had been
still. "As still as a mouse—you'll have seen it for yourself. Stiller, for three days together, than I've ever been
in my life. It has seemed to me the only thing."

This qualification of it as a policy or a remedy was
straightway, for his friend, plainly, a light that her own
light could answer. "It has been best. I've wondered for
you. But it has been best," she said again.

"Yet it has done no good?"

"I don't know. I've been afraid you were gone." Then
as he gave a headshake which, though slow, was deeply
mature: "You *won't* go?"

"Is to 'go,' " he asked, "to be still?"

"Oh, I mean if you'll stay for me."

"I'll do anything for you. Isn't it for you alone now
I can?"

She thought of it, and he could see even more of the
relief she was taking from him. His presence, his face,
his voice, the old rooms themselves, so meagre yet so
charged, where Kate had admirably been to him—these
things counted for her, now she had them, as the help
she had been wanting: so that she still only stood there
taking them all in. With it, however, characteristically,
popped up a throb of her conscience. What she thus

tasted was almost a personal joy. It told Densher of the three days she on her side had spent. "Well, anything you do for me—*is* for her too. Only, only——!"

"Only nothing now matters?"

She looked at him a minute as if he were the fact itself that he expressed. "Then you know?"

"Is she dying?" he asked for all answer.

Mrs. Stringham waited—her face seemed to sound him. Then her own reply was strange. "She hasn't so much as named you. We haven't spoken."

"Not for three days?"

"No more," she simply went on, "than if it were all over. Not even by the faintest allusion."

"Oh," said Densher with more light, "you mean you haven't spoken about *me*."

"About what else? No more than if you were dead."

"Well," he answered after a moment, "I *am* dead."

"Then *I* am," said Susan Shepherd with a drop of her arms on her waterproof.

It was a tone that, for the minute, imposed itself in its dry despair; it represented, in the bleak place, which had no life of its own, none but the life Kate had left—the sense of which, for that matter, by mystic channels, might fairly be reaching the visitor—the very impotence of their extinction. And Densher had nothing to oppose it, nothing but again: "Is she dying?"

It made her, however, as if these were crudities, almost material pangs, only say as before: "Then you know?"

"Yes," he at last returned, "I know. But the marvel to me is that *you* do. I've no right in fact to imagine, or to assume, that you do."

"You may," said Susan Shepherd, "all the same. I know."

"Everything?"

Her eyes, through her veil, kept pressing him. "No—not everything. That's why I've come."

"That I shall really tell you?" With which, as she hesitated, and it affected him, he brought out, in a groan, a doubting "Oh, oh!" It turned him from her to the place itself, which was a part of what was in him, was the abode, the worn shrine more than ever, of the fact in possession, the fact, now an association, for which he had hired it. *That* was not for telling, but Susan Shepherd was, none the less, so decidedly wonderful that the sense of it might really have begun, by an effect already operating, to be a part of her knowledge. He saw, and it stirred him, that she hadn't come to judge him; had come rather, so far as she might dare, to pity. This showed him her own abasement—that, at any rate, of grief; and made him feel with a rush of friendliness that he liked to be with her. The rush had quickened when she met his groan with an attenuation.

"We shall at all events—if that's anything—be together."

It was his own good impulse in herself. "It's what I've ventured to feel. It's much." She replied in effect, silently, that it was whatever he liked; on which, so far as he had been afraid for anything, he knew his fear had dropped. The comfort was huge, for it gave back to him something precious, over which, in the effort of recovery, his own hand had too imperfectly closed. Kate, he remembered, had said to him, with her sole and single boldness—and also on grounds he hadn't then measured—that Mrs. Stringham was a person who *wouldn't*, at a pinch, in a stretch of confidence, wince. It was but another of the cases in which was Kate showing. "You don't think then very horridly of me?"

And her answer was the more valuable that it came without nervous effusion—quite as if she understood what he might conceivably have believed. She turned over in fact what she thought, and that was what helped him. "Oh, you've been extraordinary!"

It made him aware the next moment of how they had been planted there. She took off her cloak with his aid, though when she had also, accepting a seat, removed her veil, he recognised in her personal ravage that the words she had just uttered to him were the one flower she had to throw. They were all her consolation for him, and the consolation, even, still depended on the event. She sat with him at any rate, in the grey clearance—as sad as a winter dawn—made by their meeting. The image she again evoked for him loomed in it but the larger. "She has turned her face to the wall."

He saw, with the last vividness, and it was as if, in their silences, they were simply so leaving what he saw. "She doesn't speak at all? I don't mean not of me."

"Of nothing—of no one." And she went on, Susan Shepherd, giving it out as she had had to take it. "She doesn't *want* to die. Think of her age. Think of her goodness. Think of her beauty. Think of all she is. Think of all she *has*. She lies there stiffening herself and clinging to it. So I thank God——!" the poor lady wound up with a kind of wan inconsequence.

He wondered. "You thank God——?"

"That she's so quiet."

He continued to wonder. "*Is* she so quiet?"

"She's more than quiet. She's grim. It's what she has never been. So you see—all these days. I can't tell you— but it's better so. It would kill me if she *were* to tell me."

"To tell you?" He was still at a loss.

"How she feels. How she clings. How she doesn't want it."

"How she doesn't want to die? Of course she doesn't want it." He had a long pause, and they might have been thinking together of what they could even now do to prevent it. This, however, was not what he brought out. Milly's "grimness," and the great hushed palace, were present to him; present with the little woman before him as she must have been waiting there and listening. "Only, what harm have *you* done her?"

Mrs. Stringham looked about in her darkness. "I don't know. I come and talk of her here with you."

It made him again hesitate. "Does she utterly hate me?"

"I don't know. How *can* I? No one ever will."

"She'll never tell?"

"She'll never tell."

Once more he thought. "She must be magnificent."

"She *is* magnificent."

His friend, after all, helped him, and he turned it, so far as he could, all over. "Would she see me again?"

It made his companion stare. "Should you like to see her?"

"You mean as you describe her?" He saw her surprise, and it took him some time. "No."

"Ah then!" Mrs. Stringham sighed.

"But if she could bear it I'd do anything."

She had for the moment her vision of this, but it collapsed. "I don't see what you can do."

"I don't, either. But *she* might."

Mrs. Stringham continued to think. "It's too late."

"Too late for her to see——?"

"Too late."

The very decision of her despair—it was after all so lucid—kindled in him a heat. "But the doctor, all the while——?"

"Tacchini? Oh, he's kind. He comes. He's proud of having been approved and coached by a great London man. He hardly in fact goes away; so that I scarce know what becomes of his other patients. He thinks her, justly enough, a great personage; he treats her like royalty; he's waiting on events. But she has barely consented to see him, and, though she has told him, generously—for she *thinks* of me, dear creature—that he may come, that he may stay, for my sake, he spends most of his time only hovering at her door, prowling through the rooms, trying to entertain me, in that ghastly saloon, with the gossip of Venice, and meeting me, in doorways, in the sala, on the staircase, with an agreeable, intolerable smile. We don't," said Susan Shepherd, "talk of her."

"By her request?"

"Absolutely. I don't do what she doesn't wish. We talk of the price of provisions."

"By her request too?"

"Absolutely. She named it to me as a subject when she said, the first time, that if it would be any comfort to me he might stay as much as we liked."

Densher took it all in. "But he isn't any comfort to you!"

"None whatever. That, however," she added, "is not his fault. Nothing's any comfort."

"Certainly," Densher observed, "as I but too horribly feel, *I'm* not."

"No. But I didn't come for that."

"You came for *me*."

"Well, then, call it that." But she looked at him a moment with eyes filled full, and something came up in her, the next instant, from deeper still. "I came at bottom of course——"

"You came at bottom of course for our friend herself. But if it's, as you say, too late for me to do anything?"

She continued to look at him, and with an impatience, which he saw growing in her, of the truth itself. "So I did say. But, with you here"—and she turned her vision again strangely about her—"with you here, and with everything, I feel that we mustn't abandon her."

"God forbid we should abandon her."

"Then you *won't?*" His tone had made her flush again.

"How do you mean I 'won't,' if she abandons *me?* What can I do if she won't see me?"

"But you said just now you wouldn't like it."

"I said I shouldn't like it in the light of what you tell me. I shouldn't like it only to see her as you make me. I should like it if I could help her. But even then," Densher pursued without faith, "she would have to want it first herself. And there," he continued to make out, "is the devil of it. She *won't* want it herself. She *can't!*"

He had got up in his impatience of it, and she watched him while he helplessly moved. "There's one thing you can do. There's only that, and even for that there are difficulties. But there *is* that." He stood before her with his hands in his pockets, and he had soon enough, from her eyes, seen what was coming. She paused as if waiting for his leave to utter it, and, as he only let her wait, they heard, in the silence, on the Canal, the renewed downpour of rain. She had at last to speak, but, as if still with her fear, she only half spoke. "I think you really know yourself what it is."

He did know what it was, and with it even, as she said—rather!—there were difficulties. He turned away on them, on everything, for a moment; he moved to the other window and looked at the sheeted channel, wider, like a river, where the houses opposite, blurred and belittled, stood at twice their distance. Mrs. Stringham said nothing, was as mute, in fact, for the minute as if she had "had" him, and he was the first again to speak. When he did so, however, it was not in straight answer to her last remark—he only started from that. He said, as he came back to her, "Let me, you know, *see*—one must understand," almost as if, for the time, he had accepted it. And what he wished to understand was where, on the essence of the question, was the voice of Sir Luke Strett. If they talked of not giving her up shouldn't *he* be the one least of all to do it? "Aren't we, at the worst, in the dark without him?"

"Oh," said Mrs. Stringham, "it's he who has kept me going. I wired the first night, and he answered like an angel. He'll come like one. Only he can't arrive, at the nearest, till Thursday afternoon."

"Well then, that's something."

She hesitated. "Something—yes. She likes him."

"Rather! I can see it still, the face with which, when he was here in October—that night when she was in white, when she had people there and those musicians—she committed him to my care. It was beautiful for both of us—she put us in relation. She asked me, for the time, to take him about; I did so, and we quite hit it off. That proved," Densher said with a quick sad smile, "that she liked him."

"He liked *you*," Susan Shepherd presently risked.

"Ah, I know nothing about that."

"You ought to then. He went with you to galleries and churches; you saved his time for him, showed him the choicest things, and you perhaps will remember telling me, myself, that if he hadn't been a great surgeon he might really have been a great judge. I mean of the beautiful."

"Well," the young man admitted, "that's what he is—in having judged *her*. He hasn't," he went on, "judged her for nothing. His interest in her—which we must make the most of—can only be supremely beneficent."

He still roamed, while he spoke, with his hands in his pockets, and she saw him, on this, as her eyes sufficiently betrayed, trying to keep his distance from the recognition he had a few moments before partly confessed to. "I'm glad," she dropped, "you like him!"

There was something for him in the sound of it. "Well, I do no more, dear lady, than you do yourself. Surely *you* like him. Surely, when he was here, we all liked him."

"Yes, but I seem to feel I know what he thinks. And I should think, with all the time you spent with him, you would know it," she said, "yourself."

Densher stopped short, though at first without a word. "We never spoke of her. Neither of us mentioned her, even to sound her name, and nothing whatever, in connection with her, passed between us."

Mrs. Stringham stared up at him, surprised at this picture. But she had plainly an idea that, after an instant, resisted it. "That was his professional propriety."

"Precisely. But it was also my sense of that, and it was something more besides." And he spoke with sudden intensity. "I couldn't *talk* to him about her!"

"Oh!" said Susan Shepherd.

"I can't talk to any one about her."

"Except to *me*," his friend continued.

"Except to you." The ghost of her smile, a gleam of significance, had waited on her words, and it kept him, for honesty, looking at her. For honesty too—that is for his own words—he had quickly coloured: he was sinking so, at a stroke, the burden of his discourse with Kate. His visitor, for the minute, while their eyes met, might have been watching him hold it down. And he *had* to hold it down—the effort of which, precisely, made him red. He couldn't let it come up; at least not yet. She might make what she would of it. He attempted to repeat his statement, but he really modified it. "Sir Luke, at all events, had nothing to tell me, and I had nothing to tell him. Make-believe talk was impossible for us, and——"

"And *real*"—she had taken him right up with a huge emphasis—"was more impossible still." No doubt—he didn't deny it; and she had straightway drawn her conclusion. "Then that proves what I say—that there were immensities between you. Otherwise you'd have chattered."

"I dare say," Densher granted, "we were both thinking of her."

"You were neither of you thinking of any one else. That's why you kept together."

Well, that too, if she desired, he admitted; but he came straight back to what he had originally said. "I haven't a notion, all the same, of what he thinks." She faced him, visibly, with the question into which he had

already observed that her special shade of earnestness
was perpetually, right and left, flowering—"Are you
very sure?"—and he could only note her apparent difference from himself. "You, I judge, believe that he
thinks she's gone."

She took it, but she bore up. "It doesn't matter what
I believe."

"Well, we shall see"—and he felt almost basely
superficial. More and more, for the last five minutes,
had he known she had brought something with her, and
never, in respect to anything, had he had such a wish to
postpone. He would have liked to put everything off till
Thursday; he was sorry it was now Tuesday; he wondered if he were afraid. Yet it wasn't of Sir Luke, who
was coming; nor of Milly, who was dying; nor of Mrs.
Stringham, who was sitting there. It wasn't, strange to
say, of Kate either, for Kate's presence affected him
suddenly as having swooned or trembled away. Susan
Shepherd's, thus prolonged, had suffused it with some
influence under which it had ceased to act. She was as
absent to his sensibility as she had constantly been,
since her departure, absent, as an echo or a reference,
from the palace; and it was the first time, among the
objects now surrounding him, that his sensibility so
noted her. He knew soon enough that it was of himself
he was afraid, and that even, if he didn't take care, he
should infallibly be more so. "Meanwhile," he added
for his companion, "it has been everything for me to
see you."

She slowly rose, at the words, which might almost

have conveyed to her the hint of his taking care. She stood there as if, in fact, she had seen him abruptly moved to dismiss her. But the abruptness would have been in this case so marked as fairly to offer ground for insistence to her imagination of his state. It would take her moreover, she clearly showed him she was thinking, but a minute or two to insist. Besides, she had already said it. "Will you do it if *he* asks you? I mean if Sir Luke himself puts it to you. And will you give him"— oh, she was earnest now!—"the opportunity to put it to you?"

"The opportunity to put what?"

"That if you deny it to her, that may still do something."

Densher felt himself—as had already once befallen him in the quarter-of-an-hour—turn red to the top of his forehead. Turning red had, however, for him, as a sign of shame, been, so to speak, discounted; his consciousness of it at the present moment was rather as a sign of his fear. It showed him sharply enough of what he was afraid. "If I deny what to her?"

Hesitation, on the demand, revived in her, for hadn't he all along, been letting her see that he knew? "Why, what Lord Mark told her?"

"And what did Lord Mark tell her?"

Mrs. Stringham had a look of bewilderment—of seeing him as suddenly perverse. "I've been judging that you yourself know." And it was she who now blushed deep.

It quickened his pity for her, but he was beset too by other things. "Then *you* know——"

"Of his dreadful visit?" She stared. "Why, it's what has done it."

"Yes—I understand that. But you also know——"

He had faltered again, but all she knew she now wanted to say. "I'm speaking," she said soothingly, "of what he told her. It's *that* that I've taken you as knowing."

"Oh!" he sounded in spite of himself.

It appeared to have for her, he saw the next moment, the quality of relief, as if he had supposed her thinking of something else. Thereupon, straightway, that lightened it. "Oh, you thought I've known it for *true!*"

Her light had heightened her flush, and he saw that he had betrayed himself. Not, however, that it mattered, as he immediately saw still better. There it was now, all of it, at last, and this at least there was no postponing. They were left there with her idea—the one she was wishing to make him recognise. He had expressed ten minutes before his need to understand, and she was acting, after all, but on that. Only what he was to understand was no small matter; it might be larger even than as yet appeared.

He took again one of his turns, not meeting what she had last said; he mooned a minute, as he would have called it, at a window; and of course she could see that she had driven him to the wall. She did clearly, without delay, see it; on which her sense of having "caught"

him became, as promptly, a scruple, and she spoke as
if not to press it. "What I mean is that he told her
you've been all the while engaged to Miss Croy."

He gave a jerk round; it was almost—to hear it—the
touch of a lash; and he said—idiotically, as he afterwards knew—the first thing that came into his head.
"All *what* while?"

"Oh, it's not I who say it." She spoke in gentleness.
"I only repeat to you what he told her."

Densher, from whom an impatience had escaped, had
already caught himself up. "Pardon my brutality. Of
course I know what you're talking about. I saw him,
toward the evening," he further explained, "in the
Piazza; only just saw him—through the glass at Florian's—without any words. In fact I scarcely know him,
and there wouldn't have been occasion. It was but once,
moreover—he must have gone that night. But I knew he
wouldn't have come for nothing, and I turned it over—
what he would have come for."

Oh, so had Mrs. Stringham. "He came for exasperation."

Densher approved. "He came to let her know that he
knows better than she for whom it was she had a couple of months before, in her fool's paradise, refused
him."

"How you *do* know!"—and Mrs. Stringham almost
smiled.

"I know that—but I don't know the good it does
him."

"The good, he thinks, if he has patience—not too much—may be to come. He doesn't know what he has done to her. Only *we*, you see, do that."

He saw, but he wondered. "She kept from him—what she felt?"

"She was able—I'm sure of it—not to show anything. He dealt her his blow, and she took it without a sign." Mrs. Stringham, it was plain, spoke by book, and it brought into play again her appreciation of what she related. "She's magnificent."

Densher again gravely assented. "Magnificent!"

"And *he*," she went on, "is an idiot of idiots."

"An idiot of idiots." For a moment, on it all, on the stupid doom in it, they looked at each other. "Yet he's thought so awfully clever."

"So awfully—it's Maud Lowder's own view. And he was nice, in London," said Mrs. Stringham, "to *me*. One could almost pity him—he has had such a good conscience."

"That's exactly the inevitable ass."

"Yes, but it wasn't—I could see from the only few things she first told me—that he meant *her* the least harm. He intended none whatever."

"That's always the ass at his worst," Densher replied. "He only of course meant harm to me."

"And good to himself—he thought that would come. He had been unable to swallow," Mrs. Stringham pursued, "what had happened on his other visit. He had been then too sharply humiliated."

"Oh, I saw that."

"Yes, and he also saw you. He saw you received, as it were, while he was turned away."

"Perfectly," Densher said—"I've filled it out. And also that he has known meanwhile for *what* I was then received. For a stay of all these weeks. He had had it to think of."

"Precisely—it was more than he could bear. But he has it," said Mrs. Stringham, "to think of still."

"Only, after all," asked Densher, who himself, somehow, at this point, was having more to think of even than he had yet had—"only, after all, how has he happened to know? That is, to know enough."

"What do you call enough?" Mrs. Stringham inquired.

"He can only have acted—it would have been his only safety—from full knowledge."

He had gone on without heeding her question; but, face to face as they were, something had none the less passed between them. It was this that, after an instant, made her again interrogative. "What do you mean by full knowledge?"

Densher met it indirectly. "Where has he been since October?"

"I think he has been back to England. He came, in fact, I have reason to believe, straight from there."

"Straight to do this job? All the way for his half-hour?"

"Well, to try again—with the help perhaps of a new fact. To make himself right with her, possibly—a different attempt from the other. He had at any rate something to tell her, and he didn't know his opportunity would reduce itself to half-an-hour. Or perhaps indeed half-an-hour would be just what was most effective. It *has* been!" said Susan Shepherd.

Her companion took it in, understanding but too well; yet as she lighted the matter for him more, really, than his own courage had quite dared—putting the absent dots on several i's—he saw new questions swarm. They had been till now in a bunch, entangled and confused; and they fell apart, each showing for itself. The first he put to her was at any rate abrupt. "Have you heard of late from Mrs. Lowder?"

"Oh yes, two or three times. She depends, naturally, upon news of Milly."

He hesitated. "And does she depend, naturally, upon news of *me?*"

His friend matched for an instant his deliberation. "I've given her none that hasn't been decently good. This will have been the first."

" 'This?' " Densher was thinking.

"Lord Mark's having been here, and her being as she is."

He thought a moment longer. "What has she written about him? Has she written that he has been with them?"

"She has mentioned him but once—it was in her letter before the last. Then she said something."

"And what did she say?"

Mrs. Stringham produced it with an effort. "Well, it

was in reference to Miss Croy. That she thought Kate
was thinking of him. Or perhaps I should say, rather,
that he was thinking of *her*—only, it seemed this time to
have struck Mrs. Lowder, because of his seeing the way
more open to him."

Densher listened with his eyes on the ground, but he
presently raised them to speak, and there was that in his
face which proved him aware of a queerness in his question. "Does she mean he has been encouraged to *propose*
to her niece?"

"I don't know what she means."

"Of course not"—he recovered himself; "and I
oughtn't to seem to trouble you to piece together what
I can't piece myself. Only, I think," he added, "I *can*
piece it."

She spoke a little timidly, but she risked it. "I dare
say I can piece it too."

It was one of the things in her—and his conscious
face took it from her as such—that, from the moment
of her coming in, had seemed to mark for him, as to
what concerned him, the long jump of her perception.
They had parted four days earlier with many things,
between them, deep down. But these things were now
on their troubled surface, and it wasn't he who had
brought them so quickly up. Women were wonderful—
at least this one was. But so, not less, was Milly, was
Aunt Maud; so, most of all, was his very Kate. Well,
he already knew what he had been feeling about the circle of petticoats. They were all *such* petticoats! It was
just the fineness of his tangle. The sense of that, in its

turn, for us too, might have been not unconnected with his making an inquiry of his visitor that quite passed over her remark. "Has Miss Croy meanwhile written to our friend?"

"Oh," Mrs. Stringham amended, "*her* friend also. But not a single word that I know of."

He had taken it for certain she hadn't—the thing being, after all, but a shade more strange than his having himself, for six weeks, with Milly, never mentioned the young lady in question.. It was, for that matter, but a shade more strange than Milly's not having mentioned her. In spite of which, and however inconsequently, he blushed, once more, for Kate's silence. He got away from it in fact as quickly as possible, and the furthest he could get was by reverting for a minute to the man they had been judging. "How did he manage to get *at* her? She had only—with what had passed between them before—to say she couldn't see him."

"Oh, she was disposed to kindness. She was easier," the good lady explained with a slight embarrassment, "than at the other time."

"Easier?"

"She was off her guard. There was a difference."

"Yes. But exactly not *the* difference."

"Exactly not the difference of her having to be harsh. Perfectly. She could afford to be the opposite." With which, as he said nothing, she just impatiently completed her sense. "She had had *you* here for six weeks."

"Oh," Densher softly groaned.

"Besides, I think he must have written her first—

written, I mean, in a tone to smooth his way. That it
would be a kindness to himself. Then on the spot——"

"On the spot," Densher broke in, "he unmasked?
The horrid little beast!"

It made Susan Shepherd turn slightly pale, though
quickened, as for hope, the intensity of her look at him.
"Oh, he went off without an alarm."

"And he must have gone off also without a hope."

"Ah that, certainly."

"Then it *was* mere base revenge. Hasn't he known
her, into the bargain," the young man asked—"didn't
he, weeks before, see her, judge her, feel her, as having,
for such a suit as his, not more perhaps than a few
months to live?"

Mrs. Stringham at first, for reply, but looked at him
in silence; and it gave more force to what she then
remarkably added. "He has doubtless been aware of
what you speak of, just as you have yourself been
aware."

"He has wanted her, you mean, just *because*——?"

"Just because," said Susan Shepherd.

"The hound!" Merton Densher brought out. He
moved off, however, with a hot face, as soon as he had
spoken, conscious again of an intention in his visitor's
reserve. Dusk was now deeper, and after he had once
more taken counsel of the dreariness without he turned
to his companion. "Shall we have lights—a lamp or the
candles?"

"Not for me."

"Nothing?"

"Not for me."

He waited at the window another moment; then he
faced his friend with a thought. "He *will* have proposed
to Miss Croy. That's what has happened."

Her reserve continued. "It's you who must judge."

"Well, I do judge. Mrs. Lowder will have done so
too—only *she*, poor lady, wrong. Miss Croy's refusal of
him will have struck him"—Densher continued to make
it out—"as a phenomenon requiring a reason."

"And you've been clear to him *as* the reason?"

"Not too clear—since I'm sticking here, and since
that has been a fact to make his descent upon Miss
Theale relevant. But clear enough. He has believed,"
said Densher bravely, "that I may have been a reason
at Lancaster Gate, and yet at the same time have been
up to something in Venice."

Mrs. Stringham took her courage from his own.
" 'Up to' something? Up to what?"

"God knows. To some 'game,' as they say. To some
deviltry. To some duplicity."

"Which of course," Mrs. Stringham observed, "is a
monstrous supposition." Her companion, after a stiff
minute—long, sensibly, for each—fell away from her
again, and then added to it another minute, which he
spent once more looking out with his hands in his pockets. This was no answer, he perfectly knew, to what she
had dropped, and it even seemed to state, for his own
ears, that no answer was possible. She left him to himself, and he was glad she had declined, for their further
colloquy, the advantage of lights. These would have

been an advantage mainly to herself. Yet she got her
benefit, too, even from the absence of them. It came out
in her very tone when at last she addressed him—so differently, for confidence—in words she had already used.
"If Sir Luke himself asks it of you as something you can
do for *him*, will you deny to Milly herself what she has
been made so dreadfully to believe?"

Oh, how he knew he hung back! But at last he said:
"You're absolutely certain then that she does believe it?"

"Certain?" She appealed to their whole situation.
"Judge!"

He took his time again to judge. "Do *you* believe it?"

He was conscious that his own appeal pressed her
hard; it eased him a little that her answer must be a pain
to her discretion. She answered, none the less, and he
was truly the harder pressed. "What I believe will
inevitably depend more or less on your action. You can
perfectly settle it—if you care. I promise to believe you
down to the ground if, to save her life, you consent to
a denial."

"But a denial, when it comes to that—confound the
whole thing, don't you see!—of exactly what?"

It was as if he were hoping she would narrow; but in
fact she enlarged. "Of everything."

Everything had never even yet seemed to him so
incalculably much. "Oh!" he simply moaned into the
gloom.

IV

THE NEAR THURSDAY, coming nearer and bringing Sir Luke Strett, brought also blessedly an abatement of other rigours. The weather changed, the stubborn storm yielded, and the autumn sunshine, baffled for many days, but now hot and almost vindictive, came into its own again and, with an almost audible pæan, a suffusion of bright sound that was one with the bright colour, took large possession. Venice glowed and plashed and called and chimed again; the air was like a clap of hands, and the scattered pinks, yellows, blues, sea-greens, were like a hanging-out of vivid stuffs, a laying down of fine carpets. Densher rejoiced in this on the occasion of his going to the station to meet the great doctor. He went after consideration, which, as he was constantly aware, was at present his imposed, his only, way of doing anything. That was where the event had landed him— where no event in his life had landed him before. He had thought, no doubt, from the day he was born, much more than he had acted; except indeed that he remembered thoughts—a few of them—which at the moment of their coming to him had thrilled him almost like adventures. But anything like his actual state he had not, as to the prohibition of impulse, accident, range—the prohibition, in other words, of freedom—hitherto known. The great oddity was that if he had felt his arrival, so few weeks back, especially as an adventure, nothing could now less resemble one than the fact of his staying. It would be an adventure to break away, to

depart, to go back, above all, to London, and tell Kate
Croy he had done so; but there was something of the
merely, the almost meanly, obliged and involved sort in
his going on as he was. That was the effect in particular of Mrs. Stringham's visit, which had left him as with
such a taste in his mouth of what he couldn't do. It had
made this quantity clear to him, and yet had deprived
him of the sense, the other sense, of what, for a refuge,
he possibly *could*.

It was but a small make-believe of freedom, he knew,
to go to the station for Sir Luke. Nothing equally free,
at all events, had he yet turned over so long. What then
was his odious position but that, again and again, he was
afraid? He stiffened himself under this consciousness as
if it had been a tax levied by a tyrant. He had not at any
time proposed to himself to live long enough for fear to
preponderate in his life. Such was simply the advantage
it had actually got of him. He was afraid, for instance,
that an advance to his distinguished friend might prove
for him somehow a pledge or a committal. He was
afraid of it as a current that would draw him too far;
yet he thought with an equal shrinking of being shabby,
being poor, through fear. What finally prevailed with
him was the reflection that, whatever might happen, the
great man had, after that occasion at the palace, their
friend's brief sacrifice to society—and the hour of Mrs.
Stringham's appeal had brought it well to the surface—
shown him marked benevolence. Mrs. Stringham's com-
ments on the relation in which Milly had placed them
made him—it was unmistakable—feel things he perhaps

hadn't felt. It was in fact in the spirit of seeking a
chance to feel again adequately whatever it was he had
missed—it was, no doubt, in that spirit, so far as it went
a stroke for freedom, that Densher, arriving betimes,
paced the platform before the train came in. Only, after
it had come and he had presented himself at the door
of Sir Luke's compartment with everything that followed—only, as the situation developed, the sense of an
anticlimax to so many intensities deprived his apprehensions and hesitations even of the scant dignity they
might claim. He could scarce have said if the visitor's
manner less showed the remembrance that might have
suggested expectation, or made shorter work of surprise
in the presence of the fact.

Sir Luke had clean forgotten—so Densher read—the
rather remarkable young man he had formerly gone
about with, though he picked him up again, on the spot,
with one large quiet look. The young man felt himself
so picked, and the thing immediately affected him as the
proof of a splendid economy. In presence of all the
waste with which he was now connected, the exhibition
was of a nature quite nobly to admonish him. The eminent pilgrim, in the train, all the way, had used the
hours as he had needed, thinking not a moment in
advance of what finally awaited him. An exquisite case
awaited him—of which, in this queer way, the remarkable young man was an outlying part; but the single
motion of his face, the motion into which Densher, on
the platform, lightly stirred its stillness, was his first
renewed cognition. If, however, he had suppressed the

matter by leaving Victoria he would suppress now, in a
minute, instead, whatever else suited. The perception
of this became as a symbol for Densher of the whole
pitch, so far as Densher himself might be concerned, of
his visit. One saw, our friend further meditated, everything that, in contact, he appeared to accept—if only,
for much, not to trouble to sink it: what one didn't see
was the inward use he made of it. Densher began wondering, at the great water-steps outside, what use he
would make of the anomaly of their having there to separate. Eugenio had been on the platform, in the respect-
ful rear, and the gondola from the palace, under his
direction, bestirred itself, with its attaching mixture of
alacrity and dignity, on their coming out of the station
together. Densher didn't at all mind now that, he himself of necessity refusing a seat, on the deep black cushions, beside the guest of the palace, he had Milly's three
emissaries for spectators; and this, susceptibility, he also
knew, it was something to have left behind. He only,
vaguely, smiled down from the steps—they could see
him, the donkeys, as shut out as they would. "I don't,"
he said with a sad headshake, "go there now."

"Oh!" Sir Luke Strett returned, and made no more
of it; so that the thing was splendid, Densher fairly
thought, as an inscrutability quite inevitable and unconscious. His friend appeared not even to make of it that
he supposed that it might be for respect to the crisis. He
didn't moreover afterwards make much more of anything—after the classic craft, that is, obeying in the
main Pasquale's inimitable stroke from the poop, had

performed the manœuvre by which it presented, receding, a back, so to speak, rendered positively graceful by the high black hump of its *felze*. Densher watched the gondola out of sight—he heard Pasquale's cry, borne to him across the water, for the sharp, firm swerve into a side-canal, a short cut to the palace. He had no gondola of his own; it was his habit never to take one; and he humbly—as in Venice it *is* humble—walked away, though not without having, for some time longer, stood, as if fixed, where the guest of the palace had left him. It was strange enough, but he found himself, as never yet, and as he couldn't have reckoned, in presence of the truth that was the truest about Milly. He couldn't have reckoned on the force of the difference instantly made— for it was all in the air as he heard Pasquale's cry and saw the boat to disappear—by the mere visibility, on the spot, of the personage summoned to her aid. He had not only never been near the facts of her condition—which had been such a blessing for him; he had not only, with all the world, hovered outside an impenetrable ring fence, within which there reigned a kind of expensive vagueness, made up of smiles and silences and beautiful fictions and priceless arrangements, all strained to breaking; but he had also, with everyone else, as he now felt, actively fostered suppressions which were in the direct interest of everyone's good manner, everyone's pity, everyone's really quite generous ideal. It was a conspiracy of silence, as the *cliché* went, to which no one had made an exception, the great smudge of mortality across the picture, the shadow of pain and horror, finding in no quarter a surface of spirit or of speech that consented to reflect it. "The mere æsthetic instinct of mankind——!" our young man had more than once, in the connection, said to himself; letting the rest of the proposition drop, but touching again thus sufficiently on the outrage even to taste involved in one's having to *see*. So then it had been—a general conscious fool's paradise, from which the specified had been chased like a dangerous animal. What therefore had at present befallen was that the specified, standing all the while at the gate, had now come in, as in Sir Luke Strett's person, and quite on such a scale as to fill out the whole of the space. Densher's nerves, absolutely his heart-beats too, had measured the change before he, on this occasion, moved away.

The facts of physical suffering, of incurable pain, of the chance grimly narrowed, had been made, at a stroke, intense, and this was to be the way he was now to feel them. The clearance of the air, in short, making vision not only possible but inevitable, the one thing left to be thankful for was the breadth of Sir Luke's shoulders, which, should one be able to keep in line with them, might in some degree interpose. It was, however, far from plain to Densher for the first day or two that he was again to see his distinguished friend at all. That he could not, on any basis actually serving, return to the palace—that was as solid to him, every whit, as the other feature of his case, the fact of the publicity attaching to his proscription through his not having taken himself off. He had been seen often enough in the Lep-

orelli gondola. As, accordingly, he was not, to any
appearance, destined to meet Sir Luke about the town,
where the latter would have neither time nor taste to
lounge, nothing more would occur between them unless
the great man should surprisingly wait upon him. His
doing that, Densher further reflected, wouldn't even
simply depend on Mrs. Stringham's having decided to—
as they might say—turn him on. It would depend as
well—for there would be practically some difference to
her—on her actually attempting it; and it would depend
above all on what Sir Luke would make of such an overture. Densher had, for that matter, his own view of the
amount, to say nothing of the particular sort, of
response it might expect from him. He had his own
view of the ability of such a personage even to understand such an appeal. To what extent could he be prepared, and what importance, in fine, could he attach?
Densher asked himself these questions, in truth, to put
his own position at the worst. He should miss the great
man completely unless the great man should come to see
him, and the great man could only come to see him for
a purpose unsupposable. Therefore he wouldn't come at
all, and therefore there was nothing to hope.

It wasn't in the least that Densher hoped for a visit in
that particular light; but it pressed on him that there
were few possible diversions he could afford now to
miss. Nothing in his predicament was so odd as that,
incontestably afraid of himself, he was not afraid of Sir
Luke. He had an impression, which he clung to, based
on a previous taste of his company, that *he* would some-

how let him off. The truth about Milly perched on his
shoulders and sounded in his tread, became by the fact
of his presence the name and the form, for the time, of
everything in the place; but it didn't, for the difference,
sit in his face, the face so squarely and easily turned to
Densher at the earlier season. His presence on the first
occasion, not as the result of a summons, but as a
friendly fancy of his own, had had quite another value;
and though our young man could scarce regard that
value as recoverable, he yet reached out in imagination
to a renewal of the old contact. He didn't propose, as
he privately and forcibly phrased the matter, to be a
hog; but there was something, after all, he did want for
himself. It was something—this stuck to him—that Sir
Luke would have had for him if it hadn't been impossible. These were his worst days, the two or three; those
on which even the sense of the tension at the palace
didn't much help him not to feel that his destiny made
but light of him. He had never been, as he judged it, so
down. In mean conditions, without books, without society, almost without money, he had nothing to do but to
wait. His main support really was his original idea,
which didn't leave him, of waiting for the deepest depth
his predicament could sink him to. Fate would invent, if
he but gave it time, some refinement of the horrible.

It was just inventing meanwhile this suppression of
Sir Luke. When the third day came without a sign he
knew what to think. He had given Mrs. Stringham, during her call on him, no such answer as would have
armed her faith, and the ultimatum she had described as

ready for him when *he* should be ready was therefore—if on no other ground than her want of this power to answer for him—not to be presented. The presentation, heaven knew, was not what he desired.

That was not, either, we hasten to declare—as Densher then soon enough saw—the idea with which Sir Luke finally stood before him again. For stand before him again he finally did; just when our friend had gloomily embraced the belief that the limit of his power to absent himself from London obligations would have been reached. Four or five days, exclusive of journeys, represented the largest supposable sacrifice—to a head not crowned—on the part of one of the highest medical lights in the world; so that, really, when the personage in question, following up a tinkle of the bell, solidly rose in the doorway, it was to impose on Densher a vision that for the instant cut like a knife. It spoke, the fact, in a single dreadful word, of the magnitude—he shrank from calling it anything else—of Milly's case. The great man had not gone then, and an immense surrender to her immense need was so expressed in it that some effect, some help, some hope, were, flagrantly, part of the expression. It was for Densher, with his reaction from disappointment, as if he were conscious of ten things at once—the foremost being that, just conceivably, since Sir Luke *was* still there, she had been saved. Close upon its heels, however, and quite as sharply came the sense that the crisis—plainly, even now, to be prolonged for him—was to have none of that sound simplicity. Not only had his visitor not dropped in to gossip about Milly, he had not dropped in to mention her at all; he had dropped in fairly to show that during the brief remainder of his stay, the end of which was now in sight, as little as possible of that was to be looked for. The demonstration, such as it was, was in the key of their previous acquaintance, and it was their previous acquaintance that had made him come. He was not to stop longer than the Saturday next at hand, but there were things of interest he should like to see again meanwhile. It was for these things of interest, for Venice and the opportunity of Venice, for a prowl or two, as he called it, and a turn about, that he had looked his young man up—producing on the latter's part, as soon as the case had, with the lapse of a further twenty-four hours, so defined itself, the most incongruous, yet most beneficent revulsion. Nothing could in fact have been more monstrous on the surface—and Densher was well aware of it—than the relief he found, during this short period, in the tacit drop of all reference to the palace, in neither hearing news nor asking for it. That was what had come out for him, on his visitor's entrance, even in the very seconds of suspense that were connecting the fact also directly and intensely with Milly's state. He had come to say he had saved her—he had come, as from Mrs. Stringham, to say how she might *be* saved—he had come, in spite of Mrs. Stringham, to say she was lost: the distinct throbs of hope, of fear, simultaneous for all their distinctness, merged their identity in a bound of the heart just as immediate and which remained after they had passed. It simply did wonders for him—that was the truth—that Sir Luke was, as he would have said, quiet.

The result of it was the oddest consciousness as of a blessed calm after a storm. He had been trying, for weeks, as we know, to keep superlatively still, and trying it largely in solitude and silence; but he looked back on it now as on the heat of fever. The real, the right stillness was this particular form of society. They walked together and they talked, looked up pictures again and recovered impressions—Sir Luke knew just what he wanted; haunted a little the dealers in old wares; sat down at Florian's for rest and mild drinks; blessed, above all, the grand weather, a bath of warm air, a pageant of autumn light. Once or twice, while they rested, the great man closed his eyes—keeping them so for some minutes while his companion, the more easily watching his face for it, made private reflections on the subject of lost sleep. He had been up at night with her— he in person, for hours; but this was all he showed of it, and this was apparently to remain his nearest approach to an allusion. The extraordinary thing was that Densher could take it in perfectly as evidence, could turn cold at the image looking out of it; and yet that he could at the same time not intermit a throb of his response to accepted liberation. The liberation was an experience that held its own, and he continued to know why, in spite of his deserts, in spite of his folly, in spite of everything, he had so fondly hoped for it. He had hoped for it, had sat in his room there waiting for it, because he had thus divined in it, should it come, some power to let him off. He was *being* let off; dealt with in

the only way that didn't aggravate his responsibility.
The beauty was, too, that this wasn't on system or on
any basis of intimate knowledge; it was just by being a
man of the world and by knowing life, by feeling the
real, that Sir Luke did him good. There had been, in all
the case, too many women. A man's sense of it, another
man's, changed the air; and he wondered what man, had
he chosen, would have been more to his purpose than
this one. He was large and easy—that was the great
thing; he knew what mattered and what didn't; he distinguished between the just grounds and the unjust for
fussing. One was thus—if one were concerned with him
or exposed to him at all—in his hands for whatever he
should do, and not much less affected by his mercy than
one might have been by his rigour. The beautiful
thing—it did come to that—was the way he carried off,
as one might fairly call it, the business of making odd
things natural. Nothing, if they hadn't taken it so, could
have exceeded the unexplained oddity, between them, of
Densher's now complete detachment from the poor
ladies at the palace; nothing could have exceeded the no
less marked anomaly of the great man's own abstentions
of speech. He made, as he had done when they had met
at the station, nothing whatever of anything; and the
effect of it, Densher would have said, was a relation with
him quite resembling that of doctor and patient. One
took the cue from him as one might have taken a dose—
except that the cue was pleasant in the taking.

That was why one could leave it to his tacit discretion,
why, for the three or four days, again and again, Densher

did so leave it; merely wondering a little, at the most, on the eve of Saturday, the announced term of the episode. Waiting once more, on this latter occasion, the Saturday morning, for Sir Luke's reappearance at the station, our friend had to recognise the drop of his own borrowed ease, the result, naturally enough, of the prospect of losing a support. The difficulty was that, on such lines as had served them, the support was Sir Luke's personal presence. Would he go without leaving some substitute for that?—and without breaking, either, his silence in respect to his errand? Densher was in still deeper ignorance than at the hour of his call, and what was truly prodigious at so supreme a moment was that—as was immediately to appear—no gleam of light on what he had been living with for a week found its way out of him. What he had been doing was proof of a huge interest as well as of a huge fee; yet when the Leporelli gondola again, and somewhat tardily, approached, his companion, watching from the water-steps, studied his fine closed face as much as ever in vain. It was like a lesson, from the highest authority, on the subject of the relevant, so that its blankness affected Densher, of a sudden, almost as a cruelty, feeling it quite awfully compatible, as he did, with Milly's having ceased to exist. And the suspense continued after they had passed together, as time was short, directly into the station, where Eugenio, in the field early, was mounting guard over the compartment he had secured. The strain, though probably lasting, at the carriage-door, but a couple of minutes, prolonged itself so for Densher's nerves

that he involuntarily directed a long look at Eugenio,
who met it, however, as only Eugenio could. Sir Luke's
attention was given for the time to the right bestowal of
his numerous effects, about which he was particular, and
Densher fairly found himself, so far as silence could go,
questioning the representative of the palace. It didn't
humiliate him now; it didn't humiliate him even to feel
that that personage exactly knew how little he satisfied
him. Eugenio resembled to that extent Sir Luke—to the
extent of the extraordinary things with which his facial
habit was compatible. By the time, however, that Densher had taken from it all its possessor intended Sir Luke
was free and with a hand out for farewell. He offered the
hand at first without speech; only on meeting his eyes
could our young man see that they had never yet so
completely looked at him. It was never, with Sir Luke,
that they looked harder at one time than at another; but
they looked longer, and this, even a shade of it, might
mean, in him, everything. It meant, Densher for ten seconds believed, that Milly Theale was dead; so that the
word at last spoken made him start.

"I shall come back."

"Then she's better?"

"I shall come back within the month," Sir Luke
repeated without heeding the question. He had dropped
Densher's hand, but he held him otherwise still. "I
bring you a message from Miss Theale," he said as if
they had not spoken of her. "I'm commissioned to ask
you from her to go and see her."

Densher's rebound from his supposition had a violence that his stare betrayed. "*She* asks me?"

Sir Luke had got into the carriage, the door of which the guard had closed; but he spoke again as he stood at the window, bending a little but not leaning out. "She told me she would like it, and I promised that, as I expected to find you here, I would let you know."

Densher, on the platform, took it from him, but what he took brought the blood into his face quite as what he had had to take from Mrs. Stringham. And he was also bewildered. "Then she can receive——?"

"She can receive you."

"And you're coming back——?"

"Oh, because I must. She's not to move. She's to stay. I come to her."

"I see, I see," said Densher, who indeed did see—saw the sense of his friend's words and saw beyond it as well. What Mrs. Stringham had announced, and what he had yet expected not to have to face, *had* then come. Sir Luke had kept it for the last, but there it was, and the colourless, compact form it was now taking—the tone of one man of the world to another, who, after what had happened, would understand—was but the characteristic manner of his appeal. Densher was to understand remarkably much; and the great thing, certainly, was to show that he did. "I'm particularly obliged, I'll go to-day." He brought that out, but in his pause, while they continued to look at each other, the train had slowly creaked into motion. There was time but for one more word, and the young man chose it, out of twenty, with intense concentration. "Then she's better?"

Sir Luke's face was wonderful. "Yes, she's better." And he kept it at the window while the train receded, holding him with it still. It was to be his nearest approach to the uttered reference they had hitherto so successfully avoided. If it stood for everything, never had a face had to stand for more. So Densher, held after the train had gone, sharply reflected; so he reflected, asking himself into what abyss it pushed him, even while conscious of retreating under the sustained observation of Eugenio.

Book Tenth
....

I

"THEN IT HAS BEEN—what do you say? a whole fortnight?—without your making a sign?"

Kate put that to him distinctly, in the December dusk
of Lancaster Gate, and on the matter of the time he had
been back; but he saw with it, straightway, that she was
as admirably true as ever to her instinct—which was a
system as well—of not admitting the possibility between
them of small resentments, of trifles to trip up their general trust. That by itself, the renewed beauty of it,
would, at this fresh sight of her, have stirred him to his
depths if something else, something no less vivid, but
quite separate, hadn't stirred him still more. It was in
seeing her that he felt what their interruption had been,
and that they met across it even as persons whose
adventures, on either side, in time and space, of the
nature of perils and exiles, had had a peculiar strangeness. He wondered if he were as different for her as she
herself had immediately appeared: which was but his
way indeed of taking it in, with his thrill, that—even
going by the mere first look—she had never been so
handsome. That fact bloomed for him, in the firelight

and lamplight that glowed their welcome through the London fog, as the flower of her difference; just as her difference itself—part of which was her striking him as older in a degree for which no mere couple of months could account—was the fruit of their intimate relation. If she was different it was because they had chosen together that she should be, and she might now, as a proof of their wisdom, their success, of the reality of what had happened—of what in fact, for the spirit of each, was still happening—been showing it to him for pride. His having returned and yet kept, for numbered days, so still, had been, he was quite aware, the first point he should have to tackle; with which consciousness indeed he had made a clean breast of it in finally addressing Mrs. Lowder a note that had led to his present visit. He had written to Aunt Maud, as the finer way; and it would doubtless have been to be noted that he needed no effort not to write to Kate. Venice was three weeks behind him—he had come up slowly; but it was still as if even in London he must conform to her law. That was exactly how he was able, with his faith in her steadiness, to appeal to her feeling for the situation and explain his stretched delicacy. He had come to tell her everything, so far as occasion would serve them; and if nothing was more distinct than that his slow journey, his waits, his delay to reopen communication had kept pace with this resolve, so the inconsequence was doubtless at bottom but one of the accidents of intensity. He was gathering everything up, everything he should tell her. That took time, and the proof was that, as he felt on the spot, he couldn't have brought it all with him before this afternoon. He *had* brought it, to the last syllable, and, out of the quantity it wouldn't be hard—as he in fact found—to produce, for Kate's understanding, his first reason.

"A fortnight, yes—it was a fortnight Friday; but I've only been keeping in, you see, with our wonderful system." He was so easily justified as that this of itself plainly enough prevented her saying she didn't see. Their wonderful system was accordingly still vivid for her; and such a gage of its equal vividness for himself was precisely what she must have asked. He hadn't even to dot his i's beyond the remark that, on the very face of it, she would remember, their wonderful system attached no premium to rapidities of transition. "I couldn't quite—don't you know?—take my rebound with a rush; and I suppose I've been instinctively hanging off to minimise, for you as well as for myself, the appearance of rushing. There's a sort of fitness. But I knew you'd understand." It was presently as if she really understood so well that she almost appealed from his insistence—yet looking at him too, he was not unconscious, as if this mastery of fitnesses was a strong sign for her of what she had done to him. He might have struck her as expert for contingencies in the very degree in which, in Venice, she had struck *him* as expert. He smiled over his plea for a renewal with stages and steps, a thing shaded, as they might say, and graduated; though—finely as she must respond—she met the smile but as she had met his entrance five minutes before. Her soft gravity at that moment—which was yet not solemnity, but the look of a consciousness charged with life to the brim and wishing not to overflow—had not qualified her welcome; what had done this being much more the presence in the room, for a couple of minutes, of the footman who had introduced him and who had been interrupted in preparing the tea-table.

Mrs. Lowder's reply to Densher's note had been to appoint the tea-hour, five o'clock on Sunday, for his seeing them. Kate had thereafter wired him, without a signature, "Come on Sunday *before* time—about a quarter-of-an-hour, which will help us"; and he had arrived therefore, scrupulously, at twenty minutes to five. Kate was alone in the room, and she had not delayed to tell him that Aunt Maud, as she had happily gathered, was to be, for the interval—not long, but precious—engaged with an old servant, retired and pensioned, who had been paying her a visit and who was, within the hour, to depart again for the suburbs. They were to have the scrap of time, after the withdrawal of the footman, to themselves, and there was a moment when, in spite of their wonderful system, in spite of the proscription of rushes and the propriety of shades, it proclaimed itself indeed precious. And all without prejudice—that was what kept it noble—to Kate's high sobriety and her beautiful self-command. If he had his discretion she had her perfect manner, which was *her* decorum. Mrs. Stringham, he had, to finish with the question of his delay, furthermore observed, would have written to Mrs. Lowder of his having quitted the place;

so that it wasn't as if he were hoping to cheat them.
They would know he was no longer there.

"Yes, we've known it."

"And you continue to hear?"

"From Mrs. Stringham? Certainly. By which I mean
Aunt Maud does."

"Then you've recent news?"

Her face showed a wonder. "Up to within a day or
two I believe. But haven't *you?*"

"No—I've heard nothing." And it was now that he
felt how much he had to tell her. "I don't get letters.
But I've been sure Mrs. Lowder does." With which he
added: "Then of course you know." He waited as if she
would show what she knew; but she only showed, in
silence, the dawn of a surprise that she couldn't control.
There was nothing but for him to ask what he wanted.
"Is Miss Theale alive?"

Kate's look, at this, was large. "Don't you *know?*"

"How should I, my dear—in the absence of everything?" And he himself stared as for light. "She's dead?"
Then as, with her eyes on him, she slowly shook her
head, he uttered a strange "Not yet?"

It came out in Kate's face that there were several
questions on her lips, but the one she presently put was:
"Is it very terrible?"

"The manner of her so consciously and helplessly
dying?" He had to think a moment. "Well, yes—since
you ask me: very terrible to *me*—so far as, before I came
away, I had any sight of it. But I don't think," he went
on, "that—though I'll try—I *can* quite tell you what it

was, what it is, for me. That's why I probably just sounded to you," he explained, "as if I hoped it might be over."

She gave him her quietest attention, but he by this time saw that, so far as telling her all was concerned, she would be divided between the wish and the reluctance to hear it; between the curiosity that, not unnaturally, would consume her and the opposing scruple of a respect for misfortune. The more she studied him too— and he had never so felt her closely attached to his face—the more the choice of an attitude would become impossible to her. There would be a feeling, simply, uppermost, and the feeling wouldn't be eagerness. This perception grew in him fast, and he even, with his imagination, had for a moment the quick forecast of her possibly breaking out at him, should he go too far, with a wonderful: "What horrors are you telling me?" It would have the sound—wouldn't it be open to him fairly to bring that out himself?—of a repudiation, for pity and almost for shame, of everything that, in Venice, had passed between them. Not that she would confess to any return upon herself; not that she would let compunction or horror give her away; but it was in the air for him—yes—that she wouldn't want details, that she positively wouldn't take them, and that, if he would generously understand it from her, she would prefer to keep him down. Nothing, however, was more definite for him than that he, at the same time, must remain down but so far as it suited him. Something rose strong within him against his not being free with her. She had been free enough, about it all, three months before, with *him*. That was what she was at present only in the sense of treating him handsomely. "I can believe," she said with perfect consideration, "how dreadful for you much of it must have been."

He didn't, however, take this up; there were things about which he wished first to be clear. "There's no other possibility, by what you now know? I mean for her life." And he had just to insist—she would say as little as she could. "She is dying?"

"She's dying."

It was strange to him, in the matter of Milly, that Lancaster Gate could make him any surer; yet what in the world, in the matter of Milly, was not strange? Nothing was so much so as his own behaviour—his present as well as his past. He could but do as he must. "Has Sir Luke Strett," he asked, "gone back to her?"

"I believe he's there now."

"Then," said Densher, "it's the end."

She took it in silence for whatever he deemed it to be; but she spoke otherwise after a minute. "You won't know, unless you've perhaps seen him yourself, that Aunt Maud has been to him."

"Oh!" Densher exclaimed, with nothing to add to it.

"For real news," Kate herself after an instant added.

"She hasn't thought Mrs. Stringham's real?"

"It's perhaps only I who haven't. It was on Aunt Maud's trying again, three days ago, to see him, that she heard, at his house, of his having gone. He had started, I believe, some days before."

"And won't then by this time be back?"

Kate shook her head. "She sent yesterday to know."

"He won't leave her then"—Densher had turned it over—"while she lives. He'll stay to the end. He's magnificent."

"I think *she* is," said Kate.

It had made them again look at each other long; and what it drew from him, rather oddly, was: "Oh, you don't know!"

"Well, she's after all my friend."

It was somehow, with her handsome demur, the answer he had least expected of her; and it fanned with its breath, for a brief instant, his old sense of her variety. "I see. You would have been sure of it. You *were* sure of it."

"Of course I was sure of it."

And a pause again, with this, fell upon them; which Densher, however, presently broke. "If you don't think Mrs. Stringham's news 'real,' what do you think of Lord Mark's?"

She didn't think anything. "Lord Mark's?"

"You haven't seen him?"

"Not since he saw her."

"You've known then of his seeing her?"

"Certainly. From Mrs. Stringham."

"And have you known," Densher went on, "the rest?"

Kate wondered. "What rest?"

"Why, everything. It was his visit that she couldn't stand—it was what then took place that simply killed her."

"Oh!" Kate seriously breathed. But she had turned pale, and he saw that, whatever her degree of ignorance of these connections, it was not put on. "Mrs. Stringham hasn't said *that*."

He observed, none the less, that she didn't ask what had then taken place; and he went on with his contribution to her knowledge. "The way it affected her was that it made her give up. She has given up beyond all power to care again, and that's why she's dying."

"Oh!" Kate once more slowly sighed, but with a vagueness that made him pursue.

"One can see now that she was living by will—which was very much what you originally told me of her."

"I remember. That was it."

"Well then, her will, at a given moment, broke down, and the collapse was determined by that fellow's dastardly stroke. He told her, the scoundrel, that you and I are secretly engaged."

Kate gave a quick glare. "But he doesn't know it!"

"That doesn't matter. *She* did, when he had left her. Besides," Densher added, "he does know it. When," he continued, "did you last see him?"

But she was lost now in the picture before her. "*That* was what made her worse?"

He watched her take it in—it so added to her sombre beauty. Then he spoke as Mrs. Stringham had spoken. "She turned her face to the wall."

"Poor Milly!" said Kate.

Slight as it was, her beauty somehow gave it style; so that he continued consistently: "She learned it, you see,

too soon—since of course one's idea had been that she
might never even learn it at all. And she *had* felt sure—
through everything we had done—of there not being,
between us, so far at least as you were concerned, anything she need regard as a warning."

She took another moment for thought. "It wasn't
through anything *you* did—whatever that may have
been—that she gained her certainty. It was by the conviction she got from me."

"Oh, it's very handsome," Densher said, "for you to
take your share!"

"Do you suppose," Kate asked, "I think of denying
it?"

Her look and her tone made him, for the instant,
regret his comment, which indeed had been the first that
rose to his lips as an effect, absolutely, of what they
would have called between them her straightness. Her
straightness, visibly, was all his own loyalty could ask.
Still, that was comparatively beside the mark. "Of
course I don't suppose anything but that we're together
in our recognitions, our responsibilities—whatever we
choose to call them. It isn't a question for us of appor-
tioning shares or distinguishing invidiously among such
impressions as it was our idea to give."

"It wasn't *your* idea to give impressions," said Kate.

He met this with a smile that he himself felt, in its
strained character, as queer. "Don't go into that!"

It was perhaps not as going into it then that she had
another idea—an idea born, as she showed, of the vision
he had just evoked. "Wouldn't it have been possible

then to deny the truth of the information? I mean of Lord Mark's."

Densher wondered. "Possible for whom?"

"Why, for you."

"To tell her that he lied?"

"To tell her he's mistaken."

Densher stared—he was stupefied; the "possible" thus glanced at by Kate being exactly the alternative he had had to face in Venice, and to put utterly away from him. Nothing was stranger than such a difference in their view of it. "And to lie myself, you mean, to do it? We *are*, my dear child," he said, "I suppose, still engaged."

"Of course we're still engaged. But to save her life——!"

He took in for a little the way she talked of it. Of course, it was to be remembered, she had always simplified, and it brought back his sense of the degree in which, to her energy as compared with his own, many things were easy; the very sense that so often before had moved him to admiration. "Well, if you must know—and I want you to be clear about it—I didn't even seriously think of a denial to her face. The question of it—*as* possibly saving her—was put to me definitely enough; but to turn it over was only to dismiss it. Besides," he added, "it wouldn't have done any good."

"You mean she would have had no faith in your correction?" She had spoken with a promptitude that affected him of a sudden as almost glib; but he himself paused with the overweight of all he meant, and she meanwhile went on. "Did you try?"

"I hadn't even the chance."

Kate maintained her wonderful manner, the manner of at once having it all before her and yet keeping it all at its distance. "She wouldn't see you?"

"Not after your friend had been with her."

She hesitated. "Couldn't you write?"

It made him also think, but with a difference. "She had turned her face to the wall."

This again for a moment hushed her, and they were both too grave now for parenthetic pity. But her interest came out for at least the minimum of light. "She refused even to let you speak to her?"

"My dear girl," Densher returned, "she was miserably, prohibitively ill."

"Well, that was what she had been before."

"And it didn't prevent? No," Densher admitted, "it didn't; and I don't pretend that she's not magnificent."

"She's prodigious," said Kate Croy.

He looked at her a moment. "So are you, my dear. But so it is," he wound up; "and there we are."

His idea had been, in advance, that she would perhaps sound him much more deeply, asking him, above all, two or three specific things. He had fairly fancied her even wanting to know and trying to find out how far, as the odious phrase was, he and Milly had gone, and how near, by the same token, they had come. He had asked himself if he were prepared to hear her do that, and had had to take for answer that he was prepared of course for everything. Wasn't he prepared for her ascertaining if her two or three prophecies had found time to be made true? He had fairly believed himself ready to say whether or no the overture on Milly's part, promised according to the boldest of them, had taken place. But what was in fact blessedly coming to him was that, so far as such things were concerned, his readiness wouldn't be taxed. Kate's pressure on the question of what had taken place remained so admirably general that even her present inquiry kept itself free of sharpness. "So then that after Lord Mark's interference you never again met?"

It was what he had been all the while coming to.

"No; we met once—so far as it could be called a meeting. I had stayed—I didn't come away."

"That," said Kate, "was no more than decent."

"Precisely"—he felt himself wonderful; "and I wanted to be no less. She sent for me, I went to her, and that night I left Venice."

His companion waited. "Wouldn't *that* then have been your chance?"

"To refute Lord Mark's story? No, not even if, before her there, I had wanted to. What did it matter, either? She was dying."

"Well," Kate in a manner persisted. "Why not just *because* she was dying?" She had, however, all her discretion. "But of course, I know, seeing her, you could judge."

"Of course, seeing her, I could judge. And I did see her! If I had denied you, moreover," Densher said with his eyes on her, "I would have stuck to it."

She took for a moment the intention of his face. "You

mean that, to convince her, you would have insisted or somehow proved——?"

"I mean that, to convince *you*, I would have insisted or somehow proved——!"

Kate looked for her moment at a loss. "To convince 'me'?"

"I wouldn't have made my denial, in such conditions, only to take it back afterwards."

With this quickly light came for her, and with it also her colour flamed. "Oh, you would have broken with me to make your denial a truth? You would have 'chucked' me"—she embraced it perfectly—"to save your conscience?"

"I couldn't have done anything else," said Merton Densher. "So you see how right I was not to commit myself, and how little I could dream of it. If it ever again appears to you that I *might* have done so, remember what I say."

Kate again considered, but not with the effect at once to which he pointed. "You have fallen in love with her."

"Well then, say so—with a dying woman. Why need you mind, and what does it matter?"

It came from him, the question, straight out of the intensity of relation and the face-to-face necessity into which, from the first, from his entering the room, they had found themselves thrown; but it gave them their most extraordinary moment. "Wait till she *is* dead! Mrs. Stringham," Kate added, "is to telegraph." After which, in a tone still different, "For what then," she asked, "did Milly send for you?"

"It was what I tried to make out before I went. I must tell you moreover that I had no doubt of its really being to give me, as you say, a chance. She believed, I suppose, that I *might* deny; and what, to my own mind, was before me in going to her was the certainty that she would put me to my test. She wanted from my own lips—so I saw it—the truth. But I was with her for twenty minutes, and she never asked me for it."

"She never wanted the truth"—Kate had a high head-shake. "She wanted *you*. She would have taken from you what you could give her, and been glad of it even if she had known it false. You might have lied to her from pity, and she have seen you and felt you lie, and yet—since it was all for tenderness—she would have thanked you and blessed you and clung to you but the more. For that was your strength, my dear man—that she loves you with passion."

"Oh, my 'strength!' " Densher coldly murmured.

"What then, at least, since she had sent for you, was it to ask of you?" And then—quite without irony—as he waited a moment to say: "Was it just once more to look at you?

"She had nothing to ask of me—nothing, that is, but not to stay any longer. She did, to that extent, want to see me. She had supposed, at first—after he had been with her—that I had seen the propriety of taking myself off. Then, since I hadn't—seeing my propriety as I did in another way—she found, days later, that I was still there. This," said Densher, "affected her."

"Of course it affected her."

Again she struck him, for all her dignity, as glib. "If it was, somehow, for *her* I was still staying, she wished that to end, she wished me to know how little there was need of it. And, as a manner of farewell, she wished herself to tell me so."

"And she did tell you so?"

"Face-to-face, yes. Personally, as she desired."

"And as *you* of course did."

"No, Kate," he returned with all their mutual consideration; "not as I did. I hadn't desired it in the least."

"You only went to oblige her?"

"To oblige her. And of course also to oblige you."

"Oh, for myself, certainly, I'm glad."

" 'Glad?' " he echoed vaguely the way it rang out.

"I mean you did quite the right thing. You did it especially in having stayed. But that was all?" Kate went on. "That you mustn't wait?"

"That was really all—and in perfect kindness."

"Ah, kindness naturally: from the moment she asked of you such a—well, such an effort. That you mustn't wait—that was the point," Kate added—"to see her die."

"That was the point, my dear," Densher said.

"And it took twenty minutes to make it?"

He thought a little. "I didn't time it to a second. I paid her the visit—just like another."

"Like another person?"

"Like another visit."

"Oh!" said Kate. Which had apparently the effect of slightly arresting his speech—an arrest she took advantage of to continue; making with it indeed her nearest approach to an inquiry of the kind against which he had braced himself. "Did she receive you—in her condition—in her room?"

"Not she," said Merton Densher. "She received me just as usual: in that glorious great *salone*, in the dress she always wears, from her inveterate corner of her sofa." And his face, for the moment, conveyed the scene, just as hers, equally, embraced it. "Do you remember what you originally said to me of her?"

"Ah, I've said so many things."

"That she wouldn't smell of drugs, that she wouldn't taste of medicine. Well, she didn't."

"So that it was really almost happy?"

It took him a long time to answer, occupied as he partly was in feeling how nobody but Kate could have invested such a question with the tone that was perfectly right. She meanwhile, however, patiently waited. "I don't think I can attempt to say now what it was. Some day—perhaps. For it would be worth it for us."

"Some day—certainly." She took it as a generous promise. Yet she spoke again abruptly. "She'll recover."

"Well," said Densher, "you'll see."

She had the air an instant of trying to. "Did she show anything of her feeling? I mean," Kate explained, "of her feeling of having been misled."

She didn't press hard, surely; but he had just mentioned that he would have rather to glide. "She showed nothing but her beauty and her strength."

"Then," his companion asked, "what's the use of her strength?"

He seemed to look about for a use he could name; but he had soon given it up. "She must die, my dear, in her own extraordinary way."

"Naturally. But I don't see then what proof you have that she was ever alienated."

"I have the proof that she refused for days and days to see me."

"But she was ill."

"That hadn't prevented her—as you yourself a moment ago said—during the previous time. If it had been only illness it would have made no difference with her."

"She would still have received you?"

"She would still have received me."

"Oh, well," said Kate, "if you know——!"

"Of course I know. I know moreover, as well, from Mrs. Stringham."

"And what does Mrs. Stringham know?"

"Everything."

She looked at him longer. "Everything?"

"Everything."

"Because you've told her?"

"Because she has seen for herself. I've told her nothing. She's a person who does see."

Kate thought. "That's by her liking you too. She, as well, is prodigious. You see what interest in a man does. It does it all round. So you needn't be afraid."

"I'm not afraid," said Densher.

Kate moved from her place then, looking at the clock, which marked five. She gave her attention to the tea-table, where Aunt Maud's huge silver kettle, which had been exposed to its lamp and which she had not soon enough noticed, was hissing too hard. "Well, it's all most wonderful!" she exclaimed as she rather too profusely—a sign her friend noticed—ladled tea into the pot. He watched her a moment at this occupation, coming nearer the table while she put in the steaming water. "You'll have some?"

He hesitated. "Hadn't we better wait——?"

"For Aunt Maud?" She saw what he meant—the deprecation, by their old law, of betrayals of the intimate note. "Oh, you needn't mind now. We've done it!"

"Humbugged her?"

"Squared her. You've pleased her."

Densher mechanically accepted his tea. He was thinking of something else, and his thought in a moment came out. "What a brute then I must be!"

"A brute——?"

"To have pleased so many people."

"Ah," said Kate with a gleam of gaiety, "you've done it to please *me*." But she was already, with her gleam, reverting a little. "What I don't understand is—won't you have any sugar?"

"Yes, please."

"What I don't understand," she went on when she had helped him, "is what it was that had occurred to bring her round again. If she gave you up for days and days, what brought her back to you?"

She asked the question with her own cup in her hand, but it found him ready enough, in spite of his sense of the ironic oddity of their going into it over the tea-table. "It was Sir Luke Strett who brought her back. His visit, his presence there did it."

"He brought her back then to life."

"Well, to what I saw."

"And by interceding for you?"

"I don't think he interceded. I don't indeed know what he did."

Kate wondered. "Didn't he tell you?"

"I didn't ask him. I met him again, but we practically didn't speak of her."

Kate stared. "Then how do you know? "

"I see. I feel. I was with him again as I had been before——"

"Oh, and you pleased him too? That was it?"

"He understood," said Densher.

"But understood what?"

He waited a moment. "That I had meant awfully well."

"Ah, and made *her* understand? I see," she went on as he said nothing. "But how did he convince her?"

Densher put down his cup and turned away. "You must ask Sir Luke."

He stood looking at the fire, and there was a time without sound. "The great thing," Kate then resumed, "is that's she's satisfied. Which," she continued, looking across at him, "is what I've worked for."

"Satisfied to die in the flower of her youth?"

"Well, at peace with you."

"Oh, 'peace'!" he murmured with his eyes on the fire.

"The peace of having loved."

He raised his eyes to her. "Is *that* peace?"

"Of having *been* loved," she went on. "That is. Of having," she wound up, "realised her passion. She wanted nothing more. She has had *all* she wanted."

Lucid and always grave, she gave this out with a beautiful authority that he could for the time meet with no words. He could only again look at her, though with the sense, in so doing, that he made her, more than he intended, take his silence for assent. Quite indeed as if she did so take it she quitted the table and came to the fire. "You may think it hideous that I should now, that I should *yet*"—she made a point of the word—"pretend to draw conclusions. But we've not failed."

"Oh!" he only again murmured.

She was once more close to him, close as she had been the day she came to him in Venice, the quickly-returning memory of which intensified and enriched the fact. He could practically deny in such conditions nothing that she said, and what she said was, with it, visibly, a fruit of that knowledge. "We've succeeded." She spoke with her eyes deep in his own. "She won't have loved you for nothing." It made him wince, but she insisted. "And you won't have loved *me*."

II

HE WAS TO REMAIN for several days under the deep impression of this inclusive passage, so luckily prolonged from moment to moment, but interrupted, at its

climax, as may be said, by the entrance of Aunt Maud,
who found them standing together near the fire. The
bearings of the colloquy, however, sharp as they were,
were less sharp to his intelligence, strangely enough,
than those of a talk with Mrs. Lowder alone for which
she soon gave him—or for which perhaps rather Kate
gave him—full occasion. What had happened on her at
last joining them was to conduce, he could immediately
see, to her desiring to have him to herself. Kate and he,
no doubt, at the opening of the door, had fallen apart
with a certain suddenness, so that she had turned her
hard fine eyes from one to the other; but the effect of
this lost itself, to his mind, the next minute, in the effect
of his companion's rare alertness. She instantly spoke to
her aunt of what had first been uppermost for herself,
inviting her thereby intimately to join them, and doing
it the more happily also, no doubt, because the fact that
she resentfully named gave her ample support. "Had
you quite understood, my dear, that it's full three
weeks——?" And she effaced herself as if to leave Mrs.
Lowder to deal from her own point of view with this
extravagance. Densher of course straightway noted that
his cue for the protection of Kate was to make, no less,
all of it he could; and their tracks, as he might have said,
were fairly covered by the time their hostess had taken
afresh, on his renewed admission, the measure of his
scant eagerness. Kate had moved away as if no great
showing were needed for her personal situation to be
seen as delicate. She had been entertaining their visitor
on her aunt's behalf—a visitor she had been at one time

suspected of favouring too much and who had now
come back to them as the stricken suitor of another person. It wasn't that the fate of the other person, her
exquisite friend, didn't, in its tragic turn, also concern
herself: it was only that her acceptance of Mr. Densher
as a source of information could scarcely help having an
awkwardness. She invented the awkwardness under
Densher's eyes, and he marvelled on his side at the
instant creation. It served her as the fine cloud that
hangs about a goddess in an epic, and the young man
was but vaguely to know at what point of the rest of his
visit she had, for consideration, melted into it and out
of sight.

He was taken up promptly with another matter—the
truth of the remarkable difference, neither more nor less,
that the events of Venice had introduced into his relation with Aunt Maud and that these weeks of their sep-
aration had caused quite richly to ripen for him. She had
not sat down to her tea-table before he felt himself on
terms with her that were absolutely new, nor could she
press on him a second cup without her seeming herself,
and quite wittingly, so to define and establish them. She
regretted, but she quite understood, that what was taking place had obliged him to hang off; they had—after
hearing of him from poor Susan as gone—been hoping
for an early sight of him; they would have been interested, naturally, in his arriving straight from the scene.
Yet she needed no reminder that the scene precisely—
by which she meant the tragedy that had so detained
and absorbed him, the memory, the shadow, the sorrow

of it—was what marked him for unsociability. She thus presented him to himself, as it were, in the guise in which she had now adopted him, and it was the element of truth in the character that he found himself, for his own part, adopting. She treated him as blighted and ravaged, as frustrate and already bereft; and for him to feel that this opened for him a new chapter of frankness with her he scarce had also to perceive how it smoothed his approaches to Kate. It made the latter accessible as she had not yet begun to be; it set up for him at Lancaster Gate an association positively hostile to any other legend. It was quickly vivid to him that, were he minded, he could "work" this association; he had but to use the house freely for his prescribed attitude and he need hardly ever be out of it. Stranger than anything moreover was to be the way that by the end of a week he stood convicted to his own sense of a surrender to Mrs. Lowder's view. He had somehow met it at a point that had brought him on—brought him on a distance that he couldn't again retrace. He had private hours of wondering what had become of his sincerity; he had others of simply reflecting that he had it all in use. His only want of candour was Aunt Maud's wealth of sentiment. She was hugely sentimental, and the worst he did was to take it from her. He wasn't so himself—everything was too real; but it was none the less not false that he *had* been through a mill.

It was in particular not false, for instance, that when she had said to him, on the Sunday, almost cosily, from her sofa behind the tea, "I want you not to doubt, you

poor dear, that I'm *with* you to the end!" his meeting
her half way had been the only course open to him. She
was with him to the end—or she might be—in a way
Kate wasn't; and even if it literally made her society
meanwhile more soothing, he must just brush away the
question of why it shouldn't. Was he professing to her
in any degree the possession of an aftersense that wasn't
real? How in the world *could* he, when his aftersense,
day by day, was his greatest reality? That was at bottom all that there was between them, and two or three
times over it made the hour pass. These were occasions—two and a scrap—on which he had come and
gone without mention of Kate. Now that, almost for the
first time, he was free to ask for her, the queer turn of
their affair made it a false note. It was another queer
turn that when he talked with Aunt Maud about Milly
nothing else seemed to come up. He called upon her
almost avowedly for that purpose, and it was the queerest turn of all that the state of his nerves should require
it. He liked her better; he was really behaving, he had
occasion to say to himself, as if he liked her best. The
thing was, absolutely, that she met *him* half way. Nothing could have been broader than her vision, than her
loquacity, than her sympathy. It appeared to gratify, to
satisfy her to see him as he was; that too had its effect.
It was all of course the last thing that could have seemed
on the cards, a change by which he was completely *free*
with this lady; and it wouldn't indeed have come about
if—for another monstrosity—he hadn't ceased to be free
with Kate. Thus it was that, on the third time, in espe-

cial, of being alone with her, he found himself uttering
to the elder woman what had been impossible of utterance to the younger. Mrs. Lowder gave him in fact, in
respect to what he must keep from her, but one uneasy
moment. That was when, on the first Sunday, after Kate
had suppressed herself, she referred to her regret that he
mightn't have stayed to the end. He found his reason
difficult to give her, but she came, after all, to his help.

"You simply couldn't stand it?"

"I simply couldn't stand it. Besides you see——" But
he paused.

"Besides what?" He had been going to say more—
then he saw dangers; luckily, however, she had again
assisted him. "Besides—oh, I know!—men haven't, in
many relations, the courage of women."

"They haven't the courage of women."

"Kate or I would have stayed," she declared—"if we
hadn't come away for the special reason that you so
frankly appreciated."

Densher had said nothing about his appreciation:
hadn't his behaviour since the hour itself sufficiently
shown it? But he presently said—he couldn't help going
so far: "I don't doubt, certainly, that Miss Croy would
have stayed." And he saw again, into the bargain, what
a marvel was Susan Shepherd. She did nothing but protect him—she had done nothing but keep it up. In copious communication with the friend of her youth, she
had yet, it was plain, favoured this lady with nothing
that compromised him. Milly's act of renunciation she
had described but as a change for the worse; she had

mentioned Lord Mark's descent, as even without her it
might be known, so that she mustn't appear to conceal
it; but she had suppressed explanations and connections,
and indeed, for all he knew, blessed Puritan soul, had
invented commendable fictions. Thus it was absolutely
that he *was* at his ease. Thus it was that, shaking for
ever, in the unrest that didn't drop, his crossed leg, he
leaned back in deep yellow-satin chairs and took such
comfort as came. She asked, it was true, Aunt Maud,
questions that Kate hadn't; but this was just the difference, that from her he positively liked them. He had
taken with himself, on leaving Venice, the resolution to
regard Milly as already dead to him—that being, for his
spirit, the only thinkable way to pass the time of waiting. He had left her because it was what suited her, and
it wasn't for him to go, as they said in America, behind
this; which imposed on him but the sharper need to
arrange himself with his interval. Suspense was the ugliest ache to him, and he would have nothing to do with
it; the last thing he wished was to be unconscious of
her—what he wished to ignore was her own consciousness, tortured, for all he knew, crucified by its pain.
Knowingly to hang about in London while the pain
went on—what would that do but make his days impossible? His scheme was accordingly to convince himself—
and by some art about which he was vague—that the
sense of waiting had passed. "What in fact," he restlessly reflected. "have I, any further, to do with it? Let
me assume the thing actually over—as it at any moment
may be—and I become good again for something at

least to somebody. I'm good, as it is, for nothing to anybody, least of all to *her*." He consequently tried, so far
as shutting his eyes and stalking grimly about was a
trial; but his plan was carried out, it may well be
guessed, neither with marked success nor with marked
consistency. The days, whether lapsing or lingering,
were a stiff reality; the suppression of anxiety was a thin
idea; the taste of life itself was the taste of suspense.
That he *was* waiting was in short at the bottom of
everything; and it required no great sifting presently to
feel that, if he took so much more, as he called it to Mrs.
Lowder, this was just for that reason.

She helped him to hold out, all the while that she was
subtle enough—and he could see her divine it as what
he wanted—not to insist on the actuality of their tension. His nearest approach to success was thus in being
good for something to Aunt Maud, in default of any one
better; her company eased his nerves even while they
pretended together that they had seen their tragedy out.
They spoke of the dying girl in the past tense; they said
no worse of her than that she had *been* stupendous. On
the other hand, however—and this was what wasn't, for
Densher, pure peace—they insisted enough that stupendous was the word. It was the thing, this recognition,
that kept him most quiet; he came to it with her repeatedly; talking about it against time and, in particular, we
have noted, speaking of his supreme personal impression
as he had not spoken to Kate. It was almost as if she
herself enjoyed the perfection of the pathos; she sat
there before the scene, as he couldn't help giving it out

to her, very much as a stout citizen's wife might have sat, during a play that made people cry, in the pit or the family-circle. What most deeply stirred her was the way the poor girl must have wanted to live.

"Ah, yes indeed—she did, she did: why in pity shouldn't she, with everything to fill her world? The mere *money* of her, the darling, if it isn't too disgusting at such a time to mention that——!"

Aunt Maud mentioned it—and Densher quite understood—but as fairly giving poetry to the life Milly clung to: a view of the "might have been" before which the good lady was hushed anew to tears. She had had her own vision of these possibilities, and her own social use for them, and since Milly's spirit had been after all so at one with her about them, what was the cruelty of the event but a cruelty, of a sort, to herself? That came out when he named, as *the* horrible thing to know, the fact of their young friend's unapproachable terror of the end, keep it down though she would; coming out therefore often, since in so naming it he found the strangest of reliefs. He allowed it all its vividness, as if on the principle of his not at least spiritually shirking. Milly had held with passion to her dream of a future, and she was separated from it, not shrieking indeed, but grimly, awfully silent, as one might imagine some noble young victim of the scaffold, in the French Revolution, separated, in the prison-cell, from some object clutched for resistance. Densher, in a cold moment, so pictured the case for Mrs. Lowder, but no moment cold enough had yet come to make him so picture it to Kate. And it was

the front so presented that had been, in Milly, heroic;
presented with the highest heroism, Aunt Maud by this
time knew, on the occasion of his taking leave of her. He
had let her know, absolutely for the girl's glory, how he
had been received on that occasion with a positive
effect—since she was indeed so perfectly the princess
that Mrs. Stringham always called her—of princely state.

Before the fire in the great room that was all
arabesques and cherubs, all gaiety and gilt, and that was
warm at that hour too with a wealth of autumn sun, the
state in question had been maintained and the situation—well, Densher said for the convenience of exquisite London gossip, sublime. The gossip—for it came to
as much at Lancaster Gate—was not the less exquisite
for his use of the silver veil, nor, on the other hand, was
the veil, so touched, too much drawn aside. He himself,
for that matter, at moments, took in the scene again as
from the page of a book. He saw a young man, far off,
in a relation inconceivable, saw him hushed, passive,
staying his breath, but half understanding, yet dimly
conscious of something immense and holding himself,
not to lose it, painfully together. The young man, at
these moments, so seen, was too distant and too strange
for the right identity; and yet outside, afterwards, it was
his own face Densher had known. He had known then,
at the same time, of what the young man had been conscious, and he was to measure, after that, day by day,
how little he had lost. At present there, with Mrs. Lowder, he knew he had gathered all: that passed between
them mutely as, in the intervals of their associated gaze,

they exchanged looks of intelligence. This was as far as association could go; but it was far enough when she knew the essence. The essence was that something had happened to him too beautiful and too sacred to describe. He had been, to his recovered sense, forgiven, dedicated, blessed; but this he couldn't coherently express. It would have required an explanation—fatal to Mrs. Lowder's faith in him—of the nature of Milly's wrong. So, as to the wonderful scene, they just stood at the door. They had the sense of the presence within— they felt the charged stillness; after which, with their association deepened by it, they turned together away.

That itself indeed, for our restless friend, became by the end of a week the very principle of reaction: so that he woke up one morning with such a sense of having played a part as he needed, for self-respect, to gainsay. He had not in the least stated at Lancaster Gate that, as a haunted man—a man haunted with a memory—he was harmless; but the degree to which Mrs. Lowder accepted, admired and explained his new aspect laid upon him practically the weight of a declaration. What he hadn't in the least stated her own manner was perpetually stating; it was as haunted and harmless that she was constantly putting him down. There offered itself, however, to his purpose, such an element as plain honesty, and he had embraced, by the time he dressed, his proper corrective. They were on the edge of Christmas, but Christmas this year was, as, in London, in so many other years, disconcertingly mild; the still air was soft, the thick light was grey, the great town looked empty,

and in the Park, where the grass was green, where the
sheep browsed, where the birds multitudinously twit-
tered, the straight walks lent themselves to slowness and
the dim vistas to privacy. He held it fast this morning
till he had got out, his sacrifice to honour, and then
went with it to the nearest post-office and fixed it fast in
a telegram; thinking of it moreover as a sacrifice only
because he had, for reasons, felt it as an effort. Its character of effort it would owe to Kate's expected resistance, not less probable than on the occasion of past
appeals; which was precisely why he—perhaps innocently—made his telegram persuasive. It had, as a recall
of tender hours, to be, for the young woman at the
counter, a trifle cryptic; but there was a good deal of it,
in one way and another, representing it as did a rich
impulse, and it cost him a couple of shillings. There was
also a moment later on, that day, when, in the Park, as
he measured watchfully one of their old alleys, he might
have been supposed by a cynical critic to be reckoning
his chance of getting his money back. He was waiting—
but he had waited of old; Lancaster Gate as a danger,
was practically at hand—but she had risked that danger before. Besides, it was smaller now, with the queer
turn of their affair; in spite of which indeed he was
graver as he lingered and looked out.

Kate came at last by the way he had thought least
likely—came as if she had started from the Marble
Arch; but her advent was response—that was the great
matter; response marked in her face and agreeable to
him, even after Aunt Maud's responses, as nothing had

been since his return to London. She had not, it was
true, answered his wire, and he had begun to fear, as she
was late, that with the instinct of what he might be
again intending to press upon her, she had decided—
though not with ease—to deprive him of his chance. He
would have of course, she knew, other chances, but she
perhaps saw this one as offering her special danger.
That, in fact, Densher could himself feel, was exactly
why he had so prepared it, and he had rejoiced, even
while he waited, in all that the conditions had to say to
him of their simpler and better time. The shortest day
of the year though it might be, it was, in the same place,
by a whim of the weather, almost as much to their purpose as the days of sunny afternoons when they had
taken their first trysts. This and that tree, within sight,
on the grass, stretched bare boughs over the couple of
chairs in which they had sat of old and in which—for
they really could sit down again—they might recover
the clearness of their beginnings. It was to all intents,
however, this very reference that showed itself in Kate's
face as, with her quick walk, she came toward him. It
helped him, her quick walk, when it finally brought her
nearer; helped him, for that matter, at first, if only by
showing him afresh how terribly well she looked. It had
been all along, he certainly remembered, a phenomenon
of no rarity that he had felt her, at particular moments,
handsomer than ever before; one of these, for instance,
being still present to him as her entrance, under her
aunt's eyes, at Lancaster Gate, the day of his dinner
there after his return from America; and another her

aspect, on the same spot, two Sundays ago—the light in which she struck the eyes he had brought back from Venice. In the course of a minute or two now he got, as he had got it the other times, his impression of the special stamp of the fortune of the moment.

Whatever it had been determined by as the different hours recurred to him, it took on at present a prompt connection with an effect produced for him, in truth, more than once during the past week, only now much intensified. This effect he had already noted and named: it was that of the attitude assumed by his friend in the presence of the degree of response, on his part, to Mrs. Lowder's welcome which she couldn't possibly have failed to notice. She *had* noticed it, and she had beautifully shown him so; wearing in its honour the finest shade of studied serenity, a shade almost of gaiety over the workings of time. Everything of course was relative, with the shadow they were living under; but her condonation of the way in which he now, for confidence, distinguished Aunt Maud had almost the note of cheer. She had so consecrated, by her own air, the distinction, invidious in respect to herself though it might be; and nothing, really, more than this demonstration, could have given him, had he still wanted it, the measure of her superiority. It was doubtless, for that matter, this superiority simply that, on the winter noon, gave smooth decision to her step and charming courage to her eyes— a courage that deepened in them when he had got, after a little, to what he wanted. He had delayed after she had joined him not much more than long enough for him to say to her, drawing her hand into his arm and turning off where they had turned of old, that he wouldn't pretend he hadn't lately had moments of not quite believing he should ever again be so happy. She answered, passing over the reasons, whatever they had been, of his doubt, that her own belief was in high happiness for them if they would only have patience; though nothing, at the same time, could be dearer than his idea for their walk. It was only make-believe, of course, with what had taken place for them, that they couldn't meet at home; she spoke of their opportunities as suffering at no point. He had at any rate soon let her know that he wished the present one to suffer at none, and in a quiet spot, beneath a great wintry tree, he let his entreaty come sharp.

"We've played our dreadful game, and we've lost. We owe it to ourselves, we owe it to our feeling *for* ourselves and for each other, not to wait another day. Our marriage will—fundamentally, somehow, don't you see?—right everything that's wrong, and I can't express to you my impatience. We've only to announce it—and it takes off the weight."

"To 'announce' it?" Kate asked. She spoke as if not understanding, though she had listened to him without confusion.

"To accomplish it then—to-morrow if you will; *do* it and announce it as done. That's the least part of it—after it nothing will matter. We shall be so right," he said, "that we shall be strong; we shall only wonder at our past fear. It will seem an ugly madness. It will seem a bad dream."

She looked at him without flinching—with the look she had brought at his call; but he felt now the strange chill of her brightness. "My dear man, what has happened to you?"

"Well, that I can bear it no longer. *That's* simply what has happened. Something has snapped, has broken in me, and here I am. It's *as* I am that you must have me."

He saw her try, for a time, to appear to consider it; but he saw her also not consider it. Yet he saw her, felt her, further—he heard her, with her clear voice—try to be intensely kind with him. "I don't see, you know, what has changed." She had a large, strange smile. "We've been going on together so well, and you suddenly desert me?"

It made him helplessly gaze. "You call it so 'well'? You've touches, upon my soul——!"

"I call it perfect—from my original point of view. I'm just where I was; and you must give me some better reason than you do, my dear, for *your* not being. It seems to me," she continued, "that we're only right, as to what has been between us, so long as we do wait. I don't think we wish to have behaved like fools." He took in, while she talked, her imperturbable consistency; which it was quietly, queerly hopeless to see her stand there and breathe into their mild, remembering air. He had brought her there to be moved, and she was only immovable—which was not moreover, either, because she didn't understand. She understood everything—and things he *wouldn't*; and she had reasons, deep down, the sense of which nearly sickened him. She had too again, most of all, her strange, significant smile. "Of course, if it is that you really *know* something——?" It was quite conceivable and possible to her, he could see, that he did. But he didn't even know what she meant, and he only looked at her in gloom. His gloom, however, didn't upset her. "You *do*, I believe, only you've a delicacy about saying it. Your delicacy to me, my dear, is a scruple too much. I should have no delicacy in hearing it, so that if you can *tell* me you know——"

"Well?" he asked as she still kept what depended on it.

"Why then, I'll do what you want. We needn't, I grant you, in that case wait; and I can see what you mean by thinking it nicer of us not to. I don't even ask you," she continued, "for a proof. I'm content with your moral certainty."

By this time it had come over him—it had the force of a rush. The point she made was clear, as clear, as that the blood, while he recognised it, mantled in his face. "I know nothing whatever."

"You've not an idea?"

"I've not an idea."

"I'd consent," she said—"I'd announce it tomorrow, to-day, I'd go home this moment and announce it to Aunt Maud, for an idea: I mean an idea straight *from* you, I mean as your own, given me in good faith. There, my dear!"—and she smiled again. "I call that really meeting you."

If it *was* then what she called it, it disposed of his

appeal, and he could but stand there with his wasted passion—for it was in high passion that he had, from the morning, acted—in his face. She made it all out, bent upon her, the idea he didn't have, and the idea he had, and his failure of insistence when it brought up *that* challenge, and his sense of her personal presence, and his horror, almost, of her lucidity. They made in him a mixture that might have been rage, but that was turning quickly to mere cold thought, thought which led to something else and was like a new dim dawn. It affected her then, and she had one of the impulses, in all sincerity, that had before this, between them, saved their position. When she had come nearer to him, when, putting her hand upon him and making him sink with her, as she leaned to him, into their old pair of chairs, she prevented, irresistibly, the waste of his passion. She had an advantage with his passion now.

III

HE HAD SAID to her in the Park, when challenged on it, that nothing had "happened" to him as a cause for the demand he there made of her—happened, he meant, since the account he had given, after his return, of his recent experience. But in the course of a few days—they had brought him to Christmas morning—he was conscious enough, in preparing again to seek her out, of a difference on that score. Something *had* in this case happened to him, and, after his taking the night to think of it, he felt that what it most, if not absolutely first,

involved was his immediately again putting himself in
relation with her. The fact itself had met him there—in
his own small quarters—on Christmas eve, and had not
then indeed instantly affected him as implying that consequence. So far as he on the spot and for the next hours
took its measure—a process that made his night mercilessly wakeful—the consequences possibly implied were
numerous to distraction. His spirit dealt with them, in
the darkness, as the slow hours passed; his intelligence
and his imagination, his soul and his sense had never,
on the whole, been so intensely engaged. It was his difficulty for the moment that he was face to face with
alternatives, and that it was scarce even a question of
turning from one to the other. They were not in a perspective in which they might be compared and considered; they were, by a strange effect, as close as a pair of
monsters of whom he might have felt on either cheek
the hot breath and the huge eyes. He saw them at once
and but by looking straight before him; he wouldn't, for
that matter, in his cold apprehension, have turned his
head by an inch. So it was that his agitation was still—
was not, for the slow hours, a matter of restless motion.
He lay long, after the event, on the sofa on which, extin-
guishing at a touch the white light of convenience that
he hated, he had thrown himself without undressing. He
stared at the buried day and wore out the time; with the
arrival of the Christmas dawn, moreover, late and grey,
he felt himself somehow determined. The common wisdom had had its say to him—that safety, in doubt, was
not action; and perhaps what most helped him was this

very commonness. In his case there was nothing of *that*—in no case in his life had there ever been less: which association, from one thing to another, now worked for him as a choice. He acted, after his bath and his breakfast, in the sense of that marked element of the rare which he felt to be the sign of his crisis. And that is why, dressed with more state than usual and quite as if for church, he went out into the soft Christmas day.

Action, for him, on coming to the point, it appeared. carried with it a certain complexity. We should have known, walking by his side, that his final prime decision had not been to call at the door of Sir Luke Strett, and yet that this step, though subordinate, was none the less urgent. His prime decision was for another matter, to which impatience, once he was on the way, had now added itself; but he remained sufficiently aware that he must compromise with the perhaps excessive earliness. This, and the ferment set up within him, were, together, a reason for not driving; to say nothing of the absence of cabs in the dusky festal desert. Sir Luke's great square was not near, but he walked the distance without seeing a hansom. He had his interval thus to turn over his view—the view to which what had happened the night before had now sharply reduced itself; but the complexity just mentioned was to be offered, within the next few minutes, another item to assimilate. Before Sir Luke's house, when he reached it, a brougham was drawn up— at the sight of which his heart had a lift that brought him, for the instant, to a stand. This pause was not long, but it was long enough to flash upon him a reve-

lation in the light of which he caught his breath. The
carriage, so possibly at such an hour and on such a day
Sir Luke's own, had struck him as a sign that the great
doctor was back. This would prove something else, in
turn, still more intensely, and it was in the act of the
double apprehension that Densher felt himself turn pale.
His mind rebounded for the moment like a projectile
that has suddenly been met by another: he stared at the
strange truth that what he wanted *more* than to see Kate
Croy was to see the witness who had just arrived from
Venice. He wanted positively to be in his presence and
to hear his voice—which was the spasm of his consciousness that produced the flash. Fortunately for him,
on the spot, there supervened something in which the
flash went out. He became aware within this minute
that the coachman on the box of the brougham had a
face known to him, whereas he had never seen before, to
his knowledge, the great doctor's carriage. The carriage,
as he came nearer, was simply Mrs. Lowder's; the face
on the box was just the face that, in coming and going
at Lancaster Gate, he would vaguely have noticed, outside, in attendance. With this the rest came: the lady of
Lancaster Gate had, on a prompting not wholly remote
from his own, presented herself for news; and news, in
the house, she was clearly getting, since her brougham
had stayed. Sir Luke *was* then back—only Mrs. Lowder was with him.

It was under the influence of this last reflection that
Densher again delayed; and it was while he delayed that
something else occurred to him. It was all round, visi-

bly—given his own new contribution—a case of pressure; and in a case of pressure Kate, for quicker knowledge, might have come out with her aunt. The
possibility that in this event she might be sitting in the
carriage—the thing most likely—had had the effect,
before he could check it, of bringing him within range
of the window. It wasn't there he had wished to see her;
yet if she *was* there he couldn't pretend not to. What he
had, however, the next moment made out was that if
some one was there it wasn't Kate Croy. It was, with a
sensible shock from him, the person who had last offered
him a conscious face from behind the clear plate of a café
in Venice. The great glass at Florian's was a medium less
obscure, even with the window down, than the air of the
London Christmas; yet at present also, none the less,
between the two men, an exchange of recognitions could
occur. Densher felt his own look a gaping arrest—which,
he disgustedly remembered, his back as quickly turned,
appeared to repeat itself as his special privilege. He
mounted the steps of the house and touched the bell with
a keen consciousness of being habitually looked at by
Kate's friend from positions of almost insolent vantage.
He forgot, for the time, the moment when, in Venice, at
the palace, the encouraged young man had in a manner
assisted at the departure of the disconcerted, since Lord
Mark was not looking disconcerted now any more than
he had looked from his bench at his café. Densher was
thinking that *he* seemed to show as vagrant while another
was ensconced. He was thinking of the other as—in spite
of the difference of situation—more ensconced than ever;

he was thinking of him above all as the friend of the person with whom his recognition had, the minute previous, associated him. The man was seated in the very place in which, beside Mrs. Lowder's, he had looked to find Kate, and that was a sufficient identity. Meanwhile, at any rate, the door of the house had opened and Mrs. Lowder stood before him. It was something at least that *she* wasn't Kate. She was herself, on the spot, in all her affluence; with presence of mind both to decide at once that Lord Mark, in the brougham, didn't matter and to prevent Sir Luke's butler, by a firm word thrown over her shoulder, from standing there to listen to her passage with the gentleman who had rung. "*I'll* tell Mr. Densher; you needn't wait!" And the passage, promptly and richly, took place on the steps.

"He arrives, travelling straight, to-morrow early. I couldn't not come to learn."

"No more," said Densher simply, "could I. On my way," he added, "to Lancaster Gate."

"Sweet of you." She beamed on him dimly, and he saw her face was attuned. It made him, with what she had just before said, know all, and he took the thing in while he met the air of portentous, of almost functional, sympathy that had settled itself as her medium with him and that yet had now a fresh glow. "So you *have* had your message?"

He knew so well what she meant, and so equally with it what he "*had* had," no less than what he hadn't, that, with but the smallest hesitation, he strained the point. "Yes—my message."

"Our dear dove then, as Kate calls her, has folded her wonderful wings."

"Yes—folded them."

It rather racked him, but he tried to receive it as she intended, and she evidently took his formal assent for self-control. "Unless it's more true," she accordingly added, "that she has spread them the wider."

He again but formally assented, though, strangely enough, the words fitted an image deep in his own consciousness. "Rather, yes—spread them the wider."

"For a flight, I trust, to some happiness greater——"

"Exactly. Greater," Densher broke in; but now with a look, he feared, that did, a little, warn her off.

"You were certainly," she went on with more reserve, "entitled to direct news. Ours came, last night, late: I'm not sure, otherwise, I shouldn't have gone to you. But you're coming," she asked, "to me?"

He had had a minute, by this time, to think further; and the window of the brougham was still within range. Her rich "me," reaching him, moreover, through the mild damp, had the effect of a thump on his chest. "Squared," Aunt Maud? She was indeed squared, and the extent of it, just now, perversely enough, took away his breath. His look, from where they stood, embraced the aperture at which the person sitting in the carriage might have shown, and he saw his interlocutress, on her side, understand the question in it, which he moreover then uttered. "Shall you be alone?" It was, as an immediate instinctive parley with the image of his condition that now flourished in her, almost hypocritical. It sounded as if he wished to come and overflow to her, yet this was exactly what he didn't. The need to overflow had suddenly—since the night before—dried up in him, and he had never been conscious of a deeper reserve.

But she had meanwhile largely responded. "Completely alone. I should otherwise never have dreamed; feeling, dear friend, but too much!" What she felt, failing on her lips, came out for him in the offered hand with which, the next moment, she had condolingly pressed his own. "Dear friend, dear friend!"—she was deeply "with" him, and she wished to be still more so: which was what made her immediately continue. "Or wouldn't you, this evening, for the sad Christmas it makes us, dine with me *tête-à-tête?*"

It put the thing off, the question of a talk with her—making the difference, to his relief, of several hours; but it also rather mystified him. This, however, didn't diminish his need of caution. "Shall you mind if I don't tell you at once?"

"Not in the least—leave it open: it shall be as you may feel, and you needn't even send me word. I only *will* mention that to-day, of all days, I shall otherwise sit there alone."

Now at least he could ask. "Without Miss Croy?"

"Without Miss Croy. Miss Croy," said Mrs. Lowder, "is spending her Christmas in the bosom of her more immediate family."

He was afraid, even while he spoke, of what his face might show. "You mean she has left you?"

Aunt Maud's own face, for that matter, met the inquiry with a consciousness in which he saw a reflection of events. He perceived from it, even at the moment and as he had never done before, that, since he had known these two women, no confessed nor commented tension, no crisis of the cruder sort, would really have taken form between them: which was precisely a high proof of how Kate had steered her boat. The situation exposed in Mrs. Lowder's present expression lighted up by contrast that superficial smoothness; which afterwards, with his time to think of it, was to put before him again the art, the particular gift, in the girl, now so placed and classed, so intimately familiar for him, as her talent for life. The peace, clearly, within a day or two—since his seeing her last— had been broken; differences, deep down, kept there by a diplomacy, on Kate's part, as deep, had been shaken to the surface by some exceptional jar; with which, in addition, he felt Lord Mark's odd attendance at such an hour and season vaguely associated. The talent for life indeed, it at the same time struck him, would probably have shown equally in the breach, or whatever had occurred; Aunt Maud having suffered, he judged, a strain rather than a stroke. With these quick thoughts, at all events, that lady was already abreast. "She went yesterday morning—and not with my approval, I don't mind telling you—to her sister: Mrs. Condrip, if you know who I mean, who lives somewhere in Chelsea. My other niece and her affairs—that I should have to say such things to-day!—are a constant worry; so that

Kate, in consequence—well, of events!—has simply been called in. My own idea, I'm bound to say, was that with *such* events she need have, in her situation, next to nothing to do."

"But she differed with you?"

"She differed with me. And when Kate differs with you——!"

"Oh, I can imagine." He had reached the point, in the matter of hypocrisy, at which he could ask himself why a little more or less should signify. Besides, with the intention he had had, he *must* know. Kate's move, if he didn't know, might simply disconcert him; and of being disconcerted his horror was by this time fairly superstitious. "I hope you don't allude to events at all calamitous."

"No—only horrid and vulgar."

"Oh!" said Merton Densher.

Mrs. Lowder's soreness, it was still not obscure, had discovered in free speech to him a momentary balm. "They've the misfortune to have, I suppose you know, a dreadful, horrible father."

"Oh!" said Densher again.

"He's too bad almost to name, but he has come upon Marian, and Marian has shrieked for help."

Densher wondered, at this, with intensity; and his curiosity compromised for an instant with his discretion. "Come upon her—for money?"

"Oh, for that, of course, always. But, at *this* blessed season, for refuge, for safety: for God knows what. He's *there*, the brute. And Kate's with them. And that," Mrs.

Lowder wound up, going down the steps, "is her Christmas."

She had stopped again at the bottom, while he thought of an answer. "Yours then is after all rather better."

"It's at least more decent." And her hand, once more, came out. "But why do I talk of *our* troubles? Come if you can."

He showed a faint smile. "Thanks. If I can."

"And now—I dare say—you'll go to church?"

She had asked it, with her good intention, rather in the air and by way of sketching for him, in the line of support, something a little more to the purpose than what she had been giving him. He felt it as finishing off their intensities of expression that he found himself, to all appearance, receiving her hint as happy. "Why, yes—I think I will": after which, as the door of the brougham, at her approach, had opened from within, he was free to turn his back. He heard the door, behind him, sharply close again and the vehicle move off in another direction than his own.

He had in fact, for the time, no direction; in spite of which indeed, at the end of ten minutes, he was aware of having walked straight to the south. That, he after-wards recognised, was, very sufficiently, because there had formed itself in his mind, even while Aunt Maud finally talked, an instant recognition of his necessary course. Nothing was open to him but to follow Kate, nor was anything more marked than the influence of the step she had taken on the emotion itself that possessed

him. Her complications, which had fairly, with everything else, an awful sound—what were they, a thousand
times over, but his own? His present business was to see
that they didn't escape an hour longer taking their
proper place in his life. He accordingly would have held
his course had it not suddenly come over him that he
had just lied to Mrs. Lowder—a term it perversely eased
him to keep using—even more than was necessary. To
what church was he going, to what church, in such a
state of his nerves, *could* he go?—he pulled up short
again, as he had pulled up in sight of Mrs. Lowder's
carriage, to ask it. And yet the desire queerly stirred in
him not to have wasted his word. He was just then,
however, by a happy chance, in the Brompton Road,
and he bethought himself, with a sudden light, that the
Oratory was at hand. He had but to turn the other way
and he should find himself soon before it. At the door
then, in a few minutes, his idea was really—as it struck
him—consecrated: he was, pushing in, on the edge of a
splendid service—the flocking crowd told of it—which
glittered and resounded, from distant depths, in the
blaze of altar-lights and the swell of organ and choir. It
didn't match his own day, but it was much less of a dis-
cord than some other things actual and possible. The
Oratory, in short, to make him right, would do.

IV

THE DIFFERENCE WAS thus that the dusk of afternoon—
dusk thick from an early hour—had gathered when he

knocked at Mrs. Condrip's door. He had gone from the
church to his club, wishing not to present himself in
Chelsea at luncheon-time, and also remembering that he
must attempt independently to make a meal. This, in
the event, he but imperfectly achieved: he dropped into
a chair in the great dim void of the club library, with
nobody, up or down, to be seen, and there after a while,
closing his eyes, recovered an hour of the sleep that he
had lost during the night. Before doing this indeed he
had written—it was the first thing he did—a short note,
which, in the Christmas desolation of the place, he had
managed only with difficulty and doubt to commit to a
messenger. He wished it carried by hand, and he was
obliged, rather blindly, to trust the hand, as the messenger, for some reason, was unable to return with a
gage of delivery. When, at four o'clock, he was face to
face with Kate in Mrs. Condrip's small drawing-room,
he found, to his relief, that his notification had reached
her. She was expectant, and to that extent prepared;
which simplified a little—if a little, at the present pass,
counted. Her conditions were vaguely vivid to him from
the moment of his coming in, and vivid partly by their
difference, a difference sharp and suggestive, from those
in which he had hitherto constantly seen her. He had
seen her but in places comparatively great—in her
aunt's pompous house, under the high trees of Kensington and the storied ceilings of Venice. He had seen
her, in Venice, on a great occasion, as the centre itself
of the splendid Piazza: he had seen her there, on a still
greater one, in his own poor rooms, which yet had con-

sorted with her, having state and ancientry even in their poorness; but Mrs. Condrip's interior, even by this best view of it and though not flagrantly mean, showed itself as a setting almost grotesquely inapt. Pale, grave and charming, she affected him at once as a distinguished stranger—a stranger to the little Chelsea street—who was making the best of a queer episode and a place of exile. The extraordinary thing was that at the end of three minutes he felt himself less appointedly a stranger in it than she.

A part of the queerness—this was to come to him in glimpses—sprang from the air as of a general large misfit imposed on the narrow room by the scale and mass of its furniture. The objects, the ornaments were, for the sisters, clearly relics and survivals of what would, in the case of Mrs. Condrip at least, have been called better days. The curtains that overdraped the windows, the sofas and tables that stayed circulation, the chimney-ornaments that reached to the ceiling and the florid chandelier that almost dropped to the floor, were so many mementos of earlier homes and so many links with their unhappy mother. Whatever might have been in itself the quality of these elements, Densher could feel the effect proceeding from them, as they lumpishly blocked out the decline of the dim day, to be ugly almost to the point of the sinister. They failed to accommodate or to compromise; they asserted their differences without tact and without taste. It was truly having a sense of Kate's own quality thus promptly to see them in reference to it. But that Densher had this sense was no new thing to him, nor did he in strictness need, for the hour, to be reminded of it. He only knew, by one of the tricks his imagination so constantly played him, that he was, so far as her present tension went, very specially sorry for her—which was not the view that had determined his start in the morning; yet also that he himself would have taken it all, as he might say, less hard. *He* could have lived in such a place; but it was not given to those of his complexion, so to speak, to be exiles anywhere. It was by their comparative grossness that they could somehow make shift. His natural, his inevitable, his ultimate home—left, that is, to itself—wasn't at all unlikely to be as queer and impossible as what was just round them, though doubtless in less ample masses. As he took in moreover how Kate wouldn't have been in the least the creature she was if what was just round them hadn't mismatched her, hadn't made for her a medium involving compunction in the spectator, so, by the same stroke, that became the very fact of her relation with her companions there, such a fact as filled him at once, oddly, both with certainty and with suspense. If he himself, on this brief vision, felt her as alien and as, ever so unwittingly, ironic, how must they not feel her, and how, above all, must she not feel them?

Densher could ask himself that even after she had presently lighted the tall candles on the mantelshelf. This was all their illumination but the fire, and she had proceeded to it with a quiet dryness that yet left play, visibly, to her implication, between them, in their trouble, and in default of anything better, of the presumably genial Christmas hearth. So far as the genial went this had, in strictness, given their conditions, to be all their geniality. He had told her in his note nothing but that he must promptly see her and that he hoped she might be able to make it possible; but he understood, from the first look at her, that his promptitude was already having for her its principal reference. "I was prevented, this morning, in the few minutes," he explained, "asking Mrs. Lowder if she had let you know, though I rather gathered she had; and it's what I've been in fact, since then, assuming. It was because I was so struck at the moment with your having, as she did tell me, so suddenly come here."

"Yes, it was sudden enough." Very neat and fine in the contracted firelight, with her hands in her lap, Kate considered what he had said. He had spoken immediately of what had happened at Sir Luke Strett's door. "She has let me know nothing. But that doesn't matter—if it's what *you* mean."

"It's part of what I mean," Densher said; but what he went on with, after a pause during which she waited, was apparently not the rest of that. "She had had, from Mrs. Stringham, her telegram; late last night. But to me the poor lady has not wired. The event," he added, "will have taken place yesterday, and Sir Luke, starting immediately, one can see, and travelling straight, will get back to-morrow morning. So that Mrs. Stringham, I judge, is left to face in some solitude the situation bequeathed to her. But of course," he wound up, "Sir Luke couldn't stay."

Her look at him might have had in it a vague betrayal of the sense that he was gaining time. "Was your telegram from Sir Luke?"

"No—I've had no telegram."

She wondered. "But not a letter——?"

"Not from Mrs. Stringham—no." He failed again, however, to develop this—for which her forbearance from another question gave him occasion. From whom then had he heard? He might, at last confronted with her, really have been gaining time; and as if to show that she respected this impulse she made her inquiry different. "Should you like to go out to her—to Mrs. Stringham?"

About that at least he was clear. "Not at all. She's alone, but she's very capable and very courageous. "Besides——" He had been going on, but he dropped.

"Besides," she said, "there's Eugenio? Yes, of course one remembers Eugenio."

She had uttered the words as definitely to show them for not untender; and he showed, equally, every reason to assent. "One remembers him indeed, and with every ground for it. He'll be of the highest value to her—he's capable of anything. What I was going to say," he went on, "is that some of their people, from America, must quickly arrive."

On this, as happened, Kate was able at once to satisfy him. "Mr. Someone-or-other, the person principally in charge of Milly's affairs—her first trustee, I suppose—had just got there at Mrs. Stringham's last writing."

"Ah, that then was after your aunt last spoke to me— I mean the last time before this morning. I'm relieved to hear it. So," he said, "they'll do."

"Oh, they'll do." And it came from each, still, as if it were not what each was most thinking of. Kate presently got, however, a step nearer to that. "But if you had been wired to by nobody, what then this morning had taken you to Sir Luke?"

"Oh, something else—which I'll presently tell you. It's what made me instantly need to see you; it's what I've come to speak to you of. But in a minute. I feel too many things," he went on, "at seeing you in this place." He got up as he spoke; she herself remained perfectly still. His movement had been to the fire, and, leaning a little, with his back to it, to look down on her from where he stood, he confined himself to his point. "Is it anything very bad that has brought you?"

He had now, however, said enough to justify her wish for more; so that, passing this matter by, she pressed her own challenge. "Do you mean, if I may ask, that *she*, dying——?" Her face, wondering, pressed it more than her words.

"Certainly you may ask," he after a moment said. "What has come to me is what, as I say, I came expressly to tell you. I don't mind letting you know," he went on, "that my decision to do this took for me, last night and this morning, a great deal of thinking of. But here I am." And he indulged in a smile that couldn't, he was well aware, but strike her as mechanical.

She went straighter with him, she seemed to show,

than he really went with her. "You didn't want to come?"

"It would have been simple, my dear"—and he continued to smile—"if it had been, one way or the other, only a question of 'wanting.' It took, I admit it, the idea of what I had best do, all sorts of difficult and portentous forms. It came up for me, really—well, not at all to my happiness."

This word apparently puzzled her—she studied him in the light of it. "You look upset—you've certainly been tormented. You're not well."

"Oh—well enough!"

But she continued without heeding. "You hate what you're doing."

"My dear girl, you simplify"—and he was now serious enough. "It isn't so simple even as that."

She had the air of thinking what it then might be. "I of course can't, with no clue, know what it is." She remained, however, patient and still. "If at such a moment she could write you, one is inevitably quite at sea. One doesn't, with the best will in the world, understand." And then as Densher had a pause which might have stood for all the involved explanation that, to his discouragement, loomed before him: "You *haven't* decided what to do."

She had said it very gently, almost sweetly, and he didn't instantly say otherwise. But he said so after a look at her. "Oh yes, I have. Only with this sight of you here and what I seem to see in it for you——!" And his eyes, as at suggestions that pressed, turned from one part of the room to another.

"Horrible place, isn't it?" said Kate.

It brought him straight back to his inquiry. "Is it for anything awful you've had to come?"

"Oh, that will take as long to tell you as anything *you* may have. Don't mind," she continued, "the 'sight of me here,' nor whatever—which is more than I yet know myself—may be 'in it' for me. And kindly consider too that I, after all, if you're in trouble, can a little wish to help you. Perhaps I can absolutely even do it."

"My dear child, it's just because of the sense of your wish——! I suppose I am in trouble—I suppose that's it." He said this with so odd a suddenness of simplicity that she could only stare for it—which he as promptly saw. So he turned off as he could his vagueness. "And yet I oughtn't to be." Which sounded indeed vaguer still.

She waited a moment. "Is it, as you say for my own business, anything very awful?"

"Well," he slowly replied, "you'll tell me if you find it so. I mean if you find my idea——"

He was so slow that she took him up. "Awful?" A sound of impatience—the form of a laugh—at last escaped her. "I can't find it anything at all till I know what you're talking about."

It brought him then more to the point, though it did so at first but by making him, on the hearthrug before her, with his hands in his pockets, turn awhile to and fro. There rose in him even with this movement a recall of another time—the hour, in Venice, the hour of gloom and storm, when Susan Shepherd had sat in his quarters there very much as Kate was sitting now, and he had wondered, in pain even as now, what he might say and might not. Yet the present occasion, after all, was somehow the easier. He tried at any rate to attach that feeling to it while he stopped before his companion. "The communication I speak of can't possibly belong—so far as its date is concerned—to these last days. The postmark, which is legible, does; but it isn't thinkable, for anything else, that she wrote——" He dropped, looking at her as if she would understand.

It was easy to understand. "On her deathbed?" But Kate took an instant's thought. "Aren't we agreed that there was never any one in the world like her?"

"Yes." And looking over her head he spoke clearly enough. "There was never any one in the world like her."

Kate from her chair, always without a movement, raised her eyes to the unconscious reach of his own. Then, when the latter again dropped to her, she added a question. "And won't it, further, depend a little on what the communication *is*?"

"A little perhaps—but not much. It's a communication," said Densher.

"Do you mean a letter?"

"Yes, a letter. Addressed to me in her hand—in hers unmistakably."

Kate thought. "Do you know her hand very well?"

"Oh, perfectly."

It was as if his tone for this prompted—with a slight strangeness—her next demand. "Have you had many letters from her?"

"No. Only three notes." He spoke looking straight at her. "And very, very short ones."

"Ah," said Kate, "the number doesn't matter. Three lines would be enough if you're sure you remember."

"I'm sure I remember. Besides," Densher continued, "I've seen her hand in other ways. I seem to recall how you once, before she went to Venice, showed me one of her notes precisely *for* that. And then she once copied me something."

"Oh," said Kate, almost with a smile, "I don't ask you for the detail of your reasons. One good one's enough." To which, however, she added, as if precisely not to speak with impatience or with anything like irony: "And the writing has its usual look?"

Densher answered as if even to better that description of it. "It's beautiful."

"Yes—it *was* beautiful. Well," Kate, to defer to him still, further remarked, "it's not news to us now that she was stupendous. Anything's possible."

"Yes, anything's possible"—he appeared oddly to catch at it. "That's what I say to myself. It's what I've been seeing you," he a trifle vaguely explained, "as still more certain to feel."

She waited for him to say more, but he only, with his hands in his pockets, turned again away, going this time to the single window of the room, where, in the absence

of lamplight, the blind had not been drawn. He looked
out into the lamplit fog, lost himself in the small sordid London street—for as sordid, with his other association, he saw it—as he had lost himself, with Mrs.
Stringham's eyes on him, in the vista of the Grand
Canal. It was present then to his recording consciousness that when he had last been driven to such an attitude the very depth of his resistance to the opportunity
to give Kate away was what had so driven him. His
waiting companion had on that occasion waited for him
to say he *would;* and what he had meantime glowered
forth at was the inanity of such a hope. Kate's attention, on her side, during these minutes, rested on the
back and shoulders he thus familiarly presented—rested
as with a view of their expression, a reference to things
unimparted, links still missing and that she must ever
miss, try to make them out as she would. The result of
her tension was that she again took him up. "You
received—what you spoke of—last night?"

It made him turn round. "Coming in from Fleet
Street—earlier by an hour than usual—I found it with
some other letters on my table. But my eyes went
straight to it, in an extraordinary way, from the door. I
recognised it, knew what it was, without touching it."

"One can understand." She listened with respect. His
tone, however, was so singular that she presently added:
"You speak as if, all this while, you *hadn't* touched it."

"Oh yes, I've touched it. I feel as if, ever since, I'd
been touching nothing else. I quite firmly," he pursued
as if to be plainer, "took hold of it."

"Then where is it?"

"Oh, I have it here."

"And you've brought it to show me?"

"I've brought it to show you."

So he said with a distinctness that had, among his other oddities, almost a sound of cheer, yet making no movement that matched his words. She could accordingly but show again her expectant face, while his own, to her impatience, seemed to fill, perversely, with still another thought. "But now that you've done so you feel you don't want to."

"I want to immensely," he said, "but you tell me nothing."

She smiled at him, with this, finally, as if he were an unreasonable child. "It seems to me I tell you quite as much as you tell me. You haven't yet even told me how it is that such explanations as you require don't come from your document itself." Then, as he answered nothing, she had a flash. "You mean you haven't read it?"

"I haven't read it."

She stared. "Then how am I to help you with it?"

Again leaving her while she never budged he paced five strides and again he was before her. "By telling me *this*. It's something, you know, that you wouldn't tell me the other day."

She was vague. "The other day?"

"The first time after my return—the Sunday I came to you. What is he doing," Densher went on, "at that hour of the morning with her? What does his having been with her there mean?"

"Of whom are you talking?"

"Of that man—Lord Mark of course. What does it represent?"

"Oh, with Aunt Maud?"

"Yes, my dear—and with you. It comes more or less to the same thing; and it's what you didn't tell me, the other day, when I put you the question."

Kate tried to remember. "You asked me nothing about any hour."

"I asked you when it was you last saw him—previous, I mean, to his second descent at Venice. You wouldn't say, and as we were talking of a matter comparatively more important, I let it pass. But the fact remains you know, my dear, that you haven't told me."

Two things, in this speech, appeared to have reached Kate more distinctly than the others. "I 'wouldn't say'?—and you 'let it pass'?" She looked just coldly blank. "You really speak as if I were keeping something back."

"Well, you see," Densher persisted, "you're not even telling me now. All I want to know," he, however, explained, "is if there was a connection between that proceeding, on his part, which was practically—oh, beyond all doubt!—the shock precipitating for her what has now happened, and anything that had occurred with him previously for yourself. How in the world did he know we're engaged?"

KATE SLOWLY ROSE; it was, since she had lighted the candles and sat down, the first movement she had made. "Are you trying to fix it on me that I must have told him?"

She spoke not so much in resentment as in pale dismay—which he showed that he immediately took in. "My dear child, I'm not trying to 'fix' anything; but I'm extremely tormented and I seem not to understand. What has the brute to do with us any way?"

"What has he indeed?" Kate asked.

She shook her head as if in recovery, within the minute, of some mild allowance for his unreason. There was in it—and for his reason really—one of those half-inconsequent sweetnesses by which she had often before made, over some point of difference, her own terms with him. Practically she was making them now, and essentially he was knowing it; yet, inevitably, all the same, he was accepting it. She stood there close to him, with something in her patience that suggested her having supposed, when he spoke more appealingly, that he was going to kiss her. He had not been, it appeared; but his continued appeal was none the less the quieter. "What's he doing, from ten o'clock on Christmas morning, with Mrs. Lowder?"

Kate looked surprised. "Didn't she tell you he's staying there?"

"At Lancaster Gate?" Densher's surprise met it. " 'Staying'?—since when?"

"Since day before yesterday. He was there before I came away." And then she explained—confessing it in fact anomalous. "It's an accident—like Aunt Maud's having herself remained in town for Christmas, but it isn't after all so monstrous. *We* stayed—and, with my having come here, she's sorry now—because we neither of us, waiting from day to day for the news you brought, seemed to want to be with a lot of people."

"You stayed for thinking of—Venice?"

"Of course we did. For what else? And even a little," Kate wonderfully added—"it's true at least of Aunt Maud—for thinking of you."

He appreciated. "I see. Nice of you every way. But whom," he inquired, "has Lord Mark stayed for thinking of?"

"His being in London, I believe, is a very commonplace matter. He has some rooms which he has had, suddenly, some rather advantageous chance to let—such as, with his confessed, his decidedly proclaimed want of money, he hasn't had it in him, in spite of everything, not to jump at."

Densher's attention was entire. "In spite of everything? In spite of what?"

"Well, I don't know. In spite, say, of his being scarcely supposed to do that sort of thing."

"To try to get money?"

"To try, at any rate, in little thrifty ways. Apparently, however, he has had, for some reason, to do what he can. He turned, at a couple of days' notice, out of his place, making it over to his tenant; and Aunt Maud, who is deeply in his confidence about all such matters, said: 'Come then to Lancaster Gate—to sleep at least—till, like all the world, you go to the country.' He was to have gone to the country—I think to Matcham—yesterday afternoon: Aunt Maud, that is, told me he was."

Kate had been, somehow, for her companion, through this statement, beautifully, quite soothingly, suggestive. "Told you, you mean, so that you needn't leave the house?"

"Yes—so far as she had taken it into her head that his being there was part of my reason."

"And *was* it part of your reason?"

"A little, if you like. Yet there's plenty here—as I knew there would be—without it. So that," she said candidly, "doesn't matter. I'm glad I am here: even if for all the good I do——!" She implied, however, that that didn't matter either. "He didn't, as you tell me, get off then to Matcham; though he may possibly, if it *is* possible, be going this afternoon. But what strikes me as most probable—and it's really, I'm bound to say, quite amiable of him—is that he has declined to leave Aunt Maud, as I've been so ready to do, to spend her Christmas alone. If, moreover, he has given up Matcham for her, it's a *procédé* that won't please her less. It's small wonder therefore that she insists, on a dull day, in driving him about. I don't pretend to know," she wound up, "what may happen between them; but that's all I see in it."

"You see in everything, and you always did," Densher returned, "something that, while I'm with you at least, I always take from you as the truth itself."

She looked at him as if consciously and even carefully extracting the sting of his reservation; then she spoke with a quiet gravity that seemed to show how fine she found it. "Thank you." It had for him, like everything else, its effect. They were still closely face to face, and, yielding to the impulse to which he had not yielded just before, he laid his hands on her shoulders, held her hard a minute and shook her a little, far from untenderly, as if in expression of more mingled things, all difficult, than he could speak. Then, bending, he applied his lips to her cheek. He fell, after this, away for an instant, resuming his unrest, while she kept the position in which, all passive and as a statue, she had taken his demonstration. It didn't prevent her, however, from offering him, as if what she had had was enough for the moment, a further indulgence. She made a quiet, lucid connection and, as she made it, sat down again. "I've been trying to place exactly, as to its date, something that did happen to me while you were in Venice. I mean a talk with him. He spoke to me—spoke out."

"Ah, there you are!" said Densher who had wheeled round.

"Well, if I'm 'there,' as you so gracefully call it, by having refused to meet him as he wanted—as he pressed—I plead guilty to being so. Would you have liked me," she went on, "to give him an answer that would have kept him from going?"

It made him, a little awkwardly, think. "Did you know he was going?"

"Never for a moment; but I'm afraid that—even if it doesn't fit your strange suppositions—I should have given him just the same answer if I had known. If it's a matter I haven't, since your return, thrust upon you, that's simply because it's not a matter in the memory of which I find a particular joy. I hope that if I've satisfied you about it," she continued, "it's not too much to ask of you to let it rest."

"Certainly," said Densher kindly, "I'll let it rest." But the next moment he pursued: "He saw something. He guessed."

"If you mean," she presently returned, "that he was unfortunately the one person we hadn't deceived, I can't contradict you."

"No—of course not. But *why*," Densher still risked, "was he unfortunately the one person——? He's not clever."

"He's clever enough, apparently, to have seen a mystery, a riddle, in anything so unnatural as—all things considered, and when it came to the point—my attitude. So he gouged out his conviction, and on his conviction he acted."

Densher seemed, for a little, to look at Lord Mark's conviction as if it were a blot on the face of nature. "Do you mean because you had appeared to him to have encouraged him?"

"Of course I had been decent to him. Otherwise where *were* we?"

" 'Where'——?"

"You and I. What I appeared to him, however, hadn't mattered. What mattered was how I appeared to Aunt Maud. Besides, you must remember that he has had all along his impression of *you*. You can't help it," she said, "but you're after all—well, yourself." ·

"As much myself as you please. But when I took myself to Venice and kept myself there—what," Densher asked, "did he make of that?"

"Your being in Venice and liking to be—which is never on any one's part a monstrosity—was explicable for him in other ways. He was quite capable moreover of seeing it as dissimulation."

"In spite of Mrs. Lowder?"

"No," said Kate, "not in spite of Mrs. Lowder now. Aunt Maud, before what you call his second descent, hadn't convinced him—all the more that my refusal of him didn't help. But he came back convinced." And then as her companion still showed a face at a loss: "I mean after he had seen Milly, spoken to her and left her. Milly convinced him."

"Milly?" Densher again but vaguely echoed.

"That you were sincere. That it was *her* you loved." It came to him from her in such a way that he instantly, once more, turned, found himself yet again at his window. "Aunt Maud, on his return here," she meanwhile continued, "had it from him. And that's why you're now so well with Aunt Maud."

He only, for a minute, looked out in silence—after

which he came away. "And why *you* are." It was almost, in its extremely affirmative effect between them, the note of recrimination; or it would have been perhaps rather if it hadn't been so much more the note of truth. It was sharp because it was true, but its truth appeared to impose it as an argument so conclusive as to permit on neither side a sequel. That made, while they faced each other over it without speech, the gravity of everything. It was as if there were almost danger, which the wrong word might start. Densher accordingly, at last, acted to better purpose: he drew, standing there before her, a pocketbook from the breast of his waistcoat and he drew from the pocketbook a folded letter, to which her eyes attached themselves. He restored then the receptacle to its place, and, with a movement not the less odd for being visibly instinctive and unconscious, carried the hand containing his letter behind him. What he thus finally spoke of was a different matter. "Did I understand from Mrs. Lowder that your father's in the house?"

If it never had taken her long, in such excursions, to meet him, it was not to take her so now. "In the house, yes. But we needn't fear his interruption"—she spoke as if he had thought of that. "He's in bed."

"Do you mean with illness?"

She sadly shook her head. "Father's never ill. He's a marvel. He's only—endless."

Densher thought. "Can I, in any way, help you with him?"

"Yes." She perfectly, wearily, almost serenely, had it all. "By our making your visit as little of an affair as possible for him—and for Marian too."

"I see. They hate so your seeing me. Yet I couldn't— could I?—not have come."

"No, you couldn't not have come."

"But I can only, on the other hand, go as soon as possible?"

Quickly, it almost upset her. "Ah, don't, to-day, put ugly words into my mouth. I've enough of my trouble without it."

"I know—I know!" He spoke in instant pleading. "It's all, only, that I'm as troubled *for* you. When did he come?"

"Three days ago—after he had not been near her for more than a year, after he had apparently, and not regrettably, ceased to remember her existence; and in a state which made it impossible not to take him in."

Densher hesitated. "Do you mean in such want——?"

"No, not of food, of necessary things—not even, so far as his appearance went, of money. He looked as wonderful as ever. But he was—well, in terror."

"In terror of what?"

"I don't know. Of somebody—of something. He wants, he says, to be quiet. But his quietness is awful."

She suffered, but she couldn't not question. "What does he do?"

It made Kate herself hesitate. "He cries."

Again for a moment he hung fire, but he risked it. "What *has* he done?"

It made her slowly rise, and they were fully, once more, face to face. Her eyes held his own, and she was paler than she had been. "If you love me—now—don't ask me about father."

He waited again a moment. "I love you. It's because I love you that I'm here. It's because I love you that I've brought you this." And he drew from behind him the letter that had remained in his hand.

But her eyes only—though he held it out—met the offer. "Why, you've not broken the seal!"

"If I had broken the seal—exactly—I should know what's within. It's for *you* to break the seal that I bring it."

She looked—still not touching the thing—inordinately grave. "To break the seal of something to you from *her?*"

"Ah, precisely because it's from her. I'll abide by whatever you think of it."

"I don't understand," said Kate. "What do you yourself think?" And then as he didn't answer: "It seems to me *I* think you know. You have your instinct. You don't need to read. It's the proof."

Densher faced her words like an accusation, but like an accusation for which he had been prepared and which there was but one way to face. "I have indeed my instinct. It came to me, while I worried it out, last night. It came to me as an effect of the hour." He held up his letter, and seemed now to insist more than to confess. "This thing had been timed."

"For Christmas eve?"

"For Christmas eve."

Kate had suddenly a strange smile. "The season of gifts!" After which, as he said nothing, she went on: "And had been written, you mean, while she could write, and kept to *be* so timed?"

Only meeting her eyes while he thought, he again didn't reply. "What do *you* mean by the proof?"

"Why, of the beauty with which you've been loved. But I won't," she said, "break your seal."

"You positively decline?"

"Positively. Never." To which she added oddly: "I know without."

He had another pause. "And what is it you know?"

"That she announces to you she has made you rich."

His pause this time was longer. "Left me her fortune?"

"Not all of it, no doubt, for it's immense. But money to a large amount. I don't care," Kate went on, "to know how much." And her strange smile recurred. "I trust her."

"Did she tell you?" Densher asked.

"Never!" Kate visibly flushed at the thought. "That wouldn't, on my part, have been playing fair with her. And I did," she added, "play fair."

Densher, who had believed her—he couldn't help it—continued, holding his letter, to face her. He was much quieter now, as if his torment had somehow passed. "You played fair with me, Kate; and that's why—since we talk of proofs—I want to give *you* one. I've wanted to let you see—and in preference even to myself—something I feel as sacred."

She frowned a little. "I don't understand."

"I've asked myself for a tribute, for a sacrifice by which I can specially recognise——"

"Specially recognise what?" she demanded as he dropped.

"The admirable nature of your own sacrifice. You were capable in Venice of an act of splendid generosity."

"And the privilege you offer me with that document is my reward?"

He made a movement. "It's all I can do as a symbol of my attitude."

She looked at him long. "Your attitude, my dear, is that you're afraid of yourself. You've had to take yourself in hand. You've had to do yourself violence."

"So it is then you meet me?"

She bent her eyes hard a moment to the letter, from which her hand still stayed itself. "You absolutely *desire* me to take it?"

"I absolutely desire you to take it."

"To do what I like with it?"

"Short, of course, of making known its terms. It must remain—pardon my making the point—between you and me."

She had a last hesitation, but she presently broke it. "Trust me." Taking from him the sacred script, she held it a little, while her eyes again rested on those fine characters of Milly's which they had shortly before discussed. "To hold it," she brought out, "is to know."

"Oh, I *know!*" said Merton Densher.

"Well then, if we both do——!" She had already

turned to the fire, nearer to which she had moved, and, with a quick gesture, had jerked the thing into the flame. He started—but only half—as if to undo her action: his arrest was as prompt as the latter had been decisive. He only watched, with her, the paper burn; after which their eyes again met. "You'll have it all," Kate said, "from New York."

VI

IT WAS AFTER he had in fact, two months later, heard from New York that she paid him a visit one morning in his own quarters—coming not as she had come in Venice, under his extreme solicitation, but as a need recognised in the first instance by herself, even though also as the prompt result of a missive delivered to her. This had consisted of a note from Densher, accompanying a letter, "just to hand," addressed to him by an eminent American legal firm, a firm of whose high character he had become conscious while in New York as of a thing in the air itself, and whose head and front, to the principal executor of Milly Theale's copious will, had been duly identified at Lancaster Gate as the gentleman hurrying out, by the straight southern course, before the girl's death, to the support of Mrs. Stringham. Densher's act on receipt of the document in question—an act as to which, and the bearings of which, his resolve had had time to mature—constituted, in strictness, singularly enough, the first reference to Milly, or to what Milly might or might not have done, that had passed

between our pair since they had stood together watching
the destruction, in the little vulgar grate at Chelsea, of
the unrevealed work of her hand. They had, at the time,
and in due deference now, on his part, to Kate's mention of her responsibility for his call, immediately separated, and when they met again the subject was made
present to them—at all events till some flare of new
light—only by the intensity with which it mutely
expressed its absence. They were not moreover in these
weeks to meet often, in spite of the fact that this had,
during January and a part of February, actually become
for them a comparatively easy matter. Kate's stay at
Mrs. Condrip's prolonged itself under allowances from
her aunt which would have been a mystery to Densher
had he not been admitted, at Lancaster Gate, really in
spite of himself, to the esoteric view of them. "It's her
idea," Mrs. Lowder had there said to him as if she really
despised ideas—which she didn't; "and I've taken up
with my own, which is to give her, till she has had
enough of it, her head. She *has* had enough of it—she
had that soon enough; but as she's as proud as the deuce
she'll come back when she has found some reason—having nothing in common with her disgust—of which she
can make a show. She calls it her holiday, which she's
spending in her own way—the holiday to which, once
a year or so, as she says, the very maids in the scullery
have a right. So we're taking it on that basis. But we
shall not soon, I think, take another of the same sort.
Besides, she's quite decent; she comes often—whenever
I make her a sign; and she has been good, on the whole,

this year or two, so that, to be decent myself, I don't complain. She has really been, poor dear, very much what one hoped; though I needn't, you know," Aunt Maud wound up, "tell *you*, after all, you clever creature, what that was."

It had been partly, in truth, to keep down the opportunity for this that Densher's appearances under the good lady's roof markedly, after Christmas, interspaced themselves. The phase of his situation that, on his return from Venice, had made them for a short time almost frequent was at present quite obscured, and with it the impulse that had then acted. Another phase had taken its place, which he would have been painfully at a loss as yet to name or otherwise set on its feet, but of which the steadily rising tide left Mrs. Lowder, for his desire, quite high and dry. There had been a moment when it seemed possible that Mrs. Stringham, returning to America under convoy, would pause in London on her way and be housed with her old friend; in which case he was prepared for some apparent zeal of attendance. But this danger passed—he had felt it a danger, and the person in the world whom he would just now have most valued seeing on his own terms sailed away westward from Genoa. He thereby only wrote to her, having broken, in this respect, after Milly's death, the silence as to the sense of which, before that event, their agreement had been so deep. She had answered him from Venice twice and had had time to answer him twice again from New York. The last letter of her four had come by the same post as the document he sent on to Kate, but he had not gone into the question of also enclosing that. His correspondence with Milly's companion was somehow already presenting itself to him as a feature—as a factor, he would have said in his newspaper—of the time, whatever it might be, long or short, in store for him; but one of his acutest current thoughts was apt to be devoted to his not having yet mentioned it to Kate. She had put him no question, no "Don't you ever hear?"—so that he had not been brought to the point. This he described to himself as a mercy, for he liked his secret. It was as a secret that, in the same personal privacy, he described his transatlantic commerce, scarce even wincing while he recognised it as the one connection in which he wasn't straight. He had in fact for this connection a vivid mental image—he saw it as a small emergent rock in the waste of waters, the bottomless grey expanse of straightness. The fact that he had now, on several occasions, taken with Kate an out-of-the-way walk that had, each time, defined itself as more remarkable for what they didn't say than for what they did—this fact failed somehow to mitigate for him a strange consciousness of exposure. There was something deep within him that he had absolutely shown to no one—to the companion of these walks in particular not a bit more than he could help; but he was none the less haunted, under its shadow, with a dire apprehension of publicity. It was as if he had invoked that ugliness in some stupid good faith; and it was queer enough that on his emergent rock, clinging to it and to Susan Shepherd, he should figure himself as hidden from view.

That represented, no doubt, his belief in her power, or in her delicate disposition, to protect him. Only Kate, at all events, knew—what Kate did know, and she was also the last person interested to tell it; in spite of which it was as if his *act*, so deeply associated with her and never to be recalled nor recovered, was abroad on the winds of the world. His honesty, as he viewed it, with Kate, was the very element of that menace: to the degree that he saw at moments, as to their final impulse or their final remedy, the need to bury in the dark blindness of each other's arms the knowledge of each other that they couldn't undo.

Save indeed that the sense in which it was in these days a question of arms was limited, this might have been the intimate expedient to which they were actually resorting. It had its value, in conditions that made everything count, that thrice over, in Battersea Park— where Mrs. Lowder now never drove—he had adopted the usual means, in sequestered alleys, of holding her close to his side. She could make absences, on her present footing, without having too inordinately to account for them at home—which was exactly what, for the first time, gave them an appreciable margin. He supposed she could always say in Chelsea—though he didn't press it—that she had been across the town, in decency, for a look at her aunt; whereas there had always been reasons at Lancaster Gate for her not being able to plead the look at her other relatives. It was therefore between them a freedom of a purity as yet untasted; which, for that matter, also, they made, in various ways, no little

show of cherishing as such. They made the show indeed
in every way but the way of a large use—an inconsequence that they almost equally gave time to helping
each other to regard as natural. He put it to his companion that the kind of favour he now enjoyed at Lancaster Gate, the wonderful warmth of his reception
there, cut, in a manner, the ground from under their
feet. He was too horribly trusted—they had succeeded
too well. He couldn't in short make appointments with
her without abusing Aunt Maud, and he couldn't on the
other hand haunt that lady without tying his hands.
Kate saw what he meant just as he saw what she did
when she admitted that she was herself, to a degree
scarce less embarrassing, in the enjoyment of Aunt
Maud's confidence. It was special at present—she was
handsomely used; she confessed accordingly to a scruple
about misapplying her licence. Mrs. Lowder then finally
had found—and all unconsciously now—the way to baf-
fle them. It was not, however, that they didn't meet a
little, none the less, in the southern quarter, to point, for
their common benefit, the moral of their defeat. They
crossed the river; they wandered in neighbourhoods sordid and safe; the winter was mild, so that, mounting to
the top of trams, they could rumble together to
Clapham or to Greenwich. If at the same time their
minutes had never been so counted it struck Densher
that, by a singular law, their tone—he scarce knew what
to call it—had never been so bland. Not to talk of what
they *might* have talked of drove them to other ground;
it was as if they used a perverse insistence to make up

what they ignored. They concealed their pursuit of the irrelevant by the charm of their manner; they took precautions for a courtesy that they had formerly left to come of itself; often, when he had quitted her, he stopped short, walking off, with the aftersense of their change. He would have described their change—had he so far faced it as to describe it—by their being so damned civil. That had even, with the intimate, the familiar at the point to which they had brought them, a touch almost of the funny. What danger had there ever been of their becoming rude—after each had, long since, made the other so tremendously tender? Such were the things he asked himself when he wondered what in particular he most feared.

Yet all the while too the tension had its charm—such being the interest of a creature who could bring one back to her by such different roads. It was her talent for life again; which found in her a difference for the differing time. She didn't give their tradition up; she but made of it something new. Frankly, moreover, she had never been more agreeable, nor, in a way—to put it prosaically—better company: he felt almost as if he were knowing her on that defined basis—which he even hesitated whether to measure as reduced or as extended; as if at all events he were admiring her as she was probably admired by people she met "out." He hadn't, in fine, reckoned that she would still have something fresh for him; yet this was what she had—that on the top of a tram in the Borough he felt as if he were next her at dinner. What a person she would be if they *had* been rich—with what a genius for the so-called great life, what a presence for the so-called great house, what a grace for the so-called great positions! He might regret at once, while he was about it, that they weren't princes or billionaires. She had treated him on their Christmas to a softness that had struck him at the time as of the quality of fine velvet, meant to fold thick, but stretched a little thin; at present, however, she gave him the impression of a contact multitudinous as only the superficial can be. Moreover, throughout, she had nothing to say of what went on at home. She came out of that, and she returned to it, but her nearest reference was the look with which, each time, she bade him good-bye. The look was her repeated prohibition: "It's what I *have* to see and to know—so don't touch it. That but wakes up the old evil, which I keep still, in my way, by sitting by it. I go now—leave me alone!—to sit by it again. The way to pity me—if that's what you want—is to believe in me. If we could really *do* anything it would be another matter."

He watched her, when she went her way, with the vision of what she thus a little stiffly carried. It was confused and obscure, but how, with her head high, it made her hold herself! He in truth, in his own person, might at these moments have been swaying a little, aloft, as one of the objects in her poised basket. It was doubtless thanks to some such consciousness as this that he felt the lapse of the weeks, before the day of Kate's mounting of his stair, almost swingingly rapid. They contained for him the contradiction that, whereas periods of waiting are supposed in general to keep the time slow, it was the wait, actually, that made the pace trouble him. The secret of that anomaly, to be plain, was that he was aware of how, while the days melted, something rare went with them. This something was only a thought, but a thought precisely of that freshness and that delicacy that made the precious, of whatever sort, most subject to the hunger of time. The thought was all his own, and his intimate companion was the last person he might have shared it with. He kept it back like a favourite pang; left it behind him, so to say, when he went out, but came home again the sooner for the certainty of finding it there. Then he took it out of its sacred corner and its soft wrappings; he undid them one by one, handling them, handling it, as a father, baffled and tender, might handle a maimed child. But so it was before him—in his dread of who else might see it. Then he took to himself at such hours, in other words, that he should never, never know what had been in Milly's letter. The intention announced in it he should but too probably know; but that would have been, but for the depths of his spirit, the least part of it. The part of it missed forever was the turn she would have given her act. That turn had possibilities that, somehow, by wondering about them, his imagination had extraordinarily filled out and refined. It had made of them a revelation the loss of which was like the sight of a priceless pearl cast before his eyes—his pledge given not to save it—into the fathomless sea, or rather even it was like the sacrifice of something sentient and throbbing, something that, for the spiritual ear, might have been audible as a faint, far wail. This was the sound that he cherished, when alone, in the stillness of his rooms. He sought and guarded the stillness, so that it might prevail there till the inevitable sounds of life, once more, comparatively coarse and harsh, should smother and deaden it—doubtless by the same process with which they would officiously heal the ache, in his soul, that was somehow one with it. It deepened moreover the sacred hush that he couldn't complain. He had given poor Kate her freedom.

The great and obvious thing, as soon as she stood there on the occasion we have already named, was that she was now in high possession of it. This would have marked immediately the difference—had there been nothing else to do it—between their actual terms and their other terms, the character of their last encounter in Venice. That had been *his* idea, whereas her present step was her own; the few marks they had in common were, from the first moment, to his conscious vision, almost pathetically plain. She was as grave now as before; she looked around her, to hide it, as before; she pretended, as before, in an air in which her words at the moment itself fell flat, to an interest in the place and a curiosity about his "things"; there was a recall, in short, in the way in which, after she had failed, a little, to push up her veil symmetrically and he had said she had better take it off altogether, she had acceded to his suggestion before the glass. It was just these things that were vain; and what was real was that his fancy figured her

after the first few minutes as literally now providing the
element of reassurance which had previously been his
care. It was she, supremely, who had the presence of
mind. She made indeed, for that matter, very prompt
use of it. "You see I've not hesitated this time to break
your seal."

She had laid on the table from the moment of her
coming in the long envelope, substantially filled, which
he had sent her enclosed in another of still ampler make.
He had, however, not looked at it—his belief being that
he wished never again to do so; besides which it had
happened to rest with its addressed side up. So he "saw"
nothing, and it was only into her eyes that her remark
made him look, without an approach to the object indicated. "It's not 'my' seal, my dear; and my intention—
which my note tried to express—was all to treat it to
you as not mine."

"Do you mean that it's to that extent mine then?"

"Well, let us call it, if we like, theirs—that of the
good people in New York, the authors of our communication. If the seal is broken well and good; but we
might, you know," he presently added, "have sent it
back to them intact and inviolate. Only accompanied,"
he smiled with his heart in his mouth, "by an absolutely
kind letter."

Kate took it with the mere brave blink with which a
patient of courage signifies to the exploring medical
hand that the tender place is touched. He saw on the
spot that she was prepared, and with this signal sign
that she was too intelligent not to be, came a flicker of

possibilities. She was—merely to put it at that—intelligent enough for anything. "Is it what you're proposing we *should* do?"

"Ah, it's too late to do it—well, ideally. Now, with that sign that we *know*——!"

"But you don't know," she said very gently.

"I refer," he went on without noticing it, "to what would have been the handsome way. It's being despatched again, with no cognisance taken but one's assurance of the highest consideration, and the proof of this in the state of the envelope—that would have been really satisfying."

She thought an instant. "The state of the envelope proving refusal, you mean, not to be based on the insufficiency of the sum?"

Densher smiled again as for the play, however whimsical, of her humour. "Well yes—something of that sort."

"So that if cognisance *has* been taken—so far as I'm concerned—it spoils the beauty?"

"It makes the difference that I'm disappointed in the hope—which I confess I entertained—that you'd bring the thing back to me as you had received it."

"You didn't express that hope in your letter."

"I didn't want to. I wanted to leave it to yourself. I wanted—oh yes, if that's what you wish to ask me—to see what you'd do."

"You wanted to measure the possibilities of my departure from delicacy?"

He continued steady now; a kind of ease—in the

presence, as in the air, of something he couldn't as yet
have named—had come to him. "Well, I wanted—in so
good a case—to test you."

She was struck—it showed in her face—by his
expression. "It *is* a good case. I doubt if a better," she
said with her eyes on him, "has ever been known."

"The better the case then the better the test!"

"How do you know," she asked in reply to this,
"what I'm capable of?"

"I don't, my dear! Only, with the seal unbroken, I
should have known sooner."

"I see"—she took it in. "But I myself shouldn't have
known at all. And you wouldn't have known, either,
what I do know."

"Let me tell you at once," he returned, "that if
you've been moved to correct my ignorance I very particularly request you not to."

She just hesitated. "Are you afraid of the effect of the
corrections? Can you only do it by doing it blindly?"

He waited a moment. "What is it that you speak of
my doing?"

"Why, the only thing in the world that I take you as
thinking of. Not accepting—what she has done. Isn't
there some regular name in such cases? Not taking up
the bequest."

"There's something you forget in it," he said after a
moment. "My asking you to join with me in doing so."

Her wonder but made her softer, yet didn't, at the
same time, make her less firm. "How can I 'join' in a
matter with which I've nothing to do?"

"How? By a single word."

"And what word?"

"Your consent to my giving up."

"My consent has no meaning when I can't prevent you."

"You can perfectly prevent me. Understand that well," he said.

She seemed to face a threat in it. "You mean you won't give up if I *don't* consent?"

"Yes. I do nothing."

"That, as I understand, is accepting."

Densher paused. "I do nothing formal."

"You won't, I suppose you mean, touch the money."

"I won't touch the money."

It had a sound—though he had been coming to it - that made for gravity. "Who then, in such an event, *will?*"

"Any one who wants or who can."

Again, a little, she said nothing: she might say too much. But by the time she spoke she had covered ground. "How can I touch it but *through* you?"

"You can't. Any more," he added, "than I can renounce it except through you."

"Oh, ever so much less! There's nothing," she said, "in my power."

"I'm in your power," Merton Densher returned.

"In what way?"

"In the way I show—and the way I've always shown. When have I shown," he asked as with a sudden cold impatience, "anything else? You surely must feel—so that you needn't wish to appear to spare me in it—how you 'have' me."

"It's very good of you, my dear," she nervously laughed, "to put me so thoroughly up to it!"

"I put you up to nothing. I didn't even put you up to the chance that, as I said a few moments ago, I saw for you in forwarding that thing. Your liberty is therefore in every way complete."

It had come to the point, really, that they showed each other pale faces, and that all the unspoken between them looked out of their eyes in a dim terror of their further conflict. Something even rose between them in one of their short silences—something that was like an appeal from each to the other not to be too true. Their necessity was somehow before them, but which of them must meet it first? "Thank you!" Kate said for his word about her freedom, but taking for the minute no further action on it. It was blessed at least that all ironies failed them, and during another slow moment their very sense of it cleared the air.

There was an effect of this in the way he soon went on. "You must intensely feel that it's the thing for which we worked together."

She took up the remark, however, no more than if it were commonplace; she was already again occupied with a point of her own. "Is it absolutely true—for if it is, you know, it's tremendously interesting—that you haven't so much as a curiosity as to what she has done for you?"

"Would you like," he asked, "my formal oath on it?"

"No—but I don't understand. It seems to me in your place——"

"Ah," he couldn't help from breaking in, "what do you know of my place? Pardon me," he immediately added; "my preference is the one I express."

She had in an instant, all the same, a curious thought. "But won't the facts be published?"

" 'Published'?"—he winced.

"I mean won't you see them in the papers?"

"Ah, never! I shall know how to escape that."

It seemed to settle the subject, but she had, the next minute, another insistence. "Your desire is to escape everything?"

"Everything."

"And do you need no more definite sense of what it is that you ask me to help you to renounce?"

"My sense is sufficient without being definite. I'm willing to believe that the amount of money's not small."

"Ah, there you are!" she exclaimed.

"If she was to leave me a remembrance," he quietly pursued, "it would inevitably not be meagre."

Kate waited as for how to say it. "It's worthy of her. It's what she was herself—if you remember what we once said *that* was."

He hesitated, as if there had been many things. But he remembered one of them. "Stupendous?"

"Stupendous." A faint smile for it—ever so small—had flickered in her face, but had vanished before the omen of tears, a little less uncertain, had shown themselves in his own. His eyes filled—but that made her continue. She continued gently. "I think that what it really is must be that you're afraid. I mean," she explained, "that you're afraid of *all* the truth. If you're in love with her without it, what indeed can you be more. And you're afraid—it's wonderful!—to be in love with her."

"I never was in love with her," said Densher.

She took it, but after a little she met it. "I believe that now—for the time she lived. I believe it at least for the time you were there. But your change came—as it might well—the day you last saw her: she died for you then that you might understand her. From that hour you *did*." With which Kate slowly rose. "And I do now. She did it *for* us." Densher rose to face her, and she went on with her thought. "I used to call her, in my stupidity—for want of anything better—a dove. Well she stretched out her wings, and it was to *that* they reached. They cover us."

"They cover us," Densher said.

"That's what I give you," Kate gravely wound up. "That's what I've done for you."

His look at her had a slow strangeness that had dried, on the moment, his tears. "Do I understand then——?"

"That I do consent?" She gravely shook her head. "No—for I see. You'll marry me without the money; you won't marry me with it. If I don't consent, *you* don't."

"You lose me?" He showed, though naming it frankly, a sort of awe of her high grasp. "Well, you lose nothing else. I make over to you every penny."

Prompt was his own clearness, but she had no smile, this time, to spare. "Precisely—so that I must choose."

"You must choose."

Strange it was for him then that she stood in his own rooms doing it, while, with an intensity now beyond any that had ever made his breath come slow to him, he waited for her act. "There's but one thing that can save you from my choice."

"From your choice of my surrender to you?"

"Yes"—and she gave a nod at the long envelope on the table—"your surrender of that."

"What is it then?"

"Your word of honour that you're not in love with her memory."

"Oh—her memory!"

"Ah"—she made a high gesture—"don't speak of it as if you couldn't be. *I* could, in your place; and you're one for whom it will do. Her memory's your love. You *want* no other."

He heard her out in stillness, watching her face, but not moving. Then he only said: "I'll marry you, mind you, in an hour."

"As we were?"

"As we were."

But she turned to the door, and her headshake was now the end. "We shall never be again as we were!"

NOTES

P. 1, LL. 1–2. *Preface to the New York Edition:* James wrote the preface specifically for the 1909 edition.

L. 3. *The Wings of the Dove:* James took the title from Psalms 55 and 68: "My heart is sore pained within me: and the terrors of death are fallen upon me. Fearfulness and trembling are come upon me, and horror hath overwhelmed me. And I said, Oh that I had wings like a dove! for then I would fly away, and be at rest" (Psalms 55: 4–6, King James); "Though ye have lien among the pots, yet shall ye be as the wings of a dove covered with silver, and her feathers with yellow gold" (Psalms 68: 13, King James).

L. 3. *published in 1902:* Charles Scribner's Sons, in New York, and Archibald Constable and Company, in London, published the first American and English editions of *The Wings of the Dove* in the same month, August 1902.

LL. 8–11. *a young person . . . enamoured of the world:* Scholars of James have long believed that the character of Milly Theale was at least in part inspired by the tragic death of James's first cousin, Mary (Minny) Temple, who succumbed to tuberculosis at age twenty-four, in March 1870. James had been close to Minny and was apparently very deeply affected by her loss; upon learning of her death, he wrote to his brother, William, on March 29, 1870, that: "to the eye of feeling there is something immensely moving in the sudden & complete extinction of a vitality so exquisite & so apparently infinite as Minny's." Minny is thought to have inspired a number of James's heroines, most notably Isabel Archer, of *The Portrait of a Lady* (1881), and Daisy Miller, of *Daisy Miller* (1878). In his same March 29, 1870, letter to William, James expressed his sense of how incomplete her life had been: "How far she may have been considered up to the time of her illness to have achieved a tolerable happiness, I don't know: hardly at all, I should say, for her happiness like her unhappiness remained wholly incomplete." In late 1880, when his good friend Grace Norton wrote to James to point out a resemblance between the fictional Isabel Archer and Minny, James replied, on December 28, that "Poor Minny was essentially *incomplete* & I have attempted to make my young woman more rounded, more finished. In truth everyone, in life, is *incomplete,* & it is the mark of art that in reproducing them one feels the desire to fill them out, to justify them, as it were." Through his fiction, James may have attempted to complete his cousin's tragically short life.

P. 3, LL. 25–26. *Ralph Touchett in "The Portrait of a Lady"*: the cousin of the heroine of James's 1881 novel; he dies in his mid-thirties of tuberculosis.

P. 5, L. 19. *Lorelei:* legendary siren whose songs lured boats toward the rocks along the Rhine River where she resided.

P. 6, LL. 27–28. *"heir of all the ages"*: See P. 133, LL. 23–24, where the text of the novel first calls Milly "the potential heiress of all the ages."

P. 8, L. 7. *the Rhine-maiden*: See "Lorelei" (Note to P. 5, L. 19).

P. 9, L. 29. *circumvallations*: surrounding fortifications or entrenchments.

P. 10, LL. 13–15. *the work had ignominiously failed, in advance, of all power to see itself "serialised"*: It was common practice in James's day for novels and short stories to be serialized, i. e., published first in magazine installments, and then later as a book. James had been quite successful earlier in his career at deriving the maximum revenue possible from U.S. and British serial and book rights for his novels, but by the time he wrote *The Wings of the Dove*, his novels were not selling very well, and his agent, James Pinker, was unable to find a magazine willing to serialize *The Wings of the Dove*.

LL.17–18. *as "The Golden Bowl" was to be, two or three years later*: James's novel *The Golden Bowl* was first published by Scribner's, in two volumes, in New York, in November 1904, and by Methuen, in London, in February 1905.

L. 23. *arête*: mountain ridge (French).

P. 15, L. 4. *Hermes*: Greek god of luck and wealth, the patron of travelers, merchants, and thieves. He led the souls of the dead to Hades, the land of the dead, and he was the messenger of the gods.

L. 16. *her fairly choral Bostonian*: James compares the relationship between Susan Stringham and Milly with the one between the chorus and the protagonist in classic Greek drama.

P. 16, LL. 11–14. *I should have to consent . . . the one reflector:* In
most of his fiction, James avoided using omniscient narrators, preferring either first-person narrators (in many of
his short stories and novellas) or limited-consciousness
third-person narrators (in most of his novels). As a result,
readers can only know what happens in this fiction as a
particular character's point of view perceives it. In some of
his longer novels, most famously *The Ambassadors* (1903),
James's narrator could only tell about events as perceived
through the point of view of one single character, but in
other long novels, like *The Wings of the Dove,* the narration would alternate long sections between the different
points of view of a small group of central characters. James
uses the terms "reflector" and "register" to signify the
central character through whose point of view the narrator
tells the story.

L. 26–P. 17, L. 3. *There is no economy of treatment . . . that
doesn't rather scatter and weaken:* James is saying that,
while he can acknowledge exceptions to his preferred
practice, in most cases, he cannot imagine a narration
without its particular, correlative point of view and that
truly omniscient narration is inherently weaker.

P. 17, LL. 11–13. *the long passage that forms here before us the
opening of Book Fourth:* See PP. 167–189; this first chapter
of Book Fourth, like the other two chapters of the book, is
narrated entirely through Milly's point of view.

L. 16–P. 18, L. 9. *This passage . . . the scene at Lancaster
Gate:* James states that "it is Kate Croy who is . . . turned
on largely at Venice" and that "It is in Kate's consciousness that at the stage in question the drama is brought to a
head," but in fact the sections of the book that take place in

Venice are all narrated through the consciousness of either Milly (see 449–486) or Densher (see 487–620). The "stage" at which "the drama is brought to a head," James tells us in his Preface, is "the occasion on which, in the splendid saloon of poor Milly's hired palace, she [Kate] takes the measure of her friend's festal evening." This passage occurs on pages 530–546.

P. 18, L. 9. *Lancaster Gate:* London street and garden, one block north of Kensington Gardens.

P. 23, LL. 15–17. *There is an hour of evening . . . in this direction:* See pages 146–150.

LL. 22–24. *The whole actual centre of the work, resting on a misplaced pivot and lodged in Book Fifth:* James refers to, presumably, either the scene in which Milly views the Bronzino portrait that resembles her (see pages 237–249) or the account of Milly's visit to Sir Luke Strett, which occurs in the following chapter (see pages 249–266).

P. 24, LL. 4–5. *coigns of vantage:* places allowing a good view.

P. 31, L. 1. *Chirk Street:* an invented name.

P. 33, L. 12. penetralia: innermost recesses or shrine (from Latin).

P. 34, L. 12. *straitness:* revised in 1909 edition to: *straightness.*

L. 16. table d'hôte: in a hotel or restaurant, a dinner table where all the guests sit together and share the same fixed menu meal (French); no italics in the 1909 edition.

P. 35, LL. 4–5. *Lexham Gardens:* street and small square in the Kensington neighborhood of London.

L. 17. "n'en parlons plus": let's not talk about it any more (French).

P. 39, LL. 17–19. *It all makes up . . . a hundred to Marian:* The late Mrs. Croy's estate yields an annual income of two hundred pounds a year for each of her two daughters, though from her share, Kate gives one hundred a year to her sister. In the nineteenth century, two hundred pounds was worth a thousand dollars (U.S.), which was a modest income at the time.

P. 52, L. 10. *the Park:* Kensington Gardens and Hyde Park; *South Kensington:* upscale neighborhood of London, bounded by Cromwell Road and Brompton Road.

L. 19. *Cromwell Road:* major street in the Kensington neighborhood of London, separating Kensington proper from South Kensington.

L. 20. *Kensington Gardens:* the large London park situated between Kensington Palace and Hyde Park. From 1886 to 1898 James lived at 34 De Vere Gardens, just off the southwest corner of Kensington Gardens.

P. 53, L. 8. ultima Thule: Thule was the name given by Pytheas, a fourth-century Greek explorer from Marseilles, to what may have been Iceland, Norway, or the Shetland Islands of Great Britain, hence *ultima Thule,* meaning the most distant place attainable.

P. 55, L. 19. *at times circulate more endlessly:* The 1902 Scribner's edition left out the word *circulate;* the 1902 Constable edition reads: *at times move endlessly.*

LL. 21–22. *the great grey map of Middlesex spread beneath her lookout:* Middlesex County is located on the north bank of the Thames River and consists mostly of the current limits of Greater London.

P. 57, L. 1. *twinkling bugles:* sequin-like glass beads.

L. 7. *Britannia:* name of the female personification of Britain.

L. 18. *philistinism:* In Biblical times, the Philistines were a foreign nation that warred with the Israelites; in an essay in *Essays in Criticism* (1865) on the German poet Heinrich

Heine (1797–1856), English poet and critic Matthew Arnold (1822–1888) used the word to designate an "inveterate inaccessibility to ideas"; James knew Arnold and shared several of his views.

P. 59, L. 22. *Chelsea:* London neighborhood situated between the Thames River and South Kensington. During the last three years of his life (1913–16), James kept an apartment at 21 Carlyle Mansions, Cheyne Walk, in Chelsea.

P. 73, L. 13. *the north side:* the side of the park closest to Lancaster Gate.

P. 79, LL. 20–22. *that, after all, would have been a small affair, if there hadn't been something else with it:* revised in 1909 edition to: *that in itself after all would have been a small affair for two such handsome persons.*

P. 80, LL. 12–13. *the Underground Railway:* Work on the London Underground, the world's first urban subway or underground rail system, began in 1862, and James first used it in 1869.

L. 14. *Sloane Square:* a square in London's Belgravia neighborhood, and also a stop on the Circle and District underground lines, west of Victoria Station; *Queen's Road:* Today's Queensway, the large street that runs north from Kensington Gardens, so named because Queen Victoria had been known to ride in it. What is today the Queensway station, the Central Line underground stop just east of Notting Hill Gate, was called Queen's Road (Bayswater) at the time the novel takes place.

P. 81, L. 3. *High Street, Kensington:* Kensington High Street, a major east-west street through the Kensington neighborhood; it is the western extension of Kensington Road, which runs along the south side of Kensington Gardens. It is also a stop on the Circle and District Lines.

L. 18. *Notting Hill Gate:* western extension of Bayswater Road, which runs along the north side of Kensington Gardens and Hyde Park, and the stop on the Central and District Lines north of High Street, Kensington.

P. 84, LL. 1–2. *implications:* revised in 1909 edition to: *implication.*

P. 88, L. 22. *a coach-in-four:* a carriage with four horses.

P. 91, L. 17. *a middy:* a midshipman, an apprentice officer in the navy.

P. 94, L. 10. *I knew—it was true:* The 1902 Constable edition reads: *I understood it was true;* revised in 1909 edition to: *I knew it was true.*

P. 102, L. 28. *huge, heavy objects:* The 1902 Constable edition reads: *awful ornaments;* revised in 1909 edition to: *huge heavy objects.*

P. 107, LL. 17–18. *advantage:* Both the 1902 Constable and the 1909 editions read: *adage.*

P. 112, LL. 23–24. *Fleet Street:* street in the City of London, where most of London's newspapers were located.

P. 116, L. 17. *the car of Juggernaut:* an enormous processional car that carries an idol of Juggernaut or Jagannath, eighth avatar of the Hindu god Krishna. Devotees were believed to throw themselves in front of it as it was dragged in procession; hence the expression can refer to any practice or institution to which people blindly sacrifice themselves.

P. 118, LL. 1–3. *and it put him, for half an hour, on as much of the picture of his early years abroad:* revised in 1909 edition to: *and it perched him there for half an hour, like a cicerone and his victim on a tower-top, before as much of the bird's-eye view of his early years abroad.*

L. 26. *"Murray":* In the nineteenth century the London

publisher John Murray produced a leading series of tourist guides.

P. 119, LL. 22–23. *his Cambridge years . . . his father's college:* Densher had studied at Cambridge University. As is typical of the classic English university, Cambridge consists of several colleges, among the more famous of which are King's College and Trinity College; Densher studied at the same Cambridge college as his father.

P. 120, L. 16. *having tasted of the tree:* reference to the tree of knowledge of good and evil in the Garden of Eden (see Genesis 2:9–3:23).

P. 127, L. 1. *in advance of the Swiss season:* The "Swiss season" took place during the summer months of June through September, when wealthy travelers would have sought the cooler, mountain air.

LL. 8–9. *the Italian lakes:* the area north of Milan, on the Swiss-Italian border, where such lakes as Lugano, Maggiore, Como, and Garda offer some of Italy's most beautiful scenery.

LL. 14–15. *Villa d'Este:* villa built in 1568 by the Cardinal of Como on the Lake of Como; in 1873 it became a luxury hotel; *Cadenabbia:* Village on the west shore of the Lake of Como, which James first visited at the end of August 1869; *Pallanza and Stresa:* Villages on the west shore of Lake Maggiore; James first visited this shore at the end of August 1869.

L. 19. *the Brünig:* the Brünig Pass, Alpine pass (1107 m.) on the main road between the Swiss cities of Interlaken and Lucerne, which James crossed in early August 1869.

P. 130, L. 27. *Burlington, Vermont:* the principal city of the state of Vermont, on the east shore of Lake Champlain.

P. 131, LL. 16–19. *She wrote short stories . . . in the kitchen:* James may have modeled Susan Stringham's career on that of Vermont author Mary Wilkins Freeman (1852–1930), whose stories and novels James admired.

P. 132, L. 21. *her "Transcript":* The *Boston Evening Transcript,* sometimes entitled the *Daily Evening Transcript,* started in 1830 and continued until 1941.

L. 25. *the Public Library:* The Boston Public Library was the first public, municipal library in the United States; it was established in 1848. The current central research library, on Copley Square, designed by McKim, Mead, and White, was built in 1895.

P. 133, LL. 23–24. *the potential heiress of all the ages:* See P. 6, LL. 27–28, where James uses this phrase, in reference to Milly, in the Preface.

P. 135, L. 25. *Maeterlinck:* Belgian author Maurice Maeterlinck (1862–1949), who published in French and who won the Nobel Prize for Literature in 1911; the 1902 editions misspelled the name: *Maeterlink; Pater:* English author Walter Pater (1839–94), best remembered, perhaps, for his 1873 work *The Renaissance: Studies in Art and Poetry* (originally entitled *Studies in the History of the Renaissance*); *Marbot:* Baron Jean-Baptiste Antoine Marcelin de Marbot (1782–1854), French colonel under Napoleon I and general under King Louis-Philippe. His *Memoirs* were published posthumously (1891). *Gregorovius:* Ferdinand Gregorovius (1821–91), German author of numerous historical works, including books on Corsica, Lucrezia Borgia, Rome's Jewish Ghetto, Athens in the Byzantine era and in the Middle Ages, Rome in the Middle Ages, the Roman Emperor Hadrian, and Corfu.

P. 138, LL. 21–23. *a trio of penny whistles . . . a Wagner overture:*
The operas of German composer Richard Wagner
(1813–83) used large orchestras, thus increasing the volume of the loudest passages and making it impossible to
hear "a trio of penny whistles."

P. 143, L. 6. *Vevey:* resort town on the north shore of the Lake
of Geneva; James set the first part of *Daisy Miller* (1878)
there.

LL. 24–25. *cycles of Cathay:* The phrase is an allusion to
line 184 of "Locksley Hall" (1842) by English poet Alfred
Lord Tennyson (1809–1892): "Better fifty years of Europe
than a cycle of Cathay"; *Cathay* is a legendary name for
China, and *cycles of Cathay* refers to the great length of the
history of civilization in China.

P. 146, L. 5. mode du jour: fashion of the day (French).

L. 9. *Tauchnitz:* German publisher of economical reprint
editions of English-language books, including a number
of James's novels.

P. 149, LL. 6–7. *She was looking down on the kingdoms of the
earth:* Taken from the devil's temptation of Jesus (Matthew 4:1–11, King James), especially verse 8: "Again, the
devil taketh him up into an exceeding high mountain, and
sheweth him all the kingdoms of the world, and the glory
of them."

L. 25. à bientôt!: See you soon! (French).

P. 156, L. 29. diligence: stagecoach (French); given in the plural
in the 1902 Constable edition and in the singular but without italics in the 1909 edition.

P. 159, L. 16. *"letters":* letters of introduction.

P. 160, LL. 3–4. *her interlocutress:* revised in 1909 edition to: *the
partner of these hours.*

P. 169, LL. 22–23. *the Bishop of Murrum—a real bishop:* No such bishop existed.

P. 172, LL. 9–11. *She was real, none the less, and everything and everybody were real:* revised in 1909 edition to: *She was the amusing resisting ominous fact, none the less, and each other person and thing was just such a fact.*

P. 173, L. 5. *as great a reality as:* revised in 1909 edition to: *as packed a concretion as.*

P. 184, L. 25. *blasé:* bored (French).

P. 190, L. 7. *make:* revised in 1909 edition to: *made.*

P. 192, L. 25. *the stoutest Cunarder:* The Cunard Line of passenger steamships was founded in 1839; it was the first to offer scheduled, trans-Atlantic crossings.

P. 194, L. 7. Punch: British satirical illustrated weekly magazine founded in 1841.

P. 195, LL. 15–16. *of English, of eccentric, of Thackerayan character:* One of James's favorite English Victorian novelists, William Makepeace Thackeray (1811–64), was the creator of a number of marvelously eccentric characters in his satires for *Punch* and his most famous novels: *Vanity Fair* (1848), *The History of Pendennis* (1849–50), and *The Newcomes* (1853–55).

P. 196, L. 30. *Bayswater:* neighborhood north of Kensington Gardens and Lancaster Gate.

P. 197, L. 22. *Wigmore Street:* street parallel to and just north of Oxford Street, which is one of London's major commercial streets.

P. 200, LL. 26–28. *He had been a short time in the House, on the Tory side, but had lost his seat on the first opportunity:* Lord Mark was a Tory, or member of the Conservative Party in Parliament. Although he is an aristocrat, he is not an hereditary peer—he is only the "uncle to a duke" (see

P. 380, L. 7), which means that Mark was the younger brother of the duke's late father. Therefore he would have been a member, not of the House of Lords, but of the House of Commons.

P. 205, L. 15. *Battersea Park:* London park on the south side of the Thames River, opposite Chelsea.

P. 210, LL. 17–18. *a labyrinth:* This is the 1909 reading; the 1902 Constable edition reads *labyrinthine;* and the 1902 Scribner's edition gives the presumably erroneous *labyrinthe.*

P. 213, LL. 5–6. *the quarter of the famous Carlyle, the field of exercise of his ghost:* Scottish historian, philosopher, and critic Thomas Carlyle (1795–1881), lived, after 1834, in Cheyne Row, Chelsea.

P. 214, L. 9. *Trollope:* English novelist Anthony Trollope (1815–82).

L. 10. *Dickens:* English novelist Charles Dickens (1812–70).

L. 14. *the adored author of* The Newcomes: William M. Thackeray (see note to P. 195, LL. 15–16).

LL. 17–18. *a certain possibility of Pickwickian outline:* a reference to Dickens's long, comic novel *The Pickwick Papers* (1836–37).

LL. 19–20. *another Mrs. Nickleby:* mother of the title character of Dickens's novel *The Life and Adventures of Nicholas Nickleby* (1838–39).

L. 22. *Mrs. Micawber:* character in Dickens's novel *David Copperfield* (1849–50); like Mrs. Nickleby, she is penniless.

P. 221, L. 26. " *'beaux moments'* ": beautiful moments (French).

P. 224, L. 2. *volage:* fickle (French).

P. 228, LL. 25–26. *an almost extravagantly grand Watteau-composition:* a reference to the style of French painter Antoine Watteau (1684–1721).

P. 230, LL. 19–20. *a "rush"*: James presumably uses the word *rush* in the sense of a high demand for or a run on something, although Northern English dialects did use *rush* to signify a feast or merrymaking.

P. 231, L. 17. *sward*: an expanse of lawn.

L. 20. *"durbar"*: an Indian ruler's court, or alternatively, the public levee of an Indian prince or of a British Imperial governor.

P. 233, LL. 13–14. insupportables: unbearable people (French).

P. 234, L. 17. beaux yeux: beautiful eyes (French).

L. 28. *tone? Since*: revised in 1909 edition to: *tone"? "Since.*

P. 236, LL. 5–6. *Her interlocutress*: revised in 1909 edition to: *The young person under her protection.*

L. 30. *unmistakably free*: revised in 1909 edition to: *comprehensive.*

P. 237, L. 20. *the wonderful Bronzino*: Florentine painter Angiolo Torri, called Bronzino (1503–1572), created the portrait of the sixteenth-century Venetian noblewoman, Lucrezia Panciatichi, which is in the collection of the Uffizi Gallery in Florence and which scholars have identified as the painting James describes in this scene.

P. 240, L. 17. à peu près: more or less (French).

P. 243, L. 14. "Les grands esprits se rencontrent!": Great minds meet! (French); the italics were removed in the 1909 edition.

P. 246, LL. 26–27. *the wisdom of the serpent*: reference to Matthew 10:16, King James (from Jesus' missionary sermon to the apostles, 10.5–11:1): "Behold, I send you forth as sheep in the midst of wolves: be ye therefore wise as serpents, and harmless as doves."

P. 253, L. 9. *the great square*: revised in 1909 edition to: *the great contiguous square*. If Sir Luke's office is indeed at 143

Harley Street, London (see "A Note on the Text"), this square would be Cavendish Square.

P. 254, LL. 13–14. *London fairly fatigued . . . its story all told:* High Society would reside in London for the "Season" of May, June, and July, when Parliament was open, and then would leave London for its country houses from late summer to late autumn, until Parliament reopened. James, here, writes of "London" as if it consisted only of its upper-class inhabitants and of the "Season" as if it were a "dance."

P. 261, L. 11. *its:* revised in 1909 edition to: *his.*

P. 264, LL. 11–12. *voyage to the north pole . . . the north pole:* The Arctic explorations of Robert Peary (1856–1920) were much in the news at the time, although Peary would not reach the North Pole until 1909; in the 1909 edition, *North Pole* is capitalized.

P. 269, L. 8. *Regent's Park:* a large London park between the boroughs of Camden and Westminster.

P. 275, LL. 3–4. *Gibbon:* English historian Edward Gibbon (1737–94), best known for his *The History of the Decline and Fall of the Roman Empire* (1776); *Froude:* James Anthony Froude (1818–94), English historian and disciple and literary executor of Thomas Carlyle (see note to P. 213, L. 5); *Saint-Simon:* Louis de Rouvroy, duc de Saint-Simon (1675–1755), French courtier whose *Memoirs* (composed 1694–1755) offer a detailed account of life in the royal court at Versailles.

L. 8. *Byzantine:* The Byzantine Empire (641–1461) was originally (330–641) the eastern half of the Roman Empire; its capital was Constantinople. The text refers here to the artistic and architectural styles typical of the Byzantine Empire, which influenced, for instance, the architectural style of Venice, especially of the Basilica of San Marco (see note to P. 505, L. 28).

L. 16. *a mosaic at Ravenna:* Ravenna, the Italian city south of Venice, near the Adriatic coast, is especially known for its fifth-century Byzantine mosaics.

P. 276, LL. 4–5. *a shilling:* There were twelve pence to a shilling and twenty shillings to a pound; a shilling was therefore equal to a quarter of a U.S. dollar.

P. 279, L. 3. *"you are well.":* revised in 1909 edition to: *"you are well?"*

L. 11. *Engadines:* the Engadine, a valley in eastern Switzerland, location of the popular mountain resort St. Moritz; *Rivieras:* the Riviera, the Mediterranean coast of southeastern France and northwestern Italy.

P. 280, LL. 27–28. *People were by this time quite scattered:* another reference to the members of High Society leaving London at this point in the summer (see note to P. 254, LL. 13–14).

P. 296, LL. 26–27. *inespérées:* unhoped-for (French); *manna from heaven:* the miraculous food God provided for the Israelites while they wandered in the Sinai desert in the Book of Exodus.

P. 301, L. 12. *"Because you're a dove.":* See note to P. 533, LL. 11–13.

P. 305, L. 3. *the National Gallery:* famous London art museum in Trafalgar Square built in 1832–38 and expanded in 1876 and 1885–87.

L. 29. *the Titians:* paintings by Tiziano Vecellio, called Titian (c. 1488–1576), a Venetian painter whom James much admired; *the Turners:* paintings by Joseph Mallord William Turner (1775–1851); early in his career, James criticized Turner's distinctive and atmospheric style of painting.

P. 308, LL. 2–3. *Baedekers:* Coblenz publisher and travel author Karl Baedeker (1801–1859) created an extremely successful series of travel guides, published in many languages; Baedeker and Murray (see note to P. 118, L. 26) guides were the guidebooks of choice of most American and British travelers in the nineteenth century.

P. 314, L. 18. *Fifth Avenue:* a principal Manhattan north-south street; it runs along the east edge of New York City's Central Park.

P. 324, L. 7. *Euston:* Euston Station, London terminus of many northwestern railway lines.

P. 331, LL. 10–11. *This in fact now became for him so sharp an apprehension:* revised in 1909 edition to: *That appearance in fact, if he dwelt on it, so ministered to apprehension.*

P. 332, L. 29. *with his special:* revised in 1909 edition to: *with this special.*

P. 334, LL. 6–7. *it will be the end, just now; therefore it's nothing to ask:* revised in 1909 edition to: *it will be the end; just now therefore it's nothing to ask.*

L. 13. *Brook Street:* a fashionable street in Mayfair, off Grosvenor Square. The hotel would have been Claridge's, at 49–55 Brook Street, on the corner of Davies Street, one of the finest hotels in London.

P. 339, L. 12. *had:* misprinted in 1902 Scribner's edition as: *has.*

L. 28. *solid:* revised in 1909 edition to: *ever so intimately appreciable.*

P. 341, L. 11. *Sèvres:* porcelain made in the Paris suburb of Sèvres.

P. 352, L. 18. *brummagem:* a counterfeit, cheap, and showy object, named for *Brummagem*, a contemptuous dialéct form of Birmingham, the English city where such articles were supposed to have been made.

P. 360, LL. 3–5. *with a pleasant spirit, though whether for his own or for Mrs. Stringham's benefit:* revised in 1909 edition to: *with much gay expression, though what it expressed.*

P. 365, L. 11. *Guy de Maupassant:* French writer (1850–93) who associated with the French realist and naturalist novelists, such as Gustave Flaubert, Emile Zola, and Alphonse Daudet, whom James met when he lived in Paris in 1875–76 and about whose work he was often ambivalent.

P. 366, LL. 16–18. *the gentlemen . . . not to sit too tight:* The practice at upper-class dinner parties was for the women to leave the dinner table first, leaving the men to brandy and cigars (and conversation intended only for male ears), after which they would rejoin the women, in a drawing room, for coffee or entertainment or both.

P. 369, L. 13. *ces dames:* these ladies (French).

P. 371, L. 16. *Well, she had it ready. "You can console her.":* The 1902 Scribner's edition misprinted this phrase as: *"Well, she had it ready. You can console her."*

P. 388, L. 26. *Bayswater Road:* eastern extension of Notting Hill Gate (see note to P. 81, L. 8).

LL. 27–28. *the modern church, in the middle of the square that, going eastward, opened out on his left:* probably Christchurch, Paddington, at 27–28 Lancaster Gate, demolished—except for its spire and tower—in 1977.

P. 396, L. 19. *sovereignty:* revised in 1909 edition to: *supremely.*

P. 401, LL. 13–14. *"Do you begin to rush about on visits to country-houses?":* Because the "Season" is over (see note to P. 254, LL. 13–14), Densher assumes that Kate and Aunt

Maud will spend their autumn making visits to country estates.

P. 406, L. 23. *rococo:* an ornate artistic and decorative style popular in Europe in the mid-eighteenth century.

P. 445, L. 4. *the Tyrol:* a mountainous region of northeastern Italy and western Austria.

P. 448, L. 2. entourage: set of friends (French); not italicized in 1909 edition.

P. 450, LL. 15–16. *the palace:* James modeled his fictional Palazzo Leporelli on Venice's Palazzo Barbaro, which is situated on the Grand Canal and which his Bostonian friends Daniel and Ariana Curtis had bought in 1885. James visited the Curtises there on several occasions (see note to P. 487, LL. 18–19). John Singer Sargent (1856–1925), who was a friend both of James and of the Curtises, was also a frequent guest. One of his more famous paintings, *An Interior in Venice* (1898), depicts the Curtises, with their son and their daughter-in-law, in the Palazzo's grand salon.

L. 20. *Eugenio:* James gave the same name to the Millers' courier in *Daisy Miller* (1878). A courier was employed to make travel arrangements for foreign travelers on the European continent; Milly's Eugenio is a very high-class courier.

L. 23. pourparlers: negotiations (French).

P. 453, LL. 6–7. *Charming people, conscious Venice-lovers:* i.e., like James's friends, the Curtises (see note to P. 450, LL. 15–16).

L. 13. *Palazzo Leporelli:* Milly's rented palace (see note to P. 450, LL. 15–16).

P. 454, LL. 7–10. *the Empress Catherine's famous progress across the steppes of Russia; improvised settlements appeared at each turn of the road:* Catherine II, known as Catherine the Great (1729–96), was Empress (or Czarina) of Russia from 1762 until her death. One of her favorite courtiers, Gregory Potemkin (1739–91), while he was Governor of the Ukraine, organized a tour for the Empress during which he is supposed to have erected prosperous, temporary, inhabited villages—subsequently called Potemkin villages—along her route in order to cast the best light possible on his administration.

L. 16. *Dolomite:* The Dolomites are a mountain range north of Venice.

P. 457, LL. 15–16. *some dim scene in a Maeterlinck play:* Maeterlinck's (see note to P. 135, L. 25) plays are known for their mysterious atmosphere and their reliance on allegory.

P. 462, LL. 15–16. *those moments of his showing her the great portrait at Matcham:* See pages 237–249.

P. 463, L. 8. *Carlsbad:* Carlsbad or Karlsbad, today Karlovy Vary, a city in the western Czech Republic, but at the time of *The Wings of the Dove,* part of the Austro-Hungarian Empire.

LL. 25–26. *the Rialto:* major foot bridge across the Grand Canal in Venice; *the Bridge of Sighs:* covered bridge connecting the Doge's Palace in Venice to the palace's prisons.

P. 465, L. 24. *Veronese:* Venetian painter Paolo Veronese (1528–88).

P. 466, L. 6. *sala:* the large, central room in a typical Venetian floor plan (Italian); not italicized in 1909 edition.

P. 470, LL. 29–30. *"Do you remember something I said to you that day at Matcham":* See pages 237–249 and especially p. 240.

P. 476, L. 8. moyens: means (French).

P. 487, L. 10. *pure Attic:* the form of ancient Greek spoken in Attica, the region of Athens.

LL. 18–19. *He had in each case made terms for a lodging more private and not more costly:* James visited Venice seven times before he wrote *The Wings of the Dove:* in September 1869, when he stayed at the Hotel Barbesi; in the spring of 1881, when he rented rooms at 4161 Riva degli Schiavoni, on the Basin of San Marco, to the east of the Doge's Palace, and where he wrote much of *The Portrait of a Lady;* in the winter of 1887, when he stayed at Casa Alvisi, the Venetian home of his friend Katharine de Kay Bronson, and then again in June 1887, when he stayed at the Curtises' Palazzo Barbaro; in June 1890 and July 1892, when he again stayed at Palazzo Barbaro; in the spring and early summer of 1894, when he stayed at Casa Biondetti, in San Vio, which is across the Grand Canal from Palazzo Barbaro; and in the spring of 1899, when he again stayed at Palazzo Barbaro (James would visit Venice one more time after writing *The Wings of the Dove,* in 1907, when he again visited Palazzo Barbaro). Densher's lodging probably most resembles James's rented rooms on the Riva degli Schiavoni, which he described in an April 20, 1882, letter to Edmund C. Stedman as: "a little fourth floor (4 rooms) which were meagrely & hideously furnished, but where the rent was so low, the view so divine (four windows on the lagoon,) & the situation so convenient, that it was a very tolerable habitation."

P. 488, L. 1. *campo:* literally, a field, but in Venice, a small square (Italian).

L. 4. quartiere: neighborhood (Italian).

L. 10. *traghetto:* ferry (Italian).

P. 492, LL. 12–13. *to be . . . bon prince:* acting benevolently (French).

LL. 25, 30. *direct:* revised in both instances in 1909 edition to: *pure.*

P. 494, L. 18. padrona: landlady (Italian); not italicized in 1909 edition.

P. 495, L. 12. *Gianbellini:* Giovanni Bellini, sometimes called Gianbellini or Giambellini (1430–1516), Venetian painter and son of Jacopo Bellini (1400–1471).

P. 499, L. 28. campi: plural of *campo* (See note to P. 488, L. 1).

P. 502, L. 21. *as if it had been:* misprinted in the 1902 Scribner's edition as: *as if had been.*

P. 505, LL. 20–24. *the Square . . . Piazza San Marco:* Venice's largest and most famous square, at the end of the Grand Canal.

L. 28. *the great mosque-like church:* the Byzantine-style Basilica of San Marco (begun in 1063), Venice's most famous church, in the middle of Piazza San Marco.

P. 506, L. 8. loggie: covered galleries, open on at least one side, in this case the ground-floor arcades of the buildings surrounding Piazza San Marco (Italian).

P. 508, L. 24. *the closer:* revised in 1909 edition to: *them closer.*

P. 509. L. 16. *the flutter of the doves:* Piazza San Marco is known for its many pigeons.

P. 515, LL. 20–21. *under the arcades:* under the arcades around the perimeter of Piazza San Marco (see note to P. 506, L. 8).

P. 518, L. 25. *There had practically:* misprinted in the 1902 Scribner's edition as: *There had had practically.*

P. 521, LL. 2–9. *"It's a Veronese picture . . . perch on my thumb for the evening:* Scholars have identified two paintings by

Paolo Veronese (see note to P. 465, L. 24) to which this passage appears to refer: *The Supper in the House of Levi*, which is in the collection of the Accademia in Venice and which depicts the dinner described in the Gospel of Luke (Luke 5:27–35), and *The Marriage Feast at Cana*, one version of which is at the Museum of the Louvre and which depicts the wedding feast described in the Gospel of John (John 2:1–11). Both paintings include a dwarf with a bird.

P. 522, L. 4. *Tasso:* Italian poet Torquato Tasso (1544–95); his sonnet "La Regina del Mar" ("The Queen of the Sea") is about Venice.

L. 29–P. 523, L. 2. *that weight, on his heart, of conscious responsibility which these very moments with Mrs. Stringham caused more and more to settle:* revised in 1909 edition to: *that weight as of expected performance which these very moments with Mrs. Stringham caused more and more to settle on his heart.*

P. 523, L. 2. *conscious responsibility:* revised in 1909 edition to: *the expectation of performance.*

P. 528, LL. 17–18. *the Veronese picture of which he had talked:* See note to P. 521, LL. 2–9.

P. 532, L. 1. *She looked at Milly:* revised in 1909 edition to: *Almost heedless of the danger of overt freedoms, she eyed Milly.*
L. 4. *native freedoms:* revised in 1909 edition to: *native humours.*

P. 533, LL. 11–13. *such wings could in a given case—had, in fact, in the case in which he was concerned—spread themselves for protection:* This passage completes a complex series of connected references, involving the novel's title and Kate's calling Milly "a dove" at the end of Book Fifth, chapter VI (see note to P. 301, L. 12).

P. 534, L. 15. *gay:* revised in 1909 edition to: *in great feather.*

P. 536, LL. 10, 12; P. 540, LL. 27–28; P. 545, L. 21; P. 546, L. 3.
Lady Mills: revised in 1909 edition to: *Lady Wells.*

P. 541, LL. 19–20. *I was to read:* the 1902 Constable and 1909
editions read: *he was to read.*

P. 544, L. 4. justesse: accuracy (French).

P. 548, LL. 20–21. *he must not know:* the 1902 Constable and
1909 editions read: *he must now know.*

P. 550, L. 6. *lightly:* the 1902 Constable and 1909 editions read:
slightly.

L. 27. portone: main entrance or door (Italian).

P. 552, L. 28. *there:* misprinted in 1902 Scribner's edition as:
three; the 1902 Constable edition reads: *thus.*

P. 566, L. 6. *which they found themselves concerned in, a boon:*
misprinted in the 1902 Scribner's edition as: *which they
found themselves concerned, a boon.*

P. 569, L. 15. piano nobile: the main floor, usually the one
above the ground floor (Italian).

P. 570, LL. 21–22. loggia: Covered porch or gallery (Italian);
the singular of *loggie* (see note to P. 506, L. 8).

P. 572, L. 4. fondamenta: quay (Italian).

L. 26. *Molo:* a pier or quay for tying up boats (Italian), in
this case, the Grand Canal edge of the Piazza San Marco;
the old columns of St. Mark and of the Lion: columns separating Piazzo San Marco from the Molo; revised in 1909
edition to: *the old columns of the St. Theodore and of the
Lion.*

P. 573, L. 26. *Florian's:* a famous café-restaurant on Piazza San
Marco, facing the Doge's Palace.

P. 574, L. 4. *the* Figaro: Parisian newspaper founded in 1826; it
became a daily in 1866.

P. 575, L. 22. a fortiori: more conclusively (Italian).

P. 608, L. 1. *Victoria:* Victoria Station, the London terminus for many southern railroad lines.

P. 609, L. 3. felze: A *felza,* in the Venetian dialect, is the cabin of a gondola, but James has given the plural instead of the singular form.

    L. 16. *saw the boat to disappear:* revised in 1909 edition to: *saw the boat disappear.*

P. 611, LL. 24–25. *that Densher hoped for a visit in that particular light:* revised in 1909 edition to: *that Densher invoked this violence to all probability.*

P. 637, L. 5. salone: drawing room (Italian).

P. 643, L. 16. *that the events:* misprinted in the 1902 Scribner's edition as: *than the events.*

P. 652, LL. 27–28. *the Marble Arch:* a triumphal arch designed by John Nash, situated at the northeast corner of Hyde Park, where Bayswater Road meets Oxford Street.

P. 663, L. 17. *couldn't not come:* misprinted in the 1902 Scribner's edition as: *could not come.*

P. 669, L. 14. *Brompton Road:* a street south of Hyde Park.

    LL. 15–16. *the Oratory:* Brompton Oratory, a Catholic church opened in 1851 and enlarged in 1888, on Brompton Road, next to the Victoria and Albert Museum (called the South Kensington Museum in the late nineteenth century).

P. 685, L. 25. procédé: procedure (French).

P. 690, L. 26. *but she couldn't:* the 1902 Constable and the 1909 editions read: *but he couldn't.*

P. 694, L. 18. *to:* deleted in the 1902 Constable and 1909 editions.

P. 699, L. 25. *Clapham:* a suburb south of the Thames River; *Greenwich:* a suburb east of London, location of Green-

....

wich Park, the Old Royal Observatory, and the Royal Naval College.

P.704, L.14. *made him look:* misprinted in the 1902 Scribner's edition as: make him look.

P. 707, L. 20. *she had covered:* revised in 1909 edition to: *he had covered.*

READING GROUP GUIDE

1. In his Preface to the New York Edition, James consistently invokes theatrical language, referring to his story and its momentum as the "drama," the setting for it the "stage." His evocation of lush settings, florid language, and imminent tragedy is almost operatic in tone. Describe a few points in the novel where the theatricality of a situation comes notably into play. What effect does this technique have on your perception of the story and its characters?

2. The conflict between the concepts of Fate and Agency permeates the novel. There is a sense from the book's outset that a course has been set in motion, its outcome ominous and inevitable. To what extent do you think Milly Theale, Kate Croy, and Merton Densher are the puppets of a preordained Fate, or willing, conscious agents of their own fortunes?

3. Weakness and illness is a trope in literature with a variety of interpretations. Often, physical infirmity can be interpreted as a symbol of moral frailty. Milly Theale, however,

exhibits all the qualities of a fine, righteous woman. Why
might James have conferred this malady upon Milly, and
how does her physical weakness reflect upon the characters
of Densher and Croy?

4. There are several strong female presences in *The Wings of
the Dove*, and they all serve distinct and separate literary
purposes for James. Describe the main female characters.
How do they function in the story? What roles do they per-
form when the novel is interpreted as a "morality play"?
How do they function for you, as a reader, on an emotional
level?

5. An ongoing feature in James's writing is the conflict between American and European values, often exhibited
through certain characters and situations. Milly Theale, in
the case of *The Wings of the Dove*, is his young American as
the "heir of all ages" (both literally and figuratively). Surprisingly, however, this archetypal golden child is doomed
by both fate and circumstance. What impact might this
have on James's discussion of American vs. European values? Also, how might one view the character of Mrs. Stringham in this particular context? Of what values and qualities
might she be an illustrated representation?

6. Kate Croy is a conflicted and perpetually conflicting character. She is driven by qualities that seem, at first, amoral
and inadmirable: greed, ambition, unflinching desire. One
is, however, compelled to forgive her a bit when it becomes
clear that her father is the primary impetus behind her
rather devious actions. Lionel Croy, though, is conspicuously absent for most of the novel. What impact does his

absence as a tangible character have on your perception of Kate? Does his looming presence in her life make her a more or less sympathetic figure? In what ways can her designs and actions be justified? In what ways might she also be considered a protagonist?

7. Amy Bloom notes in her Introduction that *The Wings of the Dove* is an "intimate" novel, in which "the voice of the narrative itself . . . is the intimate voice of conversation, of people living and sorting out their lives." This intimacy is conveyed through a rather roundabout narrative technique, one by which James conveys the story from "windows and balconies." Describe some instances in which a character is presented through the perceptions of others. What effect does this indirect method of storytelling have on the overall impact of the novel and its characters?

MODERN LIBRARY IS ONLINE AT
WWW.MODERNLIBRARY.COM

MODERN LIBRARY ONLINE IS YOUR GUIDE
TO CLASSIC LITERATURE ON THE WEB

THE MODERN LIBRARY E-NEWSLETTER

Our free e-mail newsletter is sent to subscribers, and features sample chapters, interviews with and essays by our authors, upcoming books, special promotions, announcements, and news.

To subscribe to the Modern Library e-newsletter, send a blank e-mail to: sub_modernlibrary@info.randomhouse.com or visit www.modernlibrary.com

THE MODERN LIBRARY WEBSITE

Check out the Modern Library website at
www.modernlibrary.com for:

- The Modern Library e-newsletter
- A list of our current and upcoming titles and series
- Reading Group Guides and exclusive author spotlights
- Special features with information on the classics and other paperback series
- Excerpts from new releases and other titles
- A list of our e-books and information on where to buy them
- The Modern Library Editorial Board's 100 Best Novels and 100 Best Nonfiction Books of the Twentieth Century written in the English language
- News and announcements

Questions? E-mail us at **modernlibrary@randomhouse.com**
For questions about examination or desk copies, please visit
the Random House Academic Resources site at
www.randomhouse.com/academic